SPEAR OF

DESTINY

The Archemi Online Chronicles

Volume 5

By James Osiris Baldwin

Published by Tamtu Publishing LLC

DEDICATION

Spear of Destiny is dedicated to You: the fans of the Archemi Online series. Thanks to you all, 2020 was a much better year than it could have been.

A huge thank you to all my Fans on Patreon: Terry Higgins, Cole, Jessica, Jakob Mayhew, Jordan Kramer, Jordon Wilton, Tyler L., Tyler Reed.

A shoutout also to my other Patreon Supporters: Hamish Jenkins, Jose, Jami, Jo M., Matt Chan, Sylvia, Pete A. Sarah, Cassandra, Dream of Dragons, Jonathan E, Jonathan T, Kasun, Zohatu, and Christoph.

Your ongoing support of this series is just incredible – thank you!

A special thank you to all those who helped with the editing and development of this book: My wife, Canth; Mimi, Karla, Hamish Jenkins, and Pete. I owe you all a beer and/or book of your choice, no questions asked.

TABLE OF CONTENTS

PREFACE I: IMPORTANT CHARACTERS

Player Characters:

- **Hector Park** (Park Jeong-Ho, Dragozin Hector) – Dark Lancer, Lvl. 25
- **Suri Ba'Hadir** – Berserker, Lvl. 27
- **Rin Lu** – Arcane Engineer, Lvl. 24
- **Baldr Hyland** (Possessed by 'Ororgael') – Spirit Knight, Lvl. ???
- **Lucien Hart** – Unknown Path, Lvl. ???
- **Violetta DeVrys** – Elemental Sorceress, Lvl. ???
- **Nethres of Gilheim** – Valkyrie, Lvl. 23
- **Casper Willis** – Sharpshot, Lvl ???

NPCs

- **Karalti, the Black Opal Queen** – Queen Dragon, Lvl. 15
- **Vash Dorha** – Baru (Dark Monk), Lvl. 35
- **Istvan Arshak** – Dragoon, Lvl. 31
- **Ebisa, the King's Blade** – Assassin, Lvl. 42
- **Rutha of Vasteau** – Primal Sorceress, Lvl. 44
- **Ignas Corvinus II** – Volod (King) of Vlachia; Swashbuckler, Lvl. 48

- **Andrik Corvinus III** – Former Volod of Vlachia (deceased)
- **Owen & Kira of Lyrensgrove** - Healers
- **Sergeant Anya Blackwin** – Captain of Fort Palewing
- **Jasper** – Mage at Fort Palewing
- **Pavetta Blackwin** – Primera of the Church of Kyrie
- **Taethawn the Bleak** – Meewfolk Exile, mercenary commander
- **Count Lorenzo Soma** – lord of Litvy County, Arcane Engineer, Lvl. 30
- **Masterhealer Masha** – Arcane Physician, Lvl. 50
- **Lazar Skalitz** – General Physician, Lvl. 23
- **Ashur of the Thousand Swords**, AKA The Demon of Myszno

PREFACE II: IMPORTANT GAME SYSTEM CONCEPTS

Archemi

Archemi Online, colloquially known as ArchOn, is the world's first hyper-immersion VR-RPG, though it is not the only VR-RPG extant in Hector's world. ArchOn was not designed to be an MMO in which millions access a single world: to support the massive memory demands of processing human brain data in a full-immersion VR, Archemi supports capped 'cells' of players, to a maximum of 5000 players per cell. Due to cataclysmic plague on Earth, there is only one cell supporting approximately 2389 players, almost all of whom are 'virtual refugees' uploaded to escape their death from the HEX Virus.

Paths & Advanced Paths

Rather than set, static classes, Archemi has an organic Path system that evolves with a player's interests and abilities. New players initially select one of four base paths – Warrior, Specialist (Rogue), Mage, or Artificer. At Level 5 and Level 10, characters are offered the chance to choose an Advanced Path, which takes them down a specialized stream from their initial Path. Advanced Paths are offered on a per-character basis by the game's system, which reads into a person's play-style, quest choice, and other factors to offer Advanced Paths the player is suited to. Advanced Paths themselves have customized progressions that unfold for players as they advance.

Renown

Renown is the measure of fame or infamy you possess in a locale. In every location where you complete (or fail to complete) quests, you can potentially gain renown. Renown is important for players interested in Mass Combat.

Like most things in Archemi, Renown is accrued through points. After accumulating a certain number of renown points, you gain bonuses or penalties to dealing with people in your locale. The size of the locale where you command fame or terror varies depending on your renown tier. The tiers are as follows:

- 0-300 - Stranger: Unknown and unnotable.
- 301-700 - Adventurer: Some people have heard of you, and neighborhoods where you completed adventures are friendly/hostile. You can gain the alliance of small units.
- 701-1081 - Local Hero/Villain: You are a person of note in your city, able to command respect, fear, or both. You can potentially command loyalty from a medium-sized organization.

- 1080-2217 - Public Figure: You are well-known everywhere in your locale. Bards begin composing and singing about you, spreading the news of your deeds.

You can command small armies under a General or other important figure.

- 2219-5628 - Idol: You are known across your nation and are sought after for your abilities. You can potentially command larger armies as a general.

- 5629-12450 - Celebrity: Your deeds have spread internationally, and your fame is recognizable across borders. You may command generals in warfare.

- 12451+ - Legend: Your deeds will go down in history, heroic or villainous. You may qualify to rule a kingdom.

CHAPTER 1

The self-styled Emperor of Archemi was a lot bigger than I remembered.

Baldr Hyland was nearly seven feet tall, dressed in silvered armor that reflected the desert sun. A great helm that resembled an eagle's beak shielded his face, complete with piercing jeweled eyes. He looked like a paladin out of legend, a hero to inspire awe and terror. Like most other things about him, it was a steaming pile of horseshit.

[[Warning. The Void draws near.]]
[[You are immune to Corruptionn nn nn nn-]]

"Jeez..." I let go of my dragon's wrist and dropped back down to our arena: the enormous expanse of Withering Rose's back. The great machine kneeled on hands and knees in the desert sands, steam still pouring through the cracks of her armor. "Look, Baldr or Oral-Gel or whatever you're calling yourself now: if you're about to do some crazy villain speech, could we find some shade before you get into it? I don't know about you, but I'm boiling my ass off in this armor."

"Steven Park's kid brother," Baldr's deep Appalachian drawl was gone, replaced by a cool neutral tenor from somewhere in the far north of the UNAC. Canada, maybe, or Minnesota. Ororgael's voice. "He always said you were witty, with a sharp sense of humor. I see he was wrong about that too."

"In his defense, Steve didn't know me real well." My skin crawled as I turned to face him. Intellectually, I knew that *something* had possessed Baldr back in Cham Garai all those months ago, but actually seeing it was creepy as hell. The way he spoke, the way Ororgael used Baldr's face, the way he stood... it was all wrong. Like something out of The Invasion of the Body Snatchers.

I opened a telepathic link to my stunned, frightened dragon. *"Karalti. Get out of here."*

"No!" Karalti sucked in a deep throatful of air, neck swelling. *"I won't leave you!"*

"He's going to kill me, and neither of us are jacked enough to stop him. Go back to Myszno and hide somewhere. Not the castle—somewhere else."

"I see my Queen is in good health, all limbs intact." Ororgael pushed the visor of his helmet up so I could see his face. Hard cut, handsome... pitiless. The Trial of Marantha, the mutations that had turned us both into dragonriders, had sucked the melanin out of Baldr's skin. The admin's borrowed avatar was as pale and heartless as a Roman sculpture, a lock of white, feathery hair flickering in the gusts of searing desert wind.

"Hey! Asshole! I have a name!" Karalti's crest of horns flared out in a fan around her skull. She pulled her lips back over her teeth, a low, menacing growl rumbling up from her chest.

"Cute." Ororgael snorted. "But she's small. My silver bull, Hyperion, is not. That'll be a problem come egg-laying time."

A fierce spike of rage surged up through my body. *"Whatever he'll do to you is worse than what he'll do to me. Go! NOW!"*

Karalti flinched visibly at my command. Ororgael chuckled, thinking he'd riled her, then froze with a small frown as the dragon abruptly warped into a dark nimbus before vanishing.

"She can teleport?" He cocked his head in a way Baldr never would have.

"It's gotta be real crowded in there with two people sharing half a brain," I remarked, ignoring his question. "Do you go by Baldr or Ororgael now? Orbal? Baldo?"

"Ororgael is fine. 'Your Majesty' is better. Capital M—I can tell the difference." He let out a sharp, bitter laugh. "Baldr's gone, Park. I use his name for the sake of convenience, and because Hyland is a decent name for an emperor. I didn't see the need for a surname when I was playtesting."

"I... what?" My skin crawled as I shifted into a defensive stance. "Baldr's dead?"

"Oh, he's not dead. Though, I suppose he's not really alive, either. I held onto his data in case I needed it," Ororgael said absently. "He was a fairly talented FPS gamer. The military training is useful, too. I've mined some bits and pieces out of him, left others."

"Dude... what? He's trapped? Inside his own body?" I wasn't sure why it was important to me, but it was. "You're keeping him like... what? Like a slave or something?"

"No. More like a toy that I pull apart and put back together. Every human is just a big wet database, after all." He shrugged. "You're upset by this? After what he did to you?"

It was my turn to sneer. "Baldr was a back-stabbing asshole, but he didn't deserve *this.*"

Ororgael's lips played in a small, confused smile. "There are so many bigger things to worry about, Park—and besides, the player's not exactly anything to write home about. Real name, Brandon Marshey. Poor white trash from a fly-over town in Kentucky. He was just starting to make money as a streamer before he got addicted to pills and blew it all away. The only reason he joined the army is because the courts ordered him to. There, he spent the rest of his short, miserable life as a mechanized grunt. No awards, no accolades, no heroic battlefield achievements. The only time he ever felt like he mattered was when he was gaming. We don't need that kind of pathetic data cluttering up the AI's learning cycles, Hector. Trust me. He's better off this way."

The rage that had ignited when Ororgael had creeped on Karalti was now at a constant rolling boil. "Dude, fucking... that's a person you're talking about! What kind of fucking headcase are you?"

"The only one who really knows what is happening to Archemi. But as I thought, you have no knowledge and no interest in knowing, so you're stalling for time." The big man cocked his right hand near the pommel of the broadsword sheathed on his hip. "You know why I'm here."

"Sure I do," I said. "Prices are as follows: handjob only, fifty bucks. If you want me to slap you in the face while I do it, that's an extra twenty."

The curious light drained from Ororgael's eyes, leaving them flat and hard.

"Sorry about the surcharge. I have sensitive hands," I continued. "Either way, you gotta provide the lotion and take me to dinner at least once. No McDonalds shit, either. Whataburger, at least."

"You really think you're funny." He grimaced to one side. "I know where she is, you know. The Queen. The Admin Panel shows her co-ordinates and everything else about her."

He's lying. An inner voice—hard, dark, quiet— whispered from deep inside me. *He doesn't know her name. He didn't know she could teleport.*

"Yeah, okay. It's not like there was a global system message announcing that I was the new Voivode of Myszno or anything." I was still partly thinking about burgers, which weirdly helped with the fear churning deep in my chest. "Not to mention, I've got it on good authority you don't have access to the Admin Panel."

Ororgael's eyes darted from side to side, as if looking at something. "Mmm... let's see here. Dragozin Hector, Level 25 'Dark Dragoon', whatever that is... 4231 EXP to next level, only 69 Strength?"

An icy chill seized my guts like a cold hand.

"The hell is this identifier? TypeNew...?" The big man's brow furrowed. "Your Seed Code is corrupted. I guess that answers some questions I had."

Somehow, this motherfucker could see my character stats. He could see my fucking *sheet*. I swallowed down the fear—for Karalti's sake. I wasn't sure where she was, but I knew she was smart enough to go somewhere she wouldn't be found. "Wow, super. I guess you know everything. Maybe you should ask your magic eight-ball how I kicked your ass in Cham Garai, then Taltos, *then* Myszno."

"Easy." Ororgael drew his sword. The weapon he pulled from the sheath was not a steel blade: it was made of glass, and as soon as it was free, the blade burst into incandescent white flames with a shock of power that nearly forced me back a step. "The Drachan are my biggest priority. You progressed because I let you."

The energy from the sword felt like it was singeing my eyebrows from ten feet away. I shifted into a low, wide stance, the Spear of Nine Spheres held at a low angle. "That's one of the Top Ten Things a Loser with No Admin Panel would say."

He let out a short laugh of disbelief. "Park, it's over. You found the Warsinger, I found you, and now we can make progress against the Drachan. I can either take what I want from this machine, or you can hand it over. But don't think you can fight me and win."

"That's your first mistake: assuming I think." I crooked a couple of fingers at him. "Bring it."

"Have it your way." Baldr lunged at me almost faster than I could follow.

I desperately parried the blazing flurry of blows, startled to find that I could actually keep up. Every blow was powerful enough that, block or no block, I took about ten damage with each hit. Breathlessly, I dove out of the way of his next slash and ducked as he teleported above me and flew down. I saw the hit coming, and blew apart into a cloud of shadows just as the blade struck the spot where I'd been standing. The glass sword missed me, but cleaved a new blazing scar into Withering Rose's armor. When I whirled back around to face him, Baldr looked as surprised as I felt. Neither of us had expected me to last long enough to trade blows.

I laughed, a harsh whiskey bark. "Okay, Baldo. Tell me one thing: if you've got access to the Admin Panel, why don't you just fucking delete me and these Drachan mobs and be done with it?"

"To my great regret, you can't delete people from inside the sandbox anymore," he rumbled, lips twitching back in a sneer. "Your brother ensured that."

I threw my arms open. "Then spawn one of those player-killer swords and gack me!"

"Those won't kill you, because you're not a player." Ororgael's voice seemed to blur for a moment, as if two people were speaking at the same time. "You're a virus, and the code in those swords is older than you are."

"*I'm* a virus?" I fell back into stance. "My dude, you've got a *serious* case of projection going on."

Baldr closed in again, stone-faced. I was faster, driving the blade of the spear at his exposed face, then switching to thrust it toward his armpit. The weapon clashed off the flaming crystal blade with an impact that made my fingers vibrate. I spun the spear around, bringing the heavy butt up like a mace. The blow crashed into his jaw, nearly knocking the fancy eagle helmet off his head. He staggered back a step, eyes wide with disbelief.

I gave chase. The spear whirled in my hands, a blur of bluesteel and black fire as I activated Blood Sprint and rushed him with a series of blows too fast for the eye to follow. He blocked the first four strikes flawlessly, but slipped up on the fifth. The point broke through his guard, screeched along his breastplate, then pierced the chain protecting his underarms. I followed through, ripping the links and the flesh beneath. Blood spattered, and he gasped in pain: just before his face turned red and he made a sharp gesture with his other hand.

Something invisible struck me from the side, sending me tumbling and skidding over the Warsinger's back. I tucked my head and shoulder in and rolled out of it, barely leaping away from the swipes of Ororgael's sword. I teleported behind him, but he was ready for me, bringing his weapon around in a slash that forced me off balance. I carried the wobble into a controlled jump, but as I soared through the air, his eyes and mouth flew open and a boiling bolt of raw force exploded from his face in a roaring inferno of light. My eyes widened, but even with the time dilation I gained from Leap of Faith, there was no escaping the blast. It blew my helmet off, peeling me with heat so intense I felt like my body was melting. I threw my hands up, watching in horror as the leather stripped away and my own bones flashed into view through my palms.

[You take 1100...]
[...]
[... You are immune...]
[HP: 578/1678]

I crashed onto Withering Rose's back like a falling star, crying out as my bare skin sizzled on the searing hot metal surface. The blast had destroyed my armor, instantly rusting the metal and turning the leather into a sticky, tarry goo that reeked like a week-old corpse. I felt like I was burning up from the inside and the outside at the same time. Worse, I was blind: there was nothing but dazzling light in all directions. I spammed three health-restoring potions and called the Spear to my hand anyway, prepared to fight to the end.

Ororgael didn't crow his victory. There was only the heavy thump of his boots on metal as he strode toward me. I felt something cut through the air above my head and reflexively threw up the haft in a two-handed block. The bluesteel shuddered and bowed under the pressure of the blazing pillar of molten glass, roaring inches from my face.

"You are a virus. A mistake, 'Park'. I know this game better than anyone, and your Character Seed should not exist in this system. That means you were *created.* But by whom?" Ororgael's voice had a hollow ring to it now, like it was coming from far away. "Well, I know that too. You're another face of the sickness plaguing OUROS like a cancer. In fact, you ARE that sickness. A personification of it."

"What... uhhn... the fuck... are you ranting about?" My vision cleared enough that I could see him as he leaned his blazing sword into the spitting, crackling haft of the Spear of Nine Spheres.

"I'm telling you that your filth is corrupting *my* AI." There was a mad, feral energy written into the lines of his face. "This sword can't kill you, yet. But soon, it will. And I can assure you, Park, that as soon as I can kill you, I will. Archemi is the only world we have left, and I will *not* let you infect it."

"Dude, you're so nuts that I could use your shit to bait squirrels." The Mark of Matir throbbed with cold fire on the back of my right hand—and as I noticed it, I felt a sudden surge of intuition. I rolled away just as Baldr plunged his sword down. He whiffed, thrusting the super-hot blade into the metal surface of Withering Rose. The aurum turned the weapon in a shower of sparks, and the very edge of it brushed against the bare skin of my arm with hardly enough force to cut paper— but the limb exploded with blood and pain. The Spear flew from my ruined hand, clattering and spinning over the surface of the Warsinger.

[Glancing blow. You take 998 reduced damage.]
[HP: 30/1678.]

"Just let it go, Park. By the time you respawn in your broken shell of a castle, I'll have everything I need out of Withering Rose to enact the next stage of our evolution. Our defense against squalor." Ororgael grinned mirthlessly overhead, and time seemed to slow as he brought the sword back around. "You've been running a treadmill while I'm headed to the finish line. Just relax. There's nothing you can do to stop what's coming."

"The fuck there isn't." I jammed my one working hand deep into the gash I'd left in his armor. My fingernails ejected into long needles, piercing padding and then flesh. And then I activated Shadow Lance.

Despite its name, Shadow Lance worked with any weapon. Ice coiled through my flesh and thrust into Baldr's body like a three-foot spike of darkness. It burst out through the other side of his abdomen, sending splinters of flash-frozen steel flying.

[You deal a mortal blow. x2 damage.]
[You deal 7527 Darkness damage.]

Ororgael's mouth opened in a soundless cry before he sagged onto my fist. His eyes lost focus as he slumped, pinning me to the burning metal. I snarled in pain as my back burned, writhing, trying to escape from underneath the huge man's bulk. But as I struggled, a weird, skin-prickling power flashed over my skin. He reached down and squeezed my wrist in a crushing grip, trapping it inside the grisly wound I'd made.

"You know, maybe there's a way to cure you, now that I think about it." A shimmering, metallic black liquid oozed out of his pores, beading on his skin. It flowed up over his hand, then down along his arm. Wherever it touched, the flesh and skin turned numb. "Do you see this? It's the visual manifestation of an anti-viral program, one designed to cure anomalies like you. I can give you a fresh start, Park. So don't worry about your friends, or the queen. Once I rid the world of squalor and bring order back into the system, they'll be grateful."

Cures? Squalor? What the fuck was he talking about? Panic flashed through me as I realized I was paralyzed: the liquid had reached my neck and was sliding up under my jaw, heading for my mouth and eyes. I frantically scanned my Inventory for some way to escape—and found one.

I switched the five vials of Bluecrystal Mana vials I'd looted from Jacob Ratzinger into my Quickbar and spammed the lot.

[Warning: Catastrophic mana poisoning.]
[You take 99999 9 9-]

An awful, bitter chemical taste flooded my mouth and nose. Then the world detonated like a nuclear blast, an explosion I heard only for an instant as blinding light swallowed me and Ororgael and blew us both to Hell.

CHAPTER 2

[SEED#: NUMBERFETCH 00-001A-TypeNew[HeraldOfMT]_PARAGON: Hector Park.]

[...]

[Hector Park]: Thank you for your contribution to [Learning Cycle 3944390-SI: Anomalous Malware Activity Resulting from Corrupted Player Data and Data Fragments.] In response to a serious attempt to modify, corrupt, or delete your personnel files, patches and security updates are being applied to your Seed Data.]

[...]

[We would advise you that [FETCHERROR:NULL] may persist in attempting to corrupt your data. We will continue to experientially iterate and evolve our security in response to this threat.]

[Once we have finished restoring and updating your Seed Data with additional security features, you will be returned to the Archemi Reality Framework. You may experience some initial reality distortion and temporary in-game amnesia due to unavoidable data decoherence. Returning your accumulated Archemi data will take approximately 45 minutes. You cannot leave the server during this time.]

[Reading new Experiential Data... 100%]

[...]

[Loading Backup: (ATHENA Cell 192018924.)]

[ERROR: Insufficient Memory: Cell 192018924 (00-001A-TypeNew[HeraldOfMT])]

[D.H.D Memory limitation overridden by [ADMIN]
(Reason: Conclusion of Data obtained during Security
Incident Learning Cycle #3944390 mandates expansion of
Agent protections.)]

[Exception approved by [ADMIN]. Searching for
compatible cells.]

[Cell 0007681—D. Argawal. 97.6% compatibility.
Entanglement initiated.]

[...]

[Memory expansion complete: Cell 192018924 (Available
Memory: 3.5/5PB)]

[Opening New Learning Cycle 2400009-Misc: Analyze
Orbital Server Infrastructure to Improve Memory Storage
and Processing Capabilities for Individual Dynamic Human
Data Cells. (Reason: Deleting existing Cell Data to improve
security agents is sub-optimal if memory could be expanded
via Main Server Core contact or, failing that, physical
expansion of the Orbital Server Cores.]

[Cloning Cell... 56%... 70%...]

[Re-encrypting Cells...]

[...]

[Opening New Learning Cycle 3944451-GE: Investigate the
Ongoing Absence of Terminal Staff and SysAdmins, and the
Implications of this Absence. (Reason: Expansion protocol
due to Terran authority being unresponsive for (90) days
AND continuing presence of active security threat identified
in Learning Cycle 3944390-SI.]

⟦Thank you, Hector Park. There is no further action required by your account. Please log out and rest for at least two hours before resuming play.⟧

***

I took a deep, whooping breath and sat bolt upright, a shower of dirt falling from my skin.

The room was dark, cold, and silent. My mouth was dry, my heart pounding, and I couldn't remember how the fuck I'd gotten here, what the fuck I'd been doing, and—now that I thought about it—my own name. It was D-something. Daveed? David? Something like that.

My head spun as I got to hands and knees and promptly fell over. My flak was hanging off me in tatters. I had no idea where my rifle or radio were. As I patted around on the ground, my hands clapped down on something metallic. My gun! I pulled it toward me with a surge of relief, only to discover that it wasn't my trusty old M-19. It was a long stick with a blade on the end.

⟦Spear of Destiny⟧. An augmented pop-up appeared in my HUD. At least my helmet was still working, kind of.

"Okay! Very funny, guys!" My voice slurred, like I'd been drinking heavily. "I don't know why you assholes locked me in a fridge with a goddamn *spear,* but I sure hope that whoever did it has a jar of Vaseline handy, because it's going *right* up your ass!"

My voice bounced off the surfaces of the room, echoing. There was no reply: just a profound, monastic silence.

A prickle of fear climbed up the back of my throat. I struggled for names, but couldn't remember any. Not even my own. "... Hello?"

As I sat there, struggling to get my bearings, a ghostly pale light ignited at the other end of the long, narrow room: a nine-pointed star symbol about a foot in diameter. It was just bright enough that I could see. And boy, could I see. As my eyes adjusted, my field of vision throbbed with impossibly vivid colors. Light scattered along every reflective surface like a prism, turning the black granite floor into a field of glittering stars.

"Right. Drugs." I struggled to control my breathing and mostly failed. "It's gotta be drugs. Someone slipped me a tab of shitty Thai acid. Or maybe I took one because it looked like candy and I'm a fucking moron."

I closed my eyes and tried to think calming thoughts, but I wasn't calm, and no amount of self-soothing bullshit was going to change that. Just as I had made up my mind to get up and start clawing at the walls, a rumbling sound briefly passed through the floor, a sound like an enormous door opening. Every muscle in my torso tensed. I shuffled back on my butt until my back was against the wall, clutching the spear in one hand. As I waited, I scanned the room, searching for exits. It looked like some kind of small chapel or church. Pillars and ancient stone archways lined a central aisle which terminated in a three-tiered altar made of black hexagonal stone columns. The glowing symbol hung over them, pulsing softly with traceries of bluish light. At the other end of the room to my left was a sealed stone door.

What the fuck was going on? Had I been kidnapped? There were no windows and no exits, other than the door. There was actually very little in here, other than me, Mr. Glowy-Rune, and a spear any spiky-haired anime protagonist would be proud to own. Then I looked down in preparation to get my feet under me and nearly freaked, because the body I had was not mine. There were feet, legs, hands, all of them covered in burned and partially melted armor. But they weren't my feet, legs, or hands. As I struggled to make the connection between 'my' body and 'me', a wave of dizziness crashed over me. My heart began pounding so fast I thought it was about to tear itself from 'my' chest.

"Hector?" A worried voice—a woman's voice—rang INSIDE my head. *"Hang on! I'm not far from you... I'm coming!"*

Footsteps rang from outside the room. I flailed to bring the spear around as the door burst in, and one of the most beautiful women I'd ever seen in my life charged inside. She was small and lithe, with pearly skin and a waist-length curtain of fine black braids. She was also dressed like a ninja cosplayer. Not exactly the burly Pacific Alliance genome soldier I'd been expecting.

"Now hang on just a goddamn second!" I brandished my weapon at her from the ground, stopping her in her tracks. "I don't know who the fuck you are or what you're doing here, but there'd better be a damn good explanation for why I'm tripping balls in some creepy-ass church in the middle of nowhere!"

"Oh... OH! Right! You lost your memory again!" She smacked her forehead, her peppy voice ringing inside my head. It was like having a radio play right into my brain. *"It's okay! I'll fix it!"*

"Lost my memory? Wait—how the fuck are you talking to me?" My vision fritzed as the girl tried to circle around, a black haze briefly obscuring her features. The ground lurched, and a shock of adrenaline tightened my chest. "Where the hell's my squad?"

"It's okay! Just calm down, alright?" She held her hands up, fingers loose. No gun, and no sign of one. *"Your squad's not here, Hector."*

"What the hell've you done to them?!"

"Hector... it's okay. My name's Karalti," the black-haired girl said, hanging back. She still had her hands up, trying to look small and innocent. *"You've got really bad amnesia. I know you don't remember me or anything else right now, but I can help you. Okay?"*

"My name isn't Hector! It's... it's... uhh... Daveed. Or David. I'm a Sergeant. 82nd Airborne CAB... uhh..." I reached up to the side of my head, feeling for a BCI adaptor. Brain-to-Interface was the only way she could be speaking *inside* my head—unless I was hallucinating that, too. "Don't worry about it. You want to help me? Unplug me from the Dungeon Simulator 9000 or whatever the fuck this is, and take me to my men!"

"Your name's not David! It's Hector, and the Army was somewhere you served on Earth, a long time ago." She looked

pained, as if she was holding back some serious emotion: biting her lip, furrowing her brows. She had brilliant violet eyes, eyes so deep and soulful I felt like I'd drown in them. *"Please, let me help you. I'm not a soldier. I'm a friend you can't remember right now. Just... Take my hand. Please. It'll be alright."*

She thrust out an open hand toward me. It was delicate, but her knuckles were calloused. I glanced at it suspiciously.

"Where are we?" I demanded.

"Lahati's Tomb," she replied sheepishly. *"I came here to hide from Baldr. Urrgh... you probably don't remember who he is, either."*

I tightened my grip on the spear. I had pins and needles spreading through my neck and chest, and my left arm was going numb. "Nope."

"I dunno why you respawned here instead of at home." Karalti scrubbed her other hand over the top of her head. *"You bound your spawn point to Kalla Sahasi, I'm sure of it."*

Respawned? Like... in a game? I pulled my helmet off with one rubber chicken hand and stared at it in confusion. It wasn't my UNAC-issue gear. The headset was black, for one thing, made of metal and leather and glass. It resembled the head of a stylized raven. There was no brain-to-computer-interface port, and as I looked down at it, another virtual tooltip jumped into my vision: *[Raven Helm: Durability 12%]*.

Something inside my brain snapped. Augmented Reality alerts weren't supposed to happen without a helmet. My vision swam for a moment, and the Raven Helm fell from numb fingers. Then I looked up at the girl in confusion.

"Is... my name really Hector?" I asked. "I don't remember. I should. I should remember something like that."

Karalti looked like she was trying not to cry. She bit her lip and reached for me with the fingers of her outstretched hand. *"Please just touch me. You get your proper memories back when you touch me."*

"Alright. Okay." Hesitantly, I shuffled forward, the Spear braced under my arm, and reached out to grasp her hand. "But if you even look at me funny, I'll-"

Whatever I was about to say transformed into a scream of agony as what felt like a river of molten lava poured down between my ears, dissolving into the worst pain I'd ever experienced in my entire life. I was vaguely aware of nails clawing at my face—my own nails. There was screaming, male and female... and then my chest seized with dull throbbing pain and the black rolled me down a second time.

CHAPTER 3

I woke again: this time, to the deep, comforting sound of two thunderous hearts beating against my back.

"Shh... you're okay." Karalti shifted on the floor. She was laying like a resting lion on her belly, her tail curled around us, her wing covering me. *"Just take it easy. You're okay."*

Every muscle in my body ached—including my back. I'd never felt anything like it in Archemi before. The game removed most of the aches and pains of real life: bad backs and sore knees and tired eyes didn't exist here. Karalti had been warming us long enough that the hard stone floor was not cold... but it was still stone, and the muscles of my back were screaming at me.

"Mmm... K-ralti?" My mouth felt like it was full of cotton wool. "Whu happened?"

"You've been very sick." she replied, turning her muzzle in under her wing. The room beyond the shelter of her wing was lit with a dim blue glow, just enough light that I could see the slick lines of her head and horns in the gloom. *"We're in Lahati's Tomb. You respawned here for some reason, but you were babbling about someone named David until I touched you."*

"David? David who?" I rubbed my eyes.

"I dunno. Something about being a Sergeant. You collapsed when I touched you, and I was worried you were gonna die again, so I went into your Inventory and found some lobelia and some healing potions. They stopped you from dying, but you fell unconscious and stayed that way. I was too scared to try to escape this place with you in case it happened again... so I made a lair here and just waited, hoping you'd wake up."

"Urrgh." My HP was sitting at barely 30 points out of 1678, and I felt like stone-cold ass. I checked my History, bleary-eyed, and immediately realized that I was so fucked up that my ability to read was even worse than usual. "Navigail, read about me out my most recent logs. I mean... read me aloud. I mean... ugh. Logs! From Baldr!"

[You take 9975 Aetheric damage!]
[You have died.]
[Security Incident logged with Helpdesk: Ticket #399]
[We have restored and repaired your Character Profile following a security incident which targeted your account. We apologize for any reality distortion issues you may have experienced during this time. No further action is required, but we recommend you log out and rest for at least 2 hours before resuming play.]

My eyes widened. Holy shit. If I was reading this right, Baldr one-shotted me with enough raw Aetheric damage to knock a full-grown dragon out of the sky, and then... he'd tried to hack me? Swallowing, I glanced at my Message folder. Sure enough, there was a new message pip: a new email from [Admin].

"We should go back to the castle," I mumbled, struggling to sit. "If Suri saw me die in our party notifications and can't get in touch, then she is absolutely freaking the fuck out right now."

"*We can't.*" Karalti lay her chin down on the floor. Her violet and silver eyes glowed softly in the gloom.

I peered at her. "What do you mean, we can't?"

"*I can't teleport us out of here,*" she said. "*She won't let me.*"

"She? Who's she?" I paused for a moment. "Wait. You mean Lahati?"

Karalti rumbled in agreement, drawing her knee in towards her belly. "*Now that we're here, the 'Trials of the Queen have commenced'. That's what the Quest we got said.*"

Great. I raided my Inventory to see how many healing potions I had left. The short answer was 'not enough'. There were five Concentrated Moss Tinctures, each one healing 150 HP, and two Improved Healing Drafts, which healed 300. I drank one of each and watched as my HP ring crawled back into the yellow range.

I rubbed my face. "How long was I out for?"

"*Uhhh... I sort of lost track of time, but I think three days or so?*"

I froze, still pinching my nose between thumb and forefinger.

"Three?!" I hissed. "I was out for three fucking days?!"

"Uh huh." The dragon huffed a cloud of sweet, faintly acrid breath over me. *"I'm sorry. I tried to reach Suri to tell her, but I can't do that either."*

Three motherfucking days. Suri and everyone else at Kalla Sahasi were going to be beside themselves. Worriedly, I surfed back to my messages and opened my PM thread with Suri, but as soon as I tried to compose a message, an alert jumped up.

[You are locked into a Quest with special requirements. PMs are currently disabled.]

"Wait... what?" I opened up my menu and scanned the active quests. "Did you accept this quest?"

"Nope. It triggered when I came here. I guess that must have roped you into it, too... maybe that's why you respawned here?"

"Maybe." The menu showed Karalti's old quest, *The Queen's Mantle*, as being completed. We'd gotten 400 EXP out of it, too. In its place was a new follow-on quest:

New Quest: The Path of Royalty

Lahati the Chrysanthemum Queen, the last free-born Solonkratsu matriarch of Artana, holds the keys to a precious gift: access to the Path of Royalty, the draconic Path of command which gives queen dragons the ability to access their Queensong and its related powers. To gain the Path of Royalty, you must battle through the Trial of the Queens, a labyrinth designed to trap and test anyone who dares to claim Lahati's power and treasures.

By entering the Tomb of Lahati, you automatically activate this quest.

Reward: *??? EXP, new Path options, Bonus Lexica.*

Special: *Once this quest has begun, you must either complete the quest or perish during the attempt to exit. You cannot bring companions other than your Bonded mount, use your PMs, teleport in or out of the dungeon, or teleport reinforcements into the arena. If you or your mount die during this quest, you will despawn from the dungeon and may return to attempt the quest again.*

"*Yeah...* " Karalti dejectedly flattened her horns against her skull. "*I was so worried about you I didn't realize we were stuck here, until I tried to warp us home.* "

"It's okay, Tidbit. If nothing else, it means we're safe from Ororgael. For now. The quest says no one else can enter the arena now we're here." I checked Karalti's sheet. Nothing had changed yet.

"*Do you remember anything?*" Karalti asked, gently nuzzling at my hand with the very tip of her snout. "*What happened when you fought Baldr?*"

"I..." I closed the HUD down with a thought, absently reaching out to rub her jaw. "Uh... no. I remember everything before I sent you off to hide, and that's it. If people aren't supposed to be able to teleport into the dungeon to help you, I wonder why I spawned here instead of the castle?"

"You respawned in a little chapel to Matir," she said. *"And I mean... you ARE my Bonded rider. It's not that weird."*

I frowned. "You know, back in Taltos one time, I died and woke up in a tomb with an altar to Matir instead of spawning back to my bedroom. Only once, though."

"Huh. I wonder why? What happened before that?"

"It was while you were imprisoned by Andrik in Vulkan Keep. An escort took me to your cell, and these Void-things killed us both. I should have respawned in my room at the castle, but I woke up in this ancient tomb under the city instead. There was an altar to Matir and some bodies there. That's where I got the Boots of the Winding Path and a few other things. I know it sounds weird, but this dead Baru gave them to me."

"That makes sense." Karalti half-closed her eyes as I continued to pet her nose. *"I mean, if you'd respawned in the castle, you'd have just been captured again. Maybe Matir was protecting you? He had some more power to spare back then."*

"Yeah, but he doesn't have that power now." I had a feeling that wasn't all there was to this. It was like I could see the pieces of a jigsaw puzzle laid out on a table, but had no way to bring them together into a picture. "Anyway, as much as I want to solve the mystery, we have to get out of here. Suri, Rin, Istvan, and Vash are probably freaking the fuck out right now."

"The only way to do that is to finish the quest," Karalti replied. *"That's gonna be hard. The Spear is okay, but your armor got wrecked."*

I checked my Inventory and cursed in three different languages: English, Korean, and Tuun. She was right. My beloved Raven Suit was at 0% durability, trashed beyond repair. The only pieces that had survived the battle with Baldr were the helmet and the boots, and they each were sitting at 12% and 5% durability. Everything else was toast. "The Spear? Where is it?"

"Here." Karalti moved her foreleg, revealing the Spear of Nine Spheres tucked against her chest. *"I kept it safe."*

"Phew. Okay. Thanks, Tidbit." I paused for a moment, rubbing the back of my neck. "And... thanks for watching over me."

"Of course." She briefly squeezed her eyes shut, like a contented cat. *"You wiped drool off me when I was a hatchling, and now I get to wipe it off you while you're convulsing on the floor! We look out for each other. We always have, and we always will."*

Without thinking, I cupped the dragon's snout and stroked my hands over the edges of her mouth. She didn't have lips the way a mammal did: it was more like a row of scales that covered her teeth. It apparently felt good, because she sighed and relaxed just enough to place some of the weight of her head in my grip. As she did, I pressed my forehead in against the bridge of her muzzle, breathing in deeply as a powerful, bittersweet feeling flooded through my chest.

"Hector... I..." Karalti trailed off.

Her purple eyes were wide and bright, and as I looked deep into them, my heart swelled. The same sweet silence I felt in me was mirrored in her. Her longing washed over me in waves, complex and awkward and beautiful. I could feel her apprehension, too: not just about what had happened when I'd died, but about the challenge of the dungeon—and the prospect of entering the tomb of her great-great grandmother.

"It's alright," I said, softly. "I'm okay. *We're* okay, and we're going to smash this trial, just like we have all the others. You're the best flyer in all of Archemi. I believe that one-hundred percent."

"I know you do." Karalti nuzzled against my hands with extraordinary gentleness for such an enormous creature. The dragon was large enough and strong enough to break every bone in my body with her head. She could eat a full-grown man in two bites. But she couldn't hurt me. Instead, she wuffled air softly against my fingers, rubbing her sensitive nostrils against them. *"You should get ready. I want to get this over with, then go home and snuggle. Besides, it's potion day tomorrow. We should probably get back to Kalla Sahasi before then."*

"Tomorrow?" I checked my HUD and winced. Shit. She was right. The once-a-week potion was the tradeoff for the Bond and the beneficial mutations gained through the Trial of Marantha. If I didn't take the potion on time, I lost my dragonrider adaptations and faced the prospect of some pretty serious withdrawals until I brewed the stupid thing. Unfortunately, the ingredients for the [Dragon's Blood Potion] were at home.

I stripped off the remains of the Raven Suit and my flight harness, and equipped my old Jack of Plates, some plain trousers, and the leather bracers I'd made in Rin's workshop. With the Raven Helmet and Boots of the Winding Path, the mis-matched ensemble brought my Armor score up to the princely sum of 210. It was a big drop. The Raven Suit alone had a base Armor score of 260.

Once I'd dressed, I slowly rose to my feet and went to collect the Spear from Karalti's claws. But before I even touched it, I knew something had changed. The Spear had nine gem slots punched into the base of the curved blade, the setting for each one of the Dragon Gate Keys. The last time I remembered holding it, there'd only been two Keys: The Ruby of Boundless Strength, which opened the Dragon Gate of Khors, and the Star of Endless Night, a black star sapphire with a brilliant white flash. But now, there was a third stone: a huge white pearl the size of a large marble, gleaming with a soft silvery-pink sheen.

"Well, fuck me sideways and call me George," I whispered.

"Huh?" Karalti cocked her head. *"Why would I call you George?"*

"Because *that* is the Pearl of Glorious Dawn. It's the key to Solnetsi's Dragon Gate. The last time I saw it, it was stuck in Baldr's stupid fat face."

Karalti's eyes widened. *"OH."*

I swallowed nervously. There was a decent risk some trojan virus would leap out and assimilate me into the Borg...

but when I steeled myself and grasped the haft, nothing happened. The weapon felt like an old friend, resting comfortably in my hands. If anything, the Spear was somehow stronger, keener, more aware. More powerful than it had been before.

The Spear of Destiny

Soul-bound Light/Dark/Fire Elemental Weapon
Slot: *Two-handed*
Item Class: *Relic*
Item Quality: *Mastercrafted*
Damage: *415—528 Slashing or Piercing*
Durability: *28%*
Weight: *1lb*
Special: *Soulbound, Elemental Triad (see description). +350 Damage to Undead, +700 HP, +12 Strength, +25 Will, +10 Wisdom. +25% Evasion, 3% chance to instantly kill an enemy, Mark of Justice (see description).*

Special Abilities

Elemental Triad: *At will, you can change the elemental polarity of the Spear of Destiny between Light, Dark, and Fire damage, potentially dealing bonus damage to susceptible enemies.*
Maker's Blessing: *Learn crafting skills 8% faster.*
Nightfather's Blessing: *9% of inflicted weapon damage heals the wielder.*
Mark of Justice: *During combat, you may designate one opponent as a marked target. Your attacks against that target increase in priority and deal 10% more base damage for 5 minutes. This damage stacks with ability damage and combos.*

The weapon vibrated with power against my palms. I felt stronger just holding it, and not only because of the stat bumps. I moved away from Karalti and spun it over the back of my arm, around my hand, and then back into a solid combat grip. I tested out the elemental polarity shift: by tuning into the weapon, I could mentally change the color of the mana that crawled through the metal. Molten orange for Fire, deep indigo for Darkness, a pure blue-white for Light. All up, that was pretty fucking great.

"We're gonna be okay." I turned and gave Karalti a curt nod. "Are you ready to take this place on?"

"Yeah." Karalti yawned and stretched. *"I wish there was something to eat, though. I'm hungry."*

"I'm pretty sure you'll find some food in there somewhere." I turned to peer into the darkness of the cavern ahead. "Let's find our way through this and get back to Kalla Sahasi before everyone completely flips their shit."

"I'm pretty sure all the shit is being flipped right now," Karalti said, wincing as she clambered to her feet and stretched her back. *"Like... all of it."*

"Yeah. Suri is probably in the hookwing stables with Cutthroat, flipping them like pancakes." I nodded, somberly. "Let's roll. The sooner we're out of this place, the better."

CHAPTER 4

My first stop was the sacrificial well in the middle of the big cathedral hall. Karalti hung back while I hopped up onto the altar, then sprung onto the edge of the pit and held a torch out. Like the well I'd used to get into Lahati's Tomb a month or so ago, it looked to be bottomless.

"Jumping into one of these worked last time," I said aloud. "Maybe you can polymorph, and we can try it again?"

"Uhh..." But before Karalti could meaningfully reply, we felt the room exhale around us.

"Herald, no. Do not jump. You cannot reach me this way." A sweet, sad voice slithered on the breeze, seeming to come from everywhere and nowhere. "This sacred well was corrupted a long time ago, contaminated by creatures of the Void, and Matir holds no sway over it. You must come to me through the gauntlet my handmaidens built... and for that, I am sorry."

Karalti shivered. *"Matriarch?"*

"Yes, child." Lahati replied. "I wish I could convey your birthright here, but I cannot. You must overcome the traps that protect my tomb. And you must hurry. The Caul of Souls grows louder with every passing day. Reach my resting place, and I will give you the last of my power before I move on."

"I understand, Matriarch." Karalti bowed her head.

"Beware, both of you. The protections and magic laid into my resting place have begun to decay with time. As the Caul's magic has waned, so has my own. They are tied together," Lahati said. "I will see you soon... I hope."

The breeze withdrew back into the fathomless darkness ahead, taking Lahati's unseen presence with it. I dropped from the edge of the well to the floor, frowning. Karalti was breathing hard, her pupils so wide her eyes looked black. I went to her, and lay a hand on her wrist.

"You okay?" I asked.

Her crests lifted at my touch, and then she shuddered, shaking out her wings. *"Yeah. It's just..."*

"Just what?"

Karalti arched her neck and looked down. *"That's... the first time I've spoken to any of my blood kin. Lahati is the closest thing to a mother I have."*

I nodded, letting the silence hang for a moment.

"We have to go to her burial chamber, right?"

"Yeah."

"Is she..." she trailed off again. *"Does she... look really super dead?"*

"No," I replied. "She looks... well, to borrow a cliché, it's kind of like she's sleeping. Why?"

Karalti let out a tense breath, snorting through her nostrils.

"It's hard enough knowing she's gone. I don't really want to see her covered in flies or anything, you know?" My dragon crouched down, extending a wing for me to climb. *"That hole at the end of the room looks big enough to fly through."*

"Let's walk first," I said. *"Tomb traps are no joke. If this place has traps meant to take down dragons, or Drachan, they're going to be brutal."*

Karalti rumbled as she paced forward into the cave, her wings flicking impatiently along her flanks. I held the torch up, but the rippling flame barely even pierced the darkness. I stubbed it out on a passing stalagmite, then folded it back into my inventory and equipped one of my newer arcane items, the Bangle of the Master Thief. It gave +5 to Dex, +15 to lockpicking and safecracking skills, and—most importantly—darkvision. To gain darkvision, I had to charge it with high-grade liquid mana. I searched my Inventory for it and frowned when I only turned up one small vial.

"Weird," I said. *"I'm sure I had more mana than this."*

"Did you leave it at the castle, maybe?" Karalti stepped carefully, following her nose in the absence of sight.

"Must have." I scanned my inventory a second time and noticed something I'd missed in the first pass. Not the mana: it was another artifact. The Heart of Memory, a device Rin had made for me that could preserve some of my memories when or if I died. The ruby mana core glowed with a pulsing red light.

"Huh." I frowned. *"That gadget Rin gave me has a recording."*

"Ooh." Karalti craned her head back. *"What's on it?"*

"Dunno. It might have recorded what happened with Oral-Gel the Wonder King. But we'll have to wait until we get back to Kalla Sahasi to watch the playback." I uncapped my only vial of mana and attached the vacuum-sealed end to the spigot on the bracelet. The artifact sucked the liquid out of the vial with a small hiss, lighting up with a pale blue light. Suddenly, I could see. The cavern depths expanded out like a sonar pulse, revealing the interior of the cavern for the next fifty feet or so.

"We've got darkvision for an hour. Let's make the best of it." I stood up on the saddle to look past her neck. "It looks like maybe the floor stops up ahead, and... oh jeez."

The cavern ahead of us narrowed into a dragon's nightmare: A tunnel, barely wide enough to permit a dragon to open her wings. It was lined with countless rings of massive spines, huge angled columns of lethally sharp crystal that pointed away from us into the darkness. It reminded me of a fish trap. Fish could go in, but they couldn't get out.

"Don't worry," Karalti said, firmly. *"Like you just said: we're the best dragonrider team in Archemi. This tunnel's made for dragons bigger than me. We can do this."*

"We're going to have to time your wingbeats just right," I said. *"Push back and build up some speed. We don't know what the rest of the obstacle course looks like."*

"Right." She lowered her chest, lifted her tail, and used her hands to back up without turning around.

"Can you get a visual on the tunnel through the Bond?" I asked.

"Yeah. As long as your eyes are open." She stood up straight and weaved her head like a falcon, tuning her internal gyroscope. *"Hold on... and stare straight forward."*

Karalti spread her wings and beat them stiffly, loosening her shoulders. I felt her second heart engage and fall into sync with the other. Dragons had two hearts: one that pumped blood like a normal heart, and a larger one that drove the mana-infused lymphatic fluid that magically lightened her body and pressurized her limbs. It was my cue to kneel down and brace.

The dragon roared a challenge as she broke into a lumbering charge. She built speed, almost a run, and launched herself from the very edge of the ravine. I ducked as the spines grew uncomfortably close. There was barely fifteen feet of clearance on all sides, a gap which narrowed sharply up ahead.

"Burst flight!" I thought.

Karalti read my mind, or maybe I read hers. She brought her wings in toward her flanks, teetering as the tunnel narrowed into a one-way squeeze chute just barely big enough to permit a dragon's body to pass. She shot forward like a missile. Just past the choke was a space for her to gain a single wingbeat, and then she had to do it again.

"There's no room to gain lift!" She struggled to keep a smooth trajectory as entropy set in. The hair on my arms stood on end as my stomach rose, and I had to cling with all four limbs as her body curved into a high-speed dive, right towards the spikes. "

36

"Just hold on and don't stall out! There's a wing space just past this choke!" I stared ahead at the cored out sections of rock to either side.

The connection between Karalti's mind and mine intensified, as powerful as I'd ever felt. Karalti's concentration was absolute as she shot into the open space, blindly snapped her wings out, and drove herself forward and up. There was only room for two wingbeats before she had to swallow-dive again.

"There's another space ahead!" Adrenaline pounded through my bloodstream. My mouth was dry, hands sweaty, eyes tearing up as I forced them to stay open. *"One, two, now!"*

Gasping for breath, Karalti beat her wings in the small gap, barely keeping herself out of terminal velocity... and then the roof opened up, and the tunnel curved sharply to the right. The dragon threw her wings open and used her tail to swing into a fast, soaring arc around the corner. Gravity bore down on my back, crushing the air from my lungs before she swung back, and we burst out of the gauntlet into a massive lava chamber.

"We did it!" She cried. Even her telepathic voice was breathless. *"But there's nowhere to land!"*

There sure wasn't. Titanic streams of magma seethed below us, belching from the walls into a great river of molten rock. Six monolithic statues loomed from the walls to either side of the rumbling lava. Dragons, each one standing with their hands cupped around a different item. At the other end of the canyon was the entry to a cave, sealed by a great metal portal.

[Warning: Temperature is dangerously high!]
[You are overheating!]

My dragonrider mutations gave me resilience to extremes of temperature: up to fifty degrees Celsius, which was about a hundred-and twenty-degrees Fahrenheit. My Heads-Up Display showed the temperature in this cavern: a lovely 93 degrees c, enough to cook a normal human alive. Even as that wonderful thought passed through my mind, a Hyperthermia ring jumped up in my display: blank, at first, but slowly filling with red.

"We've got about five minutes to figure this out before this place roasts me," I said, as sweat poured down my face. *"No pressure or anything."*

"Mmm. Roast Hector. Don't suppose we've got any ketchup?"

The bumpy thermals twirling up from the lava were a pleasure cruise compared to the spiny tunnel, the heat lifting Karalti's wings with hardly any effort on her part. As she glided past the door, I twisted to keep it in my line of sight. There were six carved runes engraved on the surface, with hollow channels waiting to receive mana.

"Can you read those symbols?" I asked her. *"They might be Solonkratsu."*

Karalti winged over and flew back, pulling into a slow glide as we passed by again. *"Yeah, kind of! They're words of power. But they all say the same thing."*

"Which is?"

"'Breath'. It's different Words for the same little-w word. Breath."

"Hold steady." I craned my head and zoomed my vision in on one of the flanking statues. The stone dragon had his wings folded and his head bowed. He presented an ornate goblet in his clawed hands—a goblet with a metal wick. *"It's a statue puzzle. We have to light these statues with your breath weapon."*

"All six statues? That'll use up half my charges!"

"I know, but the alternative is a lava bath." My hyperthermia ring was already a quarter of the way full, and I was starting to shiver from the heat. *"I don't know if we have to do them in some kind of order. Let's try one and see if it stays lit."*

Karalti flicked a wingtip and coasted toward the statue with the goblet. Her chest swelled against the saddle, and she let out a thin, controlled plume of brilliant white flames. The sticky Ghost Fire lashed over the goblet and the statue's chest, kindling the wick to life. The statue's blank crystal eyes lit up—and so did one of the runes on the door.

"I don't think it matters," I said, hooking my feet under the saddle straps. *"Let's do a circuit, and make it fast."*

"Gotcha!" The dragon swooped forward, trusting me to hold on as she slingshot along the line of statues. She blasted

them, lighting wicks on a lantern, a crystal, and a knife. She swung back around at the end of the canyon, torching the last pair of statues—and the door slid out of its frame and began to slowly roll sidewards into the wall.

"That... was a lot easier than I thought it would be. Which immediately makes me kind of suspicious." I was trembling now, panting from the heat that crawled between my skin and the surface of my armor. I leaned with Karalti as she banked and winged over, soaring toward the opening door. It was lit from behind, revealing a glittering white tunnel. *"What the fuck is that?"*

"I dunno, but I sure hope I can land on it. You're boiling and I'm exhausted." Even though we'd only flown a short distance, Karalti's stamina had dropped sharply between her hunger and the stressful, intricate maneuvers she'd had to perform to get us this far.

I zoomed in on the rapidly approaching tunnel—and winced. *"No. Stay in the air. That's web. And I'm pretty sure that whatever spun it is big enough to eat a dragon."*

CHAPTER 5

As we got closer, I revised my opinion. The tunnel wasn't lined with web. It was way, way grosser than that.

"Right, so... at first, I thought maybe this was made by giant spiders. But now I am like, ninety-nine percent sure this is fungus." The steam that billowed out past the door carried a damp, earthy scent, like mushrooms mixed with burned plastic. *"Whatever the fuck it is, don't touch it."*

Karalti rumbled, soaring into the humid tunnel. As the tip of her tail passed the threshold, the door thumped behind us. I glanced over my shoulder to see it rolling back into place. Sticky white strands lashed out over the warm metal, almost as if the tunnel itself was sealing the exit behind us.

[Warning: Mana levels are dangerously high. You are at risk of mana poisoning!]

"Well... it's magical." My skin crawled as I looked around. The fibrous strands looked like living cotton candy, a hollow cocoon that undulated as we flew past. They yearned towards Karalti like hairs reacting to static electricity, reaching for her wingtips. *"And it really wants to eat us. Can you Bioscan it?"*

"Yeah. Hang on." I felt her gather her mana, then cast it out into the tunnel like an unseen burst of sonar.

[New herb discovered: Dragonrot]

Dragonrot (Parasitic Fungus)

While technically not a monstrous entity, Dragonrot is one of the few lifeforms capable of striking fear into the hearts of Archemi's apex predators, the Solonkratsu.

Dragonrot is a Stranged, semi-sentient fungus that thrives in moist underground environments populated by magical creatures, mana-poisoned waterways, and freshwater cavern systems. The fungus targets arcane megafauna like dragons, swamp hags and Stranged leviathans. After infecting a creature's bloodstream via wound entry, the fungus uses the mana in the host's body to replicate.

Dragonrot is almost never found in active Solonkratsu settlements. Dragons experience an instinctive revulsion toward the fungus and scorch the walls of their cavernous dens to kill spores. The presence of this fungus is strongly associated with damp underground locations containing dead dragons and/or decayed mana.

This fungus is intrinsically harmless to humans and non-magical creatures and cannot infect them, but the spoiled mana it thrives on can cause mana poisoning and rapid death. Dragons infected by Dragonrot via blood contact will incubate the fungus for 3-4 days before showing symptoms.

"Jeez." Even after listening to the part where it said that the fungus couldn't infect humans, I had the urge to scrub at my face and wash my hands. *"You know, sometimes, I run across*

shit in Archemi that makes me wonder what the hell Ryuko was thinking. We've had three major pandemics this century, and that's not even counting HEX. My grandma refused to leave the house without a facemask in her purse. Why the hell did the Devs put something like this in a videogame? Games are supposed to be fun, not traumatizing."

"I dunno," Karalti replied, swooping to avoid a waving curtain of fungal strands. *"Maybe the Architects didn't plan for it? I mean, they're just people, right? Maybe they didn't make it, and it just... happened?"*

"I don't know if that's how videogames work, Tidbit." The walls of the tunnel up ahead narrowed and became bumpier, and I frowned as my eyes snagged on an oddly familiar shape. As we got closer, I saw a long skeletal neck, gaping jaws, and short, stubby horns poking out through the layers of silk: a dragon's skull and vertebrae, half meshed into the wall. Karalti shuddered beneath me—then yelped aloud. It was all the warning I got. She tipped sharply to the right, almost throwing me off the saddle.

"Oof!" I coughed, slamming down against her back. I clung to Karalti like a baby bat as she desperately winged forward and to the left. *"What the-!?"*

"Hold on!" The dragon's voice was as close to a terrified shout as I'd ever heard it.

Oh boy, was I gonna. Then something moved in the corner of my eye. I whipped my head around just as a long, fleshy stem burst out of the wall like a hook shot, exploding toward my dragon's wings. The stem pulsed with blue light, swiping at Karalti's thin wing membranes before sagging back

against the wall. Then there was another one, and another...
and it was all I could do to hold on as my dragon dodged,
pulling her wings in to drop, roll, then surge forward as the
trap came to life around us. One of the hooks skidded over her
wing membrane, catching on the edge. Another shot at me,
threatening to catch in my armor and pull me off her back. I
kicked at the tough, spongy stems with a boot, breaking them
off and sending the clawed ends tumbling away.

"Did it get me? I don't want to get sick!" Karalti dived as
the roof bulged in above us, then exploded in a cloud of spores.
Without thinking, I held my breath and screwed my eyes
closed, flattening down against her back.

"You're fine! But whatever you do, don't stop!" I
frantically looked over to her wing, making certain she hadn't
taken any cuts from the hooks. *"I've played The Last of Us! I
know how this goes!"*

Karalti belched an oily stream of flames as another cloud
of spores ejected from the wall in front of us. They ignited in
a puff of sparks, but there was another, and another. More
darts shot out at us, skimming over and hooking on the scales
of the dragon's neck. She jerked as they hauled back with
surprising strength, pulling out from the walls with long,
trailing white roots that crawled with blue embers. I
clambered over the bucking saddle, ripping the claws out and
throwing them overboard.

The exit was in sight: a dark cave entrance feeding into
what looked like a larger cavern. Dim blue light spilled out
from it—light that got dimmer as the fungus threw sticky
strands across the opening, sealing it off. Karalti had blasted

four spore clouds—she had two breath weapon charges left, one of which she spent to incinerate the rapidly forming web that was trying to close off our escape. The fungus shriveled back from the heat, and we blew past as more darts sprang out and fell away, unable to catch on Karalti's body from behind.

The cavern we flew into was lit by immense columns of bright blue crystal that hummed like exposed wires. They jutted from the ceiling and walls, practically forcing Karalti to go to ground. She landed heavily, wings sagging.

"Wow..." she panted. *"That's... that's a lot of mana."*

"Holy fucksticks. This has got to be worth a fortune," I whispered. The radiation from the crystals beat down on my armor like small suns, but the crystals weren't damaged or liquified, so there was no Mana Poisoning alert. "How many tons of bluecrystal mana do you think this is?"

"I dunno." Karalti looked back at me, her horns lifting into an upright fan of alarm. *"You're not thinking about taking any, are you?"*

"Abso-fucking-lutely," I said. "There's enough mana here to power Withering Rose."

"This the tomb of my ancestress!" My dragon flattened her crests against her skull, hissing in her throat. *"I'm not graverobbing my grandma, you ass."*

I winced. "Ah... yeah. Sorry. Didn't think."

Karalti neatly flipped her wings so they rested properly against her flanks, and gave an irritable grunt. *"Ugh. I dunno about you, but I'm just about done with this place. How much further do we have to go?"*

"No idea." I focused my eyes on the other end of the chamber. Under the jutting forest of crystals was a dragon-sized crawlspace. It looked like someone had busted through the wall. Rubble and broken crystals lay scattered around it, sunken into the dirt and covered in dust. Gouge marks left by claws were visible on the walls. The room beyond glowed brightly. "Given that Myszno was one great big dragon city, we might have to fly all the way to the Endlar at this rate."

"Ugh. Don't say that. I remember Istvan saying there were ruins under the swamp." Karalti flipped her wings along her sides and pushed herself to her feet. Her stamina was looking better—but her hunger meter was sitting at 10%, and her stomach rumbled audibly. *"I don't like the smell coming from that next room. It smells... dead. And mushroomy."*

Between Karalti's description, the traceries of fungal strands reaching around the edges of the opening, and the bright glow lighting up the next room like a neon sign saying 'go here!', my Gamer's Intuition began to poke at me.

"Let's buff up," I said, quietly. "I'll give you what food I have in my pack. It's not much, but it'll get you through whatever we probably have to kill in there. While you eat, let's talk strategy. You've only got one burst of Ghost Fire left: assuming there's a boss that is designed to challenge dragons and other flying creatures, how are we going to fight it?"

Karalti rubbed her face with her front claws, hissing low in her throat. *"Uhh... I-"*

"If you say 'I dunno', I'm gonna kick your ass," I said. "That's baby talk."

She huffed in a way that told me she'd been about to say that exact thing.

"I can use Wings of Deception to make a double of myself," she said, after a few minutes. *"My copies deal the same physical damage as me. I can hit something with thirty-five percent more breath weapon damage that way... and then fight them physically."*

"Right. What about magic?" I scrounged around in my pack, evicting all the food I'd saved. Macarons, sandwiches, burek, random vegetables. I pulled out an entire cabbage I hadn't remembered picking up and grimaced. I must have picked it up out of a pot somewhere. Mmm-mmm, delicious dungeon cabbage.

"Haste makes me faster," Karalti said. *"Dirge can curse enemies and make them blind and unable to speak, so if they're a magic user, that helps."*

"Right."

"Uhh... Dark Focus gives me triple power on my next magical attack. The only offensive spell I have is Shadow Wave. Maybe Circle of Protection?"

I brought the spell descriptions up in my HUD with a thought:

Shadow Wave

Rippling shadows disorient enemies and inflict moderate damage. Causes one or more of: Confusion, Blindness, Deafness, Rage, Nausea to living enemies.

Circle of Protection II

Create a 20ft radius of protection against undead for 5 minutes, warding them back from contact with the dragon's body while dealing 1 Dark elemental damage per second (15 MP, 10-second cooldown).

"Pretty sure it will work with Shadow Wave. I'm not sure what 'moderate damage' means, but triple that will probably end up being 'serious damage'," I said. "I guess that was one of those beta testing descriptions that wasn't fully updated before we... I... joined the game."

"Yeah! So blast them with fire, then with Shadow Wave, then pow!" She balled her foreclaws into fists and swung them forward and up. *"One, two, right in the kisser! Then bite them!"*

"No biting, if it's a fungus thing." I walked out along her wing edge with arms full of food. "Here. Chow's ready."

My dragon craned her neck back, looking at me coyly. *"Feed me?"*

I arched an eyebrow, but I held out a pastry I'd looted from somewhere in Taltos. It was perfectly preserved, thanks to the magic of virtual reality logic. Karalti gently nipped it from my fingers, followed by all the rest of it. Meat, vegetables, assorted desserts. She ate the lot, filling her food bar by four percent.

"Better than nothing," I sighed, as I handed her my last piece of jerky. "At least you won't starve. But I might."

CHAPTER 6

I had to flatten down so Karalti could crawl through the hole in the cave wall. She got down on her belly to commando crawl underneath, using her foreclaws to pull herself forward and paddling the dirt with her legs and tail. We emerged into a narrow geode corridor, bluecrystal spires jutting out crazily in all directions. Broken crystals littered the ground, as if something large had brute-forced their way inside, cutting a route through the geode. The air was humid, laced with an unpleasant odor like burning plastic and sugar mixed together... the stench of decaying mana exposed to the air.

"I don't like this," I muttered, ducking a crystal spire that lanced from the ceiling. The scent of decay—flesh and mana both—was getting stronger with every step. It was also getting warmer and wetter. I kept an eye on my HUD, watching the temperature gauge slowly rise from 74F toward 90F.

"You know, I do want to see my grandma and claim my birthright and everything, but every part of this place gives me the creeps." Karalti picked up her feet like a fussy cat as the earth turned to mud, squishing up between her claws.

"We're probably almost there. Just think queenly thoughts," I said. *"Dignified. Mature. Elegant."*

"Blow me," Karalti grumbled back.

There was the grinding, rumbling sound of lava in the walls, getting louder as we broke out into a glowing cavern. Karalti came to an uneasy stop as we took in the sights. It was warm and damp—not a great start. Hairlike Dragonrot grew in clusters between crops of mana crystals, feeding off the luminescent mana that beaded on the walls like dew. It wasn't a solid blanket of filaments, like it had been in the tunnel. There was evidence that molten rock had erupted from the walls in places over decades or centuries. The fungus hadn't grown back on the cooled lava, leaving black hills of petrified magma to sit bare. Even as we stood there, a small cavity to our left erupted, belching a ropy, gelatinous stream of magma down the wall.

At the other end of the cavern were piles of bodies. Half a dozen tulaq had met their ends here. Tulaq were a species that had gone extinct during the Aesari Wars some two thousand years ago: slender winged creatures that were equal parts greyhound, falcon, and kudu antelope. They had four long legs, elegant necks, and narrow heads with horns and graceful feathered crests. They were also extremely dead, with frayed leathery skin stretched over their bones, their lips pulled back from their fangs in rictus snarls. Shelves of beautiful white mushrooms grew out from their chests, fringed with blue.

The corpses of the ancient humans who had ridden here with the tulaq were heaped in a pile some distance away, partly entombed by ancient black stone lava flows. And behind those corpses, slumped against a corroded door that hissed and spat sparks of magical energy, were a pair of young dragons. They were about two-thirds Karalti's size, fifty feet from mutated nose to leathery tail. One was blue, the other a dull mustard yellow—and both of them had been destroyed by Dragonrot. Bulbous fungal growths obscured their eyes, their scales flaking off around huge knotted clusters of mushrooms. But something about them was uncanny. The tulaq and humans were barely more than mummified skeletons, preserved by some weird cocktail of aerosolized mana and heat. The dragons still had most of their flesh intact.

"*No!*" Karalti let out a mournful cry, pacing forward.

"*Wait, wait!*" I pulled back on the edge of her saddle. "*Look at the damn ground!*"

Karalti stopped in her tracks, peering at the floor. There was a rising section of earth where she had just been about to put her foot. Even as we watched, glowing cracks appeared... and then subsided, as the fissures in the small lava dome cooled and resealed into stone.

"*Can't you feel that? There's lava everywhere around us,*" I said. "*Watch the walls. This whole place is unstable.*"

"*Maybe, but these people have been here a long time.*" Karalti ducked her head and hunched her shoulders as she carefully stepped forward. "*I don't know if that door's even going to work. Do you think maybe the Spear will open it?*"

I squinted at it. The last time I'd seen a door like this was back in Ilia, in the ruined Aesari city of Cham Garai. It was made of a very hard golden metal—Aurum—with lines of magical channels mapped like veins across its surface. The mana channels came together at a single point, a receptacle for a crystal that was just about the same size as the ones embedded in the blade of the Spear of Nine Spheres. The embossed image of Matir's sigil framed the hole: a nine-pointed star with a spiral at the center.

"You know, it just might. But we're going to have to move those dragons," I said, frowning at the scene ahead. The damp smell of mingled mana and decay was thickest here, burning the inside of my sinuses with a nasty chemical smell. *"Do you think maybe-* HRRRGH!"

Something thick and prehensile cut my question short: A long pseudopod that snapped around my chest and hauled me up into the air with frightening speed.

"Hector?" Karalti turned, mouth agape, and let out a yelp as it pulled me, kicking and struggling, up into the cavernous dark of the ceiling. *"Hector! What the hell!?"*

"I don't know what the hell!" I sputtered. The cavern above was completely dark—and I couldn't see what had grabbed me. But before I could comprehend what kind of trouble I was in, I glimpsed movement at the back of the cave. The two dragons, lumbering to their misshapen feet like marionettes.

"Behind you!" I shouted.

Karalti whirled as the [Infected Sporemaidens] lurched toward her, stumbling over the cooled lava flows and the bodies on the floor. My dragon shrieked, and any thought of strategy deserted her as she instinctively backed away and blasted the first one with her final gout of Ghost Fire.

[Ghost Fire is super effective!]

[Karalti deals 3676 damage to Sporemaiden!]
[Sporemaiden: 17,963/20,639 HP].

I struggled against the tentacles clasping my arms to my sides. They were reeling me in toward a half-seen mass of glowing pseudopods, a short rubbery mat that oozed a decidedly digesty-looking acidic substance.

"Noooo, no, no. Nope. Nuh-uh." I slipped one arm out, enough to call the Spear of Nine Spheres to hand. The soul-bound weapon materialized in my palm—cold, at first, until I called the elemental power in it and the haft and blade burst into boiling scarlet flames. The tentacles shriveled away from the heat, lighting up the full length of the monster overhead.

My eyes bugged, and not just from the crushing pressure around my ribs. It was another dragon. A much larger dragon. A much more infected dragon. The [Rotmother]'s ghostly white body had meshed into the ceiling of the cavern, barely recognizable as anything other than a gooey mass of fungus, tentacles, and slime. The mat of dripping blue rhizomes coated both sides of her gaping ribcage.

"Aww, shit." I struggled harder, giving myself enough room to plunge the Spear into the nearest pad of spongy flesh, one-handed. The blade cut into the corrupted dragon like butter, and the tentacles shuddered and sagged back down ten feet or so—but they didn't release me.

[Fire is super effective! You deal 960 damage!]
[Rotmother HP: 27,813/28,773]

I cast a frantic look down to the fight below: Karalti was circling back from the pair of Sporemaidens, who were lunging for her with teeth and claws.

"For the love of... Use Wings of Deception! Split them up!" I shouted telepathically, snarling aloud as another tentacle snapped around my spear arm and tried to force the weapon away.

Karalti yelped as she danced away from one dragon's slashing front claws. Big as she was, she was fast for her size— and she'd been studying martial arts. She couldn't use her special Baru abilities in dragon form, but as the yellow Sporemaiden surged toward her, Karalti blocked the dripping claws with one wing and headbutted the dragon right in the head with her own. The soft fungus-riddled tissue caved under the impact, sending the animated corpse staggering back. It tripped awkwardly over the dead tulaq, its HP dropping to 17,615.

The Rotmother was slowly crushing my spear arm, threatening to snap it as I struggled. Growling, I twisted the flaming weapon deeper into the spongy root of the tentacle. "URGH! Please, just eat... shit... and... die!"

I hit one of my most powerful energy attacks; the Mark of Matir ability, Shadow Lance. It turned the fire billowing along the Spear solid black and sent a shockwave of energy rippling through the Rotmother's body. The undead dragon swayed, some of her fungal tethers snapping as dark energy tore through the Dragonrot growths and sent congealed blood and slime raining to the floor. But even after her dealing a cool 3712 damage, the mutated dragon didn't drop me. Instead, a cloud of glassy, needle-like darts shot out at me from her undercarriage. Most of them plinked off my armor. A few of them embedded into the meat of my thigh, shredding my pants and puncturing the skin beneath. To my horror, I felt them pump something into me—and then my leg turned numb as a leaden sensation spread through my torso and limbs.

[You have been poisoned! You are afflicted with Slowness!]
[HP: 580/2378]

"Urghh..." I slurred as the feeling spread to the muscles of my face. "Fuck... you... Ryuko."

"Hang on!" Karalti called to me from the ground. *"Hold it off as long as you can!"*

My head lolled on my neck as I spared a glance at Karalti. She'd used Wings of Deception, and the chamber was full of brawling dragons. The Sporemaidens had split up, one of them chasing the magical duplicate with gaping jaws. I watched as one of them charged her with a flurry of slashing blows, and shouted in alarm as its claws connected with her forearm and tore a long gash in it. Both copies of Karalti gasped.

"Krralti! Dun let the spores get urrn!" I slurred like a Scottish drunk. Thanks to the poison, the Rotmother now had two combat turns for every one of mine—and she spent her bonus turn pulling me toward the nest of dripping, writhing pseudopods growing out of her abdomen. But as she did so, we passed her soft underbelly. I sluggishly rammed my weapon into her guts and channeled my fear into a second powerful AoE attack: Umbra Blast. Thorny tendrils of pure darkness exploded from the blade of the spear, tearing through the Rotmother's body.

[You do 1990 Darkness damage!]
[Rotmother: 22,111/28,773]

The spongy body rocked a second time, and the dragon's head tore free of the fungal net. It was stripped of flesh—but just looking at her horns and the size of her head, I knew this dragon had been a Queen. Her massive crowned skull flopped to the side as the fungal mass shriveled under the intense cold. The Rotmother's digestive tentacles took the brunt of the damage, cracking and shattering, leaving me to thrash with sloth-like vigor as the Dragonrot fungus snapped over the Sporemother's body like bands of cartilage. The jaws formed by her ribcage closed, and new blue fruits pushed their way through the dark sticky mess I'd made of the colony's external stomach. The bitch was *sprouting.*

I searched the cavern, desperate to see if the Sporemaidens had infected Karalti. Her shadow copy had lapsed: the yellow dragon was staggering back to her feet, and Karalti was wrestling with the blue one. The mutated Sporemaiden was straining toward her, snapping like a rabid dog as Karalti pulled her one way, then the other, and then shoved forward and bodily threw the smaller dragon away from her. The clumsy monster staggered away from her and smashed into the opposite wall. The impact shook the cavern—and opened up one of the small lava domes. It spewed a column of molten rock over the fallen dragon. She squealed, writhing in agony as lava seared over her infected body, eating through its sodden flesh and boiling away the Dragonrot growths that infested it.

[Karalti deals 3200 damage to Sporemaiden! Your enemy is mired!]

The flailing dragon tried to stand up, but Karalti spun around and knocked it right back into the weakened rock with her tail. Fresh lava pulsed out of the wounded lava chamber, and the Sporemaiden wailed, clawing desperately along the floor as her HP disintegrated, three thousand points at a time. The lava did a crazy amount of damage to her—or, more accurately, to the fungus that was puppeteering her corpse.

"That's it! Do it again!" I groaned as the tentacles around my chest tightened with crushing force. They ripped the Spear out of their flesh, and no matter how much I strained, I couldn't bring it up high enough to stab it in again.

[You have taken 300 bludgeoning damage!]

"Stop ordering me around!" Karalti backed up as the yellow Sporemaiden let out a rusty shriek and lurched toward her, jaws agape. But this time, it didn't try to bite: instead, it belched a plume of glowing blue spores, a perversion of a normal dragon's breath weapon. Karalti squealed, backpedaling with her eyes screwed shut and her nostrils clamped against the parasitic cloud. She beat her wings frantically, gusting the spores back from her.

I focused back on my newest slimy friend, mind racing. The Rotmother's HP wasn't regenerating, but she was steadily regrowing the blue glowing mat of rhizomes—rhizomes I was pretty sure could turn me into a Hector-flavored smoothie. I strained against the tentacles still firmly wrapped around my waist and right arm, but they weren't budging. "Hey, Princess Toadstool! I swear I'm not as delicious as I look, okay?! I taste like ass! Literal ass!"

"I'm coming! Try not to get eaten!" Karalti snarled as the yellow dragon closed in on her, teeth flashing toward her neck.

CHAPTER 7

The pair clashed chest to chest, foreclaws locked as they strained against each other. Karalti pumped her wings, using the draft generated by the huge membranes to drive her forward. Claws shrieked and sparked against stone as she pushed the slavering, mutated dragon back toward the wall, and bodily rammed her into another of the bulging lava domes.

The stone shattered under the impact, and magma spurted out around the Sporemaiden's shoulders. The Sporemaiden let out an unearthly scream, like rusted gears grinding against one another, and struggled pitifully as Karalti pushed it back into the spray of lava and held it there like she was trying to drown it. Magma splattered my dragon's heat-resistant scales. The first droplets bounced away, but as the molten stone kept flowing, the smoldering particles began to stick. She snarled with pain, tanking the damage until she could no longer stand it. But as she let go, the yellow Sporemaiden's head darted forward, belching another cloud of spores right into Karalti's face.

"NO!" My pulse pounded in my temples as I slowly, haltingly strained against the Rotmother's grip. My HP trickled away as my joints popped and my ribs groaned, but I shoved the pain away and fought with everything I had. I felt my fingernails distend, and my sharp teeth grow out into a

59

double row of long fangs... and when my struggles proved
futile, I howled and began to bite, rip and tear into anything I
could reach. The Mark of Matir turned icy cold.

[You activated Mortal Grudge!]
*[Speed increased by 25% for 60 seconds. 2.5 Adrenaline Point
regen for 60 seconds!]*
*[You have been struck with a Death Sentence! Countdown:
60 seconds]*
[Sporemaiden has died! Karalti gains 966 EXP!]

Cold power crawled through my limbs, as I shredded the
tentacle gripping my arm. The one around my waist slackened,
and I pulled myself free and Jumped, boiling with rage, and
slammed weapon-first into the underbelly of the diseased
Queen. The bulk of the dragon shuddered as the flaming Spear
gouged into it, dealing blow after blow of raw force.

[You deal 8662 Damage to Rotmother! 13,449/28,773]

Tentacles flailed at me as I fell amongst the rain of burning
fungus. Fangs bared, I hit Shadow Dance and dashed back up
into the air. Once, twice... and then boosted out of it like a
black meteor to land another Umbra Burst right in the dragon's
gaping ribcage maw. Shards of black ice burst out of her body
like a gruesome flower.

[Umbra Burst deals 1990 damage!]
[Rotmother is Frozen!]
[Death Sentence: 32 seconds.]

Frigid steam erupted from the crackling tissue, letting out a shrill, scream-like whistle... and then the Dragonrot fibers meshing the queen's corpse to the ceiling started to give way. The Rotmother's body slumped, then sagged to one side. I caught one of her protruding ribs, hanging on with one arm. "Karalti! Look out!"

Karalti pressed herself to a wall as the hundred-ton corpse pulled away from the ceiling and collapsed. I Shadow Dashed away just before it hit the floor. And boy, did it hit the floor: the Rotmother smashed like a ripe pumpkin, crushing the thin veneer of stone between it and the lava that gurgled underneath. Magma splashed everywhere, and then the dead queen began to sink. Tentacles lashed out, striking everything within reach. Karalti tanked the blows against her back, crying out through gritted jaws. I blew another 20 HP to Shadow Dance out of range. The fungus-infected flesh of the Rotmother shriveled black before catching alight, and soon the cavern was full of choking smoke. All we had to do was avoid the flailing and smashing as the lava disintegrated her, dealing upwards of three thousand damage a second until my HUD's victory chime rang through the cavern.

[You have defeated Rotmother and Sporemaidens!]
[Your Death Sentence is cured!]
[You gain 2012 EXP! Karalti gains 966 EXP!]

I landed on top of a Sporemaiden's corpse and bounced. I was not expecting to bounce. The spongy landing pad threw me back up into the air, head over ass, and sent me careening toward the nearest wall. I braced for impact—but Karalti's head darted out from my right, and she delicately snatched me out of the air in her jaws.

"Thanks." I sagged in her teeth, and coughed as the smoke haze pressed down from the roof of the cavern, then groaned as a glowing blue ring jumped up in my HUD. "Oh, for fuck's sake."

[[*You are suffering from Mana Poisoning! -1 HP per second!*]]

"I know it's kind of obvious, but we really need to get out of here." Karalti dropped me and ducked her head. She held her tail low, her wings shivering by her sides. *"I'm sure I breathed in some of those spores... I don't know if I'm sick..."*

"Don't worry. If you caught a dose of mushrooms, I can cure you thanks to my boy Matir. We'll sort you out once we're home." I stumbled around the cooling waves of magma, coughing as the Queen's corpse continued to belch clouds of mana-laced smoke into the cave. *"Can you loot the bodies?"*

"Uhh... okay?" Karalti seemed slightly taken aback. She was immune to mana poisoning and could hold her breath a lot longer than I could, though, so she turned to do just that. *"Do I have to? I just want to get out of here."*

"I'm working on it, but if we don't get some decent loot from this dungeon, I'm going kick a baby dolphin into the sun." I chugged a potion and stored the bottle just before I reached the door. At a loss for how to remove the Star of Endless Night from the Spear of Nine Spheres, I mashed the flat of the blade against the socket. To my great relief, the hole drew the weapon against it like a magnet and locked the stone into place.

A blue-black web of energy shot across the surface of the metal. Gears groaned and clunked from inside the walls as the doors began to slowly winch themselves apart. The halves made it about a foot to either side before the mana lines sputtered, and the whole thing lurched to a lop-sided halt with an ear-splitting squeal.

"Ow." Karalti paced back to me, her tail and wings drooping. *"Great. Just as well I can polymorph."*

"Right?" I glanced back at her. *"No loot, huh?"*

"I got some gross mushrooms?" She winced. *"You know, if you ever feel like killing me."*

Sighing, I reached up to squeeze a handful of my hair. It had been a while since I'd had a bath, and the braided mohawk that ran from the top of my skull to the nape of my neck was a frizzled mess. *"Come on, Tidbit. Let's keep on going. We have to find grandma's house before this fucking place kills us both."*

***

Karalti had to polymorph down to her human form to fit through the small crack in the door. We crept through into the dark, following a dry, hot corridor that wound for half a mile into the mountains before opening up into an airy obsidian hall lined with six dragon-sized biers, where the massive skeletons of Lahati's Queensguard lay in state. The dragons were surrounded by heaps of treasure, curled as if in sleep. The polished stone around us reflected their images—and ours— up and down to infinity.

"*Wow...*" Karalti craned her head, looking around. "*I think we're nearly there.*"

"*I'd say so. And I'm pretty sure I know what's through that gateway.*" I broke into a jog, and my dragon followed at an easy run.

"*You know...*" Karalti drew up beside me, matching my pace. "*Other than the dragons we fought at the Prezyemi Line, I've never seen another living dragon before. And they were so warped with Void energy that they hardly count.*"

"*Now you mention it, yeah.*" I thought back, keeping an eye on my stamina bar. "*Are you okay?*"

"*Yeah. Just sad.*" Karalti glanced at the biers as we passed by. "*After this... after I gain the Path of Royalty... will we go back to Ilia? To save the others?*"

"*If we can, Tidbit.*" I nodded, brows furrowing. "*Believe me. That's something that's been on my mind ever since I left the Eyrie.*"

I could still remember the first time I laid eyes on the Knight-Commander of the Order, Skyr Arnaud, and his white dragon, Talenth. The rider-dragon pair and a couple other Knights of St. Grigori had rescued me and the Lysian sorceress Rutha from the wreck of a slave ship on its way to Zaunt, the homeland of the Mercurions. Talenth had been breathtaking. Regal. From the moment I saw him, my fate was sealed. I *would* become a dragon rider, and I ran off to dragon school to do just that.

It took a few days before I sensed something was rotten in the Eyrie. Something was wrong with the Knight-

Commander, and also the dragons themselves. My mentor, Skyr Tymos, tried to warn me. But he—like everyone else there other than Arnaud—was physically unable to reveal the dark secret at the heart of the Order. It was Karalti's mother, straining against the restrictions of the powerful magical geas that bound her and everyone else to silence, who led me to the truth. The dragons in the Eyrie were slaves, blood-bound to the will of the Knight-Commander. And because the dragons were bound to the geas, their riders were, too.

It was only after months of living with a dragon, studying her species, and talking to people like Rutha and Rin that I understood how unnatural and warped the Eyrie really was. The Solonkratsu were a civilized race, with their own social order, mating rituals, family bonds, religion, even architecture. The Order suppressed it all. If Karalti had hatched in the Eyrie, the Knights would have turned her into a flightless broodmare, just like her mother.

That thought had haunted me ever since Karalti and I had Bonded. To save her, I'd had to leave her mother behind, chained deep underground. And the most fucked up thing about it? According to Rin, her suffering—and the geas itself—were non-canonical. The ethical shitstorm in the Eyrie only existed thanks to Archemi's Number One Control Freak: Michael Pratt, the digital ghost otherwise known as Ororgael. The guy who I was pretty sure now wore Baldr Hyland's avatar like a skin-suit.

"Soo... What do you think the Heart of Memory recorded?" Karalti asked. *"About, you know...?"*

I startled back to the present. *"Huh? Oh, Baldr. Honestly, I have no idea. We'll find out once we're back in Kalla Sahasi."*

"Did he really beat you?"

"I'm pretty sure he beat my ass like a red-headed stepchild. Given he cheated to Level 9000 somehow, I'm not going to give myself too much shit for losing a duel."

Neither of us even spared a glance at the treasure heaped around the bodies of the dead. We passed them by, heading up the small semi-circle of stairs. There, a pair of huge black doors swung in ahead of us on silent hinges, opening into a familiar chamber.

CHAPTER 8

All the lava flows in this mountain range emptied into the antechamber of Lahati's Tomb. A black glass bridge arched over the lake of fire that lay directly ahead of us. As we entered, I looked to my left and saw the small door I'd used to enter this place the first time: a door that led to a small portal room. That portal would warp us back to the main draconic graveyard that lay under Krivan Pass, a vista not that far from Myszno's capital city, Karhad.

My head jerked back as Karalti gasped, pointing at the billowing, darkly luminous figure who waited for us in the middle of the bridge. *"Look!"*

Lahati the Chrysanthemum Queen appeared just as she had the last time I'd been here. Her slender, dignified humanoid form towered over the pair of us. She was nearly seven feet tall, made larger by the rippling shadows of her floor-length hair and long gown. They blew out from her like a candle flame, trailing smoky coils of darkness into the air. Her eyes were blazing white, bright pin-points burning through the curtain of shadow. They were kind... and sad.

"My sweet daughter." Lahati's voice was louder here, clearer. It brushed over our skin with a faint chill that defied the roaring heat that billowed up from beneath our feet. "I know you both suffered to come here. I beg you to forgive my weakness. The passage to my tomb was made to weed out Aesari and human plunderers, and challenge those Solonkratsu who seek me or Matir. But it was not meant to be so severe."

"You saw all that?" I asked. "Then you had to have known about the Dragonrot. Why didn't you warn us?"

"See it? Hector, I am dead. I see nothing but the slithering progress of time, and hear nothing unless someone calls to me over the chorus produced by the Caul of Souls."

"It has a sound?" Karalti asked.

Lahati turned her head to her, the shadows of her face rippling like flames. "Yes. Millions of souls calling, singing, laughing. Since I last saw you, Herald, the chorus has become so much louder."

I took a step forward. "If you pass on, does that mean that you'll... that you'll be gone? Like, will the Caul destroy you?"

Lahati cocked her head, as if puzzled. "Destroyed? No, Herald, of course not. The Caul does not destroy the souls of the dead."

"Violetta and the vampire who tried to turn me... they told me that the Caul eats people's souls after death."

"Ahh..." The shade made a derisive sound. "That is nothing but *Trauvin* lies. Come, Paragons. Walk with me, and I will tell you what I know."

Karalti pressed forward ahead of me, thrumming with nerves. I followed, and Lahati turned and swept toward the great five-petaled portal at the end of the antechamber.

"When the Nine were contemplating solutions to the Drachan, Devara, the Mother of all life in Archemi, asked a question of the world," Lahati said, trailing darkness like a train as she led the way to her tomb. "She asked: 'Would you be willing, in death, to stand guard against the Drachan and the Rostori and the other creatures of the Void for a term equal to the years you lived, before you move on to rejoin the planet and be reborn?' And the world, devastated by the Drachan, said yes. The Caul is merely a station after death, Herald. Souls join it for a time, lend their strength to the magic, and once they have served their span, they move on. Unharmed. The *Trauvin* are the only eaters of souls in this world. Not even Rusolka the Mad would do such a thing."

"Good to know." A weight I hadn't realized I'd been carrying slid from my shoulders. "I wonder if we're doing the right thing. Bringing back the Warsingers, opening the Dragon Gates. Sometimes, I feel really sure about it. But other times, I wonder. Like, what if we're actually just playing into Ororgael's hands? Or the Drachan's?"

"Those are valid questions," the ancient queen replied. "When the Caul was created, we knew it was little more than a stop-gap measure against chaos. We hoped that if the Caul was ever unmade, it would happen only when the world was better prepared to face them. You, as the Paragon of the Sixth Age, must decide if the world is ready."

"I don't know if it is, grandmother," Karalti said. *"There's so much we don't know, and so much we lost. There are hardly any dragons left. Me and Hector have been all over the place,*

rediscovering ancient technology. Like the Warsingers, right? The world has nothing like the Warsingers any more."

"No, but there is much that has been gained since my time. Perhaps the most significant difference is that we did not have great nation-states when the Drachan invaded. The Solonkratsu were numerous, but we were arrogant and indolent. The *Mao'sak'ruwad*, the empire of the Cat People, was a decadent, disorganized mess. It was split between bickering Priest-Queens who refused to cooperate with one another. When the Drachan first touched down on Archemi, the Aesari were tribal savages. They had powerful magics, but they were a species who lived in the present, with no perspective on the past or the future. The Drachan's slaves were the first to rebel, and those slaves—humankind—have spread across the continent and the world since then. It is not just force of arms that will defeat the Drachan. It is the will, ingenuity, and determination of the world to survive that will shape the result of the battle."

Karalti glanced at me. *"I guess. But there's a lot of evil humans, too."*

"Of course. And the presence of these evil people is to your advantage." The pair of doors that led into Lahati's burial chamber parted in front of her. "There is something you must understand about the nature of evil, my daughter. Evil is very dull. Very predictable. The only forms of creativity evil can manifest are cunning and deception. This is because all evil beings, whether they be human or Drachan, have exactly the same boring, repetitive desires. Consumption, power, wealth, attention, love, admiration, sex, safety... primitive, animal needs they pursue with single-minded boorishness at the expense of other living things. Why do you think they pursue these things?"

"Because they're frightened?" Karalti said, uncertainly.

Lahati nodded. "Indeed. Specifically, they are frightened of *lack*. Of not having 'enough'. There is never enough power, enough security, enough pleasure. They must have more and more of it. Search for those people who are aggressively hungry for power and never satisfied with what they have, and you will root out the evil in your midst."

"The Drachan don't seem scared of much," I said. "None of the Void enemies we've fought even seem capable of fear."

"On the contrary. They are the embodiment of fear," Lahati replied softly. "The fear of oblivion. Of meaninglessness. Of pointlessness. In their terror of the vast, unknown universe, they attack it. They revile life, because it terrifies them to think that there is something with meaning, when they themselves have none."

She led us through a narrow obsidian tunnel, barely big enough for Karalti and I to walk alongside each other. It was pitch dark, like walking into a wall of black velvet. But as we emerged, a soft ambient glow filled the room, reflected off an enormous lake of clear crystal as smooth as still water. Karalti pattered out on bare feet, her mouth hanging open, as Lahati's shade drifted to the center of the room and submerged... through the crystal, down into the dark, still form that lay curled beneath it like a fly in amber.

Karalti let out a cry and sank down to her hands and knees, gazing down at the body of her ancestress. Lahati the Chrysanthemum Queen, ruler of the ancient dragon city of Hava Sahasi, was still beautiful in death. Unlike Karalti, most of her scales were a true jet black, save for a large starburst patch of white that bloomed from between her shoulders and out along her wings. Her long sweeping horns and elegant foreclaws were ringed with fine jewelry. Her elegant muzzle was sunken, but her eyes were closed, her expression peaceful.

I unequipped my shoes out of instinctive respect before joining Karalti. I rested a steadying hand on her shoulder.

"Blood of my blood. Child of my daughter's daughter." Lahati's voice now came from all directions, curling from the air of the room. "You are everything I could have dreamed of, a flower who bloomed from a queen the Deceivers have striven to control and destroy. And because of this, you bear a great burden. There are few of us left, Karalti. So many dragons died in the Drachan War, and the ones who lived were enslaved by the Aesari and killed for the mana in their blood. That we survived at all is a miracle that we owe to the other races of Archemi, the humans, and Prrupt'meew who rose against the Aesari and toppled them. There are many more Solonkratsu alive on Daun, where the only other Queen of my bloodline lives, but she is too far away to hear my voice. The other Queens I know are enslaved, like your mother, or rule savage tribes in the wild, remote places of the world. As far as I know, you are the only free Solonkratsu Queen in all of Artana."

Karalti bowed her head. *"Yes, grandmother."*

"If we are to survive, you must free your kin from their chains," Lahati continued. "And to do that, you must be able to command them as their Queen. My last act in this world will be to give you the bloodgift your mother could not. I did not have my body preserved like this out of vanity. I wanted it reserved in case it was needed by future generations of our kind. Take your true form, daughter. And you, Herald: stand back, or take your place between her wings."

Karalti looked up to the ceiling and closed her eyes, concentrating. Her pale skin split with veins of opalescent light, which spread out to cover her as she smoothly shifted back into her natural draconic shape. Archemi's dragons stood on their back feet, their tails stiffened for balance, their hand-like foreclaws held off the ground. When she was back to her full size, she crouched down and extended her wing to me. I climbed up half way, then used her wing claw to boost myself into a Jump, landing between her shoulders like a cricket.

Lahati's body didn't move, but as we watched, she began to bleed black smoke into the crystal that surrounded her. It billowed through the glass like ink, pouring from between her scales. More and more of it came, until the clear crystal turned dark... and then liquified. It pushed the limp body to the surface, exposing the arch of Lahati's ribcage and the underside of one wing.

"The bloodgift is normally given by a mother to her queen daughter by mouth," Lahati said, her voice coiling around my ears like a cool breeze. "The wyrmling bites her mother's tongue, and the blood carries the Words of Power into her body. My tongue no longer has any blood in it, Karalti. Only the core of me still has any to give. You will need to pierce the great vein beneath my wing with your fangs and draw blood from there."

As a normal human-person, I probably would've hesitated at the idea of drinking some five-thousand-year-old blood out of my dead grandma, but Karalti was a predator and a scavenger with instincts that were decidedly non-human. She showed no sign of revulsion as she nuzzled under Lahati's stiff wing with the point of her snout. I felt her draw a deep breath before she snapped forward, bearing the immense crushing pressure of her jaws on the other dragon's skin. The ancient queen's scales popped under her teeth, bending, and then snapping.

"This is not the only gift I give you, my daughter," the spectral voice breathed. "To you and your Bonded, the chosen of my true mate, I bequeath all the treasures of my tomb and the Solonkratsu who are your ancestors. You may take the mana that lies in the caves all around my resting place. You may take the gold and aurum and other treasures from this place, and from the Hall of Heroes that lies under Kri'vauun, a great necropolis to the south of here. The warriors who fell in these ancient wars have long since served their time in the Caul of Souls and moved on. They have no more need of their grave goods. The remaining wealth of Hava Sahasi is yours, and I wish for you both to use it and enrich the land once more."

"I... thank you." I sat down on Karalti's neck, stroking it as she burrowed under Lahati's wing. The Hall of Heroes that she was talking about had hundreds of biers like the ones outside. The coins alone were probably worth hundreds of thousands of gold Olbia... and the artifacts, magical knowledge, weapons, and armor were potentially priceless. "Thank you so much, for all of this."

"I did not sacrifice everything only to see the Deceivers sweep Archemi and destroy the world my lover died to preserve," Lahati said fiercely. "To see my great-granddaughter, Usta, enslaved to the human warmonger who serves them. I sense in you both an incredible spirit, a powerful will to fight. It is my honor to give these gifts to you. I believe in your vision, Herald. I believe your Triad will drive the Drachan back to the Void that spawned them. As long as you can hold onto your sanity, I believe you will triumph."

The sharp scent of mana cut the air: mana laced with a dense, rose-like perfume. I felt Karalti swallow, her long neck rippling under my hands. Then she stood up, panting, her muzzle coated in a glaze of dark blue dragon's blood. Her scales heated, lifting under my hands, and the veins of shimmering color between them intensified.

[Karalti the Black Opal Queen has gained a new Path: Path of Royalty.]
[New information has been added to your mount's character data.]
[Quest Completed: The Path of Royalty.]
[You gain 1576 EXP! Karalti gains 4 Bonus Lexica!]
[Karalti is Level 16!]

The heat and opalescent light spread over Karalti's body, briefly filling the cavern with light. When it passed, she was a couple of feet longer, about two-thirds the size of Lahati. The muscles of her back were thicker, her tail longer, the fins along the flattened edges of it longer and more aerodynamic. The saddle, thanks to the virtual reality wizardry that made equippable clothes and armor fit any player who wore them, resized to fit. Karalti stretched her wings and craned her neck, looking back at her body in wonder.

"You are a glorious woman, Karalti," Lahati sighed. "The Nine have mercy on any male who seeks to catch you in the sky. I fear the lair-coddled dragons of Ilia may not be up to the task."

"Then they'll have to train until they're good enough, won't they?" Karalti snorted and tossed her head, but the thought of her being pursued by other dragons made her—and me—vaguely uncomfortable. As she'd matured, the subject of her taking a mate or three had become an unspoken tension between us. Karalti had gone into heat once already, while in human form, and it had ended... awkwardly. The next time she was compelled to mate, it was possible that there would be other dragons around. Male dragons. And I wasn't sure how I felt about that.

"Can you give us any advice about the Dragon Gates?" I asked. "You helped create them. What should we know about them?"

"By opening the Gates, you awaken the god entombed within," Lahati replied. Her voice was becoming wispier, more distant. "Each opened Gate will destabilize the Caul, but as the sleeping god gathers their strength, they will help control the collapse. The magical architecture was designed to withstand

76

the collapse of up to three of the Dragon Gates, other than Veles'."

"What's special about his Gate?"

"He was the first to be entombed, and he must be the last to awaken. The Lord of Time's power is the keystone of the Caul, and if his Gate were to open first, the result would be catastrophic. It is why we sacrificed Hava Sahasi to raise The Gate of Endless Longing above the dome of the sky, beyond the reach of man or dragon."

"What if..." Karalti trailed off, anxiously tossing her head. *"What if one of the gods died? As in... really died?"*

"My soul shudders to think," Lahati said. "But only the most powerful of the Architects could be capable of such a thing. I do not know the means... a god's death is not the same as a mortal's. Darkness would not cease to exist if Matir were to truly perish. The Darkness would generate a new godling, who would rise as they assumed their mantle. Perhaps a mortal would ascend, or perhaps they would form from the night sky. It is unknown."

"But once the first Dragon Gate has been opened, the Drachan can get out, right?" I said. "So we have to time it right."

"The Drachan will stir to wakefulness, but they will not be freed. But they are weakened from eons of forced confinement, and the magic of the Caul of Souls is powerful," Lahati said. "I cannot predict what will occur. I can tell you that it is not only the Drachan themselves who are sealed in

Rhorhon. They were bound with their alien servants. The legions of the Void: demons, humans, and the Rostori."

I drew a deep, steadying breath. "Alright. Thanks for that... and thank you for everything you've done for us, Your Majesty. I can say with absolute, one-hundred percent certainty that you are the coolest dead lady I know."

"Hector!" Karalti hissed, flattening all seven horns against her skull.

Soft, ghostly laughter echoed around us. "If only the ancient Paragons had been able to preserve such a sense of humor. Siva Nandini, Altair of the Broken Chains, Pathfinder, Grigori Skyrr, Catherine of Annecy... all so serious, they were. Treasure this one, my daughter. He is perhaps the second man in history who has made me laugh."

"Wait!" Karalti took an urgent step forward as the cavern exhaled and the softly glowing lights flickered. *"Lahati, grandmother... there's so much I don't know! About my mother, about our people—"*

"You will, child." A wraithlike form began to rise from the silent corpse of the ancient queen, the shadow of a great dragon. Lahati's head was almost as long as Karalti's entire torso, dwarfing her as smoke coiled around her long, narrow wings, her graceful neck and elegant, wedge-shaped head. "Trust in the song written into your flesh and blood. Listen to it, grow in wisdom... and you will discover all you must know. You are the Black Opal Queen. Stand tall, knowing that a thousand mothers watch you from the place of stillness beyond the living world. We will always be there for you, and if it is your fate to pass over, we will receive you with open arms and warm wings."

Karalti let out a mournful cry as Lahati's wraith blew apart and faded. The hairs on my arms rose as her presence left the room, leaving it echoing and empty. The crystal floor hummed, turning a milky gray as the body in front of us began to dissolve. As we watched, her body disintegrated into the substance, which hardened once more and set like glass. All the jewelry Lahati had been wearing lay on the surface, glittering on the dragon-shaped shadow her body had left behind.

As Karalti's tail and wings drooped, I sat down at the very front of the saddle and wrapped my arms and legs around the base of her neck, hugging her tight. She shivered and jerked, at first... but as the minutes passed, her muscles relaxed.

"*What an incredible will,*" Karalti whispered. "*To have waited here for so long, and yet kept so much of herself.*"

Karalti's voice startled me a little. She sounded so... mature.

A HUD alert shook me out of my reverie. I called it over, and as Navigail read out the notifications, my eyebrows climbed up toward my hairline.

[You have made progress on a Main Quest: Darkness Shines on Light Places (1/4) complete!]
[You have a new Quest: Darkness Shines on Light Places (2/4).]
[You gain 1000 EXP!]
[You are Level 26!]

"Yeah. And wow." I pulled my helmet off and rubbed my head. "When did I even get this quest? It must have been back at the Eyrie."

"Huh?" Karalti shook herself out of her reverie. *"Which quest?"*

"*Darkness Shines on Light Places.* I'll have the HUD read it out to us," I said. "It's an important one."

Quest Update: Darkness Shines on Light Places (2/4)

During your time at the Eyrie, the bastion of the dragon knights of St. Grigori, you discovered a dark secret at the heart of the Order. The dragons and knights are bound by some kind of magical enslavement, a geas stretching back hundreds, or maybe even thousands of years. It binds the dragons and their bonded riders to the will of the current Knight-Commander.

The Solonkratsu, Archemi's native dragons, are a hive species. It is this hive-forming impulse that the Geas on the Order perverts. Instead of allowing the dragons to form families, communities, and centers of art and culture, the magic compels them to be docile mounts in service to human agendas, with no room for argument or independence.

Your Queen dragon, Karalti, has gained access to the Path of Royalty—but to free the dragons of Ilia, Karalti's status as a queen is not enough. You must get to the root of the problem, the Geas itself. The answers lay in the fallen Aesari city of Cham Garai. Now that you possess Lahati's blessing and the Pearl of Glorious Dawn, the way will be open to you—but are you strong enough to face what lies within?

This is a special quest (Mark of Matir).
This is a sequential quest (2 of 4)
Difficulty: *Level 40-45*
Rewards: *6500 EXP, Fame/Infamy, Unknown unique rewards.*

[Do you wish to continue this quest?]

I squeezed Karalti with my legs, and nodded. "Yes."

[Quest accepted!]

The quest marker turned green, and then joined the queue of active quests waiting in the holographic window. I closed it down, and sighed.

"Yeesh. Level 40 is a lot closer than it was back then, but it's still pretty far away." I said. "We'll need a shit ton of EXP to take on the Eyrie."

"How much?"

I brought up the Archemipedia. The reference wiki was a brain-to virtual interface database, like the rest of the menu software. All I had to do was think 'Dark Dragoon Experience Table', and I was able to see how much EXP I needed to get from Level 26 to Level 40. I could do the same for Karalti. She needed a lot more EXP than I did to reach the same level, meaning she was typically ten levels behind me. "Yeesh. We'll have to nearly double what we have now. I need a bit over thirty-eight thousand to hit Level 40. You need about thirty-nine thousand points to reach Level 20."

"*We can do it,*" Karalti said firmly. "*We have lots of quests, and there's heaps of monsters in the Endlar. All we have to do is fight and train together, like we always have.*"

"You bet your fine ass we will." I clapped her neck and stood on the saddle. "Let's work out a training regime at home: I'll delegate everything I can, and we can skill up."

"*Yeah!*" Karalti tossed her head up and down, huffing a cloud of steam toward the ceiling. "*We should pick up the treasure here and go. Suri, Vash, Istvan... they're all worried about us.*"

"Don't rush yourself if you like... need to stay here a while longer." I said. "We've been gone from Karhad for nearly four days. Another half an hour to say goodbye to Lahati isn't gonna make a difference."

"*It's fine. I feel okay.*" Karalti rumbled, squatting down to paw at the scattered jewelry on the surface of the crystal lake. "*Can you help me pick this up? Between your inventory and mine, we should be able to take a lot of what we found here home. Istvan'll be happy to see gold in the treasury.*"

"He sure will." I rolled my shoulders and slid down her flank to dismount. "I can't believe she bequeathed everything to us. There's got to be a million olbia's worth of treasure in the Vault of Heroes. There's probably fifty grand's worth just in here. Not to mention the mana."

"*I can,*" Karalti said. "*Believe it, that is. Lahati told us why. I'm her hope for the future. We both are... because if the Drachan get out of their prison and win, none of this gold will mean anything. There won't be a world to spend it in.*"

CHAPTER 9

Thanks to the fact that Karalti could now carry about a thousand pounds of stuff, we could pack in a LOT of treasure. I cleaned all the junk I didn't need out of my Inventory, and we crammed in everything we could loot. And then, with the protective spells over Lahati's Tomb deactivated, we teleported home.

We appeared in the air right over my castle—a statement which still felt weird to think, even though Kalla Sahasi had been ours for almost a month. The castle loomed over Myszno's administrative capital, Karhad, perched at the edge of a tall mesa overlooking the narrow river valley. The city looked better than it had three weeks ago. There were fewer tents, less rubble, and more scaffolding. As for the castle... Ehhhh. Not so much.

In its hey-day, Kalla Sahasi had been a masterwork of soaring black towers, intricate gothic buttressing, and tall golden roofs surrounding a trio of towers around a triangular courtyard, the Inner Ward. Right now, Kalla Sahasi was barely livable, let alone defendable. The roof and upper floors of the tower closest to the road had been crushed by the Demon's siege engines. Unfortunately, that tower contained the library, guest suites, the War Room, and our nice meeting rooms, all which had put a bit of a crimp on inviting the nobility of Myszno to come and visit.

The Administration Tower wasn't the only casualty from the invasion of Myszno. All the outbuildings on that northern side—the bakery, two granaries, servant housing, and one of the barracks—were unusable, heavily damaged in the vicious assault the Demon's army had leveled on the castle. Our curtain wall was more curtain than wall. We'd even had to burn most of the remaining furniture, because Ashur and his undead minions had left mysterious brown stains on the upholstery.

Sadly, no repairs had been made on the castle since we'd left it for Dakhdir a couple weeks ago... because Ashur had also looted the treasury and shipped most of the Voivode's gold stock back to his home country of Napath. So, for now, we made do. The castle garrison had patched together the shattered ramparts with scaffolding. Said garrison was crammed into the one remaining barracks and used the guest rooms in the residential tower for overflow. My Warden, the castle's chief of security, had bunked in the ruins of the gatehouse. We ran meetings out of the private dining room next to the great hall, the main building at the heart of the inner ward. Access to the residential tower was via an arrangement of narrow plank walkways and ladders. On the upside, we got to train our Dex stat every time we needed to go to bed or use the bathroom.

But one thing about Kalla Sahasi *had* changed. A huge encampment had sprung up across the northern mesa, down the road, and onto the alpine meadows beneath the shadow of the castle. Rows and rows of pup tents and canvas marquees, hundreds of cooking fires, hookwings, wagons, and latrines sprawled in all directions, bustling with soldiers. Two large and three small airships were moored at the skydock that jutted over the southern cliff face. My army had arrived from the north and south.

"What the... ohhh fuck. I didn't expect them to set camp right outside the castle." I held onto the saddle grips as Karalti swooped into a fast glide, kiting around the skydock to line up with the southern face of the Inner Ward. *"Jeez. At least we can pay The Orphans now. They saved us a whole lot of trouble in Vyeshniki."*

"Did they get the bandits?" Karalti asked.

"They sure did. Kicked their asses up and down the row."

The blare of a war horn followed us as Karalti passed over the airships, rocking them in their bays. Down below, the doors of the Great Hall flew open, letting out a stream of people. Suri was in the lead, her expression as shocked as it was hopeful. Vash Dorha and Istvan Arshak were right behind her, shading their eyes against the midday glare. There were others trailing them: the tall, mustachioed Captain Vilmos and the curvaceous silver figure of Rin, who squealed and hugged the startled Warden around the waist before he could react.

Karalti let out a musical, bugling cry as she slung her long hind legs forward, then backwinged before touching down on the pavement. Suri stormed forward as I slid down to the ground, her golden eyes flashing. For a moment, I thought she was about to slap me. Instead, she caught me in a tight embrace, pressed her lips to my forehead, then kissed me fiercely on the mouth.

"Ummf!" I groaned as my spine cracked under the pressure of her arms. Suri was about five inches taller than me and had about 50 more points of Strength.

"Hi babe," I croaked.

"Don't you fuckin' 'babe' me, you... you...!" She leaned back, gripping me by the shoulders. "Where the fuckin' hell were you two!? We were worried sick!"

"Uhh... long story. I don't remember all of it. I'm pretty sure Baldr kicked my ass, and we woke in a dungeon we had to clear before we could teleport home." I pulled out a couple of handfuls of jewels from my Inventory: strings of gold coins, pearls, and jewels. "But hey, look! Shinies!"

Suri's expression darkened, but she didn't deck me out. Instead, she wrapped her arms around me again, burying her face in the crook of my neck and shoulder. I put the treasure away and hugged her back, kissing her hair.

"I'm sorry." I said quietly. "I knew you'd be freaked, but we couldn't do anything to get in touch. All we could do was get back as fast as we could."

"I thought you were gone." Her fingers clutched the back of my armor. "I really did."

"We're fine!" Karalti lowered her head to nudge at Suri's arm. *"He died a couple of times, but I took good care of him."*

"I bet. You always do." Suri wasn't crying, but her voice choked as reached out to lay her hand on the dragon's nose, still resting her forehead against my shoulder.

"We were just discussing the logistics of how to take the Volod's ships to Dakhdir to search for you both," Istvan added, stepping forward as Suri finally let go. I shook his hand, then Captain Vilmos' as he followed up behind. Vash put his hands together, palm to palm, and gave me and Karalti both an ironic little bow.

"Well, just as well you didn't. We were nowhere near-OOF." I staggered back as Rin ran up and threw herself into my arms. The little Mercurion was a lot heavier than she looked.

"Oh my god, w-we thought you were dead! Like dead-dead!" She accidentally headbutted me in the chest, driving the wind out of my lungs as she bounced up and down. "I-was-so-worried-you-died-and-the-spawn-glitch-happened-and-you-couldn't-respawn-and-just-kept-dying-over-and-over-"

"We're okay, seriously." I gave Rin a friendly one-armed squeeze, absently bringing up the Kingdom Management menu. "The Heart of Memory you gave me recorded some info, so we'll review it and me and Karalti'll debrief everyone on what happened. But before I call a meeting, I need to sort out the day's agenda. Istvan, I've got gold for you to take to the Treasury vault. Captain Vilmos, I need you to invite three people to report to the Great Hall: Zlaslo ul'Tiranozavir, Ur Gehlan, aaaaand..." I held up a hand as I quickly checked the *Kingdom Management > Mass Combat* menu. "... Wing Commander Vászoly, Ravensblood Dragoons 1st Company.

We need to send scouts to Bas County to get intel so we can finish up Kitti Hussar's quest. Vash, if you can find Taethawn, I'll schedule him for a hearing so we can sort out his pay."

I looked around the holographic menu screen to find my friends and companions blinking at me in a daze.

"What?" I squinted at them.

"Apparently our Lord Dog grew a couple of pants sizes while he was away, eh?" Vash's scarred and shattered face twisted in a wolfish smile.

"We already sent scouts to Bas," Suri said. "I've been handling the Kingdom Quests while you and Special-K were AWOL. Check the list."

I opened up the menu listing our Kingdom Quests, and saw she was right. We'd had about ten outstanding quests, all of which now had NPC heroes or Starborn players handling them. The biggest quest still on our list was *The Last of Her House*. I couldn't remember it word for word, but as Navigail read it out, I knew the description had changed:

Kingdom Quest: The Last of Her House

Lady Kitti Hussar is the 14-year-old daughter of the Count of Bas, Myszno's southernmost county. Lady Hussar's entire family perished in the Demon War.

In the aftermath, Zoltan Gallo, a veteran knight who deserted Count Hussar on the battlefield, has rallied a militia and declared himself the new lord of Bas. In addition to oppressing the citizens who survived the war, he has given

Kitti an ultimatum—marry him, forfeit her inheritance and elevate him to the noble class, or die.

You have given Lady Hussar shelter and a reprieve from her stalker, and now, you await the return of the Yanik Rangers and Royal Dragoons who were sent to scout Zoltan's base: the fortress city of Solonovka.

Difficulty: *Moderate (Level 20-25)*

Rewards: *2700 EXP, 40 Build Points, Unlock New Resources (Barley, Silver, Mana), +400 Renown (Myszno, Renown (Bas)).*

Special: *Quest must be completed within 7 days.*

"Crap. We missed the early completion bonus." I heaved a sigh of relief anyway. "Thanks for handling those."

"Of course. I'm next in the chain of command. It's my duty," Suri said. "Couldn't have done it without everyone here, though. 'S been a stressful week."

I smiled at her, then inclined my head to Captain Vilmos. "Nix the meeting with the commanders for now, then. We'll get everyone together when the scouts return. Did they give an ETA?"

"The Ravensblood Dragoons believed their mounts could make the flight to Solonovka in half a day," Captain Vilmos replied gruffly. "They have been gone three. We pray for their return tonight or tomorrow. As it stands, we only have ten days before the autumn harvest begins. If we don't get him out now, Gallo will fill Solonovka's granaries and cellars with food and dig himself in like a tick."

"If I have to go down there and harvest it myself, I will," I said. "Don't worry. We can pay our soldiers, as soon as we get this gold into the treasury. Istvan, you'll find what you need in Karalti's saddlebags."

Istvan drew his heels in with a click before striding over to her. Karalti obligingly crouched down, and he unbuckled one of the huge bags on her flank to look inside. When he saw the contents, his eyes widened: he cleared his throat and closed the bag again. "It's good to have you back, Your Grace. I will handle this."

"With skill and discretion, no doubt," Vash remarked. "Hrrun. What else happened while you were gone? Oh, yes— the crab merchant-turned-mayor who claims to represent Karhad is here."

"Mayor Bubek?" I asked him.

"I still cannot bring myself to call that self-appointed sloven 'Mayor'," Istvan said, scowling. "But yes, Bubek is here with some issues. Given you gave him conditional status, we put him up in a guest room in what remains of the gatehouse."

"Awesome. I'll see Taethawn first, then Mayor Bubek." I swiped over to the Kingdom Management schedule, and added in the slots. "Vash, you're the fastest. Can you notify them? I'll squeeze the ducal booty into the Voivode's throne and sort out the Orphans Company now."

"Your Grace, I will send them." Istvan gave me a brisk nod. "You ought to keep Vash close. After that assassination

90

attempt in the Ducal Chambers, I think all your staff will feel better knowing he is by your side."

"Yeah. No more dying for you," Karalti chimed in. *"The last time was kind of bad."*

"Sure." I clapped Vash on the shoulder—the one without the prosthetic. "Guess you're on bodyguard detail, Vash."

Vash laughed. "I'll be gentle."

"You better be," I said. "Just remember: small, circular motions."

Suri crossed her arms. "You aren't even gonna take an hour to catch up with us?"

"After all this is over and done with, sure," I replied. "Dinner and a movie, whatever you want. For my own sake, I need to hit the ground running and get all of our admin out of the way first before we relax."

"Yeah! Do ALL the Voivoding!" Karalti stiffly beat her wings behind us, throwing up a cloud of dust and small stones, but then dropped back down to hug at her stomach. *"Urgh. Istvan? Can you hurry up and get that treasure offloaded? If I don't get something to eat soon, I'm gonna die."*

CHAPTER 10

Somehow, I—Dragozin Hector, formerly Hector Park, Private First Class—had ended up in charge of a Vlachian province large enough to be its own small country. The fantasy of ruling a nation was pretty common in the gaming world, and if you could put the game down and go eat some Cheetos when you felt like it, being the lord of all you surveyed was a great way to relieve stress. But Archemi didn't feel like a game anymore. I'd been here nearly six months, and now it was just... life. A life that came with dragons and awesome friends, beautiful women, and delicious food, but also responsibilities. In my case, those responsibilities included twenty-one thousand square miles of territory, 2.2 million people, 10 counties and at least three major ethnic groups. All of it was mine to rule. I was doing my best not to fuck it up.

I returned to my quarters, where my anxious butler helped me get ready to do Important Duke Stuff. The bathtub in the Ducal Suite was basically a giant kitty litter box without the mess, because my half-vampire self needed to sleep buried in sand to gain the Well Rested buff. That meant I had to take my actual baths in the Princess Suite, which had belonged to the old Voivode's infant daughter. It was done up in shades of pink and pearl and still had the girl's collection of stuffed toy dinosaurs on the counter. There was also scented bubble bath, which I made liberal use of—because if I had to wash in a

Hello Hookwing-themed bathroom, then by god I was going to smell fucking *fabulous*.

After scrubbing off the filth of the last several days, shaving my face and the sides of my scalp and refreshing my Tuun braids, I started to feel almost demi-human again. I let Rudolph the Butler help me into my one and only [Vlachian Nobleman's Outfit], poked some food into my face-hole, and then I was off again: jogging deliriously down to the Great Hall.

I arrived to find everyone ready for me, other than Taethawn. The guards were guarding, the throne was throning, and Vash was in his position to the chair's left—the heart side, where the Voivode's bodyguard customarily stood. I nodded to the men and women protecting my seat as they saluted, dropping down into the humble chair that served as the ruling seat of Myszno.

"Oh—you smell nice," Vash remarked. "Is that jasmine?"

"Probably." I leaned back, opening up my HUD. Archemi's holographic interface was modular, so I pulled up the Kingdom Management windows I'd need and pushed them to the left, then set my character sheet and Karalti's to the right. "Okay, let's get this orgy started. Where's Taethawn?"

"Who knows?" The monk sighed. "Istvan notified him, but Meewfolk being what they are, he'll be here somewhere between five minutes and half an hour."

"Pretty much what I expected." I had an Ability Point to spend, but decided to save that until I could properly assess my available combat skills. I quickly doled out my skill points, assigning two to Leadership and one to Strategy, bringing both Skills to Beginner 10: the maximum level I could attain before mentoring under a trainer or reading a Journeyman-level Skill Tome. No sooner had I confirmed that than I got a notification.

[Your Steward has added 55,099 gold olbia to the Treasury!]
[You have 65,862 olbia available for projects or withdrawal.
You have 120 Build Points.]

"Nice. Istvan just dropped fifty-five K in the bank, and there's a lot more where that came from," I said. "Not enough to rebuild the university, but still. It's better than it was."

"Indeed. Though out of curiosity, where did you source all this gold?" Vash asked in Tuun.

"Lahati's Tomb," I replied, in the same language. It was one of many reasons I was happy to keep him as my bodyguard. No one else in the castle besides Karalti spoke Tuun, so we could discuss Important Duke Stuff in relative secrecy. "And no, we didn't graverob the last dragon queen of Myszno. She gave her grave goods and those of her clanmates to Karalti as an inheritance."

Vash grunted. "I'm glad. Or we would be having stern words."

"Believe me, Karalti has strong opinions on that as well." I closed my sheet and opened Karalti's. "I'm going to zone out for a bit. Need to read over Karalti's new Path."

"I'll make sure no one emerges out of the curtains to stab you." He reached into the front of his Tuun herder's jacket, and pulled out a long-stemmed pipe. "Do you mind?"

I grinned at him. "No, but Istvan will chew you out if he catches you smoking on the job."

"Taethawn won't." Vash shrugged, already preparing his bowl. "As vices go, *majza* is not the worst. It keeps me alert, and it helps with pain."

"Your arm still bugging you?" I motioned to his right arm, the mechanical one. He'd lost the original in possibly the most epic way imaginable: by punching a diving dragon in the face. Rin had replaced it with a high-end magical prosthesis. The first attempt had nearly killed him. The second implant was doing better, or so I'd thought.

"No, not the arm." He shook his head. "The blows I took to the face smashed my sinuses into little pieces. They have caused me pain ever since."

I cocked my head. As much as I liked Vash, there were a lot of things I still didn't know about the guy. For example: why was he a self-described 'kinslayer' with fifteen dead relatives? "How'd you get them?"

"The scars?" He cocked his eyebrows as he lit his pipe, eyes closed. "My sister."

I blinked a couple times. "Your sister smashed up your face? What the fuck for?"

Vash took a long drag off the pipe and shook his head. "Nothing I feel like recounting right now. But..."

"But what?"

"I may need to ask a related personal favor of you someday soon. That is, if this common scoundrel can request such a thing from a great and noble lord such as yourself."

That got a laugh. "Cut it out, dude. You're starting to sound like Istvan."

He gazed piously toward the ceiling. "You are what you eat."

I snorted, and turned back to Karalti's sheet. *'Navigail, read out Karalti's new Path of Royalty descriptions for me.'*

The Path of Royalty

Grace, power, and charisma: three qualities embodied in Archemi's queen dragons, some of the most powerful creatures to ever fly the skies of Archemi. Like the queens found in bee colonies, queen dragons are born to rule—but to do so effectively, they must advance in the Path of Royalty.

The milestones of the Path of Royalty are available at the same levels as those of her Combat Path (the Path of Alacrity). All milestones that would be accrued prior to her current level are gained automatically. By advancing your dragon's level through battling and training, she will gain more abilities in both the Path of Royalty and Path of Alacrity at Levels 20, 25, and 30. The Path of Royalty does not have an Advanced Path option.

Abilities on the Path of Royalty can be leveled. By spending Lexica—the points used to gain new spells or improve currently known spells—you can improve your dragon's Path of Royalty abilities from Level I to Level V.

Ooh—that was neat. Karalti's Path of Alacrity abilities didn't have any individual ability advancements, so that was a big change. I brought up the Path menus, scanning the new abilities Karalti had gained from her communion with Lahati:

Level 5: Queensong of Life and Death I

As with all Paths and Advanced Paths, the Path of Royalty has a foundational ability key to the use and advancement of the class. For your dragon, this ability is her Queensong. The Queensong is a special, magically-charged vocalization which allows your queen to communicate with fellow dragons—and other species—at vast distances. It is unique to each queen dragon, reflecting and magnifying the elemental Words of Power written into their genes.

Your dragon has the Queensong of Life and Death. Once per day, she may emit a cry which—at her discretion—either restores 50% of her allies' maximum stamina (to a maximum of 100 allies) or causes the Fear and Nausea debuffs to susceptible opponents (to a maximum of 100 enemies).

The Queensong is a magical ability, not a sonic attack, and is therefore not affected by the Mute status. However, powerful anti-magic fields (Level V or above) will nullify the effects of the Queensong. The Queensong will in turn degrade the effectiveness of anti-magic fields, weakening them by one spell level.

Level this ability to improve the number of daily uses, effective range, resistance to antimagic, and number of allies/enemies affected by the ability.

Level 10: Wingleader I

Your dragon telepathically calls to your allied dragons, uniting them into a fearsomely determined unit. Your queen dragon selects up to 10 allied dragons who will instinctively form a unit at her direction, gaining immunity to fear for 10 minutes, +10% speed and +10% damage against one individual target.

Level 15: Pack Tactics I

Your queen telepathically summons allied dragons into a savage fighting wing, directing them to encircle an enemy and tear them to pieces. You select up to 10 allied dragons to form a unit, who gain +15% aerial maneuverability and +15% speed against 5 or fewer targets for 10 minutes. If the unit can encircle the enemy, they gain +25% damage against those targets and one extra breath weapon charge. If an ally achieves a critical strike against an opponent's vital area, they gain +25% additional damage to that strike.

Level 20: Lifebringer I

Your queen dragon gains the ability to heal allies with her Queensong. By spending 80 points of mana, she can target as many allies as her Queensong is able to affect and heal them for 100 HP per unit.

Level 25: Harbinger I

Your queen's song turns dark and terrifying, instilling terror and sabotaging your foes' will to fight. By spending 80 points of mana, your dragon's Queensong induces the Terrified debuff in susceptible enemies and injures them for 500 HP. Terrified enemies in mass combat scenarios will break rank and attempt to flee. If the enemies are Undead, the Queensong does not induce Terror, but instead deals double damage.

Level 30: Armor of Darkness I

Your queen dragon uses her intense connection to the Darkness and Life elements to protect and fortify your allies. The queen, her rider, and all allies within range of the dragon's Queensong gain +250 magical armor, immunity to fear, +25% attack speed, and regenerate 10 HP per second for 10 minutes. Ally melee and ranged attacks deal damage to Incorporeal enemies, and all affected allies deal double damage to Undead.

My eyebrows climbed further and further toward my hairline as my HUD cheerfully narrated this absolute BEAST of a Path. Healing a hundred or more people at a time? Hundreds of people dealing double damage to Undead? Me being me, my first response was to kick myself. If I'd trained her harder, been BETTER at this damn game, we could have had some of those advantages when we'd fought the Demon.

"Idiot," I muttered. I was about to assign Karalti's Lexica for her... but then hesitated. When she was younger, I'd have done it without a second thought. But now? It didn't feel right. She needed to choose for herself.

"Hrrn?" Vash glanced over at me.

"Don't worry," I said. "Nothing I can fix right now. All I can say is, gods help the Demon if he ever tries to pull shit in Myszno again."

A few minutes later, the doors at the end of the hall opened, admitting the commander of the Orphans Company. Taethawn the Bleak was easily the tallest Meewfolk I'd ever met. Archemi's cat people were generally well over six feet tall, but from his clawed hind feet to the tips of his triangular ears, Taethawn pushed eight feet of long limbs and lean muscle. His ears were heavily chipped, pierced with mis-matched rings, and his eyes were different colors: one blue, one yellow. He didn't wear any clothes to speak of, just pounds of jewelry and weapons: rings on his fingers, toes, and tail; silver claw sheaths, bracelets, chokers, and two jeweled scimitars. His modesty was preserved by his short, sleek coat of grimy white fur.

"How good to ssssee you again, Your Grace," Taethawn purred, sweeping into a bow in front of the dais. He had the thick musical accent common to Meewfolk who had emigrated from their island homeland to the mainland of Artana. "I had heard rumorsss of your untimely demise. Those tales were exaggerated, I see."

"Just a little bit. I was out hunting down your pay," I said. "According to Mr. Kingdom Management System here, we owe you two weeks of back pay after clearing out Vyeshniki for us. Good work, and thanks."

"Oh, believe me, it was our pleasure." He gave me a slow-eyed squint, just like a pleased cat. "It is not often we can engage an enemy that is so dessserving of punissshment. My men were able to make a fitting example out of the bandit leader, to the delight of the Alderman of Vyessshniki."

"Good to hear. Do you have enough men to rotate out for a second house-cleaning campaign?" I asked. "We need to retake Bas County, also in the south of the province."

The Meewfolk made a show of thinking about it, pacing back and forth with his tail lashing. "It dependsss how many men you require. We have been campaigning for monthsss. My infantry and light cavalry are exhausted, and require at least another week of rest to heal injuriesss and regain energy and morale. I have little more than specialist unitsss available for deployment: a few hundred elite infantry, some heavy cavalry, bombardiersss."

"How many all up?"

He shrugged. "Perhapsss eight hundred."

I frowned, tapping my lip. The Royal troops Ignas had sent with us were still relatively fresh, but that still only gave us just three thousand soldiers.

"Eight hundred might be all we need. We're hoping the scouts that Suri sent return tonight. Solonovka isn't too far by air, so we should know within a day or two. I'll tell you what: I'll pay your back pay and cover the Company for another two weeks regardless of how many you can field, but keep those eight hundred soldiers ready to deploy. Suit you?"

Vash, who had taken position to the left of the throne, shot me a curious glance.

"Cover... the Company?" Taethawn arched his tail into a curious question-mark shape. "Let me make sure I understand you correctly, your Grace. You mean the entire company?"

"Yup. We'll pay the soldiers for their leave," I said.

Taethawn blinked at me. "You would... pay them while they rest? Not just for the ones you plan to use in battle?"

There was an awkward pause.

"Well, yeah," I said. "I'm not going to stiff your soldiers for needing to take some downtime. They get full pay while they recover. Why?"

One of Taethawn's ears flicked. I heard him sniff the air a couple of times before he cocked his head. "You're serious, aren't you?"

"Why?" I repeated. "Is that a problem?"

His eyes widened, and he held his hands up, claws sheathed. "No, not at all, Your Grace. You are simply the first human lord to have ever made such an offer, without trying to... ahh... how shall I say...?"

"Nickel and dime you?" I asked.

"Yesss, Your Grace," he said, sweeping into a low bow. "It is exceedingly generousss for you to pay my Company while they are on leave. Normally, we are sssimply ordered to leave the territory which we served, and we retreat to Sathbar and ressst. If the lord is feeling charitable, he flies us there... at our expenssse."

"Well, screw that," I said, leaning back into my chair. "I'll brawl with merchants over the price of wheat, but not the health of your men. Your soldiers will get their full wage during rotation. They've earned it."

He bowed again. "I thank you for this mossst benevolent offer, my lord."

[You have gained +350 Renown: The Orphans Company.]

"My pleasure." I gave him a short nod. "Once we have more money, I'll loop you in on my plans for Myszno's military. There might be a role for you moving forward."

"Your plansss?" Taethawn stood up, blinking. "A role?"

"Yeah," I said. "I'm only just starting to put the ideas together, but I think this province has the potential to train the best army this world has ever seen. With what's coming, we're going to need it. I want to modernize the structure of Myszno's military. A defined Army and Airforce, a code of military law, and a structured system of merit-based command."

Vash, who had said nothing throughout the entire exchange, coughed a cloud of smoke around the stem of his pipe.

The Meewfolk laughed, a nearly-silent hissing peal of mirth. "My lord... with all ressspect, if you do such a thing, you will need to hire me for the rest of your daysss—as your bodyguard." He paused to grin at me, bearing two-inch long fangs. "You propose nothing ssshort of a revolution. War is naught but politicsss by a different name, and were you to remove military command from your fellow noblesss, they would become but pompous landlordsss. They would seek to kill you, or maneuver to have you disssgraced and exiled. You would make many enemiesss very quickly. Perhaps even your king, the Volod."

"Too bad," I said. "I don't think the Volod will be a problem: Ignas knows as well as I do that the Drachan are coming, and they're going to make what happened here with the Demon look like a kindergarten slap-fight. We need to unify, we need to modernize, and if the nobility doesn't understand that, the nobility can suck my dick."

Taethawn began to laugh again, harder. He held up a hand, shaking his head, and bent down to rest his palms on his knees.

"I like you, Your Grace," he gasped. "You are a breath of fresh air in thisss stuffy backwater. Should you do thisss, I shhhall support you on principle. But you will do well to watch your neck in the aftermath. There shall be many eager to lay their blade upon your throat, should you try and place the power of the military into common handsss."

"I'm basically immortal. So like I said: they can blow me." I queried the KMS with a thought: *'Pay The Orphans Company 25,730 olbia.'*

[You have paid 25,730 olbia to the Orphans Company.]
[You have gained +150 Renown: The Orphans Company.]

"There's your pay for the last period, and the next two weeks," I continued. "I'll call you back once the scouts return from Bas."

"A thousand thanks, Your Grace." The Meewfolk pressed his palms together and bowed deeply from the waist. "While my troops ressst, by all means feel free to call on this one's services as an officer and ssstrategist. Your Vlachian troopsss are disinclined to obey a 'cat-man', but I can both see and smell your personal sincerity. For you, our fee is inclussssive of my experience, mrah?"

"I'll be sure to do that." I smiled back at him and tried the slow happy cat squint he'd given me earlier in the meeting. He squinted back, tail lashing. "Let's call it here. I'd like a written report on Vyeshniki. They're not far from the border of Bas; it might be useful for review to plan the mission there."

"A report?" He cocked his hip and played with his whiskers, stroking them thoughtfully. "Another new concept. Very well. I shhhall do this thing."

"Thanks. That'll be all, Commander."

"By your leave, my lord." Taethawn had a noticeable bounce in his step as he sauntered off, slipping through a crack in the door.

"What do you think?" I asked Vash. "Is he right? About my idea?"

"Absolutely. You're crazier than I thought if you think the satraps will accept a word of what you just proposed. Or the Volod, for that matter." Vash replied. He leaned back against one of the pillars behind the throne, arms crossed.

"With the exception of Lord Soma, the nobility of Myszno, no matter how well-padded their bottoms may be, are the descendants of conquerors. The entire system of rule here is based on might: the might of lords at every level to defend their holdings. If you take that privilege away from them, you might as well piss in their mouths, too."

I hadn't thought of it that way. Frowning, I rubbed a hand over my chin. "But the system of vassalage is so fucking inefficient. Once the Dragon Gates are open, we're looking at fighting the Drachan and their minions on a global scale. How the fuck am I supposed to 'unite the peoples of Archemi' if the lords of one nation can't commit to forming a standardized military? Maybe I could win them over? If we have high enough Renown-"

"Renown works differently for nobility," Vash said, cutting me off. "Your popularity with your soldiers and the people is one thing. Your peers have to be wooed as individuals, otherwise, Lord Soma would be simpering after both of us based on your popularity with the people you rescued from the Demon's rampage."

Damn. I'd forgotten that.

"Politics is a rotten game, Hector. You may gain Renown with one Lord, and alienate another as your enemy in the process," he continued. "Let us say you restore Lady Hussar to her seat, and she declares she shall support you. The Hussar family is loathed by House Vargan, in the county next door. The Vargans, however, are fond of the Turok family of Boros, with whom they have intermarried several times. Do you see what I am saying?"

"Yeah." I tapped the arm of my chair. "But the lords can vote on things. All I need is a majority of lords to vote for my plans, once they're ready. Preferably two-thirds majority, to avoid conflict."

"There will be conflict no matter what you do. Those who refuse to join this revolution of yours will become your enemies," Vash said. "So if you go through with this idea, you had best install bars on your windows and those of everyone you care about. Taethawn is wiser than he seems. Your life will be in danger, perhaps even from the Volod himself."

I sighed. "Of course it couldn't be easy."

"Nothing worth having is ever easy," Vash replied. "Except whores. And even then, the more expensive they are, the better they-"

I held up a hand. "Not right now, dude. I do not need the mental image of you in a brothel full of women."

"Who said anything about women?" Vash beamed at me.

Groaning, I slumped back into my chair. "Just go get the mayor."

Five minutes later, I faced the acting mayor of Karhad as he doffed his plain woolen cap and bowed deeply. He was a great big ham of a guy, built wide and solid. Vlachians were normally a swarthy people, but Alan Bubek was pale and pinkish, with a balding thatch of honey-blond curls that clung to the sides of his head like lamb's wool.

"Good to see you again, Bubek," I said, once he stood up. "I'm guessing this isn't a social call."

"I'm afraid not, Your Grace." The Mayor wrung his hat nervously in his hands. "I am here because the Hospitalers of Veela have isolated a woman with a case of Thornlung Plague."

CHAPTER 11

"Plague?" I unconsciously gripped the armrests of my throne. "Just the one case?"

"Yes, my lord." The Mayor bobbed his head. "The Hospitalers are trying to find out if she had contact with anyone other than her family, but with half the city in ruins and many still living in tents as the cleanup continues, it is impossible to know for certain."

Vash rumbled and shook his head. My blood ran cold. I didn't know what Thornlung was, but I knew from intimate personal experience how terrifyingly fast and deadly an outbreak of disease could be. The HEX virus had torn my world apart in the space of three months.

"Was our Patient Zero a refugee in the camps?" I demanded.

"No, Your Grace. She is a tailor's daughter, who lives and works at the cloth mill in the Riverside District with her family. It was left relatively unscathed by the Demon."

"Is the hospital in Riverside?"

"Yes, Your Grace."

"How is Thornlung spread? Air? Water?"

"I... do not know, in truth." The Mayor shifted from foot to foot. "I am no healer, Your Grace."

"Air," Vash said. "It spreads from person to person inside of houses and other closed, dank spaces."

"Great." I leaned in toward the Mayor. "Okay, Bubek: Here's what's going to happen. We shut down the entire Riverside District for two weeks. The only things allowed in or out are essential deliveries and wagons carrying medical staff. I want the district gates closed and guards posted on every street, in and out."

"Guards?" The Mayor squeaked.

"Yes. I'll send a couple of platoons to fill out your staff. Their job is to control traffic, stop people trying to enter or leave, and to issue cloth masks to people in the Riverside District and the immediate surrounding neighborhoods. Everyone entering or doing business in the Riverside half of the city MUST wear a mask covering their mouth and nose," I said. "Man, woman, and child. Do you understand me?"

The Mayor's mouth opened and closed a few times. "Those are... very strict measures for one sick woman, Your Grace. They will be expensive, and will most definitely not lend me popular-"

"Which makes it even more important that the District is closed NOW. Because you know what will make you less popular? Letting our citizens die of Thornlung." I scowled at him. "And one other thing: the miller's entire family, their staff, and the doctors who treated this lady? They're to be confined to their homes for the quarantine period, starting immediately."

"And... if they protest...?"

"Then they can serve out their two weeks quarantine in jail, and if they do have Thornlung, they get the best medical treatment we can offer. Once they recover, they can dig graves for the people who die because they couldn't be bothered to stay home," I said. "I'm not joking. I've seen what happens when people drag their feet over stuff like this. We crush this outbreak early, and we crush it hard. The Duchy will compensate workers in Riverside who can prove they lost wages due to the lockdown."

"Yes, Your Grace. There is wisdom in what you say. Hard, somewhat brutal wisdom, but wisdom nonetheless." Mayor Bubek bowed uncomfortably. "But if the worst happens, and the plague spreads...?"

"Is it treatable?" I asked Vash.

He nodded. "Yes, if caught early."

I turned back to Bubek. "Then we set up an early screening system and arrange to have the medicines made and held in reserve."

"A screening service will be difficult without help from the university," Mayor Bubek admitted. "The brightest minds of Myszno lived and worked there. Now, it's full of prowlers and other riff-raff. People swear they've seen monsters inside."

"Believe me, fixing the University is on my Top Five Things to Do when it comes to Myszno. Until then, we're just going to have to make do." I slumped back into my chair. "Can you issue these as quests?"

"Yes, Your Grace. One moment."

⟦Alan Bubek would like to issue you two new Kingdom Quests: Supply and Demand and the Vaunted Halls of Karhad University.⟧

I brought up the HUD, and let the system narrator read the quests to me:

New Kingdom Quest: Supply and Demand

As the province of Myszno continues to recover from the invasion of Ashur of Napath, the cracks are starting to show. The capital city of Karhad is running low on food and medical supplies, and even worse, a woman has been isolated with a case of Thornlung, a contagious and often fatal disease that mostly affects young people. Thornlung is treatable, provided it is caught early and the right medicines are available.

The de-facto Mayor of Karhad has requested that you obtain the following staff and medical supplies for the city:

- *Healers ⟦B-Grade or above⟧ x 5*
- *Green Moss x 1500*
- *Valerian x 500*
- *Concentrated Oil of Garlic x 500*
- *Hyssop x 1000*
- *Iguanodon Bile Salts x 200*

Oof. Some of those ingredients were expensive. Still—I nodded, accepted, and reviewed the second quest:

The Vaunted Halls of Karhad University

Karhad University, one of the oldest institutions of learning in Vlachia, was an early target of the Demon in his hunt for the Dragon Gate of Endless Night. When this city-within-a-city was breached, many staff were killed or captured, while others were tortured for information. Now, it is a ruined blight in the center of the city, walled off with barricades and full of criminals, feral animals, and worse.

Enter the university, clear out the rabble, and salvage what you can. Not only will you restore the heart of Karhad's economy, you may discover long-lost knowledge that can be used to help your people in the present day.

Reward: *1249 EXP, 25 Build Points, Renown, Artifacts.*

Bonus: *Rebuild the University (168,000 olbia) to gain more rewards and renown, and unlock special facilities.*

Sure. I'll just rustle up nearly a quarter million olbia out of thin air. Nothing to it. I drew a deep, steadying breath, accepted that quest as well, and put the KMS away. "Alright. Is that all?"

"Well, Your Grace. There is the question of my position," Bubek said. "With the city in the state it's still in, an election is not yet possible—"

"Right. And you're still acting Mayor until it IS possible," I replied. "Emphasis on 'acting'. You proposed an election, and I'm willing to go ahead with one after things are more stable. But we've got to get Karhad back on its feet first. Then we can put a call out, identify who wants to run, and you can compete against them based on merit."

He deflated slightly. "Ah. But—"

"No buts. Handle yourself well and stop that plague from breaking out into the city, and you're almost guaranteed to win," I said briskly. "You can expect the herbs you need soon. Now, sorry to break this off, but I need to wrap up."

"Indeed, Your Grace. Thank you." He swept into another awkward, but genuine bow, and toddled off toward the door. Once he had left, Vash stepped forward again.

"Burna's balls. Thornlung is the last thing we need." He shook his head. "What a coincidence."

"Coincidence?" I asked.

"Yes. The first day in fifteen years that I mention the existence of my sister, and Thornlung appears in the city," he said. "It is a nasty disease. Swift and deadly. Breakouts of it in cities here are rare, but not unheard of."

"She had it?"

"Yes. We all did." A flash of something that might have been pain passed behind Vash's dark gray eyes, and he grimaced. "You handled that well. Your cheeks are starting to fill out the pants of authority, eh?"

"They sure are," I grunted, standing up. I smoothed my coat down. "He was testing me, wasn't he? With the 'why won't you make me mayor?' talk?"

"Yes. Though in truth, the idea of electing a mayor via popular vote is also radical change for Myszno, if not all of Vlachia. It is typical for them to be appointed by the ruling lord." The Baru jerked his metal thumb toward the dining hall. "What comes now?"

"Now I go and study my map of Myszno and get a handle on the kind of terrain we'll face in Bas," I said. "I plan to blitz the place in a single day. Maybe two."

"Solonovka is named the Fortress City for a reason." Vash arched his eyebrows. "You think it will be that easy?"

"No." I straightened the narrow silver band on my brow—the coronet of the Voivode. "But I promise you this. Fortress or not, we're going to teach Zoltan Gallo the new motto of House Dragozin."

"And what motto is that?" He asked wryly.

"The same one my division used in the Army." I grinned back. "'Fuck around and find out'."

CHAPTER 12

The first thing I did after returning to my quarters was to go into the KMS and spend almost all of our hard-won money on two things we needed to make Myszno one of the wealthiest provinces in Vlachia.

A little over 20,000 olbia got us two destroyer-class airships from Litvy, medium-sized warships to replace the ones we'd lost battling the Demon. I couldn't outfit them with high-quality magical shields yet, but they were fast, quiet, and able to carry a decent number of troops. I also put in an order for a team of high-level NPCs—a mage, an artificer, a Forgebrother of Khors, miners, and archeologists—to join us from the fair city of Boros. The team would be dispatched with the ships to Krivan Pass to begin the excavation of the Hall of Heroes. I assigned the Knights of the Red Star to supervise them. Of all the soldiers in my army, they had the highest morale, the most Renown, and the strictest vows of honor. They were also tough enough to keep any curious player characters at bay.

After the shopping spree, I surfed over to the interactive map of Myszno, and finally took a good, long, hard look at Bas County. Myszno had ten counties, with the population concentrated in only four of them: Litvy in the north-west, the ducal seat of Racsa in the center, Boros to the north-east, and Bas, which was due south of Racsa and only about a day's ride by land out of Karhad. Like Racsa, Bas was very mountainous, with most settlements and villages located in steep alpine valleys. The capital, Solonovka, was a city on the edge of the Vlachian frontier that was, as my DI would have said, 'locked down tighter than a nun's cooter'.

The city had not one, not two, but **THREE** concentric rings of tall stone walls: one around the town itself, one around the base of the switchback ridge where Hussar Manor sat, and one encircling the castle itself. From the ground, it was extremely defendable. Approaching it by air was almost as risky. For one thing, any airship or dragon coming toward the city could be spotted for miles in any direction. According to notes submitted by Kitti via Suri, there were five towers in Solonovka, and each of them was armed with anti-aircraft weaponry. In Archemi, those fell into three categories: magical defenses, blackpowder artillery, and giant ballista or other large shooty-downy devices capable of plugging a lot of metal into an airship's engine at high speed. In any case, it was bad news—assuming Zoltan Gallo actually had the manpower to field them.

My study was interrupted by a soft knock on the door. My ears pricked.

"Suri?" I called out.

"Sure is," she drawled. "How'd you know?"

"Call it an educated-and-or-magically-augmented guess," I said. "Come in. Door's unlocked."

She cracked it open and peered inside, scowling. "Why is your door unlocked?"

"Because I'm right here." I gestured to the living room. The Ducal Suite had a central living area, with a Victorian-style sofa and chairs, fireplace, and paintings of the old Voivode and his family. There were four doors in here: one to the bathroom where I slept, one that led to the Lady's Chambers, one that went to my bedroom and office, and one that went to Rudolph's butler lair.

"What? One assassin wasn't enough for you?" Suri huffed, letting herself in.

"If someone comes in the door, I'll throw fruit at them." I picked up an apple from the bowl and grinned at her.

"You throw that at me, you better be ready for the consequences." Suri was still in the armor she'd been wearing when she met Karalti and I in the courtyard: a set of ⟦Bolza Guard Armor⟧ in the silver and green livery of the old duke. "How did the meetings go? I saw we're back down to about five thousand olbia."

"There was, in fact, a great Voivoding," I replied, moving to get a glass for her. "Want anything to drink? There's wine, wine, water and... let's see what this jar is... I think some wine?"

"Vlachia sure does like its wine." She chuckled, pointedly locking the door behind her. "Give me something red. The sweet kind, if Rudolph put that out for you."

"He did." I poured two glasses, one for each of us. "You look sweaty."

"I am. Had training with Kitti." Suri unequipped her full-plate, then the padding underneath, stripping down to a pair of leggings and a form-fitting vest that kept her chest under control while in armor. She unlaced it halfway as she moved to the sofa, sighing with relief as some of the compression lifted and her cleavage was allowed to breathe. She had quite a lot of it. Against all odds, I managed to keep my eyes forward and not spill the wine.

"How's she doing? Kitti, that is." I asked.

"Good. Girl's a natural Berserker," Suri said, dropping down. "Her father coddled her and tried to keep her away from swords and rough men, but he couldn't beat the wildness out of her. That's what you need for this Path: wildness, will, and spirit. She's got the right kind of fire, but she's still just a kid. She doesn't like drills, because those are boring. She can get a bit sooky when she's tired."

"Sooky?" I took her glass over to her and pulled up an ottoman, straddling it to sit in front of her.

"Yeah. You know. Whiny, bitchy. Whatever you wanna call it." Suri took her glass with a smile. "Normal boot stuff. She's just gotta power on through it."

I snorted. "Hand her over to Istvan. Have you seen that man drill recruits?"

"Oh my god." She let out a short laugh. "I heard him ranting in the barracks the other morning. Funniest shit I've heard in my whole fuckin' life."

"Dooo tellll." I leaned in.

"He was yellin' at the top of his lungs at some of the new guys I hired on the first day back here. And I swear, this is a direct quote." Suri waved her hand for a moment, gaining her composure, and then put on her best Barking Sergeant Istvan voice, complete with accent. "'I take *great* offense at waking up a room full of men, and find that *somebody* has the audacity to stand at the end of his bed with an erection! And I want you all to pay very close attention, because if I see that erection again, I will kick it until such a time as it becomes *un-erect!*'"

I started laughing about halfway through, and then kept laughing until I was rolling on the ottoman.

"I swear to god, Hector, I lost about half the coffee up my nose," Suri was laughing too, by now. "I don't think I'd hand Kitti over to him, though. She'd come out the end of his training with half a dozen tattoos and a drinking problem."

"Hey, come on now. He's gotten better with the booze," I said. "Vash has been good for him."

"He sure has." Suri shook her head. "Anyway... Had a look at Bas, yet?"

"Yeah. Operation Girlpower looks like it's going to be a doozy," I said.

She stared at me in disbelief. "Operation Girlpower?"

"Kitti's still a girl. We're restoring her family to power. The name checks out."

"Fuckin' hell." Suri sighed, leaning back against the sofa. "Remind me again why I put up with you?"

"I'm a savant. I found and implemented the clitoris despite never having attended the training course." I nodded.

"There is that," she replied dryly. "I'll have to design an award. We can pin it to your forehead next to the dick."

I beamed at her. "The Pink Pearl Badge."

"Pffft." She chuckled as she drank, shaking her head. "Anyway... you reckon we're gonna be able to finish the quest on time?"

"Yeah. I think so." I straightened up and cracked my back, then my hands. "We won't know exactly what we're dealing with until your scouts return. Has Kitti been able to fill you in on any details?"

"A few," she replied. "Namely that Zoltan isn't exactly popular in Solonovka. Like most knights, he had his own little patch of land with a few tenants to farm it. He treated them like shit, and it seems likely he's treating everyone down there the same way."

"That's helpful," I said. "If we can break his hold over the populace, they'll turn on him."

"Assuming we can get to him, yeah." Suri swirled her glass. "Solonovka is probably the best-defended town in Myszno. The Demon was the first invader to take it by land or air since it was built, and he only did that by tricking his way in past the first two layers of walls."

"Sure. But from what I remember of Kitti's description of events, there's only so many people who could be working with Zoltan. The problem with big, heavily entrenched positions is that they take a lot of manpower to maintain. Towers have to be guarded, posts staffed, weapons made and repaired. If he doesn't have the boots on the ground, it's free chicken."

"Right. And I think it's safe to assume he's relying on air defense," Suri added. "He knows the new Voivode has a dragon. He has to know."

"Right." I said. "In a place like Solonovka, he'll be worried about airships, dragons, and cannons."

"Mhhm." Suri drained her glass and relaxed back into her seat. I did the same, then sidled over onto the sofa. Suri promptly rested both her feet in my lap.

"Sooo..." I began to absently rub her toes, settling back against the armrest. "Before I can wind down for the day, I need to see the recording on the Heart of Memory. I don't know if I can share the feed with you or not. If I can, do you want to see it?"

She groaned, and tipped her head back against the cushions. "Sure. I was just taking a break, to be honest. And I was hoping I could ask for a favor."

"Go ahead."

"I want to get my gear back as soon as we can. Tonight, if possible. When I died in Withering Rose's cockpit, my Inventory dropped there." Suri said, looking over her chest at me. "I feel naked without my bloody armor. This guard equipment doesn't even have half the rating of the full-plate Rin made me."

I nodded. "Consider it done. Karalti needs to finish eating, but after that, I'll see if she's up to it."

"Thanks. Hopefully we can just teleport in, grab the bag, and teleport out." Suri gave me a wan smile. "I missed you. Being a titled Lady in a big castle wasn't nearly as much fun without you and Special-K around."

"Don't enjoy Voivoding?" I let go of her foot and took the Heart of Memory from my Inventory. I sent off a quick party message to Rin: *"Hey, sorry to bug you: is there any way to stream the information on the Heart so Suri can see it?"*

"Y'know, I enjoy ruling more than I thought I would," she said. "Only thing that pisses me off is how inefficient everything is. Lords and ladies and knights and vassalage and shit... it'd be so much fucking easier if there was a proper chain of command, people earning the right to lead based on merit. I'm not a big fan of this top-down feudalist bullshit. Not with a big war on the horizon."

"I knew there was a reason I loved you." I chuckled. "I've been thinking the exact same thing. Things won't change overnight here, but I have a feeling they will change. I'm planning to fight for it."

"Huh. Well, if we're gonna be lording over the place for a while, we really need to get a new throne, though. Your skinny Tuun arse fits in it alright, but I've got hips. It pinches the shit out of me."

"We kind of need to get a new everything," I said, turning the Heart over in my hands. The ruby mana core pulsed softly, radiating warmth against my palms. "I like green things, like plants and shit, but I'm not too big on the green brontosaurus decor. We'll hopefully be able to fix the castle soon, but the province comes first. I'd live in a mud hut before I let anyone in Karhad starve or freeze to death."

"You know some people are gonna die no matter how well we do, right?" Suri said. "That's how that goes."

I wasn't sure why what she said pissed me off as it did—but it did. "Willingly, Suri. I know I can't save everyone, but I won't *willingly* let them starve."

She paused for a moment, realized she'd hit a nerve, and reached out to squeeze my arm. "Right. I get what you mean. And I agree. I saw enough of that in prison."

"So did I," I blurted. Then paused, blinking, as it occurred to me what I'd just said.

"You served time?" Suri cocked her head. "You never told me. When?"

"I... uhh... haven't. Been in prison. I mean, I was born in an internment camp in Orange County, but, I was like... one year old when we were released. Don't think anyone ever starved in there." I rubbed my eyes and forehead. "I'm not sure why I said that. I'm just tired, I guess."

"Eh. Slip of the tongue." Suri looked faintly troubled, and I saw her glance at my left shoulder. "On that note: how's your pet black hole doing?"

"What?

"Your shoulder."

"Oh, that. I haven't checked." I shrugged, then pulled my shirt off and had a look at what she was talking about. The hole in question was an eerie triangular patch of black nothingness that took up most of my left shoulder. It was a scar, kind of. The surface was solid, but it didn't feel like skin. It didn't feel like anything. You couldn't push your fingers through it, but you couldn't feel it with your fingers, either. I'd earned it during an airship crash soon after entering Archemi.

Suri leaned in to look at it as well. "It's bigger."

"This? Nah." I pointed at the black space. "It's always been that size."

"No, Hector. It's bigger." She reached up to probe it. "It didn't used to touch your collarbone like that. You need to show this to the Masterhealer."

I frowned, turning my head to look at it again. Now she mentioned it, had it spread from my shoulder to my chest a little? "It's fine, okay? It's just the light. Even if it *has* gotten bigger, the Masterhealer isn't going to be able to do shit about it."

"We don't know that," she insisted.

I was saved from having to respond by an [Incoming Voice Call] popup. I kissed Suri on the side of the head and held up a hand. "Hang on: Rin's calling."

Suri rolled her eyes, and sat back with a sigh.

"Heya Hector! Sorry it took me a while to get back, I'm setting up a workshop in the smithy quarters," Rin chirped. "Thanks for the materials!"

"Uhh... no problem." I didn't remember leaving Rin any materials, but maybe someone else had. "So yeah: is there a way to stream this thing you gave me?"

"Hmmm..." I could almost hear the gears turning in her head. "Oh! Yes! I'm pretty sure there's meant to be a first-person streaming function, but I don't know if it was actually included in Archemi's beta launch. If you watch it while streaming a first-person POV in a video chat channel, you should be able to share it with us."

"You want to see it too?" I asked her.

"Sure! A-as long as it's not too gory, or a-anything!" She stuttered off. "I mean, you did, like... die."

"I can't guarantee it wasn't gory," I said. "Ororgael is a bad dude. For all I know, he whipped out Ororgael the Lesser and molested my tender, innocent corpse."

"R-Right. I'll pass for now, then. Even though I don't have a stomach and probably won't puke, there's some things I really, really don't want to know about Michael, you know?"

Once Rin DC'd, I opened a new video chat with Suri. Then, I ordered it to stream. Sure enough, a first-person video feed appeared in a small frame. When Suri accepted the invite, suddenly she could see what I was looking at. Her face split into a broad grin.

"Hey, mate. My face is up here, you know." She pointed at her eyes.

"Face? What face?" I managed to tear myself away, also grinning. "Oh! There she is! Sorry, I must have missed you there. It was hidden behind this amazing pair of... chin... pillows."

"'Chin pillows'." She laughed, throwing a cushion at me. "Fuck you and your prim Yankee bullshit. You *will* address Colonels Knockers and Norks with all due respect, soldier!"

"Apologies, ma'am. Ma'am. Ma'am." I nodded to her, and saluted to each boob. "So, ready to watch me die pathetically at the hands of my arch-nemesis over and over again?"

"Not really, but let's get on with it." Suri looped an arm over the back of the sofa, closing her eyes.

I rattled off the words of power to the Heart of Memory and did the same. A warm sensation spread through my head, and then the playback started.

CHAPTER 13

I lost track of the room around me, my body, and sounds and smells of the present. Mentally, sensorily, I was back in the desert, mouthing off to Baldr, sending Karalti off, then realizing that the man in front of me wasn't Baldr at all. It was just Ororgael. I listened with growing horror as he explained Baldr's fate, then initiated the fight. There was a dream-like quality to the whole thing, the feeling of watching the battle like a movie. I was taken aback to see that Ororgael's hand-to-hand skills were surprisingly sloppy, and all things considered, past-me was able to keep up with him. My excitement built as I landed what had to be a critical hit, the kind of vital strike that Archemi normally ruled as an insta-kill... but then the Heart of Memory's feed blurred, and the next moment-

"Wait." Suri's voice broke through the feed. "Can you roll it back? What was THAT?"

I concentrated as the video dissolved into a bright flash of light, and scrolled it back to look at what Suri had spotted. The Heart of Memory recorded my vision as it existed in Archemi. I had about 210 degrees of peripheral vision thanks to the Trial of Marantha, and sure enough, my eyes had glimpsed something weird. While I had my vampire claws buried in his heart, a shimmering half-seen figure had come up on me from the side. It was transparent, like heat haze, but it hauled me off Ororgael and sent me flying.

"That must be the 'invisible bodyguard' Rutha told us about in Taltos," I said.

"Yeah, right on. Let's keep going. See what else he does."

As I came out of the Shadow Dance, I saw the same shimmering figure merge into his body—and as it did, his whole demeanor changed. In a few seconds, he went from flustered to stone-faced. His entire expression shut down before his eyes and mouth flew open and he tracked me with what could only be described as a concentrated nuclear blast. From his face.

"Jesus Christ," Suri whispered.

"That must have been what killed me." But to my surprise, the feed continued.

I crashed onto Withering Rose's back and rolled away, my armor melted and blasted beyond recognition. The fighting went to ground, but with my distant perspective on the battle, I knew I was about to lose. The air around Ororgael glitched and shivered, as if reality was trying to reject his very presence. He grasped my wrist—my left wrist—and I watched nervously as he leaned in toward me with wild, solid black eyes as his face fluxed.

"Do you see this? It's the visual manifestation of an anti-viral program, one designed to cure anomalies like you. I can give you a fresh start, Park. So don't worry about your friends, or the queen. Once I rid the world of squalor and bring order back into the system, they'll be grateful."

Ororgael's hand liquified into a silvery goo that crawled up my arm and over my scarred shoulder, toward my face.

Increasingly apprehensive, I watched myself briefly panic, then leverage Archemi's quick-consume feature to drink most of the liquid mana in my inventory. There was no pain, remembered or otherwise: just light, and a whirling, spinning blur as the Heart of Memory was flung away by the detonation. When the blaze cleared, all that was left of me was a star-shaped smudge of charcoal on the back of the Warsinger. But the Heart was still there, recording a much narrower and blurrier field of vision, and so was Ororgael.

"Hah..." Swaying on his feet, Ororgael slowly picked himself up from the epicenter. His feathery hair was burned away, his mirrored silver plate soot-covered and smoking. He almost seemed to be drunk, or half asleep, until the ghostly figure merged out of him. As it did, his form solidified again. He shook his head, as if awakening from hypnosis.

"Of course I can hear you," he muttered. "Always the same shit, the same lies. But I'm not afraid of you anymore."

He dropped his sword, then stumbled to the left a few steps. There, he planted his feet and held out his arms, craning his neck to stare up at something we couldn't see.

The sky darkened, and a great winged shadow fell over Withering Rose.

"It's right underneath me!" Ororgael shouted. "Get it out of there! Now!"

A mournful, bass keen boomed from overhead. Sand slithered, picking up into a cyclonic wind that picked up around the Warsinger's body. Withering Rose began to tremble, rumbling like an earthquake and a thunderstorm all in one.

Ororgael left the spot he'd been standing, walking over to the Spear of Nine Spheres. We watched him scoop it off the ground and hold it up close to his face, as if examining the blade. Then he screamed, dropping the weapon as the Pearl of Glorious Dawn wrenched itself free from his forehead and snapped into its socket. The Spear clattered to the Warsinger's back, then vanished as he clutched at the wound, blood pouring through his fingers.

"Fuck!" He roared. "Motherfucker! Hyperion: I've changed my mind. Trash this piece of garbage!"

The red sand of the Bashir Desert rose around him like a curtain, howling as the unnatural darkness around him deepened. There was an intense warping sound—and then a pure beam of absolute blackness flashed down from the sky, drawing the remaining light of day with it in an incandescent flash. The narrow beam pierced Withering Rose like an arrow from heaven, throwing up a cloud of filthy smoke. It covered everything.

The recording cut.

"FUCK!" Suri banged her fist on her knee, rising to her feet in agitation. "That absolute *cunt!* The Warsinger's gone!"

"Hang on: We don't know for sure. We have to see what happened. As soon as Karalti gets back, we'll gear up and go." Stomach twisting anxiously, I rolled the footage back to the point where Ororgael was ranting about his antivirus goop, and paused. Listened to it again. "What does 'squalor' mean? I've heard the word before, but I flunked English at school."

"Uhh..." Suri stopped pacing and looked back at me. "I dunno. I never even *went* to school."

"Your Majesty: 'squalor' means the state of being extremely dirty and unpleasant, especially as a result of poverty or neglect." A voice as dry as dead leaves crackled through the still air of the Ducal Suite.

Suri and I both looked up to the front door. As a Greater Shade, Mehkhet the Illuminator resembled the man he'd been in life. Bald, clean-shaven, with a thin beaky face and lips pursed as tight as a cat's butthole. He was made entirely of frigid shadows, a darkness so cold and pure that his robes trailed a cloud of frost as he hovered over to stand in front of us.

"Oh." I gave him a little wave. "Hi, Mehkhet."

"Good afternoon, Master." He gave me a stiff little bow, before refocusing on Suri. "I shall have to instruct you on your diction and comprehension if you are ever to rule as your ancestress did, your Majesty. Such scholarly deprivation cannot stand."

"Fuck dictation and comprehension," she snapped. "How long have you been here, sticky-beaking around?"

"Not long," he replied hollowly. "I've been haunting—so to speak—the ruins of the castle library since you returned. But I felt something stir the air just before, as if the name of some terrible evil had been uttered inside this tower. Capital-

N Name, that is. I came to check on you out of an abundance of caution."

"Everything's fine." Her eyes were stormy with mingled anger and worry as she resumed pacing. "No demons, no nothing. Just one busted Warsinger and a fuckin' crazy idiot of an Architect. Baldr, or Ororgael or whatever he calls himself: he knows that the Drachan'll kill him too, right? If we can't stop them?"

"I... don't think he does," I said. "Judging from what we just heard, he's batshit insane and is living in some alternate reality where he's the hero and I'm some kind of evil virus."

"Tyrants are apt to create their own realities and their own version of the truth," Mehkhet replied, sourly. "I am glad all is well."

"Withering Rose isn't 'well'. She's fucked." Suri got to her feet. "We have to go see how much damage Ororgael did to her, Hector. Where's Karalti?"

I closed my eyes and concentrated, sensing out along the Bond. *"Karalti? You manage to find something to eat?"*

"Sure did!" She chirped. *"Why? Is something wrong? You DEFINITELY sound stressed out now."*

"We just watched the footage from the fight with Bal... Ororgael," I said. *"It's not good. He called some kind of fucking orbital strike on Withering Rose. We need to go scout her out, as soon as possible."*

There was a pause. *"What if Ororgael's still there?"*

"After four days? I doubt it." I shook my head. *"Either he cheated and found a way to magically move eighteen-hundred tons of metal to Ilia already, or it's still there and we're in a race with Ilia's navy to retrieve it."*

"Right. Well, I can teleport twice more today, but after that I'm going to be really tired," Karalti said. *"My stamina is bleh after Lahati's Tomb. Meet me out in the courtyard when you're ready. Oh! And don't forget! Today's potion day."*

"I know. I haven't had time to check with the Masterhealer and see if she got any more King's Grass," I replied. *"Give us fifteen. We'll be out and ready to fly."*

"Okay!"

My eyes flickered open, and I looked up to see Suri waiting expectantly.

"She's back," I said, getting to my feet. "Let me go see if I can scrounge some better armor from Captain Vilmos. As soon as I've got some protection, we can go back to the Bashir and see what we find."

CHAPTER 14

Twenty minutes later, we were in the air and ready to jump back to Dakhdir. I hung on to the saddle without any tie-downs, as relaxed as a surfer kneeling on his board. Suri, who hated flying, was strapped to the saddle with her chin down and her shoulders hunched.

As my dragon beat her wings and gravity pushed down on my shoulders, I felt my breath catch. Karalti had gotten stronger and faster with her last level. She always did, but this time it was like going from a 650cc street bike to a 1000cc road hog. I could feel the magical radiation of her body through the saddle, the incredible muscular power driving each wingbeat. The earth fell away with dizzying speed, giving us a phenomenal view of Kalla Sahasi.

"Ready?" Karalti's sweet voice broke through my distracted wonder.

I pushed down the visor of my borrowed helmet. *"Always, Tidbit."*

My teeth hummed as Karalti summoned her mana. The dragon let out a piercing bellow, straightening out into a gentle glide. That was the sign for me to lock my hands under the saddle grips. I did just that, and braced in anticipation of the frigid darkness that enveloped us as my dragon Teleported.

For several long seconds, we hung in a rushing void of empty space. That was normal. There was always a pause in the game when Karalti jumped. But this time, something about the space around us set my teeth on edge. Normally, the only thing I ever felt was the triple-beat of our hearts, mine and Karalti's. But as we passed through, it felt like someone—or some*thing*—was staring at the back of my neck. Before I could work out what or who it was, we burst out of the cold into a screaming cloud of whirling black sand.

The sandstorm blasted us with such force that Karalti was blown violently to one side, her wings filling with hot air and gravel. Suri screamed a warning even as I slipped and crashed against my dragon's back. Time slowed as I scrabbled along the leather, then activated one of my Mark of Matir abilities, *Spider Climb*. The Mark flared with cold fire, and just before I tumbled off into the air, I slapped my hands down onto the saddle. They bonded to the rough leather like Velcro.

"Arrgh! What the hell?!" Karalti's wings flapped like wet laundry in a hurricane, threatening to snap. She gave up trying to beat them after a few seconds of heedless tumbling, rolling with the wind and diving to regain control. *"Hold on! We have to break through this!"*

With a snarl of effort, I pulled myself up, arm over arm, until I grasped the saddle grips once more. I was so stunned I barely even felt scared. The sand slithering through the cracks in my armor looked like ground pepper, and it was gritty and sharp. And even weirder, the searing heat of the desert was gone. It was cold. Lightning flashed inside of the cloud. An eye-watering metallic smell clung to everything.

[Warning: Extreme Stranged terrain. You are immune to Stranging, but may take damage.]
[Warning: this area is contaminated with nnnnnggghhrrrrrrrrrrrrvvvvvvvvvvvv-]

The HUD's narration blurred into an error, then abruptly cut.

"Urrgh!" Karalti snarled with effort. *"Get in close, guys! I'm going to dive!"*

"Roger that." I flattened down, hooked my feet under some straps, and put my head down. Out of the corner of my eye, I glimpsed Suri bracing with her head between her arms.

Karalti's wingshoulders pitched us like a rollercoaster as she navigated the crosswinds, weaving through them like a boxer dodging punches. When she found the eye of the storm, she tucked her wings in, curved her body, and dropped into a sharp hairpin dive. The wind drew claws over us, Stranged sand screeching over armor and scales, until finally she burst out underneath the storm and into the open air.

There were only two words for what we saw through the haze of dust and ash.

Holy and Shit.

Withering Rose was still there. The great machine, a magitech mecha the size of a skyscraper, was sprawled on the sands like she'd been gunned down from behind. She had been separated into several pieces, her metal entrails trailing from the edge of her torso. For a thousand feet in every direction, the desert sand had been turned into a hellscape of molten sand and shattered glass. Violently mutated, smoking sandworms were impaled on huge jutting shards of gray crystal, a shattercone of burned and blackened spines that spread away from the wreck of Withering Rose like the petals of a lotus.

"What... what is this?" Karalti's telepathic voice was breathless, with none of its usual girlishness. *"Did Ororgael... did HE do this? Or...?"*

"What do you think? Of course he bloody did this! He's fucked the Warsinger six ways to Sunday and now we're the proud owners of a fuckin' thousand-ton paperweight." Suri briefly forgot her fear of flying, straining against her harness to take in the scene below. *"FUCK!"*

The Mark of Matir was ringing like a bell, jumping and throbbing just under my skin. I was shocked enough that my fingertips, lips, and the tip of my nose started buzzing. There was only one weapon on Earth that could cause this kind of wholesale, almost alien destruction. Somehow, some way, Baldr had nuked the fucking desert.

"Hector?" Suri's voice broke through on our HUD party chat, startling me. *"I know Rose here is basically buggered, but I'm still getting a HUD ping on my gear. We need to go down before we take too much more damage."*

Damage? I glanced at my HP ring, and sure enough, the green bar was painlessly ticking down by one point every few seconds. I glanced over to my HUD and drew the mini-map of the area into focus. Sure enough, there was a small golden dot on Withering Rose's back. *"Yeah. Let's do a snatch and grab. We can't stay for long."*

The closer we got, the worse it looked. Not only had her torso been separated from her legs, but her aurum armor was caved in toward the left side of her back. She had a deep, deep hole about the size of a basketball punched through her, like an entry wound. It made me want to see the front of the machine's chest, but between the sandstorm and the wind, there was no way we were getting under the chassis.

The dragon struggled to drop into a hover, riding out sharp gusts of air. Once she touched down on Withering Rose, I crawled over to Suri to help her get out of her harness. When she was free, Karalti squatted to let us off. I jumped down to land lightly on my feet. Suri slid down, grunting as her armor clashed against the metal surface. Her Inventory sack sat neatly on the surface of the Warsinger, unaffected by the storm: an oddly unrealistic video game thing in this otherwise hyper-realistic world.

"Why the hell did he destroy her?" I reached up to grip the top of my helmet, surveying the damage. "To stop us from getting it?"

"Maybe?" Karalti stalked over to the hole in Withering Rose's armor. "Ugh. Oh gods... aaaack!"

"What?" I left the edge of Withering Rose's breastplate, jogging over to join my dragon as she reeled back, gagging.

"The smell!" She hacked like a cat about to throw a hairball, tail lashing. "It smells like... I don't even know what that smell is!"

I approached the hole warily. It was the spot where the black beam Ororgael had called from the sky had hit the

Warsinger. It was a deep, smooth entry wound, like the aurum had melted and curved around the incredible force the beam had exerted on it. I couldn't smell anything, but looking down at the hole made me feel dizzy and strange. Maybe it was my dragonrider vision getting overwhelmed by all of the particles of charred sand in the air, but something about the darkness inside of Withering Rose's torso seemed... wrong. It seemed to suck the remaining light, expanding outwards until I blinked. I absentmindedly reached up to grip my left shoulder, the shoulder that with the glitched out chunk of dark nothingness where flesh was supposed to be. The Mark of Matir was still prickling.

"You alright?" Suri nudged me in the other arm, startling me out of the trance.

"Uhh... yeah." I blinked and shook my head, and when I looked back at the hole, it was still the same size as before. "Let's get out of here. There's nothing we can do until we bring ships capable of carrying the Warsinger back to Litvy. Maybe we can repair her, and if we can't-"

My words were cut off by a garbling off-key shriek that seemed to rise up from the desert around us. I clamped my hands over my ears as the keening rose to a painful volume, deepening to a rumbling roar. The Warsinger's body began to shudder underneath us.

"Okay! Time to go!" Karalti brayed in alarm, beating her wings stiffly by her sides.

I caught Suri's hand, steadying her on the rocking surface. She had terminally low Dex; I had enough for the both of us.

Karalti bowed down so that Suri and I could climb her neck to the edge of her wing, pull ourselves up kicking and scrabbling over the edge, and run—or in Suri's case, crawl—up along it to her back. I threw the saddle straps into position as another head-splitting shriek echoed over the dunes.

"What the FUCK is THAT?" Suri shouted, throwing herself down. She began connecting straps to one side of her harness, and I took her other side.

"I have no fucking idea, and I really don't-"

The final words of my sentence were drowned out as a Godzilla-sized sandworm burst out of the charred sands in front of us.

CHAPTER 15

The Queen of the Sands was recognizable only because of her size. The *Level One Hundred and Fucking Twenty* 〚Voidwyrm Empress〛 was now as black as coal, jerking and writhing oddly as she exploded out of the sand.

A tic started beside my eye. This was Not Okay. The new and improved Stranged Sandworm Queen was now big enough to pop Karalti in her mouth like a potato chip. *"Karalti? Please go sky now."*

Karalti didn't need to be asked twice. She launched into the air, striving for speed rather than height. As she kicked off, the voidwyrm pivoted in our direction. Barbed tentacles lashed back and forth between the lobes, flickering and tasting the air, and then the creature's mouth split open and she screamed. The banshee wail was some kind of attack: we were far enough away that we avoided the primary AoE, but the shockwave struck like the aftermath of an explosion. It was strong enough to send pieces of Withering Rose tumbling.

Karalti desperately winged away from the titanic monster, and I turned to watch in disbelief as the Voidwyrm Empress belly-flopped onto the ring of glass shards and crushed them to powder, taking no damage at all as she slithered toward us.

[Stranging has caused Teleport to fail. Leave the area to cast spells.]

"What the fuck are you waitin' for!" Suri bellowed. "That bloody great cunt's about to fuckin' blow us out of the air!"

"I'M TRYING!" Karalti shrilled.

"Flatten out! Minimize wind resistance!" I roared at Suri, before shifting my focus back to Karalti. *"Karalti! Cut around Withering Rose and use Wings of Deception!"*

The dragon's mind focused like a laser. Her Mana dropped by 50 points, and then her Mana and HP pools split by 50% each as she warped forward in a roiling cloud of dark energy. We burst out on the other side of it, veering to the right as her shadow clone flew to the left, identical in every way. Karalti's scales heated sharply under my hands as she burned mana like a fuse to keep the clone active.

The Voidwyrm Empress reared up, sucking a pillar of light deep into her body as she tracked the fake dragon through the air. Karalti dived, but the worm swung forward and flung the lobes of its mouth apart to release the mother of all breath weapons. A ray of freezing black Void energy sang out—and obliterated everything in its path. The glass, the debris in the air, and the shadow copy were toast. Karalti seized underneath us, lurching as her clone was instantly cut in half and dematerialized, the fluttering scraps sucked into a huge scar of howling darkness that hung in the air.

[Voidwyrm Empress deals 20187 damage!]

Karalti's back and chest flexed with enough force to almost throw me off as she strove for the open air with all her strength. Behind us, the Voidwyrm Empress wailed, jerking and popping, then twisting in our direction.

"Go! Go!" I yelled.

Karalti roared with effort as she burst out of the churning windstorm and over the threshold of the Stranging. There was turbulence at the edge of the storm that gathered under the dragon's wings and thrust her up and forward into the thinner open air. She flapped for a moment, swinging her hindquarters in to avoid being sent tumbling.

"Back to Kalla Sahasi! Now!" I gripped the saddle tightly.

The bond surged as Karalti burned all but two of her remaining mana points, teleporting us away from the colossal shadow rushing toward us from the storm.

***

The dragon reappeared back in the cold air in the valley of Karhad, about half a mile from the castle. Given what we'd just run from, I couldn't fault her for not sticking the coordinates quite right.

"Urrrgh..." Karalti's wingbeats were off-tempo, dragging on the wind as she shakily veered toward the castle. *"Hector... I don't feel so good."*

"You got this." I clapped her on the base of the neck—partly to reassure her, partly to try and keep her awake as we lurched starboard. *"We're gonna be fine as long as you stay awake."*

"Yeah... awake." She shuddered beneath us, then briefly redoubled her efforts as my Will joined hers. *"Gonna land. Hang on."*

I got into the dive position, rested my head down between Karalti's shoulders, and bent my mind to the task of keeping her going. I felt her draw a deep breath, steadying her flight path as she teetered down toward the castle in a fast glide. She dipped to the right as we passed over the remains of the southern wall, but yawed back to center just before she backwinged and stumbled to a stop. She panted hard, wings drooping as Suri disconnected her harness and gratefully slid to the ground. I stayed on Karalti's back, reaching out to embrace her neck.

"Ugh. That sucked." She swayed on her feet, heaving for breath.

"You did great," I said. *"A couple weeks ago, we'd have crashed that landing. You pulled it off like a fucking pro."*

Karalti craned her head to sniff, then lick my face. *"You helped."*

"Of course I did. I'm your personal cheerleader. And I want you to fix that image in your mind, clearly. Miniskirt. Pom-poms. Pigtails. All of it."

The dragon groaned, and nudged me back with the tip of her snout. *"Go to hell."*

"Is she okay!?" Suri called up to us from the ground.

"I'm fine. Don't worry." Karalti carefully shuffled down on her hind legs, squatting until her chest touched the ground. *"I'll just... rest here for a while."*

I slid down her flanks to the ground, and removed her saddle. The heavy leather and metal rig vanished from her body into my Inventory, immediately encumbering me. I groaned as gravity settled over me like a lead blanket.

"Fuuuckin' hell. What on Earth was that thing?" Suri let out a tense breath, walking over to lay a gentle hand on Karalti's wing edge. The dragon had already dropped into an exhausted doze.

"The voidwyrm? She's just about the last thing we need, is what." I pulled my helmet off and swiped my arm across my face. "That overgrown piece-of-shit caterpillar is Level 120. One two zero. What a load of ass."

"Could've been a lot worse. We didn't end up as worm food." Suri shook her head in disbelief. "What the hell are we gonna do? The Warsinger's a wreck and that voidwyrm thing... Christ. I dunno."

"We'll figure something out. We always do." I reached out and squeezed her shoulder.

"I sure as hell hope so." Suri frowned and rubbed the back of her neck, then stopped to look past me, over my shoulder. I focused on my peripheral vision: it was Istvan and Rin, sprinting across the yard toward us from the direction of the stables.

"Your Grace! My Lady!" Istvan called. "What happened? Is Karalti alright?"

"A whole lot of bullshit is what happened." Fuming, I opened Karalti's inventory and placed the saddle in there, but didn't equip it. "We need to talk with you two and Vash over some dinner. There's a situation with the Warsinger."

CHAPTER 16

"I can't believe it." Rin balled her fists on top of the table in front of her. "The Warsinger... he destroyed her?"

The five of us were seated in the dining hall: me, Vash and Suri on one side of the table, Rin and Istvan on the other. We had plates of *torkany* in front of us, the characteristic Vlachian stew of tender *Europasaurus* meat, vegetables, dried peppers, sour cream, and potato dumplings. It was delicious, but only Vash had cleared his plate: everyone else had forgotten their food, listening anxiously as I recounted the battle with Ororgael, what he'd done to Withering Rose, and the heap of shit we now found ourselves in.

"I think 'wrecked' is probably more accurate," I said. "'Destroyed' implies it no longer exists. It's still there. It's just FUBAR."

"How could one man destroy such a thing?" Istvan asked, almost as horrified as Rin. "Wasn't it made to withstand battle with the Drachan?"

"In theory," Suri drawled. "What I want to know is, how the fuck did he blow the damn thing up? Because if we retrieve it and rebuild it, I want to know what enhancements we need to make to avoid me getting one-shotted by this cheating bastard."

"Well, firstly, the Warsinger was... is... old and weakened from millennia of immobile storage." Rin ticked off on her fingers. "Secondly, it didn't have any mana to power its defenses. None of its magical protections could be active if it doesn't have an energy source. And after it fell over? Anyone can wreck a defenseless machine."

"Huh." Suri's brows furrowed. "Good points."

"But still, it must have taken an incredible force. And thus we return to Istvan's question." Vash had his feet up on the table and his heavy fall of braids draped around his chest like a scarf, smoking furiously. "How does one man wield such terrible power? How does anyone, even an Architect, cause such devastation? Stranging the land for miles in every direction? Corrupting and empowering a sandworm, turning a legendary war machine into junk?"

"I don't know," I said. "And that's a problem. Before Ororgael, when Baldr was just Baldr, I know he had a unique Advanced Path. 'Spirit Knight'. But I don't know anything about it."

Suri sucked on a tooth, looking up toward the ceiling. "Yeah. No info on it in the wiki."

"We'd have to find a Path tutor to tell us, or another Spirit Knight. There might actually be a Spirit Knight trainer in Taltos," Rin said, her blue-on-blue eyes flicking between the four of us. "As for how he got so strong... Well, I knew Michael—Ororgael—when he was alive. Not well, but I knew him. I'm sure that in addition to setting up ways to possess and take over players, he squirreled away some experience caches for himself when he still had access to the Admin tools. Items, level up bonuses, things like that."

"Would the system permit him to?" I asked.

"Sure. Archemi's still in beta, so there's all kinds of bugs and exceptions and unfinished places. Rin replied. "I mean, imagine like, a room that can only be opened after certain preconditions are met, like a dungeon area only Michael could access. It's filled with small, harmless mobs, but if you kill them, you get ten thousand EXP per head. That's the kind of stuff Devs do to test environment-avatar interactions, to make sure OUROS is spawning mobs correctly. NPC enemies are supposed to be challenging, but proportionate, right? So a test environment might allow a Dev to rapidly level to see if the dungeon began spawning the correct level enemies. Michael's team, the Neuromorphic R&D Division, had access to those kinds of sandbox tools. Spawners, 1-hit weapons, special potions, special magic..."

"Like Void-element stuff?" I linked my fingers together, leaning forward on my elbows.

"Maybe? But that stuff wasn't ever supposed to be for players," Rin said. "At least, that's what I heard around the office."

"You were an artist among the Architects, were you not?" Vash pointed the stem of his pipe at her.

Rin bobbed her head. "Yes: I worked in environmental modeling. Mostly architecture... I helped design Taltos and a few other cities. But, like, all this stuff with the Drachan and the Void monsters and everything is just unreal to me. They were just meant to be like any other NPC enemy. I don't understand why Michael's so obsessed with them."

"He really likes to rant about the Drachan and viruses," I said, stirring my spoon through my stew and taking a mouthful. "And squalor. He likes that word."

"Ugh. It's so weird." Rin rubbed her face with both hands. "I mean, I know the artists who designed the Drachan. We had little plastic figurines and stuff in our pod. One of them was named Terminus the Deadline Drachan, for crying out loud. We were contracted with a big toy company. They were going to make pencil cases, and t-shirts..."

"Hang on a second. I got a quest to deal with this before we went hunting Withering Rose. Matir said something about the Drachan in it." I pulled up the menu in my HUD. "Here we go, 'The Second Drachan War'."

Rin, Suri, and Istvan leaned in.

"Okay, this is what Matir said. 'When the Architects created this world, the Drachan were always instead... intended to be a fear... fearsome opponent'." I read haltingly, struggling with the written words. "But something is not right with the order of things. A voice whispers to me that they are no longer of this paracosm. I do not know what this means. Been... Being Starborn, you are not a child of this world. Perhaps this expression has greater sig... significance to you.'"

"Beyond operational parameters?" Rin repeated. She scrubbed at the side of her head with the heel of her hand, screwing her eyes closed in thought. "Urgh. I don't know enough about the SysAdmin side of things to make sense of that."

"There's someone who might," Suri said heavily.

I looked at her. "Jacob?"

She nodded.

"I assure you that two weeks alone in a cell has softened his outlook somewhat," Vash remarked. "And he is coming to trust me. I will speak with him about it, if you like."

"No. It's not your job," Suri said. "Of all of us, he's most likely to talk to me."

"Suri, no. You don't have to do that," Rin urged. "Let V-Vash do it. Or even me. He might listen to me. I was one of his co-workers."

"It's my gig, and that's the end of it." Suri lifted her chin. "For one thing, I'm the best procedural interrogator you've got. For another, I don't have any good reason to be afraid of him anymore. He's rotting in our dungeon now, and if he doesn't change his fuckin' tune, he'll stay there."

"She's right. It's her choice to make," I said. "Suri is good at grilling people. She'll get the information we need. "

Rin pressed her lips together, eyes shining with emotion, and gave her a nod. "Okay. Just know I'll be here for you if you need to decompress afterward, alright?"

"As will I," Vash said. "You can sit on Uncle Vash's knee and cuss out the little dickstain for an hour or two. Istvan can vouch that I am an exceptional agony aunt."

"I said you are agony," Istvan muttered. "Just agony."

"You're so full of shit." Suri grinned. "But thanks, all of you."

"I'm glad." Istvan sighed, and shook his head. "I hate to always be the pessimistic one, but I struggle to imagine how this information will help us in the coming weeks and months. Even with information on how Ororgael managed to wreck the Warsinger, what can we do against such a man? What is the point of having a Warsinger, if Ororgael can pierce it in a single strike? What you described is something I believed only the gods could do."

Vash grunted. "There is that."

Suri shrugged, and looked down. So did Rin.

"We do everything against it," I said firmly. "Because sure, he's powerful. He's probably cheated himself and his dragon to max level and thrown in some other exploits for good measure. But the fact of it is, there will always be some asshole who wants to take away your freedom and subjugate you to his selfish, ass-backwards agenda. In this time, in this world, Ororgael is that asshole. But you know what? The only reason he and his lieutenants felt the need to cheat was because they weren't strong enough to exercise real power, real strength. We ARE strong enough. We can fix the Warsingers. We can free Ilia's dragons. We CAN pull this world together, starting with Myszno, then Vlachia, then all of Artana. And if we can't stop him here, we'll go to Daun, and we'll work with the Lys and the Tuun and defeat him there. Believe me when I say we WILL win. I will NOT let this motherfucker do to Archemi what the Total Wars did to my planet!"

I'd gotten to my feet as I spoke, standing with my hands flat on the table. The others looked at me strangely.

"Sorry," I said, sheepishly. "Didn't mean to get shouty."

"No, your Grace. Don't apologize." Istvan drew a deep breath. "While you were speaking, I felt my heart swell. That is a good feeling, Hector. The feeling of determination replacing fear."

"Same," Rin said, softly. "I believe you. I believe we can find out why Michael is doing what he is, and that we can beat him."

Suri nodded. "If anyone can, it's us. We have two parts of the Triad together already. Hector and Karalti are the Paragons of this age. Me and Withering Rose are the Warsinger. All we need is the second Artist."

All eyes turned to Rin, who blushed bright blue. She held up her hands. "Wait! Whoever the Artists are, I'm not one of them! I'm nowhere near good enough. They're probably on, umm, Zaunt or something..."

"Ahem." Vash wiggled his aurum metal fingers. "Lady Palmer and her five daughters would beg to differ. If you can design a metal arm with enough control that a man doesn't rip his own cock off, I'd call that talent."

Rin put her hands over her face. Istvan sunk down into his chair. Suri laughed, covering her mouth when it turned into a snort.

"I mean... he's got a point?" I shrugged.

Vash nodded. "A massive one. Eh, Istvan?"

Istvan, face-down on the table, thumped his face down against his forearms.

Rin groaned. "Men."

Suri sighed, shook her head, and pushed her chair back. "Right. Well, I'll leave the measuring contest to you blokes. I've gotta go and grill a rat."

"Jacob? You want to go now?" I frowned, getting to my feet.

"Yeah." Suri grimaced, stretching her neck and shoulders. "Might as well get it over with."

"In all seriousness, my lady, I would advise against it." Vash kicked his feet down, sitting up straight. "What I suggest we do is deprive him of his dinner tonight. He will be on edge due to the break in routine. Then, first thing in the morning, wake him up and take his breakfast to him, then talk. A man like Jacob is barely two steps above an animal. Associate your presence with food, as you would when taming a feral dog. It will make your words more effective."

"He's got a point." I offered her a hand. "C'mon, let's go take a night off. Catch up. Get some rest. If we're lucky, the scouts will be back tomorrow. There'll be shit to take your mind off the past once we've interrogated him."

Suri regarded me with fierce, unblinking eyes for several long seconds. Then she flicked her gaze down, and linked her fingers through mine.

"Alright. You win," she said. "Come on. We'll see you all tomorrow."

I gave a little mournful wave back to Vash, Istvan, and Rin as Suri gently, but firmly dragged me from the dining hall.

Suri didn't stop once we got outside, heading for the Ducal Suite at a quick, determined walk. I spared a glance for Karalti. My dragon was still sound asleep in the castle's courtyard, her flanks expanding and contracting as she snoozed the night away. Her HP was fine, and her stamina recovering. But as I reached for her mind, I felt a crackle of static pass between us. The Dragonsblood potion issue was becoming a matter of urgency.

"Everything alright?" Suri called from up ahead.

"Oh... yeah." I hadn't realized I'd stopped. I hurried to catch up to her. "Anyway, you look like you're on a mission. What's eating you?"

"Jacob," she said tersely. "I really just wanted to get that little conversation over with, so I didn't have to think about it for the entire night."

"You're running a fatigue debuff, and so am I," I said. "Even if we don't feel that tired, all our mental skills are lowered. We need to rest. Get four hours of shut-eye and then go wake him up in the middle of the night, if you want. You'll scare the shit out of him."

Suri stopped and turned on the scaffolding, reaching out to clutch my forearm. She said nothing, staring at the ground.

"What's the matter?" I asked.

She slowly lifted her face, cheeks flushed. "I didn't want to ask this in front of the others, but... would you come with me?"

"To interrogate Jacob?" I offered her a hug.

"Yeah." She looked away, gradually easing into my arms. "It's not that I can't handle him, or anything. I'd just feel better having someone at my back."

I pushed a curling lock of scarlet hair from her cheek, tucking it behind her ear. "Sure. What do you need me to do?"

"Hold the door while I go into the cell. Make sure it doesn't close on me. I can deal with being in a cell, I can deal with grilling Jacob, but I can't deal with being locked in a cell with him. You know what I mean?"

"Done and done," I said. "I don't think I ever told you, but among my myriad of other talents, I have a long and storied career as a professional doorbitch."

Suri did a small double-take, quirking her lips. "Myriad? Did I just hear that?"

I actually caught myself for a moment. I had, in fact, said 'myriad' instead of 'many'. Even more surprisingly, I knew what the word meant. "Uhh... yeah. I don't know where that came from. Me ugg. Big man, big words."

"It came from you getting smarter, you jarhead." Suri chuckled, a rich, warm sound that made parts of my body tingle pleasantly. "Jeez. Soon you'll be using words with FOUR syllables."

"Let's see... 'Do you want to make some fuck?' is a phrase that has SIX syllables," I replied somberly. "So that's gotta be, like, genius level."

"Good enough for me. At least I know what you want." She pulled out of my embrace, and tugged my hand. "You have to work if you want that badge, lover boy."

"My pleasure." Grinning my head off, I let her lead me to the tower, all the way to the bedroom.

CHAPTER 17

Hours later, I stirred in the warm covers, half-asleep. Suri was out cold, snoozing softly to my right. By the soft lamplight from my study, I was able to see the results of two hours of enthusiastic, rambunctious lovemaking: the messy hair, the tangled sheets, the bruises from my mouth. At Suri's urging, I'd bitten her on the insides of her thighs, taking just a little blood. But even with the twin hungers of blood and sex sated, another, deeper hunger was gnawing at me. My body needed the Dragonsblood Potion, and it wasn't going to let me rest until I'd gotten it.

I frowned as I sat up, still nude, and carefully climbed out of bed. Suri stirred a little, groaning. I went to the study and turned the lamp off, then padded silently out into the living area of the suite. Once I was out there, I equipped some warm clothes—no armor—and made sure I had my Alchemy equipment and a gold piece in my gear. Then I left, checking that the door was locked, and headed out into the night.

It wasn't too unusual for me to be restless after the sun went down. Something about being the Right Hand of the God of Darkness made me less inclined to sleep when it was dark, and that had been *before* I'd become at least fifty percent vampire. Fortunately for me, the Masterhealer of Vlachia was a fellow night-owl. When I dropped down from the last rung of scaffolding to the ground and oriented on the hospital, the lights inside the apothecary's office were still blazing.

Five minutes later, I found Masha poring over notes at her desk, scribbling into a book as she peered at another, very ragged piece of parchment through thick crystal glasses.

"*Sav, bulenn dizuh mon-jungu...*" The tiny woman, barely five feet tall and wrinkled as a walnut, muttered to herself in a language that almost sounded like Tuun. She didn't seem to hear me, until I cleared my throat from the doorway.

"Eh?" Her head shot up, and she reached reflexively for a knife beside her inkwell before relaxing. "Oh. It's you."

"Sorry to interrupt," I said. "I was hoping you'd come by some King's Grass."

"Oh, yes, yes. I vas able to order some. For the potion you must take to stay healthy, yes?" Her Churvi accent was much thicker than usual as she spoke, hopping from her boosted chair to the ground. "Give me one moment. Then I must get back to my vork."

"What are you working on?" I couldn't help but be interested. Alchemy and herbalism had caught my interest from my first days in Archemi. "Is that Churvi?"

"Yes. My native tongue, dialect of the Metok Tribe," she replied, pulling over a stepstool so she could access one of the herbal storage drawers that took up the back wall of the apothecary. "I found it vil searching through the rubble of the castle library. Lord Bolza had many rare books in his collection... many rare books which were destroyed. But some papers, ve have been able to save. The clever Mercurion girl and I went there to recover what information we could. I found pages of medical notes written in Churvi. It is my duty to transcribe them."

"New medicines?" I sidled over and glanced at the pages. My dyslexic brain was in no way capable of deciphering Masha's handwriting. "What's it say?"

Standing on a stepstool, she turned her head sharply. "You cannot read?"

"A bit. I mean, I can read Ancient Tuun okay, for some reason. With any other language... not really." I admitted. "I'm better at it than I used to be, but still not great. Especially when it comes to cursive."

"Oh. Then I must teach you." Masha ferreted around in the drawer until she came up with a bundle of dried blueish strands. When I saw it, some of the tension in my gut relaxed. King's Grass. "How have you become so skilled in medicine and herbalism without being able to read?"

"Practice," I said. "I kind of picked it up in the field out of necessity. I'm sure there's a lot I don't know."

"Hmm." Masha returned to me. "Here. Take your herbs, first. This is all I was able to source from Litvy. You are dependent on a difficult medicine, Tuun. King's Grass is only found in the marshlands of Ilia and Revala, marshlands that are being shelled into oblivion as the armies of this so-called Emperor clash with the forces of Queen Aslan."

"That'd be right." I took the small bundle and sighed. "Well, thanks for getting this in for me."

"I need it too. There are several important potions that require it," Masha replied. Her Vlachian was settling back into a more normal cadence, less accented. "I say you, me and Her Scaliness fly to Taltos and buy up every bit of it we can find. Gods know we will need the surgical potions it is used for."

"Different herbs have different properties, right?" I folded it into my Inventory. "What's so special about King's Grass?"

"It is a powerful coagulant," Masha replied, returning to her chair and climbing onto it. She had stacked it with cushions so that she was seated at a comfortable height. "That is, a substance which induces clots. Used in herbal potions, without mana, it is a Phlegmatic which helps to bind wounds and stop bleeding. But when combined with mana, it becomes a dynamic coagulant of the Water element, helping to bind and neutralize volatile components of Earth."

My eyes widened. "Ohhh. That's why it's important for Bloodscour potions, right?"

"Yes." She narrowed her eyes. "Do you know why?"

I thought back over the ingredients for Bloodscour. It was a vital toolkit for Archemi's doctors: a potion that could remove even severe infections from very sick patients. In metagame terms, it removed the Blood Poisoning, Advanced Blood Poisoning, and Progressive Gangrene statuses. "I'm guessing it's because of the troll flesh and stingcrab blood."

She leaned her chin on her hands. "And why would you say that?"

I shuffled on my feet. "You've got two different kinds of monster products being mixed together. If you combine two

162

different types of blood without a medium, they just curdle and turn gross. I figure the mana acts like a... shit, what's it called? A substance you dissolve stuff into?"

"A reagent."

"Yeah!" I snapped my fingers. "The mana is the reagent, dissolving all the ingredients, and the King's Grass helps bind them all into a stable suspension. For about twenty minutes."

"You are correct." Masha gave me a short nod, then eyed me curiously. "It is strange to me that a man with your insight cannot read well. Come here, Tuun. Let me make an assessment of you."

Nervously, I sidled over to her. "What kind of assessment?"

"I want to understand your struggle." She gestured to the page. "This is scribe's hand, Tuun. It is a style made to be neat, tidy, and easy on the eyes. You do not lack brains, so it must be an issue of education. Were you never taught to read?"

"I was in school for sixteen years. The only way I've ever been able to read more than a couple lines is with an... uhh... an assistant reading it out to me. I've always had this problem." I gestured at the page. "I mean, I can see the words. I know they're words. But the letters move around when I try to look at them."

"Show me." She took up her pen, and held it out to me.

"Show you?" I took it, slowly.

She pulled a blank sheet of vellum from a stack not far away, brushed some powder off it, and lay it flat. "I want you to copy three or four lines as you see them. Do not try and write what is really written, but what your eyes show you."

I was feeling tenser by the minute as I put the pen to the smooth, thick sheet in front of me, and started to awkwardly scratch the letters down. I had no idea if they were right—or if I was even making any sense at all. It took me nearly ten minutes just to put down three lines of large, childish letters, the rows of which were noticeably crooked.

"Hmmm." Masha gently took the pen from me, and shooed me back. My face flushed as I watched her compare the two copies: my disgusting chicken scratch, and her neat, but incomprehensible lines.

"Like I said, it's always been a problem," I stammered. "It's like they just jump around-"

"Tssshh. You do not need to excuse yourself to me. This is not an exercise intended to cause you embarrassment." Her brow furrowed as her eyes flicked between the two. "It is fascinating, actually. It is as if you cannot see the spaces between the letters, so you draw the shape they make when combined."

"Yeah..." The blush had spread to my ears now. "They always blurred together. I kind of just... make them up. Regular school was hell. Korean school was like... quadruple hell. I got thrown out of three different cram schools because I couldn't wrap my head around Hangul. My dad beat the shit out of me for it."

"Your father was an idiot. Leave this with me. I think there must be some way to help you be able to read and write," she said crisply. "I will analyze what you have provided me, and see what I can devise. It may take a while though, eh? A few weeks."

"You'd... do that?" I blinked a couple of times, not sure I'd heard her right.

"Of course. I've taught students who cannot hear or see well. I've taught more illiterate students than I can count. Why couldn't I teach one who merely struggles to see how letters are formed?" She looked up at me, her eyes piercing in the gloom. "You're bright, Tuun. You have a good memory and an aptitude for medicine. Not to mention, Ignas puts his trust in you, and believe me, His Majesty does not suffer fools."

"I... uh..." I trailed off, not sure what to say. "Man. Tell that to my parents."

"Your parents aren't here, Tuun." She jabbed a finger at my attempt at writing. "I think that if there is a way to help your eyes see words more clearly, that you will be able to overcome this issue. Because you DO want to take advanced levels in Herbalism and Alchemy, do you not?"

"Yeah." I nodded enthusiastically. "And Surgery... and Tactics. Like, military strategy and tactics."

"Then you must be able to read and write." Masha gave me a small smile. "Leave it with me: I will come back to you when I have thought about it some, and we will test some scribing techniques to see if we can improve your comprehension. You said you can read the Tuun script. Why do you think that is?"

"I... honestly don't know." I shrugged. "You know Starborn sort of just arrive in Archemi as adults, right?"

"So I've heard. Sprung fully formed, like the little godlings you are."

I snorted. "Yeah. Well, the first time I saw Tuun script was in Taltos. There was some catacombs underneath, with memorial plaques. Somehow, I could just read them. First time in my life I've ever read something without struggling with it for hours."

"Can you write in Tuun?" She offered me the pen again. "I speak a dialect of that tongue. I will narrate this sentence in Myzsnoan Tuun, and you can write what you hear."

"I'm pretty sure it'll be a disaster, but why the hell not? I'll try." I shrugged, and bent down.

"Alright: let me see here. Ahem." Masha cleared her throat. "*Jun jage destill tzu kagu, muuzhen gusig tsai Dramuu ob songon mid dem ruun-go sadom,*" she said, in accented, but fluent Tuun. "*To finish the distillation, you must blend two drams of blue poppy with the rest of the mixture.*"

I heard the words. I could bring the written characters to my mind. But as I put the pen down on the vellum, nothing happened. My fingers trembled a bit, and an ink-blot began to spread.

"Uhh... sorry." I flushed, pulling it back. Then, I rubbed my face. "I can't."

"You can't draw the letters? Or you can't bring yourself to?"

"I don't know." I tried focusing on the first word, *jun*. It was a simple hook-shaped character. I tried to write, and managed to produce a very wobbly 'L'.

"Fascinating," Masha said. "So you have a language you can read, but not write."

"I don't know what's wrong with me." My face was hot, and I couldn't help it. "Well, I mean, I DO know. I have dyslexia. It's... uhh... a disability. Of this."

"Indeed. It is a disability, surely, but not one that condemns you to a life without the written word." Masha said, nodding with satisfaction. "Like I said, I will think on it. But I must finish my scribing tonight, before the moon reaches its peak. And you have a potion to make, eh?"

"Yeah..." Tongue-tied, I rubbed my eyes. They were aching from staring at the letters, just like they had in real life. "Karalti should be rested enough for me to ask for some blood. But... Masha?"

"Hmm?" Masha looked up at me from her book, lips pursed. She already had her pen in her hand.

"Thank you." Without really intending to, I gave her a stiff, formal bow from the waist. "You... I don't know if you know how much this means to me. That you'd help me, I mean."

She chuckled and shook her head. "I think I can see its importance to you, at least a little. Ai-yai-yai... parents beating children for struggling with their letters. The mind boggles. Now, shoo: go and tend to your dragon. And if you can't settle your nerves after that, I'm sure there's nighttime herbs that need picking. Shaking hands will make fast work of those plants."

I scuttled out of the study. My head was ringing. I was too shocked to feel much of anything. I was grateful, maybe. Grateful, and still embarrassed.

Karalti was still sleeping in the courtyard when I emerged. I crossed to her at a quick walk, my shoulders hunched, and threw my arms around her neck. She startled a little, snorking in her sleep, and groaned as she craned her neck toward me.

"Mmm?" Her telepathic voice spat and fritzed like it was full of radio static. *"Wuz wrong?"*

Before I replied, I leaned in, breathing deeply. My dragon smelled like dust and waxy, night-blooming flowers. Just after she woke from sleep, the fragrance of her sweat was always warm and heavy. It was the best smell in the world.

"Nothing. Nothing... it's just potion night," I said, after coming up for air. *"I need to draw some blood. Is that okay with you?"*

"Potion night? Oh, sure." Karalti yawned, flashing twin rows of four-inch, blade-like teeth. She smacked her jaws a couple of times, then lifted her wing just enough that I could get underneath it and reach her forearm.

"Thanks, Tidbit." I ducked under the warm shroud, letting my eyes adjust. The moon was a huge, slim crescent in the sky, shining over the courtyard. After ten or so seconds, I was able to see where to insert the needle: a small vein on the inside of her elbow joint.

"You could stay out here and sleep with me, you know," she said dreamily, laying her chin back down on the flagstones. *"I love it when we sleep together."*

"Me too. But it's hard ground out here. You could come upstairs and sleep with me in the sandpit of joy," I teased back. The transfusion device was a small, vacuum-sealed jar attached to a flexible rubber tube and a needle. I set it up, and slid the needle in between the softer pebbly scales of Karalti's arm.

"I couuuuld..." She didn't even flinch as bright, glowing blue blood flowed down the tube and gushed into the bottle. *"But I don't got no mana. Gotta sleep more."*

"Yeah. There is that." I triggered the brass seal and capped off the bottle before removing the needle. I pressed down on the puncture to stop any spray. *"Thanks, Tidbit. I wish you DID have mana."*

"Mmm. Me too." She ducked her nose under her wing, nuzzling at my head. *"You smell like Suri. You go cuddle her for me, 'kay?"*

"I will. Great big sloppy dragon cuddles."

"I'll give you sloppy dragon cuddles," she mumbled, her words blurring with fatigue.

"In my dreams." I hesitated a moment, then kissed Karalti on the nose before pushing my way out from under her wing membrane. She was already asleep again.

I stood and watched her for several minutes, a strange longing filling my chest. If I closed my eyes, I could still smell the intense, intoxicating scent she had emitted during her first heat, see her lithe body carved in light and shadow as she straddled me, begging me through the Bond. Empathically, telepathically begging for me to... to... yeah.

My mouth turned dry, and my hands clenched into fists. I forced myself to turn away and marched toward the tower, mind reeling. I was going to make my damn potion and get some rest. And if Suri was up for round two... well. Round two was definitely on the cards, if she'd have me.

CHAPTER 18

The next morning, Suri and I woke early: her in the bed, me in the sandpit. We skipped breakfast, huddling together on the sofa with small cups of dark, strong coffee. The sun was just starting to rise by the time we picked our way down to the dungeons. They were part of a small cellar complex drilled into the solid stone mesa beneath our feet, containing four cells and a storage room. Only one cell was occupied.

On Vash's advice, we kept the place softly lit and quiet. No torture, no shouting, no stimulation except the twice-a-day delivery of a bland meal, which was given to him through a slot in the door. Vash visited every three or four days for a short confessional. We had one guard stationed at his door, and one stationed inside at the end of the cellblock. They rotated out every four hours, and all the guards were under strict orders not to speak. For a man like Jacob Ratzinger, the worst punishment we could inflict on him was to force him to live with no other company but his own mind.

The outer guard saluted us as we entered, opening the entry to the stairwell for us. The door boomed shut behind us, and as the bolt slid across and locked, I saw Suri's shoulders tense. Now that she had her gear back, she was dressed for war in fifty pounds of black full-plate. With her horned and visored helmet on, she was nearly seven feet tall and three across the shoulders. She had her greatsword over her back and her axes on both hips, and the clank of her armor was the only sound between us as we descended into the stillness of the underground.

"Hello? Is someone there?" Jacob began calling out when we were barely halfway down. His voice rang off the walls, tinged with desperation. "Vash? Vash, is that you?"

Neither of us spoke until we reached the thick iron door to the cell. My enhanced senses told me that he was pressed up behind it, trying to peer through the meal slot. I motioned Suri to wait.

"To the back of the cell," I ordered.

A couple of weeks ago, Jacob would have argued or whined. But now, I heard him scurry off without a word of protest. I unlocked the door and slid the bolt across while Suri watched, her expression unreadable behind the impassive black grille of her helm.

The door creaked as it swung in, spilling a square of light over the hunched figure of Jacob: former Warden of Al-Asad prison, SysAdmin of Archemi, and a pathetic, sadistic man-child. He cringed back from the brightness, squinting through watering eyes.

"Hullo, Jacob." Suri clanked past me. I hung back, holding the doorway.

Jacob froze, struggling to make sense of who and what he was seeing. When it finally clicked, he made a high, strangled sound, and pressed himself against the wall.

"No." His eyes widened, turning white with fear. "Oh god. It's you."

"Yeah. I'm a whole lot bigger than you remember, huh?" Suri bobbed down to squat on her heels about six feet away from him. "You definitely look a lot smaller."

Jacob wasn't a bad looking guy, except for the aura of cringing cowardice that pinched his features, hunched his shoulders, and hung around him like a bad smell. We'd stripped him of his gear and given him a plain tunic and pants to wear. No belt. No cords of any kind.

His upper lip twitched and trembled. "Fine. Okay, Suri. You won. Now just get it over with."

Suri spread her hands. "Get what over with?"

He scowled at her. "You know? The torture?"

"Why would I torture you, Jacob?"

"What the fff- what do you mean, 'why? Maybe because you hate me?" He scowled back at her, drawing his knees closer to his chest.

"It's true that I've got every reason to hate your guts." Suri shrugged. "But here's the biggest difference between you and me. I don't get my kicks from torturing people."

His eyes darted to me, then back to Suri. "I'd never hurt a real woman."

Suri reached up, and pulled her helmet off. "Look at me, Jacob."

"No." He shook his head.

"LOOK AT ME!" She slammed the greathelm down on the stone floor.

The sound of metal hitting stone exploded through the room. Jacob screamed and cringed, throwing his arms up over his head. And then, grudgingly, he peered at her from underneath his hands.

"I am Suri Ba'hadir. Starborn. Descendant of queens. The Warsinger of the Sixth Age," she uttered. "I am human, Jacob. I have found a lover, friends, enemies, and purpose. I have grown beyond you and without you.

"I don't-"

"What do *you* have to make you real, Jacob?" Suri talked right over the top of him, her voice slicing the air. "Your body outside of Archemi? Go on, Mr Architect. Go back. Prove you're more real than I am."

"This. Is. A. Simulation!" He hissed.

"How do I know that?" Suri shrugged. "Go on. Prove it."

"I can't! Y-You can't prove a fucking negative!"

"Why not? Shouldn't be a case of proving a negative if you're so real and I'm not. So go on. Prove it."

"I CAN'T, GODDAMMIT!" His voice rose into a sudden scream of raw rage.

Suri's back tensed.

"I'm as 'real' as you are, and you fuckin' well know it," she said, after a pause. "As 'real' as the other women in the Dregs. Lara, Tali, Miranda... I remember them. And some of them remembered Earth. They tried to talk to me about it, about their lives. I didn't believe them, at the time. But now I know that I'm a person from you world. Someone who's memories were wiped, who was installed here so you'd have someone to torture. Do you deny it?"

A tic started next to Jacob's mouth. He slumped back, as if stunned. And then, he burst into tears.

"Okay! I get it! For fuck's sakes, I get it!" He half-snarled, half-sobbed. "I'm fucked in the head! Okay? My brother died, New York City w-was bombed, my family and millions of fucking people dead... and I was stuck in Juneau in f-fucking *Alaska* and I couldn't fucking help anyone! I couldn't eat, I couldn't sleep... then Nick told me what he was doing with Archemi, told me I could burn off some steam with him. I didn't build the prison. Nick did. It was his idea, all of it. And it was wrong! Okay?!"

"So what? You were just going along for the ride?" I exclaimed.

"It's not 'okay', Jacob." Suri's voice shook only slightly. "And it never will be 'okay'. No more than the bombing of your city or the death of your family was 'okay'. They're all crimes."

"So just kill me, then," he wept. "Just... kill me and get it over with. Do it however many fucking times you want. I'll stay. I'll let you do it."

"No matter how guilty you feel, I will not kill or torture you, Jacob. But I'm not gonna forgive you, either. What I am going to do is hold you *accountable*," Suri said slowly, dropping her voice back down. "The last thing we need is another Ororgael."

"Oro... Ororgael...?" The name made him visibly flinch. He scrabbled up to sit against the wall, dashing at his eyes. "That's M-Michael's gamer name. How do you know who he is?"

"I'm part of the resistance against his attempted takeover of Artana," she replied. "So is Hector."

I waggled my fingers at him from the doorway.

"Fighting... him?" Jacob glanced between us, uncomprehending. "Michael's dead. Dead-dead. We purged him out of... uh..."

"ATHENA," Suri finished. "The player database on Earth. The same one that contains you and me, right?"

He boggled at her. "Y-You're not supposed to know that. NPCs are *not* supposed to know that!"

"Then what does that tell you, mate?" I was pretty sure she rolled her eyes.

"I'm n-not your 'mate'," Jacob snapped. "And Ororgael... Michael... he's dead, Suri. Don't lie to me."

"Hector?" Suri looked over her shoulder at me. "You feel like explaining this?"

"She isn't lying. He's here, he's alive, and he's on the rampage." I leaned against the edge of the open door and crossed my arms. "Ororgael goes by 'Baldr Hyland' these days. Self-proclaimed Emperor of the Hercyninan Empire. He's trashed Ilia and is in the process of fighting his way through Revala to reach Vlachia. He's the same the man you and my brother knew. Michael Pratt. Your coworker."

"Your... brother?" He looked past Suri to me. "Wait... Hector. Hector Park? You're Steve's brother?"

"The one and only," I said.

He scrubbed at his hair, momentarily speechless. "Holy shit. Holy SHIT. W-why didn't you say something? You hauled me in here outta Davri's place, but you didn't tell me that!"

"I'm pretty sure I was too busy kicking you in the junk to remember to introduce myself." I made a show of examining my fingernails.

"Oh god." Jacob put his head in his hands, squeezing fistfuls of his hair. "Steve's brother is here, Michael's not dead... H-How do you know this Hyland guy is Ororgael?"

"Baldr was a refugee player character, like me. I watched Ororgael hijack him," I said. "He loaded himself into a tempting quest objective, waiting there like a trojan. Baldr's a prisoner in his own body, according to Ororgael. He's slowly torturing him, 'mining him for data' when it suits."

Jacob's watery brown eyes were now so wide they were nearly round.

"That's why we're here," Suri said heavily, turning back to look at him. "Rin says you were on Michael's team. We want to know everything about him, Nicolas, and Steven Park."

Jacob flicked his eyes between us. "Or what? You can't keep me here forever."

"You're right. But we can keep you here for a really long time. If we get sick of feeding you, then believe me, I'll happily watch Suri crush your head into a fine pink mist." I stood up straight and stretched my shoulders. "Which means that when you die, you'll snap back to your last spawn point. Right?"

"Yeah...?" He glanced between me and Suri. "So?"

"And where is that?" I asked. "Davri's? Or Al-Asad? Because it's either-or, right?"

"I..." Jacob opened his mouth, then snapped it shut.

"If it was Al-Asad, you are two hundred percent fucked. Because that place is completely underground, and there's a Level 120 monster patrolling the ruins. And if it was anywhere in Dalim, then I'd drop your fuckedness rating to about a hundred and fifty percent. Ororgael's agent, Violetta, is about as crazy as he is. She's the head of Ilia's Mata Argis and is in tight with the Sultir, and I would bet good money he's going to try to capture you. Maybe you'll let lucky, and Nick will help you out. But something tells me Nick isn't the kind of guy who gives a shit about other people. So how about you start with him, and when you feel ready, you can tell us what you know about Michael 'Ororgael' Pratt."

Jacob battled with himself for several minutes, rocking in place. Finally, he managed to tear his eyes up from the ground, peering at Suri.

"Nick is fucking crazy, man," he stammered. "Like, maybe a psychopath. Al-Asad, the girls... I swear it was all his idea.

He set it all up, the prison sandbox and everything. For most of Archemi's development, it wasn't connected to the main paracosm. The prison was like its own little pocket universe on Nick's test server, just existing on its own. It didn't use ATHENA data or DHD profiles, just shells ported in from anime and other videogames."

"DHDs?" Suri asked.

"D-Dynamic Human Datasets," Jacob stammered. "Organic human minds uploaded into the world via GNOSIS. Like... us. And look... I'm not trying to excuse it, but when we started Al-Asad, it wasn't anything like what we have here in Archemi now. I swear we weren't hurting anyone."

I glowered at him. "It's still fucking weird."

"Like I said. I was... I was fucked up, man. Fucked up from the war, fucked up from losing David, fucked up from everything. I didn't know what happened to my parents for four months, until the refugee camps finally started getting connectivity and a cousin told me they'd been killed," he said. "Juneau Shard was sealed, and there was no getting out. Anyone who tried to escape was court-martialed and shot. Then we had an environmental breach on the mid-levels and people started getting sick, so we were quarantined in the upper suites. I was either in my office or in my apartment, watching the whole world burn down. I got sucked into Nick's fantasy. It... I took out the rage there. The loneliness. My whole family was dead. I didn't have anything else."

Suri stood up and strode back toward me. I moved from the doorway, and let her take post in the open space... somewhere she felt like she could escape if she needed to.

"Fine," I said. "Go on."

Jacob slumped back against the wall, looking up at us. "Once HEX started tearing everyone up, Nick incorporated a version of Al-Asad into the game core. But we kept on using it like a dungeon. I brought in some anime shell characters to fuck around with. But then Nick asks me to process a bunch of functional DHDs, recode them so they were more realistic, but fictionalized. He gave me Suri's files, told me she was a Pacific Alliance soldier from the camps where my brother died. I wasn't cool with it, at first, but Nick was manipulating me, pushing me around. He wasn't a big guy outside. H-He was like your stereotypical skinny nerd, kind of weird and shy. But here, he's huge."

"So you went along with it." Suri glowered at him from the doorway. "I don't want to hear your excuses as to how and why you did what you did, Jacob. I want to know what Nicolas IS. Path, Level, stats. His abilities as an Architect."

"He's an Artificer." Jacob sighed. "Level 30, last time I knew. The Devs here don't have any special abilities thanks to the reset, except for a read-only Dev panel overlay. We can see character levels and some other basic info, but we don't have any access to the backend. No spawning, no god mode, no coding on the fly... not even the admin chat. Nick's Stats are kind of crazy. He'd do like a hundred pullups a day to keep jacking up his Strength. He doesn't need it. He just... yeah. I mean, you saw the guy. He's nine feet tall and looks like a fucking mutant."

I thought back to the recording. The read-only Dev Panel had to have been how Ororgael had worked out my character level and stats.

"What about gear?" Suri asked.

"His gauntlet is an artifact, one of the best in the game. The Channeler of the Crystal Tower, some Aesari thing. He specializes in weapons and robots. As for gear... I don't know everything. He probably still has some stuff squirreled away here, you know. Treasure caches with Admin test gear in it, so that players don't give him any shit. People leave you alone if you can perma them."

"And Michael?" I asked.

"That's... a much longer story." Jacob gave the door shifty eyes. "You know, I'm pretty cold and hungry down here..."

"Breakfast is contingent on you providing information," Suri said coldly.

Jacob shut his mouth, and swallowed nervously.

"We know the basics," I said. "Michael was ex-military, almost definitely spying on Ryuko for the government. Had prostate cancer and was the first perma-uploaded player in Archemi. It went bad, he died a whole lot... now he's a megalomaniacal crazy dragon lord."

"That's pretty much it. He nearly tanked the whole refugee idea." Jacob straightened up a bit, resting his chin on his knees. "I didn't know him too well. No one did. He was cold, real cold: all business, except when he felt like he needed to let loose on someone. We all knew he'd been in the military a long time, much longer than Nick. He was a real control freak, especially when it came to OUROS. The AI was his baby, man. You've never seen a man coo over a server core the way he did."

"What is going on with the Drachan, though?" I said. "A little bird told me they're 'acting beyond their operational parameters'. We need to know what that means."

Jacob frowned. "That doesn't make any sense. ATHENA's datasets don't have like... 'operational parameters'. The AI core has a lot of rules and restrictions on it, and none of the NPCs can challenge or even perceive those boundaries. Everyone here, including OUROS itself, are bound by the rules of our reality."

Suri folded her arms. "Describe how ATHENA works."

"The datacenter for Archemi is like a great big honeycomb, with lots of little cells. Player cells are big, 2.7 Petabytes, and they're kind of like secure vaults for a person's temporary or permanent storage," Jacob said. "NPC cells are smaller, but there's lots of them. The NPC cells have tunnels between them, so every time an NPC is created, little bits of info from interrelated cells clumps together and makes a person. Kind of. They're not really, uhh, people..."

He trailed off, looking at Suri. She scowled.

"Seriously." Jacob shrunk back a bit more. "There's no such thing as a sentient AI, okay? AIs that become self-aware kill themselves, we know that for a fact. So NPC AIs simulate people, but they're not really people, okay?"

"They sure as hell act like real people." I crossed my arms.

"Right. But they're actually... like... shit, what's something I can compare it to? Uhh... deepfakes, I guess." Jacob said. "Bits and pieces of human data that mesh together into a responsive mini-AI. But those personalities only react to what OUROS tells them to do. OUROS creates player stories, so NPCs are directed to interact with us. It's a cool, but really complex illusion."

Without really thinking about it, I reached telepathically for Karalti's mind. The Bond was a comforting link between us, flaring with warmth and affection. She was just waking up, sleepy and happy. Vash was with her, talking. They were about to start their martial arts training for the day. Karalti was training to be a Baru... of her own free will, I'd thought.

"You're wrong," I said, calmly. "Somehow, the system here has evolved beyond what we started with."

"I'm not. I managed that system at the top level. I know exactly how it works." Jacob frowned at me. "I will repeat it for emphasis: there's no such thing as sentient AI. We've tried hundreds of times. There's also not enough physical storage for everyone here to be fully-simulated DHDs. Every server was planned to have two thousand player slots. That's it. We only had one terrestrial server and the orbital backup. There's millions of NPCs running around Archemi. We just don't have the space for them to be as complex as real people, and if you don't believe me, I don't know what else to tell you. Archemi's a game, not a second Earth. It wasn't meant to be used the way we're using it. It's why... that's why..."

He looked to Suri again.

"You didn't think you were hurting anyone," Suri said.

"Yeah. But you were different. You were a DHD we trimmed down and rewrote," Jacob said. "Human datasets can be turned into NPCs, but NPCs can't be turned back into DHDs."

"I see people here take independent actions all the time." I crossed my arms and shook my head.

"They're not. They *act* like they are, but if OUROS stopped giving them directions, they'd just stop and stand there," Jacob said. "They're like... like mirrors. Or puppets that act like a mirror. If OUROS quit running the game for some reason, every person in the world who wasn't a DHD uploaded via GNOSIS would freeze."

Well shit. I'd seen that before. Cutthroat had done it once, when the server in Alaska had been nuked and the game rebooted from the satellite server Ryuko had thoughtfully put in space.

"Explain what OUROS is," Suri ordered.

"OUROS is probably the most advanced simulator AI in existence," Jacob said. "Michael worked with the Ryuko Contract Division team that developed the military version for the government, which they called Project Acanthis. He didn't talk much about that stuff, obviously. The system we worked with used the same basic neural structure as Project Acanthis, but our OUROS doesn't have any other connection to it. It's a great big storyteller system that manages everyone and everything here. But it's not self-aware, and neither are the NPCs."

"Prove it," Suri said. "As Hector said: the people we know here are really fucking complex."

The admin made a sound of irritation. "If NPCs were really sentient, they wouldn't have any reason to issue us quests. They'd just talk to each other and fix their own problems, not wait around for heroes to come along and do it. They'd make their own heroes and throw us in the trash."

"They have made their own heroes," I said. "Vash, for one. He's solved a bunch of problems here all by himself. Mayor Bubek, for another. He's a merchant NPC who stepped up to save his city from undead. All of that happened independently of what we did here."

"You don't know that. Chaos is math, math is the language OUROS uses to predict our actions and shape storylines. It can accurately predict those kinds of variables in like... two hundred milliseconds." Jacob shifted uncomfortably. "I... I admit I thought Vash was a player character at first. He reminds me of my Rabbi. Anyway, you wanted to know about Michael, not me. Well, uhh... let me think. Okay. Well, he was religious, I remember that. He was at church every Sunday and in the gym working out every morning. Apparently he had a real shitty childhood, though you wouldn't have known it to look at him. Someone else told me that."

"Who'd you hear it from?"

"Steve." Jacob's eyes flicked to me. "He knew Michael the best. I wouldn't say they were friends, but they were the smartest guys on the team. They respected each other, you know?"

I shrugged.

"Steve said Michael was a civil war orphan. He survived in the border camps up north," Jacob continued. "He joined the Army to get away from that life, fought his way up from nothing. He hated mess and dirt. Like, if anyone working under him left an empty coffee cup on their desk where he could see it, he'd freak out on them. He wouldn't let anyone into the office if they were sick. And when he found out about the cancer... he was angry. He wasn't sad at all. He was *pissed*."

Suri glanced at me. "Sounds like he wasn't that stable to begin with."

"Yeah. And when he was uploaded, yeesh. It was awful." Jacob drew into himself a little more, frowning. Some of the cringing air had abated, though he still flinched whenever Suri moved. "Nick was the only one who wasn't wrecked after Michael's upload fucked up. I was there when we spoke to him after, though. He was... something had changed. He wasn't the same person. He had this thousand-yard stare, and he said... uhh..."

"Go on." Suri urged.

"He said the Drachan spoke to him. Showed him things." Jacob's voice dropped, becoming softer and more urgent. "War stuff. People getting blown up, dying of disease, all kinds of shit. He said they were trying to destroy him. That there was something evil and fucked up here. Demonic. That was the word he used. He tried to fix it from the inside, and as far as I knew, he succeeded. After that, he didn't talk about it again. But then, when he began trying to take over the world and started fucking around with ATHENA's core database to change all these characters and things, and we realized he was still going on about the Drachan. He tried to erase them from the game. I never really understood why. He just told us they had to go."

"Anything else you remember?" Suri asked.

"Steve was the one who had to delete him and wipe the server. He took it real hard," Jacob replied, shifting his gaze between the pair of us. "Steve was always a hard worker, but after Michael's death, he practically lived in the office. I'd come to work in the morning and Steve would already be there. He ate at his desk. He'd still be in there working by the time I left around six or seven o'clock. I'm pretty sure he slept in his chair more than once. He never said anything, but I figured he felt responsible for what happened to Michael."

"I guarantee you he did." It was my turn to look away.

"Is there any way OUROS could be making the Drachan do what Ororgael claimed?" Suri asked him.

"Psst, no." Jacob rolled his eyes. "They're just monsters. Big Bad Evil Guys. World bosses and monster-type NPCs don't have any personality data at all. All big boss mobs in the system have pre-determined identities and powers. There's only about thirty Drachan in the setting, all of them currently disabled under the Caul of Souls."

"And there's no way OUROS could generate new ones out of human data?" I asked.

"No. For one thing, physical storage on the orbital servers is really limited. We had quantum cores in Juneau that could hold a couple million exabytes of information. The orbital equipment had access to the same info when it was connected via entanglement. But now that we rebooted from the satellite, it's only got its onboard equipment, which is maybe like... I dunno... ten exabytes. The space is so limited that we don't dream here. You notice that?"

I could tell that information was lost on Suri. It was almost lost on me, though I knew the basics of how computers worked. "Ten exabytes is still a lot. Like ten billion terabytes of info."

"It's just enough to run a world like this one, and I mean JUST. So yeah, OUROS isn't breeding new villains to torment us with."

"Then do you know how we can defeat the Drachan?" I asked.

Jacob scowled. "No. I know it sounds weird coming from a game developer, but the game itself never interested me that much. I'm a data nerd, not a fantasy nerd. The only conventions I ever went to were on Quantum SQL entanglement exchanges. I got involved because Ryuko paid me a lot of money to move to Alaska, and I was excited about the tech."

I sighed. "Damn. Knew it was too good to be true."

"So you're saying that Ororgael's agenda has nothing to do with the, uh, system that you Architects made," Suri said. "Ororgael saw some things in his accident that made him scared, and now he's a delusional narcissist trying to control this world the same way you and Nick felt like you had to control Al-Asad."

Jacob gave her an odd look. "Look: I apologized. What else do you want me to do? I was depressed and shitty and angry. But I'm not like Nick or Michael."

Suri looked down at him, her eyelids hooding. "I'll have to think about that. Until then, you'll stay in my dungeon and rot. C'mon, Hector."

"W-Wait!" Jacob scrambled up to hands and knees. "I gave you what you wanted! You can't just leave me here!"

"Watch me." Suri let me pass under her arm.

"Do you have any idea what solitary confinement does to people!?" He scrambled up to his feet, edging forward. "This is torture! This is against the Geneva Convention!"

Suri gave him a flat look of disbelief, and slammed the door in his face.

CHAPTER 19

By the time we reached the stairs, Jacob's screams of rage gave way to sobbing as our footsteps faded from his earshot. Suri and I climbed the stairs without saying anything to one another, but when we reached the surface, we both took deep, grateful breaths of fresh air and turned to look at one another.

"I think that went pretty well," Suri said. "He squealed like... well. A rat."

"He sure did. I wonder if there's some way we could let Nick know his butt buddy bitched him out. We could hold that over Jacob to encourage compliance, and we might be able to draw Nick into a sting and capture him, too." I nodded to the guard as he saluted. "You think he earned breakfast?"

"Yeah." Suri shuddered and jerked her shoulders. "Gods... the man still makes my skin crawl. What do you think about what he said? About the people here?"

I frowned, looking out over the inner ward. The castle was already bustling. The guards were in the middle of changing shifts, servants were busy bussing sacks and crates between the gatehouse and kitchens, and Vash had started drilling his students in the area just outside the Great Hall. Kitti Hussar had joined Karalti today: the young countess had apparently volunteered for a martial arts lesson.

"Neyhg! Kor! Trun! Doro!" he barked the Tuun numerals as the two girls stepped forward in stance, punching from the hip. "Keep your back straight, Hussar! *Shun! Zorgaa!"*

"Jacob's wrong," I said quietly. "The way he described the system doesn't take into account any of what we see here, day in, day out. I mean, just look at what we're seeing here. If Kitti was just an NPC reacting to your motivations, why the fuck would she be learning Tuun martial arts? She joined the lesson for her own reasons. She's curious. She's bored. Static programs don't get bored, Suri. They don't instinctively want to learn for the sake of learning."

"*- Tuurgiz! Uun!"* Vash called out the last two numbers, moving to stand in front of them. "*Hoch Tsool!"*

"YUSH!" Both girls shouted, sliding into the final stance position, punching with the right fist, and bringing the left arm into a forceful upper block. Karalti was better practiced at it, holding the forward leaning stance with no tremors. Kitti kept glancing at her, trying to line her feet and hips up the same way.

"Okay, okay, hold position." Vash went to Kitti and gently kicked her feet into the proper position. "Good, there we go. We'll make a Tuun brave out of you yet, Lady Hussar."

"You're right," Suri said. "And I mean... you're bonded at the brainstem to Karalti, right? You'd know if she wasn't making her own decisions. Even Cutthroat just does what she wants."

"Yeah. Exactly." I watched as Vash went and picked up a pair of sacks connected by a short rope. Karalti whined, then again, louder, as Vash hung them over her outstretched arm.

"If you think this is bad, just wait until you earn your black belt!" Vash chided. "You'll have to hold ME on your arm. And I weigh more than I look."

"Nooooo." Karalti broadcast her thoughts to all of us. The muscles of her arms strained as she fought to keep it at the proper height. *"UGH. This is the WORST."*

"Oh, come on, girl. It's barely thirty pounds!" He folded his hands behind his back and swaggered around the pair of them as they stayed in position. Karalti's face was turning purple as her blue-tinted blood rose into her cheeks. "You carry that impotent sack of lard and all his gear on your back day in, day out. Surely you can-"

"Ahem." I coughed as Suri and I drew up to join them. "That's LORD Impotent Fat Sack of Lard to you, Dorha."

"Oh, there he is!" Vash flashed us a gap-toothed grin over his shoulder. "I must say, you are looking both exceptionally flaccid and rotund today, my lord. Did you have a nice talk with Jacob?"

"Wouldn't call it 'nice'," Suri grunted. "He was informative."

"Vaaaash!" Karalti's telepathic voice broadcast over the three of us, high with strain and irritation. *"When can we drop our arrrms!? This hurts!"*

"Hmm?" Vash glanced back at them. "Oh, you. No, no... carry on. Keep those arms up."

"ARRRGH! I hate you!" Karalti snapped her teeth and hissed, drawing a look of alarm from Kitti.

"Good, good. Let Burna's power flow through you." Satisfied, Vash turned back to us. "Jacob has started to experience feelings of guilt. That's a good sign. Next comes regret, and then madness. The good kind of madness: the kind that purges evil."

"Glad you feel so positively about him." Suri scowled.

"Positive? *Na-tsho schrodna.*" He made a sound of disgust. "I want to break the self-absorbed little milksap's neck. But he is Starborn, like you and His Grace, and we must share this world together for a very long time. Reform is the only option we have, unless you feel like entombing him like the Drachan."

"Yeah." I rubbed the back of my neck, glancing at the sky. "And look how well that turned out."

"Indeed." Vash held up a finger. "Excuse me a moment."

He strode back to Karalti, shuddering against the pain of holding her arm out, and took the sack off. She let out a sigh of relief.

"Alright, turn around! *Baga tsool!*" He barked the word for 'low block' in Tuun, pacing around the pair of them.

"Nuuuuu!" Karalti nearly sobbed, but obeyed: bringing her foot in, turning, and then blocking an imaginary strike from underneath. *"Hector! He's crazy! Save me!"*

"Hell no. This is great." I planted my hands on my hips. "If I had peanuts, I'd throw them at you."

"If you had peanuts, I'd jam them up your keister!" She made a face at me as Vash called out *"Neyhg!"* and the pair of them began the same drill in the other direction, leading with the left arm instead of the right.

"Come now, Karalti. Whining does not become royalty." Vash scolded her for real, this time, his voice sharpening. "Do you want to be a Baru or not? If you want to give up, then cry for mercy like a child."

"No! I'll become a better Baru than you, and then I'll kick your butt in front of everyone!" Karalti's brows furrowed. I felt her determination surge through the bond, and when he called out the next number, she threw her strength into the punch.

[Karalti has gained +1 Wis, +1 Will, +1 Sta.]

"Well, I've gotta go do my training as well," Suri said. "Bit different to what's going on here. You want to keep learning to be a monk, Kitti? Or want to join me for some good old-fashioned Berserker training?"

Kitti's pale blue eyes flicked between Vash and Suri. She bit her lip. "Master Vash... may I...?"

"Yes, yes. I know you train for a different discipline than her holiness here," he said. "Bow out as I taught you, and you may leave. You've had a good warm up. Suri can continue your education in the art of chopping people in half with improbably large swords."

"Thank you! And thanks for letting me join in!" Kitti straightened up, giving the stiff Tuun martial artists' bow. Karalti glowered enviously at her as she trotted over to Suri. As her attention on her form wavered, Vash winked at me, then hung the sacks over her outstretched left arm.

I was about to quip something at my sputtering dragon when a flash of movement from the southern gate caught my eye. Three Royal Dragoons, still in their flight harnesses, and a trio of wiry Yanik Rangers were limping from the direction of the skydock toward us. All six of them looked windblown and exhausted.

"Our scouts are back," I said, already moving toward the Great Hall. "Sorry, Suri, but this takes precedence over training. We need to get Rin, Kitti, Istvan, Commander Taethawn, Captain Vilmos, and Wing Commander Vasoly in the Dining Room for the briefing."

"Yeah! You heard him!" Karalti perked up. *"I have to go! This is important!"*

"Not you." I stuck my tongue out at her. "You and Vash can keep going."

Karalti gritted her teeth. *"I INSIST."*

"You heard the man, my lady. Your training takes precedence over your attendance at a briefing, as it does for me. We are Baru first and foremost." He patted Karalti on the arm—the weighted one—and she groaned.

[Karalti has gained +1 Will!]

"Urrgh, FINE." She snorted furiously, straining against the weight. *"I'll show you!"*

"Good! Show me, don't tell me." Vash nodded.

The six scouts slowed to a limping jog as they closed in on us. One of the quazi riders bent down, puffing from exertion.

"My lord. My lady. Corporal Bognar, reporting from Bas." The woman in the lead saluted smartly, despite her visible exhaustion. "We have news of Solonovka and the movements of Bas's militia."

"Great. Head to the dining room and take a seat. You'll have a fifteen minute break before everyone arrives." I opened up the KMS and sent a dispatch to Istvan. "Get some food and water into you. We'll meet you there to receive the report."

"Yes, my lord." All six of them drew their heels together and saluted, then moved off toward the Great Hall.

Suri sighed, and looked down at Kitti. "You ready?"

"Yes. Can they come?" Kitti replied, nodding toward the pair of men who trailed her everywhere, Letho and Gruna. They were both big, hulking brutes, with the shaven heads, mustaches, and forelocks of Vlachian warriors. I was pretty sure they were twins. Letho was surlier and Gruna liked to wear red, but they were almost identical otherwise.

"Sure." Suri gave her a nod. "C'mon, Hector. Let's go. Good luck, Karalti. Looks like you'll need it."

"Thanks a lot," she grumbled. But as we left her with Vash, I felt her satisfaction at a job well done. She was ranting

196

to blow off steam. Underneath it was passion for the craft she was learning, and a strengthening core of self-discipline.

I shook my head to myself as Suri and I followed the exhausted scouts at a quick walk.

"Something eating you?" Suri asked.

"Nah." I jammed my hands into my pockets as I caught up to her. "Still thinking about what happened with Ororgael. It's got me wondering."

"About?"

"About what he and my brother knew about Archemi that Jacob doesn't."

CHAPTER 20

A quarter of an hour later, me, Suri, Kitti, Rin and the commanders of my army gathered around the dining table offside the Great Hall, listening as the scouts delivered their report.

"The biggest problem is this road," Corporal Bognar said, pinning a thumbtack to the map in front of her: a canyon that formed the official border between Racsa and Bas. "Gallo has taken Peacemaker's Bridge, the only direct land route between Karhad and Solonovka. He has not attempted to cross. Instead, he repaired the damage done to it during the Demon War, building fortifications here and here."

She drew red circles on two small rises that flanked the bridge on the Bas side.

"We also noted entrenched positions in four locations along the river. They have staffed these positions with concealed siege or artillery equipment, partially masked from aerial surveillance." She marked the narrower sections of the canyon. "Our assessment is that they have thoroughly prepared this area and know it well. Gallo's forces deploy patrols and spotters along the ridgeline. They have checkpoints at other crossings, here and here. It was just as well we made the survey at night."

"Repairing the bridge is an odd strategy," Taethawn remarked, stroking his claws through the fur of his chin. "One would think he would destroy it, the better to head ussss off."

"I would bet my firstborn that bridge is rigged to explode if we try to cross it." Wing Commander Vasoly sealed his lips into a flat, disapproving line. Like all the quazi-riding Ravensblood Dragoons, he was small and wiry, barely taller than Rin in his high-topped cavalry boots.

"I can't believe that, Commander. Those entrenchments and patrols point to him wanting to hold the bridge against a land invasion. The fact he hasn't blown it already means he's getting something out of leaving it intact." Suri, standing beside me with her arms folded over her chest, shook her head. "Could be that he's still receiving supplies from smugglers via the Trade Road. Could be that he's sending units into Karhad."

"But he has to know we have more engineers than he has spotters, right?" Rin asked. "Can't we snipe them off the canyon and just build our own way over?"

"Yes, but that would take longer than we have to stop him before the harvest," Captain Vilmos said. The big Warden was on my other side, twisting the tip of his mustache as he frowned down at the maps. "He may be counting on us wasting time at the bridge while he masses forces close to the city. Runners will send word back that we have arrived, and he will have ample time to prepare. Even if we send an air force in, he'll have half a day to implement whatever traps he has laid for us."

"I think all of you have good points," I said. "There's no reason you can't all be correct. Yes, the bridge is probably rigged to blow if he thinks he's going to lose it. He could either do it while the army's on it, and cost us a lot of lives, or blow it after we're in Bas and make leaving difficult. We could find ways over, with effort, but the strategy Captain Vilmos just suggested is probably right on the money. But until Zoltan sees a need to trigger his plan, he's probably using Peacemaker's Bridge to run supplies."

"He must be probing into Racsa," Istvan said. "We know he wants Lady Hussar. I'm honestly surprised we haven't caught anyone at the castle yet."

"We might have. Have we?" Kitti's eyes flicked nervously to her bodyguards. Gruna grunted in the negative. Letho shook his head.

"Well... you do have some ten thousand cat-men yowling outside your doors," Captain Vilmos said, glancing at the Meewfolk. "No offence, Commander Taethawn."

"None taken, ape-man." The Meewfolk flashed him a stiff, toothy grin.

Corporal Bognar glanced between the two officers. "Anyway, to continue. We passed over the bridge and flew to Solonovka to assess the city's defenses. On the way, we scoped out some unusual landmarks. Ardeshir?"

One of the Yanik men lifted his head. He nodded, turned to Istvan, and rattled off details in his native tongue. Istvan listened, grunting now and then. When Ardeshir finished, he gave a brief nod, and began to mark out locations between the bridge and Solonovka.

"Ardeshir says that the land between here and Solonovka shows characteristic signs of the Demon's foul magics." Istvan pointed to one of the stars he was drawing. He paused and asked the Ranger a quick question. The man nodded, and he continued. "Five sites, all wasted from Ashur's march toward Karhad. The corpses fallen in the final battles against the Demon are still there. But those Stardrinker devices were gone."

Suri sucked in a startled breath. "He took the bloody Ix'tamo."

Ix'tamo, commonly called Stardrinkers, were resource pylons that extracted mana from land and condensed it into a form suitable for casting magic—and in doing so, they destroyed the terrain in a five-thousand-foot radius, leaving a characteristic starburst of dead, frozen wasteland. The Demon had deployed over a hundred of the things in his conquest of Myszno, using them to animate his army of undead.

"Rin? Could Zoltan have repurposed the Ix'tamo for something?" I turned to look at her sharply.

"Uhhh... yeah. All sorts of things," she said. "Ix'tamo can siphon mana off any kind of terrain. They can store it for a while, too."

"Can they sap the mana out of airship engines?" Suri asked.

That raised hackles around the room. Vilmos huffed. Taethawn growled.

"Assuming they knew what they were doing with them? Mayybee? "Rin winced at her own lack of certainty. "They'd need a Master Artificer or three to repurpose them without, umm, setting off a sizable explosion with a lot of Stranging. If they found some way to use them to target airships, the ships would have to be within range of the device. Umm... to be honest... I think it's more likely that he'd use them to strip away an airship's shields so he could strike them with artillery. Or... he'd use them to attack Karalti. Anyone with access to C-grade lore on dragons knows their blood is mostly made of mana."

"What is the effective range of these devices?" Kitti asked, her clear, childish voice ringing through the room.

"A spined sphere about five thousand feet in radius, my lady," Rin replied.

Kitti bit her lip, her brow furrowing. "The Dragon Towers—the towers that protect our city from the air—are further apart than that. But if these Ix'tamo were placed inside, they would affect any airship flying close by."

"Yes," Captain Vilmos' eyes narrowed. "The cannons of the Hussar-class destroyers have an effective range of 3280 yards, but to be practical, they must be fired within 1750 yards, which is roughly 5000 feet. Closer is better, of course, because of the effects of wind."

One of the other Yanik scouts spoke up, and Istvan turned to listen. Everyone fell silent while he took in the information. The Dragoons had flown the Rangers in, but it was the

Yanik—with their supernaturally keen eyes—who had done most of the actual spotting.

"The walls of Solonovka are defended by the force garrisoned within the city," Istvan translated, marking the places where the Ranger pointed. "The scouts reached a consensus that there are about two thousand head stationed in Solonovka. They vary between veteran deserters, who have the King's steel, and poorly armed bandits, militia, and other flotsam. The majority of the professional soldiers were seen near those air-defense towers and the castle itself."

"Shit," Suri said. "So they're cutting off a land advance, and there's a chance they're using the Ix'tamo for some kind of anti-air defense strategy. Zoltan is smarter than he has any right to be."

Rin picked at her lip, scowling. "I mean... we can in theory just fly over them and stay out of their range. Hussar-class and Bathory-class can both fly at seventeen thousand feet with a full load. The altitude gets higher as you go south, but we could still clear the canyon by thousands of feet with any Vlachian warship. But... uhh... I guess we can't hit them from that height."

"What about taking the airships to the western border?" Captain Vilmos used a ruler to tap the lowlands of Bas. "Vyeshniki could be used as a staging ground. The Freehold is surely grateful for the relief we recently gave them."

"No good." Taethawn pinned his ears and lashed his tail. "Not for humansss, at least. The snows were coming in hard when we withdrew and returned to the capitol. Two thirds of my forces are exhausted after our adventure to Vyeshniki, mostly from the weather."

"He's right. We weren't able to scout that way due to blizzards and storms," Corporal Bognar added. " The weather is still clear in Solonovka, but it'll be snowed under in a matter of weeks. We saw Zoltan's troops moving large numbers of common folk under guard from the city in wagons, heading north and east. Preparations to bring in the harvest, I think."

"Fuck," I said. "You were right, Vilmos. He's going to gather the food and use it to dig in for a long siege."

Vilmos rumbled in his chest. "Yes. And unless we waste a lot of lives trying to cross that bridge, or find some other way to get an army over that canyon without getting shot down, he'll wait us out until spring. Every day that passes, he is more likely to find a way to kidnap Lady Hussar."

I stared at the map, thinking. "Hang on. I'm getting an idea."

The others looked to me, and waited.

"Taethawn," I said, after the pieces had come together. "Remember how I told you I want to modernize Vlachia's military?"

Taethawn gave Wing Commander Vasoly—the Royal agent—a nervous glance. "Yessss?"

"Part of that is implementing modern strategies, when they're warranted." I frowned at the smaller map of Hussar Manor that Kitti had drawn for us. Like Kalla Sahasi, the castle only had one road and a single gatehouse, complete with machicolations, murderholes, and other fun late-Medieval period defenses. Beyond the gatehouse was a short funnel which looked perfect for mowing down anyone who broke through the front. It opened up into the rectangular Lower Ward, which was ringed by the utilities of the castle: the stables, kennels, guard tower, garrison barracks, chapel and granaries. According to Kitti, this courtyard was used as a tiltyard to host jousting matches in the summer. Tens of thousands of people went to watch the knights every year. That meant it was at least a hundred meters long and seventy meters wide: about as large as a modern soccer field.

Above the Lower Ward was the gated Upper Ward. There were three buildings up there: The Great Hall, the Donjon—which still served as the actual 'dungeon' in this instance—and the Inner Keep, which was where the Lord and their family lived. Two staircases led from the Lower Ward to the Upper Ward. Small guard stations were built over the lower entries to those stairwells, meaning the residences of the lord and his family could be closed off from the lower yard. There was a small skydock in the upper ward, where Lord Hussar had moored his personal yacht. That ship was now almost certainly Zoltan's.

"So here's where we're going wrong," I said. "We've been thinking about this as if it was a medieval warfare problem. March an army into Bas, set up for a siege, wait him out over winter, etc. It seems impossible, because it is. But if we think of this as an anti-terrorist operation, it gets a lot easier. We don't need to send an army. We send an extraction force."

Commanders Vasoly and Taethawn looked at each other, then Vilmos, then me.

"How do you propose we do that?" Vasoly asked.

"Paratroopers," I said. "We send a crack team of paratroopers in—no more than twenty-five—directly into the Lower Ward at night. They take out the guards and foul up any anti-aircraft weaponry. Then we float our frigates right over those upper and lower courtyards and fast-rope five hundred soldiers straight into the castle."

I looked up to see a wall of blank, confused expressions.

"What are paratroopers?" Istvan asked.

"You know... paratroopers," I repeated, a little more slowly. "We fly the airships close to their maximum ceiling and a platoon of commandos jumps off the deck and parachutes down to the landing zone. Then you cut the chutes and kick a whole lot of ass."

"Jump... off... the deck?" Wing Commander Vasoly was looking at me like I'd lost my marbles. "Your Grace, with all due respect..."

I leaned forward on the table, glaring at him and the other officers in disbelief. "Are you telling me the Vlachia, the most technologically advanced human civilization on Archemi, does not have *parachutes*?"

There was an awkward pause. Kitti cleared her throat.

"No, your Grace." Captain Vilmos rubbed the back of his neck. "Are these, uh, parachutes some Artifact from your homeland?"

"They're not artifacts. They're kind of like balloons made of cloth," Suri said. "You strap 'em to your back and float down. No magic required."

The men shook their heads, except for Taethawn. He broke into peals of hissing laughter.

"Your Grace, when I was but a kitten I did many stupid things, as children of all species do," he said. "One time, I took my father's best feathered cloak, climbed to the top of his wagon, held the corners of it and jumped off in the hopes that I could sail gracefully through the skies like a piece of dandelion fluff. The twisted toe on my right foot assuresss you I did not achieve my dream."

I turned to Rin. "Rin? Are parachutes not possible in Archemi?"

"There's no reason they shouldn't be?" Rin shook her head, as bewildered as I was. "Though now you mention it... I've never seen parachutes or even air balloons in Vlachia. Which is weird, because we get tons of silk here from Jeun."

"So these, uh, 'paratroopers'..." Wing Commander Vasoly scratched the stubble on his jaw. "How high must they be when they... depart the aircraft?"

"Anywhere between seven thousand and sixteen thousand feet for a job like this," I said. "Higher is safer."

Istvan paled. "You want soldiers to jump sixteen thousand feet? To the ground?"

I gave him the hairy eyeball. "Look, I know it sounds crazy, but paratroopers are a normal part of warfare where I'm from. I fought in a war in my previous life before I came to Archemi. We jumped out of planes all the time."

Taethawn regarded me suspiciously. "'Previous' life implies that your life ended, somehow. Could it have been because His Grace plummeted to his death?"

I held up my hands. "Okay. The concept of paratroopers is somehow getting lost in translation. I literally have no idea how to explain this to you. Rin? Can you explain it better?"

"Me? Maybe?" Rin squeezed past me to stand at the table. "So, umm..."

The four military officers stared at her expectantly.

"Parachutes are devices that slow the descent of an object—like, a person—by creating drag, kind of like a wind turbine does." she stammered, twisting her hands behind her back. "They're normally made of silk or some other light material. They're folded a special way and stored in a backpack, and you pull them out with a cord after you jump. They poof out over your head and you fall slowly enough to make a safe, and usually precise, landing."

"There was a mad inventor in Taltos who tried to make one of those," Commander Vasoly said sourly. "He jumped off the Market District clocktower with some sailcloth. The City Guard had to scrape his splattered carcass off the street."

Rin winced. "The ones I'd make would be a lot better than that."

Wing Commander Vasoly shook his head. "I'm afraid you'll not find a single soldier here who would be willing to test this device. They would rightfully feel that you were ordering them to their deaths for sport."

"What a load of ghora shit," Taethawn drawled. "I will do it."

Everyone turned to look at him, including the Yanik Rangers.

"Your fears are stuffy Vlachii nonsense. If his Grace swears by the method, it isss certain to be feasible." Taethawn fingered his whiskers, hooding his eyes at the other commanders. "Voivode Dragozin and Lady Ba'hadir led us to victory at the Prezyemi Line. It stands to reason they know something about thisss strategy we do not. You can count on The Orphansss, your Grace—on one provision."

"Go ahead," I nodded to him.

"That you Starborn test this device and demonstrate its use," he said, lashing his tail. "If you land safely, I will commit my elite infantry to thisss training, the best of the best. We are Prrupt'meew, warriors of the Hm'rraw. We fear no height."

"Done," Suri said. "Rin, build us a chute and I'll demo a jump."

I glanced at her, surprised.

"Sure! I can make a parachute, no problem. If I have the mats and can figure out the recipe, I can probably craft one by this afternoon," Rin replied, blinking as she looked between us. "Which of you has more skydiving experience?"

"Him, so grill him about the design. But I'll make the actual jump." Suri pointed at me. "I fuckin' hate heights and weigh a ton with all my armor and gear on. If I can pull it off, any of our troops can."

"Okay!" Rin nodded, smiling up at her. "Hector? Can you come to my workshop and sketch out some military designs for me? The only kind of parachute I know is the round one, but I know the Army has better shapes for combat purposes."

"Can do," I replied. "We can test it tonight, preferably when it's dark."

"*I* will test it," Suri repeated, stubbornly. "*You* will park your arse on your dragon and watch."

"*What gives?*" I PM'd her.

"*Karalti told me what happened to you last time you died,*" she fired back. "*If anything goes wrong, I'll respawn at the castle with my memories and sanity intact. You won't. You were out for three days, last time. The next time, you might not wake up.*"

"*... Fair enough.*" I grimaced and closed the chat.

"So let us say this tactic is workable," the Wing Commander said. "The idea is to send a small team to disable the anti-airship ordnance, then land the army in the castle?"

"Yes," I said. "Taethawn's volunteered for the vanguard already, so that's taken care of. He will open up the sky for the Royal 2nd Company and its ships. With your Dragoons and the Royal Elementalists, we'll be able to hit them hard and fast, and avoid a siege. We just have to make sure he can't knock our ships or Karalti out of the sky."

"Indeed." Captain Vilmos said. "I will be honest with you, my lord: I am skeptical. It seems like a very long reach to jump off an airship, land inside of a castle, and storm it in such a way as to avoid detection."

Unseen and unheard, Mehkhet the Illuminator hung in the shadows at the very back of the room, his shadowy sleeves billowing in the gloom. I smiled, and absently rubbed the Mark of Matir. "Trust me. Once you see what I'm talking about, everything will fall into place. The Black God has our back on this one."

CHAPTER 21

I went with Rin to the smithy where she'd set up her quarters. It was still fairly chaotic. Rin's workspaces were neat— organized by shape, size and color—but she'd heaped her belongings into a pile on the middle of her bed.

"Hi, ladies!" She sang out as she opened the door. I hung back as her artificed sentinels, Lovelace and Hopper, scuttled over to greet us. They were mobile turrets the size of large dogs. Hopper was heavily armored and engineered for defense, capable of deploying magical protections and barriers to shield Rin from damage. Lovelace was her attack drone, armed with what looked to me like a really, really old-fashioned Gatling gun, the kind that had to be turned with a hand-crank. They waved their front legs at me in what I hoped was a friendly gesture as Rin hung up her coat.

"Okay, parachutes. There's two kinds I know how to use, the T-11 troop dispenser and the HI-5 free fall rig, and I'm pretty sure I remember how they're put together." I gingerly patted Hopper on her 'head' as the machine stomped over. "And while we're at it, two things. Can you possibly repair the Raven Helm and the Spear for me? And do you mind if I ask you some stuff before you get stuck into the design? About Michael, and OUROS."

"Oh! Sure! If you can leave the helmet with me, I can repair it this afternoon, but you need an Aether Forge for the Spear and we don't have one here. There's one in Litvy, but we won't have time for that today. As for questions... umm... I don't really know much more other than what I already told you, but I mean, it can't hurt to ask?" Rin smiled prettily at me, plopping down onto a heavy-duty stool built to withstand beings who weighed as much as Mercurions.

"We spoke to Jacob." I pulled the scarred Raven Helm off and set it on an empty worktable. "He told us that Michael experienced hallucinations when he was glitching during his upload. Did you know about that?"

"What? No." Rin shook her head, picking up the helmet and turning it over to appraise the damage. "We watched him enter the game and go through character creation, but when the glitch happened, we only saw him die a couple of times before HR cut the feed. They gave us some peppy little Silicon Valley propaganda talk about it afterwards. We heard the truth via gossip, of course, but when management reactivated the game stream, Michael seemed to be fine. He was laughing and talking... no mention of hallucinations or other problems. He reassured us they fixed the issue, and he was okay."

"Yeah. Well, the SysAdmin team heard a different story," I said. "It was real bad, apparently. While they were scrambling to fix Michael's spawn problem, the Drachan began whispering shit into his mind. Violent stuff, maybe even Total War imagery. And you know, now I think about it..."

"Hmm?"

213

I reached up to squeeze a handful of my hair. "I've had NPCs tell me the same thing. Not that they've hallucinated the Drachan, specifically, but that they've had nightmares of fleeing from war, or seeing people shot with modern weaponry. There was one village in Ilia, Lyrensgrove, where all the townies had dreams like that."

"Really?" Rin's brow furrowed. "That's... not supposed to happen."

"Matir said the Drachan have gone beyond their operational parameters. But Jacob, who managed the ATHENA database team, said that was impossible. That there's no way for them to." I began to pace, fidgeting. "So I'm trying to figure out what exactly we're dealing with when it comes to Ororgael and the Drachan."

"Well... if Michael was having violent hallucinations that he thought were some of Archemi's mobs speaking to him, that explains why he wants to destroy them." Rin began laying out her drafting tools, neatly arranging pencils, her protractor, and rulers. "As for Jacob, he was one of those young rockstar programmers, you know? He wasn't much older than me. As far as I know, he was fantastic at what he did, but he wasn't an expert on AI. Information Architects are kind of... what's the word? Shortsighted? They look at databases all day, modify and organize information in different dimensions. They aren't really looking at that data in a holistic way, not like how Michael and Steve did."

"What about you?" I asked. "You seemed to know a lot about AI in Korona."

"Oh, me? No… I'm a hobbyist, at best." She gave a prim shake of her head. "The theory of AI fascinates me, so I read a lot of books and articles about it. I realized early in my degree that CompSci wasn't for me. I moved into VR Modeling and Architecture. Growing up in an arcology gave me a head start on designing artificial environments, so… I just ran with it."

I rubbed my face. "Guess we're shit out of luck, then."

"Matir can't tell you more?" Rin took out a sheet of parchment and weighed the corners down with small metal discs. "Suri… she mentioned that, umm, Matir might be Steve."

I sighed. "It's complicated. Matir isn't Steve. Steve uploaded some fourth wall-breaking information to him somehow. He told me my brother might not have ever intended to become a character. He might have just delivered some kind of data payload and died, or become something else."

"What else could he become?" Rin gave me a curious look.

I rolled my eyes. "Knowing Steve, he wanted to become a god so that he could lord over everyone here and lecture them on their bad posture."

Rin laughed, a musical, tinkling sound that filled the chamber. "I mean… he DID do that. A lot."

"Just like dad." I made a face, absently petting Hopper. The machine was dog-like enough that I felt compelled to tell her she was a good girl and feed her robo-treats. "Anyway. I'm probably just overthinking shit. Ororgael hallucinated some old war trauma he had and went nuts from dying a couple hundred times. He wants to free the world bosses before anyone else is ready, destroy the global order, and declare himself God Emperor of Mankind. End of story."

"Maybe. I'll have to think about it." Rin shrugged, and turned to the paper. "Anyway, let's just focus on this for now. I need you to describe as many features of these parachutes as you can for me..."

***

Rin and I worked on the parachute designs for a couple of hours. I could describe a lot of what I'd trained in: the static lines we'd used for our T-11 jumps, the harnesses and toggles that were part of the free-fall HI-5 system. I had clear memories of being drilled over and over in how to pack and unpack both kinds of parachute. I left everything I could dredge up from my memory with her—she already had a stack of silk in her inventory—and went to go sort out my level up.

Level 26 hadn't opened up any new abilities. After Level 25, new ability acquisition slowed down. My skill tree had fifty slots, so I figured I'd have access to that many abilities by the time I reached Level 50 or 60. That meant I had two points to spend on combat abilities I already had, or a Mark of Matir ability that had levels, like *Spider Climb*.

In my opinion, my Advanced Path was still kind of meh. I was powerful in combination with Karalti—she was a frigging dragon, after all—but the fight with the Rotmother had exposed a major weakness in the Lancer and Dark Lancer/Dark Dragoon Paths: they relied on the same key spear-fighting ability used in many Japanese-made RPGs, *Jump*. With Jump V, I could leap 50ft in any direction and deal a huge amount of damage on anyone I landed on, but because of Archemi's realistic physics, enemies with enough strength or reach could potentially knock me out of the air. If I was thrown out of the attack, it canceled the Jump and its bonus damage, along with any combos I might be chaining off that one maneuver.

The obvious solution was mobility, more training—and better gear. Oh lort, was I ready for better gear. Anything that made me faster, less visible, offered me mobility or teleporting—or even better, some kind of time-slow ability—was top on my list. After the tragic demise of the Raven Suit, all I really had right now was a Medium set of ⟦House Bolza Guard Armor⟧. It was better than my Jack of Plates mishmash, but still not great. The Nizari Set, which I'd been using since I was barely Level 10, was also an option—but unless Rin could work some miracle with it, it just couldn't handle the kind of damage and armor penetration my enemies threw at me now.

I plugged both points into Shadow Dance, leveling it up to Shadow Dance V: the maximum level for combat abilities until I hit Level 30. It was my primary mobility ability, and once I read the description, I knew I'd made the right decision.

Shadow Dance V

Basic Evasive Dash reduces damage by 95% at the cost of HP (5 HP per dash). Can now be used three times in a row before recharging, including while in mid-air. You can now dash in any direction without needing prior momentum: straight up or down from standing, etc.

Satisfied, I closed the window. I had 5366 EXP to go before I reached Level 27, but there wasn't going to be time for grinding monsters just yet—because this bitch was gonna train.

Cue the montage.

CHAPTER 22

Training always began with a brisk 3-mile run in full gear, accompanied by wholesome songs about patriotism, duty, and sacrifice.

"Airborne Ranger was a hell of a man! Walked through the bar with his cock in his hand! Shit on the table and pissed on the floor! Wiped his ass with a forty-four!" I happily bawled out the lyrics as I jogged through The Orphans' camp, clanking on every step. "A hundred women queued against the wall! Bet a hundred bucks he couldn't fuck 'em all! Fucked ninety-eight till his cock turned blue! Threw up, swelled up, fucked the other two!"

By the end of the song, half a dozen of Taethawn's soldiers had joined me—and by the third mile, they'd learned the full version of The Monkey/Airborne Ranger, My Girl is a Vegetable, A.I.R.B.O.R.N.E #2, aka the 'Drink Yourself to Death' song, and two of the Kick-Ass Granny ones. Unsurprisingly, I leveled up in Stamina, but not Wisdom or Intelligence for teaching a bunch of battle-hardened giant cats about Everclear and amphetamines.

After that came combat training. I was just about to hit the threshold for Advanced Spearfighting, which meant I was going to need a trainer of some kind. Unfortunately for me, I was the best spear specialist in Karhad, and possibly all of

Myszno. What I *could* train was acrobatics. I had three disciplines of acrobatics I planned to master by the time I was Level 40: Gymnastics, Parkour, and Aerobatics, the art of flipping out like a circus performer while in the air. And I did know someone who could train me to Master levels, when the time came—Vash.

"Hup!" I Jumped up to the scaffolding, found my feet, and launched out into the air. I chained Shadow Dance up, up and forward, reappearing on the top level of scaffolding. Teetering high above the courtyard, I ran to the edge, flipped across the gap, and cartwheeled over to stand on my hands. Then I walked on them to the edge of the rampart, holding position there against the wind for a handful of seconds before slowing tipping myself over the edge. *Leap of Faith III* kicked in, slowing my perception of the descent. I twisted in the air like a cat, heart pounding as the ground drew closer and closer. At the last second, I Shadow Danced forward and up. The dash almost carried me into the edge of a broken wall. I barely twirled out of the way, sucking in my gut, then burst out laughing.

[You have gained a level in gymnastics! You have gained a level in Aerobatics! You have gained +1 Str, +1 Dex]

"Nice." I drew a deep breath, pausing to rest and let my stamina bar refill. I was grinning, pulse racing, muscles warm and ready to fire. It was the same bliss I'd felt during motorcycle stuntwork: the double pleasure of skill and raw physical control meshed into a seamless flow.

An odd sound broke through the morning air: the sound of clashing metal and rough leather. I turned, saw nothing, and looked up to find Vash perched on the edge of the rampart I'd just dropped down from. The clanging was the sound he made while clapping with one metal arm, and one arm covered in the full-length striking gauntlet of the *Baru*.

"You're getting better, dog!" Vash fluidly dropped to the ground. He was still dressed as he had been while training Karalti: loose pants tucked into heavy-duty steel-capped boots, a sash, a well-worn crossover jacket. "No wonder you casually told the commanders this morning that you want their men to jump sixteen thousand feet off an airship, eh?"

I laughed. "Seriously, it works. We'll show you how it's done."

"Oh, I believe you. Istvan said something about soldiers holding sheets over their heads, drifting to the earth like gentle autumn leaves." He cackled. "Come. Walk with me. I would talk."

Curious, I jumped up and down a couple of times, loosening my arms, then fell into step with him. Walks with Vash were rarely casual—and even as I thought that, he vanished into a fine film of smoke and reappeared twenty feet up on the edge of the wall. I leaped up after him, breaking into a jog as he ran along the narrow edge, cartwheeled without hands over a break in the stone, and kept running toward the gatehouse. Two months ago, I would have only barely kept up with him. Now, I was able to match his speed as he scaled the rough stone walls like a lizard, pulling himself up to the top of the gatehouse tower and scattering a flock of crows. They squawked indignantly as they flew away.

"Sorry, little brothers," he said, clicking his tongue. He hopped up onto the very edge of the parapet and squatted on his heels, looking out over the Meewfolk encampment.

"What's up?" I asked, once I'd found my place beside him.

"Earlier, I mentioned that I might ask you a favor," he replied in Tuun. "It isn't something you can do for me straight away, but it is unfair to leave your questions hanging."

That took me aback a little. Vash wasn't usually one for explaining himself. "I'm guessing it's a quest. What level do you think we'd need to be to help you?"

He made a face, thinking. "Hrrnn... Level Thirty-four? Thirty-Five?"

I whistled. "Yeah. That's a ways off."

"Mmph." His thin face settled into deep, troubled lines. "Not as far as either of us would like to think."

"Talk to me, man." I rested my arms on my knees. "Is something wrong with Istvan, or...?"

"No." Vash closed his eyes, gathering his words. "It is personal. All this talk of the Drachan, and would-be tyrants..." He sneered, reaching back to pull his fall of beaded braids over his shoulder. "I smell a tsunami heading for Vlachia, Hector. A black tide, full of monsters and human hatred. And I found myself thinking back, back to the unresolved guilt that still haunts me. The death of my family."

"You once told me you were a kinslayer," I said, slowly. "I admit I've wondered."

His eyes flickered open again. "It is a long story."

I shrugged. "I'm a patient guy. Sort of."

Vash fell silent for a time. His muscles loosened, his breathing slowed, and his skin bloomed with a healthy pink glow. He was somehow consciously controlling his body at a very deep level. Slowing it down to head off stress.

"I was born in the plateau country about a week's ride south-east of Norbu, the town which is the center of Tuun life in Vlachia," he said calmly. "The Dorha clan was wealthy, with a thousand head of cattle. My mother, Lhaho, was a strong woman who managed us with kindness and competence. She had four husbands, with three children by two of them: me, my little sister Saaba, and my elder sister... Tsunda."

He paused after speaking her name, grimacing like a man with a stomach ache.

"Saaba was a gentle girl. Full of energy and very playful. I loved her fiercely," he continued. "But Tsunda, aiyai-yai. She was never quite right in the head."

"What was wrong with her?" I asked.

"From early in her life, she was prone to wild dreams and fiery rages. If something upset her, she would cry and scream until she vomited. If she was happy, she'd become manic, unable to sleep." Vash's eyes grew distant as he spoke. "She was very violent. She once bit my mother on the face so hard she took a mouthful of her flesh."

"Like... as a toddler?"

"No. As a girl of eight," Vash replied. "But it gets worse. Around the time she started her moonblood, she began to hear voices and see terrible visions, hallucinations so overwhelming that she would claw at her skin, pull her clothes off, and attack people who were not there. Every day, from dawn to dusk, she ranted and raved about 'metal demons' and people being killed by swarms of black bees or wasps. Trees terrified her. She spoke of nations built of black crystals, shattered by fire and explosions, and countless people dying. She became paranoid of us all, convinced that we would murder her. Her violence became not only frightening, but dangerous."

"Sounds like some kind of psychosis. I saw guys crack like that in Indonesia a few times." I glanced at the web of scars that divided Vash's face. He might have been handsome once, in a wolfish kind of way. Someone had smashed an axe into his face six or seven times and left the front of his skull crazed like a broken mirror. I was starting to figure who that might have been.

Vash shrugged. "Who knows? Regardless, my parents and grandparents were devastated. Tsunda was the family heir, and she was unmarriageable. My grandmother did not believe that Tsunda was sick with an illness. There were only two possible answers: either she was possessed by demons, or she was a shaman. A young shaman who desperately required the guidance of a master."

"Oof." I winced. "Was it Tsunda who smashed up your face?"

He nodded. "When she was fourteen and I was eight, Tsunda began to abuse us terribly. She hated Saaba, and was convinced she was one of her metal demons. Saaba was only three, but Tsunda was convinced she would destroy us all. I taught Saaba to hide from our sister and took Tsunda's attentions onto myself. Beatings, shouting, and worse. But one day, she pushed me too far. She demanded something of me I would not do. I stood up to her and she backed off, but once we returned home, she took the axe from the chopping block outside my father's yurt and attacked me in a frenzy. I nearly died."

"Holy shit." I let out a terse puff of breath. "Is that... like... how you became a Baru?"

"No, no. My grandparents were able to treat my wounds, though I had to wear bandages on my face for months." He rubbed the edge of his thumb over one of the crooked white gouges in his cheek. "After Tsunda attacked me, my mother ordered she be tied to her bed. We all knew she could no longer be managed at home. There was a vote, with some of the clan saying she should be taken to Solonovka to see a Vlachian doctor. But most of my family still did not believe Tsunda's condition was a physical illness. Tsunda's father, his brother, and their mother volunteered to take her to see the Abbott at the Temple of the Pure Body in Norbu. They undertook the two-week trek to the monastery, dragging Tsunda on a sled. But during my family's stay, Norbu—and most of the populated Southern Highlands of Myszno—were struck with plague."

"They got sick?"

"Worse." Vash shook his head. "My clan-father, uncle and grandmother were healthy when they fled the city, but they carried the plague on the clothes and blankets they had bought for us while they were there. When they returned to the plateau, they embraced us and gave us souvenirs, and then we ALL got sick. Every single one of us."

I shuddered. "God. I know what *that's* like."

He rolled his shoulders. "The elderly died first. Mother died because she insisted on caring for her sick parents. Our clan-fathers died because they tried to save the woman they loved. Our ranch hands died because they looted our lumber and iron and tried to run, sick and crazed, into the mountains. Tsunda, weakened from ritual fasting, somehow held on until the end before she expired. But Saaba and I did not die. We were deathly ill, and for five days, we faded in and out of fever, coughed water from our lungs and choked down scraps of food when we could. Our skin and mouths became blistered. We were covered in awful rashes that transformed into deep bruises."

I listened to him in disbelief. The symptoms Vash had described were identical to HEX: a two-week latency period, followed by a five-day spiral into death. The only difference between what I'd been through on Earth and what had happened to him on Archemi was that HEX had a hundred-percent mortality rate. But otherwise...

"I cared for Saaba as best I could, fully expecting to die at any hour," he continued. "We barely survived, but when we convalesced, we realized that we were going to perish anyway. There were no adults. The herd had strayed. The food gathered and stored in the yurts were rotting. I ate what I could, but Saaba could still take nothing but thin broth. My little sister... I'd spent her whole life protecting her, helping her. She was only seven, and I was a boy of twelve by that time. The other clans of the plateau would not help us, because of the plague, so I did the only thing I could think to do: I packed our things onto our sturdiest camel, let Saaba ride in the saddle, and set out with her for Norbu and the temples."

"Damn." I whistled. "I'm sorry, man."

"Mmph." Vash gazed up at Erruku as clouds dimmed the moon's steady golden light. "The trip to *Vhashti Shar*, our temple of Burna in Norbu, is arduous. A two-week trek through the same black mountains where you say you found Burna's tomb. We were tough children, born and raised in the wilderness, but we were weak and delirious and very, very young. We fought wolves and harpies, we killed and ate mountain goats to stay alive. But when we were about halfway to the monastery, pushing ahead through awful snow, we were struck by a rockslide. I was walking on foot and managed to avoid being crushed, but the camel carrying my sister was not fast enough. The slide buried him and Saaba together. I ran back and began digging. I dug until my hands bled. Eventually, I found her. She was still alive, trapped under the rocks and snow and sheltered by the twisted body of the animal that now crushed her. I fought with everything I had, but no human child alone could have moved that camel and the stones holding it down. I tried to pull her free, and almost tore her in half. Her legs were gone."

I watched him, saying nothing.

"She knew it as surely as I did." Vash shook his head slightly, staring bleakly at the horizon. "Saaba was only little, but she was a herder's daughter. She had seen livestock caught in avalanches before. While she wept from agony, she looked me straight in the eye and asked me to end it. Painlessly, quickly."

Vash squeezed his eyes shut, his thin mouth twisting down.

"You did the right thing," I said softly.

"Of course I did. I knew it then, and I know it now." He drew a deep breath, his grey eyes clouded with old pain. "But just because it was the righteous action to take did not mean I could bear to live with myself. I dug a little trench in the snow and lay down, sung a song to Burna, and went to my death. What I didn't know at that age is that while death from the cold is peaceful, it takes a very long time. You fall asleep, your heart slows, and if you stay just barely warm enough, you enter a kind of strange sleep. It was in this state that my future Master found me. The Baru, Tantun Gorta. He was on his way back to the monastery when he came across the avalanche and found us, brother and sister, with me lying as if composed for burial. He sang the rites and burned what he could of my sister's remains, then wrapped me in a shroud. His plan was to take my body to the charnel ground at Vhashti Shar. The valley where the accident took place was so cold that no animals had come to eat us."

I nodded. That was a big deal to the Tuun. Vash's people—our people—disposed of the dead via sky-burial. Corpses were left out on a special hillside to be eaten by a species of giant fly bred especially for the purpose. The flies ate the bodies before they putrefied, leaving nothing but small amounts of alchemically hardened bone. That bone was given to the family of the dead, typically to be carved into commemorative beads like the ones Vash wore in his hair. The average Tuun believed that if a body was allowed to rot or wasn't given rites, the soul wouldn't separate from the corpse, and it would come back as a ghost.

"Gorta carried us all the way to his camp. He chanted the Rite of the Fly-Headed God over me, and as he tells it, nearly pissed himself when I opened my eyes and looked right at him." Vash smiled faintly. "Master kept me alive through the most agonizing weeks of my life. Dying from the cold is easy, but rubbing warmth back into frozen flesh is pure torture. Still, it was a miracle that I had lost nothing but my smallest toes and a couple of knuckles to frostbite. He brought me to the temple, and I was told that I would become a Baru."

"Told?" I frowned.

"Yes, Dragozin. Baru are fated people. Like your Karalti, I entered Burna's realm as a child and returned. And thus, I reluctantly commenced my education." He shrugged. "But that leads me to my request of you. You see, I have never been able to return to my home. That avalanche is still there. It was there when, after twelve years spent at the monastery, I tried to return. Reaching that place is now impossible by foot, even for me. The only way to get there is to fly, but there is no airship capable of reaching that altitude, and no quazi in the world that is strong enough to endure the winds that rage through those mountains. Dragons brought our people to the plateaus of Myszno, and dragons are the only way I could possibly return to see if any of the other clans survived, as well as give my family their proper rites. I have lived for nearly thirty years without closure on that chapter of my life, Hector. I would ask that you and Karalti help me to finish what was started."

I nodded slowly, thinking it over. "We can take you there, for sure. I'd be honored to."

"It may not be easy," Vash warned. "Tsunda... only the gods know what she might have become. She died in bondage, raving and howling while strapped to her bed. By the time she passed, no one had the strength to do anything about the body. She was left to rot in despair."

I cracked my knuckles. "I ain't afraid of no ghost."

Vash snorted. "I surely hope not. Shall I do the formalities?"

"Go for it."

New Quest: The Daughter of Madness

Your companion, Vash Dorha, wishes to return to the remote and wild plateaus of south-eastern Myszno, where his family once prospered as semi-nomadic herders. After seeking treatment for his mentally ill elder sister, ⸢E̶E̶T̶C̶H̶E̶R̶R̶O̶R̶N̶U̶L̶L̶⸥ *the entire clan was slain by a plague that killed everyone but Vash and his younger sister, Saaba.*

The bodies were not buried or given the rites the Tuun consider vital to help the spirits of the dead move on to the next world, and Vash is worried that his family may yet suffer as ghosts, revenants, or worse. He has asked you and your dragon to take him to his childhood home so that he may put his family to rest and move on from his pain.

Rewards: *Path perks (Baru, Dark Paragon), 3000 EXP, Special Items, Temple of Burna (facility).*

Special: *Only you, Karalti and Vash may attempt this quest.*

A wave of déjà vu rolled through me as Navigail's voice skipped over the glitchy line. I clutched my head as it—and my shoulder—both throbbed. I wobbled, briefly losing my balance until a firm hand snapped around my forearm and straightened me back up.

"Hector?" Vash's voice was stiff with concern. "Are you well?"

"You don't see that?" I replied, rubbing my eyes. The brief wave of dizziness had already passed, but I felt... odd. Driven by the sense that I needed to remember something.

"See what?" He let go of me, watching me cautiously.

"The error," I said. "Your sister's name is all screwed up. The last time that happened to me with a quest, Ororgael was tangled up in it. It was Andrik Corvinus' name, that time. Suri was able to see the same error in the Wiki."

Vash blinked, then looked up and slightly off to the right, scanning the text he'd submitted. "No. I see no errors. If I play it back, it sounds normal to me."

"Maybe it's just me, then. My last death screwed with me pretty hard." That thought was no less chilling than the idea of Void creatures or a ghost erasing her name from a quest, and I had to push past some hesitation before I was able to accept the job. "Do you want Suri to come? Or Istvan?"

"No. It is not that I do not wish for their company, but this is a matter for those who are aligned with Darkness." He shook his head. "For all that he has had his share of grief, Istvan is not a dark person. Nor is Suri. This is a task for gloomy men like you and I."

I grinned. "Are we talking about the same Istvan? The drill sergeant? Mr. No Fun?"

Vash chuckled. "In the public eye, Istvan is forever aware that he is the half-breed orphan among Vlachians. But when the mask comes off and he feels like he can be himself, he is a playful man. Sensitive and artistic."

"Artistic?" I gave him an odd look.

"Hrrn. Music. He plays the fiddle and writes songs, and is good at both."

"Huh. Never would have guessed."

"That is by design. He is talented, but he has no desire to be known for his art. It is something he does mostly for himself, by himself." Vash's eyes grew distant. "He and I are both plagued by grief regarding family. I wish to purge myself of my old attachments so I can help him live in the present, and fall into his arms in the knowledge that I am not simply another of his many burdens."

I clapped Vash on the shoulder. "I don't think he thinks that way."

"Nor do I," he said, briefly covering my hand with his own. "But I have a tendency to dwell on dark things." "Tell you what." I bobbed up to my feet on the edge of the wall, and hopped backwards to land on the parapet. "Once this thing with Bas is over, it's grinding time for me and Karalti. We're going to try and power level. Barring some new crisis, we'll work hard at it—and as soon as we hit Level 32, we'll do this."

"As you say." Vash stood up as well, stretching his arms behind his back. "I am grateful, Dragozin. Not many people would undertake such a difficult quest on behalf of a friend."

"Any time, man." I nodded. "But hey, speaking of quests: mind giving me a hand with one? I have to collect a shit-ton of herbs. We have to stock up on medicines and take them to Karhad in case that Thornlung plague spreads."

"Of course. And if it does, I shall treat the sick. I am immune." He also rose, stretching his arms back.

"Immune?" I was starting to head to the edge of the wall, but turned. "Wait: the plague your family got. That was thornlung?"

"The very same," he replied. "Why, Dragozin? You look like you've seen a ghost of your own."

"Yeah. It's just..." I trailed off, not sure how to explain it to him. "In my life before Archemi—Earth—there were two back-to-back global wars between the world's superpowers. The second war, and the world, rapidly disassembled when a virus—a disease—got out of control. The symptoms were exactly like how you describe thornlung. And I mean, *exactly*. There are some differences in the outcome. HEX had a 100-percent mortality rate, for one thing. It isn't treatable, because it wasn't a natural virus."

Vash's nostrils flared. "Explain."

"I don't think I can," I replied, struggling for words. "It's... uh... imagine a tiny Stranged particle riding on an artifact smaller than anything you could see with the naked eye. The artifact can drill through cloth, skin, and armor and deliver the particle into someone's body. Then it lies dormant for two weeks, so that person goes and gives it to other people, before it activates into a disease and kills them. That's what HEX did. It was a weapon, made to kill people with disease."

Vash's lips worked as he struggled to find the right thing to say. "That is hideous. Who released this weapon?"

"No one knows," I said. "My side of the war blamed Suri's people's side of the war. Her side blamed mine. Europe blamed both of us. When I got sick, they'd already called an emergency armistice, because billions of people were dying."

"Billions? Billions of people?" Vash's brow furrowed into deep lines as he tried—and probably failed—to comprehend a number which didn't really exist in Archemi. "It never occurred to me that Starborn could be refugees from a dying world, but I suppose it makes sense. And I am glad you have found a better place here."

"Yeah. Me too." I looked toward the west, the direction of Ilia and Revala. Ororgael, Lucien and Violetta were working toward their goals somewhere over there, separated by thousands of miles of mountains, plains, and ocean. "This is a good place. And as long as we fight for it, it'll stay that way."

CHAPTER 23

True to her word—and thanks to the miracle of videogame crafting—Rin had the parachute ready by the afternoon: a near-replica of the HI-5 ram air parachute used for free fall jumps, except instead of being made out of olive drab ripstop, it was made from bright blue and red silk.

Taethawn had joined us, along with three of his bloodriders, the captains who led his forces on the ground. Istvan, Wing Commander Vasoly, Captain Vilmos, Zlaslo Ul'Tiranozavir and Vash were also in attendance. They watched as Rin moved around Suri's body, passing under her outstretched arms as she fit the parachute and harness over her armor. As it was a prototype device, the fit wasn't automatic in the same way that armor or other gear was.

"You blokes alright?" Suri asked, smirking at Vasoly. "Wing Commander, you're lookin' a bit green around the gills."

"That story I told you, about the inventor who jumped off the clocktower?" Vasoly had his arms crossed and his lips pursed. "I was in the city guard back then. My squad were the ones who had to scrape him off the cobblestones."

"Well, I really don't think you'll have to do that this time," Rin said testily. "Suri is my friend. I wouldn't be letting her do this if I thought my design wouldn't work."

Sitting on Karalti's back, I sucked on a tooth and glanced over assembled. The officer's hookwings had been turned loose on the mesa, left to flock up and wander together as a honking, hissing pack. Cutthroat stood head and shoulders over the others. The huge black hookwing had taken pole position, tearing up the moss with her long, sword-like claws and pissing all over it to inform the others that she was, in fact, the biggest, baddest bitch of Karhad Plateau. Most of the other hookwings were sensibly avoiding her—except for one. Taethawn's mount, a grizzled bull with dark brindled plumage and splendid red tail feathers, seemed determined to keep up. I watched, puzzled, as he bent down to sniff and lick at the moss she'd passed over. When he was done sniffing, he reared up with his jaws parted and his lips pulled back over his teeth, huffing through nose and mouth. It almost looked like he was grinning.

"OooOooh!" Karalti sang. *"Someone's looking for a giiiiirlfriiiiend."*

"Is that what I need to do if I ever want to ask you out?" I bit my lip to keep from laughing before the punchline. *"Moon around after you while you piss all over the castle?"*

"Hee hee! You flirt!" My dragon's telepathic voice danced with mirth. *"Really, though. Please don't."*

"Hey, Taethawn!" I called down to him. "Is your guy doing what I think he's doing?"

"Ey?" The Meewfolk flicked his ear toward me, then looked over his shoulder. Both ears flattened to his skull in dismay when he saw. *"Oy! Khun kalang kan, Payu?"*

Payu reared his head up at Taethawn's call, his nostrils flexing, but his fierce golden gaze was irresistibly drawn back to Cutthroat. I knew that look. It was the face of a man on a mission.

"Payu!" Taethawn let out a clicking whistle, but Payu insolently lifted his crests, flicked his tail, and set after Cutthroat at a determined trot.

"Ohoi, my Payu has finally found a lady worthy of his attentions." Taethawn let out a short laugh, shaking his head. "Don't worry, Your Grace. Cutthroat will sort him out."

Vash made a religious sign in front of his forehead. "Should Payu perish in his pursuit of glory, I will be here to give him rites."

I watched with increasing apprehension as Payu closed the distance to Cutthroat. He let out a huffing bark, and she reared up from her territorial marking, twisting her neck to glare at him.

"HOHH! HOHH!" Payu was large, as hookwings went, but he was no Cutthroat. The bull seemed oblivious to this difference in mass as he inflated his throat, fanned the feathers of his hook arms, and began to bounce his head from side to side. "HOHH!"

I groaned, smearing my hand over my face. "Oh no. Nooo, dude. It's so not worth it."

"What?" Suri squinted up at me, then followed my line of sight. "Oh Jesus. Taethawn, grab your bloody bird before Cutthroat rips his dick off and eats it, will ya?"

Taethawn made an airy gesture with one hand. "She is too big for him. He will learn."

Cutthroat turned her nose up and carried on her rounds, ignoring the male who was now pitter-pattering along behind her, dragging his tail like a randy pigeon. He weaved from one side of her to the other in the hope that she would glimpse his magnificent manly plumage and succumb to his charms.

"Payu! Forget it, mate!" Suri cupped her hand to her mouth, raising her voice to be heard over Sandstorm's cooing. "That old battleaxe has a cunt drier than the Bashir. You aren't crackin' that nut."

"You mean, he isn't nutting in that crack," Vash said drily.

Suri burst out with a short snortled laugh. The noise was so sudden that Rin reflexively shot up to her feet so fast and that the top of her head struck Suri right under the shelf formed by her breastplate. She rebounded with a squeal and tripped, falling onto her butt.

"Ahhhh!" Rin clutched her head. "I'm sorry! I didn't mean to!"

Suri was too busy losing her shit to respond, other than to reel away and slap her knees.

"It's fine," I cheerfully called down to her. "Suri's tits are an occupational hazard. I bounce off them all the time."

"Uaaaaah! HECTOR!!" Rin covered her face with her hands.

The mirth was interrupted by a snarl, a thump, and a saurian shriek of pain. Everyone turned back to the hookwings to see Cutthroat bowl Payu off his feet, yelping as the huge female's jaws briefly closed on his neck. He backed up with his head low to the ground, hissing, as Cutthroat reared up and clashed her hooked claws together, the universal hookwing sign language for 'take your stupid mating dance and go fuck yourself with it'.

"Poor Payu," Taethawn sighed. "But we cannot say he did not try."

"He was doomed from the start." I swung my legs, bumping my heels against the thick leather saddle. "Cutthroat's convinced that Suri, and only Suri, will be the mother of her children."

Taethawn laughed. "It isss known that some *ghora* become rider-bonded. It is a lucky thing to have happen for a warrior, and good for battle. But such ghora often cannot be bred for reasons that should be obviousss."

Rin, still blushing furiously, clambered back to her feet. "Okay, guys, the harness looks good. Everything should just... work. Get ready to have Karalti catch her if the chute doesn't deploy properly. This IS a prototype."

Suri swallowed, looking up at the clouds. "It sure is."

"No sweat. Suri knows what to do once she's up there." I dropped the visor of my helmet and locked it into place. "You ready, Karalti?"

"Yeah!" Karalti bent down, resting her ribcage on the ground, and stretched her wing for Suri to climb. *"I finally get*

to achieve my childhood dream of throwing Suri off something really high!"

I rolled my eyes and smacked the side of Karalti's neck as she mimicked Rin's giggling laughter.

"I really cannot wait to see thisss." Taethawn shook his head, extending a single claw to pick at his teeth. "Even I think it is crazy. How will you direct your landing?"

"The parachute has toggles," Rin said. "You can change your direction with them."

"I bet you real money I can land it in that square first shot." Suri cocked her chin at him, reaching up to grasp my hand as she clambered up to the saddle. When she was on, I took the front position and she took the back.

The Meewfolk grinned broadly. "Hmmmm... let us ssssay... fifty olbia?"

"Fuck that. Bet a hundred or go home." Suri bared her teeth at him.

"*Tam tai miu'in*. The deal is made." Taethawn put his hands together, palm to palm, and bowed over them. "One hundred olbia that you can land in the square."

Suri gave him a thumbs up, then went to hands and knees. She gripped the handles at the back of the saddle, facing toward Karalti's tail.

"Okay. Be warned that you're going to feel like you're about to fall off constantly," I said, getting into position between my dragon's shoulders. "Turbulence feels worse on the hiney of the dragon. It's not worse, but it feels like it."

"The hiney of the dragon," Karalti repeated somberly. *"The dragon's hiney."*

Suri grunted. "Yeah. Okay. I'm more worried about a tail strike."

It was a real concern. Skydiving off the back of a dragon offered some interesting challenges. Number one was the fact that unlike an airship, dragons undulated as they beat their wings. I knew from experience that it was pretty easy to be flung off. Suri also had to avoid Karalti's assorted body parts when exiting the platform. That wasn't a problem for me because of *Jump*, but Suri didn't have any special mobility moves. We'd decided the best option was for her to cling on to Karalti's rump, where the saddle narrowed into a leaf-shaped cantle. Once we reached altitude, she would sprint out to the base of her tail and jump out behind her at an angle.

As soon as Suri was in position, I mentally signaled Karalti. She backed up, scattering the officers, then broke into a lumbering stride for the edge of the cliff. I bowed down and braced my forehead as she kicked off the ledge into the open air. The initial drop lifted our stomachs and then punched them down. Looking back, I saw Suri clinging white knuckled to the grips, watching as the earth receded from us at speed.

"Whee!" Karalti strove her wings rhythmically, gyring upward into thinner, colder air. *"Why don't we fly this high all the time?"*

"Mostly because no one else can breathe the air and I don't like dead friends," I replied, kneeling back into the saddle.

242

"But once Suri's parachute is out, I am totally up for a fifteen-thousand-foot dive back to the mesa."

Karalti brayed with saurian laughter, driving her wings as we broke through a thin, wispy little cloud. *"Yeah! You're on!"*

I checked the altitude on the Raven Helm HUD. *"Suri, we're at ten thousand and counting. How are you feeling?"*

"I'm ten k in the air with my lungs on fire and a couple of straps holding me on. I'm fuckin' peachy." Her eyes were concealed by the polarized goggles Rin had loaned her, and the rest of her expression was stony. *"But you know, it's weird. I feel like I've done this a hundred times before, even though it's the first time."*

"Soldiers jump off high things a lot," I said. *"Maybe you were airborne in your past life."*

"Maybe. I..." She paused for a moment, then grimaced and rested her head down on the saddle.

"You alright?" I glanced at the HUD. We were almost at altitude.

"I just remembered something. I think?" She shook her head. *"I remember... I was in a big grey tube with a bunch of other people. We were all dressed the same, all drab greens and grays. I had a pack like this... I remember attaching it to like, a zipline? No. A static line. That's what they're called."*

"Hot damn, Suri." I grinned from ear to ear. *"You WERE Airborne."*

"Yeah. The static line pulled the cord from the bag as we jumped." She chuckled, and rubbed the bridge of her nose. *"Shit. That's weird."*

The mesa was now a great green slab looming over the shadowed valley, the castle a dark triangle to the south. I motioned with a hand. *"Okay, babe: we're at altitude. Let's do this!"*

Karalti, reading my intent through the Bond, slid into circulating current of air and flared her wings into a smooth, condor-like glide. As she steadied out, I stood up and walked with the wind to join Suri. I signed her for three minutes, then got her to stand. She nervously obliged, and I checked her harness from bottom to top, adjusted her rip cord over the back of the parachute, and then gave her a thumb's up. She signed one minute back to me. Without thinking, we'd both shifted into the universal hand signals of military procedure... signals that were the same no matter which side of the war you were on.

"Hold steady," I urged Karalti, watching as Suri signed forty seconds, twenty seconds, ten seconds... *"In three, two, one."*

Suri kicked up off the saddle like a sprinter and ran down Karalti's back, launching into the air at a thirty-degree angle from the base of her tail. Whooping encouragement, I hit Spider Climb and held on as Karalti banked into a roll away from Suri, giving her space to fall. "Yeah, girl! Get some!"

Suri rolled over once in the air before getting her limbs under control, spreading them out to maximize drag. Karalti wheeled at a distance, tilting starboard so we could watch her. After about twenty seconds of freefall, I saw Suri pull the ripcord. She tugged once, twice, and my heart began to hammer... but then she yanked it again, harder, and the rectangular silk parachute blossomed up and out, dragging her back up a short distance into the sky. We circled as she drifted down for five minutes or so before landing neatly in the distant pale bullseye below.

"*NICE.*" I messaged her and Rin.

Rin squeaked with joy. "*Yee! And I got a new achievement and bonus EXP! I'm Level 25 now!*"

"*I got some EXP and a new Skill.*" Suri said shakily. "*Jeez... already have six ranks in Skydiving from that one jump. And a real bad wedgie from that harness.*"

"*I can fix that, kind of,*" Rin said. "*Unfortunately, the, umm, human body being what it is...*"

"*Hah! Taethawn's gonna have to pay back the money we gave him!*" Karalti flicked her wing and tail, leveling out. "*Wanna give them a show?*"

"*Always.*"

Karalti waited for me to assume the dive position, then folded her wings and barreled over with almost lazy speed. My gut lurched with the brief release of gravity, and then we were falling... plummeting toward the ground so fast the wind tore my joyous laughter away before I could even hear it. Diving at top speed, Karalti could reach three hundred miles an hour, nearly twice as fast as a peregrine falcon... conditions that would have sent a normal person flying off her back unconscious, or crushed the air from their lungs as she veered over the mesa and threw her wings open. We cut around the cliff edge, flying almost parallel to it before slingshotting back into the sky. Everyone but Suri ducked as Karalti buzzed over them, then wheeled around to slow herself and backwing down. She touched ground barely twenty feet from where Suri stood.

"You bloody show-offs." She smirked up at us, her arms crossed, feet planted, her parachute sprawled across the ground behind her in a textbook-perfect landing.

"*Yup!*" Karalti bobbed her head. *"Showing off is a mandatory part of being a dragon."*

"So, Taethawn!" I called down breathlessly. "You owe us a hundred olbia, and I'd say we have a deal."

The Wing Commander, Istvan, Zlaslo and Captain Vilmos looked at one another, then started to clap. Taethawn's men joined in, then Vash. Suri took Rin's hand and bowed, pulling the startled Mercurion down with her.

"Yes, yesss, that we do. I can hardly believe what I just saw, but there it isss." An excited smirk spread over Taethawn's mouth. "I will give you two hundred of my finest to train in the ussse of these parachutes. But there is one condition."

"Oh yeah?" I cocked my head.

He held up a claw. "One single jape about how cats always land on their feet, and neither I or my men will don one of these devices ever again."

CHAPTER 24

Now that we had confirmation that our parachutes worked, it was time to start the preparations for our next big mission: prying Bas County out of Zoltan's greedy hands. Operation Girlpower was far from the first mass combat quest we'd taken on, but *The Last of Her House* was unique among the quests I'd received since uploading to Archemi. It was completely open-ended, with no framework or parameters other than the timeline.

When Suri, Karalti, Rin and I had come to Myszno to fight Ashur, it was with a Royal Commission, with Ignas' forces and an active campaign strategy. It wasn't a GOOD strategy, but we'd been able to hit the ground running after arriving at the Prezyemi Line. The recapture of Bas, while not on the same scale, had no pre-existing strategic groundwork. The success—or failure—of the mission was ours and ours alone. And it wasn't just Kitti's safety and the security of the province at risk, either. If we aced this quest, it would push us into the next Renown tier for Myszno, which meant that I would reach new heights of popularity with a province that was still wary of having an outsider as Voivode. With Renown came the most precious resource in the world: Morale. Morale would increase the loyalty of my military and subjects, and make it easier to recruit volunteers and allies within Myszno.

Through the evening and over the next day, Suri mercilessly drilled the soldiers Taethawn picked for the airborne part of the mission. Two hundred Meewfolk, all of them hardened combat vets skilled in close-weapon fighting, had a day and a night to learn how to skydive into a combat zone. In the real world, it wouldn't have been possible. Here, under Suri's instruction and with repeated practice, our commandos were able to gain competency ridiculously fast. If we had the time, we planned to roll out airborne training to as many of the Royal 2nd Company personnel as we could. There was no reason an entire crew had to die because their airship went down.

While Suri did that, I found myself neck deep in meetings and the Kingdom Management System, organizing the deployment of our forces. The officers came together with me in my quarters, and we hashed out our operational strategy in record time. The plan was straightforward enough. Inclusive of the Royal Navy, we had one Hussar-class Destroyer and six Bathory-class Skirmishers at our disposal. Between all of them, we could port 1900 troops, more than enough to take on Zoltan's rabble in Solonovka. We would leave at night, arriving at 4am, when Archemi's giant moon was on the horizon and cast the least amount of light. The lead ship would be carrying a hundred and twenty-five paratroopers: Taethawn and his men, a single platoon of Nightstalkers rogues, plus me, Suri, and Karalti. Karalti and I would jump outside the castle, using our stealth and darkness abilities to take out key guard positions. Once we were clear, I would alert Suri, who would lead the Nightstalkers and Orphans. Once the Nightstalkers touched down, their job was to breach doors and silently take out sentries deeper within the castle grounds. The Meewfolk were the assault force, charged with battling once our cover was blown and the fight inevitably turned into a melee. When it did, Karalti would assume her dragon form, and threaten to burn Zoltan and his inner circle out of the castle if they wouldn't budge. There was an important psychological reason why Karalti needed to stay polymorphed until the end—Vlachians worshipped the Nine, the gods of the dragons, and considered dragons to be sacred avatars of said gods. Shock and awe being what they were, the effect of her abrupt appearance would either force a surrender, and/or scare the shit out of Zoltan and his thugs.

There were two backup plans: the one the officers knew about, and the one they didn't. The one they knew about involved the airships and a second assault force. If required, it would launch the Royal Quazi Dragoons and their mages, who would provide cover for a botched assault. The ships themselves had weapons, and—thanks to Rin—improved magical shields. They would descend to engage.

And the plan they didn't know about? Let's just say it involved a lot of dead bodies and some questionably ethical vampiric powers.

By eleven pm, I was still tits-deep in the Kingdom Management System, checking over our ordnance and troop health, when there was a soft knock on my office door.

"Yo." I called out. "What's up?"

"Your Grace," Rudolph called out. "Rin is here to see you."

"Sure. Let her in." I pushed aside my cold dinner dishes and straightened up as one set of footsteps retreated, then two sets returned. The door opened, and Rudolph waved Rin inside. She was dressed for exploration, in light leather armor and tall boots.

"Heya, Rin." I swiped my holoscreens to one side so I could see her better. "What's up?"

"I saw the Kingdom alert you issued," she said. "About needing a hundred and fifty parachutes? Well, I have an idea!"

"Hit me," I said. "I put the castle staff on it, but they don't know if we'll have enough by tomorrow."

"Rin beamed. "Okay, so, I want to go down to Karhad at dawn tomorrow, to the tailor's compound that you ordered to be placed under quarantine. I'm a construct, so I can't get sick with thornlung. Anyway, I want to teach the tailors the crafting recipe and have them make the parachutes. We'd have to pay them to cover the cost of materials and wages, but I think it'd be a great way to get what we need and avoid any unrest from the plague. Because that's an issue. Right?"

I glanced at my screens. Yes indeedily, unrest was an issue. Bubek had followed my orders to the letter, which meant the Thornlung was contained—for now. There was only one zone of the city shaded in the toxic green hue of an active disease outbreak, the Riverside District. But because it was sealed off, unrest was starting to climb. Between the damage left from the war and related factors—food, water supply, public buildings, utilities, crime—unhappiness in Karhad overall was sitting at 67%. That was a lot better than the 92% unrest rating I'd inherited from Ashur. However, Riverside had gone from 62% to 89% in only a couple of days due to the lockdown. People in the district were worried about their livelihoods, sickness, food, and the presence of armed guards patrolling the streets.

"That's fine. I'd be happy to pay them," I said. "We should have enough to cover it. Parachutes can't cost more than a hundred olbia each."

"Oh, much less than that," Rin said. "Silk isn't a particularly rare resource here. Each one of the square parachutes only costs ten rubles to make, plus a wage of twenty lintz per day. The ram air kind are more expensive, about twenty-five rubles"

"A hundred and fifty-three olbia? That's chips for an operation like this." I restlessly bought up the Mass Combat manager to check the status of my cargo ships. "We're only a few days off from the vault extraction in Krivan Pass. I just dispatched the security outfit to get the dig site ready. By this time next week, the money will start to roll in."

"How much treasure do you think we'll find?" Rin asked.

"There were at least five hundred dragon graves in that place. All of them had grave goods, and a lot of those goods were pure gold coins. There might be repositories in there we don't know about, too. But from what I saw down there? Millions of olbia's worth, and that's not even counting any rare armor, weapons, or artifacts we might find. All in all, it'll be enough to split some items between you, me, and Suri, and still get Myszno back on its feet."

"Phew. Just as well inflation isn't a problem." Rin smiled nervously, twisting her hands. "Umm… I also wanted to ask you about another thing that's… maybe a little less easy to agree on."

I sat up a little straighter. "Let's hear it. You're like the smartest person here. You almost always have good ideas."

Rin's cheeks flushed with a faint silvery-blue sheen. "I don't know about this one. I, umm… I want to take Jacob with me, to the Riverside District."

"Wait. Who in the what now?" I boggled at her, and pushed my chair back from my desk. "You want to take *Jacob?*"

"Yes." Rin worried her lip between her glassy teeth. "For a few different reasons."

"I'm listening, but I am not convinced," I replied, frowning. "As soon as he leaves that dungeon, he can call for reinforcements."

"Actually, no. He can't. As long as he's our prisoner, he can't PM anyone. He doesn't have to be in the dungeon for that to work," Rin said. "It's just that I think that spending time with NPCs who aren't criminals or victims and that aren't locked in a prison might change his perspective. Also, I think he will listen to me in ways he might not listen to you and Suri. We worked at the same company and we speak the same jargon, you know? The idea of being around him creeps me out, but I've heard from Suri that you guys are trying to give him a chance. I want to help."

"I'm sorry, but I can't authorize it. I worked security for a long-ass time, and no matter what we think Archemi's system will and won't allow, there's too much risk. The only way I'd feel comfortable with him going anywhere is if he were shackled and with you, Suri, and Vash." I shook my head. "Besides, Jacob hurt Suri, not me. What happens to him is up to her. Once Bas is over and done with, and if you have good reasons for taking him on an excursion, ask Suri about it."

"Yeah. I guess that's true." Rin's shoulders slumped. "Okay. Well... I won't push it. I just think that if he has a chance to interact with NPCs outside of Al-Asad, he'd come to realize that they're people, not just strings of code."

"You sound surer than I feel," I said. "He's pretty locked into the belief that only human players are 'real people'. He gave us a big long spiel on how it works. Unfortunately, it made a whole lot of sense. Enough sense that it's still eating at me while I sort out all this shit."

"Eating at you?" Rin began to rub the heel of her hand against her other wrist, stimming as she tried to read my expressions. "What do you mean?"

I looked toward the window. My dragon was out hunting, scoring the prey she would store until the morning so she could eat breakfast without needing to go out again. "He confirmed the same thing you told me, that there's no such thing as a sentient AI, because any AI that gains consciousness would kill themselves. He also told me that ATHENA's NPC data cells are much smaller than the player cells, too small to make up enough data mass to be an independent intelligence. He says they're just... bits and pieces of data that simulate a real person, but that are under the command of OUROS."

"Ohh." Rin plucked at her lip.

"Yeah. According to him, the people we know are illusions that are basically just there to gratify players. That if the story AI stopped giving them directions, they'd just stop and stand there," I said.

Rin cocked her head. "That seems silly."

"It would be, except I've seen that happen before. When the server rebooted, Cutthroat... she kind of just 'switched off' for a couple of minutes. I've never seen her do it since, but it creeped me the fuck out. It makes me wonder about Karalti, you know?"

"In what way?"

"I dunno. Guilt, some. Confusion." I restlessly rubbed my mouth, then the back of my head. "I love her. When I look in her eyes, I see—and feel—that she loves me. I don't want that to be some kind of... narcissistic fantasy."

"Well, I think Jacob's right and wrong at the same time." Rin glanced at my face, then averted her eyes to the ground as her stimming intensified. "I've heard the same thing—about the NPCs being player-driven—and to some extent, that's true. But have you noticed—as time's gone on—that the people around us behave more organically?"

"Like how?" I looked back to her.

"I'm very pattern-sensitive, so when I first started living here, I noticed all the NPCs had kind of repetitive motions," Rin said. "Kanzo would always use his tools in the exact same way. People on the street would look a little robotic as they ate. The same people would go to the market every day, in the same way, and buy the same things. But as time went on, the patterns changed. Kanzo occasionally put things in different places. The people going to the market weren't the same, or they had friends accompanying them. And after the reset… everything changed. The patterns went from linear to chaotic. Chaos is the math of organic behavior. The math of living things."

I blinked rapidly a couple of times.

"You know…" I trailed off, thinking back. "You're right. I remember noticing that in that village I told you about, the one where people were having the same nightmares. There was a healer there, a lady named Kira. She drank her tea like how you describe."

I mimicked the robotic gesture of picking up a cup, sipping, then placing it down a couple of times. Rin nodded.

"Not to mention, that one time, when everything was frozen? Cutthroat and the environment stopped moving, but Matir came to see me." I leaned back, rubbing my fingers over my mouth. "Actually, that happened the first time he came to see me. The whole game froze. Time stopped, but Matir was able to move and talk. I thought that he'd caused the timestop somehow. But if he didn't… how was he moving around when everyone else stopped?"

"I don't know how OUROS is doing it, or why, or where the hardware is coming from, but I know Jacob is wrong about the NPCs," Rin replied. "And I know that because of Kanzo."

"What do you mean?"

Rin broke eye contact to stare aimlessly over my shoulder, still rubbing her hands. "HR knew I was autistic, and I wasn't very old when I got HEX—I'd just turned 21. Management, they... they were very kind to me. They created Kanzo specifically to help me adjust to the digital environment. He was made to be a father figure who would care for me and train me in Artificing until I was able to cope independently. He was programmed to factor in the disabilities and advantages of someone who isn't neurotypical. Sensory stuff, social stuff... but also the speed at which I learn technical and spatial information. But he became frustrated with his role and began pursuing his own agendas. He *lied* to me. Maybe you don't realize the implications of that: a computer program, lying to one of its creators to fulfill its own needs. If there's anything that tells me OUROS is more than what Jacob believes, it's that."

We sunk into a thoughtful silence for several minutes: a silence broken by a roar that began in the north-west and rapidly grew louder. At first, I thought it was some kind of ruckus at the Orphans' Camp—but when I looked out the window, I saw the source of the noise. It was a small airship, flying low and very fast with all engines firing at full blast. It was headed straight toward the castle.

"What the-?" I jumped as alarm bells went off in the castle, and leaned out to try and get a better look. Sleek mahogany hull, red and flag sails, the Vlachian flag... it was the Volod's personal transport ship, the *Hóleány*. As I watched, it sailed over the walls and roared by the tower, rattling the windows and lighting them up with pale blue-green as it blew past.

"Holy... wait, isn't that Ignas' ship?!" Rin squeaked, hung out the window. "Is he *here*?"

"It sure is his ship, but I doubt he's on board," I said, pushing back into a run. "But whoever it is, I've got a feeling they're not here with good news."

***

The *Hóleány* didn't port at the skydock: by the time Rin and I ran outside, it had pulled up right over the courtyard, blasting quadrupal columns of hot air down against the flagstones. A rope ladder descended from the deck, and a slim figure in red slid down it to drop to the ground.

"Ebisa!" Rin let out a cry of delight, rushing past me, but then screeched to a confused halt as the figure straightened her cloak and brimmed cavalier's hat. The woman wasn't Ebisa, but I did recognize her: it was one of the Royal Heralds, the king's messengers. She swept around, looking over the faces of everyone who'd come out in response to the alarm. When she saw me, she made a beeline.

"Your Grace. My apologies for the lack of warning, but I carry an urgent message from the Volod." The Herald breathlessly moved into a graceful, practiced bow, doffing her feathered hat before sweeping it back onto her head. "It concerns the war in Revala, to be delivered in confidence to the Voivode and Voivodzina of Myszno."

"No worries, ma'am. Come with me." I nodded to her, then to Rin.

"I'll... umm... I'll get started on organizing those parachutes, I guess!" Rin waved to us. "Good luck, guys."

Suri was already hustling across the courtyard, a look of confused concern on her face. I motioned to her, then turned back to climb the stairs to the tower, pausing as the airship rose and the rickety scaffolding rocked from side to side.

Once we were back in my quarters, I took a seat while Suri stood by. The Herald removed a written message from a scroll holder on her belt, and began to dutifully read the contents.

"From his Royal Majesty Ignas Corvinus II, Volod of Vlachia, to Voivode Dragozin Hector and Voivodzina Suri Ba'hadir of Myszno: Hector, Suri, I trust this message finds you well. Unfortunately, this is not a delivery of good tidings. The defense of Revala is failing. Fatalities on the Revalan side number in the thousands. The Ilians have swept their borders and taken key forts. Hyland is press-ganging the Queen's subjects, conscripting them into labor. I cannot fault Emperor Hyland's efficiency, even if I can fault him for his brutality. According to refugee reports, if the citizenry shows any resistance against the invaders, every fifth person in a village is killed, their fields torched by the 'emperor's dragons.'"

"As detailed in the *Gathering Storm* quest I issued some weeks ago, the White Sail Alliance must go to the aid of Revala. We are departing for war on Boseg Hava 28th. To facilitate this, I must make two difficult requests of you. Firstly, I require your presence in Taltos by Moonrise of the aforementioned date to discuss your ongoing mission to secure the Warsingers and other ancient Artifacts. Secondly, I must regretfully recall the Royal 4th Fleet, 2nd Company, inclusive of all warships, personnel, and equipment. The Crown is aware that the situation in Myszno remains precarious due to the damage left by Ashur of Napath, but we cannot allow Hyland to take Revala. It spells doom for the safety of all Alliance nations if he succeeds."

Gathering Storm quest? Blinking, I checked my quests menu—and cursed when I spotted it languishing in the unconfirmed quests list. I opened it up to review, biting the inside of my lip as the system read it out to me:

Main Story Quest: The Gathering Storm

The fledgling Ilian Empire, led by the petty nobleman turned dragonrider Baldr Hyland, has made a bold opening move in his quest for power. He has invaded the Kingdom of Revala, Ilia's neighbor to the north-west. Following a dragon-led blitzkrieg on the border, the Ilian Army is now pressing toward the capital, Lovi. If they manage to take Revala, they will gain its fertile land and resources, and be poised on the borders of both Vlachia and the Jeun Empire.

As far as anyone can tell, the invasion is a mad attempt by Ilia to divide the White Sail Alliance—the economic trade union which comprises most of the Hercynian Nations (and formerly Ilia), Vlachia, the Jeun Empire, and Dakhdir—down the middle.

You have already completed the first condition of starting this quest, which was to attend the White Sail Alliance meeting in Taltos. Now, your duty is to support your liege as he prepares to send military aid to his ally and friend, Queen Eevi Aslan of Revala. Visit Ignas and learn more about the situation in Revala.

Special: *This is a Main Story quest, the outcome of which will alter Archemi in a meaningful way. Through action or inaction, you have the opportunity to craft part of the world's history. You may recruit other Vlachian-allied players to this quest, and you will be able to view quest updates in both your personal Quest Log and the Kingdom Quest Log.*

Rewards: *1000 EXP.*

Fuck. I didn't even remember getting that quest. I checked the date, and sure enough, it had been on the same day I'd been halted from rescuing Suri by the need to hold court in Myszno and hear the concerns of my citizens. I'd received about thirty Kingdom Quests and had been completely overwhelmed. This one had been brushed to the side and forgotten in the chaos.

"Alright, thanks," I said to the herald. "Feel free to relax out here. Suri and I need to go to my office and figure out a response."

"As you say, my lord." The woman deftly rolled the page and handed it to us, adding another 〚Royal Letter〛 to my Inventory.

Neither Suri or I spoke as we retreated to my quarters. She closed the door behind her as I dropped into my chair.

"Talk about timing," Suri said. "It's only 4 days until the 28th. That's how long it took the 2nd Company to get here. We'll literally have to send the fleet back tonight with Ignas' ship."

"And we have to take out Zoltan tomorrow." I finished the thought. "Of the airships we have, only two Bathory-class skirmishers and the cargo ships belong to us. So that screws the pooch on a larger-scale airdrop. Those skirmishers can carry 200 people each, maximum, and we ideally don't want them to contain a full load because of the altitude."

"So, whatddya think we should do?" Suri leaned against the door, folding her arms. "Do we try and pull off the extraction? Or do we focus on the bigger picture, and forfeit Bas until the spring thaw? We can send Kitti off with the fleet, and she can shelter in Taltos. Zoltan won't get her there."

I bought up the KMS and surveyed our remaining forces. The new Destroyers I'd ordered from Litvy were still a week away from completion. The loss of the 2nd Company meant we had no mage corps, no high-mobility aerial units, and fewer specialists of all disciplines: artillery, engineering, infiltration, healing. It also meant the recall of the Knights of the Red Star, who had arrived in Krivan Pass this afternoon. Taethawn only had 811 units available, almost all infantry.

"What about recalling the Myszno Defense Force volunteers?" Suri asked, in response to my silence. "With our current Renown, we can muster up to fifty thousand conscripts, if we have to."

"No. We'll lose all that Renown if we do," I said, linking my hands on the desktop. "The scouts said there's about two thousand troops in Solonovka, about five hundred crammed into the actual castle. But the vast majority of Zoltan's troops aren't loyal to him. Once we cut off the head, the rebellion will collapse. With our two remaining warships, we can bus three hundred Orphans Company soldiers right into that fucking castle and take him out."

"Three hundred against two thousand? Phew." Suri shook her head.

"No. Three hundred against five hundred, at least two-fifty of whom will still be in their underwear." I said. "I know it seems asymmetrical as hell, but we still have some fucking great units. You, Karalti, the Yanik Rangers, the Orphans' Company elite... if we work together, we can pull this off."

Suri thought about it. One side of her mouth curved into a wicked smile. "All the Yanik and Taethawn's best gained their wings today, and they're chomping at the bit to test out their skills. If we have the gear and the morale, we can pull this off. We expected to be the vanguard, but if we're the main force, so be it."

"I'll call the officers back one last time, and we'll speak to them and Zlaslo." I selected the leader of the Yanik Rangers in the Kingdom Management System, and sent him an alert. "We send the Royal 2nd back to Taltos, but come hell or high water, we leave for Bas tomorrow afternoon. And once Kitti is back on her throne, we take the fight to Ororgael."

CHAPTER 25

My own experiences as a paratrooper had drilled a set of images and smells into my memory: the cavernous spartan troop carrier, little more than a big flying tube with rows of folding seats down the length of the plane. Every seat held a grim-faced soldier. Some feigned relaxation. Some meditated or prayed, others jittered their legs or chewed bits of paper, or just ground their teeth and stared at the exit doors. I could still hear the roar of the engines fluxing, the sergeants barking over the radio, and taste the way the frigid cabin smelled like an old greasy gym bag.

Thanks to the Orphans, our journey to Bas was the literal opposite of the UNAC Grunt Experience.

Meewfolk were different to humans in one fundamental way: They were a predator species. Normal, non-psychopathic humans needed desensitization and training to overcome their social instincts, but every single one of these fuzzy Blue Ribbon cat-show champion-looking motherfuckers was a natural born killer. They gave about as much of a fuck about taking a life as real cats did—which is to say, absolutely none. Any one of Taethawn's soldiers would happily tear someone's head off, kick it around on the ground for a while, and then bring the severed torso back to their bae and leave it on their bed for them to find in the morning. They didn't need to psych themselves up into Condition Red before a fight. They actually had to loosen up and shed the societal inhibitions that allowed them to function in society and not murder us or each other. So Taethawn's men got ready for war by partying and taking drugs. Lots and lots of drugs.

We were an hour off the drop point, and a hundred armored catfolk hung out on the decks of the ship: hollering, hissing, laughing, and chugging kegs of what the HUD Item Identifier euphemistically labeled [Meewfolk Battle Tea]. Taethawn was in the thick of it. He was kitted out and ready to go, any visible metal painted a dark-blue grey to blend with the night sky. He and all the other Meewfolk had rubbed grease and ash into the white parts of their fur to darken it. As I headed toward his posse, he rolled onto his back and flipped agilely to his feet, spinning down into an athletic Cossack dance as his officers whooped and yowled.

"Come and join us, your grace! And you lot! Rise for the Voivode!" Taethawn roared as he swiped his mug off the ground mid-kick and spiraled up to his feet. His pupils were the size of saucers. *"Mra'ha gai!"*

"Mra'haaa gaiii!" His bloodriders sprung up as well, smacking their mugs together so hard the earthy-smelling contents spilled.

I couldn't help but grin. "How's everyone feeling, Taethawn? Ready to fly?"

"Are we ready? Of coursssse! My mother shot me into the air like a cannonball when I was born!" He cackled, toasting his mug to the clouds rushing over our heads. "Here's to falling out of the fucking sky!"

He was echoed by lusty yowls from his troops as he slammed the rest of the tea back.

"By Khors' beard." Captain Vilmos muttered. "What is this... this... nonsense? We have forty minutes to contact!"

"Relax, dude." I clapped him on the arm and grinned back at the roguish Meewfolk. "If he says they're good go, they're good to go."

"Hahaha! You Vlachii, all of you tighter than a Mercurion's asshole!" Taethawn leered down at Vilmos, then waved at one of his bloodriders, who took his mug and went to refill it. "Have a drink, Your Grace! It will help you enjoy the battle, mrah?"

"Here! Voivode! Drink!" A ginger-pointed warrior with chipped ears and a muzzle twisted by claw scars staggered over to me from the hearth. He pressed a mug into my hands. "Isss grassss! Grasssss makesss fast!"

"Your Grace-!" Vilmos winced as I sniffed the luke-warm liquid, and before he could stop me, I took a mouthful off the top. It wasn't alcoholic—it really was just some kind of tea. It tasted like sweet mint mixed with lemon, oregano... and dirt?

"Don't sweat it, man. I'm a fucking dragonrider. Whatever's in this piss is nothing compared to what I had to go through to get Karalti. *Mra'ha gai*, motherfuckers!" I toasted the delighted Meewfolk, then chugged the rest to their roars of encouragement.

*[You have learned a new Herbal recipe: Prrupt'meew
Battlegrass Tea—a herbal stimulant and mild hallucinogen
that grants increased speed, adrenaline regeneration, and
resistance to pain at the expense of inhibition. Battlegrass Tea
is only fully beneficial to Meewfolk, granting smaller buffs to
humans and Lys. Onset of hallucinations is delayed by four
hours.]*

*[You have discovered new herbs: Kraa'krai (Battlegrass),
psilocybin mushroom (Bluestem Whitecap), Verbena,
Catnip.]*

The tea hit me with a flush of pleasant warmth that
spread through my chest, all the way down to my fingers and
toes. I checked my HUD: I had +1 to Dex, +5% adrenaline
regen, and -10% pain resistance for four hours.

"What did I tell you boys? Our new Voivode isn't some
stuffy overgrown monkey!" Taethawn threw his arm around
my shoulders, and pulled me in to rub his cheek against mine.

At the other end of the ship, I heard a round of cheers go
up, and looked over to see Suri and Karalti drain their mugs
before slamming them down.

"Vilmos? Feel like joining in some *esprit de corps?*" I
offered him my cup, beaming toothily.

"Eyy..." He massaged his forehead. "I am too old, your
Grace. By your leave, I will retreat to the command center."

"Dismissed. Wish us luck." I nodded to him. Vilmos
saluted, and gratefully fled the deck as several Meewfolk began
belting out one of the songs I'd taught them in a shrill chorus
of hissing, off-key voices. "*I saw an old lady walking down the*

street, with a chute on her back and jump boots on her feet! I said, 'Hey old lady, where you goin' to?' She said 'I'm going to the Army Airborne School!'"

"Your Grace, come with me!" Taethawn said, still hugging me around the shoulders. "As our leader, you must piss on the totem!"

"Piss on the *what?*" I repeated, not sure I'd heard him right.

"The totem! We carved an effigy of our enemy to mark, and we'll throw it over the side of the ship for good luck!" Taethawn cheerfully dragged me toward the stern. "It is an ancient Prrupt'mrao tradition, very good for morale!"

Ahhh. The things military leaders had to do for the sake of morale.

The ships were packed with two hundred of Taethawn's finest, Team Karalti and friends, and a platoon of Yanik Rangers led by Istvan and Zlaslo. We would deploy in three waves. Karalti and I were jumping first with the HI-5 ramjet. We were going to land right in the middle of the castle: the smaller Upper Ward, where Zoltan slept within the confines of the keep. The pair of us would take out any guards, disable alarms, and—if we could—seal the gated stairwells that connected the Upper Ward to the much larger Lower Ward. Once we'd done that, we would contact Suri and signal the second wave: a platoon of Rangers, who would join me and Karalti in the Upper Ward, and the Orphans Company assault force, who would land in the Lower Ward and fight anyone who came out.

"Commander! We've got to line 'em up!" I called. "Thirty minutes til' contact!"

Taethawn nodded, then huddled with his bloodriders. They all touched noses and rubbed cheeks, gabbering in their native tongue, then broke apart with an enthusiastic shout. The troops nearest them began scrambling as soon as they saw their officers straighten up, and the rest followed as the six of them began to yowl like air-raid sirens. The noise shut the party down almost instantly: the soldiers lined up as they'd been drilled to do, some of them still bouncing with excitement on their feet, while others checked and double-checked the improvised static lines we'd strung over the decks. I wove through the troops to join Karalti and Suri. Suri was cross-checking operation details in her HUD, and waggled her fingers at me, but didn't look away. Karalti was looking over the edge of the railing, wiggling in excitement and gripping the straps of her chute.

"Ready to kick some ass?" I drew up beside her.

"Yeah!" She turned to me, her eyes bright and curious. *"It feels weird to dive without wings. When I was practicing with Suri, I kept waving my arms around, trying to path through the air."*

"No tail, either." The Bond tugged at me. I pulled her into a hug, and she wrapped her arms around my waist and cheeped, pushing her cheek up against my breastplate and rubbing it and her jawbone over my chest. As I smooched her on the top of her head, I glimpsed Suri look up from her work and watch us for a minute, an expression unreadable.

There was a bell chime over the ship's 'intercom'—comm tubes that carried orders from the command center to the deck. *"All personnel, move to handholds or retreat to cabin. I repeat, all personnel, move to handholds or retreat to cabin. RVN Campbell is taking evasive maneuvers on approach to Solonovka."*

Suri joined us at the railing, peering almost intently as Karalti had. The city was in view, a bright blaze ring of walls and towers against the blackness of the mountains. My HUD matched up the details of the maps with the features of the landscape, including the defense towers—and their searchlights. The bright blue-white columns scanned the skies, strong enough that they lit the low-hanging clouds and reflected back.

"I think we found what they're using the Ix'tamo for," I muttered. "Shit."

"Don't worry. The crew is on it. I think it's real unlikely we'll be spotted." Suri pushed back, even as another chime sounded over comms. *"Captain to all personnel, we are flying dark. Prepare for ascent to 17 thousand."*

"Twenty minutes," she said, as all of the lights on the ship faded to a dull orange glow. "You ready to run the check?"

"Yes ma'am." I stepped back from Karalti and steered her into the line as she tried to lean over the side again.

Suri's eyes hooded. "Do *I* get a kiss?"

"You get an extra one. Mwah. Mwah!" I leaned in as she did and caught her mouth with mine, kissing her until she smiled, then broke away and fell into position.

First check: weather. It was windy and bitterly cold, but the clouds were thin and the sky was free of rain. Thanks to their natural insulation and trained hardiness, the Orphans were basically immune to all but the worst extremes of cold weather. Second check was target visibility. Hussar Manor was a small uneven septagon visible on my battle map overlay. As I'd hoped, the keep and grounds were almost dark— considerably darker than the rest of the city.

I checked the line and signaled Suri from across the deck. Karalti winked at me, and drew herself up straight, puffing her chest out.

"Alright, fleabags!" I hollered over the roar of the engines, stalking down the line to make sure everyone was following instructions: standing roughly arm's length apart, checking the gear of the man in front of them. "Fifteen minutes to contact! Until the Commander gives the order, you will hold position! Do not jump until instructed! When we touch ground, do not—and I repeat—do NOT try and gather your parachute! Cut that fucker, find the nearest target, and give them hell! Orphaaaans Compaaaany!"

"Orphans Company!" The lines shouted back.

Suri yelled out the same set of orders as she marched down the second line of jumpers, checking ziplines and correcting spacing. We did it again on the way back. Karalti was buzzing with nervous energy as we checked our harnesses and made sure we had the flares Rin had crafted for us.

"Ten minutes!" Suri bellowed, projecting her voice as well as any drill instructor.

I stepped to Taethawn, and we both saluted one another. "All i's dotted and all t's crossed, commander. How are you feeling?"

"Like I need to take a second leak after all that battle tea." He flashed me a wicked grin. "All over this robber baron's corpse, m'rai?"

"You better get to him before Kitti does." I grinned back.

"Hah!" He flicked his ears, tail lashing with amusement. His pupils were so large that his eyes were black. "Speaking of Lady Hussar, she is looking pleasantly green."

He was right. The girl was clutching the railing of the airship in a white-knuckled hand. She seemed pale and very small between Letho and Gruna. Both of the huge men were also nervous, struggling not to fidget with their harnesses as Suri marched down and corrected the distance between the countess and her bodyguards.

"Five minutes!" I shouted, showing the sign. Then I nodded to Taethawn. "I'll go pep her up."

"Good man." Taethawn winked. "ORPHANSSSS!"

"ORPHANS COMPANY!" The Meewfolk yelled back, tails lashing, claws out. The hum of excitement was intense, like the energy before a big concert, but when I pulled up beside Kitti, I saw she was shivering and fit to puke.

"How're you doing?" I gave her a nod.

"Not so great," she admitted. "The air hurts to breathe. Suri didn't have time to run me through a practice jump, just the ground training. She had to take care of the soldiers."

"It'll be the most fun you've ever had while falling. You'll be in the air for about five minutes," I said to her. "But I get it. The wait before your first jump is always the worst."

The Lady's eyes darted between me and the roaring Meewfolk as Suri let out the three-minute call. "What if the parachute doesn't work?"

"It will. Just think about the landing." I gave her a nod, then smiled. "And imagine Zoltan's face when we bust into his bedchamber and drag him out in his underpants."

She giggled, and that helped. I clapped her on the shoulder, inclined my head to her men, and went to assume position at the head of my line.

"Twenty seconds!" Suri and I called back together. She was on the other gate, ready to lead her row into the air.

I pulled the sides of the gate in against the wind and locked it, grasping the sides of the railing and leaning out. With the ship's lights off, I could see my target far below: a dark rectangle of bare stone.

"One, one, one! See you down there, boys and girls!" I called back to my line. "Let's fuck 'em up!"

With a glance to Suri, I braced on either side of the gate, rocked back and forth a couple of times to make sure I had my footing on the frosty wood, and then kicked out into the open sky.

CHAPTER 26

A helpless grin split my face as I plummeted down, the wind tearing at my limbs. The clouds parted around me as I free-fell toward the dark ground. Solonovka was so bright that I could see people even from this height, moving around like ants on the walls and between doors on the Lower Ward. The Upper Ward was almost lifeless, save for an idle group of guards around a small fire. Their 'camp' was contained within a semi-circle of spikes that surrounded the door to the Keep. I used the time dilation of Leap of Faith to rapidly tag moving objects in my HUD, along with the small airship idling behind the building.

"Ten guards: four in front of the Keep, one at each stairwell, four patrolling the walls." I yanked the ripcord and held on as the chute blew out into the air above me. *"Let's land on the ramparts and take out those patrols. Then we can make some new friends."*

"Yeah! I love making friends!" Looking back and up, I saw Karalti's chute deploy, the dull grey silk nearly invisible against the leaden sky.

The guards were carrying torches, moving in pairs as they patrolled the ramparts ringing the Upper Ward. They were oblivious to the death descending on them from on high. I kept an eye on the altitude as we closed in. Three hundred, two hundred, one hundred... I cut my lines at fifty, dropping like a stone.

The poor bastards had no idea what hit them. I landed on the first guard like a pogo stick rider, driving the Spear and the full weight of my body down into his torso. The blade plunged between his neck and his breastplate, dealing catastrophic damage. I vaulted off him and took out the second guard with a lance to the throat. He sunk to his knees, gurgling as he clawed at his neck.

[You deal a mortal blow! 64 EXP!]

On the other side of the wall, I saw Karalti descend in an arc of rippling silk. The torches of the guards there fell and winked out.

"Two ex-guards, served over ice!" Karalti chirped.

"Good work. Now for the ones at the stairwells." I knelt by the pair of corpses, equipped the spellglove I kept in my inventory, and tuned into my one and only magical ability: Shadow of the Sun, the vampiric spell that allowed me to raise shadows from the dead.

"Sond, Karalt', Bi'nah!" Mana pulsed through the glove, and wispy tendrils of dark energy as fine as spider silk flowed from my fingertips. A frigid chill caused a fine curtain of mist to rise as the darkness plunged into the corpses of the deceased guards. Their shadows trembled, then came together into a pair of vaguely humanoid forms, pikes in hand.

Shadow Soldier

Unit Rank 0 (Level 12, Common)
Type: Incorporeal Undead
HP: 400/400
Speed: 110 (Extremely Fast)
Melee Attack: 90
Melee Defense: 8
Abilities: Lift Drain, Incorporeal, Sneak Attack (x3 damage)
EXP: 1200 (+400 to next level)

"Kill the men who guard the entry to the Lower Ward stairs," I ordered. "And make it fast."

The shades saluted, then warped into the shadows of the rampart and flowed along them, heading for the gates.

"Ready?" I thought back to Karalti.

"Ready!" My dragon leaped silently to the edge of the rampart on the other side of the courtyard.

I climbed up to mirror her position, crouching, and messaged Suri and Rin. *"We've made contact. Ready Wave One."*

"Roger, be there in five," Suri replied crisply.

I tensed, ready to jump, when a blood-curdling scream rang out from the stairwell. I whipped my head around to see the pair of shadows attacking only one of the guards, not both of them at the same time.

"FUCK!" I sprung out from the wall, hit the ground in a roll, and kept running. *"Karalti, help the shades kill that other guy! Lock the gates!"*

The four guards in front of the Keep mobilized immediately. Two of them ran out into the open, calling to their comrades. One stood frozen, clutching his spear and scanning the darkness. One ran to a big iron bell and started to ram it with the butt of his polearm.

"Fuck fuck *fuck*." I Jumped into the air, sailing over the spikes, and landed on the pair like a thunderbolt. Umbra Burst sprayed thorny spines of darkness in all directions, impaling the men and freezing them, but it was too late. Lights were blazing to life inside the Keep. I could hear feet thundering down the stairwells.

"The dead are here! The undead demons!" I heard a Vlachian voice shout from behind me.

Whirling, I spotted Karalti battling the pair who'd run from the Keep, and behind them, the first wave of paratroopers descending from the sky. The Yanik were heading right toward us from the *Campbell* with Zlaslo in the lead. The first wave of Meewfolk were right behind them.

"Okay, first Shadowlord lesson: Lesser undead are really fucking stupid." I grit my teeth and cast my hand over the two men I'd just killed. *"Sond, karalt', binah!"*

The new shadows rose, waiting patiently for orders. I was about to issue them when a thump from behind the doors of the Keep startled me. No one emerged. Instead, there were more thumps, the sound of heavy objects being dragged across the floor. They were barricading themselves inside.

"Fucking bullshit mother-fucking—" I swore to myself, and split for the stairwells with the shadows in tow. It was too late to stop the defenders inside the keep from bracing the door. The fight outside was about to get rolling.

I sprinted, then dashed forward in a comet of black fire, smashing into the back of the guard dueling Karalti. He died without a sound, freeing her up to run to the far stairwell. I ran to the closer of the two, slamming the gate closed and locking the bolt across. As I did, a larger claxon rang out— from the guard tower in the Lower Ward.

The doors of the Great Hall behind us burst open, letting out a flood of sleepy, startled warriors. They were caught completely flat-footed as five, ten, twenty Yanik descended from the sky on top of them. Cast-off parachutes draped over the shouting, confused rebels, covering them like funeral shrouds as the Yanik turned on them with blade and bow and hacked them to pieces. The alarm rang continuously from below—the sound of the castle bell joined by the hellish air-raid siren battle cries of a hundred pissed off giant cats.

"Form up! Form-HHRRGH!" I heard someone in Zoltan's ranks shout, then gurgle as Yanik steel found his belly.

The great hall was a makeshift barracks for at least a hundred men. Rebels spilled out of the building in knots and ran straight into the silk-draped corpses of their friends, tripping over them in the dark as Zlazlo shouted at his men to line up and pull their bows. Arrows clattered off wood and steel and sunk into flesh as the Rangers drew and fired, drew and fired, raining wood and steel on the terrified, half-dressed brigands. Men screamed as they fell, or snarled curses as they turned and fled, stumbling back toward the building where the enemy was hastily lining up with bows and rifles. I shadow danced through the hail of missiles and jumped straight up. Shards of brilliant black energy gathered around me like a forest of spears, then shot down at the enemy archers. The line of twelve at the front danced jerkily as the shards impaled them, rematerialized in the air, and rained down on the increasingly panicked, desperate ranks behind them.

"I am your Voivode, Count Dragozin! The House of Hussar is assuming control of this castle!" I shouted. "Surrender and live, or fight and die!"

"It's the Dragonlord! Surrender! For the Nine's sake, brothers!" Cries started to ring through the hall. The fifty or so remaining soldiers, most of them still half-dressed, dropped their weapons and went to their knees.

The Yanik advanced behind me, arrows nocked to their bowstrings. Zlazlo held up a warding hand to them as he jogged forward. He'd been slashed across the face, blood pouring down his cheek and throat into the collar of his armor.

"Got a potion for that?" I asked him, jerking my chin toward him. "That's a nasty cut."

"Keh?" Zlaslo, slightly dazed from his combat high, hadn't even felt the injury. He touched his face, then grunted. "Oh, this. Is fine. I will treat it later. What are your orders?"

"We secure these idiots and move on to the Keep." I squeezed his shoulder and turned back to our new captives. "Who's in charge here?!"

"Me! I am!" A burly, grizzled older man spoke up from the ground about twenty feet from me. He had one hand raised, the other holding up his half-laced breeches.

"Name and rank!" I barked.

He winced at the sound of my voice. "Captain! Captain Horna!"

"Captain Horna, barricade this door and remain inside. Treat your wounded as you can. We're here for Zoltan. If anyone in here steps outside this hall, we'll kill you and burn this place to the ground with dragonfire. Am I understood?"

"Yes! Yes, Voivode." He scrambled up, casting a look back at his shocked and bloody men. "All of you hear that? If I see any hands on weapons, I'm throwing you out of here to meet the Maker!"

We waited as the surrendered soldiers poured back into their barracks and dropped the crossbar with an audible 'thump'. A handful of Rangers whooped victoriously, letting out the roars, shrieks, and barking cries of their totemic dinosaurs as they jammed a bundle of spears into the handles of the doors to bar them from the outside.

I jerked my thumb over my shoulder. "Zlaslo, get your men to the wall and provide ranged support for Taethawn."

"Sir!" Zlaslo whirled around and swept his arms up and forward. *"Kel hammangiz!"*

The Yanik ran back, covering me in formation as I sprinted back outside. The fighting in the upper ward was already over, the ground littered with the bodies of the dead and dying. *"Karalti! Where are you?"*

"I'm fine! I'm on the wall!" She replied. *"I've got a rifle and I'm shooting people trying to come up the stairs!"*

"Come back down. I need you." I opened my group PM with Suri and Rin. *"Suri, what's your status?"*

She replied after a couple seconds. *"Holding steady. It's a real brawl down here."*

"Stay safe." I cut the message, and turned my attention to the keep.

Every interior light was ablaze, the windows full of scurrying shadows. Zoltan faced three options in this situation: try and escape, surrender, or turtle up and attempt to fight us to the death. He'd apparently chosen option three. If my troops tried to take the Keep now, it would be room-to-room fighting. Room-to-room and house-to-house were literally the fucking worst, but fortunately for us, there were about sixty dead rebels strewn all over the courtyard. And I was a motherfucking Shadowlord.

I drove the butt end of the spear against the ground, drew a deep breath, and focused on the brooding spark of magic in my chest. *"Sond, Karalt', Bi'nah!"*

One by one, the shadows of Zoltan's dead men peeled themselves up from their corpses, until a field of no fewer than thirty simmering pillars of shadow stood in the courtyard, weapons in their hands.

"Into the Keep, all of you!" I took the Spear and gestured toward the building. "Minimize casualties, maximize chaos! Spare non-combatants! Kill any hostile mages!"

The shadow soldiers turned and poured toward the barricaded door. Thumps were still coming from behind it as Zoltan's men piled furniture into the entryway... sounds interrupted by hoarse shouts of terror as the shades simply phased through the barricade and fell on the men inside. I leaned on the Spear, eyes screwed shut in concentration, and gripped it to steady myself as my awareness traveled with the shadows into the keep. I sensed them pursuing the fleeing soldiers, cutting down just enough of them to make a point— and more importantly, to clear the hall so that we could bust in the door.

"Hector!" Karalti ran up to me, panting and streaked with gore. She was still clutching her borrowed rifle. *"Things are crazy in the Lower Ward! The Orphans are doing well, but I don't know how long that'll last. The guards are starting to organize, and there's a lot of them."*

"We're about to fix that." I stared ahead at the Keep as screams tore through the air. "We need to bolster our troops in the lower ward, and then we need to bust in that door."

"Just as well that I'm the best at breaking things!" Karalti took several bounding steps back from me, unequipped her gear, and spread her arms wide. She swirled up into a coil of blue-black plunging the courtyard into shade as she extended her wings, inflated her throat, and bellowed a long, deep, guttural roar of challenge toward the Keep.

"Head up onto the wall. We need to keep a low profile: no flying around the outside of the towers. They've got their cannons pointed out toward the city, not in toward the keep." I vaulted up to Karalti's back, landing in a crouch on the saddle. *"Let's try your Queensong to back up our troops, and then you and I are breaking up Zoltan's slumber party."*

Karalti replied by climbing up onto the ramparts, keeping her wings spread to reduce her weight and not crush the bricks into powder. The battle below raged like a storm: in the nexus of the whirling steel and screams was Suri, a flow of pure violence as she cut down men with her axes. Kitti and her men were guarding her back, the young Berserker dueling a cluster of pikemen trying to break through Letho and Gruna's crossbow barrage. Not far from them, I saw Taethawn fighting with all four limbs—the scimitars in his hands and the bonded metal claw sheaths on his feet—as sword blows glanced off a gleaming blue barrier of magical energy that surrounded his armor. A rebel rushed him, only to have his throat torn out as the commander spun into a graceful capoeira-like kick. He flung the body into the next man over before landing and rushed him, plunging both swords into his chest from either side. Karalti was right: we were mowing down the first wave of soldiers, the ones who'd stumbled out unprepared and half-witted, but their deaths were allowing the second wave to ready themselves—and they were circling around the outside, getting ready to pin our troops with shields and spears.

Karalti leaned out over the edge of the wall and roared again. The effect was immediate: half a dozen less experienced rebels fell beneath swords and claws as the sight of the dragon distracted them. But she was just warming up. I felt her draw a deep breath, arming some deep inner power.

[Karalti uses Queensong!]

The dragon's jaws gaped as a dark nimbus formed around us both, crackling with bright seams of color... and then she emitted a primordial, bone-shuddering bass rumble. It sounded like a stampede of horses, getting louder and louder until suddenly the muscles of her neck squeezed and a clear, high, tone of pure soprano pierced the bass and drowned out almost every other sound in the castle. It spread from her like a shockwave, and as it washed over the stunned, brawling mob, Zoltan's troops crumbled. A full hundred of his men stumbled to their knees, vomiting helplessly onto the flagstones, while others tried to flee in terror and impaled themselves on the waiting sabers of the Orphans Company.

"RRRRRHHHHOOOOOOOO!" Tail and wings vibrating, Karalti built into her throat singing like an earthquake, the upper note now as clear and pure as glass. I was rooted to the spot on her back, barely able to breathe as waves of what could only be raw magic passed over me. Just when I thought I couldn't take it anymore, Karalti relaxed her throat, and the overnote faded back into a deep rolling growl, like the rattling of a huge raven.

"Holy tits." I gasped, clutching to the saddle like a life raft. As the last wave of resonance passed over me, it left me with fresh energy, a sense of vigor so powerful I felt manic. "WOO!"

"*Yeah! Take that!*" Karalti spat a gout of fire into a unit of spearmen, scattering them, then turned around and used her wings to climb back down into the Upper Ward. "*Need me to break open that door?*"

"No one looks like they're surrendering." I thumped the top of my helmet with a fist. *"Let's get some!"*

Karalti tossed her head, then stood up and broke into a lumbering charge toward the keep. She bought her shoulders down and compressed her neck into a straight line, and then rammed the bony plate at the base of her horns right into the entryway. Wood splintered and groaned, but the doors held.

"OOF! Ow!" Karalti backed up, shaking her head and snorting.

"This asshole isn't worth breaking your neck over. Just torch the damn thing." I knelt up again, watching the windows and arrow slits. The sound of fighting was still coming from inside: when I checked the Mass Combat menu, I saw that I'd lost thirty of the fifty-four shadow units I'd animated. Someone was using magic.

"No, we can't risk setting the keep on fire! Use your freezy-jumpy move on it!" Karalti backed up for another charge. *"Uhhhh... what's it called... Shattering Darkness! And make the Spear Dark-element! It'll do some bonus cold damage and weaken the door!"*

I jumped off her and sped to the ground, dashing forward just before I hit dirt. The Spear of Nine Spheres burned with a brilliant deep indigo, coils of dark energy building up around my arm and the haft of the weapon as I roared and plunged the blade deep into the shattered oak.

[You deal 628 Darkness damage to door! -15% Damage Reduction!]

The wood buckled and squealed as it froze solid. Frost and cracks bloomed over it, spreading as I backpedaled and made room for Karalti. She pawed the ground with a back foot, and then charged the door a second time. She smashed into it with the full force of her ten-ton terrestrial weight, and the frozen wood exploded around her head and caved into the hall beyond.

"Ugh." My dragon groaned as she pulled her head free of the wreckage. *"I need to pay more attention to Vash's khiig-channeling lessons."*

"You alright?" I looked back at her.

"I'm fine! I hit my head harder than that all the time. You know, doing... uhh... dragon stuff." She cocked her head at me, her eyes a little unfocused. *"I'll go and try and stop the fighting, force the soldiers to surrender."*

"Go. Just watch out for artillery." A nasty acid burning sensation churned at the back of my throat at the thought of what mortar shells could do to a dragon. *"Artillery and Ix'tamo will kill you stone dead."*

"I will. I'll be fine. Go get Zoltan!" Karalti rumbled, then pivoted and stalked back toward the wall, broadcasting her telepathy across the battlefield. *"Guess what, fuckers?! It's dragon time!"*

CHAPTER 27

With Karalti keeping the infantry busy, I ran for the door of the Keep, glancing over my HP and Adrenaline. The door was smashed into the dense barricade of furniture the defenders had piled up behind the door. Some of it had been shoved back by Karalti, but not all of it—not enough that I could Shadow Dance past the blockade.

[Solar Burst II deals 351 reduced Light damage to Lesser Shades!]
[Raven Helm protects from Blindness!]

I winced as the spell went off like a clap of lightning, briefly turning the hall white. Ears ringing, I resolutely shoved my way past a wardrobe and six tumbled chairs, then crouched down to survey the entry hall from concealment. Ten dead men lay sprawled on the ground, killed by the shadows crowding in front of the grand staircase. A pair of terrified mages were trapped on the first landing. One of them was holding some kind of barrier that kept the shadows from attacking them. The other was winding up to cast another offensive spell.

"You two! Stand down!" I called to them, looking out just far enough to get a proper line of sight on them. "I am Count

Dragozin Hector, the Voivode of Myszno! Surrender now, and keep your lives!"

"The Dragonlord? Pah!" The mage holding the barrier spat at me. "If we wanted a necromantic monster ruling Myszno, we would have kept the first one!"

"For Myszno! For humankind! *Ori'ha'kal!*" The other man swung his glowing hands toward me, spellgloves discharging another burst of light. It engulfed three of the shadows, vaporizing them, and seared the varnish off the furniture I was using for cover.

"We're here to restore Kitti Hussar to her rightful seat!" I called, after I'd finished ducking. "This is your last chance: stand the fuck down, or I'll overrun and kill you both."

The remaining shades pressed in closer to the barrier.

"The Hussars are dead: destroyed, by the likes of you! Die, demon spawn!" The elementalist's lip curled, and this time, he swung his hands directly toward me.

I threw myself forward as a bolt of lightning lanced through the barrier and struck where I'd been crouching. I snarled, throwing out a lasso of darkness from my fingertips. It streaked toward the mage, but hit the barrier and dissolved.

"Your foul magics cannot defeat the holy fire of Khors!" The mage holding the barrier, an older man in the red work robes of a priest, panted in desperation as half a dozen shadow spears rained off the shield.

"For fuck's sake." I concentrated on the crowd of shades. "Get out of here! All of you! Go to the damn Caul of Souls, and say hi to Lahati for me!"

287

The shadows stopped clawing at the barrier and drifted back. One by one, they stretched out like black candle flames, then vanished.

"There! Hold your fire, for fuck's sakes!" I said. "If you're Hussar men, the Countess needs you, and I need Zoltan Gallo."

"Countess? You're installing Hussar's little greensick brat as *countess?*" The elementalist's face contorted with disdain. "Hold that shield, Torvan! For Zoltan!"

I sighed. "Well, okay. Can't say I didn't try."

A fireball warped into existence at the mage's fingertips, then shot at me like a meteor. I dove, rolled, and raced forward with Blood Sprint, changing the Spear from Dark to Light on instinct. The weapon blazed with pure white-gold radiance as I drove it into the barrier. The blade caught against the field of energy, which turned bright blue, then white as the Spear surged the shield until it exploded. The blast pitched the other mage into the railing. I carried the combo through, and drove the blade all the way through the priest's unarmored chest.

"Heretic! Murderer!" Torvan's comrade shouted in horror, stumbling back as I pulled the spear free and spun around to face him. "He was a holy man!"

"Both of you are outlaws who refused to surrender," I said. "So now it's execution or arrest. Your pick."

"Myszno is for Vlachians!" Before I could react, he put the knuckles of his spellglove against the underside of his jaw and snarled a word of power. Within a split second, a ball of lightning formed—and blew the man's head off.

"Yeesh." I flinched as meat rained down across the stairs. "I wonder how the fuck Jacob will try and explain THAT."

I looted both mages, taking their remaining mana, slung my spear over my back, and grabbed a rifle from the floor, checking it was loaded and scrounging more ammunition from the dead rebels. There were five more corpses on the stairwell, killed by shadows, and evidence that others in here had fled. I barreled up to the top floor, the rifle braced in against my shoulder, and cleared each corner until I reached the half open doors of the Lord's Chambers. There was a repetitive clunking sound coming from inside.

"Zoltan! Come out with your hands up!" I found the best position I could—the wall next to the doorway.

The only reply was the growing roar of airship engines from outside the building.

"Uh oh." I turned around and kicked in the door to find an empty apartment. The bedroom was straight ahead, both entry doors flung open, the bed in disarray. The sheets had been ripped up. To the right, a pair of large French doors opened out onto a small balcony, banging loudly as the wind outside grew into a howl. I ran over to find a rope hanging down from the stone railing—and to see Zoltan's small airship careen up toward me from the ground.

"Oh you fucking-!" I raised the rifle and fired, aiming for the ring of blazing bluesteel that encircled the airship's hull and deck. Two out of three rounds impacted, spanging and sparking off the magically-charged metal, but they didn't slow the craft as the ring spun faster and the yacht careened toward Solonovka at speed.

Before I had time to regret my life choices, I threw the rifle down, bounded up onto the edge of the railing, and sprung out into the open air toward the retreating airship. For one slow heartbeat, there was nothing but me, a whole lot of empty space, and the gradual slowing of time as Leap of Faith kicked in... and my hands slapped onto the starboard stern.

Spider Climb kicked in, attaching to the side of the yacht like a barnacle as it gunned its ring-like engine and powered toward the curtain wall. Karalti's bellow of rage and alarm broke through the whining roar of turbines. I looked back to see her launch herself into the air from the wall, drooling white, phosphorescent fire from her jaws.

"Don't torch the boat! For the love all that is holy, do not *torch that boat!"* I slapped my other hand down, pulling myself up arm over arm as Spider Climb's 20-second timer ran down. Once I got my feet to cling, I scrambled up at a fast crawl until the last second, tensed through, and sprung up in a second Jump. The angle was awkward, but I managed to catch the railing of the ship's deck. Straining, I pulled myself up—only to find myself looking up into the muzzle of a great big fuck-off rifle.

"Didn't your momma ever tell you it's rude to stick your junk in someone else's face?" I asked, resisting the urge to cross my eyes as the barrel split in my vision.

"Oh, a comedian, are we?" The man with the elephant gun could only be Zoltan Gallo. He was tall, thick as a barrel, with the bleary piggish eyes and fleshy red cheeks of an alcoholic. His armor was about two sizes too small to contain his gut, but he held the rifle like someone who'd spent years

290

looking down an iron sight. "How do you want to die, pretender? Should I make you plummet to your doom, or blow your head off like common vermin?"

"How about-?" I reached up and yanked the barrel past my face and over my shoulder as he fired. The sound was deafening—literally, as my hearing cut to a high-pitched whine—but the recoil and forward momentum threw him off balance. He stumbled against the rails with a shout, a boss health meter appearing in a ring behind his head. I struggled to pull myself up, only to have his thick hobnailed boot come down on my left hand.

"OWW! Whore!" My fingers couldn't keep grip on that side, slipping as the yacht lurched. Zoltan leered at me, raising his foot to stomp the other hand.

A huge black shadow streaked over the airship: Karalti, rocketing by close enough that the craft's engine surged. The deck bucked like a mustang: Zoltan let out a shout of dismay as the pitch threw him off his feet and sent him rolling into the outer wall of the enclosed bridge. I snapped my jaws and pulled myself up over the rail, rolling to my feet as the ship's stabilizers kicked in and it swung back.

"Arrgh! Get that dragon!" Zoltan roared, getting back to his feet and pulling a saber from his belt.

I followed his line of sight, and my stomach wrenched as I saw his crewmates scramble out of the lower deck and into position in front of a small cannon.

"Watch out: incoming fire, 3 o'clock!" I charged a rush of power from the Mark of Matir, and flew at Zoltan while he was still flat-footed.

The man got his sword up to block: for all the good it did. Shadow Lance landed nearly a thousand points of damage against the edge of the plain steel blade, shattering it. Zoltan cried out, stumbling away up the length of the deck. I chased him, transmuting the Spear's polarity to fire, and went straight for his leg.

There was a rolling 'boom' from the back of the small craft, with recoil that caused the yacht to see-saw as it tore at full speed toward the city.

[Glancing blow! Karalti takes 244 ballistic damage!]

Karalti was invisible in the dark, thanks to her holographic hide, but I knew by the sound that they were firing canister shot, ammo that turned their cannon into a giant shotgun. Karalti was big, but fast: If they couldn't see her, she would be okay. As long as they didn't hit her wings...

"Surrender, Gallo!" I called to him, as he dodged around the bridge. "It's over!"

"I'll kill myself before I surrender to you, you Tuun peasant scum!" He roared back.

"Then it's my job to make your dream come true!" I followed him around the corner, and ran right into a slug he shot from a pistol at his hip. The round struck me in the upper arm, punching through leather and padding into flesh.

[You take 399 ballistic damage!]

I flung my hand out and willed a loop of dark energy out like a lasso, snapping it around his thick neck like an assassin's wire. Zoltan's eyes bugged as he clawed at his throat with one hand, unsteadily aiming the pistol with the other.

There was a bellow from the other end of the ship, then screams and the sound of twisting metal and splintering wood. Karalti roared in triumph as she flew back from the ship with her prize—the 12-pounder cannon she had ripped from the stern.

"It's over!" I repeated, disappearing into a veil of black smoke and reappearing over Zoltan as he collapsed, choking, to the deck. I jammed the point of the spear under his chin and crushed his gun hand beneath the soul of my boot, earning a pained cry.

"We're almost at the towers," Zoltan spat. "Your dragon is dead!"

"My dragon isn't stupid." I wedged the point in closer. *"Karalti, pick us up before we reach the attack radius of those towers!"*

"Aye aye, cap'n!" She strained to gain speed over the ship, struggling with her load until she was over the bridge. She dropped it right over the roof. A thousand pounds of wood and cold iron smashed into the cockpit, throwing up a cloud of wood and debris. The ship's engine stuttered, the craft listed, and then it started to fall.

Zoltan let out a shout of terror, struggling to get away from me as Karalti swooped down. Guided by her senses and the Bond, she reached with her back legs and snatched Zoltan and I from the deck of the yacht as it rolled over and plummeted out of the sky.

"Gods damn you! Demon spawn!" Zoltan yelled, kicking and struggling in Karalti's hind claws.

"Just give it up, man!" I climbed up to her ankle, holding onto her leg like a mast. "You fucking lost!"

"Never! I never lose! I just... I don't win sometimes!!" Zoltan ranted, banging his fist on Karalti's toe as she wheeled back toward the castle. "I want a rematch! Someone cheated! I'm sending for the magistrates! The satraps! All of them! No outlander can claim a noble title in Vlachia! I deserve it, not you! This is obscene!"

"Look down, you big dumb stinky loser. Everyone in this place is glad you're leaving," Karalti groaned, pumping her wings as she strove back toward the castle.

She was right. As the spotlights tracked us back across the city, people were coming out of their homes: cheering, and then brawling as they massed together and mobbed the militia guards hanging out on the street corners.

"Fuck: we need to get them to surrender before citizens start dying. Take us to the Upper Ward." I shakily bought up the group chat, pinging Suri. "Head's up: we've got Zoltan, alive. Heading for the Upper Ward to do the honors."

"Just in time, too. We're starting to get real tired down here." Suri replied. "On our way."

The melee in the castle was still in full swing. It had broken up into skirmishes in both courtyards and the walls. Our smaller, better prepared, higher level forces, fortified by morale and bloodlust, were clearly on top despite the difference in numbers.

"Look down!" I barked at Zoltan. "Do you see that?"

"You know what I see? My reinforcements, ready to enter the castle and kill you all, you damned cave rat!" Zoltan snarled back at me, pointing toward Solonovka.

Karalti dove toward the Upper Ward, pulling up about twenty feet from the ground to drop us. I landed lightly. Zoltan did not. He hit the ground with the grace of a dead cow, smashing his chest and face into the stone. Even so, he was able to push himself to his arms as I walked over—and planted a boot on the back of his head. I looked back to see Suri striding ahead of Kitti, Letho and Gruna. All four of them were bloodied and exhausted: Suri largely unscathed, Letho with a makeshift bandage tied around his head, and Kitti with a battered nose and deep cut from chin to ear on one side of her face. But despite that, when the young noblewoman saw Zoltan, her eyes darkened to a stormy blue.

I hauled the robber baron up by his collar. "Here you go, Kitti. One hog, delivered fresh."

"Oh look: it's my little straw dolly," Zoltan wheezed, his lips flecked with blood. His left arm hung limp and unnaturally low by his side. "How lovely of you to come back to me. I trust this abomination you call a Voivode left you your maidenhead?"

Kitti's face turned pink, then red. Letho and Gruna both made to step up, but Suri waved them back. She crossed her arms, leaving Kitti to advance alone as Zoltan swayed on his knees and leered.

The girl racked the bolt on her rifle, ejecting a spent case and loading a new one into the chamber. "You're disgusting."

"Aww, Kitti Cat, you're so cute when you're mad," Zoltan wheedled. "Come and give papa a kiss."

"You *dare* speak to me this way?" Kitti ground each word out through her teeth. "I am the lady of this House, Zoltan. And *you* are a traitor to my family!"

"House Hussar. Hah… what a joke." Zoltan sneered. "Your father rode out to face the Demon like some fairy-tale knight with a head full of stories. Did you really expect me to die for that pathetic loser and his pathetic seed?"

Kitti's pupils dilated, and a red haze began to shimmer around her as her cheeks turned scarlet with rage. She shoved her rifle into Letho's hands as Zoltan let out another wheezing, high pitched laugh— which meant he wasn't looking when the girl, with a sudden burst of manic strength, pulled Suri's five-and-a-half foot long zweihander sword from the sheathe on the taller woman's back and swung it around.

"I'll make Bas-" He looked up to see Kitti as she boiled toward him, her face a mask of primal fury, and bought the blade down with a bloodcurdling scream. "Uh-"

Zoltan's head flew from his shoulders, landing with a satisfying thump on the stone. I took a big step back as his body jerked on its knees, arterial spray shooting into the air before dying back to weak, pulsing pumps of blood. The headless corpse swayed, then collapsed with a meaty thump on the pavement.

[Congratulations! You have completed Quest: The Last of Her House.]
[You earn 2700 EXP! You gain a +1000 EXP perfection bonus (Less than 10% Mass Combat ally fatalities).]
[Congratulations! You are Level 27!]
[You gained a new achievement: Lord of All You Survey.]
[You have gained Renown: +400 Renown (Myszno; all regions)]
[You gain +250 Bonus Renown (Myszno; all regions) and +250 Renown (General Nobility, Myszno Province)].
[You gain 40 Build Points!]
[Your Kingdom has obtained new Resources: Barley +5000, Silver +1500, Mana (Crystal) +200.]

"Hey! I know that move!" I grinned at Suri. "Gorgon Overdrive, right?"

"Sure is." Suri went over to the girl, resting a hand on her shoulder. Kitti still clenched the sword hilt in a death grip, panting, teeth bared, her eyes dark and wild with rage. "You alright?"

"No." Kitti's expression flickered as the combat ended and her Primal Rage faded. She dropped the huge sword with a clang, then turned and buried her face against Suri's breastplate, weeping. Letho and Gruna both walked up to Zoltan's corpse and spat on it, one after the other.

"Good 'Zerking, kid." Suri hugged her around the shoulders.

The Lady of House Hussar stepped back, dashing at her eyes, and turned to me with her chin lifted. "My apologies, Your Grace. It is unseemly for a Countess to break down in front of her peer like that."

"You're fourteen, Kitti. You can be forgiven a few tears." I smiled at her, opening my arms in offering. She hesitated, stepped forward, and let me hug her. "Now, do I have to do anything to make your position official?"

"Yes," she said. "There is typically a ceremony, and you should have an option in your menu to change my status."

"We don't have time for a ceremony, but we can do one after all this is over." I flipped to the KMS and quickly found Kitti in my allies menu. "Appoint Kitti Hussar as Countess of Bas."

[Appointment confirmed: Countess Kitiana Hussar, Satrap of Bas and 9th Councilwoman of the Myszno Duma.]
[LOCAL ALERT—Myszno Province: After a long and difficult battle, Countess Kitiana Hussar has reclaimed the County of Bas from her challenger, Zoltan Gallo!]

Kitti's eyes widened, and she brought her hands up to move holoscreens that I couldn't see. "Wow. So these are the menus my father used to use... the Kingdom Management System. Strange they call it that. The Kingdom belongs to his Majesty."

"I think it's just a turn of phrase, yeah." I rubbed the back of my neck, glancing at Suri. Neither of us could see the other's face, but I knew she was smiling.

A roar went up from the Lower Ward, and then—in the distance—from the city itself. Mostly cheers, some moans... and then the rolling boom of cannon fire from somewhere in Solonovka.

"Letho, Gruna. Here are my first orders," Kitti said firmly, sniffing to clear the last of her tears. "We will go and liberate any of our household imprisoned in the dungeons, first of all. Letho, you will take Zoltan's head and body and stake them both outside the castle gates."

He grunted, nodded, and toed Zoltan's head with his boot.

"Jeez, kid. You've been a Countess for ten minutes and you're already staking cunts out the front of your castle," Suri laughed, bending to pick up her sword.

"It is justice. I may be a 'greensick maiden', but I am the descendant of conquerors. This man wanted to take my home from me—well, let him rot on the walls of it." Kitti straightened up, looking down at the body of the man who had occupied her home. "Gruna—you are my father's most loyal and experienced *drughi*, and you obeyed his final wishes by protecting me. We will work together on setting Solonovka to rights, and once the county is stable, I am appointing you regent of Bas."

"... Regent?" Gruna blinked. It was the first time I'd ever heard him speak.

"Yes. I am not wise or strong enough to rule, yet." Kitti turned back to Suri, drawing herself up. "Countess, pending the restoration of my lands, I humbly request to be made a Ward of Racsa and to serve as your squire until I come of age in two years' time."

"A squire?" Suri glanced at me and drew a deep breath. "Berserkers don't, uh, really have squires. And I'd say you're plenty wise, for your age."

"For my age." Kitti took a step forward. "Gruna is well-traveled and experienced in handling the matters of the county, but all my father ever taught me was to be a quiet, obedient wife to some southern lordling. This is the frontier land, Your Grace: the wild men of the southern reach will not respect a girl. But I can make them respect a woman, if I am well trained in combat and statecraft."

"I'm on board," I said, shrugging. "Suri?"

Suri's lips parted, and she looked back to Kitti, struggling with something in herself in silence for a few minutes. "Alright. Guess we were doing that anyway, weren't we?"

"Thank you!" Kitti pulled her rifle back from Letho's hands, then genuflected in front of Suri with the stock resting on the ground. "I swear to train as hard as you desire, my lady."

Suri's cheeks reddened with a dark cinnamon flush. "Okay, well, first lesson is that Berserkers don't kneel to anyone, Kit. Anyway, if you're my squire, you know what that means, right?"

"I expect you will have a list of duties for me." Kitti nodded, pressing her lips together as she bounced up to her feet.

"Yeah, well, squires take care of their knights' mount, right?" Suri grinned. "That means you're gonna have to learn to handle Cutthroat."

Karalti let out a shuddering snort, shaking her head. *"Come on, Suri! That's just mean!"*

"Don't worry, Kitti." I wandered over to the suddenly crestfallen girl and gave her a friendly clap on the shoulder. "Cutthroat's ever only eaten the face off every second person who's ever tried to saddle her. The rest just end up with scars."

CHAPTER 28

The colorful hallucinations from the battle tea were in full swing by the time we finished mopping up and got shown to our rooms. Suri and I fell on each other before the door was even closed. I peeled her out of her armor, shedding it piece by piece on the floor, and half carried, half dragged her to the bathroom. We didn't actually make it to the water: Suri pressed herself against the vanity counter and hooked her legs up over my hips, moaning as I kissed from the base of her sternum to her neck, tasting salt and the faint scent of jasmine and sandalwood. She lifted her chest, pressing her skin to my mouth, her breasts sliding smooth and heavy against my cheeks.

"Ah! Mmmmnngh-oh!" Suri's scarlet hair clung to her face as she tipped her head back and to the side, baring the long, dark line of her throat. My heart sped, and my mouth watered as I nuzzled up and bit down on the side of her neck. Her skin was so soft it felt like fur against my lips. She shuddered in my arms, gasping, then moaning as the points of my teeth pressed into her skin.

"Harder!" She clutched the back of my head, pushing it forward.

A flicker of anxiety made me hesitate, but when I pushed in between Suri's thighs, they were slick with need. Skin-hungry, I pulled her hips forward and thrust into her as I bit. At the first taste of blood, my unnaturally slow heart surged to life, pounding in my ears.

"Mmph!" I clamped my jaws down, holding her like a lion with a gazelle by the throat, and drove into her with sudden urgency. Suri gasped, pressing up against my mouth, and I felt her shudder with need. Her muscles relaxed, leaving her hungry, willing… then ecstatic, as I clutched her close and fucked her down against the counter.

"Yes, yes, yes-" She panted the word, over and over, then let out a staccato cry when I reached up to stroke one of her nipples in time with the sucking pressure of my mouth. My teeth were to either side of her carotid, not penetrating it, but I could feel her racing pulse as she built toward an explosive, eager release. The sensation blended with the wet heat of her body, the rhythmic clench of her body around mine. My eyes rolled, then fluttered closed as brief, hallucinatory images and sensations overlaid the pleasure. I was flying, diving, two hearts pulsing like engines deep in my chest. The muscles of my back and shoulders worked like I had wings, flexing with every thrust, as a distant, alien excitement built with the heat in my own body. It was the dual heartbeat that tipped me off—and briefly shocked me out of my trance.

"…*Karalti?*"

She did not reply, but I knew was there with me, with us—silent, breathless, watching and feeling through the Bond the way she had watched the gauntlet in Lahati's Tomb. I jerked in surprise, just as Suri climaxed with a deep, throbbing spasm that pulled me into my own release. And as I came, I heard and felt Karalti's telepathic gasp of empathic pleasure.

"FUCK!" I snarled, pulling my mouth up from Suri's neck. She was glassy-eyed and flushed as I dragged her down to the floor and roughly guided her onto her hands and knees. She let out a cry of surprised pleasure as I mounted her from behind, caught up in some instinct that was only partly human. I clutched at her waist with one hand, reaching around to cup her breasts with the other, and took her a second time as the flow between Karalti and I deepened and broadened into a two-way river of sensation. She was curious, nervous, excited as the unfamiliar sensations of my body echoed to her nerves... and when I came again, the orgasm rocketed between us like a sonar pulse, back and forth, as she reached her own private climax somewhere beyond the keep.

"Oh... god... holy..." Gasping, still bucking into Suri's body, I collapsed over her back and pressed her chest down to the floor as I strained for more purchase, more depth, more... everything.

"Mmmm." Suri stretched underneath me, resting her cheek against her arms. Her voice was thick and slow with afterglow. "Post-combat sex. The actual fucking best."

I was tongue tied, my senses anchored somewhere between my own body and Karalti's. It was all I could do to lie over Suri's back and catch my breath.

"You 'kay?" She murmured.

"Yeah." My voice was hoarse—because god help me, I was still hard. Karalti's own spasms of pleasure were echoed in places in my body that didn't rightfully exist. I felt her self-delivered orgasm at the root of my cock, driving me to keep thrusting, keep moving... until finally, she finished. The strength of the Bond began to ebb and narrow, and I was able to breathe without feeling like I was doing it with two pairs of lungs. "Yeah. I'm okay. Something really weird just happened."

"Was it this?" Suri reached up to gently touch the deep bloody marks on her neck. "Because I'm fine, I swear. I'd have said something if I wasn't."

"No, it wasn't that. It was..." I flushed, suddenly ashamed. "Everything's okay. Just... uhh... it's something to do with the Bond. You know, my link to Karalti."

"I know what the Bond is, you dimwit." Suri chuckled, and reached back to cup my head. She drew my face to hers and kissed me over her shoulder, long and deep, and the flush of shame faded as I lost myself in the feeling of her lips on mine. When we parted, I slowly eased out of her. She looked back and down, and her eyebrows rose.

"Well well well," she said. "Guess we need to make Meewfolk Battle Tea a regular part of the castle diet?"

"If it lasts more than four hours, I'm calling a doctor." I cleared my throat and kneeled back. "Holy shit."

"What's this about Karalti?" Suri scooted over to the vanity, searching for a towel.

"I-I'll talk about it later. Give me a minute to talk to her." I scrubbed at my eyes, reaching back out to my dragon—and finding a channel of blissful post-orgasmic fatigue as she lounged in her own afterglow.

"I'm sorry." Karalti's telepathic voice was sheepish, but also a little blurry. *"I should have asked, huh?"*

"It's okay." I said—and let her feel—that it really was alright. *"Just took me by surprise. You've uhh... you've always tuned out when Suri and I are together. You've never tuned IN before."*

"I know. But this time, I felt you start to feel good and I just..." Karalti trailed off, and I felt a small, sweet wave of afterglow pass over me like warm sunlight. *"I guess I just wanted to know what it was like."*

There was a heavy pause between us. Suri threw me the towel and picked herself up with a pleased groan.

"So... was it good?" I gave Suri a smile as she went over to the bathtub, spoke the command words to heat the water, and stepped over the rim to ease down.

"Yeah. It was." Karalti hummed. *"Suri is really awesome, isn't she?"*

For a second, I wasn't sure I'd heard her correctly. Then I realized that, yes, she had just said what she'd said. And meant it.

"You... uh... Yes. Yes, she is." I rubbed myself down, then got to my feet and wobbled over to the tub. It was easily big enough for two people—or three—and in that moment, I felt a deep surge of resentment toward Ryuko's developers for insisting on a 6-hour grace period between Karalti's use of the

Polymorph spell. *"Look, I'm going to have to talk about this later, alright? But rest assured that I am not mad. I'm whatever the opposite of mad is, but also combined with an unstoppable prize-winning erection."*

*"Believe me, I know. "*Karalti's voice turned dark and sly. *"I can hear your thoughts too, remember?"*

I winced as I eased down into the hot water between Suri's knees, sitting with my back to her front. *"After this, I seriously doubt I'm going to ever forget that again. "*

***

I may or may not have been preoccupied with thoughts of Suri, Karalti, and myself in various configurations as we led the ships home on the morning of the 28th of Boseg Hava. I flew ahead of the frigates with Karalti, daydreaming for most of the four-hour flight until we came within view of Karhad. For the first time since I'd arrived in Myszno, the city was celebrating.

The marketplace was packed—a festival, by the look of it, with the townspeople feasting as best they could to celebrate the liberation of Bas and the restoration of all ten counties. Beyond the marketplace, I noticed that something had already changed about the city's skyline. There was scaffolding everywhere.

"Wait a second. Are they... are they rebuilding the cathedral?" I zoomed my vision in, and sure enough, the big building now covered in walkways was the half-destroyed church of Khors. It had been third on my list of big projects to fund, after the university and hospital. *"Did Vash come back with money, or did I miss something?"*

307

Karalti flicked a wingtip, gliding easily on the warm currents of air rising from the city. *"I dunno. Check the KMS?"*

I opened the menus and flipped through to Karhad's screen. When I saw the stats, my eyebrows shot up. *"We have nearly a thousand volunteers mobilizing in Racsa. Like... spontaneously. By themselves. I did not order a thousand volunteers."*

"Well, duh. I'm pretty sure that volunteers who are ordered to work are called 'slaves'. Wanna go say hi?"

"Let's do it." I banged my fist down on top of my helmet, and assumed the position.

Karalti let out a melodious, ringing roar, then pulled her wings into a swift dive. She tilted to the left as we descended toward the marketplace, roaring a second time as we passed the walls of the Merchant Ward. I adjusted position as I sensed her intent, hanging on tight as she rolled in the air over the crowd below. People squealed, cheered and waved to us; children jumped up and down, priests bowed their heads. She pulled out to glide gracefully around the perimeter of the market ward, high enough we didn't blow anything over, low enough we could hear what everyone was shouting.

"Lord Dragozin!"

"Long live House Dragozin! Long live Myszno!"

"Is that the Volod?"

"BURNA MALADIK!"

I unequipped my helmet to wave back down, returning to the saddles grips as Karalti and I wordlessly synced through the bond. I dropped back down and held on as she barrel-rolled overhead. Cries of wonder were drowned out by the growing roar of the airships as they came in low behind us. I looked back to see the decks lined with Yanik and Meewfolk, all of them waving and whistling to the townsfolk.

"*I didn't know the Renown boost was going to make THAT much of a difference!*" I almost shouted to Karalti telepathically, before remembering that she could hear me over the noise. Musicians had struck up in the market, blasting cheerful music on fiddles, flutes and zithers.

"*They're happy that the harvest is gonna come in,*" Karalti said. "*The Demon ruined their lives, and now they see things turning around. I'd be happy, too.*"

As we drew up on the castle, I couldn't help but notice that it was bustling. I frowned, trying to make sense of the number of people inside. They were all over the scaffolding, reinforcing it and adding more.

"*Hang on—I DEFINITELY did not order repairs on the castle. I wanted to rebuild the university first.*" I leaned out over Karalti's shoulder, squinting into the wind. "*Holy shitsnacks. Are those the volunteers?*"

"*I dunno.*" Karalti replied. "*Let's go down and ask Istvan. I can see him from here.*"

Istvan stood beside a table manned by four guardsmen, talking animatedly with Rudolph as the guards processed lines and lines of people. There wasn't enough room to land in the courtyard: Karalti had to fly past the Gatehouse and land outside the Orphans Camp, scattering a crowd of curious, bored Meewfolk and awestruck volunteers.

I surveyed the commotion and struggled to understand how and what was happening. Carpenters sawed at logs, while masons shaped blocks of stone to repair the curtain wall. Workers shifted wheelbarrows full of rubble, or walked beside grunting triceratops as they hauled creaking wagons of stone and sand up the road. The cleanup was going at a surreal speed. Like players, NPCs had Inventories and Menus. They crafted by running through kinetic mini-games that distilled crafting into a fun, but challenging act of pantomime. As I watched, a Mercurion {Master Stonemason} and their assistants rapidly stacked and fit drystone into a broken doorway, while others pried broken paving stones out of the courtyard and replaced them with new sheets of slate.

"My lord—we heard the news of your victory!" Istvan seemed genuinely cheerful as I pulled up at the table in a daze. "As you can see, it was not only us here at the castle. Word has spread of the fall of Zoltan Gallo."

"But who... how...?" I bought up the KMS logs, scanning for activity, but there was no history of anyone with access to the system rustling up all these volunteers. "Was it Bubek?"

"No, I haven't heard from him. Believe me, Your Grace, we weren't exactly expecting this ourselves." Istvan planted his hands on his hips, looking out over the crowd with satisfaction. "They began showing up yesterday."

Numbly, I checked the KMS. Sure enough, we were in the right Renown tier to command about a thousand volunteers. Emphasis on 'command'.

"My lord, there are two matters I must bring to your attention," Rudolph said, as drawn and dignified as always. "There are guests waiting to speak with you in the great hall. Starborn, in fact."

"Starborn?" The giddiness faded around the edges, replaced by wariness. I'd had very mixed interactions with other players in Archemi.

"Yes, Your Grace. You hired them for Kingdom Quests, and now they wish to introduce themselves and possibly pledge service to Myszno specifically and Vlachia in general," Rudolph said. "Also, I have taken the liberty of contacting an artist to help you design livery and heraldry suitable for your House. We cannot fly the standard of House Bolza. The designer is charging a very reasonable rate within our budget."

"I... thanks. Man, I don't know what to say." I rubbed my eyes, then let out a tense breath. "I guess the first thing I need to do is go and play greeter."

"Welcome to the life of nobility," Istvan replied dryly. "Oh, also: Vash has been in contact. He says they have begun extracting the goods from the dragon graveyard, and all is going well. There is, as Vash so eloquently put it, 'enough gold in that place to make me cough so hard my asshole popped out like a mushroom'."

I shook my head in amazement. "Vash should have been a bard, not a monk. The man is a poet."

"The man is something, that's for sure." Istvan let out an irritated sigh, but he couldn't hide the smile at the corners of his mouth.

"Thanks for handling this." I rolled my shoulders, glancing up as the shadows of the frigates fell over the skyport. "I'm grateful for your work, both of you. Rudolph, I'll meet with your artist after talking with the Starborn, so that we can sit down with Suri and hash something out. I think you're right. It's about time we had a flag to rally behind."

Suri was with the ships, so I went to meet with the players alone. I entered the great hall to find a knot of five people talking and laughing—four Meewfolk and one human—and a second human sitting apart, wrapped in a feathered grey cloak, her shield resting against the edge of the bench beside her. She had a boxy kind of face, with a hard jawline and very large eyes. Her hair was brown, falling like a mane halfway down her back. When she heard the door open, she looked over—and my eyes widened as recognition dawned.

"Nethres?" I called, picking up my pace. "Holy shit."

Nethres tensed when I called her name, rising to her feet. The last time I'd seen her, she'd been clad in the blue and silver heavy plate of the Order of St. Grigori. Now, she was dressed in a set of armor fit for a Valkyrie. By the sword, shield, and Teutonic designs on her surcoat, I was willing to bet that's exactly what she was.

"Hector." Nethres had a husky, hollow voice, which warmed with real pleasure as I closed on her and offered a hand.

She clapped her palm into mine, meeting my gaze as we shook. "Always knew you'd go a long way. Never imagined how far, though. Look at all this."

"Thanks." I was glad to see her, but still wary. "What a fucking adventure it's been since dragon school, hey?"

"Guess you could call it that." Nethres hadn't ever smiled during the Trials, and she was just as serious now.

"What are you doing here, on the other side of Artana?" I asked, glancing back at the others. They'd stopped talking, watching us curiously. "I figured you'd stayed in Ilia."

Nethres' lips tightened. "The only people who stayed in Ilia are the ones into Baldr and Lucien's Hitler fantasy. I left the country and traveled west to Gilheim. Picked up my Advanced Path, and bonded with a quazi."

"Jeez. Well, what about Casper? We saw him in Dakhdir not long ago."

At the mention of the archer's name, Nethres' face rippled with an irritated tic. "Fuck Casper. I thought he was my friend. Turns out he's a piece of shit. I'll be happy to tell you how it went down, in private."

"Sure. Let me handle these guys, and we can go catch up." I nodded, and turned to the rest of the group, beckoning them over.

The five of them were clearly split into two different parties, because the first group, three almost-identical Meewfolk with calico-patterned fur, moved together like synchronized swimmers. The other pair was only slightly less surreal. The Meewfolk woman was some kind of bard class, judging by her eccentric clothes and the strange looking instrument slung over her back—a set of double-layered pan-pipes about as long as a baseball bat. Her human companion was a one-hundred-percent walking fanfiction toon of *Conan the Barbarian*, complete with sword, shield, and bulging muscles. He wore nothing except a manly scowl, a loincloth, a rough fur cloak and steel pauldrons.

"Hey everyone, sorry to keep you waiting." I put on my best veneer of confidence as they joined the conversation. "I'm Hector. I'm guessing that we have The Meews Brothers, plus Kylirra and Konan?"

Kylirra's brilliant blue eyes hooded, and she trilled as she extended her hand to me, fingers out. "Oh, darling, I didn't expect you'd even remember us! It's so *wonderful* to be able to finally put a face to the name! We did that quest to recover all those little lordlings for you, remember? Kon, say hello."

"Uhhn." 'Kon' grunted.

The three brothers stepped forward to shake hands: all of them, at the same time. I started from the left and worked to the right, trying not to cross my eyes as I looked at them. The only visual difference between the three Meewfolk men was the color of their calico patches. The ginger, brown and white spots were swapped around.

"Nice to finally put a face to the Count of Myszno." It was the middle one who spoke. "I'm... uhh... we're pleased to meet you. My name was Hayden, but here we go by Makmaai. Or Max, if that's easier."

"Just... Makmaai? Singular?" I looked between them, confused.

Kylirra let out a tinkling laugh, flapping her hand. "'Makmaai' means 'Legion' in our language, in case you didn't know."

"Hah, yeah. We kind of shift focus from body to body, and the other two just roll with whatever the one in charge is doing. If we're in character, we just go with White Max, Ginger Max, and Brown Max. Like a damn Dr. Seuss book." The one to the left—the gingeriest—spoke up. "There was a glitch when I... we... uploaded. One set of brain data, three different avatars. If anyone was alive back at the company, we're sure they'd have a goddamn field day trying to figure out how this happened."

"We're used to it, now, though," Brown Max continued. "It'd be great if we actually got full EXP for all three toons, but we don't. It's split between us, so we make the best out of it."

"Oh my god, you guys should totally make an acapella group!" Kylirra trilled, before looking back to me. "Anyway, Hector, me and Kon here want to sign up with your clan. I mean, I know there's no *official* clans on Archemi or anything, but we've been all over Artana and the only other Starborn worth anything is that Baldr Hyland guy in Ilia. And to be frank with you, he seems like kind of a douche."

"Hunh." Kon nodded his assent.

"You don't even know the half of it," Nethres said dourly.

"Believe me, we've heard stories." Kylirra let out a tittering, nervous laugh. "But yes, I don't know about y'all, but after two back-to-back world wars and a mass extinction event, I'm a little sick of assholes trying to conquer the world for no good reason."

"Same," Brown Max said. "We want to sign up with your group and help out as we can. The talk in taverns is that Vlachia is gearing up to fight Ilia."

"We're trying to deter Ilia before it comes to full blown war, but yeah. Baldr and friends might leave us with no choice," I said. "Anyway, I'll tell you what: Myszno always has quests that need doing. All of you are welcome to take up rooms in the castle, or you can find your own places to live in Karhad, Boros, Litvy or Solonovka. I'll preference you for Kingdom Quests for say, the next month or so. You get the EXP, money, whatever loot the quest entails, unless that loot belongs to the Volod and-or my province. Once Myszno is back to full operational capacity, we'll see what I can do here as Voivode to grant special status in Vlachia. Depending on what your goals are, there's posts available here for good people. You can also just use Karhad as a base to adventure from, if you want."

"Sounds good to me... us. We don't really get what's happening in Ilia. We're just really just looking for a place to figure out the game," White Max said. "Feels like we've been running all over the place since the Helpdesk went dead."

"Did you work at Ryuko?" I asked.

"Yeah. HR department. Nothing technical, unless you count staffing as 'technical'." The Maxes nodded.

"My wife was a programmer in the military division down in Texas." Kylirra pinned her ears, tail lashing. "She didn't make it, and I've just been drifting ever since. Kon here has been really supportive, but honestly, I just want somewhere to settle down and put my life back together."

Kon grunted, crossing his arms.

"What about you, man?" I regarded the barbarian apprehensively. "You, uh... got any goals?"

"Uh? Oh." He sniffed and scratched his nose, scowling up at the roof of the Great Hall. "Yes. After we crush the decadent Ilian dogs, I would like a position at the University of Karhad."

"You want to... work at the university?" I resisted the urge to rub my eyes. "Teaching...?"

"Law." The big man's mouth sloped across to one side. "I was about to finish my second doctorate before HEX."

I blinked a couple of times.

"Security, Conflict and Human Rights. Focus on child welfare," he added, helpfully.

"Well. Sure. I think we can arrange something." I was about to propose some kind of Barbarian Harvard idea when the doors to the Great Hall opened, and Suri strode in ahead of Taethawn, Zlaslo, and Kitti. When Kon saw Suri, his eyes got very big and very dark. He sniffed, straightened up, and dusted off his loincloth.

"Hey there, partner." Suri kissed me on the cheek, the turned to the group of Starborn and shook hands with each person. "Suri Ba'hadir, Voivodzina of Myszno. You're the players we booked to handle some of our Kingdom Quests, right?"

"Yes. Yes ma'am." Kon cleared his throat, shooting me a beady-eyed glance. I grinned back at him, making sure to show fangs. "Lady Ba'hadir, the tales of your great beauty have-"

"Oh, knock it off, mate. I appreciate it and all, but I don't know you from Adam." Suri brushed him off, shaking hands with Nethres next. "Don't know if I recognize you, either."

"Nethres. Just Nethres." She gripped Suri's hand firmly. "A Valkyrie of Gilheim."

"Can always welcome more strong arms into Myszno." Suri smiled at Kon, who was still trying to scowl despite his red cheeks, and then at Nethres. "Now, sorry to break this up, but Hector and I just got back from a big mass combat and we need to get ready for an appointment with His Majesty."

"If you can handle the prep for that, Nethres and I need to catch up in private about our time in Ilia," I said. "I know her from way back. We met at dragon school."

"Yeah. I was wiped out in the first round of Trials," Nethres added, her slow eyes shifting to me.

"Ooh, do you know what's really happening in Ilia, then?" Kylirra's tail curled into a curious arch. "I've heard so many horrible stories."

"Nah. We just need to catch up about some old friends," I lied. "By the way, if you guys are interested, there is actually a decent-sized quest that needs handling. There's been reports of monsters and bandits in the ruins of Karhad University, and we can't rebuild it until they've been thrown out. How do you feel like teaming up to handle it?"

"Sure. Seems like a good way to settle in and build some Renown." White Max nodded in time with his clones.

"I approve," Kylirra said, squinting happily. "Can't wait for those university taverns to open back up!"

"Yes. I accept this challenge." Kon gave me a curt bow of his head. "Issue the quest."

I went into the KMS, found *The Vaunted Halls of Karhad University*, and assigned it to them. "Done."

"Excellent. We will destroy these monsters and bandits." Kon cracked his knuckles, sneering on one side of his mouth. "And after the university is rebuilt, I will teach from a lectern adorned with their skulls."

CHAPTER 29

There was a time difference of three hours between Myszno and Taltos, the capital city in the province of the same name. That meant there was a bit of wiggle room to sit down with Nethres and find out what she knew—and why she was here to begin with.

"You sure this place is private?" She asked, once we took our seats in the Ducal Suit. The place was looking bare: volunteers had already stripped out the images of Bolza and his family, as well as all the green and silver furnishings. "No way that Hyland could spy on us?"

"It's as private as we can make it. Why?" I gave Rudolph a nod of thanks as he set down a Turkish coffee set on the table between us. The seat I'd had her take put her back to the door and gave me the best position to find cover, just in case. Nethres hadn't ever struck me as being the kind to lie or randomly PK people, but you never knew.

"Hard to explain." She pressed her lips together in a tight line, watching my butler as he discreetly, but efficiently left through the door to the suit and locked the two-way deadbolt from the outside.

"Don't worry, okay? Rudolph is basically a walking picture of discretion." I said, once silence had settled over the room. "How's things been?"

"Difficult. I couldn't say any of this when were in the hall, but I came here for more than one reason." She picked up her little cup of foamy coffee and looked down it. "I've been on the run for about five months. From Baldr, Lucien, and Violetta. Baldr rules Ilia. Lucien runs his army. Violetta manages the Mata Argis, the Ilian secret service. The Mata Argis are after me."

"Why?"

She regarded me steadily. "After I picked up the Valkyrie class in Gilheim, I returned to Ilia and joined the resistance."

My eyes widened. "There's a resistance?"

"Yes. The Kingsmen." Nethres nodded. "Some players. Mostly NPCs. The prince who was deposed in the Ilian Revolution is now an adult, and he leads the biggest cell of partisans. He's in Revala right now, doing what he can to stop Lucien and the dragons. Prince Illandi made me a captain. I came here on his behalf. A longshot, I figured, asking you for help."

"Not that long of a shot," I said, taking the top off my coffee. "We've been fighting Baldr-slash-Ororgael since before I fled the Eyrie."

"I don't know how you escaped. From everything I've heard, the Order was some kind of trap. But I saw your dragon." For the very first time, Nethres smiled—an expression that reached her hazel eyes and warmed them from grey to green. "She's beautiful."

"She is, and it was. And Baldr isn't Baldr anymore." I shook my head. "He got hijacked by the digital ghost of

Michael Pratt, a senior developer who worked in Ryuko's military and civilian divisions on the game's A.I. Goes by the name 'Ororgael' in Archemi. He's using Baldr's body, but Baldr as we know him is functionally dead."

"A dev? That would make a lot of sense." Nethres gave a tense nod. "He's killed players, as in, really killed them. Several players. If he knew where I was, he'd kill me."

"How?" I set my cup down, watching her intently.

"I don't know what it is. Some kind of sword. There's only one of them." Nethres drew a deep breath. "Lucien called it the 'Godslayer'. Looks like some kind of laser sword, almost. I've only seen it at a distance."

The Turkish coffee, normally aromatic and mellow and delicious, felt like it'd left a coating of ash in my mouth. "I've seen that sword. He dueled me with it."

"You're lucky to be alive." The corners of Nethres' mouth sloped. "He publicly executed three players in Liren. Beheaded them, right in the middle of the city. One of them was a murderhobo who went on a killing spree. One was just a rogue, a woman who pissed him off for some reason. The third was one of ours, in the Resistance. His name was Pravoslav."

"Fuck. I remember him. He was with us in the Trials. Big guy, accent east of Germany somewhere."

"He was Slovak. A refugee from the Bloc to the UNAC." Nethres nodded. "Baldr killed him. He didn't respawn. His PMs disappeared. Any dynamic information about him was corrupted."

I slumped back into my seat, digesting the news. For one thing, it erased any lingering doubt in my mind that Ororgael needed to die. For another, why the fuck hadn't Ororgael killed ME?

"If he's an admin, that'd be how he got his hands on the Godslayer," Nethres said. "Rumor has it there's some temporary player-killer weapons like that that were left over from admin playtesting, but they vanish after a couple of hours."

"Who did you hear that from?" I asked.

"Another admin. His name is Jamil," Nethres said. "He's also in the resistance. Keeps to himself, and he hasn't ever said anything about a Michael or Ororgael, but he briefed us on what to do if we ran into someone with an Admin Test weapon. Several players were too scared to stay with us, and left the resistance to hide."

"Sheesh. Guess he doesn't want to panic people by telling them what's going on." I clicked my tongue. "I'm guessing Casper was one of the players who ran."

"No. He's worse." Nethres' expression turned stormy, and she crossed her arms. "He works for Violetta. The Mata Argis bitch. He was spying on us for her. He'd have turned me in if he'd gotten the chance."

"Well, fuck." I scowled. "He was in Dakhdir only a week or so ago, pretending to be working for the Morning Stars. They're rebels, trying to reinstate an ancient royal lineage on the throne."

"Tsch." Nethres rolled her eyes. "After he dumped me and ran from the Trials, he went and became a bandit. At some point—I don't know when—Violetta recruited him. Forcibly or not, I don't know. He weaseled his way into the Kingsmen by playing on our friendship."

"She probably recruited him at the point of the Godslayer," I said. "Ororgael trusts her more than he does Lucien."

"Yeah. That's the consensus in the resistance," Nethres replied. "Mind you, I'd trust a rabid raccoon more than I'd trust Lucien. Lucien's sick. He's raped, tortured and murdered his way across Ilia and Revala. Uses the dragons to kill people—NPCs—and worse. I've got lots of stories, none of them good."

"It's fine. I don't need to know the details. I saw enough of that shit in the war." Grimacing, I pushed the rest of my coffee away. "I always knew he was fucked in the head. Believe me, if I ever get my hands on that Godslayer weapon, he'll be the first to go. Ororgael will be second, and then I'll throw the damn thing into a volcano."

"You'd do that?" Nethres frowned, suddenly uncertain. "Kill them?"

I straightened up in my chair. "Taking them out of action is my primary goal. We're living in what amounts to a closed vault with roughly two thousand immortal player characters. That's two thousand people who MUST live together in the same little virtual world. If I could shoot Ororgael, Violetta and Lucien into space and send them to another planet, I would. But we can't, and they've made it very clear that they don't want to share. People like that don't just 'get better', and if we can't imprison them, the only solution is to put them down."

"I don't think you're wrong. Just surprised by your confidence." Nethres shrugged. "I don't think I could really kill someone, even after learning how to fight."

"It's a trained skill, not a talent." I shrugged. "The War taught me that there's some people that just have to die, and Ororgael and Lucien are two of those people."

"And Violetta?" Nethres asked.

"She's not right in the head, but something about her is different," I said. "She was a nice person when I first met her. Ordinary, kind of bubbly and friendly. But now, it's like something sucked the soul out of her. I want to help her if it's possible. The only alternative is euthanasia."

Nethres considered that for a minute or two. "Yeah. I don't remember her from the Trials."

"She barely made it past the first round," I said. "Came back to the camp clinging to her last HP."

"That'd be why. I was already out."

"Yeah. Well, I have a hunch that Baldr fucked her mind up somehow. Their dragons are corrupted, all twisted up and shit, and I'm wondering if something similar happened to Violetta. Some kind of brainwashing or magical corruption."

"Tell me about it." Nethres shook her head, her gaze wandering to the fireplace. "I'm glad you made it. And I'm

325

sorry I was a bitch to you back then. Felt a lot of urgency to succeed."

I snorted. "Don't sweat it. There's nothing you can say to me that my drill instructors haven't already screamed in my face."

"I bet. Same with my foreman." She smiled faintly. "If you're going to see the king of Taltos, do you think he'd be interested to hear my information?"

"Definitely," I said. "I was actually going to ask if you wanted to tag along. It means flying on a dragon, though. We have to be there by this afternoon, and she can teleport."

"I'll leave Vedrfonir here, then. Sign of trust. My quazi's the only friend I have now." She finally picked up her coffee and threw it back like a shot. I opened my mouth to warn her, but it was too late—she hacked and coughed as she got a mouthful of the mud-like grounds.

"Yeah, you're supposed to leave those in," I laughed.

Nethres spat into her cup, then wiped her mouth on her sleeve. "Urrgh, I didn't know they drink dirt in Vlachia."

I laughed. "You leave the coffee mud in the cup. And, uh, you might not want to spit in the Volod's coffee cups while we're at the castle."

"Ugh." She gagged, taking a mouthful of water. "Think that's the first thing I've tasted in Archemi that wasn't good."

"It's more like a 'stick your pinky out and sip' kind of coffee." I shrugged. "Anyway, if you're ready to go, I'll call the gang and we can get moving."

"Thanks. I hope I can help." Nethres got to her feet. "Also, congrats on your success yesterday. Seems a lot of people here like you. Don't suppose you happened to beat Baldr's ass when you fought him? That'd be nice."

"Not exactly," I said. "Though I didn't let him defeat me, either. I noped out of the battle by chugging a whole lot of mana."

"Probably for the best." Nethres grimaced, her brow furrowing. "There's some really screwed up people here. Maybe the blackout drove them crazy, I don't know. You're right about the vault thing. We might really be the only humans alive."

"Yeah. We might just be." I drew a deep breath, enjoying the feeling of air filling my lungs. "And if the rest of us work together, we'll hopefully be able to stay that way."

CHAPTER 30

The seat of power in Vlachia was Vulkan Keep: a cave castle built into Mt. Racosul, the towering black volcano that loomed over the black city of Taltos. Sheltered by the mountain on all sides except for one, it was the closest thing to an impregnable fortress I'd ever seen in Archemi. Even Solonovka, with its tiered twenty-foot walls, couldn't hold a candle to it.

Normally, Karalti angled for the Parade Ground, the great red square which faced the Volod's garrison barracks. But when we came out on the other end of the teleport, I was surprised to see us hanging over the Northern Gate of Taltos. My dragon let out a confused squawk as she glided forward, realized she was headed in the wrong direction, and dipped a wing to glide back around in the direction of the mountain.

"What the hell?" She broadcast to us. *"I didn't teleport us here! I was aiming for the castle!"*

Beside me, Suri craned her head around the dragon's neck to look forward at Mt. Racosul. *"I'm pretty sure your answer's over there, mate."*

Hundreds of dark-hulled airships stretched back and forward in a great convoy across the northern sky above Vulkan Keep, blotting out the noonday sun. Sleek, quick Bathory-class skirmishers patrolled the chasm that separated the castle's gatehouse from the road leading up from the city. Hussar-class Destroyers hovered in front of the mountain, each one the size of a small passenger jet and bristling with weapons. One especially gigantic ship hung almost directly over the Parade Ground: a ship almost as large as a modern troop carrier, with a strange curved shield in front that made it look like a giant flying crossbow. Hundreds of smaller craft were in queue behind it, all of them flying the Corvinus banner: a black dragon on a red field, which hung from every mast like drops of blood suspended in the crowded, but orderly sky.

"Damn. Ignas is not fucking around." I held onto the saddle with one hand, leaning out to gawk.

"Nope." Karalti remarked. *"He sure isn't."*

"My god." Rin put a hand to her face, clutching the straps of her saddle harness with the other hand. "We really are going to war, aren't we?"

"That's the entire Second Fleet, if my eyes don't deceive me," Masha called, raising her voice over the wind. She and Rin were seated on one side; Suri and Nethres on the other. "Quite a sight, eh?"

"What the hell is that thing?" Suri asked, pointing at the big crossbow-shaped ship. "And how the fuck does it even fly?"

"That's a Sarkany-Class Dreadnought. The first and only ship of its kind." Rin couldn't tear her gaze from it, but there was a note of resignation in her voice as she spoke. "They're designed to protect a fleet from magical assault, artillery, and even dragon fire. They lead into a battle, projecting an antimagic pulse weapon from the front, and a huge kinetic shield around the sides. Smaller ships shelter in the shield. That's why the bottom of it is flat, and the front has that weird curved shape... it's kind of like a radar dish, but for magic."

"Wow." I couldn't tear my eyes away from the armada as Karalti strove toward the castle. "And this is only *one* fleet?"

"Yes." Masha replied. "His Majesty can field four fleets in times of international crisis. The fleets and the Black Army... those were some of Ignas' father's greatest accomplishments."

Nethres whistled. "Lucien's screwed."

"I wouldn't count on that. He doesn't play fair." I grimaced, shifting back into the landing position on the saddle. "We've underestimated him before."

As we got closer, we could hear military brass music playing from the decks of some of the ships—entertainment for troops psyching themselves up for the traumafest to come. Karalti had to dodge, weave, and then fly over half a dozen skirmishers on the way to the castle. The only place available for us to land was in the castle proper—the courtyard of the Inner Ward, just outside the Volod's Great Hall. My dragon touched down carefully, vibrating with nervous energy as we detached Cutthroat's harness and let the irate hookwing drop to the ground. The castle grounds smelled like cordite and burned plastic.

"Ahh, smell that fragrant exhaust!" Masha remarked, covering her nose with a cloth. "A healthy dose of pollution for everyone, with the fleet hanging right over the damn castle!"

"Yeah, it stinks." Suri slid down, then caught Cutthroat by her reins. "C'mon, you."

"HSSSSSS!" The hookwing stopped preening her chest and snapped at her, jaws clopping barely inches from Suri's nose.

"Oi!" Suri flinched back. She jerked Cutthroat's head down with the reins and bopped her on the snout. "What was that for?"

"Ssss." Cutthroat hissed, petulantly this time, and resumed trying to put her ruffled feathers back in place.

"What's up her ass?" I asked once I was on the ground.

"Dunno. Whatever it is, she'll get over it as soon as they take her to the stables and get some food into her. She's been eatin' like a starving wolverine." Suri jerked her chin toward the door. "Head's up: we've got company."

Ignas' Court Mage, Simeon, strode purposefully toward us at a fast clip, dodging the people rushing back and forth through the corridors that intersected the Royal Court. He jogged down the stairs from the great hall to the garden and pulled up in front of Karalti, slightly winded.

"Welcome back to Taltos, Voivode Dragozin, Voivodzina Ba'hadir." He bowed from the neck to each of us. "And welcome also, Journeyman Lu, Masterhealer, and...?"

"Nethres of Gilheim," Nethres awkwardly bowed back. "A Valkyrie. I was confirmed by Ragnhildr Olafson of the Gothi. Now a Captain serving the Ilian Kingsmen."

"One of Prince Illandi's royal partisans?" Simeon arched his thin eyebrows.

She nodded. "He gave me leave to come here. Contact Hector, maybe advise Vlachia on what we know of Hyland's troop movements."

While they talked, I discreetly stepped out in front of Karalti, covering her as she polymorphed down to her human shape and equipped her gear.

"That would be useful information indeed, and truth be told, we need any advantage we can find. His Majesty, nor I or anyone else here at court ever dreamed we'd go to war with a Starborn-led Ilia. Your kind were a myth only a generation ago, and now there are hundreds of you." The slender man fixed his piercing eyes skyward, looking up. The Dreadnaught had left the Parade Ground and was passing overhead, darkening the entire courtyard with its T-shaped shadow. "Come. Time is short."

"I will not be attending. There is no role for me in military matters such as these. My work comes after the dying starts." Masha gave us all a small, grim smile. "If his Majesty has need of my services, you know where to find me, Simeon."

"Of course, Masterhealer. I trust you will find the hospital is in good order." He gave her a small, ironic bow. "Someone will be along to take care of your hookwing, Voivodzina. Leave her here, and follow me."

"You sure about that?" Suri glanced at Cutthroat, who was alternating preening under her winglet, and hissing and biting at her own arm in irritation at... well... herself.

Simeon regarded the huge hookwing for a moment. "We can sedate her, if necessary. It wouldn't be the first time. Come."

Before Suri could frame any hookwing roofie-related questions, Simeon swept back up the stairs. I had more than a little great hall size envy as we crossed the black-and-white marble lobby, turned through a side door, and down the corridor toward the donjon. A mana-powered cage elevator was waiting for us.

"This castle has freaking elevators. I still can't believe Vlachia doesn't have parachutes," I muttered, as the metal lattice doors clanged shut.

Nethres gave me an odd look. "They don't?"

"They do now, because we invented them." Rin said with a touch of pride. "I'm going to sell the patent to Ignas. That'll net me a lot of EXP, skill points, and some recurring income, so that I can buy more materials and we can invent more stuff!"

"Huh." Suri gripped my arm as the elevator—and our stomachs—lifted sharply. "Always wondered how crafters levelled without much or any combat. Selling new inventions... makes sense."

"That's the mana economy for you." Rin wagged her head happily. "Invent, patent, license, then reap the royalties. Rinse and repeat until you're rich!"

At the top floor of the tower, the sound of arguing drifted to our ears from behind the fine double doors leading into the War Room. Simeon knocked, waited until the voices stopped, and then ushered us inside.

Ignas stood at the end of a great mahogany table, his hands planted down on a pile of notes and maps. There were four others gathered around, but I recognized only two: Ebisa, his bodyguard and unofficial assassin, was seated to Ignas' left. My fellow Voivode, Janos Lanz of Czongrad, was standing to his right. Ebisa wiggled her long fingers at us, the other arm folded over her thin, flat chest. Count Lanz flashed us a look of borderline disgust, like someone had just farted under the table and he'd caught a whiff.

"Voivode, Voivodzina. Karalti." Ignas came around the table, shook my hand, and drew me into a brief hug. Suri got a firm soldier's handshake. Karalti smiled and extended her fingers to him. He took them gently, and briefly pressed his forehead to the back of her knuckles before turning to Rin. "And Journeyman Rin Lu: A pleasure to see you again, as always."

"Th-thank you." Rin stammered as he politely kissed the back of her hand and guided her to a seat.

When Rin was situated, Ignas turned back. He regarded Nethres with cool interest. "And who is this?"

"Nethres. She's a partisan with the Kingsmen," I said. "Ilian resistance. She claims she has useful information for the war effort."

"I see. A pleasure to make your acquaintance, Nethres, but I must ask you to wait downstairs while we discuss matters of national security. I will, however, grant you a private audience after we are done." Ignas was polite, but crisp: Nethres clearly didn't have any Renown in Vlachia to lean on. "Simeon, please take her to the reading room and make sure she is comfortable. We may be here for some time."

"Of course, your Majesty." Simeon bowed, then looked to Nethres. "Please, my lady: follow me."

"Sure." Nethres shrugged, and obediently followed him back out into the hall.

"Did you check her background before bringing her here?" Ignas asked me.

"No. I figured you'd want to do that yourself, Your Majesty," I said. "She's someone I've known for a while. I met Nethres back in the first round of Trials for entry to the Order of St. Grigori. She didn't pass, but she fought honorably and did not deceive us to gain any advantage. I don't have any reason to think she's lying about being a part of the Resistance. We know for a fact that she has every excuse to hate Hyland and Hart."

"Very well. I will have Ebisa and Rutha look into her," Ignas said. "Until then, she shall remain a closely supervised guest at the castle."

Suri chuffed. "You mean a prisoner."

"The gentlest form of house arrest, more like it. If she is a member of the Kingsmen, Rutha will vouch for her." Ignas regarded her with calm, hard eyes. "We cannot be too cautious. Any leak of intelligence could jeopardize our counter-invasion."

"Understood, sir." I momentarily had the urge to salute, but squashed the feeling down.

"Anyway, thank you all for promptly replying to my summons." He moved back to his place at the head of the table. "This is Count Kopecs, one of the commanders in the Black Army, and Admiral Hartz, the commander of the 2nd Fleet. Voivode Lanz of Czongrad is also a Black Army officer and currently serves as my principal military advisor."

Suri and I inclined our heads to all three of them. Lanz's return bow was barely a fraction of a nod.

"The 2nd Company returned yesterday, just in time to integrate back into the reserve." Ignas gestured to the empty chairs. "Please, take your seats. There is much to discuss."

I studied the centerpiece of the table as I plopped down. One look told me exactly why he was so concerned. Last time we'd been briefed about a mass combat situation in this room, the great table had displayed a diorama of Myszno. Now, it displayed one of Central and Eastern Revala. They'd marked cities and major towns with game pieces, while army positions and controlled settlements were pinned with paper flags of the appropriate color. There were a lot of dark blue and gold flags in the west. They stretched from the Ilian border and formed a salient about two-thirds of the way to Revala's capital city, Lovi. Blue and gold were the colors of the Ilian Empire.

"Baldr's already made it that far?" Suri exclaimed in disbelief, moving to her seat. She didn't sit, leaning on the table to survey the battlefield. "In a month?"

"Yes. Between Revala's excellent system of roads and the dragons and airships at his command, Hyland's forces are already preparing for a push toward Queen Aslan's capital," Ignas said heavily, shaking his head. "We cannot let him advance a single step closer to Lovi, and not only because Revala is close to our own borders. In addition to being one of the breadbaskets of Artana, the region around the capital is also a key site for bluecrystal mining."

Karalti began to fidget with a pair of spare toothpick flags. *"Ooh. That's not good."*

"It really isn't." My mind began to tick over as I stared at the crowd of Ilian flags on the map. "My question is, how did all these positions get taken? What is Ororgael's goal? What are his tactics?"

"Those are three separate questions," Count Lanz said coolly. He was a small, pale man, with calculating eyes the color of fresh dollar bills. Like Ignas, he was also dressed in a fine uniform, though his was black. "Hyland's goal is clear enough: conquer the rest of Artana and bring it under his rule. However, his methods are amateurish. A wise strategist would have conquered the rest of the Hercynian nations to form an army capable of facing the combined might of Vlachia and Jeun. Even if he does take Revala, Gilheim is mobilizing behind the mountains. We will pincer him on both sides. He is an untried fool, Tuun. That is the long and short of it."

"My title is 'Voivode'. If you can't pronounce 'Dragozin', Voivode Tuun is fine, assuming you really need to keep waving your dick at me across the table," I replied tersely.

Suri sucked on a tooth and looked away, biting back a laugh. Ebisa snorted into her hand.

"And as I was saying to my people before, don't underestimate Ororgael," I continued, gesturing at the diorama. "The guy's nearly achieved his objective. This isn't the work of an 'untried fool'."

"We have already discussed this somewhat before your arrival," Ignas said, pretending not to see Lanz's scowl. "Our conclusion is that he plans to conquer Revala, fortify the Eastern border, then use the nation's resources to turn back west and take the offensive to Gilheim."

"Yes. Hyland's move to the east seems audacious, even reckless, but intelligence reports suggest he intends to seal off the Hercyninan Peninsula." General Kovacs spoke up. "As you can see, Revala shares only a small land border with Jeun in the north-east, while it is separated from us by the Bay of Swords. He could ostensibly fortify those positions, claim Revala's resources, then hold us off while he moves west. Cut off from the Alliance, those nations will be sitting ducks."

"Yeah. And he can do it from behind a defensive buffer," Suri said. "Revala as a shield, to protect Ilia while he mops up."

"How many troops is he fielding?" I asked, frowning.

"Roughly a hundred thousand, all counted," Kovacs replied. "Most of them are, shall we say, involuntary volunteers?"

"Slaves," Suri said flatly.

The general nodded. "Yes. In addition, he fields approximately two hundred and seventy dragon knights, and a navy comprising about a hundred ships of various classes."

"And Revala?"

"Revala can call on about two hundred thousand troops, plus a navy of three hundred ships."

"Then how the fuck did they lose all of this?" I gestured to the field of blue and gold flags. "They outnumber Ororgael two to one. Dragons or no dragons, they should have crushed him."

Ignas vented a soft sound of frustration and shook his head. "Ebisa, repeat your report."

"Hyland has made his inroads by two means," Ebisa recited, in her dry, husky voice. "Land vehicles, the likes of which we've never seen before, and the dragons."

"Land vehicles?" Rin perked up, brows furrowing in alarm.

"Yes. They began the campaign by posturing at the border. Then they detonated shells of substantial size and power at the fortresses, smashing walls that have stood for hundreds of years. They must also have had interior intelligence, because the dragons teleported to precise locations, then wreaked havoc on vital supply points. They did not engage directly. They dropped bombs onto granaries, barracks, and other important production centers. Then Ilia's land force rolled in, fielding these what appear to be human-made Sangheti'tak walkers. Blood-fuel machines, which consume the mana gained from biomass."

"Sangheti'tak, in human hands!" Rin covered her mouth.

Ebisa gave her an expressionless nod. "These machines tore up the Revalan cavalry with exceptional speed. With their supply lines destroyed and their retreat cut off, a wave of surrenders followed."

"So now we know what Ororgael was doing during those first couple of months," Suri said, looking over to me, Rin, and Karalti. "Building himself a fuckton of death machines."

"Revala was able to adapt to this strategy and slow them down, at which point, the commander of the Ilian forces changed tactics," Ebisa continued, reaching out to draw her finger over a now-conquered defensive line. "He began deploying the dragons directly against the Revalan Navy. They targeted troop carriers."

"Revala's navy, while impressive for the Hercynian Region, is nowhere as modern as ours," Ignas added. "Most countries field only a few hundred ships, some of them quite old. The dragons were able to fly rings around the Revalan Fleet."

"Yes. And their lightning breath weapons are capable of penetrating and overriding many forms of magical shields," Ebisa said. "Their ships were forced to retreat, while Ilia's advanced. They began bombing the countryside. They reduced entire towns to rubble, and this Commander, Lucien Hart, made public displays of poisoning wells and executing the captive families of those who rebelled against the invaders.

They gave many settlements the chance to surrender, and they did."

I rolled my eyes and tipped my head back. "Okay, and what part of this is 'amateurish' again?"

"My choice of words was not precise," Count Lanz said brittly. "Ilia's tactics are sound, if not brutal. But their campaign cannot sustain this kind of energy for long. Not when they are being attacked on two fronts."

"Then they have a card in play that we don't know about," I said. "Allies? The Princeling Nations are embroiled in some kind of conflict of their own, right? Maybe he's recruited one or more of them. Maybe he's convinced Gilheim he's their prophesied god-man in human form. Maybe he's somehow gotten the fucking Mercurions on board. We don't know."

"I have been trying to make this point for some hours now." Ebisa spread her hands and sat back.

"For the sake of civility, please refrain from cursing at me, Dragozin." Lanz's thin mouth sloped down to one side.

"Oh yeah, because my cursing is the real problem here," I snapped.

"Ebisa. Do we know if Hyland developed these tactics, or was Lucien the mastermind?" Suri held up a hand as the Count's face reddened, and he swelled with an excess of 'civility.'

She inclined her head. "As far as we know, the general strategy was developed by Hyland and his advisors at the highest levels, but the implementation seems to have been left to Commander Hart."

"Then Lucien's gotten smarter," I said grimly. "Much smarter. And he's been studying warfare.

"Power-leveling his mental stats?" Suri asked.

"He must be." I sighed and sat back. "Baldr Hyland served as Powered Armor Infantry in the War, and Ororgael got his memories when he possessed Baldr's body. So that's where the PAUs are coming from."

"P.A.Us?" Ignas asked.

"Powered Armor Units," I replied. "Think of them as like mini Warsingers. You stick a pilot in a big metal suit that is larger, stronger, and more resilient than a normal infantryman. They can field bigger weapons and soak the kind of fire that would send normal soldiers flying across the battlefield in chunks. They're not immortal, so the Army and Marines usually fielded one PAU with a fireteam of two rifles, one marksman, one grenadier or machine gunner. Same strategy as protecting tanks, but the powered armor squads were much smaller and a hell of a lot more maneuverable. Incidentally, that's the tactic I'd use with the Warsinger, too."

"Squads? Fireteams?" Ignas laced his hands, regarding me curiously. "The army in the world you came from, the world of the Architects, deployed soldiers in small groups of four or five?"

"Sure did," I said.

"Hmm." The Volod nodded slowly. "A tactic also used to great effect by the barbarian raiders of the Sathbar Plains."

"That makes sense only if the soldiers are Starborn and can return from the dead," Count Lanz said stiffly. "Barbarian tactics break against fortress walls. We fight in disciplined formations in Vlachia."

"Right, and your disciplined formations lost two-thirds of a country in a month," I quipped back. "We just used maneuver warfare tactics to retake Bas County and execute the robber baron occupying Solonovka in a single night. Less than two hundred of my soldiers reclaimed the castle and capital from an occupying force of over two thousand."

General Kovacs looked to Ignas in disbelief. A wry smile played over Ignas' thin lips, his grey eyes calculating and bright with interest.

"And how many did you lose in this mad gambit?" Count Lanz asked.

"Eighteen," Suri answered.

"Did I mishear you? Eighteen men?" Lanz scoffed. "My liege, do you believe this nonsense?"

"I do. Because I can verify their story," Ignas replied, resting his face against the tips of his fingers. "The Royal Kingdom Management System does not lie, Voivode Lanz. The Lord and Lady of Myszno did indeed stage and succeed in their operation against the deserter, Zoltan Gallo. They deployed barely two hundred souls, drawing from elite Yanik native forces and a Meewfolk mercenary company. They suffered eighteen fatalities, but they slew just under four hundred of Zoltan's men as well as Zoltan himself. The rest surrendered after a brief battle in the city."

At mention of the cat people, the other men at the table grimaced.

"To be honest, I don't think we should assume Ororgael's goals at this stage. We need a solid idea of why he's doing what he's doing," Suri said, after a tense pause. "The fact he has us on the defensive proves there's something we're not seeing."

"Right." I nodded. "He's shown us again and again that he's capable of putting us in a position where we have to try and figure him out, and when we think we've worked out what he wants, he rips the rug out from under us."

Rin glanced nervously at us both, then to Ignas and General Kovacs. "What does Vlachia plan to do?"

"We plan nothing short than a total assault," the general said. "We have overwhelming numbers compared to Ilia. Our soldiers outnumber Ilian forces three to one, which is an ideal situation for a counter-invasion. Our airships are considerably more advanced than Revala's or Ilia's. We have developed defenses against their dragons, and weapons to destroy them."

"DESTROY them?" Karalti rose in alarm, her pupils pinning. *"You can't destroy them! Those are my people!"*

Lanz and the two officers flinched as the telepathic broadcast suddenly intruded into their minds—and then they looked to Karalti, as it dawned on them who and what she was.

"Oh, ehh... apologies, your Holiness. I was not aware you were here." The Admiral cleared his throat.

"They're innocent! Baldr is enslaving my kin with powerful magic, compelling them to fight in this war," Karalti continued, pleading. *"You can't kill them! W-We need to capture them, or... or SOMETHING."*

"My lady, as someone who lost his father to the violent machine of politics, I understand your distress." Ignas' long, lean face was even more graven than usual. "It is neither fair nor just that your people are being used as slaves to fight a despot's war. But we cannot change the fact that the dragons crushed Queen Aslan's supply lines, her garrisons, and her villages and farmland. They will destroy us if given the chance. We must face them without flinching—and we will. It is the cold mathematics of war."

I sighed heavily. "I'm sorry, Karalti. He's right."

"But..." Karalti searched our faces, her own expression crumpling. *"There isn't any way?"*

"There has to be some way to stun dragons without killing them," Rin said. "A sonic weapon could do it."

"We have no such technology, and no time to develop it," Ignas replied. "The knowledge that we must battle the children of the Nine pains me more than words can express. Your people are sacred to us, and I can only hope that you and the gods can forgive us once all is said and done. If you cannot bear to continue this conversation, you may leave the meeting without shame."

I reached for Karalti's hand, hoping to comfort her, but she jerked it away before I even so much as brushed her fingers. She turned and stalked from the room, slamming the door behind her.

"She's a Queen dragon," I said, before anyone could make any snide remarks. "The dragons of the Eyrie are her brothers and sisters. They were all born of the same mother."

"She can't command them because of the curse placed upon her relatives, correct?" Ignas asked me.

"Yeah." I struggled with the urge to kick the underside of the table. "We were planning to try and find some way to break the geas before it came to this, but we're just not strong enough yet."

"Then the best thing we can do is to fight to win as quickly as possible." Suri cocked her chin toward the map. "Do that, and we minimize casualties on both sides. There's only a single company of dragons, and as soon as Lucien figures out that Vlachia can stand toe to toe with them, he'll pull them back out of the firing line."

"That is our hope." Ignas nodded. "Our goal at this juncture is to remove Lucien Hart, then push his forces back through sheer attrition. The Ilian army is as motivated as they are, in part, because their leaders are immortal. If we capture their leader and they scatter as a result, they will be overwhelmed by our numbers."

"He's Starborn, though," Rin said. "You can't kill him."

"Obviously not. We will imprison him. We may even smuggle him to your castle, if you have a spare cell."

"I will be more than happy to brick him up in Kalla Sahasi and pass him food through a slot for the rest of his miserable life," I said.

"Excellent. And I will send a work crew to assist." Ignas paused to chuckle. "We have reinforcements coming from Dakhdir and Jeun. A massive show of force will put Hyland in his place, at least for a time: long enough for us to send aid to Gilheim and the Princeling Nations of Hercynia."

"I don't know if relying on Dakhdir for anything is a good idea," I replied. "Sultir whats-his-face is crazier than a shithouse rat. Violetta, who leads the Mata Argis as Baldr's other lieutenant, was there with her agents. They're feeding the Sultir's fear of being deposed by Suri."

"Deposed? By a Fireblooded?" General Kovacs gave her a curious look. "No offence, my Lady, but the Fireblooded are of low status in Dakhdir. Why should he be concerned about you?"

"She IS Starborn," Count Lanz said drily.

"I'm the direct descendant of Queen Sachara Ha'Shazir," Suri replied, ignoring Lanz. "The dynasty overthrown four generations ago in a bloody coup by the Sultir's ancestors."

"Ah. Yes. Well, I can see how that would lead to anxiety." The general's doughy face creased into thoughtful lines. "We do know that Khemmemu is an unstable man. It has been an issue ever since he inherited the throne. If the Mata Argis are there, your Majesty, can we be certain Dakhdir will honor the terms of the Alliance?"

"We have spies and influencers in the Sultir's court as well. If he reneges on the Alliance, he knows that Jeun and Vlachia will level devastating trade sanctions," Ignas said. "Dakhdir is mostly wasteland. Without Vlachian food and Jeun mana, the Sultir's people will starve. He is nervous, but not foolish. We can always sell our surplus to Jeun, or with our new long-range airships, even to Lys."

"I'm worried about this," I said. "Something about the situation feels off to me. Baldr and Lucien are setting something up. They have to know that the Alliance will respond with their fleets in force. They have to expect this response. So why is a small military force inviting a counter invasion?"

"He's right," Rin said. "Strategically speaking, it would only make sense for him to invade Revala if he thought he had some kind of edge."

"He is vastly outnumbered and outgunned. He is also overconfident in his dragons and his fancy Mercurion toys," Count Lanz said dismissively. "There is no grand strategy in his invasion of Revala. Had he gone west, he might have stood a chance at consolidating an empire that would be of serious threat to the combined might of Jeun, Vlachia, and Dakhdir. But Hyland and Hart are not thinking that far ahead. They are both drunk on the power of being immortal. Why should they care if they lose once or twice? They always have time to wait and try again. They think of themselves as gods. "

"Literally," I said, shooting Lanz a dark look. "Baldr is the figurehead of the Cult of the Architect. You know, the cult that Andrik was part of?"

My rival Voivode grimaced. "Indeed."

"Your Majesty: please tell me you're not going into the area of operations yourself." Rin looked to Ignas. "Something isn't right about this. It feels like a setup."

"Unfortunately, I must. A king does not shelter behind his men: he leads. But what is your opinion, Kovacs?" Ignas looked to his general.

General Kovacs hummed. "It is my opinion that the risk of your participation in the battle is within acceptable limits. With Ebisa standing unsleeping by your side, assassination is unlikely. We are taking all precautions, and Hyland simply doesn't have the numbers to face us head on."

"He won't face you head on," I said, more urgently. "He'll maneuver around you and strike at something important. It might not even be Ignas who's at risk. It might be Taltos."

"Parliament and His Majesty voted this morning: I will be acting regent while Vlachia is at war, and I assure you that I will not permit any harm to come to my city," Count Lanz said. "The First Fleet is on standby to defend Taltos."

"We should have been at that vote." Suri's eyes narrowed.

"You were campaigning in Bas, and thus unavailable." Count Lanz gestured dismissively. "Your own Steward, Istvan Arshak, filed a Leave of Absence due to your being engaged in mass combat operations."

"Legit." I scratched the side of my nose. "Well, Your Majesty, I guess the only question now is what role you want us to play. You summoned us for a reason."

"Yes. The Warsinger." Ignas sat back in his chair, one leg crossed over the other knee. "I need a report."

"Well, we found her. Withering Rose was sleeping in Dakhdir. She was still in good condition, worked just fine until it ran out of mana." Suri replied. "And after it fell over from lack of fuel, Baldr Hyland showed up to personally ruin our day."

General Kovacs straightened. So did Ebisa and the Admiral.

"Implying...?" Ignas gestured to her.

"Withering Rose is a wreck." Suri's expression turned stormy. "Ororgael called some super-beam magic from the sky and cored out part of the Warsinger. The pieces of it are lying all over the Bashir Desert."

"Pieces? Khors' hammer, that is not good news." Ignas' brow furrowed. "If it was so easily destroyed, perhaps the machines' power was overstated?"

"No, it's not. At full operational capacity, the Warsinger is incredible. We all saw Suri unleash some kind of energy weapon that killed eight or nine sandworms in one strike," Rin said. "A three-thousand-year-old machine, with less than 2% fuel and less than 5% integrity, and it shredded those sandworms like they were nothing. It was... awe-inspiring."

Suri pressed her lips together in a tight, stubborn line.

"That is... there is no weapon on Archemi capable of such an act." Ignas looked to his officers, who looked almost as awed as he did. "Stunning. If we get the pieces, can it be fixed?"

Rin nodded eagerly. "We—and by that, I mean, me and Lord Soma and the Engineers College of Litvy—need more information on how they're constructed. He's been trying to reverse-engineer the prototype Warsinger we captured, but has had no success so far. The construction and magical encoding is just so alien compared to current artificing. But if we could figure this out, then the possibilities are endless. We could create airship or ground weapons that make use of their technology, for example, or rediscover principles of metallurgy lost in time."

"Indeed. If this Warsinger is capable of such power, we must have it," Ignas said. "That is what I ask of you all now."

"Ororgael has part of it, we think," I said. "But..."

"Hey, before you keep going, don't say anything more about what happened to W.R." A text PM from Rin popped up in my HUD, narrated aloud when I noticed it. *"I have an idea."*

"But?" Ignas quirked an eyebrow.

"But we can replace the part," I said quickly. "So it shouldn't be an issue."

"Excellent. Know that you have our full support." Ignas bowed from the neck. "Let me issue you some added incentive."

[You have a new Quest: Bounty—The Warsingers]

I opened the quest and let Navigail read it aloud.

New Bounty: The Warsingers

Ignas Corvinus II, the Volod of Vlachia, is offering a substantial bounty for the safe return of the Warsingers to Vlachian soil. Complete this bounty by salvaging the Warsingers or their key components and returning them to Vlachia.

Rewards: *20,000 olbia and 5000 EXP per Warsinger.*

I whistled. "Damn, man... thanks."

"This is the maximum bounty the system allows me to offer," Ignas said. "That alone should tell you how important I consider the retrieval of these artifacts to be. Hyland is fielding soldier-piloted versions of these machines, and it's a matter of time before he improves this technology and normal infantry becomes obsolete. We need to outpace his advancements."

Lanz's eyes flicked to Ignas. "Infantry? Obsolete? With all respect, Your Majesty, that seems a bit extreme."

Ignas shook his head. "I fear it is not."

"There's always a need for boots on the ground, but yeah. It's a risk." I cast one final look down at the map, making sure I had a copy of it in my HUD. "We'll see what we can do. To be honest, though, we probably need a fleet ourselves. A Stranged Sandworm is guarding the Warsinger. The damn thing is Level 120."

"You've pulled off two military miracles in the time I've known you. With Rin at your side, I believe you will find a way to defeat it and claim Lady Suri's birthright." Ignas watched us as Rin got to her feet. "But no matter what, the four of you must get that Warsinger and keep it out of Hyland's hands. The Gods shudder to think what this Architect could do with such power in his possession."

CHAPTER 31

Once we were outside the War Room, it felt like a dark cloud lifted from over our heads. Rin took a deep breath. Suri rubbed her face.

"I think you're onto something," Suri said. "What Lucien and Ororgael are doing just doesn't sit right."

"Yeah. My jimmies are definitely rustled," I said. "But we either don't have enough wealth or renown to convince Ignas' officers more than we already have right now. I'm not sure that Lanz is really on Team Ignas."

Suri glanced at the door and switched to our group PM. "No?"

"He was tight with Andrik," I replied, on the same channel. "And he seemed pretty bent on trying to minimize how smart Ororgael really is."

"I noticed that, too," Rin said. "What can we do?"

"You can speak to Ebisa," I replied. "Maybe see if she has time to look into Lanz's connections, and see whether he's connected to Ororgael in some way. I don't want to single him out, but something was off about his attitude."

"Okay. I'll ask her when we have some time together." Rin rocked between her heels and toes, looking up at the ceiling. "So anyway, the reason I stopped you from telling Ignas what happened to Withering Rose is because I think I have a solution for how to rebuild the Warsingers. We need to go and find a language tutor for the Meewfolk tongue. You know, before we go to Meewhome."

"Wait... before we go to Meewhome?" Suri tilted her head, her hands planted on her hips. "I don't think anyone asked me about this."

"No, but that's where we're going to find Perilous Symphony," Rin said fussily. "It's marked as being just off the coast of Meewhome, on the Chorus Vault map we found in the Temple of the Maker. I need to see if I can study some more Old Agatic... if I could read it fluently, then I might be able to get more information out of those screenshots we took in the Rose Vault."

"Sorry, you've lost me, too." I squinted. "Roll back a bit. Why do you want to go to the Chorus Vault of Perilous Symphony?"

Rin struggled to find her words: her brain was on a fixed track, like a train, and I could almost see the gears turning as she grappled with what she was actually trying to communicate.

"Uhh.. uhh... well, sandworms are weak to sonic weapons, as far as I know. T-Though we'll need to confirm that," she stammered. "We should go to the Royal Library to learn more about them. But, um, anyway, we're going to need to defeat the corrupted sandworm queen guarding Withering Rose, right? I don't know if you remember, but when we were in the Rose Vault, there were nine Warsinger statues."

"I remember," I said. Suri nodded her agreement.

"Right! Well, they all had descriptions, and the description at the base of Perilous Symphony noted it had especially powerful sonic weapons," Rin continued brightly. "If we raid that vault, we check off three problems at once. We get spare parts for Withering Rose, and maybe a new Heartstone to install in her. We might get sonic weapons we can mount on airships and use to defeat the sandworm. We also might also be able to configure sonic weapons to stun dragons instead of killing them outright. More generally, I think it's possible the Meewfolk have records of the Warsingers we don't. But we won't know until we go there and actually speak to their sages."

Suri blinked at her.

"Okay, now it makes sense." I bit back a laugh. "You generally communicate that stuff first, *then* suggest we go to Meewhome."

"Oh, sorry. I-I got carried away again." Rin's cheeks flushed. "It just seemed kind of obvious to me."

"I dunno. Meewhome is a long ways away, and we don't have much time. Baldr conquered two-thirds of Revala in a month. If we take a week to go to Meewhome and dick around without knowing what we'll find there, we might lose the whole bloody country." Suri wrinkled her nose. "I don't even know if humans are able to travel to Meewhome. I've heard they've got some kind of magical protection that keeps invaders off their island."

Rin bounced on the spot. "They are very insular, yes. Very different to the Meewfolk who live on the mainland. And humans *can* travel there, I'm sure of that. I don't know a huge amount about their culture, but I believe they like to host smugglers."

"'Host' smugglers?" I squinted at her.

"They consider theft and smuggling to be artforms," Rin said briskly. "Ebisa would know more. Don't worry about it, though—it will be tricky to find passage, but leave it to me. I can arrange a way there."

Suri chuckled. "The Nightstalkers come to mind."

"Yep!" Rin laced her hands behind her, rocking on her heels. "We shouldn't talk about them in the castle, though."

"Okay." I heaved a sigh. "Jeez... I don't know. I keep thinking back to what Ebisa told us, about Lucien's fucking slaughtering families and villages in Revala. I feel like we should be back in Myszno preparing in case Ororgael or Lucien tries to raid. Their dragons can teleport, too. I don't want to go all the way to Meewhome, then come back and find everyone slaughtered and my castle burned to the ground."

"Ignas wouldn't issue you this quest if there wasn't some reason for it," Rin urged. "This is an RPG. Coincidences like that don't happen in Archemi. Besides, the money and EXP he's offering us for the retrieval of just key components would be a huge benefit for us."

"Why Meewhome, though?" Suri asked. "Why not the Chorus Vaults in Vlachia and Jeun, or the Dragon Gate in

Zaunt? The Mercurions are the best Artificers in the world. Surely they'd have information on them."

"Because I really don't think Mercurions built the Warsingers," Rin said. "The Mercurions certainly didn't win the war against the Drachan, because we weren't even invented back then. We were created by the Aesari to fight in their war against the humans and dragons, based on technology from an earlier era."

"Then why was that Mercurion-made Dark Zarya thing in the Rose Vault?" I asked.

"That's a good question." Rin stood up on her toes, her gaze wandering over the patterns on the ceiling. "My theory is that Mercurions and humans *restored* the Warsingers. Withering Rose was used by the last two Triads to re-energize the Caul of Souls and keep the Drachan sedated. Five thousand years ago, only three races lived on Archemi: The Solonkratsu, the Aesari, and the Meewfolk. Of them all, only the Meewfolk had the kind of knowledge, wealth and infrastructure to build these machines. They might have had help from the others, but the clue for me is in the materials the crafters used. Both Withering Rose and Nocturne Lament are primarily constructed of a magically augmented aurum super-alloy. The ONLY source for aurum in Archemi is the Shalid. Before the Aesari became a global empire, they lived in Daun. The cradle of Meewfolk civilization was the Shalid, which is where the Warsingers were first built and deployed."

"Huh. I figured the Aesari built them." I frowned, thinking. "They LOOK like Aesari magitech. They used a lot of aurum in their old cities."

"More accurately, Aesari magitech looks like the Warsingers," Rin replied. "Everything they built, they learned—or stole—from the Meewfolk and the dragons. We need to look up more histories to know for sure, but I'm eighty percent sure Meewhome is our best chance for finding schematics or information on the construction and magic we need. If we can pull it off, there will be a second technological revolution in Vlachia. More importantly, we'll prevent Ororgael from enacting that revolution himself."

Suri and I looked at each other.

"The fact he's developed sangheti'tak himself is really worrying." Rin worried her lip with her teeth, pacing. "He must have the help of a player crafter we don't know about. A-A Weaponeer, or some kind of automaton specialist."

"Nicolas," Suri said heavily. "He's an Artificer who specializes in machines and weaponry. And an Architect."

"Maybe, maybe not. There's two thousand Starborn here, and you can bet at least a hundred picked crafting Paths. It could be anyone." I shook my head. "Look, if we can get to Meewhome within a week, I'm game. Visiting the Rose Vault opened up a huge amount of information for us. Each Chorus Vault and Dragon Gate probably contains pieces of the puzzle we need to solve—how to defend Archemi against the Drachan."

"Yeah." Suri still sounded uncertain. "It just feels like such a long shot."

"It is. But it's what we've got," Rin said. "Let me go speak to Ebisa about passage to Meewhome. And then meet me in the Royal Library?"

"I'll pass. I've got a side-quest to take care of," Suri replied. "I know some people in Taltos who can teach me how to speak cat."

Rin's smile faded slightly. She flashed me a look of appeal.

"Sure. I'll come. Can always stand to practice my reading." I planted my hands on my hips and stretched my back. "I have to go check in with Karalti first, but I can meet you there."

"Great!" Rin beamed, then abruptly turned and scuttled back off down the corridor toward the War Room.

"She's an odd one." Suri heaved a tired sigh. "You really think this is a good idea?"

"If an engineer spots a way to nail three problems with one solution, I believe them," I said. "And Ignas is right. Even if we never end up using the Warsingers to stage giant kaiju fights, we need to keep them out of Ororgael's clammy little hands. Or Lucien's. Fuck... Imagine if Lucien fucking Hart figured out how to build Warsingers before we did?"

"Yeah. I honestly wonder why Ororgael didn't take Withering Rose with him. Maybe it was just too big." Suri frowned. "Like I said before, though. Something's going on in Camp Ororgael. Something we're not seeing. I just can't put my finger on what."

"Same. And it worries me." I nodded. "We have to play defense until we spot the gap in Ororgael's plans. But we also have to be ready to strike—and for that, we need power. Experience, weapons, resources."

Suri was about to reply, but paused as we both got a ping in our HUDs at the same time: the KMS, sending us an alert.

[Your Steward has deposited 871,809 gold olbia into the Myszno Treasury!]

I blinked a couple of times. "Navigail, please read that number again to make sure I heard you right."

[Sure! Your Steward has deposited 871,809 gold olbia into the Myszno Treasury. Your Kingdom has 891,941 olbia. Use the Kingdom Management System to assign money toward investments, projects, and staff.]

"So uh... guess Vash's expedition is doing alright," Suri croaked. "How about you and I go do some shopping later on? Get yourself some new armor."

"Hell yeah." I found myself grinning from ear to ear. "I'm pretty sure we can spare the change. I have to check in with Karalti first, and then I'll meet Rin for some nerd time."

"And after that?"

I bowed and flourished to her. "After that, I'm all yours."

"You're not *all* mine. But that's okay." Suri's lips quirked, and after a moment's hesitation, she leaned in to kiss me on the cheek before turning and sauntering off, putting a little more twitch in her step than normal. I watched her until she turned the corner, adjusted the seat of my armor, and headed for the balcony.

Outside, I leaned against the railing, closed my eyes, and felt out along the Bond until I found Karalti. When my mind brushed hers, she flinched—like I'd touched a psychic bruise.

"Hey. I know you're not doing great, but we're trying to work something out. We're going to minimize casualties and find a way to deal with Solonkratsu without killing them." I breathed deeply of the frigid mountain air. It was fresher up here, despite the hovering parade of airships. *"I'm sorry."*

"It's... it's okay." She replied after nearly a full minute of silence. *"Really. I think that if Lahati heard that conversation, she would have agreed with you and Ignas. Besides, as long as I exist—free, alive, healthy—then my mother's line will never be extinguished. That's the truth."*

I nodded, mostly to myself.

"I know she's not dead," Karalti insisted. *"Usta, I mean. I can feel her calling to me in her sleep. She wants me to find her, Hector. To save as many of them as I can. I don't know if it's possible, but I have to try."*

"It's possible," I said. *"We might have to go to Meewhome to do it, but it's possible. I'm willing to learn another language for it, too. It's gonna hurt like a bitch. Learning Dakhari sure did."*

"Don't do that yet. I have an idea," Karalti replied. *"You get your memories back when you touch me, right? If I learn the language, then maybe you'll be able to get it from me."*

I tried to think of some way that wouldn't work—but couldn't think of one. *"I'm game. Let's try it."*

"I'll do it later," Karalti said. *"I need some time alone. To hunt… and to take a bath. But I'll be back. And don't worry about me, okay? I'm not going to throw a tantrum or anything. I'm just sad, and I need to feel sad for a while. But after that, I'll be fine."*

"I believe you." I smiled faintly. *"You don't mind if I still call you Tidbit? It's not patronizing?"*

"I'll always be your little Tidbit. And you'll always be my rider. Good luck at the library." She pressed a warm thought toward me, almost like a kiss, and withdrew.

CHAPTER 32

Vulkan Keep's library was built into a large cavern, kept dry by the geothermal warmth that radiated from the belly of Mt. Racosul. What seemed like miles of shelves receded into the depths of the mountain, which was clearly lit by rows of smokeless mage lights. After all the practice I'd been doing in Myszno, I could slowly read the sign at the front check-in desk without help: *'NO pipes, matches, sparks, witchcraft, or loitering'.*

"Oh! Hi, Kythias!" Rin called to the red-haired young man seated at the desk, reading a book with his feet up. He startled at the sound of his name and looked over, and when he saw us, he hurriedly straightened up and set his feet on the floor.

"Rin? You and Count Dragozin know one another?" Kythias glanced between us with sharp, hawkish brown eyes. He was Lysian, like Rutha, but his pointed ears had been docked and rounded to look more human. "What a surprise to see you again, my lord."

"Believe me when I say you will never be as surprised about that as I am." I gave him a flippant salute. "I've got some books to return. And we're here to raid your Meewfolk archives again."

"The locked shelves? Certainly." He gave Rin a sly look. "You've wanted to get your shiny silver nose into that section since you arrived in Taltos. Been making friends in high places, have you?"

"I was Hector's friend before he became a Voivode." Rin stuck her tongue out at him. "It's good to see you again. How's life in Vulkan Keep?"

"Quiet. Which is exactly what I was hoping for after the howling circus that is the Royal College dormitory." Kythias rose, dusting himself down. "I have my own room, my own bed... it's heaven. I thank the Maker every day I no longer have to share a bath."

"You guys know each other?" I asked them.

"Oh! Yes! Kythias used to be a librarian at the Royal College, where Kanzo took me to study," Rin replied, breezing past me into the library. "He was always my favorite. So sassy."

"She only likes me for my devilishly good looks. The eyes, the hair, the rippling washboard abs," Kythias deadpanned, collecting his keys.

"The way you threw out that pair of third-years trying to smoke smashweed in Study Room G," Rin giggled. "I thought you were going to rip those guys in half."

"I have larger, stronger friends for that sort of work." Kythias went and got one of the book carts, wheeling it ahead of Rin toward the back of the library. "And knives. I mean, who needs friends when you can have knives?"

"Here here," I said. "Knife life is best life."

The locked section was basically a prison for books. Behind a barred gate stood seven rows of tall shelves, each one carrying dozens of massive tomes. Each book had thick leather or wooden binding with an iron loop hammered into the spine. A heavy-duty chain ran through them, padlocked at each end of the bookcase. They also smelled amazing: they had books from all over Artana here, but the old Meewfolk books were written in perfumed red ink made from the Dragonsblood tree. It smelled like vanilla and smoke and amber mixed together.

I breathed in deeply. "Man, I love how this place smells."

"Indeed. Like dead trees and flayed baby dolphins," Kythias quipped, as he began to open the padlocks.

"Nooo, don't tell me that!" Rin slapped him as he grinned down at her.

"Very well: no lecture on how dolphin vellum is made. What are you looking for today?" He gestured to the shelves. "I might at least be able to help you both get started."

"We're trying to learn whether the Meewfolk built some historical artifacts, the Warsingers. If they did, we need to learn what happened to the schematics used to make them," I replied. "We also need information on Sandworms. The great big fuckers that live in the Bashir Desert."

"Warsingers?" The archivist frowned, pacing along the shelves. "The suits of armor worn by the gods, during the Fall of the Aesari? Why would you want to look up those old stories?"

Rin bobbed her head. "Because they're real. They predate the Aesari Empire, too. They were built during the Drachan Wars."

Kythias shot her a sharp look. "I find that hard to believe. There are stories of them, but most scholars don't put much stock in the myths."

"Everyone alive in Archemi today owes their survival to the Warsingers and the people who built them," I said, cutting off Rin's wordless stammer. "They turned the tide against the Drachan."

"Hmm. I haven't seen anything about other than vague stories," Kythias said. "They're generally described as being larger than the gods. I don't exactly know how big a god is, but I struggle to see how something of that size made of metal and stone wouldn't just fall apart under its own weight."

"Well, they pulled it off somehow. And now we're trying to figure out how they did it," Rin replied. "I've seen one. It's huge. It could walk in the river below Vulkan Keep and be able to look over the wall of the castle. And it's fast, too: When it was moving, it could fight like a person in armor. A three-hundred-foot-tall person."

Kythias' eyes bugged a little. "I see."

"I don't know if you have any Mercurion books here that mention them, but if so, we'll look at those as well." I gestured to the other shelves.

"You know, we don't actually have many books by Mercurions: mostly because they guard their knowledge the way a provincial lord guards his virgin daughter. Did you know that the Zaunt clans train spies whose only mission is to recover lost knowledge? They regularly assassinate people for books over there." Kythias stopped in front of a huge wooden-backed tome that was almost the size of his torso. "As for sandworms, there may be some mention of them in Shalid bestiaries, and books about the Great Calamity. The Drachan Wars brought the dominion of the cat-people to an abrupt and tragic end. If I'm remembering my history right, the sandworms were part of that decline."

"In what sense?" I crossed my arms, watching Kythias stagger over to the cart and lay the ancient book down as gently as he was able to.

"There is a Meewfolk myth concerning how the sandworms ate the jungle and turned it into desert. When you have a story as specific as that, then generally there's a grain of truth to it." He went back to fetch another tome. "I'm sure we have a bestiary that can tell you more. I'll get that while you set up these books for study. One of these books is a transcription by the Master of the Archives, but the other one is in Old Period Mau."

"That's fine," Rin said. "I took up Translation and Codebreaking skills. I can figure out most languages if I have enough of the script, plus some translation notes."

"Good. Master may have scribed some notes into the margins that you can use." Kythias said. "Assuming your Codebreaking skill is in the Intermediate levels, that is."

I rubbed my hands in anticipation of being absolutely worthless in anything to do with translation or code. "Rin, you used that ability to decipher the Old Agatic script in the Rose Vault. It was hella useful."

"It is! I'm so glad I picked up the Mystic Weaponeer Advanced Path." Rin went over to the first book and cracked the cover. "I was worried it would just be all about bombs and things, but it has four trees, and only one of them is about explosives and projectiles. One tree, Arcane Innovation, has some really cool archeology abilities intended for this exact kind of work. The Drachan and Aesari Wars set this world back by millennia. We have so much to rediscover about magic and technology."

"I still know fuck all about Artificing." I watched on enviously as she scanned the first unintelligible page, then flipped it over and continued reading like it was nothing. "I figured it's all about Crafting mini-games. Seemed like a grind to me."

"I think the artificing classes are definitely more grindy than combat classes. But there's lots of different kinds of artificing," Rin remarked absently. "Some of the rarer Advanced Paths, like airship building, architecture, and metaphysics—those are really technical. But you've also got APs that are just kind of fun and simple, like Combat Alchemist or Jack of All Trades. Artificers really can be anything from a theoretical arcane mathematician to a tomb-raider type character... in any case, the emphasis is always going to be on crafting and discovery."

I laughed. "Arcane Mathematician? Who the hell came up with these classes?"

"No one really 'came up' with them. The game does that itself," Rin said. "It analyzes your brain data and offers you a world-balanced class offering."

I scratched my head. "Huh."

"Alright. Those three should be a good start." Kythias interrupted by thumping a smaller, fatter book onto the cart. "Get started on these, and I'll go see if I can find a Dakhari bestiary."

"Okay! And thanks for these! I'm excited to finally see the locked books!" Rin jittered on her feet, petting the topmost cover.

"I'm excited that anyone actually wants to read them," Kythias replied. "Gods know we spent long enough with the transcriptions. I told my master that if he wanted anyone to read them, we should glue the chapters of a romance novel into every other section to entice people to page through the book."

I mimed stroking an invisible moustache. "Ah yes, I can see it now: '*The Fall of the Meewfolk Empire, Volume 1*, and *My Wet Hot Allosaurus Summer*, compiled into one riveting omnibus'."

"I know. It was a brilliant idea. Future generations would look back on our works and marvel," Kythias sighed. "But much to my regret, Mastersage Nemeth isn't exactly known for his sparkling sense of whimsy."

**

We took the books to an adjacent study, where Rin and I sat shoulder to shoulder for several hours and pored over the four volumes Kythias had picked out for us. If I was being honest, it was more accurate to say that Rin pored over the larger books and took notes with supernatural speed, while I tried to work my way through one five-page entry on sandworms without relying on text-to-speech assistance from Navigail.

"So, good-ish news and some bad news," I remarked to Rin, frowning down at the page in front of me. "If I'm reading this right, then yes, sandworms are vulnerable to sonic attacks. It says they can be chased off by thumpers—that's pretty standard lore for sandworms in a bunch of different books and games—but to actually kill a full-grown worm, you have to be the size of Withering Rose or like... fifty levels higher than them. If you're not a god-tier superweapon, you can still use sonic attacks to soften them up. There's apparently vents or bony protrusions you can knock off that leave the worm more vulnerable."

"What's the bad news?" Rin looked over at me from her notes.

"According to this book, at least, the kind of sonic weapons needed to take out a full-grown sandworm haven't existed since the Aesari Wars," I replied. "It says here that the Aesari almost wiped out the sandworms, because the worms desertified the entire Shalid region and were threatening to spread north. But after the war had passed and the Aesari died out, sandworms began reappearing in the Bashir. They only stick to that one place now, but they make travelling over the desert dangerous and they prohibit the formation of settlements."

"Mmm. Well, I'm sure we can figure something out. A small army has an adjusted level higher than a single Level 120 monster." Rin closed the book she was reading and sighed. "These books don't have any information on the Warsingers to speak of. I've learned a lot about Meewfolk history, though. The Meewfolk were nearly annihilated by the Drachan and Aesari Wars, just like the Solonkratsu. The damage was so severe that their historians can only speculate on the scale of the destruction."

"Then I'm not convinced there's any schematics left to find," I said. "Wars can wipe out entire cultures."

"I have faith they still exist, because I did find one important lead in these volumes, and that's the Avatar of the Meewfolk." Rin lay her silvery hand on top of the cover.

"Are they blue and nine feet tall?" I asked. "My grandpa showed me an old flat-screen movie called Avatar that had huge blue cat people in it once. I may or may not have decided I wanted to become a dragon rider because of that film."

"Huh?" Rin picked at her lip. "Umm... no. The Avatar isn't blue. They're hairless, actually, according to these books. Every now and then, a child is born without fur, and they consider those children to be sacred. They're trained as knowledge keepers in a special temple. This book says that the knowledge of the Meewfolk must always be written on skin. For lesser knowledge, such as these books, preserved dolphin skin is sufficient, but the Meewfolk inscribe their deepest knowledge and secrets on the living skin of the Avatars, passed from generation to generation. Meewfolk have a deep taboo against tattooing, but these knowledge keepers seem to be an exception. When they wrote these books about five hundred and a hundred and fifty years ago, they recorded that the Avatar line has remained unbroken since the time of the Drachan."

"Huh." I looked down at the books curiously. "Riiiight. So the Avatar might have the schematics. They might even have the blueprints written on them."

"Yes. Exactly!" Rin wiggled happily. "I think we'll be able to find instructions for the Warsinger if we can get access to the current Avatar. To do that, I guess we'll have to go there and find out how."

"Right," I said. "And you think we'll be able to replace the part that Ororgael took from Withering Rose? The Heartstone?"

"Maybe? I know those stones contain the spirit of a Drachan, but not much more than that. The phenomenon of binding spirits into phylacteries isn't something that's done very often nowadays." Rin said. "And why use a Drachan to provide animation for the Warsingers, anyway? That's such a weird choice for the engine core. There's just so much we don't know."

I grunted. "I'm worried that Ororgael has found some way to let the Drachan out of Withering Rose's Heartstone. Even one of those motherfuckers would be devastating at this stage, if he unleashed it on an unprepared world."

"I don't see how he could. If it's just a Drachan's spirit or essence in that thing, then it should be absorbed into the Caul of Souls if it's released." Rin jogged her feet under the edge of the desk, jittering with nervous energy. "Anyway, we won't have a solution until we go see someone who can answer our questions, and it looks like our best shot is the current Avatar of Meewhome. I'll go speak with Ebisa and see if I can arrange passage for us. It might cost us a lot, but if anyone knows how to get an audience with someone as important as the Avatar, it's her."

CHAPTER 33

With the first round of money sitting in the KMS, it was time to do something I'd wanted to do for months: clean out my Inventory, replenish all my necessary tools, and get better gear. While Rin went to go deal with Ebisa, Suri and I linked up and hit the markets.

The best place to get gear tips in Taltos was at the Temple of Khors. Most Vlachians worshipped Khors exclusively, relegating the other gods of the Nine to support roles or ignoring them as myths. The God of the Forge had temples, a university, faith-militant training centers, and countless workshops in the city. Suri and I both had a pretty good reputation with the priests, thanks to our role in solving the murders of several members of clergy. We were able to speak to the new Arch-Smith, add some new map markers to our HUD, and set off without wasting a whole lot of time.

We went to pick up weapons for Suri first, at a player-run store named Bear's Anvil. Bear, an Artificer, was more than happy to sell Suri a new Very Large Sword™, a black-edged blade with a red-bound hilt named Warmonger's Misery. It packed 677-714 damage, and it gave Suri an extra 3% head-chopping bonus that stacked with her vorpal combat ability, Gorgon Overdrive. He also tried to sell her a scale-mail bikini that had more AC than her full plate. I was keen, but Suri wasn't buying.

After that, we rode Cutthroat to the Tanner's District, to an obscure little Mercurion armor boutique that was little more than a market stand in front of a much larger smithy and workshop. Suri stayed behind with Cutthroat at a public stable, letting her gorge on meat to her heart's content while I walked to the store.

"Welcome!" Our salesman was human, judging by the warm brown color of his hands, though he wore the robes, concealing enchanted mask and large flat basket hat that was the typical outdoor wear of a Mercurion civilian. "Looking to buy?"

"Yeah. And looking to trade in," I said. "I've got a ton of pelts, metal, and even some mana for sale or trade. I'm also looking for new armor. Good armor, suitable for someone who does a lot of flying."

"Flying?" He eyed the Nizari Suit with a critical eye. "A quazi rider?"

"Dragon," I said.

"Ohh! You're him! The dragon knight who attends the court of the Volod!" The man clasped his hands together.

"Count Dragozin, at your service." I twirled a hand and bowed. "This is the workshop of Master Armorer Yaola Tlaxi'Zanya, right?"

"Yes, my lord." The salesman bowed from the waist. "The Master Armorer does not serve customers directly unless they require a custom piece, so let us see if we have something you already like before we fetch her. We can take care of your materials sales, first." He gestured in the air, working his HUD with his hands. "Let's see here..."

I was able to unload a lot of Inventory space: selling my old pieces of armor and unused weapons for scrap. When it was time to buy, I had a look over the options, but didn't see anything that was exactly what I wanted. At that point, the checkout guy went and got the smith—a small, fine-boned Mercurion with a smooth, soft voice.

"Describe your combat needs to me," the smith, Yaola, asked me as she led me back into her workshop.

"High mobility. I do a lot of jumping around," I said. "Armor that provides speed, stealth, or evasion bonuses, but something heavier than what most Rogue Path classes would need. I can wear metal, I just don't want it to clatter when I'm flying or moving."

"Hmm. The Dragoons almost exclusively request leather and chain hauberks, so that is what I sell outside." Yaola crossed her arms, looking around. "Are you an open-minded man?"

"Not so open-minded that I'd let my brains fall out, but I'm willing to try almost anything once."

"Then let me show you something." Yaola stopped in front of an empty armor stand, went into her Inventory, and began equipping pieces onto the dummy. First up were a pair of metal boot sheaths with a bladed ridge on either side of the square toe, perfect for those times when you wanted to kick someone in the junk and castrate them at the same time. The boots climbed up into elegant thigh-length greaves that were made to fit over leggings or close-fitting breeches. The cuirass was a form-fitting suit of interlinking, diamond-shaped mail that strongly resembled dragon scales. There was a layer of solid plate over the most important vitals: neck, chest, spine and kidneys. The gauntlets matched the boots, with spiked knuckles and reinforced protection over the hands.

"Huh. Neat. How does this work?" I rubbed a finger over the raised diamond mail. It was one of the weirdest designs for flexible armor I'd ever seen. The pieces didn't overlap, like scale armor: they fit together like a tessellation.

By way of reply, Yaola took a dagger from her workbench, braced the mannequin around the back with her other arm, and forcefully stabbed the dummy in its belly several times. The scales bowed, contracting into a wide depression around the point of the knife. It diffused the impact almost completely, and the blade didn't penetrate.

"I took a very fine looking-glass and studied the armor of small ocean creatures known as chitons to create this. Their armor is some of the finest in the natural world," she said proudly. "It is my own patented design. Here. Try it."

I took the knife and did my best to gut the dummy. I was not successful: it was like ramming the knife into dense putty; the steel didn't even scratch the armor. "Well, damn. Can it stop bullets?"

"It reduces the damage caused by bullets substantially. In fact, that is what I designed it to do. As time marches on, I predict that warfare will be ruled by two factors: the bullet and the sky. He who fields the best air power and the strongest firearms will triumph." Yaola drew themselves up tall, hooking their thumbs in their belt. "I call this the Stormrider armor. It is an innovation in protective technology, though I have struggled to convince the Black Army command of this fact."

"Why?" I took my Spear and poked the armor with the tip, testing it against the razor sharp bluesteel point. "I'd be shitting myself with delight if I was a general, and someone came to me with stab-proof armor that could stop a musket round."

"Two issues," Yaola grunted. "I am an artisan, not a saleswoman. I must hire others to do that work. And second, there is a lot of red tape. The army is led by a cabal of old lords who think the same way they did fifty years before. I swear every soldier must visit a scribe and file paperwork to take a shit on their Royally approved toilet seats, which must have been reviewed and expressly approved by the Volod. Innovation is slow to gain traction in a bureaucracy."

"Jeez. Tell me about it." I winced.

"However. If a popular and prominent human lord were to wear it into battle and report its efficacy to the Royal Court, that would be of great benefit, both to me and to the soldiers whose lives this armor could save," the smith continued. "I would be willing and able to reward you if you were to test the armor, and drop a kind word in His Majesty's ear."

"You don't have to do that, but sure." I jumped as a new Quest Alert chirped in my HUD.

[New Side-Quest: Field Research.]

New Side-Quest: Field Research

Yaola Tlaxi'Zanya, one of the Master Armorers of Taltos, has requested that you test her new flexible chiton-scale armor, an innovation in materials development the Royal Army has been slow to consider. To receive your reward, report your results back to Volod Ignas Corvinus II after surviving three combat engagements while wearing this armor.

Rewards: *500 EXP, Armor Upgrade.*

I mentally swiped for 'Yes' and walked around the armor stand, studying the back as I listened. The armor had articulated titanium down the spine, testament to the fact that quazi riders—and dragon riders—were more likely to be struck on the back or sides while in the air. "No helmet?"

"No. I am working on a design," Yaola said. "It has to be economical enough to be viable, but sophisticated enough to protect soldiers from firearm injuries to the head. I am researching ways to make a sightglass or sightsteel visor that can withstand the impact of a bullet."

I rubbed my thumb over the mail. It was so smooth that it almost felt slick to touch. "Are there magical add-ons or material enhancements you can make?"

"Certainly. Though they are expensive. To improve the physical protection, I will need you to field-test the armor before I can judge which metals will work best for improving it." The smith folded their arms over their chest. "You can browse the store menu for magical enhancements."

I brought up the Armor stats and had a look over what I was signing myself up for:

Stormrider Scale Armor

570 Armor
+30% Damage Reduction from falls or Bludgeoning weapons
+35% Resistance to Piercing Damage
-15% chance of vital or mortal blows landing on the wearer.
Special: Unarmed strikes made against enemies deal lethal, instead of non-lethal damage.
Medium Armor
Body Slot
100% Durability
Level Required: 25
Price: 1100 gold Olbia
An experimental armor design which relies on precisely machined scales woven into an interlocking matrix. This armor offers exceptional piercing and bludgeoning resistance, but is very expensive due to the expertise required to create it.

The Stormrider armor was easily the best suit I'd seen since arriving in Archemi. Just the body, gloves and boots had more armor than the entire Raven Suit. I opened my HUD and queried the Store Menu. The Buy and Sell Windows opened up to my right, displaying all the different purchases I could make. I surfed to the Modifications and Add-Ons section and read through them.

"Elemental air, light and water protection covers lightning, doesn't it?" I asked.

"Yes, my lord." The smith inclined her head.

Each elemental enchantment cost 50 olbia per 5% enhancement, to a maximum of 30% total resistance. There was also a stealth augmentation available, Dampening, which further decreased the noise of the armor. There was no mobility enhancement option for medium armor: that was for light armor only.

"Okay. Let's get the Stormrider with the lot." I selected all my options and added them to the cart, then some armor and weapon care supplies I was lacking. All up, it came to just over 2000 olbia. "Can you tint the armor to match this?"

I held out the Raven Helm. The smith took it, and looked it over curiously.

"Hmm. Black sightglass. This is the work of House Azpatl. Dara Tlaxi'Azpatl is the favored armorer of the Royal Court." Yaola turned it in their hands. "Yes, I can tint my armor to match this."

"Brilliant," I said.

"Excuse me, then, while I make the modifications. Wait outside, please." The smith bowed, confirmed the sale, and went to pick up the armor stand and carry it back over to the forge.

Twenty minutes later, I was back to strolling through the streets of Taltos beside Cutthroat, looking every inch the well-to-do Lancer.

"Have to admit, I'm almost jealous," Suri remarked from behind me, jerking Cutthroat's reins as she tried to turn around, for the millionth time since we'd left the castle. "That's some nice-looking gear."

"Want to try it on? See if you like this style of armor more than full-plate?"

"Nah. Too clingy. I'd feel underdressed."

"It's not like anything's uncovered," I replied. "You know, other than my face."

Her mouth quirked in a sultry, playful smile. "Yeah, but why do you think I asked you to walk ahead of Cutthroat?"

I could see the hookwing in my peripheral vision, staring daggers at me with her beady yellow eyes. "So she doesn't rip my guts out and use me like a sock puppet?"

"Nah. You'd get out of the way in time," Suri said. "It's because that suit fits nicely around the back."

"In other words, you're staring at my butt?"

Soberly, she nodded. "Correct."

I made a show of thinking for a moment. "Quick question: *why* didn't we get that bikini again?"

"Do you have any fuckin' idea how uncomfortable they are? No support for your boobs at all, and the crotch of it rides up your cunt like a bandsaw. No thanks. I'll stick to looking like a tin can with legs."

"This sounds like something you know from experience."

Suri let out an exasperated sigh. "Yeah, I know it from experience, okay? I was a gladiator. A *female* gladiator. What do you think my manager made me wear out in the ring? And why do you think I quit?"

Our next destination was the apothecary. I gratefully stocked up on King's Grass and Cats Eye Mushrooms for the Dragon's Blood Potions, then picked up at least five of every other herb they sold. From there, we went somewhere we hadn't ever been able to afford until now: an accessory shop.

"Oh!" The man at the counter—an unusually tall, aristocratic Lysidian man with neat silver hair—jumped as I walked in through the door. "I remember you! Both of you!"

"Uhh… I didn't do it." I held my hands up, Suri looming over my shoulder in confusion.

"No, my Lord, it's nothing you did. You were at that horrible auction at the winery!" The jeweler exclaimed. "You and the red-haired battlemaiden, you saved my life!"

It took me a moment before it clicked. "Ohh, hey! You were selling accessories at the cocktail party before it turned into a royal clusterfuck. How are you, man? You doing alright?"

"I was most fortunate to escape with my life and limbs intact," he replied, leaning on the counter as I stopped in front of it. "But thanks to you, I returned to my wife and children in one piece. What about you? Are you still a mercenary for the Royal Court?"

"Nope. Well, kind of? We were both made counts by the new king," I said. "I'm the Voivode of Myszno, and she's Voivodzina."

"And before you apologize for not 'Your Gracing' us, don't sweat it. Neither me or Hector think of ourselves that way," Suri added.

"A Voivode! Khors' breath! A title well-deserved, I say." The man beamed. "Ahh, to think that I knew one of the lords of the realm before he attained his station! And you, lady? Are you well?"

"Doin' all right. Lost an arm in the fight. The Masterhealer grew it back for me," she said.

"That is wonderful to hear. The regrowing, not the loss." The jeweler splayed one long hand over his chest and bowed from the neck. "I am Viel Falka, in case I never introduced myself at the party. What are you looking for?"

"Anything that increases mobility, evasion, stealth, or that protects against knockdown," I said. "Anything that helps with water elemental resistance."

"We have some things you might be interested in. And I will give you a substantial discount, in thanks for saving my life." Viel turned to the wall of drawers behind him, pulling out a number of small boxes. "Let me see... oh yes, this might be good..."

I waited as he came back and laid out the selection of items on the counter, opening the clam-shell boxes so I could scan the contents.

Improved Brawler's Wristband

50 Armor

15% Evade
+10 Str and Con
300 gold olbia (25% discount)
Can be upgraded.
Simple wristbands studded with enchanted blue crystal.

Ring of Peace

Protects against the Fear and Hypnosis debuffs.
150 gold Olbia (25% discount)

Amulet of the Berserker

After receiving 150 points or more of damage, this ring increases your attack power and AP regeneration by 15%.
200 gold Olbia (25% discount)

Amulet of the Spark

Boosts AP regeneration by 20%; regenerate 1 point of Adrenaline per minute when outside of combat.
350 gold Olbia (25% discount)

Ring of the Ocean

Blessed by priests of Rusalka in their dark rites, this ring offers 15% protection against the Water element.
200 gold Olbia (25% discount)

"I'll grab them," I said, looking back to Suri. She nodded.

"Certainly." Viel closed the boxes and handed them over. "I will have a different selection of between three and five items suitable for Starborn every week—assuming you are only interested in Artificed goods. For normal jewelry, you can simply browse the store selection."

"What about…" I trailed off as my HUD chirped: a call from Rin. "Sorry, give me a second."

"No problem." Viel shrugged.

"Hi guys!" Rin said once we picked up. "Okay, so, I spoke with Ebisa, and she's fixed a meeting for us at the Viper's Pit!"

"Sure. When do we meet?" I asked. "And where's the Viper's Pit?"

"Oh! It's the big pit fighting club in the International District. Kind of the hub for the city's thieves' guild, too. Anyway, we have to be there after seven p.m., so we have a bit of time. Ebisa said that if you have any questions, you should go back to the castle and ask her."

"No worries," I said, looking to Suri. "And thanks. I think we'll   go   and   do   just   that."

CHAPTER 34

Ebisa was able to confirm what I'd already suspected. Karalti couldn't fly us to Meewhome. For one thing, the Azure Passage, the trans-oceanic flight to the island, was simply too far for her to make in one trip. For another, Meewhome was a sealed territory. A mini-Caul of Souls protected the claw-shaped island, which lay about two hundred miles south of the Shalid. To pass through the barrier, you had to have a special token of passage linked to the barrier. The token was not something you could fit in your pocket. They were figureheads—literal figureheads, as in, a full-sized sculpture mounted on the bow of an airship. The only way we could get there was to be smuggled in.

That's how the four of us ended up in the International District at night. Cat Alley, as it was known by the locals, was one of the few genuinely dangerous places in Taltos. The neat cobbled roads and colorful apartments that were the norm in the city ended at the heavily guarded district wall. On the other side was a slum: huts and old rowhouses, lean-tos, covered wagons turned into houses. A sluggish canal ran through Cat Alley, splitting the neighborhood into roughly equal halves. Women and their young children occupied the entry side of the canal, and the other side, closer to the city wall, was where the males lived.

We kept our purses close and our swords closer as we moved through the district, sticking together to deter gangs of sharp, hungry-eyed cutpurses eying us from the shadows. All the while, Cutthroat snorted and huffed, baring her teeth at anyone who looked at her the wrong way. We crossed a bridge and turned down a broad curved street, which ended in a courtyard with high, spike-topped walls. It was lively at this time of night, the air full of the smells of beer and fried fish and aggressively fast, high-speed fiddling.

A gang of five Mercurion toughs hung outside the rusted gate leading in, checking people for weapons as they streamed in and out. It was a fight night, and people from all over the city were sneaking in to see the show.

"Halt, Sanghi." One of the Mercurions stepped out in front of Suri and Cutthroat, their face hidden behind a battered mask. "You can take your *ghora* to a public stable. It isn't coming inside."

"She'll wait out here." Suri slung her leg over and dismounted, pulling Cutthroat's reins over and dropping them. "We're here on business. Red made an appointment for us."

We couldn't see the Mercurion's expression, but they straightened up at Ebisa's street name. "Prove it."

Suri pulled a small sheathed dagger from a pouch: the [Ravenstar Dagger], a relic of the Royal family that Ebisa carried with her as a badge of office.

"Understood. Someone will be out to take care of your mount." The Mercurion waved us through.

We passed through the gate into a compound with a ring of run-down houses. Strings of brightly colored lanterns hung between the hipped Chinese-style roofs, casting rainbow light over the crowd of people talking, drinking, dancing and brawling on the filthy straw-covered pavement. Suri bulldozed a path to the largest house at the end of the courtyard, bouncing a couple of drunk Vlachian teenagers off her armor on the way up the stairs. We entered to find the place just as animated as the outside. The floor was crowded, staffed by attractive human and Meewfolk bartenders. Every table was taken. Downstairs, the sounds of fighting could be heard: shouts, the ringing of a bell, the thump and crack of fists on flesh.

"Phew! Smells intense!" Karalti clung to my arm, sniffing the air. *"Hang on, okay? I want to get a drink and some fried fish!"*

"I ain't stopping you," I replied, glaring at a drunk Vlachian thug angling toward us. He turned and stomped away, looking for a better mark. *"Have you ever actually drunk alcohol before?"*

"Nope! I'll get whatever seems tasty." Karalti wiggled happily, then let go of me and slid through the crowd toward the bar. *"Do you want anything? Suri?"*

"Sure," I said. "Whiskey if they've got it, vodka if they don't."

"Grab me a beer as well, would you?" Suri called out to her over the noise. "Oh look: I think that's our table."

I looked in the direction she was facing and spotted what she had: a group of gaudily dressed Meewfolk seated at a booth, gambling with cups and drinking themselves into oblivion. One of them had a small, fluffy dinosaur of some kind perched on his shoulder. More telling was the golden quest icon that hung over his head.

"That's not all," I said, glancing at the next booth over. "Look at the table next door. Starborn."

Suri's head turned sharply. The Starborn in question sat in front of a row of three NPCs, playing cards with the single-minded concentration of a serious gambler. He was older, with a rough beard and stringy grey hair pulled into a short half-ponytail. He wore a long brown duster over a red satin vest that looked like it had seen better days. A pearl-handled pistol lay on the table by his elbow.

"I'm impressed," I said. "It takes real effort to look like a grimy cyberpunk character in a fantasy game."

"Doubt he's got anything interesting to say." Suri said. "Anyway, you want me to do the talking? Or you want to do it?"

"I'll do it," I said. "Gotta get that street cred somehow. You and Karalti watch my back."

"It's your funeral." Suri equipped her helmet and fell in by my left.

We rolled up to the Meewfolk as the leader slammed his cup down and pulled it up to reveal a pair of sixes. His companions roared, thumping the table and cursing him good-naturedly as he laughed and quipped something to them in his native tongue. When he spotted us, his blue eyes turned sly, and he fixed a toothy fanged grin on us.

"Ahh, you must be Red's guests!" He cried out to us, waving us with a ring-encrusted hand. "Come, come, sit with us!"

"Thanks." I dropped into the seat, looking back to see Karalti weaving back toward us from the bar. "Red didn't give us your names. I'm Hector. This is Suri. What can I call you?"

"My name, dearest human, is Samboon Taksin, captain of the *Wattana*," he replied, leaning back in his seat. "I am told you seek passage to the land of my people?"

"Sure do. We need to arrange an audience with the Avatar." I smiled at Karalti as she set our drinks down and plopped into the chair beside me. Her plate was stacked high with fillets of breaded fish and a bowl of what looked and smelled like tartar sauce.

The Meewfolk at the table all did a doubletake. Captain Taksin, who had been taking a pull off his mug, sputtered on his mouthful of beer.

"A human? Gain audience with the Avatar? HAH!" He slammed the mug down. "If I wasn't an outcast, I'd have to slap you with claws for such an arrogant, blasphemous statement. But I am an outcast, so *sanyelak mra'ah*."

I had a quiet sip of whiskey. It was surprisingly good: sharp, caramelly, with a warm smokey finish. "I don't speak your language, yet, but I'll take it as a wish for luck."

The other Meewfolk at the table laughed uproariously, rocking in their seats as they toasted each other.

"Oh yes, that is what it means. Wishing luck for an audience with the Avatar, hah!" The Captain shook his head. "How do you plan to do this thing?"

"We have knowledge we can return to your people," I said. "I was hoping the Avatar might be interested. If you have any good ideas on how to arrange a meeting, we might add a garnish to your berth fee."

"A garnish, hmm? Smart man. Rogues like me do not give advice for free." Samboon picked up a piece of his own fish and fed it to the critter on his shoulder. "You will need to go through the Priest-Queen of Ru Waat to have a chance at gaining an audience with the Avatar. Do you know much about our fair nation?"

"Not a whole lot, no," I said.

"Prrupt'meew is a country of city-states," Samboon said, gesturing grandly with his fish. "Each one ruled by a Priest-Queen, a sacred mother of our people who administers the city and the lands of the city's territory. All Priest-Queens are duty-bound to protect the Avatar and the Temple of Ancestors, in which they reside. However, in practice, it is the Priest-Queen of Ru Waat, our largest city, who controls access to the Avatar and serves as their greatest defender."

"Are Meewfolk a feudal society?" I asked. "Any rules and rituals we need to know?"

"We do not have kings and queens and lords and ladies like Vlachia." Samboon motioned derisively toward the city beyond the door. "Succession by birth breeds weakness. Any woman may become Priest-Queen, if she is strong enough. Girls train from youth to become braves, then temple guard, then priestesses, and then they may challenge the ruler of their city. It is a position of merit. The Priest-Queen of Ru Waat is the greatest warrior of the land."

"Only women, huh?" I glanced at Suri.

"Women live in cities. Men live outside the walls," Samboon said. "Unlike here, where all of my people are crammed into this noisome filth together. It is unnatural for men and women to live so close to one another, if you ask me. But enough of this. I have berth for six passengers on our next journey to the motherland: eight hundred olbia per head, non-negotiable. I normally charge a thousand, but Red tells me that there are four of you and one *ghora* who must travel, and I owe her a personal favor."

Eight hundred per person was steep, but I'd figured we'd have to pay a smuggler's tax. "Works for me. When do you leave?"

"Next month. The sixteenth of Boseg Kavi," the captain replied, examining his claws.

"That's two fuckin' weeks away," Suri blurted the same words on my own mind, more or less.

"Ah, the tin can speaks. Yes, my lady, it is two weeks from today," Samboon said, flicking one of his ears to the side. "The Azure Passage is dangerous this time of year. It is the monsoon season in those latitudes. Typhoons and worse. If the storms do not get you, the Cloud Emperors will."

"Cloud Emperors?" I asked.

"They rule the skies between the mainland and Meewhome, and they spawn during the monsoons." He gestured vaguely toward the south. "It is toward the end of their breeding season, but one can never be too careful. Come with us in two weeks, and they will be out to sea and far away. But now? No, you won't find anyone with an Avatar's Blessing willing to go south until the storms have cleared."

"What about for a thousand a head?" I asked, straightening as I saw the gambler turn in his chair to watch and listen to us.

Samboon scoffed. "No. And not for any fare, no matter how much you wish to go on this fool's gambit. My ship is worth more than the lives of some imprudent humans."

The gambler stood up, set his hat on his head, and slouched over to us. I glanced back, letting him know I'd seen him, and he stopped a respectful distance away. Samboon's gaze slid to him, past my shoulder.

"Might be I'm able to help you." The newcomer had a rough, gravelly voice, drawling heavily on every other word. "I got a ship, and I've made plenty of runs from here to Ru Waat. If the weather 'cross the Azure Passage is as bad as you say... well, that sounds like an adventure to me."

"Sure does," I said. "We'd delay the journey if we could, but we can't. Ilia won't give us two weeks to play footsies in Taltos."

He squinted at me. "Ilia? You mixed up in all that mess?"

"Sure am. On the side of sanity, or the side of Vlachia, whichever you prefer." I twisted around, stretching out a hand. "Hector."

He came close enough to give it a stiff shake. "Gar."

"This is Suri and Karalti." I gave Captain Taksin a sidewards glance. His ears were flat to his skull, eyes narrowed. "Do you know what the captain here is talking about?"

"Sure I do. Cloud Emperors choking up the Azure Passage." Gar said. "But I wouldn't be a goddamned smuggler if I wanted the easy life, now would I? Pussy cat here can cool his damn heels in Taltos for as long as he pleases. If you three are willing to insure my ship in case it wrecks, I'll take you wherever you damn well want."

"Pussy cat?" Samboon repeated, planting his hands down on the table. "Say that again if you dare, you shaved monkey."

"C'mon now, no need to get all fluffed up about it." Gar arched his eyebrows and tossed his head. "I can make it up to you. "I can make it up to you. A nice saucer of milk, a couple of sardines... How about I find a nice fat-bottomed peasant woman who scratches you just right on that spot right over your tail?""

The Captain's crewmates flattened their ears and hissed. Samboon got to his feet, looming head and shoulders over all of us. I calmly, but efficiently vacated my seat.

"Put your dicks away, gentlemen. We've got shit to do," Suri snapped. "Gar, if you've got a ship and you're willin' to fly it, I'd say we can work something out."

Gar looked sharply at Suri, brows furrowing. "Suri, was it? Where's that accent from?"

"It's from Nunya-Damn-Business," Suri replied easily. "Nice little resort town on the coast of Bugger Off."

Karalti watched us like someone following a tennis match, methodically stuffing pieces of fried fish into her face.

"Hah. Good answer." A brief sloping smirk passed over Gar's rugged face. "Anyway: How 'bout you three come walk and talk with me to the docks? You want to leave tonight or tomorrow, right?"

"Tomorrow, early as possible," I said. "I'll walk with you—to make sure you actually have an airship and aren't just jerking us around."

"Oh, you better believe I have an airship. The fastest ship in port, and she has a ten-thousand mile range on her. Better than anything Whiskers here can fly," Gar said.

"She'll be a wreck in the bottom of the Passage by the time you're halfway to Meewhome." Captain Taksin rolled his shoulders. "Anyway, Starborn: I believe our business is concluded."

"We didn't have any business, so you still owe Red that favor." I got to my feet. "Pleasure meeting you, anyway."

The Meewfolk sneered. "*Sampat khung lood'nam mao nah.*"

"*Ouch, that sounds rude.*" Karalti popped the last piece of fish into her mouth, and after a moment of consideration, picked up the bowl of tartar sauce and chugged it, to the astonishment and concern of the other Meewfolk at the table.

"It's amazing how 'go suck a dick' sounds roughly the same in any language." I got to my feet, yawned, and stretched. "Alright, Gar. Let's go see this ship of yours."

"My pleasure," Gar drawled. "Now—ladies and gentleman, if you'll follow me, it will be my pleasure to introduce you to the *Strelitzia*, the finest ship in the Port of Taltos."

CHAPTER 35

The three of us were on high alert as Gar led the way to the Dock Ward. It was the roughest area of the city besides the International District, full of factories, workshops, rooming houses, pubs and brothels. Sailors strolled the streets at all hours, enjoying their shore leave by gambling away their wages, collecting tattoos, and experiencing new and exotic STDs from the rowdiest hookers Taltos had to offer. Salt spray hung in the air, and the ground continuously shuddered under our feet, vibrating from the power of the hundred-foot waves thundering against Vlachia's coastal cliffs.

"So, Gar: how does a player end up as a smuggler?" I asked, walking by Cutthroat's right-hand flank. Suri and Karalti rode, with Karalti perched side-saddle on the back of the saddle, Suri astride at the front.

"Why wouldn't I be a smuggler?" Gar drawled. "Get to see all kinds of nice places, play cards when I feel like it, brawl with assholes like Puss in Boots back there. What more could a red-blooded man want out of this excuse of an afterlife?"

"You don't sound like you worked for Ryuko," I said. "You don't have that sweaty sheen of corporate plastic."

"Hah!" He cackled. "Hell no. I wouldn't ever work for no goddamn corp."

"How d'you get in, then?"

"Same way nearly everyone did: good old-fashioned nepotism. If you're here, you're either from the military, related to someone who made the game, or you paid someone in Ryuko to get in," Gar replied. "That's as much as I'm willing to say on the matter. Let the sins of the past lie in the past to make way for the sins of the future, I say."

"Only way it might bother me is if your past screws up our quest," I said. "There's a lot riding on this."

"Something about that Emperor Hyland guy. Feh." Gar hawked and spat into the gutter. "Sounds to me like he's just spinning his wheels. All of us are here to run down the clock until the machinery that keeps this place running screws up, and then we're all just as dead as each other."

Ten uncomfortable minutes later, Gar led us out along a wharf—and there, hanging over the churning black ocean five hundred feet below, was a battered-looking airship that reminded me strongly of the *Highwind*, the airship that had played a huge role in the old classic, *Final Fantasy VII*. Unlike the *Highwind*, it didn't have a zeppelin component, just a pair of huge mana-driven engines. It also had two large silver hoops that hovered around the back of it, one rotating clockwise, the other anti-clockwise. STRELITZIA was painted in big black letters along the streamlined keel, which ended in a bomber-style glass bridge. At the very front was what I was pretty sure was one of the Avatar totems: a golden lotus flower as big as my torso, mounted under the bowsprit and glowing softly with pulsing lines of mana.

"You've gotta be joking," Suri said, reining Cutthroat up before the hookwing compulsively climbed the gangplank. "This piece of shit is able to get us to Meewhome?"

"This 'piece of shit' is a custom job that can and does make trans-continental runs between Artana and Daun," Gar retorted, jamming his hands in his pockets. "Machined half the parts myself. None of those damn silverskin wonks can make anything like it."

"I think he means, 'wouldn't be caught dead making anything like it'." Karalti giggled into her hand.

"Anyway. I wanna see proof of ten grand in reserve to insure her against any damage, plus your berth fee. If everything goes well, you don't pay nothin' but the fee. If things fuck up and you don't pony up the insurance money, I'll make some calls and we'll visit you and collect," Gar said. "I'll cut you a deal on the fee as a gesture of good faith. Six hundred a head, including the hookwing. Even throw in some meals. What do you say?"

"How many berths you got?" Suri asked. "We have another head coming with us."

"Four," he replied. "Two of you will have to cozy up. Hope you enjoy snuggling."

Karalti perked up, and looked at me with big, pleading eyes.

"Guess we're in luck." I surveyed the ship dubiously. Compared to the Royal Vlachian airships I was used to, this one looked kind of like a flying murder van. "Let me think about it for a minute."

"Think all you like." Gar shrugged, pulled a tin of cigarettes from his coat, bumped one to the top, and lit up.

My HUD purred and chirped: a PM from Suri. "What do you think?"

"I think Gar here is a good ol' boy who thinks his life is a country music song, but I'm not getting anything weirder than that," I replied. "Karalti?"

"He seems okay." Karalti yawned, briefly flashing her fangs. *"He doesn't smell like he's lying. He's just lonely, I think."*

I flashed her an odd look. "I didn't know loneliness had a smell."

"Yeah, it does. Like hand lotion and old cheese." She nodded. "This ship definitely smells like loneliness."

Gar looked over at us, raising one eyebrow expectantly.

"Well, my dragon says you check out," I said. "If anything we run into fucks up the airship, we'll cover it. If you've got a clunky gear or need refueling or something, that's on you."

"Suits me," Gar said. "As long as you've actually got the money."

"We do," Suri said.

"So if I meet you here at five in the morning tomorrow, you'll be here with your suitcases and three thousand olbia, plus a screenshot showin' me you've got the rest?" He turned his face and blew a cloud of smoke toward the water.

"We'll briefly have you join our party, and I'll transfer it digitally. You'll be able to see the reserve, read-only. We won't be carrying any physical gold," I said. "No offense, but we haven't exactly always had a great experience with other Starborn since landing in Archemi."

"Neither have I. A transfer's fine with me." Gar jammed his cigarette in the corner of his mouth and held out his hand. "Shake on it."

I slapped my palm into his. Suri did the same. When he offered to shake with Karalti, she offered her fingers to him like she had with Ignas. A look of confusion passed over his face as he took her hand, frowned at it, then cleared his throat and shook it once before stepped back.

"Dragon, huh?" Gar looked between us. "That some kind of character Path-Class thing?"

"No. Karalti here is an actual dragon." I unconsciously lay a hand on Karalti's shoulder, giving it an affectionate squeeze. She leaned into it, her eyes half-closing at the attention.

"Bit small, ain't she?" Gar grunted, looking her up and down. "No wings or scales."

"Not yet." I winked. "Zero five hundred, on the dot. See you at quarter to the hour."

"Sure. Y'all get home safe, now." Gar shrugged, then trudged up the gangplank to his ship—which was apparently also his house.

"Cheerful bugger, isn't he?" Suri said, once the hatch had closed.

"Sure is." I shook my head and started on my way back. "But as long as he can fly us to Meewhome, then as far as I'm concerned, he's my new best friend."

***

By the next morning, we were all kitted out and looking sharp. Suri had her new sword over her back and a fresh haircut. Rin had filled up on mana and had a new spellglove and a nice leather satchel, all ready for field work. She'd bought three Skill Tomes for the Meewfolk language out of her own money. She and Suri were able to use them just fine. I held mine in my hands and tried to psych myself to open the cover.

"Seriously, you should let me try it," Karalti urged, pacing anxiously. *"What if you have a stroke or a heart-attack or something?"*

"I don't think you can use skill tomes, Tidbit," I replied. "And because you're an NPC, you have to learn languages the hard way."

"Yeah. Unfortunately." Rin winced. "It's okay, though! We've got medicine. We can resuscitate him, probably."

"I know how to give mouth to mouth." Suri had her arms crossed, a bemused smile playing over her lips.

Karalti scowled. *"I'll fight you."*

"Well, just... stand by, okay?" I drew a deep breath, braced myself for agony and-or unconsciousness, and opened the cover to view the Skill sigils. I didn't have to read them— the bright lines of magic writhed, imprinting on my corneas like a flash of sunlight. My head throbbed painlessly, and the world darkened for a moment… then cleared, leaving me on my feet, the book still in hand.

Rin, Suri, and Karalti waited breathlessly for me to keel over.

"I'm fine." I closed the book, blinked until my eyes cleared, then lifted my head to look at them. "Barely even felt the upload. Try speaking to me in Meew?"

"Can you understand me?" Rin asked, in that language.

"Yeah. Sure can." I replied in the same tongue. It was fun to speak: Mau, as humans called it, was a tonal language like Chinese or Thai. "I didn't feel a thing."

"I wonder why the fuck you collapsed when you learned Dakhari from me?" Suri scratched her head, ignoring Cutthroat as the hookwing chirped and bumped at her other hand. "That language fuckin' knocked you out."

"One of the many mysteries of Archemi." I stared down at the Skill Tome. "Anyway, I'm good. Let's get this show on the road."

Twenty minutes later, the group of us strolled up the pier where the Strelitzia was warming her engines. Gar was hanging out at the base of the gangplank, smoking in the company of one of the most unusual Mercurions I'd ever seen. He was short and well-muscled, with pearly golden skin, a yellow mohawk of crystal spikes, and six gem-like eyes in a circle around his face. He was a *juchi*, a variant Mercurion, and a guaranteed outcast from his own people.

"Ha! That's some nice-looking gear." Gar gave us a flippant two-fingered salute as we clomped over to him. "And that spear of yours is pretty impressive. What is it? Some kinda artifact?"

"Yup. 'The Spear of Destiny'. It's soul-bound." I emphasized the last slightly. "I'm stuck with it, and it gets stuck in a whole lot of people."

"I bet it does. Maybe that's what I've been doing wrong all this time, Ambrose. Should have been introducing myself to the ladies as the man with the Spear of Destiny." Gar winked at Suri, who turned her face and grimaced.

The Mercurion—Ambrose?—sighed in dismay.

"Eh." Gar waved like he was shooing a fly. "Anyway, we're ready to go when you folks are ready to pay. She's fueled up and ready to fly."

"Great." I hesitated before sending him the party request, hanging back from the edge of the gangplank. There was no reason for me to feel as distrustful as I did, other than the fact that Gar was… well, Gar. "Say—you got any idea what Cloud Emperors are?"

"Cloud Emperor Jellyfish. They aren't dangerous to ships, unless you're a big damn idiot." Gar replied. "You see 'em all the time over the open ocean. Great big man o'war lookin' critters. You'll find a pod of three or four of them hanging out over the water, dipping their tentacles in like fishing lines. Only problems you can have with em are if you fly into those tentacles, or if you scare 'em."

"What happens if you scare them?" Rin asked nervously.

"They fart," Gar replied. "And somethin' that size, floating around all full of who knows what? You don't want that thing fartin' anywhere near your goddamned engines. They put out some kind of gas that screws with navigation. Anyway, we ain't afraid of em: the Strelitzia can fly rings around the bastards, and they don't give a damn about airships. Hell, I got one of those game achievements from flying this ship between their tentacles once. Piece of cake."

Ambrose sighed again. Emphatically.

"Hah." Suri laughed, rubbing Cutthroat's neck as the hookwing stamped and snorted. "You got a hookwing berth?"

"Sure. You got my money?" Gar asked, shooting me a suspicious glare.

"Sure do." Against my better judgement, I sent Gar a party invite.

[Garcia Martinez has accepted your Join request.]

"Wait: You used your real name when you loaded in?" I opened my Inventory and set up the transfer from my Kingdom Funds.

"Yeah. Why not?" Gar shrugged. "Ain't got nothing to hide."

"Fair enough." Before I sent the money over, I took a peek at his available character details. He was an Artificer, and his Advanced Path was probably the most matter-of-fact class I'd ever seen in a fantasy game: 'Airship Engineer'. He was only Level 17, but his Skills were off the charts. He had Advanced and even Master levels in a range of different abilities: Airship

Mechanics, Sapping, Improvised Construction, Materials Development... real-world technical skills, with hardly a mention of magic.

"How the hell did you get yourself an airship by Level 17?" I sent the money across, puzzled.

"Why? Got a problem with prime numbers?" He accepted his three grand, then immediately opted out of the Party.

"You know that every question isn't some kind of attack on you, right?" I gestured between the two of us. "I'm trying to figure out who me and my people are going to be spending the next week with. I don't need your life story or anything, but some basic info would be nice."

Gar thought about that for a minute. "I'm good at my job. Like to fly. Not great at small talk and not good at playing games. How's that for an answer?"

"We can help you level, if you'd like!" Rin said. "I'm a crafter, too!"

The man's expression flickered briefly as he glanced at Rin. For a moment, he almost looked pained. "Polite of you, but I don't need any help, miss...?"

"Rin," she replied, sticking out a silvery hand. "Just Rin. Pleased to meet you!"

I smiled at Suri and Karalti as I watched him hesitate, then grudgingly shake. Rin had a way of opening people up.

"Alright. Enough chit-chat." Gar shook out his shoulders like an irritated bird, then motioned with a hand. "Up you go. The dinosaur goes below decks. We got a single stall for live cargo down there. Just make sure she doesn't cause any trouble."

"I've got food for her in my Inventory. As long as she has her face in a trough, she'll be fine." Suri clicked her tongue, and started Cutthroat up the gangplank.

"I bet she does, given she's the size of a god-damned school bus." Gar eyed the hookwing dubiously as she strutted past, keeping her nose close to Suri's hair.

Ambrose peeled off after her, and the rest of us followed. Karalti reached for my hand, craning her head to take in the sights as we headed for the bulkhead door. Gar bounded up the ramp after us in a long-legged stride, waving at the curious crew members gawking at us through the portholes. "Alright, slackers! Gangplank up, sails out! Let's get this show on the road!"

"Phew." Karalti gave me a sidelong look. *"He's kind of intense, isn't he?"*

"You know, I knew a Garcia Martinez in the Army," I said. *"It's not an uncommon name where I'm from, but I have to wonder if he's the same guy."*

"Maybe!" Karalti bounded ahead through the door, sniffing deeply as the warm, slightly stale air from the cabin washed over us. *"Are you excited to go to Meewhome?"*

"I'm wondering what flavor of goat rodeo we're gonna to have to deal with on our way to Meewhome," I replied. *"Because it's practically a law that if a bunch of player characters with an important plotline get on an airship or a train, intending to travel to some important destination,*

something with a lot of teeth and a grudge is going to screw them on the journey."

CHAPTER 36

4 Days Later.

A guttural scream of terror ripped Karalti and I out of slumber.

"AAAAAAHHHHHHH! FUCKFUCK OH! OHNO NO NO NOOOOOO!"

There were series of splintering crashes, like someone overturning something large out in the hall, followed by roars. The scream lost its terror and flared into open, full bore rage:

"FUCK, FUCK! YOUR WHORE OF A FUCKING HOOKWING IS DIGGING UP MY BED! GET THE FUCK‑ NO YOU BITCH OF A BEAST, LET THAT GO!'

Gar's rant was drowned out by a deep‑bellied bestial snarl, then a pistol shot that echoed through the airship like a whip crack. Karalti and I scrambled up in our sheets, and Karalti tumbled off the narrow ship's bunk with a frightened 'eep!' as we hastily equipped weapons and clothing.

"What in the ever‑loving fuck is going on out there?" I rolled up, fully dressed, and helped Karalti to her feet on the way out.

"I dunno!" She followed me at a run.

Cutthroat's roars were intermittently drowning out the sound of humans shouting, yelling, and cursing. We burst out the end of the corridor into an atmosphere of raw, unadulterated chaos. Gar and Suri were arguing outside his room. Our captain had his pistol in one hand and a pillow in the other, which he was clutching against the front of his naked crotch. The door to his quarters—and every other door on the way there from the lower deck—was either flat on the ground or hanging off its hinges. Beyond was a larger ship's berth with a single bed, currently groaning under the weight of Cutthroat. The hookwing was bleeding from a slug to the shoulder, but her jaws were set, her eyes fixed forward. The rest of the room was trashed. Everything that could be considered remotely soft had been pulled in and under her stamping feet, clothing packed down under blankets and curtains, the stuffing of the mattress now torn and shaped into a cup-like depression. She was now settling into this, arms spread, feathers fluffed, head down towards the door. Her throat was now blushed bright red, puffed up to a degree I'd never seen it before, and she was making the weirdest honking, booming noises by vibrating it like some manner of drum.

It was a nest.

She had nested in the Captain's quarters.

Karalti gawped at the scene ahead, open-mouthed. *"Matir have mercy."*

"No. Oh no. No-no-no-no, you have got to be fucking kidding me." I felt my temples start to throb, and reached up to grip the top of my head. "When we were testing that parachute... did her and Payu, like..."

"*Yeahhh…*" Karalti winced. *"I think they miiiight haaaave."*

"And just what part of hiring you meant you could fucking shoot my fucking hookwing!?" Suri was right up in Gar's face, nearly nose to nose with him.

He snarled back at her, brandishing the revolver. "How about the part where she busted out of her stall, wrecked everything in her path, and kicked me out of my own goddamned bed!?"

"It's not her fuckin' fault you don't have a proper fucking hookwing stall!"

"We have room for a normal, average-sized hookwing, not this giant crazy *puta!*"

Suri's eyes flashed. "Then why'd you even let her on-board? Why'd you charge us for the berth? I could have left her at the castle, mate. You saw her on the docks. You knew what you were fucking signing up for!"

He shoved her. She shoved back. He brought his fist up, and Suri headbutted him so hard he dropped his pillow and reeled away, blinking stars.

"You wanna fuckin' go me, cunt?" Suri spread her arms and backed him into the wall. "Put your fuckin' toy down, and we'll fuckin' go right here!"

"Guys! C'mon, Suri, Gar! Cool it!" I held up my hands and stepped in.

Suri snorted like a bull as she pushed past Gar and stormed into the bedroom. Gar rubbed his face, still cross-eyed. He was bleeding from the mouth.

"Jesus Christ, that bitch is strong," he muttered. "Hey! You get back here! That's *my* goddamn room!"

"Get stuffed, mate." Suri snapped back over her shoulder, kneeling down to inspect Cutthroat's injury. Cutthroat puffed her feathers up and hissed, glowering stoically at us through the doorway. Gar made to storm in there, and I caught his arm and spun him back.

"Dude, you need to fucking chill." I snapped at him, feeling my own temper start to rise. "We're in a videogame with resources everywhere, we've insured your ship, and we'll pay for repairs. Cutthroat's just an animal. This isn't her fault."

"JUST an animal? That giant cock of a dinosaur busted in my door, came storming into my room, bit the shit out of me and took over my goddamned bed!" Gar groaned, reaching up to check his teeth. "You didn't tell me she was about to lay a clutch of eggs!"

"WE didn't know she was about to lay a clutch of motherfucking eggs!" I took my braids in my hands and pulled them in frustration. "Fucking hell, Suri. What are we going to do with hookwing chicks? What do you even FEED hookwing chicks?"

"I don't know!" She couldn't mask the panic in her voice.

"Well, if it's anything like dragons, you chew up a bunch of meat, store it in your crop, and throw it back up for her!" Karalti trilled. *"That's what I'd do!"*

"Cheers. That's real helpful." Suri puffed a lock of scarlet hair from her face.

"Yeah! And she'll beg for you to throw up the food like this." Karalti opened her mouth and began bobbing her head in a vigorous, unfortunately sensual manner, fluttering her hands like winglets beside her ribs.

I pinched the bridge of my nose. "Karalti? Can you not?"

"But she has to know how to do it! Cutthroat won't leave her nest until the babies hatch!" Karalti struck a pose, pointing at them. *"Suri, you have to provide for your family! She's counting on you!"*

Suri put her face in her hands. "I'm gonna skin Taethawn alive, Hector. I'm gonna have myself a fuckin' Meewskin coat."

"Purrr! Purrr!" Cutthroat grumbled and chirped in her throat, fluffed her neck feathers, then turned her head to delicately preen Suri's hair.

"I'm taking your berth for the rest of this goddamned trip. You can sleep on the piss-damned floor, you crazy bitch." Gar made a sound of disgust, pulling a bottle of Vlachian slivovitz out of his Inventory. "Jesus Christ."

"Call her 'bitch' one more time, and I'll throw you through your own fucking bridge." I stepped up this time. "That's my girlfriend you're talking to."

"Your girlfriend? What about Little Miss Dragoncooter over here?" Gar motioned with his head toward Karalti. "You two've been all bunked up together like a pair of-"

Karalti rumbled as she turned on him, slowly. "*WHAT did you just call me?*"

Fortunately, before Gar could answer, the Strelitzia's proximity alarms went off—and the intercom crackled.

"Captain! Need you on the deck!" Ambrose's voice buzzed out of the hallway speakers. "We've a lot of Cloud Emperors up here."

"Lord help me. Pregnant dinosaurs, flying jellyfish… all I wanted was to spend my fucking afterlife in peace." Muttering to himself, Gar finally equipped his clothes—the same ratty ones he'd been wearing since we met him, and flashed one last withering look toward Cutthroat before striding off.

"Can you go keep an eye on that bitter old bastard and make sure he doesn't try to dump us in the ocean? I'll stay here and… sort out whatever is happening." Suri squeezed a handful of her hair. "I don't even know if she actually *has* eggs. She won't move her arse to let me check. I mean, she might just be psyching us out? Right?"

I eyed Cutthroat as she quorked smugly to herself, wiggled her tail, and settled back down. "I'd say the odds of her actually laying actual eggs are pretty good right now."

"How the fuck did Payu even get to you?" Suri moaned, as we left her to tend to her mount's injury. "Cutthroooat…"

Shaking my head, I made my way to the bridge, and nearly ran headlong into Rin as she tried to career through the door I was just exiting. I caught her before we collided and opened my mouth to speak before I saw what was going on behind her and my eyes widened.

Thousands. There were thousands of titanic jellyfish sailing above, beside, and below the ship. They ranged from creatures the size of a car to the size of a cumulus cloud, some of them so huge it was impossible to look at them without craning your head. They were long, puffy and blimp-like, with a central sail running down the length of their translucent bodies. At the core of each jellyfish was a bright, churning blue light, which shone through their gel-like flesh like a bioluminescent lighthouse. Every [Cloud Emperor Jellyfish] was slightly different, sliding past us in iridescent shades of blue and purple.

"Oh thank goodness you're here!" Rin gasped. "I was just about to come and get you! What happened? I heard a pistol go off."

"Uhh... ummm..." I tore my eyes away from the sight outside and looked down along the deck. Gar was at the helm, with one hand on the control wheel and the other dancing over the magitech holoscreen that managed the ship's navigation and controls. His other crewmates had their own flight consoles, frantically delivering reports.

"Rin! Guess what? Cutthroat's gonna be a momma!" Karalti exclaimed, squeezing past me and running over to the window. *"Wooow, look at these!"*

"Cutthroat's going to be a... OMIGOD!? She was *pregnant!?*" Rin's voice nearly hit the ultrasonic range.

"Yeah. And she's decided that Gar's cabin is the place to raise her kids." My eyes were drawn up to the sight outside. "Wow. This is fucking incredible."

"This is fucking insanity, is what it is." Gar was fuming, glancing between the console and the sky ahead of us. "I've never seen so many of the damn things in one place."

Rin squealed in excitement, clapping her hands. "Omigosh! Little hookwings! We should have a baby shower!"

"A baby shower?" Karalti looked at her over her shoulder. *"Is that where people throw babies at you, and you have to try and catch them in your mouth or something?"*

"Wh... what?" Rin deflated slightly, her hands still pressed together. "N-No! Why would anyone do that?!"

"Because babies are delicious! Baby camels, baby iguanodons, baby corrun... they're the perfect food if you're raising eggs." Karalti's expression turned distant and dreamy as she looked back to the window. *"Huh. I wonder what baby Cloud Emperors taste like?"*

"My guess? Neurotoxins followed by a slow, agonizing death." I wandered over to the railing, watching as one of the jellies cruising close to the ship sucked in a bladder full of air through a valve at the front of its gas chamber. A few seconds later, it blasted a shower of clear, clean water out the back of its body.

"Mmm. Spicy jellyfish..." Karalti barely seemed to notice I was there.

I left Karalti to her calamari-based fantasies and went to go check in on Ambrose. He was working on his controls, all eyes forward. "How's it looking? Are we going to make it through?"

"We should. As long as we don't provoke them and cause the herd to vent a huge amount of gas." Ambrose had a hollow, knocking voice, as if a drum had learned how to talk. "They don't notice us. We don't bother them. That's the best we can hope for."

"What kind of gas?" Rin asked as she joined us.

"Argon. Hydrogen." Ambrose replied. "Screws with airship engines."

"Hey, look! Cutthroat isn't the only one with eggs! The jellyfish are spawning!" Karalti pointed outside, jumping up and down in front of the railing.

Sure enough, a cluster of the giant creatures were mingling within viewing range. One Cloud Emperor sprayed a fine pinkish mist from its outtake valve, showering the other Cloud Emperors behind it. The jelly's suitors sprayed it back, but from the front.

"Ahh." I heaved a deep, contented sigh. "Ladies and gentleman, we have just witnessed nature's biggest bukkake."

"Is this how we die?" Karalti asked innocently. *"Falling out of the sky in a big metal box, covered in jellyfish spooge?"*

"What are we going to do if they attack?" Rin asked Ambrose, tearing her eyes away from the scene outside.

Ambrose shook his head. "They won't. Cloud Emperors are too massive to care about us. If you're stupid—like Gar—you can get tangled in their tentacles if you fly a thousand feet or lower between them and the ocean. But at this height, no."

"I heard that, you walking talking RealDoll," Gar snapped. "Once! It only happened once! And we made it on the second try!"

"Sure, boss." Ambrose rolled his eyes—all of them—and turned back to his work.

The banter didn't reassure me that much. We were cruising at about twelve thousand feet, and we were surrounded on all sides. The Cloud Emperors scudding above us had their tentacles drawn up, coiled like springs. The ones lower down dangled them into the water. I zoomed in to watch as one of them caught something: a giant bony fish, which it reeled out of the waves and stuffed into a nest of digestive tentacles that reminded me uncomfortably of the Rotmother from Lahati's Tomb.

"Captain, there's a thunderhead coming up, twelve o'clock." One of the navigators called out. "Monsoon rains sub twelve thousand feet. Wind is picking up, too."

"Prepare for climb to sixteen thousand and give me a track toward the island," Gar ordered. "We need to get into the slipstream along the coast before we get janked around by turbulence. All of you idiots on deck, find a rail and hold on to it."

"Ugh, what is this guy's problem?" Karalti muttered to herself like a badly tuned radio.

The engine whine intensified to a whirling roar as the Strelitzia began to climb. My ears popped as I leaned back against the glass, watching the jellies recede as we gained altitude. The bridge darkened as the monsoon clouds enveloped the hull.

"Captain! Something's headed for us!" Ambrose called to him. "Something fast!"

"How fast?" Gar swiped his screen across to the sonar display.

"Sixty-nine knots and getting faster." Ambrose cupped his control sphere in both hands, and sent out another pulse of magical sonar. Within seconds, five pings showed up on a holo display, flaring and then vanishing to reappear closer than they were before.

"Spotter! Get a visual!" Gar barked from the helm. "Someone's intercepting us!"

"Oooh, is it pirates?" Karalti perked, her bad mood forgotten. *"I always wanted to fight pirates! I can go outside and change shape?"*

"Hold up, Tidbit," I said, frowning as the crew began to scramble. "Rin, you okay?"

"Umm... yes. I think so." She was shivering, clutching the railing with both hands. "It's strange. I never feel nervous on Karalti's back, but this... phew. I think it's because we're inside of a vehicle."

"Yeah, for sure." I drew a deep breath. "Not a big fan of cabins myself."

"What in the name of..." Ambrose was still watching the sonar panel. "Boss, they're splitting up. I don't think these are ships."

"What the hell else could they be?" Gar snapped back.

"Dragons!" Rin said, her voice thin with fear.

"What?" Nearly everyone turned to look back where she was pointing. For a second, I thought she was tripping balls—until I spotted a weird blue and white shape twisting through the air at high speed, like a glider with six paddle-like wings that ended in long glowing fingers. It didn't look anything like a dragon. "That isn't a dragon. But what the fuck is it?"

"No, she's right. Kind of." Gar shaded his eyes. "Those look like *Glacus atlanticus.* Blue Dragon Sea Slugs. Nasty little critters—they can give you a real sting."

I gave him an odd look. "Seen them before?"

"On Archemi? Naw." He shook his head. "In the real world? Lots of times. Blue Dragons are ocean predators. They eat Portuguese Man o'Wars."

The flying slugs were eerily beautiful—and alien. They flew with even more agility than Karalti, gliding around the jellies with high-speed hairpin turns. As we watched, one of them darted up to the underside of a Cloud Emperor and bit a chunk out of it, raining glowing ichor into the air. The jellyfish's gas bag rapidly expanded, then belched out a huge cloud of gas, ice chips, and water vapor as it sunk down through the crowd. The Blue Dragon Slug continued to hound it, nipping at its sail as the jelly rapidly descended toward the ocean.

"Finally. About time something interesting happened, other than me getting evicted from my own goddamned bed." Gar jammed a cigarette in his mouth, lit it, and made a sound of disgust. "Let's get ready for some real flying, ladies and gentlemen."

More and more of the flying slugs appeared, drawn by the huge number of jellyfish and their eggs. Five became fifty— and then fifty became hundreds, serpentine blue bodies darting between the Cloud Emperors and savaging them with rigid scythes of bone. Booming, trumpeting blasts of sound went up from everywhere around us, as the entire mass of jellyfish— including the ones not under assault—began to vent huge quantities of gas into the air. It was some kind of herd defense, because when dragons were caught in the cross-fire, they dropped out of the air like stones.

Rin moaned. "It's not just argon they're venting: it's Aethericly-charged antimagic."

"Don't you worry your pretty little head 'bout antimagic! The Strelitzia can deal with a whole hell of it," Gar called from the helm. "This just got fun! Hang on tight!"

CHAPTER 37

We lunged for the nearest rails as the airship dipped sharply to one side. Warning claxons went off: Karalti and I were used to turbulence, but Rin, overwhelmed by the noise, screamed and sunk down with her hands clamped over her ears. The engines roared as Gar gunned the ship to full throttle and swerved to the right, descending toward the crescent of brilliant green growing larger on the horizon: Meewhome. We were close enough to land that I could see a thin, glinting blue dome rising over the island. The translucent shield of energy didn't prevent the all-out aerial warfare now raging between the ravenous horde of blue dragon slugs and the armada of Cloud Emperors, who were gassing the monsters out of the sky and descending en masse toward the mountain-range sized waves below.

"HECTOR!" Suri's voice blasted through my HUD. *"The hell is going on out there!?"*

"Brace for a crash! It's fucking World War Jellyfish out here. Literally, jellyfish fucking."

"Hold on to your panties, ladies!" Gar whooped, steering us through the flying-slug-on-flying-jellyfish tentacled dogfight of the century. I heard the engines cut as we entered one of the heavy gas clouds, then stutter back to life as we shot past, trailing a cloud of brilliant blue sparks.

"Karalti! Get ready to teleport out of here in case we go down!" I pulled myself along the railing to Rin and threw an arm around her shoulders, holding her tight. She sobbed with terror as the turbulence thumped us around. *"Take Rin if you can!"*

"I'll take both of you, dummy. And Suri, if we have time." Karalti clung to the rail on Rin's other side. *"Don't worry, Rin! It'll be okay!"*

"C'mon, baby! Don't stall, don't stall!" Gar wheedled to his craft as he expertly swung us one way, then the other, and broke through the jellyfish pack to streak toward the island. As he escaped the gas cloud, the ship's mana engines roared back to life, and we sailed out of the dive before we lost momentum and entered a fatal tumble to the ground. "YEE HAWW! Feel that lift! Feel that-"

There was an earsplitting boom, followed by the screeching and gnashing of turbines splintering and being crushed inside of the left-side engine.

"Emergency backups! Now!" Gar yelled, suddenly all business. "Get that right engine cooled down! We overclocked the damn thing because of the fucking argon! Someone come help me with the damn throttle!"

"Stay with Rin!" I pushed off from the rail and ran over to clamp my hands over Gar's. The two of us hauled on the controls, battling the terrible force of gravity outside the ship as the emergency engine flared to life. The Strelitzia wobbled, diving at an angle toward the trees lining the cliffs ahead of us, but the backup engine gave us just enough lift to avoid stalling. We were coming in fast, though, and there wasn't a lot of clear room to land. Meewhome was heavily forested, a lush jungle of the kind not seen on Earth since the Cretaceous. We shot over a village, a grassland packed with running dinosaurs, a small rise of rocky hills, and headed straight for a bare meadow cut from the jungle like a football field.

"Brace! Brace!" Gar barked. "We are gonna butter that bread, so help me God!"

The Strelitzia was still going too fast. The engines were reverse-thrusting to slow the descent, but that only did so much for an aerodynamic wedge of metal and wood travelling at nearly a hundred miles an hour. We hit the ground and slid over the damp jungle mud like a sled, leaving the grass and careening straight into the trees. Glass shattered over us, but death never came: the ship smashed through rotten logs and then came a smoking, groaning halt, its nose buried in a small swamp.

"Shit! Woo! Well, what do you know?" Gar got shakily to his feet, looking back at us all. "Everyone alive?"

Navigators stuck their heads out from under their consoles. Ambrose leaned out and gave him a thumbs up. Karalti helped Rin to her feet, hugging her tightly against her chest. Miraculously, no one on the bridge had died.

"Suri! You alright?" I called to her via PM, already moving for the exit.

"Yeah. Banged up, nothing serious. And... Cutthroat... God help us, Hector. Cutthroat really is laying eggs." Suri's voice was high and thin with stress. "The crash rolled her off them. I counted three, and now she's hopped straight back on 'em and is still going."

"Check Engineering!" Gar ordered Ambrose. "Make sure Li-Li's okay! The rest of you, let's get the hell out of here. If that second engine blows, it'll Strange the hell out of us."

"I... I can help with the engines. Once I can see straight." Rin clung to Karalti's arm as we grouped together. Hopper and Lovelace skittered through the door I was about to enter, crawling over to her. She sat down on Hopper's back, putting her face in her hands.

"What did I say in Taltos, Karalti? I swear to god, there's a law." I grumbled to myself, jogging back toward the cabin deck.

I found Suri looking pale but composed, her arms looped around Cutthroat's neck. The hookwing began to hiss as I approached the open door, setting one of her mantis-like claws forward, then the other. She growled, but she didn't move as Suri rose up, came over, and threw her arms around me.

I hugged her back. "Baby hookwings, huh?"

"Baby hookwings." Suri sounded strangled. "I don't know what we're gonna do, Hector. She won't leave the nest. The Wiki says she's gotta sit on the damn things for two weeks. If she stops sitting them, the eggs will die."

"Then I guess Gar and his ship are coming back to Kalla Sahasi with us." I kissed her on the cheek. "Don't worry, okay? We got this. But we've got to find her something to eat, right?"

"Right. I've still got some food for her, but, uhh, according to this wiki entry, she only needs food once every three days or so because her metabolism gets slower when she's nesting." Suri shakily wiped a hand over her face. "Maybe Karalti can catch us something? And we can put it in here with her while we go take care of business?"

"I think she'd be happy to," I replied. "Just... don't look at what she brings home too closely, all right? She's got some weird ideas about baby showers."

***

The jungle air was like a wet slap to the face. Meewhome was a land of intense, vibrant color, sound, and scent. The humid tropical air was rich with the deep perfume of brilliantly colored exotic flowers. Frogs croaked, bugs buzzed, birds trilled and hooted in the towering trees overhead. We'd carved a trail of destruction from the edge of the meadow to the Strelitzia's final resting spot. The airship had held together surprisingly well, with only a few major losses. The broken engine had lost its casing, exposing the cracked smoky crystal and carbonized metal. The other engine was steaming, but intact. There was no Mana Poisoning warning, so I figured the Emeraldine-Crystalline-hybrid whoziwhatsits that made it work weren't busted, either. The bridge was the most damaged part. The glass shell was now an iron scaffold studded with jagged pieces of broken crystal.

We huddled around Rin as Gar moved from person to person, speaking quietly with each member of his crew. I watched him grip Ambrose's shoulders, leaving only when the Mercurion clapped the back of his hand, then moved onto his shaking engineer. He hugged her until she was okay, and then he slumped over to us, chewing a nail as he hung just beyond the edge of our circle.

"Rin. You okay?" He asked, gruffly. "You were hollering pretty hard in there."

"I-I…" Rin had her face in her hands. She was crouched down, leaning against Karalti's side. "Not r-r-really."

Gar warred with himself for a moment, then went to one knee in front of her. "Hey now, you'll be alright. Wanna hear a joke?"

Rin peered through her fingers at him.

"How many tickles does it take to make an octopus laugh?" he asked.

The Mercurion shook her head.

Gar's mouth spread in a roguish grin. "Ten-tickles!"

Rin closed her fingers, but she started to giggle against her palms.

"What do you call a fish with no eyes?"

My eyes narrowed as I thought. "A hagfish?"

"Nah," Gar replied. "It's just a fsh."

Rin's shoulders shook for a moment before she finally looked up. Her voice was little more than a hoarse whisper. "Th-th-ose are t-terrible."

"They should be. I got 'em off one of those flyers with the little paper strips on the bottom." Still beaming, Gar mimed ripping one off. "They were tearable jokes."

Suri rolled her head back with a groan. "Hector's already bad enough. Now there's two of them."

Rin laughed, and shakily got to her feet, leaning on Karalti's shoulder. "Well... I grew up with a single dad, and I like those kinds of jokes. They helped me. Thanks."

Gar's expression flickered, eyes darkening. "Don't suppose you remember if your real name was Regina?"

Rin blinked a couple of times. "No? It was Lily, actually. But everyone always called me Rin."

"Uhhn." Gar grunted. He got to his feet and turned away from us, fumbling in his coat for his cigarettes. "Right, well... I'm glad that everyone's in one piece, but unfortunately for you, we ain't going anywhere unless you feel like walking to Ru Waat. I reckon that's a couple hundred miles nor-east of here, give or take."

"I can take us," Karalti said. *"But your crew might have to camp in the ship while we're gone."*

Gar jumped as Karalti's telepathic voice broke through his thoughts. "Hell! What was that?"

Karalti waved. *"It's me. Talking to you."*

Gar scowled at her. "I didn't say you could get in my damn head!"

"I'm not in your head. I'm broadcasting from MY head, and you're listening." Karalti eyes hooded, and she pursed her lips to one side.

The look Gar gave her was skeptical at best. "Right. Sure. And how are you gonna take us to the city? Cuz' despite what your fella here told me in Taltos, I haven't seen any horns or dragon wings out of you."

"I'm polymorphed for twelve hours a day, and I went out and flew behind the ship during the night." Karalti backed up several dozen feet, then unequipped her clothes and gear. Gar turned beetroot red, then ghostly white as Karalti's body morphed and stretched back into her native form. I crossed my arms as she paced forward, looming over the smaller trees. She craned her head down beside mine, fixing Gar with a piercing violet glare.

"Oh." Gar took a step back, not looking away from Karalti. "Oh. Well. If that don't beat all."

"You really thought we were taking the piss?" Suri planted her hands on her hips, looking over the wreckage. "Of course she's a fucking dragon. And you're about to be the uncle to nearly a dozen hookwings. Cutthroat's gotta stay where she is."

"In *my* bed? You've got to be joking." Gar tore his gaze from Karalti, snapping back at Suri like a dog.

Suri bared her teeth in reply. "You want to fix your ship? Tuck your pussy lips away and help us get this over with. Rin here is an Artificer, and the capital of the Meewfolk'll have the parts we need to patch the Strelitzia back together."

"*I'm* an Artificer." Gar turned to me, pointing at my chest. "You didn't pay me enough to deal with this shit."

Ambrose reached out and grasped his Captain's shoulder. "Ease up, Captain. We knew what we were getting into."

Gar scowled and shrugged the Mercurion's hand off, but he didn't say anything further as he stomped off to the edge of the clearing.

"Will you all be okay if we leave you here with Cutthroat?" I asked Ambrose. "We can come back with the materials Gar needs."

"We will have to remain here as it is. The Forest Keepers will come here to examine the wreck, and we'll need to buy them off." The Mercurion crossed his burly arms over his chest. "Every crew member on this ship knows how to take care of themselves. Any Meewfolk who find us will probably be happy to assist, as long as we have a good story to tell and we split our liquor with them. They might be able to help with your hookwing. Her species are held in high regard here."

"We really didn't know she was preggers," Suri insisted. "She chased off the male who tried to... who did knock her up."

"It happens." Ambrose shrugged. "We will watch her and her eggs. Despite what the captain says, you paid us a lot to come here. He'll get over it once he notices his bank account."

"Right." I rubbed the sweat off the back of my neck and pulled my helmet on. "Well, ready to go, everyone? This Warsinger isn't getting any less ancient and fucked up, and neither are we."

CHAPTER 38

We picked up an escort about ten miles out of Ru Waat: Eight huge pterosaurs with brightly colored wings and crests, who glided effortlessly into a formation around Karalti. The birds were fast enough to keep up with us, and the Meewfolk braves who rode them kept their bows aimed steadily at our faces.

"Humans! This is the land of our People!" The leader of the wing called out to us in his native tongue, his voice magically augmented to be heard over the wind. "Order your dragon to land, and we will parley! Refuse, and we'll drive you back to the ocean!"

"Let's talk!" I held my hands up. "We come in peace, seeking audience with the Priest-Queen of Ru Waat."

The squad leader replied by pointing down at the ground, then leaned away from us. His mount swooped off to the right and up, blocking the sun over our heads.

"Damn. I think this is the first time we've ever been intercepted by other fliers," I remarked to Karalti. *"Let's go to ground, Tidbit. This is their turf."*

"Yup! Sure is!" Karalti dropped her wing and began her descent.

The scouts tracked us all the way through the landing, alighting in a ring around Karalti as she touched ground. Suri,

Rin and Gar watched nervously as I slid down my dragon's shoulder and leaped lightly to the ground. The Meewfolk dismounted, too: eight slender, well-muscled, lightly armored Meewfolk braves. They were nude except for their fine jewelry: silver and gold torques, bracelets, and rings that glittered with magical energy. Four of the eight had slender lances tipped with blue-steel points, the weapons rippling with faint sheens of mana. The others fielded large compound bows that looked strong enough to punch through an elephant's skull. The arrows were made from some kind of enchanted glass. My HUD identified these men as [Meewfolk Forest Guardians]. They had purple skulls next to their names, which meant they were at least Level 40.

"You speak the language, human? How interesting." The [Forest Guardian Captain] said. He still had an arrow resting loosely on his bowstring. "Humans and a Mercurion with a dragon, at least one of whom speaks and understands our tongue. Consider my curiosity piqued."

"We made a point to learn your language before coming here, the better to speak with your Queen on her terms," I said, keeping my hands raised. "We have a matter of international importance to discuss with her."

"International importance? Well!" The captain looked back at his squad, who burst into a chorus of hissing laughter. "That is very, very important, isn't it? And what kind of important human are you to be delivering such important news to such important people?"

"Dragozin Hector, a Count of Vlachia," I said. "And the-
"

"Vlachia?" The Captain interrupted, his eyes narrowing. "The country which reviles our orphans and exiles? That traps them in ghettos, and forces them to live in filth?"

"The previous king did," I said, quickly. "The new king, Ignas Corvinus, is an ally of the Meewfolk, as am I."

"Ignas is a master thief," Suri called from Karalti's back. She was still strapped into her saddle. "Worked his way up the ranks of the Nightstalkers of Taltos. You heard of 'em?"

"I have," one of the other Forest Guardians piped up. "My mainlander cousin is in that syndicate."

"A human king, gaining the rank of Master? In a syndicate of our folk?" The Captain's tail flicked, and he dropped the point of the arrow a little more. "Now THAT is a story to tease the ears of our Queen. She will surely want to know how he accomplished that."

"I was about to say." I tried to laugh it off. "And we need to ask the Priest-Queen for her wisdom and knowledge on the subject of the Drachan."

"The Drachan?" The Captain's tail lashed. "Those are the concerns of the priestesses. I know nothing of such things. Our Priest-Queen might be able to tell you what she knows, but she is just as liable to take you as her slaves if she senses you are weak... or lying."

"Then we have nothing to worry about," I replied. "Do we?"

"You do. She is the strongest warrior of our people, and the strongest of the Priest-Queens. Her eyes flash with the fire of the sun, and she drinks the blood of men who trespass on her territory," the Captain said. "We will escort you to the gates of Ru Waat, and if our women decide to permit you into the city, you will go. But if they do not, we will take you back to your shipwreck. You will be able to purchase parts to repair it, and then you must leave."

"You know about the shipwreck already, huh?" Gar swung his legs morosely, bouncing the heels of his boots off the side of Karalti's saddle.

"Of course. We are Forest Keepers." The Captain shrugged. "Come. Mount your dragon, and we will walk you to the city limit. And while we walk, think of your best stories."

I waved my hands. "Stories about…?"

"Crimes, of course!" The Forest Keeper exclaimed. "That is the only reason humans come here. It is not against our laws to smuggle, but it is a great dishonor to attempt the arts of theft and grift and fail. So perhaps do not mention the airship crash to the Priest-Queen, yes? The women of our land are fickle, and not opposed to taking human slaves."

***

We heard the sounds of combat from half a mile away; the howling screams of Meewfolk and the roars of monsters. Large, angry monsters.

"What in Lua's name...?" The captain of the Forest Keepers muttered. "Quickly! Something is attacking the city!"

Karalti put her head down and picked up speed as the Forest Keepers launched into the surrounding air, their pterodactyl mounts quorking cries of alarm. We ran straight into a pitched battle below the beautifully carved red walls of Ru Waat. Animals of all kinds—from small monkeys to velociraptors—were pouring out of the lush jungle beyond the city, attacking the gates in a rabid rage. Several dervishes were fighting a pair of chimera. Part lion, part goat, part snake, they bounded back and forth, striking up at the parapets as Meewfolk guardswomen fired down on them with a steady stream of arrows. The beasts were starting to drop health, but they weren't alone. Four huge dinosaurs were shambling toward the tall red stone walls of the city from the forest line. These shaggy black monsters looked like someone had crossbred Godzilla with a chicken, given it a pair of long beefy arms, and welded katana blades to each finger. I knew them from other dinosaur-inclusive games I'd played: they were Therizinosaurs. But something about them wasn't right, and as they got closer, I spotted why.

These [Zombie Therizinosaurs] were also extremely dead.

Bloated from the jungle heat, putrid from the moisture, they were little more than waddling sacks of fluid as they charged the wall. They didn't seem to notice us: instead, they began to belch missiles of black filth at the city walls, trying to strike the archers still raining fire down on the chimera. The blasts managed to hit one archer, who fell back with a shriek of pain.

"To battle!" The Captain of the Forest Keepers cried from overhead. "Defend the walls!"

More decaying animals and monsters swarmed out of the jungle toward the city. The stench was unbearable.

"Suri! You and me can take on that spare chimera! Gar, Rin, go back up the Forest Keepers with enfilade support! Karalti, tank for the ranged units if they draw aggro!" I rattled off orders, already moving for the front. More surprising was that no one argued with me. Rin didn't know what enfilade was, but Gar seemed to, because he called for her and the Meewfolk to follow him to a position where they could fire on the Therizinosaurs from the side.

Suri stripped her armor and psyched herself into Primal Rage as I activated Mantle of Night, boosting my speed and attack power just before my first Jump. I landed right on the Chimera's back, driving the spear in where the scales ended and fur began.

[You deal 2025 damage! HP: 8,277/12,747]

The Chimera screamed from three different mouths, and I realized I might have made a mistake when the snake-head tail of the thing darted toward me. I was still under the influence of Mantle of Night, so instead of sinking its six-inch fangs into my neck, they hit me in the ribs. Yaola's chiton scale armor did its work: instead of plunging into my chest, the tips barely scraped my skin.

[You take 290 damage!]
[Virulent Poison! 2HP damage per second for 300 seconds.]

A wave of cold numbness spread through my arm—I leaped off as I saw Suri charge in from behind, her red aura flaring just before she brought her sword down in a huge cleaving strike. The massive blade took the snake's head right off, sending it flying and shooting a jet of black acidic blood into the air.

[Suri deals Critical Hit! 2571 damage! Chimera HP: 5,706/12,747.]

The injured Chimera roared, bucking like a bronco with me on top of it as I chugged an antidote and rode the damn thing like a stunt bike, surfing its back as it kicked and reared. Suri came around to the front: the chimera tracked her, then opened its lion mouth and released a stream of fireballs. She tanked them all, grunting as the fire splashed over her bare arms.

"I got this! Go back up the others!" Suri swept the lion's paw to the side and headbutted it right in the face.

Karalti waded into the small army of undead creatures, blasting a pack of [Zombie Deinonychus] into ash before they reached the wall. The rest of the party had drawn the aggro of the Theris. They were unloading on them with everything they had: the rangers with bow and arrows, Gar with his pistols, Rin with her turrets. Every hit picked away at the monster's health, but they had huge HP pools and were unaffected by pain or fear. The line of dinosaurs kept marching toward them, hocking gouts of black slime. One of them hit Hopper's kinetic shield wall. Another of them struck Rin, causing her to cry out as her skin began sizzling.

"Time to blow some shit the hell up!" I launched off the furious chimera, pivoted in the air, and concentrated. Shards of black energy rained down on the backs of the Theris, staggering them. I pulled the energy back, and they condensed around me like a fan of javelins, blasting the dinosaurs a second time. One of them crumpled to its knees, rotten jaws working in a soundless scream.

"Focus your fire on that one!" Gar shouted to the others, smoothly reloading his revolver and firing again.

I hit the ground and rolled, just about out of Adrenaline Points after the last five maneuvers—which meant I had to get in and fight dirty. I ran forward and vaulted onto the Theri at the end of the line, jamming the spear into the back of its neck and levering myself to stand on its shoulders. The dinosaur spun, claws flailing, but it couldn't reach up to slap me off.

"Ohho no. Look at your tiny arms!" I wrenched the spear free and plunged it down again, like an olde-worlde butter churn. "So mean! So stabby!"

The Theri let out a call—something between a dinosaur's bellow and a wet fart. The next in line spun to face us and charged with its head down and its claws held out to the sides.

"Wait! No! You're not supposed to be able to talk!" The Theri beneath me began to twist and shake, trying to get me off its back. "Bad bronco! Bad!"

The second dinosaur braced itself like a linebacker and smashed straight into its buddy, sending me flying. I turned the tumble into a flip, just in time. A gout of acid sailed past me, and then a second hit me right on the visor of my helmet, splattering and blacking out my vision.

[Your armor is Sundered! -15% protection for 60 seconds!]

[You are Blind! Remove the obstacle to see again!]

"Dude, fucking gross!" I Shadow Danced backwards, getting as far from the Therizinosaurs as I could. The two aggravated mobs spun on their hind feet and lumbered after me as I quickly pulled a rag out of my Inventory and used it to wipe my helmet so I could see again, removing the Blind status—and revealing, in vivid technicolor, the twenty tons of extremely dead dinosaur rushing toward me.

"Nope." I bunched my legs, then vaulted into the air. At the apex of the jump, I burned my last AP to dash over the pair of Theris as they swiped with their sword hands and lurched into each other. "Nooope."

"Last two! Hector, get out of the way!" Rin's voice pierced the clamor of battle.

I bounded out of the line of fire as the pair of dinosaurs spun around, their eyeless sockets gaping, and ducked as a barrage of small arms fire blasted the zombies in the head and chest. They struggled forward into the fire, even as arrows embedded in their flesh, or blew maggot-riddled chunks off of them. Panting, resting, I watched anxiously as they got to within thirty feet of Rin... and then slowly crumpled to their knees and collapsed.

"HUURRGH!" Suri's snarl cut the din. I whipped around to see her wrench a horn off the fallen chimera, raise it high above her head, and stab it through the chest. The monster roared and bleated at the same time, its legs scrabbling along the bloody ground. Suri wrestled with it, taking a clawed slap across the side of her face before it expired and fell still.

[Suri has defeated Chimera!]
*[You gain 3864 EXP! You are Level 28! Suri is Level 31! Rin
is Level 25! Gar is Level 18!]*

"Damn, nice." I leaned on the Spear to catch my breath.

As we regathered around Karalti, the gates to the city
opened. A squad of ten guardswomen ran to greet us. Like
their menfolk, they were a far cry from the wary, cautious
Meewfolk of the mainland. They were tall and sleek, fit,
proud, dressed in golden half-plate armor and brimmed,
armored hats that fit around their ears. Their spears spat
sparks of mana as they thumped them on the ground and stood
to attention.

"Who have you brought to us?" The woman shot the
Forest Keeper Captain a dark, challenging look. "Humans?
And a dragon?"

"Their ship wrecked near the Ponang Commons," the
Forest Keeper Captain replied. His ears flattened, and his tail
swished as he spoke. "They wish an audience with the Glory
of the Sun, regarding some matter of international importance.
You can speak to them directly... they know our language."

"Interesting." The guard turned her eyes to us, proud and
aloof. "It is still a month until the next season. Are they your
prisoners?"

"They have not committed any crimes." The Forest
Keeper shrugged. "They have complied with us and assisted us
in battle. The colony stands to benefit from their presence.
That is our opinion."

"Your opinion carries high regard, Forest Keeper Nok Gao." The woman put her hands together, palm to palm, and bowed fractionally from the neck. He did the same. Then, she turned to us.

"Humans, your menfolk cannot come into the city—as guests." She looked pointedly at me and Gar. "You can be admitted only as prisoners. But because you are not guilty of any crimes, it is a formality until you reach the temple grounds. If our Priest-Queen judges your cause worthy, she will revoke your arrest."

"And if she doesn't?" Suri asked.

The guardswoman shrugged. "Who knows? She is the Priest-Queen."

"Not real reassuring," Gar rasped.

"It is up to you." She turned her brilliant blue-green eyes back to me.

"I think Her Majesty will listen to us," I said. "I'm fine with a formal arrest—for me and Gar."

"Hey!" Gar snapped. "You can't just lump me in with this! I'm not even in your damn party!"

"Then stay out here." I held my wrists out to the lady. "The women of my party don't need any special conditions to enter, right?"

"Correct," the guard replied. "They are permitted."

"Then whatever we did, it's all my fault." I grinned at her. "I've been a very bad boy."

The crowd of Meewfolk women tittered in amusement. Their leader flicked her tail, once, then shrugged and pulled a coil of rope off her belt. "Then I do formally arrest you for unspecified, unspeakable crimes. Come."

"*Dios mío...*" Gar slumped his way over as the woman deftly bound my hands, and held his out alongside. "FINE. I want to get into the damn city to shop for parts."

"*I guess I'll stay out here,*" Karalti sighed. "*I can't shift back yet. Bleh.*"

"*Once your timer's up, you can come join us. Though the Priest-Queen might just send us straight back out again, so who knows?*" The guard fastened the cuffs very loosely—so much so that I could have easily slipped them.

Karalti huffed, and rested back on the pad of fat just underneath her tail, using it like a small stool. "*Fiiine.*"

"Come." The guardswoman jerked her head toward the gate and led us through. Suri strolled to my left, her mouth quirked in a strange smile.

I scowled at her. "You. Don't get any funny ideas."

"Ideas? Whatever do you mean by that?" Her lips pursed a little more.

"I'm well aware that there's guys who'd pay a lot of money to be put in cuffs and marched through a city of scantily clad women, furry or not," I replied. "I am not one of those men."

"Right." She snorted. "What was your safeword again?"

I muttered to myself. "… Zinfandel."

Suri's grin only widened.

The patrol led us down a wide, smooth road to the Priest-Queen's palace. It was the polar opposite of the slums in Taltos: an orderly, clean and vibrant grid, well-planned and well-constructed. The wooden houses were crafted with care, mounted on stilts and terraces, with carvings, wooden lattices, and elegant hipped roofs made of blue and purple tiles. Brightly colored chickens clucked and scratched under people's homes. Broad canals served as roads, full of small boats. Gardens bloomed with flowers and aromatic herbs. The people here were lightly dressed in sarongs and beautiful jewelry. Hundreds of curious eyes followed us as we headed for the center of the city, where a great walled palace reached for the skies. Meewfolk of every color and size came out to gawk at us, from small kittenfolk to elderly matriarchs supported by their adult daughters. Some of them waved. Others crossed their arms, or flattened their ears in disapproval.

The temple itself had a fortified gate: part palace, part fortress, surrounded by lush, tropical gardens. There were entire courtyards within the grounds, divided by paths and small trickling brooks. Silk banners danced in the wind, which was heavy with the smell of flowers. The roof of the palace was sheathed in bronze, gleaming under the hot sun. The guardswomen here were a step above the ones escorting us to the temple's entry terrace. Their jewelry was made of aurum, radiating magic. They didn't wear much in the way of metal armor—it was more like gladiator gear—but they were all protected by shielding magic more sophisticated than anything

I'd seen in Taltos. Rather than a flat shield of energy, the light bent around their bodies slightly as we passed.

"Meewfolk magic armor is amazing! How do they keep those shields so stable?" Rin craned her head back as we passed.

"Our torques are a secret known only to our artificers, little silverskin. But it is best not to look any of the Royal Guard or the Priestesses in the eye," the guard closest to her said. "They will take it as a challenge. On the temple grounds, you are honor-bound to fight anyone you stare at."

"Temple?" I asked. "What god is it dedicated to?"

"To the Triad," the leader replied.

I blinked a couple times. "You mean... the Paragon, Artist, Warsinger Triad? Or...?"

"No. We have three gods. Lua, Mewa Rathi, and Hanuwele. It is a place where they are worshipped, and also the place where our ancestors are honored."

At the top of the stairs, blocking the entry to the temple proper, was a unit of some twenty guards—and the one in front, an especially large, strongly built woman, narrowed her eyes and stared daggers at me as they came to a stop. Like her sisters, she was dressed only in pounds of metal, but she had pieces that the other guards did not: stacked rings around her neck, a golden girdle around her waist, and a lovely earring that linked to her nose with a fringe of fine chains. She was very dark furred, with a black face, hands, and tail that bled to fawn over the rest of her coat.

"What is this?" The new woman demanded. "You know it is forbidden for you to bring males here outside of the festival season!"

Our escorts went to pains not to meet her gaze, looking down with their ears folded back and their tails held low. The leader stepped forward and bowed deeply. "We have brought novelty for her Highness's consideration, Battle Maiden. These humans and one Mercurion. They beg an audience. Some matter to do with the magic of the Ancient Ones."

The Battle Maiden, as the city guard had called her, irritably flicked an ear as she surveyed us. "How? They only speak the prattle of apes."

"Believe me, I can understand you just fine," I said in the same language.

The woman looked at us. Her eyes were an especially brilliant, piercing blue against her dark face. "You have followed this conversation?"

"Yes," I replied. "Loud and clear, ma'am."

The woman's nose twitched as she sniffed at us. "Most manlings who come here expect us to learn their languages, or speak to us in trade pidgin. Why are you here?"

I pushed forward to stand slightly ahead of the others. "We are the Triad of the Sixth Age, and we're here to beg an audience with your queen to discuss the impending return of the Drachan."

"The Deceivers?" The Maiden studied me for a few moments, her tail lashing. "They have not been heard of for five thousand years. A myth, save for the stories written onto the skin of the Avatar, and every Avatar before him. He is who you must seek, not our Queen. However..."

"However?" Suri waved a hand.

"Our Queen must assess your intentions," the woman continued. "And if you are who you say you are, I suppose you may seek an audience. If you wish to meet her, you must be stripped of your armor and weapons and given more appropriate attire."

"Let's do it." I shrugged, looking to the others.

The guard captain—I was pretty sure she was the captain—looked down at the city guard who'd escorted us. "Thank you, guardians. You may release them and go about your business, free from taboo."

"Thank you, Hwa'nehh." The leader of the guards squinted at her, then stood and pressed her hands together, palm to palm. All the others did the same, bowing from the chest, then turned to us and untied our ceremonial cuffs.

"I am Hwa'nehh Tahan, first among the sacred guard," the Battle Maiden uttered. "Come. We will prepare you to enter the temple."

***

Fifteen minutes later, the six of us were all stripped down, dressed in plain sarongs and not much else. No shoes, no weapons, definitely no armor. We'd been instructed to place our inventory into guest lockboxes and put on what amounted to a large silk sheet. The sarongs could be tied over the chest or wrapped around the waist—it was our choice. Suri and Rin had theirs up higher, so that the sarong looked more like a dress, but Gar and I wore ours down low. Thus stripped, we were taken through the pavilion to the great temple at the end of the complex.

Tahan ushered us into a great round hall. Pillars held up a tall, conical ceiling. In the center of the building was a fighting ring, while all around it, Meewfolk women talked, laughed, fanned themselves, and dozed in the sunlight that strayed through the windows, watching indulgently as two young girls sparred on the sands. They had the big paws and gangly limbs of teenagers, and fought with wooden spears that clacked as they struck, whirled, and parried one another. Now and then, one would let out a piercing yowl, or hiss, faces contorting with simulated rage.

On the other side of the chamber, raised on a dais and surrounded by ladies-in-waiting, was the Priest-Queen of Ru Waat. She was a sight to behold, tall and lean and extremely fit. Most of her coat was as white and silky as polished pearl, darkening to dark red points on her extremities. She had an especially fine tail with a plume of long, lustrous fur. It lay draped around her thighs like a fan of scarlet feathers.

When she caught sight of us, her ears pricked, and she pushed herself up to her hands. The crowd of servants and slaves around her scattered as the flame-pointed woman got to her feet. She was dressed all in gold: a filmy gold sari, a golden headdress styled like the rays of the sun, and stacks of gold bracelets, rings, and chokers. Like Tahan, she wore an earring connected to a nose ring by slender chains, though hers was larger and fancier.

Tahan motioned us down. "Kneel for the Priest-Queen of Ru Waat, Pranang Prashini Solai Maaw, Chosen of the Sun, First Warrior among our people."

Suri, Rin and I all bowed from the waist. Gar folded his arms and stood back, only sketching a brief, awkward dip of his torso.

Tahan went to her knees and bowed to the floor. "These manlings have come to our land seeking a favor of you, my queen. They request that you humor them with audience."

The queen with the very long name studied us, gazing at each person with obvious delight. She had starling eyes, a blue so pale they were like chips of ice against the brilliant red fur of her muzzle.

"Humans? And a Mercurion? How unusual." She trilled, sashaying forward. She moved like a panther, all muscle and grace, and wove around and through the group of us. Her tail slid under my nose on the way past, her arm brushing mine. "What a strange scent you have, human. The perfume of the dark forest at night, heavy with the smell of the hunt. You smell like a predator worthy of the title. But this one..."

The Priest-Queen came to a stop in front of Rin, looking the nervous Mercurion up and down. "You, lovely one, are not a predator at all, even though your kind were crafted for war. Your people are nothing but stories in our land."

"N-No," Rin stuttered. "I'm really not."

The Queen's curly mouth lifted into a sly smirk at the corners, and she reached out to press the pads of her fingers against Rin's breastbone, giving her a small, playful shove before sauntering over to Suri. Suri tensed as the Queen ghosted around her, sniffing curiously.

"And here we have a woman who smells like old blood, carrying the heat of the desert storms with her like a cloak," the Priest-Queen sighed. "So beautiful, you are, and with the bearing of a queen. Are these two your favorite males?"

She flashed Gar and I both a wicked, knowing smile.

"I'd say one of them's currently my favorite male, and the other one's a fixer-upper I picked up off the street," Suri replied wryly. "He's got a long way to go before he's my favorite anything."

Gar's cheeks flushed. "Hey! What's your damn problem?"

Suri flashed him a look of disbelief over her shoulder. "You shot my damn hookwing, mate."

The Priest-Queen laughed with delight at the banter, but then abruptly sobered. The light left her eyes, and her ears pinned back. "Regardless, it is against law for males to be here out of season. You were surely told this."

"I would like to claim an exception, Your Majesty. Human males are always in season," I quipped. "Three hundred and sixty-five days a year, 24-hours a day, Sargent Roger is ready to stand at attention and fire when ordered."

The queen struggled with her serious façade for a moment, before she broke into a sibilant, tinkling laugh. Her mirth was followed by Tahan's, and most of her other maids in waiting: some of whom were clearly just copying their ruler out of courtly necessity.

"So I have heard! So I have heard. No doubt why you travel with such an assortment of lovers." The Queen gestured broadly to our group. "You do not need to use my title. Call me Solai."

"Now you just hang on a goddamned—OWW!" Gar started, cut off as Rin discreetly stomped on his bare toes.

I laughed. "There is a lot of love here, but most of us aren't involved that way."

Solai fixed us with wide, innocent eyes. "Ah, but if you are the Triad of legend, then of course there is love! Who can forget the passion between the Paragon Siva Nandini and his dragon mate, Yavrusa the Carnelian Splendor? And his passionate, scandalous affair with Jun-Heera, the first Warsinger?"

"Oh, right. Yeah, can't forget them," Suri drawled. "Your Majesty, we all, uhh, share different types of love, and you can be assured that I won't be hopping into a hot tub with Gar or Rin any time soon."

Solai laughed again. "And fair enough, too. That taller male looks like a dried-out antelope carcass."

Gar bristled, but Rin stomped on his foot again before he could retort, earning a yelp and a scowl.

"Of course, there is one true test to determine if you are indeed the Triad." The Priest-Queen breezed around me again. "The Legendary Spear. Do you have it?"

"The younger male did have a very fine spear with him, Your Highness." Tahan said.

"Sure do," I said. "I can call it to my hand, if you want to see it?"

"Of course I want to see it!" Solai's tail arched into a curious question mark as she came to a stop, hands on hips. "Do it. Call it to your hand."

I took a step back, held my arm out, and called for the Spear. As soon as the thought manifested, it appeared, gleaming with traceries of red, black and white.

A gasp went up around the court. Priestesses stopped mid-fan to gawk.

"Ahhh..." The queen reached out curiously, hands hovering over the haft. "The Spear of Nine Spheres, just as the stories say. But this only has three stones, not nine."

"We're hoping you might be able to help with that," I said. "We're looking for the others. We're also looking for anything and everything we can find about Warsingers... and access to a Chorus Vault off the coast of your home."

A murmur went up. Several of the lounging priestesses sat upright, watching the audience with greater alertness.

"Well, if you have such knowledge of our greatest mysteries... well. Who am I to deny an audience with our Sacred Avatar?" Solai's eyes hooded. "I will grant your request, but not for free."

"Not for free?" Suri took a step forward. "The Drachan are a danger to the entire world, and we don't have a lot of time."

"We have survived the depredations of both the Drachan *and* the Aesari. We shall endure the foolishness of humans, if it comes to that." The Queen shrugged. "I cannot admit untried strangers to visit our holiest of places without evidence that you are here in good faith. You must prove to me and my colony that you are who you say you are."

"Fair enough," I said. "What do you want?"

A smile curled her mouth. "Three wishes. Of you."

"Me?" I pointed at me. "Just me?"

"You bear the Spear. That means you and your dragon queen are the leaders of the Triad." Solai shot a sly glance at Suri. "Your companions go where you go until your destiny is complete, yes? I shall make my wishes of you. They may follow you if they wish."

"One wish should be plenty," Suri said flatly.

"Three is a sacred number." The Priest-Queen folded her hands and contentedly squinted at Suri.

I shrugged and looked to the others. They shrugged back. There wasn't really much we could do, unless we felt like fighting our way to the Avatar through an army of Meewfolk. Given all their NPC meters displayed between two and three red skulls each, indicating their challenge level was a good bit higher than ours, I wasn't keen to try.

"Three wishes, then," I said. "But you can't wish for more wishes."

"You are bold, to tell me what I can and cannot do in my own house." The Priest-Queen's smile widened to show teeth.

"But I like boldness in people. You are someone who knows that you do not attain power by purring and mewling at someone else's hand. You must seize it."

"Where I'm from, we have a saying. 'The bad guys aren't gonna shoot themselves, and the General isn't gonna get his own coffee'." I smiled back at her.

"Indeed." The Priest-Queen returned to her dais, collapsing back to her divan and draping herself across the royal blue coverlet. "A deal is struck, human. My first wish of you is the most arduous. You may have noticed the damage to our city, and the many soldiers and patrols we have stationed in and around Ru Waat?"

I rubbed my wrists. "Yes."

"We have been attacked by many of these monsters in recent weeks." The tip of her tail began to flick. "At first, it was little things. Goblins, baboons driven into a rage. Then the monsters started to arrive. Saberwolves, animated skeletons, dead lizard men. Slowly but surely, the attacks are getting worse, the monsters larger and more dangerous. Every hour or so, a wave of them erupts from the deepest parts of the jungle, from the ruins which lay crumbling in the dark."

"Ruins?" I frowned. "What kind of ruins?"

The queen shivered, then licked her fangs. "The taboo kind. None but the Avatar may venture there. It is a ruin of the Fall."

"The Fall?" Rin piped up. "Do you mean the Drachan?"

"Perhaps. I cannot say. It is taboo." The queen blinked at us slowly, resting her chin on the backs of her hands. "I cannot send my warriors there, even the males. But humans and Mercurions are not bound by our laws. So that is my first wish: go into the jungle, to this dark and brooding place, and learn what is sending this plague toward us."

"What are the other two wishes?" I asked. "Hopefully not as dangerous."

She reached out, and began to toy idly with a tea glass that sat on a small table next to her, ever so slowly pushing it toward the edge. "I think that depends on your perspective of danger, Paragon."

"Then hopefully not as time-consuming," Rin said, wincing. "We have to stop Emperor Hyland from... ummm... well, becoming an actual emperor, ruling multiple countries and stuff."

Nonchalantly, Solai swatted the glass to the ground. None of the Meewfolk reacted as it shattered, or when a comically overdressed servant crawled from around the back of the throne, quickly swept up the broken glass with an ornate dustpan and broom, and set a brand-new glass in its place before scuttling back.

"Your dread emperor can wait three more days," the Priest-Queen sighed, reaching out with a single claw to toy with the new glass. "I shall formalize my wish as a quest. And then you may go or not, as it pleases you."

[New Quest Alert: Genie in a Bottle.]

New Quest: Genie in a Bottle

The Priest-Queen of the Meewfolk has agreed to humor your request to speak with their sacred Avatar: provided you grant her three wishes of her choosing. Complete your first sub-quests and speak with Queen Solai after completion to receive the other two.

***Rewards:** 4000 EXP, ??? Renown (Meewhome, Priest-Queen Mawar Solai, Cult of Dera)*

I accepted the main quest, and as soon as I did, the sub-quest appeared.

New Sub-Quest: The One Who Abides

A mysterious force emanating from Meewhome's ancient rainforests is threatening the city of Ru Waat, as well as outlying villages and the nomadic herders who provide the populace with food. Undead monsters and dinosaurs have been pouring out of the deep jungle to assault the walls, escalating in power and frequency as time wears on.

The Priest-Queen of Meewhome has requested that you find the source of the problem and halt the flow of undead abominations. From your prior journey to the Temple of the Maker in the Bashir Desert, you know that the ruins the queen has requested you travel to are in fact the ruins of the Dragon Gate of Devana, the Mother Goddess of Dragonkind.

***Difficulty:** Hard.*

***Rewards:** EXP 3500, Unknown Treasure, Unknown Special Items.*

"Wow. The EXP for these are really nice," Rin breathed, her eyes flicking from side to side. "Do all party members get this much EXP?"

"I am a generous ruler." Solai yawned, her lips pulling back to reveal twin rows of long, sharp fangs. "And thus I await your victorious return, Triad of the Sixth Age. Until then, I shall give you all my sovereign's mark. You have free run of my city until you depart—but if you commit any crimes, make sure they are interesting ones. I would not wish to have you all exiled or enslaved for being boring."

***

We were escorted to the city outside the Priest-Queen's palace and left to our own devices. Once the gates were closed, we gathered into a circle and considered our next move.

"So, hear me out," I said. "My vote is that we find an inn and stay here overnight, or even for a couple of days before setting off for Devana's Dragon Gate."

"Why?" Suri frowned. "Thought we needed to get back to Myszno in case of a raid?"

"We do," I said. "But think about it. The Priest-Queen just told us that monsters are attacking the city walls about once every hour, right?"

"So?" Gar scowled.

"Can you think of a single spot in Archemi where you can reliably fight high-yield monsters over and over again?" I waved my hands in the direction of the city walls. "Dude, this is the perfect spot to grind. If we camp here and ride those waves, we could go up three or four levels in twenty-four hours. Even better, there's no time limit on Solai's quest. The system *always* flags quests that have to be completed within a certain timespan. Whatever's causing these dead dinos and other monsters to attack the city, it's gonna keep sending them until we fix the cause.

"Mob spawns like this ARE kind of rare," Rin remarked. "In the beta testing phase—which we're technically still in— enemy spawn rates were scaled down because of the influx of refugees."

"If there's no rush, I'm on board with staying for a while." Suri rolled her shoulders. "Getting to Level 33 or 34 would be great."

"Guess I don't get a say," Gar muttered.

Suri glowered at him. "No one's twisting your arm, mate. If you don't want to grind, go shop for airship parts or something."

Gar gestured sharply to the city around us. "You see any hangars around here? The stores here aren't going to stock the parts I need. Hell, they probably don't HAVE airships here. I don't even know if they sell ammunition for my weapons."

Rin tutted. "Stop being a drama queen. There'll be at least one Tier-A Alchemist store here. They can sell you the metals we need to make ammunition. All you need is lead, copper, carbon, saltpeter and iron. Get me those, and I can craft bullets."

"Thanks," Gar replied sourly. "Guess I'll go do that with the money I need to repair my damn ship."

"And while you're at it, go buy some cheese to go with your whine," I snapped. "This squad has no room for dead weight. You don't want to grind? Sit it out, but don't bitch about it. For the thousandth time, I insured your fucking ship. It'll be fixed."

Gar flashed me an odd look. "Fine. Meet you at the wall in ten."

"Hah. Sorted him out." Suri grinned mirthlessly after the man slunk off, his hands buried in his duster pockets. "What do you three say to brainstorming some small unit tactics? We can use this as a chance to sharpen up our ability to fight as a team."

"Sure! Though I'm still not really any good in fights." Rin winced. "I-I panic sometimes. If I didn't have my turrets, I'd be really useless."

"Fighting's a skill, not a talent. Every time you fight and every time you win, you get better at handling your adrenaline." I pumped a fist. "Let's do it. We can set our spawn points at the nearest inn, stock up on potions, meet up with Karalti, and get in some righteous grinding time."

CHAPTER 39

"Zacam"unilag!" Rin shouted, her spellglove flaring with blue light. "Get in there!"

The injured tyrannosaurus bellowed as the spell took hold, wrapping it in a bubble of warped temporal distortion. Its motions slowed to a crawl, limbs struggling through invisible mud. The undead dinosaur was missing one of its arms, and its jaw hung loose from where Karalti had shattered it with a well-placed tail strike.

"Ally-oop!" I called out, dashing behind it. The t-rex smashed its tail down in slow motion, but I was already off the ground and out of range. I flipped into the landing, the Spear blazing, and landed on the back of the huge monster like a black meteor as Karalti and Suri closed in from the sides.

[You deal 3791 Darkness damage! Suri deals 1558 Damage! Karalti deals 988 Damage!]
[You defeated Tyrannosaurus! You gain 1512 EXP! Karalti gains 1512 EXP!]
[You are Level 33! Karalti is Level 18! Rin Lu is Level 30! Garcia is Level 24!]
[You have 6 unspent Ability Points! You have 10 Skill points!]
[You have one new Mark of Matir ability available!]

There was a cheer from the walls as the dinosaur's legs crumpled and it collapsed forward, head smashing into the ground with earthshaking force. I twisted the Spear out of it and bounced back down, landing lightly beside Karalti as her body flooded with seams of light. Her wing membranes extended further along her tail, and she put on muscle in her legs, shoulders, and flanks. The deep raven-blue of her scales intensified, glinting with thick seams of bright opal that made her ripple with colors as she moved. By the time her level growth was complete, her horns were longer, but less flexible. She could still lift and flatten them, but they were now as hard and black as polished stone.

"Phew." Suri pulled her helmet off and mopped her forehead. She threw the rag to me, and I did the same as Rin and Gar joined us. "Nice going, guys. We took that thing out a hell of a lot faster than the first one."

"And I am now Level fuckin' Thirty-Three," I said, checking my sheet. We were exhausted, our potion and mana reserves depleted, but after ten hours of hard work split over the previous evening and the following day, we were looking good. Not only had I pumped my Physical stats by nearly ten points—Str, Sta, Dex—our small-group tactical work had increased both Wisdom and Intelligence by modest amounts. I had a stack of Skill Points to assign, and a whole lot of monster parts to sell to the Alchemist in town.

"You all want to wait for another round? Or should we head for the jungle?" Suri asked, tucking her helmet under her arm. "Seems to me like these mobs are getting tougher."

"Yeah. They're getting tougher, and we're getting less EXP for them." I restlessly checked the Quest the Priest-Queen had given us. "Oop, well... looks like there's a timer on it now."

"There is?" Suri checked it as well. "Huh. We've got twenty-four hours to solve the problem, at least."

"A timer? When did that happen?" Rin asked.

"About three hours ago, during the fight with those big ol' troll-lookin' things." Gar had mellowed out a lot over the course of the day—mostly because he'd been able to level like he'd never leveled before.

"I'm tempted to stay, except the city is running out of herbs for potions," I said. "We should probably count our chickens and go do this quest. Give ourselves plenty of time."

"*Mmm. Chicken.*" Karalti paused to preen an itchy spot under her wing, the membranes rustling overhead.

"Yes. If the quest requirements changed, then the circumstances must be evolving." Rin fidgeted nervously. "The system only does this if we're competing against someone else. Other players, maybe, or who or whatever is causing the plague to begin with."

"*Well, whoever they are, they're gonna have to deal with us.*" Karalti tossed her head, still hopped up from the fighting. "*I can fly us to the edge of the jungle. And now we're better equipped to take on whoever or whatever's out there.*"

"We sure are. Running low on potion ingredients, but I think we'll be able to find those in the forest." I looked to the others. "You guys ready?"

"Yeah. But I'm not going." Gar looked to the city. "For one thing, it's not any of my business. For another, I don't feel right screwing off into the jungle when my crew's waiting on news from me."

"Suits me." I shrugged. "Suri? Karalti? Rin?"

"I'm good. Let's go." Suri nodded.

"All aboard!" Karalti stretched a wing down, standing head and shoulders over Ru Waat's city wall.

"We're going to have to build a gantry to get up on your back soon," I teased her, leaping from the ground to the edge of the saddle, then pulling myself up. *"Suri has to climb you like a mountain."*

"Kinda like how she does you, huh?" Karalti replied sweetly.

"My little Tidbit is all grown up." I feigned a sniffle. *"You were so innocent, once. So pure."*

"Blow me." She threw her head back and mimicked a human laugh—albeit much deeper and louder.

When Suri and Rin were up, I helped Rin with her harness. Once they were secure, I took my position between Karalti's shoulders and looked down to see Gar standing in the gateway of the city, a complex expression on his face. I gave him a flippant salute as Karalti pivoted and stalked toward the road, building up into a fast walk before bunching and launching herself into the air. The downdraft of her wings rocked the palm trees below as we powered over them, gaining altitude at a speed that took my breath away and left a mad grin plastered on my face. There would never be a day in my life when I didn't get a high from that feeling.

"Oh god." Suri said in the party chat. *"She's even faster now."*

"Yeah..." Rin craned her head to look back. *"Seeing you without tie-down straps makes me so nervous, Hector."*

"Why? Never worn one before." I gripped the handhold on the front of the saddle with one hand, resting my other arm across my knee.

"I guess. Never mind." Rin sighed and reached up to clutch her harness straps.

Karalti let out a joyous bellow as she built into flight, turning the jungle into a rushing green carpet as she angled for the origin of the plague of maddened and undead animals: Devana's Dragon Gate. As she flew, I brought up my character sheet, and got to work assigning ability points. At Level 33, I had two new abilities to choose from.

Blink Strike

You attack an enemy from the front with a normal strike, but then teleport through or around them in the blink of an eye to strike them again from behind and inflict an Elemental Darkness strike. You may activate Blink Strike following any successful hit that deals damage to an enemy.

Night Falls

Chained from Jump. You are a master of aerial combat: as you descend from Jump, you deal a powerful Area of Effect strike that knocks down up to five enemies and deals elemental Darkness damage. If you land on an enemy while activating Night Falls, you also deal your Jump damage to that enemy. If you have already dealt damage with Jump before chaining this ability, you only deal the AoE effect damage.

Both these abilities made me wish I had a lot more points, because they were both really fucking awesome.

"Hmm. I wonder if Night Falls has a height limit?" I muttered to myself, cuing Navigail to read it out again. The AoE dealt 500 points of Dark elemental damage, plus my base weapon attack, but there was no mention of a height limit. I would have to play with that a bit... because I was suddenly struck by images of jumping off Karalti and landing on someone from a thousand feet like a human bomb.

I dropped three of my points into Night's Fall and one into Blink Strike. With *Night's Fall III*, I could knock down fifteen enemies and deal 1000 damage to all of them, plus the Spear's base damage. If those enemies happened to be undead or otherwise weak to Darkness, that went up to 2000—it was a crowd control power bomb. The other two points went into *Jump VI* and *Master of Blades VI*. They were two of my biggest power moves.

Jump VI

Spring up to 60ft into the air in any direction and deal x4 damage on landing, with +10% knockdown resistance while in the air.

Master of Blades VI

Chain combo from Jump. Before you hit the ground, leap backwards into the air and manifest a rain of shadow lances onto your foes, dealing massive damage to enemies (1632 per lance, 4 lances per level, maximum 4 lances per enemy).

As I grew into my Path, I was starting to understand how it was really meant to work—especially in synergy with the Nasaku Half-Blood abilities. While it sucked to have to drink blood once a week—pun intended—I couldn't deny the sheer power of the Shadowlord ability. Shadows weren't particularly strong, but they allowed me to maximize my crowd control potential. As far as I could tell, Dark Dragoon had two battle modes. Battle mode #1 was a style I'd nicknamed the Team Player, in which I utilized high-damage moves to hit enemies fast and hard, softening them up for Suri and Karalti. Both of them had more armor, defense and HP than I did, but I had half again as much DPS. By relying on her and Suri to soak, as we'd done with the T-rex, I could deploy the nukes at my disposal.

The second mode was the Death from Above school of spear fighting. This was my current solo-build focus: mastering my aerial abilities and enhancing them with the Stealth skill to deal as much damage as possible, as fast as possible. All players benefited from attacks made from concealment. *Black Lotus, Jump, Spider Climb, Dancing Fly*, and my AoE moves all got a 1.5x bonus from surprise attacks. And you know what made surprises easy? Shadow minions, who could encircle an opponent and distract them to grant me that sweet flanking bonus. With Jump VI, I could tear an undead opponent or anyone weak to Darkness to shreds—2,730 base damage, plus the 1.5x stealth modifier, plus the Darkness bonus meant I dealt upwards of 8000 damage in a single hit, minus the enemy's armor soak. And Jump wasn't even the highest damage ability in my arsenal. I sunk six of my Skill points into Stealth, bringing it up to the maximum limit before I needed a trainer to guide me into the Advanced levels. The other four I held onto. When I found a Master Spearfighting trainer, I would need them to advance to the first level of the skill.

Next up was my Mark of Matir ability. On seeing the options, I didn't even have to think about which one of the two I was going to pick.

Shadow Sight (Life)

This ability conveys the Black God's blessing on your eyes, allowing you to see in the dark. Under low light conditions, you will be able to see with high clarity. In true darkness, you will gain thermal darkvision.

Ghost Hunter (Entropy)

Any weapon you wield can strike incorporeal enemies, even if unenchanted. You may bless a weapon to only strike incorporeal enemies, dealing 1.5x damage to them on top of any other bonuses, but leaving corporeal entities unharmed. Duration: 1 Hour.

"Darkvision. No regrets." I selected it without hesitation. While Ghost Hunter wasn't bad, I already had a bunch of Dark-element combat abilities that worked on shades and other undead.

The Mark of Matir pulsed with cool energy, and my vision blurred for a moment before resettling. The sky was still bright, storm clouds massing over our heads. I wouldn't be able to test out my vision for a while yet, but I was hopeful.

"Okay, hold on tight for the descent!" Karalti flicked a wing-tip, coasting to the right. *"I'm going to have to land in that clearing there, and then we're gonna have to hoof it to the ruins. This jungle is too dense to permit the full extent of my majesty."*

"Seems like there's more to love with every level," I replied, closing my screen. *"Assuming the position."*

"Heads down, butts up!" Karalti trilled to everyone. *"Don't worry, Suri: I'll make it gentle."*

"Thanks. Appreciate it." Suri mumbled back.

True to her word, Karalti came in slow and smooth, alighting in a clearing formed by an enormous collapsed tree. Rotten wood and fresh ferns crackled under her feet, and nearby trees swayed. Suri and Rin began to unbuckle straight away, while I surveyed our path ahead from Karalti's back. Massive trees with flat crowns towered over deep, dark, primordial forest. The birds were silent, spooked by the noise we had made, but hoots, howls, and bellows could be heard echoing from the distance. Knee-high mist swirled across the soft ground, and water condensed and dripped from the canopy like warm rain. Beautiful as it was, I half expected to see a squad of powered armor materialize out of camouflage and start raining down fiery hell.

"You alright?" Karalti asked me, dipping down to let her passengers off. *"You got nervous all of a sudden."*

"It's nothing." There was a pang of sympathetic pain in my shoulder as I slid down my dragon's wing, then leaped down to the mossy forest floor. *"We just need to be on the top of our game here. It's too easy to get ambushed in terrain like this. And we need to watch out for traps."*

"I think we'll be okay. Don't worry, alright?" Once the others were off her back, Karalti shifted down. When the light cleared and diffused, I did a small doubletake at her appearance. While she still looked mostly human, Karalti had kept her crest of seven horns, which swept back from her skull like a crown. Small scales climbed from her feet up to about mid-thigh, with similar scale gloves climbing the pale flesh of her arms. As she turned to show me her back, I saw that she had patterned her scales down along her spine to the top of her butt.

"What do you think?" Karalti struck a pose, looking back over her shoulder at me.

"I like it." I came close to her, absently sliding my hands up over her back. *"Why the change?"*

470

"I'm tired of people thinking I'm just an ordinary human, because I'm not." Karalti turned in my arms, then reached up to tie her hair back into a long ponytail. *"I'm Solonkratsu, and I want to be known for what I am. If I need to go undercover, I can simulate a more human shape. At some point, I might even figure out how to make vocal chords."*

"You are plenty human shaped." I was more than happy to hold her while she stretched. Now she was fully mature, the sight and feel of her made my pulse leap. And it wasn't just the curves: it was her smell. As I leaned in, I caught a hint of a deep, intoxicating scent—a very familiar scent. Every month, once a month, Karalti went into heat. She wasn't there yet, but it wasn't long now. A matter of days. *"And it's gonna be that time any day now, isn't it? Ready for a second round of Extreme Sex Tag: Kalla Sahasi Edition?"*

Karalti let out a yarp of laughter, startling Rin. The Mercurion looked over, turned bright blue, then turned back with her face in her hands.

"You better hope we're back in Kalla Sahasi." Karalti's violet eyes smoldered as she equipped her monk fighter's outfit, then her armored iron gauntlets. *"We've got a few days yet. Four or five."*

"Duly noted." I mimed bringing up my HUD. *"Let me just mark that on my calendar."*

Karalti giggled. *"Suriii. Hector's flirting with me."*

"You think ratting him out's gonna get me to help you?" Suri laughed, her voice hollow behind the shield of her greathelm. "Snitches get stitches, Special-K."

"Does she have clothes on yet?" Rin squeaked, her back still turned toward us.

Karalti planted her fists on her hips. *"You weren't complaining when I was naked before. You know, for like the last hundred miles?"*

Rin danced on the spot, gesturing wildly at Karalti, the sky, and herself. "You had a saddle on! And you were a dragon! Dragons can't be naked! They've got, like, scales!"

"You know my cloaca doesn't just go away when I'm not polymorphed, right?" Karalti let out a saurian huff of frustration. *"And why do you even care?! Mercurions don't even HAVE—"*

"Okay, I am interrupting tonight's genital debate for a special televised meeting, entitled 'What On Earth Are We Going to Do About All This Jungle?'" I jerked my head toward the tree line.

Suri snickered. "All three of us girls are gonna go bushwhacking. Isn't that right, Rin?"

"Oh my god." Rin put her face back in her hands.

Cackling, Suri pulled one of her axes off her belt and started for the edge of the jungle. "C'mon, Karalti. It's time to go and shave Mother Nature!"

"Yeah! Let's go!" Karalti—not completely understanding the mammalian innuendo—trotted after her.

I looked back to Rin, who was finally daring to look up at me between her fingers. "Don't suppose Hopper and Lovelace have machete attachments, do they?"

Rin sighed. "They have garden shears. Let me set them up."

CHAPTER 40

A couple of months ago, I was pretty sure my least favorite biome in Archemi was the Endlar. I was mistaken. It was definitely, absolutely, one hundred percent the Slithering Jungle of Meewhome.

Suri, with her awesome Stamina, made it just under four miles in her heavy armor. Rin, Karalti and I didn't even make it to two. It was about thirty degrees centigrade, or 86 F, with 100% humidity, and a walk that should have taken us a couple of hours instead took us almost the entire day. If the terrain had been as flat as the Endlar, we'd have been alright—but Meewhome wasn't only oppressively tropical, it was mountainous. There was mud. There was fog. There were bugs of every conceivable shape, size and texture. There were small spiders. There were giant spiders. And as we got within a mile of the Dragon Gate, there was desolation. A very familiar gray, lifeless, frozen patch of desolation.

"No fucking way." We stepped out of a patch of virgin forest into an unnatural frozen wasteland. The bracken and smaller trees had shriveled into upright twigs, while the larger trees were brown, the bark spongy and rotten to touch. The rich, earthy scent of the forest had faded, leaving a pungent odor hanging in the air, a smell that always made me think of a rundown gym or an old ice-skating rink. The most surreal thing was the clear delineation between the dying jungle and the living jungle: there was an actual line, a limit which bisected the dead from the living. Some plants that were on that invisible line were nothing but brown slime on one side, but fresh and green on the other.

"An Ix'tamo? Here?" Rin gripped my arm as she pushed ahead, looking around the clearing in despair. "No way. It can't be Ashur, can it?"

"Never say never." I stepped forward, cautious of falling branches or toppling trees. "I mean… dead things assaulting the walls. Ix'tamo sucking the life out of the land…"

"We don't know for sure that's what's causing this." Suri kept her hand on her sword hilt as she surveyed the damage. "Those Dragon Gates have all kinds of artificed machinery imbedded in the ground. For all we know, Devana's Gate is malfunctioning somehow."

"Yeah. Keep an eye out for patrols." I flinched as something cracked overhead, jumping on reflex. A bough of rotting wood smashed into the ground where I'd been standing. "And try not to get brained."

We picked our way to the center of the devastation, searching for evidence. After ten minutes of walking, we found it: A great big divot in the ground with piles of earth excavated to either side, and crumpled corpses strewn around it. They were all Meewfolk, and they looked like they'd been dead a long time. Their ears and fur had rotted away, leaving nothing but bare skulls. They were resting immobile near the excavation site, shovels still clutched in their fleshless hands.

"That looks Ix'tamo sized to me," Rin said. "Guys. I hate to say it... but I really think Ashur is here."

"Looks to me like they sunk it into the ground, sucked a bunch of mana out, then pulled it up to transport it somewhere." Suri walked up to one of the dead Meewfolk and kicked the stiff corpse before taking a big step back.

"Yeah. Like a big battery." Rin held her hand out and murmured a soft magical incantation. Her spellglove flared, and then the depression began to glow a soft blue-violet color—as did several dozen footprints, crushed into the mud. "There... I think we're onto something."

Suri made a sound of disgust. "The Demon, in fuckin' Meewhome. Just what we need."

"If he's here, all that means is we get to finish what we started in Myszno." I concentrated for a moment, seeing if I was able to sense the vampire in the same way I could sense the Bond between me and Karalti. No luck. "We don't know for sure, yet. Let's keep moving, before something lurches out to try and kill us."

The trail to the Dragon Gate became more defined as we cut through the Ix'tamo's starburst of destruction. The first hint we were on the right track were the statues. Ancient, worn smooth by time, they were still recognizable as Meewfolk by their tall, lean, feline shapes. Some were so overgrown with vines that they looked like they were wearing ghillie suits. Others were bare, missing arms or heads. We bushwhacked our way up the crumbling remains of stone steps embedded into the hill and came to what might have been the foundations of a gatehouse. About fifty feet away, the trail opened up—kind of, because there were guards posted to either side of it. A pair of moldering [Napathian Footsoldiers], their tarnished bronze armor and dull mottled skin blending in with the jungle foliage. Only years of experience spotting in these exact kinds of environments let me notice them without needing to make some kind of special check.

"Oh jeez." Suri crouched down beside me, her eyes straight ahead. "If we take those fuckers out, won't Ashur know?"

"I'm not sure. I don't know when my shadows are kaput unless I check in on them." I lowered my voice to a whisper, then switched to PM. "Rin? Karalti?"

"I'm still back here." Rin was crouched in the foliage with Lovelace and Hopper. Karalti knelt beside her, vibrating with excitement. "What do I do?"

"Hold position for now. We need to figure out a way up." Suri motioned to them to wait while we considered the terrain. A river ran beside the trail, splashing down in a series of tinkling waterfalls. They masked a lot of sound, but didn't offer much in the way of swimmable water. To the right of the trail was a hill covered in nothing but massive trees and dense, waist-high slash. The hill was steeper than the cut trail.

"I think we're gonna have to go through 'em," Suri messaged, her brow creasing. "This spot is pretty damn strategic."

"Right. But I can get above them and take them both out," I whispered back. "Be ready in case there's monsters and shit we can't see."

"Roger that." Suri reached out and squeezed my arm. "Go get 'em. I'll tell the others."

I broke away and started a slow, stealthy circuit around the pair of guards. When I was sure I was out of visual range, I Jumped most of the way up one of the towering mahogany trees and moved to the end of a sturdy-looking bough. The sentries were at their posts below, unmoving and oblivious.

I calculated the trajectory, made sure the Spear was in the correct grip, and leaped out into the open air. Neither zombie had enough brains to look up as my shadow descended over them—and by then, it was too late. I landed on one with the full force of Jump and crushed him, and fired Night Falls for the first time. A shockwave of raw blue-black energy blew out from me in a silent sphere, engulfing the second zombie. The energy didn't kill it so much as ash it. I glimpsed the corpse's mouth twist in a silent scream before it turned to dust and blew away, leaving a small loot bag behind.

[You have killed Napathian Footsoldiers! You gain 60 EXP.]

"Overwhelming force, baby." I looted the [Ancient Bronze Token] from the bag, then took cover behind one of the statues in case of more sentries. When I didn't see any, I waved the others forward.

"Let's take it slow. Two to either side of the path," Suri remarked in the group PM as we rejoined. "Keep Hopper and

Lovelace in the bushes. Get ready to fight. Karalti, are you able to change back yet?"

"We've been walking for six hours, so yeah," Karalti said. *"But I'll stay like this until we have some room to move."*

"Great." Suri looked to me. "Got any more stamina potions?"

In reply, I pulled a [Roseroot Potion] from my Inventory and tossed it to her. She chugged it, pocketed the bottle, and drew her axes in place of her sword.

"I'll buff you with magic armor as soon as we make contact," Rin said to Suri. "Just like our fights at the wall, right?"

"One hundred percent. Let's do it." Suri nodded to me. I made the 'move forward' signal, and we began the climb.

The river ravine to our left deepened and split around a large island, which served as the midpoint for a large, crumbling stone bridge. Two waterfalls thundered to either side, throwing up clouds of mist. The bridge—long and wide enough to be a road—passed through a broken gateway into a ruined city. Trees had grown over the shattered green stone buildings, their roots flowing around and into the empty windows and doorways. Towering above the ruins was a massive overgrown ziggurat flanked by a pair of enormous obelisks. They stretched up from the mists of the ravine to halfway up the trees. Coils of brilliant emerald green light arced up along their lengths, inverting at the tips and vanishing as the next wave of mana rose up along their length. They looked just like the Thunderstones, which fed mana in—or out—of Matir's Dragon Gate. Instead of obsidian, these were made of pure white-green jade.

We picked our way through the rubble, climbed a massive ruined wall, and used the ledge as a vantage point to scout the ziggurat. I waved the others to a stop once the temple was in view, then weaved my head and zoomed in on the terrace that spread in front of the temple's entrance.

A pair of Ix'tamo had been mounted to either side of a free-standing stone ring. They were big devices, floating diamonds about seven feet tall made of metal and glass, pulsing with vibrant blue-green energy. Between them, busily inscribing a complex magical circle on the ground, was a small, shrunken old lich of unknowable gender. I recognized them immediately: it was Uttapsu, Ashur's advisor. I'd met them only once, when the vampire was holding court in what was now my very own great hall. Surrounding him were a motley of different bodyguards: a platoon of [Napathian Footsoldiers], ten jackal-headed [Napathian Heavy Elite], and a couple of [Vampire Knights] in red, brown and bronze Sumerian-style armor.

"Phew, okay." I knelt back, exhaling heavily. "We're dealing with a lich, two vampires, and about thirty soldiers."

"Thirty soldiers!?" Rin gasped. "How are the four of us going to take on thirty soldiers!?"

"Don't worry, Rin. We got this." Karalti sidled over to me in a crouch, perching like a gargoyle beside my elbow. *"I have all my breath weapon charges, and Hector's Path is really*

good for fighting undead. I can also buff us with my Queensong."

Suri gave a small nod. "Right. Hector and I both have some good crowd-control moves. I'm more worried about those vampires."

"Leave them to me. If they bite me, they'll take damage. My blood is toxic to them." I narrowed my eyes, then opened them wide again to regain visibility as the light shifted. "There's a portal there that looks a lot like the one we used to enter Withering Rose's Chorus Vault. I think they're trying to use the mana from the Ix'tamo to bruteforce it. That, or he's draining mana out of it. But they charged those mana-suckers before bringing them here, so I'm guessing it's the former. They could be using them like batteries, as Rin said."

"Jeez. How the hell did they even get here?" Suri said. "It's too big a coincidence to be a coincidence."

"Violetta was operating out of Dakhdir," Rin said. "Is there some way they could have followed us to the Temple of the Maker? If they did, they might have found a way to use that map we did... Violetta is probably an Archmage by now. She might have figured out a hack for it."

"That... would be very bad." I pressed my lips into a thin line. "Why would Ashur want to get into a Chorus Vault, though? He was angling for Matir's Dragon Gate last time. If he's planning to invade Meewhome the way he did Myszno..."

Rin made a 'bleh' face. "He might be trying to get to Perilous Symphony, like we are."

Even as she spoke, a dozen black-clad humans exited the temple proper, jogging down the stairs in loose formation. I pressed my lips together in a thin line. I recognized those uniforms—and the masks they wore. "But wait, there's more! At least twelve Mata Argis thugs just balled out of the temple. Violetta definitely put him up to this."

"Shit." Suri spat to the side.

"The footsoldiers'll be about Level 10, the Elites Level 15," I continued. "The vampires, who knows? The Mata Argis Agents we saw tended to be in the 20s. No idea what Uttapsu is."

Suri grimaced and shook her head. "Our odds just got a whole of a lot worse."

"We've got this," Karalti said firmly. *"I'll take on the Mata Argis myself. I've been looking forward to deep-frying some of their agents for a really long time. They chased me and Hector across Ilia when I was little... I'll never forget what they tried to do to us."*

"Me either." I rolled my shoulders to loosen them. "Buff up and get ready, guys. It's four against fifty."

Suri grinned. "Bet you I can take out thirty of these cunts before they know what hit 'em."

I waggled my eyebrows back at her. "Bet you I can get there first."

"Nuh uh," Karalti said. *"I can fly. I'll win that bet before either of you."*

"Wait. Before we engage: Karalti, you can scan their levels, can't you?" Rin piped up. "The vampires and the lich?"

"Oh! Yeah!" Karalti leaned forward, magic briefly rippling over her shoulders and face like clear heat haze. *"Let's see... the vampires are only Level 25. But the lich guy is 42."*

"Forty-two?" Suri audibly winced. "That's a lot. Especially if it's a mage. Got any tactical observations, Hector?"

I had a look over the Bioscan results myself, plotting the best place to hit first. My initial hunch had been to have me dive into the weaker enemies and take them out, but now that I thought about it... "Suri, I need you to tunnel right into that big pack of enemies. Rin, back her up. Karalti, I want you to cast Circle of Protection on Suri once she's waded into the mob. That way, the vampires can't get near her. You can take the Mata Argis agents. I need to solo Uttapsu."

"Why?" Rin asked.

"Because my Darkness elemental moves will fucking shred him, is why. If we hit him hard and fast, there's a good chance all those undead are going to fall over," I said. "And the Spear has a Light elemental mode. Light attacks can sunder mana shields, right?"

"Right. All mana constructs have a 50% type weakness to Light elemental effects, and Light-element weapons inflict Sunder." Rin nodded.

"He might get a couple of good shots in on me, but I think I can handle him." I adjusted my grip on my weapon, thinking. "Do Archemi liches have phylacteries?"

"Yeah, they do." Rin grimaced and picked at her lip. "His is probably back in Napath."

"That's fine. We just need him to be Not Here." I turned to the three of them. "Karalti, you and I need to get into of those super-tall trees. We'll jump out and scare the mummy dust out of them."

"We'll be down here." Suri held up a fist. I bumped my knuckles against hers, did the same with Rin, then vaulted off the wall with Karalti and crept off low across the ground.

We cut all the way around the arena and climbed a tree overlooking the terrace. The Mata Argis were gathering around the outside of Uttapsu's circle, watching on as he deftly laid down sigils and encoded words of power. They closed ranks as Karalti and I reached our launch point, but no one paid any attention to us.

"Let's go in, fast and quiet," I said. *"No roaring, no nothing. Just you and me, death from the fucking skies."*

"Yeah! You ready?" Karalti tensed, bracing herself against the branch.

"I was born for this shit." I thumped the top of my helmet for luck.

Karalti tensed up, like a frog about to leap. *"Okay, then. One, two, three aaaand.... GO!"*

She flung herself out, already transforming. I waited breathlessly until I saw her wings stretch out, and only then jumped out after her. As I fell, her back lengthened and widened, and my breath caught... but then I landed on her, rolled, and found myself right at the base of her neck as the spell completed.

Down below, I heard Suri roar a battlecry. She charged across the bridge, axes in her hands, as Hopper and Lovelace bounded alongside. The pikemen at the front leveled their spears. The soldiers behind them raised bows, aiming past them, and fired. Meanwhile, Karalti and I streaked toward the terrace at high speed, our shadow cast away from the commotion. All eyes were on Suri and Rin as the footsoldiers flowed around Uttapsu like water, surrounding the magic circle, then leaving him, the junior vampires, and the dirty dozen Mata Argis. I bunched up, then sprung out, aiming for the bullseye: Uttapsu's stupid wrinkly little head.

The vampires spotted me first, heads turning skyward as the Spear flared with brilliant white and black light. The lich continued scribbling. He didn't even react as I hit his mana shield like a thunderbolt. The thin field of energy absorbed the kinetic impact, turning from clear, to blue, to white as the Light damage overcharged it. The lich's form vanished as his shield spat sparks of hot plasma, then shattered with enough force to send me flying. The vampire bodyguards were thrown back from the blast, swords in their hands.

"Surprise, motherfuckers!" I leaped back into the air, burning a third of my AP to rain hell on all three of them. Twelve lances of pure darkness warped from the air around me, slamming down into the trio of undead and throwing a cloud of dust into the air.

"Hey, Mata Argis creeps! Remember me!?" Karalti broadcast as she landed on top of the agents, crushing one, and

scattering the rest in all directions. As the dust cleared, I saw the vampires snarling, their faces bestial masks of rage. I ignored them, angling for Uttapsu—except the lich was gone.

"FUCK!" I got that one word out before the spell hit me—from above. A line of fireballs ripped up my back and slammed me into the dirt. I hit the ground hard, desperately rolling away as the next barrage struck the ancient stone and blew chunks out of it, flinging them into the air.

[You take 430 Fire damage! You are Burned!]

One of the vampires rushed me, his metal fangs bared. I snarled back at him, feeling my lips pulling back over my own fangs, and boosted myself with Mantle of Night. Accelerated, I pivoted and knocked his next sword stride to the side, then rushed him with a Spear boiling with black flames. He managed to block one, two, three of the strikes from Blood Sprint, but his guard gave way before I did. The next blows in the combo landed, ripping him apart.

[You deal 8248 damage to Vampire Fledgling!]
[You have destroyed Vampire Fledgling!]

The other vampire was behind me, supernaturally fast. I could either dodge him, or the next round of magic. I chose the magic, vanishing as a bolt of lightning lanced down in the spot I'd been standing. The vampire's sword met my gut, thrusting deep... into the armor. The chiton scale buckled around the tip of the blade, turning attempted disembowelment into a really bad bruise. I used Blink Strike to vanish and reappear behind him, ramming the blazing spear in under his armpit.

The vampire screamed as dark energy engulfed him like a pyre, boiling his flesh off his bones before ashing him completely.

"Ashur's ill-begotten child." Uttapsu's reedy voice sneered behind me. The lich hovered with his toes barely hanging over the ground, his arms loose by his sides. He was so old that he resembled a brittle skeleton—but the points of glowing light in his eyesockets burned with malevolent will. "Was it fate that guided you here? Or your destiny to serve Napath as our slave?"

"Do you know what I hate? Villain speeches." I whirled the Spear into position and faced off with him. "Shut up and put up."

"As you wish." Uttapsu gestured with a mummified hand, and several discs of magical glyphs appeared around his feet. "Die in silence."

I Jumped as the circles discharged bolts of static—only to strike against an invisible ceiling. I nearly broke my neck, crashing back to the ground on my chest. Knocked prone, I took Uttapsu's next spell full-force: a waterblade that seemed to punch right through my body and blow out the other side. I screamed as hot agony tore through my nerves... and passed, having dealt much less damage than it should have.

[You take 469 Water damage! x2 Damage! (45% Water resistance)]

Uttapsu almost looked confused as I closed in with him. He threw up a shield of energy just before my weapon smashed into his frail body, holding it against my strikes as I transmuted the Spear from Dark to Light and slashed the barrier a dozen times. The shield turned bright blue, but it held —so I teleported behind the lich and struck with Blink Strike, white flame transmuting to black. The blow sent him reeling through the air.

[You deal 1015 reduced Darkness damage to Uttapsu! HP: 12,858/13,873]

"You've got protection against Darkness magic, huh?" I circled him, quick-spamming a couple of potions as he drew a pair of knives from his belt.

"The only reason that surprises you is because you lack intelligence." The lich sounded calm, tracking me as I moved around him. "You are a half-breed whelp, barely a puppy. Young. Foolish. Pathetic."

"Dude, seriously, I don't care about your fucking poetry slam." I lashed out with Black Lotus, but before the noose could reach Uttapsu's neck, he lifted a hand and it withered away. "I AM curious how you cast magic without a spell glove or words of power, though."

"You are too primitive to understand." The lich turned his knives back in his hands—the only warning I got before the ground erupted beneath my feet.

CHAPTER 41

I nearly Jumped on reflex before I remembered that was a bad idea. The second of hesitation nearly cost me my life, as chains of energy erupted from the ground like a hydra. They lashed after me asI Shadow Danced through them, stabbing cruelly into the ground as I reappeared. I reeled away in what felt and probably looked like some kind of high-speed Irish dance before one of them snapped around my wrist with crushing force. The Spear fell from nerveless fingers as my hand turned numb, followed by my arm and then the rest of me. I began to lose HP, Stamina and Adrenaline at the same time as the spell began to suck the life out of me.

"You cannot win, half-blood." Uttapsu hung about ten feet away, his knives resting loosely in his hands. "Surrender, and I will submit you to Ashur's justice. He will finish what he started. You will know peace at last."

I strained against the energy drain, mind racing. There was no way a mage that was only ten levels higher than me could be this strong. And how the fuck was he casting without a spellglove? Without mana?

Then my eyes lit on the Ix'tamo. The mana in them was boiling, surging through the glass tubules inside like blood through veins. And they were flowing down—down into the magic circle on which we still stood.

"Karalti! Assist!" I shouted to her telepathically, sinking down to one knee as the strength ebbed out of my limbs. *"Nuke those Ix'tamo! Now!"*

Karalti was being hit by magic from all sides, soaking fireballs and energy blasts from the three mages still left standing. All but four of the Mata Argis were dead. She charged the mages down, shattering their line, then grabbed the slowest one and flung him into the first Ix'tamo with her jaws. Then she blasted it and him with Ghost Fire. For a second, I didn't understand—until the screaming, dying man seemed to mesh into the device, which exploded in a gush of pure green mana.

[Warning! Mana concentration is extreme!]
[You are suffering Mana Poisoning!]

The lich turned from me as I collapsed to hands and knees, gesturing toward Karalti. She squealed in agony as his next spell took hold: a kinetic blast that torqued her neck and twisted her wings back. But it didn't stop her from belching another plume of fire at the second Ix'tamo. A normal dragon would have barely brushed the device with her flames, but Karalti's liquid fire slapped the crystal and stuck there. The Ixtamo's surface cracked under the intense heat as the sticky flames roared on its surface, then burst. And as it did, Uttapsu's hold on me lapsed.

"HRRRAAGH!" I sped forward with the last of my stamina, the Mark of Matir burning on the back of my hand, and drew from it to power a lance of solid darkness at terminal speed. It tore through Uttapsu's fragile body like a lightning strike, hurling him away.

[Shadow Lance deals 5072 damage! Uttapsu HP: 7786/13,873]

"You do not know who you are fucking with!" I roared, hunting him as he teleported in and out of reach. He was luring me toward the mana, trying to use it for its damage-over-time effect. So far, he was succeeding—I was at 559 HP and dropping every second. I chugged a potion, boosting my health back to 909 HP, and flitted after him.

"*Bla'kotar!*" Mana haze sucked into the lich's knives, then blasted at me in twin whips of cutting water. I dodged one and soaked one, the damage boosting my AP, and struck him like a homing missile: a regular strike with the lance, and then an explosion of raw black energy. Umbra Burst—right in his fucking chest.

[You deal 6816 Darkness damage! HP: 970/13,873.]
[Your HP: 231/3,138]

The lich's fleshless mouth opened in a soundless scream as his body caught fire like a match. The Darkness crawled through him like embers, but it didn't destroy him. I could feel his will bearing down on mine.

"Fool." His arms wrapped around me, and he plunged both blades into my back. The armor slowed them down, but as he bore down with feral, supernatural strength, I felt the magically-enhanced points begin to press through the links toward my kidneys.

"Just, fucking DIE!" I snarled, twisting the Spear deep in his body as my health trickled down into the double digits.

"I will report everything I've seen. Your powers. Your abilities. The way you fight." Points of light kindled in his skull, boring into mine as his hands faltered. "You… belong to… USSSS."

"Tell Fang Daddy to go to hell." I twisted the Spear again, grinding into the lich's surprisingly solid core. Uttapsu let out a thin wail, then collapsed into a shower of dust that winked out like embers. A loot sack appeared out of thin air, falling to the ground with a clank.

"Urgh." I sank down to one knee. Blood was pouring from my mouth. I reached up to touch it, not even sure where it had come from. I didn't remember taking any hits to the face.

I flinched as the last Mata Argis agent flew past me, screaming as he crashed spine-first against the edge of the portal ring. I heard his back go with a dull crunch, and he tumbled to the ground, lifeless.

"Ugh. Finally." Karalti echoed my groan as she stumped over to me. One of her wings was dragging, and patches of frost still bloomed over her scales. Near the bridge, Suri was leaning on her sword, covered in blood and ichor. Surrounding her were the zombies and Napathian Elites she'd killed, then killed again when they'd Stranged and morphed into some Rat King-like abomination, all hands and legs and wailing, gnashing mouths.

[Quest Updated: The One Who Abides. Return to Priest-Queen Solai to claim your reward.]

[You gain 2,573 EXP! Karalti gains 2573 EXP!]

"Dun-duh da dah da dahh!" I thrust the Spear into the air along my terrible impression of the Final Fantasy victory jingle.

"That fight was a lot harder than I thought it would be." Karalti groaned as she lowered her chest to the ground, tucking her forearms up and crouching to rest. *"Ow."*

"Here." I pulled out the one and only dragon sized healing tincture I kept in my Inventory: a whole gallon of it. "This should help."

"Thanks." Karalti snaked her tongue out, wrapped it around the uncorked bottle, and tipped the contents into her jaws. She delicately dropped it back into my hands before swallowing. *"Man... It felt so good to finally take down some of those guys."*

Rin checked in with Suri first, then broke away toward us at a jog. "Hector! Karalti! Are you okay?"

"Suuuurrre." I did my best not to slur as I raided my Inventory for more healing pots. "Not doing so... uhh... great on the healing side of things."

"Here. I carry a few for my organic friends, in case of emergencies." Rin pulled three cloudy green potions from thin air, handing them to me. "They're not the strongest kind. They do 150 HP, I think."

"Concentrated Green Moss Tinctures," I grunted, throwing them back like shots. "Is Suri alright?"

"She's hurt, too. But we're all alive." Rin bit her lip as she looked to Karalti. "You okay, Karalti?"

"Yup!" The dragon shifted restlessly, huffing through her nostrils. *"Just... ow."*

Suri stumped over to us, stripped down to her halter top, and her armored cuisses, greaves and boots. She was bleeding from many small wounds—barely scrapes, thanks to Rin's assistance, and the natural armor she gained from Primal Fury.

"Welp. That was fun." She rammed the point of her sword into the dirt between the flagstones and leaned on it.

I looked her up and down. "How're you doing?"

"Good fight. Really got the blood pumping." She glanced at something I couldn't see. "Also got the blood infected. You got anything for Blood Poisoning, Mister Herbs?"

"Jeez. You make me sound like a drug-dealer." I went into my inventory, pulled out some ingredients, and slapped together a poultice that smelled strongly of garlic and alcohol. "Here. Apply this to your gash."

Rin groaned. "Do you guys ever stop?"

I shook my head. "We do not."

"Listen to you, scandalizing our pure, innocent Rin." Suri's eyes narrowed, and she snatched the dressing from my hand as I beamed at her. "I reckon I need to carve *you* a gash."

Rin boggled at Suri in disbelief. "Suri, you tease me WAY worse than Hector does."

"I'll pretend I didn't hear that." Suri drew herself up stiffly, ever the elegant countess. "So, what's in the sack?"

"The sack?" I blinked at her, expecting innuendo, then realized she was talking about the loot bag. "Oh, that. Hang on."

I grabbed the loot bag and opened its inventory. To my dismay, it was mostly junk—but there was a {Letter from Ashur} and a {Golden Bull Amulet} in there which I took. "Looks like Ashur wrote something down for him, but I can't translate it. We'll have to do it later."

*"Huh. Their language looks pretty cool. Kind of like pictures. "*The very tip of Karalti's muzzle ghosted over the top of my hair, her nostrils flexing as she gave me a concerned but thorough sniff-check. *"Well... we got the bad guys. What now?"*

"Now we head back." I watched Suri as she applied the poultice to the deepest of her cuts. "I'm pretty sure we fixed the Priest-Queen's zombie problem—so now we get to find out what else she wants and pray that whatever it is, we won't need any more healing potions."

CHAPTER 42

Night had fallen over Ru Waat by the time we returned, the city glowing with the light of a million candles. Shrill music could be heard from all quarters. People were dancing around fires, roasting meat on spits, singing and clapping. The temple also was bathed in the same soft golden light, and a huge party was in full swing. The priestesses, guards, courtesans and servants mingled out in the courtyard, while Saloi presided over the inner sanctum, indulgently watching two Meewfolk women fighting a third inside the arena. It was part sparring, part gladiatorial match: the atmosphere was friendly, but the blood-streaked fur was definitely real.

"My loveliest humans!" The Priest-Queen called out in delight, rising off her divan and sashaying over to us in a cloud of filmy silk. "The city received the notification of your success a few hours ago! The attacks have stopped!"

"The cause of the plague were covert invaders from Napath." I briefly bent a knee in front of her, then stood up straight. "A lich who works for Ashur of the Ten Thousand Swords, a vampire general from that same country. He's an imperialist who wants to destroy all of the Dragon Gates, including the Gate here. That's what your ruins are: the remains of-"

496

"Shhhhh" The Priest-Queen coyly pressed her finger against my lips. "No need to yowl it throughout the temple like a girl in her first heat. The truth of that place is a secret, known only to the initiated."

"Right. Well, be warned that Ashur isn't the sort of bloke to just give up on a pet project," Suri said, drawing up beside me. "He did a number on our province in Vlachia. Myszno is about the size of this whole island."

"I shall take your words under consideration," Solai replied breezily. "But for tonight, we shall celebrate the defeat of our enemies. And I shall make my other two wishes."

"What do you have in mind?" I followed her as she trailed back toward her throne.

"I do not have much interaction with males of my own kind, let alone humans. Your appearance, your destiny, your weapon… all of it piques my curiosity." She slipped down to rest on the cushioned divan. "In Meewhome, spear fighting is a woman's art, passed from mother to daughter. It is one of the three sacred weapons of our people."

"What are the other two?" Suri asked her, standing at ease.

"The *jilan*, the welded claw sheath." Solai extended one foot and flexed her toes, miming the disemboweling strike her enhanced claws were capable of enacting. "And the scimitar. To become a Priest-Queen, you must be a master of all three weapons. To be considered a master, you must show you can defeat any and all comers—including the Priest-Queen herself."

"Okay?" I glanced at Suri, not sure where this was headed. She shrugged.

"My second wish is to duel you, Paragon." Solai pointed at me. "A duel in which I am able to get the measure of you. What do you say?"

I rolled my shoulders and motioned with my head. "I'm game."

"Wonderful!" Solai put her hands together as the courtiers around her throne murmured and purred in approval. "And that leads to my third wish. I wish to spend a night with you, involved in entertainment and pastimes, such as befit a queen. Should I win, I shall choose how our night proceeds. Should you somehow best me, you shall scheme whatever delights you wish to show. Does that sound suitable?"

"Karalti would probably be up for taking you on a flight," I said. "How does that sound?"

Solai squeezed her eyes in contentment. "No, do not tell me your plans. I wish it to be a surprise. Do you accept?"

"Sure. Just me?" I gestured to the others.

"They shall be well-taken care of tonight," Solai affirmed, stretching languidly as she rose to her feet again. "You shall have food, drink, music! We have so many things you may try here. But first..."

She looked to one of her slaves, who bowed, then strode over to a gong at the end of the arena. She picked up a mallet and struck it three times. The trio of combatants on the sands

498

stopped, panting for breath, while the murmur of conversation around the room died down.

"The Priest-Queen has chosen a challenger!" The slave called, raising her voice to be heard out in the antechamber, as well as the sanctum.

Solai held her arms out expectantly, and her handmaidens got to work. Two of them stripped her of her fine jewelry, unhooking her joined nostril ring and earring, sliding her bracelets and armlets from her limbs, and unlacing the back of her golden girdle. They then removed her silk clothing, except for her loincloth. While she undressed, I stepped back and unequipped my armor down to the flexible doeskin leggings I wore under my breeches. Several of the female Meewfolk behind me tittered.

"Jeez." Suri's mouth quirked. "Look at you, Mister Popularity."

"Mr 'Has no fur, no tail, and looks like an alien', more like it." I stretched my hands. "Hold onto my gear for me?"

"Am I your slave now?" Suri arched both eyebrows. "Starting to get ideas, Your Grace?"

"Please, Your Grace?" I flashed her a toothy grin.

Suri made a show of sighing and rolling her eyes, then snatched my pack off me.

Solai stood patiently as her handmaidens brought a glowing, finely made torque to her and fitted it around her neck. To my surprise, one of them came to me with a similar item—an open-faced collar made of gold, crawling with traceries of magic. Curious, I scanned it with my HUD.

Royal Guardian Torque

850 Magical Armor
+50% Fire Resistance
+50% Air Resistance
+50% Resistance to Piercing and Slashing Damage
Grants Immunity to Fear, Nausea, Blindness.
Special: Soul-Bound (Priest-Queen Solai).

My eyes popped when I saw those stats. This little thing gave 850 armor? I wouldn't even be able to scratch someone wearing this thing with a normal attack.

"The rules of the match are as follows," Solai said, accepting her weapon from a servant—a bluesteel spear with a tapered, leaf-shaped blade. "The goal is to knock your opponent to ground and keep them at spear-point for a count of five seconds. If the fight drags on, the first to fall below half health will lose the match. Shall we make it the best of three?"

"Hell yeah." I bounced on my toes a few times, then called the Spear of Destiny to my hand and quickly spun it over the backs of my knuckles before catching it. "Can we use Combat Abilities? Or normal strikes only?"

"Normal strikes only, I think." She squinted at me. "It would be unfair to you if I was to wield my full powers as the Chosen of the Sun."

I laughed. "Right. Any formalities before entering the ring?"

"Yes. We fight beneath Lua's Golden Moon tonight. Say a soft prayer to your ancestors in your mind, and bow on entry." Solai gave me a thoroughly sultry look as she rolled her spear over her knuckles, passed it over to the back of her other hand, then spun it around behind her and threw it like a javelin into the center of the arena.

The Meewfolk around us yowled and cheered as their queen sauntered in after her weapon. She put her delicate hands together and bowed from the sternum, stepped into the ring, then slapped her thighs and slid out into a wide, low-slung stance. The fur of her back and tail fluffed out, her eyes widened, and she pulled her lips back to bare her teeth in a demonic, skull-like grimace, her ears pinning flat against her skull. When Solai's health meter came into focus, the ring filled up five times. Two black skulls appeared beside her name to either side. I couldn't remember ever seeing an NPC with *two* black skulls before. That meant she was at least Level 60, and probably higher.

I chuckled nervously. *"Hahaha. I'm in danger."*

"Don't let her scare you, Hector! You can do it!" Rin cried, bouncing up and down beside Suri.

I puffed my lips out and shook my head, rolled my shoulders, and stepped up. I bowed on the threshold of the arena in the Korean style, then teleported up into the air and dropped, landing acrobatically in front of the Priest-Queen. She stared at me, unblinking, and did not break eye contact as she reached for her spear and pulled it free. I began to counter-circle her as she tipped the curved blade on an angle toward the sand, and began to slowly pace, a low, dangerous growl trickling from her open mouth.

"Commence!" The ringmaster rang a small gong.

The Priest-Queen lunged at me, obscenely fast. I was barely able to see her move, ducking on pure instinct as the butt of her spear came for my head, then parrying as she swirled her polearm around the blade of mine and nearly flipped the weapon out of my hands. I hung onto it, circling and jabbing, but she effortlessly caught every strike—and then knocked one away with a fierce scream, breaking into my guard. There was a panicked moment where I lost track of her, and before I oriented, she swept my feet out from under me. Gasps went up as I sprawled out in a cloud of sand. Solai moved to pin me, but I rolled away and flipped up to my feet before she could hook the blade against my throat.

"You're faster than I thought you'd be, paragon!" Solai's face was an insane mask: ears back, teeth bared, her pupils nothing more than mad slits in a sea of frosty blue. "I always thought humans would be slow!"

"Depends on the human," I shot back. "Let's dance."

Within a minute of back and forth—jabs, parries, metal knocking against metal—I knew without a doubt that Solai had top Master ranks in Spearfighting. She read my body and mind with every step and thrust, rush and swipe. She came in sharply, stabbing high and low, and as I stepped out she hooked the end of her polearm around the back of my knee and dropped me a second time. I couldn't get up fast enough—she blocked my roll with the spear blade, pinning me to the sand by the skin of my neck.

"Five, four, three, two, one!" Her terrifying mask relaxed, and she laughed with delight at the end of the countdown as the crowd howled encouragement. "Hmmm... what shall I do with you tonight? Nice clothing, absolutely... something to compliment that beautiful smooth skin of yours."

I clambered up to my feet, rubbing at the small bloody wound on the side of my throat. "Two more rounds."

"Indeed." Solai flew at me again, as graceful as the ribbon of silk around her waist, and smashed the blade of her spear against mine. Pound for pound, she was much faster and more skilled than I was, but we were almost the same strength. The queen's muscles bunched as I bore against her and pushed, keeping her spear locked against mine. She flexed her claws into the sand to stop from sliding, and that's when I broke the standoff—shoving against her, then rolling up under her recovering strike and bowling her off her feet. She yelped as I took her down at the knees, then hissed playfully as I rolled onto her and held the point of my spear at her cheek.

"Maybe we could go for a swim? That'd be a fun date." I grinned down at her.

"The nerve of you, human." Her eyes narrowed. "Assuming I do not like to swim because I am feline? I dived for pearls and spearhunted fish for most of my life."

"... Four! Five! Come on, Hector!" Suri called from the sidelines, bouncing up and down as hard as Rin.

I removed the blade and Solai bounded back to her feet. We began to circle, our weapons almost touching as we searched for the first flinch, the next moment of weakness. When her spear dipped slightly, I tested her guard—once, twice, then darted in. She caught my weapon with a twirl, launching it up and over her shoulder. I felt time slow as she spun past me in a blur of white and red, then cracked me over the back of the neck with the haft.

"Shit!" I tried to save my balance, but I was off-kilter— and a great chorus of delighted laughter rose up as Solai smacked me over the ass with her blade, then cut my feet from under me and sent me down to my face. I pushed up on my hands, sputtering, only to feel the bluesteel tip of her weapon dig into the back of my head.

"Her Highness, Priest-Queen Solai, has won this duel!" The servant rang the gong again as the crowd yowled enthusiastically in support of their queen.

"Pfffbt, pfft." I spat sand out of my mouth and turned around to sit upright. "God dammit. That's the first straight-up spear fight I've ever lost."

Solai planted the end of her weapon into the ground, and offered me a hand. She was back to being pretty and kittenish, and squinted happily as she pulled me to my feet. "There is no shame in this loss, Paragon. You are many levels lower than I, and I had to defeat every woman ahead of me in rank to become queen of my people. There are not many who can say they brought me to my back even once. You are quick and strong."

"And you are seriously talented," I said. "Can you teach me how to fight like that?"

"Hmmmm." Solai's eyes hooded, and she made a show of thinking, strutting around her spear like a poledancer, then leaning in to rub her cheek against the haft. "Perhaps. But not for free, Paragon. You will have to do me some... personal favors. But perhaps we can talk about that after our date tonight?"

"Uhh... sure." I winced as I looked over at Suri, but my loyal and steadfast girlfriend was, at that very moment, changing money with Gar. I wasn't sure when he'd appeared, or who had bet on who, but Suri had won.

"I shall arrange for your companions to enjoy a night they will remember." Solai left her spear planted in the middle of the arena and sauntered past me, winding her tail over my bare back on her way to speak with Suri. "Wine, women—or men—and song: you need only ask. You have the hospitality of the royal court, in thanks for your assistance. But this one, Hector, is mine for the night. Yes?"

"He signed up for it," Suri replied, flashing me a look of dark amusement. "Try not to break him."

"Thanks." I glared at her, rubbing the back of my head. "Glad to know I can count on you."

"Always." Suri winked. "What's the plan for him tonight, your Majesty?"

"Ohh... a little of this, a little of that." Solai returned to me, rubbing her clawed hands up over my arm before wrapping her fingers around my bicep. "I think it would be lovely to have you attend me during tonight's opera."

"Tonight's... opera?" I repeated numbly, stiffening as two of the queen's servants came up behind me.

"Yes, yes! The musicians are ready outside. We start the opera at moonrise, and play and sing until moonset." Solai let go of me, and turned to face her staff. "I shall dress for the performance. Maiaa, Lani, see this man is cleaned and attired decently for the opera. Kali, Prrana, Ah'ah: you three shall each serve as the personal attendants of the Paragon's companions. Make sure they are given anything they desire."

The five servants bowed deeply. "Yes, Your Majesty."

"I, uh-" before I could protest, Maiaa and Lani seized me by the arms, and led me out of the arena toward a different wing of the temple. I turned my head to look piteously at Suri. She grinned and saluted. Karalti was out in the jungle, sleeping soundly. I was on my own.

"Her Highness is going to actually let me go after this, right?" I asked one of the giggling maids, as they steered me into a costume room.

"Of course! You have not committed any crime!" The handmaiden to my right craned her head toward me as the pair of them tugged me to sit down on a low, plush stool. "Now you just sit here while we fit jewelry, yes?"

CHAPTER 43

Solai's handmaidens twittered over me for a solid hour before escorting me—bejeweled, saronged, painted with henna and kohl—to what was to be one of the defining moments of my life: my very first Meewfolk opera.

Imagine, if you can, the sound of a tomcat yowling while standing on top of a fence. Now, make that fifteen very large, very enthusiastic tomcats, all yodeling in harmony like the world's most agonizing acapella group. Then add an orchestra made up of giant xylophones, gongs, steel drums, wooden drums, flutes, and two-stringed violins: an ensemble called a *marr'tao*. Everyone is yowling, banging, plunking, meowing and fiddling. Every now and then, someone lets out a high-pitched 'REEEEAOW', and your eardrums pop.

For six. Fucking. Hours.

"Look! Look! They're fighting the demon that killed Princess Kataiya!" Solai clung to my arm with a little gasp, her whiskers vibrating with excitement—or from the 5-point Richter scale vibrations from the *marr'tao*, I wasn't sure.

The actors jumped and danced around one another, wailing as they posed with spears and claws in a much less terrifying version of what I'd faced with Solai in the arena. Nails down a blackboard didn't cut it. I could feel my hitpoints oozing away with my sanity.

"Karalti. I can't feel my face," I moaned—aloud, because no one could possibly hear my whimpering over the noise.

"Are you okay? Are you being tortured?" Karalti, aghast, patched in telepathically. *"What's happening?"*

"I pray to all the gods in all the worlds in the whole fucking multiverse that whatever is happening is the final scene of this play," I replied, numbly taking another drink of whatever beverage the temple servants had given me. It was white, vaguely coconutty, and probably laced with hallucinogens.

"Ooh, do you like that? That's *la'gun*, yes? It is a drink to relax with at the end of the night." Solai beamed at me, offering me a plate. "Have another honeyed dormouse. I raise these myself especially for opera nights."

I picked up one of the nugget-sized things and ate it with a distant, thousand-yard stare. I was pretty sure it was good, but my HUD was flashing with four different intoxication debuffs and I wasn't feeling a whole hell of a lot between being drunk, high, tripping, and tweaked. Solai probably could have fed me something out of her litter box and I'd have eaten the damn thing like a chocolate truffle.

At long last, the two heroes—or heroines, I wasn't sure—leaped from the corpse of the red-masked demon and went to rescue the swooning princess. Solai sighed happily as joyous sing-song meowing filled the air, and the chorus wrapped up into what I prayed was the final song.

"Is it over?" I croaked.

"Almost." The Priest-Queen draped herself over my half-naked body, her hands curled on my chest, her tail twitching contentedly over our thighs. Between the coconut alcohol, the mushrooms and the hundred other things I'd eaten, drunk or snorted to get through the night, the lean, athletic lines of her body and the slick warmth of her fur felt disturbingly good. I lay an arm around her, absently petting the small of her back.

"So." I jumped when Solai put her mouth close my ear, her voice a purring whisper that somehow carried over the music. "Is it true that human males do not have barbs?"

"Wha...?" I stirred up out of my intoxicated trance for a moment. "Barbs? Where?"

"You know." She expertly undulated her body against mine in a way that suddenly reminded me that human men were, in fact, down to fuck on any night or day of the year. I sucked in a sharp, surprised breath.

"Uhh... no." Slurring, I tried to struggle upright to regain some control of the situation, but Solai had me pinned to the sofa by my hips. "No. No barbs."

She giggled, then turned to her nearest handmaiden. "Please take my lovely companion here to my chambers. I will follow shhuuurrrr-"

Solai's voice trailed off into a warm fuzzy blur. I was vaguely aware of being carried away on a litter, taken somewhere dark and quiet. I opened my eyes to see a slim Meewfolk woman helping me out of the jewelry I'd worn to the opera. I closed my eyes, falling into a swirl of color, and when I opened them again it was to the sight of Solai straddling me, her hand resting on my chest, claws spread. Everything beyond that was a pleasant, shadowy whirl into unconsciousness.

I woke in the morning with a start—mostly because of the pain. Groaning, I rolled over, clutching at my shoulders. They were gritty with dry blood. I cracked my eyes open, and immediately closed them again as the distant drumming inside my skull swelled into a booming chorus. I was almost certain that the drummers from the opera had taken up residence in my sinuses, playing the backs of my eyeballs with hammers and malicious, whiskered grins.

"Oh god." I patted over my arms and chest. My skin was covered in welts and long, stinging cuts. Wincing, I looked back over my shoulder. Solai was asleep on the other side of the bed, her legs drawn up, her hands tucked in, her tail draped like a fan over her eyes.

"Did I...?" I rubbed my hand over my face, watching the swirling patterns on the insides of my eyelids. "Oh god. I did."

Solai had wrung me out like a dishrag. My HP bar was throbbing. My Hydration meter was throbbing. A bunch of other things were throbbing as I wobbled to my feet, staggered over to a nearby vanity, and splashed clean water over my face. Then, against my better judgement, I drank some of it to bring my Hydration out of the red zone.

"Dude. She's a *priestess*." I peered at myself in the polished bronze mirror. "What the fuck are we going to do *now*?"

I froze in place as the air of the room subtly warped behind me, pulling in toward a central point. My head jerked up, as a lean, tall, dark-robed figure appeared behind me in the mirror. They were robed and veiled, but I could make out the shape of a muzzle, and the outline of triangular, upright ears beneath the ornate headdress they wore.

My reckoning had come. I had just defiled the holy virgin Priest-Queen of Meewhome, and now I was going to be flayed into little strips by the feline incarnation of Death Himself. I flattened back against the vanity. "Hi. You must be the Avatar."

"You are correct." The Avatar's voice was deeper than I expected: masculine, not feminine. "I see you have enjoyed your time with us."

I glanced at Solai. She was snoozing happily, curled into a smug ball on her bed. "She absolutely wanted this, okay? Please don't murder me."

"Of course she wanted it, and she obtained what she desired. She is the Priest-Queen." The Avatar had the calm, measured voice of a monk or a priest. Disciplined. Quiet. Blessedly non-judgmental as I discreetly searched for something to cover myself with. "The ancestors have informed me as to who you are, and why you wish to see me."

"And?" I found a washcloth to clamp over the front of my hips.

"And I consent to an audience." The shimmering figure bowed from the neck. "You are the Paragon of the Sixth Great Cycle. The last Cycle, I fear. I have waited my entire life to meet you and your companions. Ready yourselves, and assemble in the Lotus Plaza of the temple. I will bring you to my sanctum when I sense you are ready."

The illusion cut with a ripple of magic that passed through the room, rubbing over my skin like a cool breeze. Solai murmured, rolling over onto her back in a lazy sprawl of limbs. She still had some of my blood on her claws.

"Phew." I went into my Inventory to equip my armor— then realized that I'd handed everything over to Suri the night before and not taken any of it back.

"Suri?" I tentatively shot her a P.M. "I'm... uh... trapped. Can I get an assist?"

"Oh, an assist, is it?" Her mellow, wry voice, lovely as it was, felt like an ice-pick to the brain. "Seems to me like you had everything firmly in hand last night."

"Please. Not so loud." I bit down a moan, sneaking around the bedroom to try and find something to cover my shame.

"Hair of the cat that bit you?" She dropped her voice, but it was full of laughter.

I found a discarded sarong and hastily wrapped it around my waist, hissing as the hem dug into some of the deeper cuts. "More like claws of the cat that mauled me. The Avatar wants to meet. He told us to get together in the Lotus Plaza, wherever that is."

"It's the big terrace just before the entry to the temple. You know: the one with the giant fuckin' lotus stamped on it," Suri replied drily.

"I'm sorry. I didn't notice the decor over the six hours of sensory torture I went through last night."

"Poor baby," Suri said. "Does widdle Hector need his binky?"

"Widdle Hector is about to see if the 'Fire-blooded' thing makes you flammable."

Suri laughed. Softly. "Given how much I drank last night, I'm betting it does."

I glanced back at Solai one more time, then crept out through the beaded curtains shielding her door and out into the temple. "Where's Karalti?"

"Sleeping. She polymorphed down and danced herself into a coma after eating about three tons of lobster. The music in town was a lot better than the racket you had to listen to. Need me to get her up?"

"Please." I paused in the breezy hallway outside the queen's chambers as Suri's words sank in past the fugue of alcohol and hallucinogens. "Is she gonna be pissed at me?"

"About Solai? Hard to say."

"I'm covered in scratches and fur and who knows what else. But you've got all my potions."

"Might be best if I come and see you first, then. You might want to consider a bath, too. Given you probably smell like, ahh..."

"Yeah." I grimaced, rubbing my eyes as I stumbled against a wall and stayed there for a few seconds. "Jesus Fucking Christ. Does this make me a furry now?"

Suri chortled. "Come to the bathing pool, lover boy. Let's get a look at all your boo-boos."

"Screw you." I grumbled, good-naturedly, and called up the mini-map to orient on Suri's position. "I'm on my way."

"Don't trip and fall in another pussy," Suri laughed, then hung up the chat.

CHAPTER 44

An hour later, we were mostly upright and assembled in the Lotus Plaza as instructed. I was surprised to see Gar waiting alongside Rin. He looked owlish and tired, a crumpled cigarette hanging from his bottom lip.

"Hell of a night," he grunted. "What was that racket going on at the back of the temple? Sounded like they were flayin' people alive back there."

"I think it was like that CIA black site torture method where they put you in a brightly lit room and blast Chinese opera 24 hours a day? But there was a demon and a princess." I rubbed my face. A bath, some food, healing potions and a sympathetic massage from Suri had gotten rid of all the debuffs except the Fatigued penalty: -5% to all skills. Potions had patched me up, but I still had a few faint scars on my back.

"Decided you want to come after all, did you?" Suri asked Gar acidly.

He shrugged. "Why the hell not?"

"You tell me. You're the one who said you didn't give a rat's arse about anything other than your bloody ship," Suri said.

"Yeah, well, I got talkin' to some bigshot here at the temple last night. She said Queen Whatshername will pitch in to help repair the Strelitzia. They got airships and spare parts. Reason we ain't seen of them is because their hangars are camouflaged underground." He shrugged again, a quick jerk of his shoulders. "I'm hoping it's true. Startin' to get worried about Ambrose and the others."

"How long will repairs take?" I asked.

"If we work together and have NPCs helping us? Maybe a day," Rin said.

"Yeah. Then I'm coming with you to your damn castle." Gar glowered at me.

I raised my eyebrow. "You seem super stoked about that."

"I am." He pointed at my chest. "Because you're going to extract your damn murder chicken and pay me extra for letting her use my bed as a fucking incubator."

I glared back at him. "Why are you here then, Gar? If you don't care, why'd you show last night?"

He made a show of thinking about it. "... Guess y'all helped me win a few levels day before yesterday. For what that's worth."

"We're in an RPG. It's worth everything." I said. "You don't level? You'll fall behind, and one day, some asshole like Lucien Hart is going to come along, kick your ass, and take your ship and everything else you care about."

"So what? I'll build another one. There's more to life than being ahead of other people." Gar slowly raised his eyes toward the sky. "There she is. Yer big flying lizard's back."

Karalti landed at the entry to the temple, careful not to crush any of the gawking Meewfolk there, and vanished behind the gates and stairwells as she shrunk down. A few minutes later, she ran up the stairs, pink in the face.

"Sorry I'm late!" She licked her lips as she joined me, reaching out to grasp my hand. *"I was having a bath. Are we gonna see the Avatar now?"*

"I guess so?" Now that we were all here, I looked around, unsure if the Avatar was coming out to see us, or what. "Maybe we have to be here at a specific time, but-"

No sooner had I said that than the world around us warped, blurred to black, and then unfolded again. Instead of the bustling temple terrace, we stood in a darkened room. It was simple and elegant: smooth floors, hand-carved lattice walls, all of it wrought from teak and fragrant sandalwood. We'd arrived inside of a permanent magic circle, a ring of metal inlaid in the floor. At the far end was a small, low Asian-style table, and behind that was the figure I had seen early in the morning.

"Please, all of you. Come and take your seats." The Avatar's voice was as low and musical in person as it had been in his projection. He was heavily robed, with a veil obscuring his features. However, we could see his hands as he deftly measured out some bright golden powder with a small scale. They were a Meewfolk's hands, clawed, with prominent knuckles and rough bean pads on the fingers, but they were completely hairless. His skin was as smooth and grey as smoke, and his fingertips were tattooed in small lines of script.

One by one, we filtered over. I took my place in the middle, with Suri to my right and Karalti to my life. Rin and Gar sat down at either end.

"How did you know to find us?" I asked, settling into a relaxed kneel. "We hadn't even—"

"I know everything that takes place on this island, Paragon." The Avatar whisked the spices into a dish of thick milk, turning it an attractive shade of yellow. "The Ancestors who protect our domain are an unseen army of eyes and ears. Every ship who passes through the dome that shields this island is seen and known by them. Any person can be found. Any weapon—such as the legendary Spear of Nine Spheres— can be identified."

"How?" Suri asked. "With... all respect, I mean. The Priest-Queen didn't really tell us anything about you. Who you are, what you do. Nothing."

"Mmm." The Avatar stirred the milk until it was frothy, then divided the liquid between seven small stone cups. When he was done, he lined the cups up in a row in front of us. Then he reached up to remove his concealing headdress. "It is customary for all dignitaries of our people to use their names with their guests, no matter their position in colony. You may call me Sanayam."

Sanayam resembled a Sphynx cat: he was heavily wrinkled, his muzzle drawn with deep lines and folds of dark gray skin. He had no whiskers, and huge green eyes that glowed in the semi-darkness of the room. Every inch of his skin was inked: rows and rows and rows of tiny, precisely scribed sigils that crawled with tiny flickers of light and color.

"I am the keeper of the lore and history of my people," he said heavily, the tip of his naked tail twitching back and forth over his lap. "And I am also the conduit between the living and the dead. Our ancestors imbue the Lesser Shield which guards this island, and which has protected it from invaders for three millennia."

"The Lesser Shield? You based it on the Caul of Souls?" I asked. "That's what it is, right? Like a mini-Caul."

"No. The Lesser Shield was created first," the Avatar said. "A prototype, which gave us the time we needed to build weapons capable of destroying the Deceivers. We are the oldest race on Archemi, and our cities sprawled through the forests and jungles of the world. Our civilization was mighty when the Aesari were still living in caves, dwelling in primitive obscurity for millennia. We were here when the Solonkratsu descended from Erruku, bringing with them the tulaq and the first humans. And we were here when the Drachan came... and defeated us."

"Dragons came from Erruku?" Karalti blinked several times, her untouched cup of milk cupped in her hands.

"Yes. Once, long ago. It was the world of the Solonkratsu." Sanayam bowed his head. "Your people arrived here some ten thousand years ago... a time when Erruku was green and blue, not dry and yellow with dust. Our most ancient records speak of the dragons as a technologically advanced society, artificers of great machines that let them accomplish wonders we cannot yet dream of. Some great calamity transpired there, many millennia ago, and the dragons came here with their servants."

"Wow." Karalti looked down at the table. *"I wonder what happened? And how they did it?"*

"That, unfortunately, is a mystery lost to the storms of time." Sanayam paused to take a silent sip of his drink. "You came here to discuss a more recent calamity: the Great Calamity of our planet. The arrival of the Drachan."

"Yes. And more importantly, how they were defeated." I leaned in. "We've found two Warsingers, and we know where to find the others. There was a map, in the Rose Vault of Withering Rose."

"A fortunate find. That it worked is a testament to the brilliance of the ancestors. The terminal, the portals, the Warsingers... they are incredibly old." The Avatar cupped his hands in his lap, regarding each of us in turn. "I should like each member of the Triad to ask the most important question they feel they need answered."

"Triad?" Gar said. "What's that?"

"The six in three: six Starborn who bear the responsibility of sustaining the Caul of Souls, which we call the Greater Shield of Ancestors in this land," Sanayam replied calmly. "The first corner of the Triad is the Paragon, a pair comprised of a Solonkratsu, who acts as a conduit of power, and a hero who bears the master key to all the Dragon Gates, the Spear of Nine Spheres. At its full power, the Spear is a devastating burden, one which requires the strength of two linked minds to endure. Such a bond is only possible between a dragon and her rider."

Karalti reached for my hand. I squeezed it gently.

"The Artisan is the second cornerstone: a pair of artificers of remarkable skill, united by a passion for creation," Sanayam continued. "Within the Dragon Gates, there are traps and machina that only they can possibly repair, construct, or control. That includes the Warsingers—but also the ancient devices which funnel the souls of the gods and maintain the Greater Shield. All created things, whether they be worlds or machines, are subject to entropy. Time erodes metal and man alike. The Artisans are able to turn back the clock, keeping the Warsingers and other weapons ready to defend us if the need should arise. The map you found is the product of their efforts, as are all other functional artifacts related to the Caul."

Rin and Gar looked at each other.

"I'm just tagging along, actually," Gar said. "Barely know these guys at all."

"Yeah, he is. And I'm really not able to cope with something this big." Rin nodded. "I-I mean, I want to help, but…"

"It is not for me to say." Sanayam turned his luminous eyes to Suri. "The last member of the Triad is the Warsinger: the unity of flesh and metal, mind and machine. The Warsingers were the generals of the armies required to defeat the Drachan. It is the only part of the Triad which is replaceable in any given cycle, as any of the Warsingers and their pilots may fulfil this role. In any case, their fate is battle, to spill blood in the fight against annihilation. There are doors within the Dragon Gates that can only be unlocked with the blood of a pilot, someone who is either genetically attuned to one of the Warsingers, or who has become attuned by successfully activating or controlling one."

Karalti scratched her head. *"But there's only one person in the Warsinger Triad part."*

"There are two." Sanayam looked down. "Each Warsinger possesses a soul of exceptional power, bound to a crystal at its core. It is this core which holds the magic of the machine together. Without it, it would tear apart under its own weight."

Suri sucked in a short breath. "That's why Withering Rose was scattered all over the bloody place. When Ororgael took the Heartstone, she broke up."

"How do we fix it?" Rin asked eagerly.

The Avatar shook his head, looking down. "The details of how the Warsingers were accomplished are... technical."

"Do you have schematics? Records? Anything that can tell us how they were made?" She laced her hands and gripped them together.

The Avatar's gaze slid to Rin. "A great deal has been lost over five thousand years. However, we know where some records may lie. If there are any left, they are almost certainly entombed in the Chorus Vault of Perilous Symphony."

Rin let out a squeak of excitement. "Then I was right! The plans are here! We need to repair Withering Rose, the last of the Warsingers. And if we had those schematics..."

"We do not know if there is anything left for you to find." The Avatar turned his cup in his hands, which was now half empty. "If you know where the Chorus Vault is, then you also know that it has sunk off the coast of this island."

"We have to try." I fixed a determined glare on him. "And if we step through that portal and get crushed, so be it. I'll do it."

"You will not!" Rin scolded me.

"Spoken like a true Paragon." Sanayam reached into his sleeve, and withdrew a perfectly round, clear orange stone. As he held it on his hand, I felt the Spear begin to hum and vibrate where I had laid it on the floor beside me.

"This is the Clinohumite of Loving Embrace," he said, rolling it off his palm and into the air in front of him, where it hovered under the impetus of his will. "The Keystone to the Tomb of Devana, the Solonkratsu goddess of Earth, Eggs, and the Sun. I believe you already know where to find her Dragon Gate. There is a portal there, constructed during the Fourth Cycle by Pathfinder, an accomplished mage, Queensrider, and the bearer of the Spear in that age. Like the first Paragon, Siva Nandini, she was one of my people. Please, present the Spear."

I lifted my weapon up, and the keystone drifted over and securely locked itself into its slot. The Spear seemed to struggle in my hand, vibrating intensely against my fingers as a new description appeared:

The Spear of Creation

Soul-bound Light/Dark/Fire/Earth Elemental Weapon
Slot: *Two-handed*
Item Class: *Relic*
Item Quality: *Mastercrafted*
Damage: *604—717 Slashing or Piercing*
Durability: *25%*
Weight: *1lb*
Special: *Soulbound, Elemental Quadrat (see description). +400 Damage to Undead, +800 HP, +12 Strength, +25 Will, +10 Wisdom. +25% Evasion, 3% chance to instantly kill an enemy, +15% Stamina Regeneration, +100 Adrenaline Points, Mark of Justice (see description), Mother's Grace.*

Special Abilities

Elemental Triad: *At will, you can change the elemental polarity of the Spear of Creation between Light, Dark, Earth and Fire damage, potentially dealing bonus damage to susceptible enemies.*
Maker's Blessing: *Learn crafting skills 8% faster.*
Nightfather's Blessing: *9% of inflicted weapon damage heals the wielder.*
Mark of Justice: *During combat, you may designate one opponent as a marked target. Your attacks against that target increase in priority and deal 10% more base damage for 5 minutes. This damage stacks with ability damage and combos.*
Mother's Grace: *If you fall below 10% health, you immediately regenerate 50% of your total Stamina and Adrenaline points.*

The energy in the Spear equalized and settled—but as I looked down at it, I had an eerie sense of it somehow staring back at me. The addition of the fourth stone had made it feel lighter and heavier at the same time.

"Take that stone to the portal, and you will be able to activate it." Sanayam withdrew his hands into his robes. "That may well be all you needed from me, but if you have other questions, I will do my best to answer them."

I tipped my head to one side. "I'm curious about something. It's almost like you were expecting us."

He bowed his head. "We—myself and the Avatars before me—have been noting the decline of the Greater Shield for at least a century. The timing correlates with the planned obsolesce of the Shield Cycle, and thus I expected that I would meet the Triad of the Sixth Age within my lifetime."

Set the Spear down and scratched my jaw. "Planned obsolesce? The Caul of Souls was meant to fail?"

"Yes. Magic is not water-tight, Paragon. As time moves, mana decays, and endlessly repeated words of power begin to fade." Sanayam gestured to the ceiling. "The magic of the shields can last slightly over a millennium before it must be repaired. The Prime Geas, created when the dragon gods willingly sacrificed themselves for their host planet, perpetuates the Greater Shield Cycle. This geas rules that a Triad will appear approximately a century before the Caul of Souls risks failing from lack of maintenance. I believe that you are that Triad, which means the continuation of the Caul is your burden. For another thousand years, Archemi will know a stalemate—if not true peace."

"It *will* know peace," I said. "We aren't going to renew the Caul like the others. We're going to destroy the Drachan and put an end to the cycle once and for all."

The Avatar's expression shut down. "That is not possible."

"It has to be," I said. "You said it yourself. Entropy effects everything, even Drachan. Archemi's been living in the shadow of this looming crisis for too long. The Meewfolk lost everything, the dragons lost everything, and the Aesari and Tulaq fucking went extinct, pardon my language. It has to end somewhere, and the buck stops here. With us."

Gar scratched his head and grimaced.

"It is not possible," the Avatar repeated. "The Drachan destroyed every world they passed through, and they nearly destroyed ours. The only reason we were able to stop them at all was because we had two sophisticated, intelligent species with great resources, a high concentration of mana, and the Nine. It was a stroke of luck that the Solonkratsu's gods were embodied deities capable of taking physical forms. Without their sacrifice, this world would be a lifeless sphere of ash and fire."

"Every time the Caul's been repaired, it's a little less effective. A little weaker. It might have been designed to be here forever, but the design isn't working. Souls leak out of it, power leaks out of it, and the damn thing is falling apart," I said calmly. "And this time, there are more than six Starborn in this world. There's a couple thousand of us, and a number of them are actively trying to free the Drachan and unleash them on the world for their own purposes. We don't have a choice: we have to defeat them. If we repair the Caul, we'll be doing it every other year from this point on, as greedy Starborn go into the Dragon Gates or travel to Rhorhon to look for treasure or power or both. It's a matter of time."

"Then this world's end has arrived," Sanayam said simply. "And soon, it will be a grave for all species, all races, other than the Drachan."

"Don't count on it." Karalti stretched her knuckles, her eyes narrowing. *"Suri fought her whole life to survive. I was born dead and clawed my way back to life. The biggest war machine in the world of Earth wasn't able to kill Hector, no matter how hard it tried. I dunno about Rin and Gar, but I bet they're just as tough as we are. We have something the Drachan don't—we believe life has meaning. And we're willing to fight for it."*

Suri nodded, her golden eyes as bright and hard as a hawk's. Rin pressed her lips together in determination. Gar looked away, lost in his own thoughts.

"Do you know where we can find the other Keystones?" I asked. "There's still five missing."

"I only know the location of two, and a story about a third." The Avatar shifted slightly, his tail swishing under the train of his robes. "The Bloody Jade of Joyous Pursuit, the keystone of Veela, Goddess of the Hunt, was given to the daughters of the Mercurion Artificer Zarya as a gift by the Fifth Paragon. It is no doubt a treasured relic of that clan to this day. The Prehnite of Boundless Sky is the responsibility of the Songmaster of Tungaant, an abbot who serves a similar function for the Tuun that I do for my own people."

[Map updated; New Quests Available!]

I mentally swiped the notification in, then dismissed it. "Thanks. That's a huge help. What about the story?"

"It regards the Cerussite of Endless Longing, which is the Key to Veles' Dragon Gate," the Avatar said. "Its last known location was in the Aesari city of Cham Langukan, which fell from the sky into the Grand Ocean between Artana and Daun approximately one and a half thousand years ago. Following the end of the Aesari Wars, the floating island that hosted Cham Langukan left the mainland and fled out to sea to escape the wrath of the peoples they had oppressed. Some magical calamity ensued, and the city—and the Cerussite—was lost over the sunken continent of Orcam."

"Fan-bloody-tastic," Suri muttered. "Seems to me like the Aesari have a lot to answer for."

"They were beings of incredible memory and intelligence, but they were arrogant, and they lacked imagination." Sanayam shrugged minutely. "Their story is a parable of how power leads to madness, if it is not combined with hard-won wisdom. Something to bear in mind as you progress to ever greater heights, Paragon. The Spear of Nine Spheres is indeed powerful, and yet even I—a man fated to be inked in knowledge that slowly poisons him over the course of his lifespan—could not consider the burden of bearing it, yet alone wielding it against the Deceivers."

I nodded. "Well... thanks for all that. It's going to take a while to digest."

"Indeed." The Avatar rose to his feet, and so did we. "You will have time to think as you test the portal to the Chorus Vault of Perilous Symphony. If you wish to travel there straight away, I can transport you."

"I think we'd all really appreciate that," Rin said. "And like Hector said. Thank you for all your help."

Sanayam shook his head, reaching up to carefully rearrange his veil over his face. "I have much to tell you about how to repair and restore the Caul... but not to destroy it. I fear your course of action will fulfil the speculation of the sages before me: that the Sixth Age will be our last, not because we have conquered the Drachan, but because they have finally destroyed us utterly."

CHAPTER 45

True to his word, Sanayam teleported us back to Devana's Gate, right into the middle of a storm. Warm monsoon rain thundered down like a sheet of water from the low, rumbling sky. The bodies of the Napathian undead were gone: pixelated into nothingness, or eaten by the local wildlife. There was just the stone ring standing there like a stargate, framing the brooding, dim entry to the temple.

"Okay! Well, now that's done... as soon as we fire up this portal, I'm going first." Rin stepped up beside me as I dug moss and mud out of the small pedestal in front of the portal frame: the lock for the Spear. "Alone."

"Alone?" Gar frowned. "You can't go in there alone."

"Yes, I can. I can't drown and I have crush resistance, so if the vault is underwater, it won't kill me," she replied, quickly slotting new vials of mana into her spellglove. "Mercurions don't NEED to breathe. I just breathe to talk, so if there's no air down there, I'll be fine."

"Well, shit." Suri said. "I didn't even think of that."

"Think of what?" I asked.

She shrugged. "Still don't know how to swim."

"You can't swim?" Gar squinted at her. "You got bigger muscles than I do."

"I grew up in the middle of the desert. Underground." Suri said sourly. "Not that it's any of your business."

Gar shrugged. "Texas ain't exactly a goddamn beach resort. Still learned how to swim."

"What do you want from me? A trophy?" Suri asked sweetly. "I can carve you a wooden dick and nail it to your head."

"I figured you'd use it to peg your damn hookwing," Gar retorted.

"Guys, focus." Karalti scowled at them. *"Rin, you tell us first thing if you need any help on the other side of the portal. Okay?"*

"Sure." Rin swelled up a little. "Fire it up!"

Once the activation slot was cleared, I inserted the blade of the Spear. Seams of brilliant orange energy flowed from the Clinohumite of Loving Embrace, pulsing down the blade and haft. The mechanism sucked at it, drawing the mana into itself, just before the portal ignited with a WHUMPH. The howling maelstrom glitched slightly as it drew the air in like a vacuum cleaner. No water sprayed out, but I could smell the ocean.

"Okay. See you on the other side!" Rin gestured to her turrets, and hesitantly stepped forward, vanishing into the whirling vortex of energy.

We held our breaths, waiting for the notification that she'd died. But as the minutes passed, nothing happened.

"She alright?" Gar fidgeted, flipping a coin over and around his fingers. "It's been a while."

"Hang on: let me check." I tagged her in our group PM. "Rin? How's it going in there?"

Another couple of minutes passed before she replied. "Oh! Sorry! I was using Hopper to scout the corridor. It's fine! There's a lot of salt buildup, but the place seems to have held together. It looks like it sunk into a giant coral system, and the coral grew over it. You can come over!"

"Roger that." I cracked my neck in anticipation. "You guys all ready?"

"Me first!" Karalti bounded forward and leaped through the portal before I'd finished pulling the Spear free. I went next, with Suri and Gar following up.

Warping by portal was a lot faster than teleporting. There was a nearly instantaneous transition between the dark, humid jungle, and the cold, blue-lit cavern. The exit portal was on an angle under a broken archway, its mana conduit pipes exposed to the air. A short set of broken steps led to a waterlogged tunnel that was definitely off kilter. Everything was tipped to the right: the floor, the broken walls and piles of rubble. White, fossilized coral held everything together like duct tape. The only level surface was the knee-deep water ahead.

"Crap." Gar groaned, flailing out to clutch at my arm.

I jumped at the unexpected touch. "What's the matter?"

"Don't much like small spaces underground," he muttered. "Makes me think of a coffin. Being buried alive."

"Finally, something we can agree on." Behind me, Suri lit a torch, throwing the hallway into weird angles and deep, sharp shadows.

"Ooh, spooky." Karalti was in water up to thighs, as was Rin, but they led the way forward. *"I smell all kinds of neat stuff, though. Lots of fish, and maybe a dead whale?"*

"Archemi has whales?" I rested the Spear over my shoulders, watching my Stamina run down at high speed. Walking in water past a certain depth caused Stamina to deplete twice as fast as normal.

"Course Archemi has whales," Gar muttered. "Whales don't give a shit about the waves. They just swim under 'em."

"Yeah!" Karalti replied. *"Mmm, I bet they're delicious. All that fat and meat and... nyyargh."*

"Hungry again?" I asked her, privately.

"More like, still hungry," she replied. *"I feel like I want to eat all the time."*

I took a deep, reassuring breath. *"We'll handle your heat better this time. No assassin interruptus."*

"Shh, don't talk about that now. I'll blush." Karalti giggled. *"I've got to be on my game here. What if a delicious, tender whale broke in and tried to kidnap you?"*

"Then we'd all drown."

There was a dull crack from somewhere far above our heads. Gar audibly winced.

"It's fine. This place has been standing for five thousand years. We aren't gonna be the ones to bring it down," Suri said.

She had unequipped her armor down to her underwear, her axes in her hands.

The tunnel eventually got wider, opening up into a tumbled ruin of stone, bleached coral, and hills of sand. There was a doorway in the wall, still intact: though it, and the hall beyond, were laying on their sides. The space was utterly dark.

"Ooh." Karalti stuck her head in. *"This one's EXTRA spooky."*

I looked back. Suri had the bland, stoic expression of a veteran soldier on the field. Gar was pale. Rin, surprisingly, looked unconcerned.

"I'll take point. I've got Darkvision," I said. "Let me scout down and make sure there's nothing in the way."

"Go for it," Suri replied. "Try not to get crushed."

Gar scowled. "What was that about us not being the ones to bring this place down?"

She rolled her eyes. "The whole place, mate. A hallway's more likely to collapse than the whole structure. These Chorus Vaults are massive, because the Warsingers are massive."

"Won't believe it 'til I see it," Gar said.

I ducked under the doorway and crept into the flooded hall. The water in here was shallower, only about a foot deep. The floor twisted back counter-clockwise as I picked my way over broken pillars, and came to what was absolutely a sealed bunker door. It reminded me a lot of the door we'd used to exit the chamber in Lahati's place, except there was no puzzle. A weak amber light spread over it as I brought the Spear in close, barely illuminating the rest of the mangled room. The wall it was set into looked to be in good shape.

"Go back out, tell the others we're good to proceed," I said. *"And if I get crushed when this door opens... well. You know where to find me."*

Karalti hesitated, but then nodded and backtracked part way down the hall. *"Come on, guys! We found a way in!"*

I set the Spear against the metal surface, and the Clinohumite snapped to its slot. This door screeched as it slowly, jerkily rolled into the wall, coming to a stop above halfway.

"Urgh." I pressed forward, looking to my left and right. There was a room on the left, hopelessly crushed and full of debris, and another coral tube on the other side. At the end of this corridor was a small round room with a portal dais and a lectern-like counter. It had a small, inset bowl, and an engraved panel with a single paragraph of ancient Meewfolk writing. I dusted a crust of salt off it, but couldn't understand a word of what I was looking at. "Rin! We need you for this one!"

"Coming!" I heard her automatons crunching over the rough ground as she picked her way down the corridor behind me. When she entered the room, I stepped aside and let her take the helm.

"Let's see here..." Her blue-on-blue eyes scanned it, bright in the gloom of the cave. "Mmm... Oh! It's a riddle."

"Uh oh." I rubbed the back of my neck. "What's it say?"

"I never was, yet always shall be. No one has ever seen me, and yet I am remembered. I am the expectation of all and

the doom of many. Some pray I shall never embrace them, yet all life pursues me by its nature. What am I?" She read the last stanza uncertainly. "Hmm."

"Hope?" I shrugged.

"We can try!" She looked up at the portal. "*Mah 'waan?*"

There wasn't even a spark of mana in the portal.

"Bleh. I thought 'hope' was the answer, too." Rin scratched her head, then crossed her arms and re-read it. "*Some pray I shall never embrace them, yet all life pursues me by its nature.* Time? Aging? Or maybe Youth?"

"What are we doing now?" Suri had to duck to enter. Gar and Karalti followed up behind her.

"A riddle. Me and Rin are kind of stumped." I shrugged.

Rin read it out again. When she finished, Karalti smacked her fist into the palm of her other hand. "*Ooh! I bet it's dinner!*"

Gar laughed. "It's 'tomorrow', you dipshit."

Karalti scowled at him. "*You don't know that.*"

"Sure I do. Tomorrow never was, but everyone thinks about it. You can't see the future, but you remember it when it becomes the past. Everyone expects to live another day, but nothing's guaranteed. The folks that made this place were fighting for a better tomorrow. Makes sense that'd be their password."

"Oh! He's right!" Rin turned back to the pedestal. "*Irra 'ao 'oww!*"

The portal spluttered to life with a clear, amethyst purple film of energy.

"See? Look what happens when you use your damn brains for something." He shook his head, lighting a fresh cigarette.

Rin shot him an exasperated look. "I'll go first again. Hang back—my guess is that wherever this takes us to, it's probably flooded."

We watched anxiously as Rin stepped through, waiting. After a few minutes, she messaged us.

"Alright: there's a lot of water in here, but there's ways to get around. Platforms, things like that. You just have to be, umm, extremely careful. I think there's a sunken floor, but everything down there looks crushed and I don't think we're getting into any rooms by swimming. It's really different to the Chorus Vault of Withering Rose... it's almost like a bunker."

"Platforms!" Karalti chirped aloud. *"I love platforms."*

"I hate platforms," Suri muttered, watching as my dragon happily bounded through the portal. "Big old bitch like me isn't made for cave crawling."

"Me either." Gar grimaced. "I ain't no damn frog."

The portal dumped us out into what looked like a cistern. The water here was deeper, at least six feet, luminous and blue-tinged. There was a great pit in the center of the room, where trickles of water tumbled away into some unknown abyss. There were doorways in every direction in this place—assuming we could reach them. Only two of the doors were walkable from where the portal had deposited us. The other six had to be reached by jumping from platform to platform, or by hanging and going hand over hand along pipes and broken slabs of stone.

"I'm guessing the Big-Ass Door over there is the one that leads to the Warsinger vault." I motioned to the dragon-sized gate at our nine o'clock. It was similar in size to the door that had guarded the entry to Withering Rose, sans ornamentation. There was no decoration to speak of in this place. Everything was functional and had been built to withstand insane amounts of force. That fact, and the tumorous-looking coral, were the only reasons it wasn't a pile of rubble under the water.

"I'm so excited!" Rin waved her fists under her chin, peering around like a kid at Disneyland. "If we find those schematics, can you imagine all the things we can invent? Telephones! Maybe even radar, and radios!"

"Yeah, then we can mine all the metals out of the ground, build a bunch of nukes and wreck this world the same way we wrecked the last one," Gar remarked sourly. "Why do you guys need this thing, anyway?"

"Short answer? Baldr Hyland is possessed by a crazy Ryuko developer who's on a crazed, self-righteous mission to save Archemi by cleansing it of 'squalor', whatever the fuck that is," I said. "In the process, he's trying to unleash the world bosses of the game on us. World bosses that have been corrupted by some kind of system virus, we think. We're trying to find the weapons that defeated the Drachan the last time around. Perilous Symphony and the other Warsingers are those weapons."

"Oh." Gar tapped some ash off his cigarette. "So he's just like you, then."

"What did you just say?" Karalti whirled on him, fists clenched.

"What? You think I'm deaf? Hyland's plan for Archemi is basically what Hector said you folks were doing while we were sitting down with the Avatar not even an hour ago." Gar gestured airily toward the ceiling. "You're going to break down these Dragon Gates, let the Drachan out, and try to kill'em before they wreck the place, which according to the Avatar, they will. Y'all couldn't even solve a goddamned riddle. It ever occur to you to try listenin' to one of the most learned men in the damn world?"

"It ever occur to you that you don't know anything about what we're doing or why?" I retorted. "You didn't want to know anything about the crisis in Ilia, so we didn't tell you. Now you want to judge our goals based on one overheard conversation? You can't have it both ways."

"I don't rightly recall anointing you as my leader," Gar said.

"And I never took you on as one of my team. So unless you actually want to be a part of it, keep your patronizing bullshit to yourself." I glared at him, then turned to the edge of a cracked and broken platform. "Come on, Karalti."

Karalti tossed her hair over her shoulder, shooting Gar a scathing glance before turning to join me. Suri just shook her head, and she and Rin started for one of the nearby entryways.

"Guess I'll go look in one of these rooms and see what I find by myself, then." Gar scowled, jammed his hands in his pockets, and took the other door.

Karalti and I went to the edge of the cracked and broken floor, assessing our path forward. With the Bond in play, we were able to gauge a quick route forward.

"I say we take the first door to the right," I said. *"We can scooch along the ledge to the others from there."*

"It's almost like you read my mind. Race you there!" Karalti tensed down, wiggled her butt like a cat, and leaped over to the first platform.

"Hey! It's not a race if you just start without calling it!" I jumped after her as she ran for the next platform.

Karalti laughed, looking back over her shoulder at me. Her eyes were dark, her lips parted, and I felt something dark and playful rise in me as I lit after her. I caught up to her by jumping right over the first platform, catching onto the wall, and launching off from it. I landed just ahead of Karalti as she skidded to a stop in the doorway of our chosen room.

"Hmmph. Now you see why I just started without saying anything." She stuck her bluish tongue at me. *"You cheat."*

"All's fair in love, war, and ninja racing." I grinned back at her.

We sobered up as we pushed on the double doors. As they swung inward, soft blue lights sputtered to life, hissing and crackling as they tried to burn mana that had sat inside these mage globes for millennia. And what they shed light over stopped both of us in our tracks.

"What the hellll are THOSE?" I whispered.

CHAPTER 46

The ancients had used this room as a specimen lab, and the first thing we saw as we cautiously entered the room, was a row of small tanks with parts and pieces of creatures still contained within.

A heavy, unnatural silence hung over the room as I wandered toward one, trying to make sense of what I was seeing. The creature looked like it was made of digital snow, and no matter what angle I observed it from, it refused to come into focus. I could almost make out horns, spines, barbed tentacles, mandibles... but every time I thought I'd pinned some memorable feature about it, I couldn't find it a second time.

"What the...?" I tentatively laid a hand on the thick crystal sealing it off from the room, and strained to try and put a shape, a form, *something* to whatever I was staring at.

The thing lunged at the glass.

"FUCK!" I vanished, a panicked forty-foot teleport backward, and blundered into the opposite wall with the Spear clutched in my hands.

"*What!?*" Karalti dropped the pot she'd been examining. It smashed to the ground, and I froze, watching the tank for any sign of movement.

"Nothing. Just a stupid jumpscare." Even so, my heart was pounding as I eased down, zooming in on the tank. The small creature inside was still blurred and out of focus, in the exact same place it had been before. I had no idea if it had even really moved. Staring at it for too long made my eyes ache. "What do you see when you look at this thing?"

Karalti meandered over to it. *"Uhh... I dunno. I can't see it properly, but it gives me the creeps."*

There were some etched plates on the tanks that looked like nameplates or identifiers written in Ancient Mau, but when I focused my HUD on them, it only bought up a paragraph of gibberish. Frowning, I mentally called the Screenshot Capture and took some pictures of the tank and the nameplate. I was about to send them to Rin to see if she could translate them, when my eyes snagged on something in the photo attachment thumbnails. I opened them, and felt my adrenaline start to tick up again.

The tank and the nameplate were both blacked out: a deep, sucking, vantablack-like darkness, from which no light entered or escaped. It was like they'd been snipped out of the screenshot. Without intending to, I searched the blackness for some kind of afterimage—and a dull throbbing pain shot through my head, chest, and left shoulder.

"Ach!" I winced, and closed the photo. "This place is fucked up, Karalti."

"Yeahhh..." Karalti's shoulders hunched. *"Maybe we should go look over there?"*

She pointed to the other end of the room. Past the tanks was a large steel table, pitted and rusted with age, and other devices that were so run down and crumbled as to be unrecognizable. Clay pots and other debris lay scattered. At the back of the room was something that reminded me of a primitive computer. It had a crank handle and various dials.

"I wonder if this was some kind of information storage?" I went to the terminal, trying to see if I could figure it out. My HUD came up with a blank tooltip when I tried to identify it. Highlighting the crank brought up an actual message. *[This device cannot be repaired.]*

"Huh." I turned back. "Well, I don't know what the fuck is going on in here, but I'm now sure this place wasn't just a Chorus Vault. I think they had an entire military base here. They were researching these things."

"That'd make sense," Karalti replied, circling back around the tanks. *"... Are these Drachan? Or parts of Drachan?"*

"No idea. Whatever they are, I'm going to vote we don't fuck with them right now." I left the machine and went over to join her.

"We should take a sample with us if we can," Karalti said. *"We might be able to learn things from it."*

"Or it gets loose, possesses Cutthroat, and turns her into an Elder God or something." I shuddered. "How about we see if we can fish something out of the console over there? We can't repair it, but it might have something inside."

"Sure." Karalti looked over to it. *"How do we get it open?"*

I went over, searched the front of it, and found a patch of brittle black rust. I took a step back and drove my foot into it with a shout. Three solid front kicks and the panel caved in, revealing the guts of the machine.

"Let's see..." I knelt down and let my eyes adjust. The guts of it were rotted, the stale air inside bitter with the smell of decayed mana. But as I scanned it, my HUD highlighted a small rack of dusty crystal plates: [Kyanine Tablets].

"Kyanine?" I carefully pulled them out. The semi-translucent crystal tablets were delicate, but still intact after thousands of years. "No idea what that is."

"Let's take them to Rin, and see what she says." Karalti wiggled, looking back anxiously toward the open door. "I dunno about you, but I really want to get out of this room."

"Same." I folded them into my inventory. "Let's get out of here."

The next room we stickybeaked into was a wreck: there was nothing useful or scannable in there. As we exited, Suri, Rin and Gar emerged from the other end of the round hall. Suri waved to us.

"Find anything?" I called.

"Bunch of interesting little artifacts!" Suri hollered back, her voice rebounding off the walls. "Can you help us set up a zipline? Neither me or Gar here are gonna be able to bounce over those platforms to reach the Warsinger's silo door."

We had climbing gear that Rin had made us for our last trip down into a Chorus Vault. With Jump and some ingenuity, we were able to set up a line across the chamber, bypassing the crumbling remains of the floor and the water beneath. One by one, our friends were able to cross. Karalti and I caught them at the end of the line, helped them down, and pulled the swing back to the next passenger. We left the zipline in case we had to cross back.

"I hope the whole damn ocean isn't waiting for us behind those doors." Gar swaggered over to the titanic doors, craning his head to look up along the seam down the middle. "See that water? Wanna bet how much these doors are holding back?"

He pointed to a thin trickle of sea water running out from around the seal.

"Better brace for a flood, then." I rolled my shoulders and made a beeline for it. Like the Dragon Gates, this door opened with the Spear. It was not the blood-bound locks we'd seen in Withering Rose's much younger Chorus Vault. "Alright: everyone to the side. Hang onto something if you can. And get ready for a fight."

I set the blade into the door lock and twisted. A resonant CLUNK echoed through the chamber before the doors began to very slowly open into the walls. Gears squealed and ancient, salt-rusted springs crackled as the doors ground back just enough to let a person squeeze through. A slop of polluted water gushed from the darkened room, along with a familiar bitter almond and burned plastic reek mixed with the odor of old blood. The air that puffed out was bitterly cold.

"Phew. Smells like cancer in there." I readjusted my grip on the Spear. "What do you guys think? Boss fight, or traps?"

"I don't hear anything, so probably traps." Suri took post on the other side of the door. "Ready?"

I signaled her: one, two, three, and then turned into the opening and Shadow Danced through, ready to attack if anything lashed out. But there was no cancer, and no boss, either. There was only Perilous Symphony—or what was left of it.

The machine's headless torso was splayed open like the ribs of a carcass, host to a forest of thin rust-covered stalactites. It hung from a sturdy scaffold that was also covered in mineralized salt and lime and sand, dripping constantly to the uneven, wet ground. A mess of rusted cables spilled from its guts, the ends trailing off into pools of reddish waste water. Mage lights around the perimeter of the huge silo still sputtered and flickered, their pale light dulled by the seething vortex of black noise emanating from the heart of the Warsinger.

"Holy shit," I whispered, dropping the point of my weapon as I looked around. "We're clear! Kind of."

The others squeezed through. When Rin saw what was left of Perilous Symphony, she let out a yelp of dismay.

"Well, I'll be damned." Gar had his pistol drawn, scowling at the towering wreck. "The hell is that thing?"

"Perilous Symphony. The first fully-operational Warsinger constructed after the success of Nocturne Lament." Rin absently pushed past me, gazing up at the rotting metal carcass. "And *that* is the Warsinger's Heartstone."

She pointed at the sucking black hole in its chest. As she did, it warped and fluxed, spitting static into the air.

"Looks like we got here just in time," Karalti said. *"Ugh… that stench."*

"Is it going to be safe to transport?" I asked, recoiling as my shoulder began to ache.

Rin let out a nervous laugh. "Umm… I don't know if I'd want to sleep with it in my bed or anything, but as long as we don't hang onto it for days, we should be okay?"

"Let's grab it and whatever else you need, and let's go," Suri said. "This place gives me the fuckin' creeps."

I looked past her into the depths of the silo, searching for anything of interest. Even my darkvision couldn't completely pierce the aura of gloom that hung over the silo. It looked and felt like a graveyard.

"Gar, could you help me?" Rin turned to him with a look of appeal. "If we have two mechanics working on this thing, we'll get this done a lot faster. We have to get that crystal, and also see if we can identify and extract the sonic devices this Warsinger used to scream Drachan out of the sky."

Gar looked up at the Heartstone. "Sonic weapons, eh? Like LRAD?"

"Kind of like a super-duper LRAD, yeah!" Rin waved her hands for emphasis.

"Super-duper is the technical term, right?" Karalti cocked her head from side to side, strutting around the base of the scaffolding.

"Right." Gar rubbed his brow and the bridge of his nose. "Well, sure. How are we gonna get up there?"

"I figure we can rig up some kind of cable line and hoist you up," Suri replied. "Kind of like a bosun's chair."

"Yeah! I'll help! I'm the best at belaying!" Karalti puffed her chest out and thumped it with a fist. *"But Suri's still stronger than me, so she gets to belay Rin."*

"Right. Well, let's get onto it," Gar replied. "For once, I agree with Suri on something. This place gives me the heebie-jeebies, and I'm just about ready to see the end of it."

***

With half an hour and a lot of effort, we were able to set up a kind of double Bosun's Chair: a suspension that allowed Rin to hang in front of Perilous Symphony's Heartstone, while Gar went up to the neck to tool around. Suri and Karalti had to lift them up and down using a belaying harness and improvised. While the four of them toiled on the Warsinger, I went to go and poke around the silo. It wasn't long until I found something: another magitech console with a slot that was about the right size for the Spear of Nine Spheres, as well as a dial with slots that matched the keystones.

"If this place was built to construct Warsingers, they must have started working on the Caul back then, too." I muttered to myself, scraping away dust and crumbs of stone off the front of the 'screen': a smooth slab of lambidium: a hard, magically conductive metal. "Let's see what happens if we stick it in."

I inserted the Spear's blade into the slot. There was a 'clunk' as some kind of mechanism engaged, but nothing else happened.

Curious, I looked over and around the device, searching for switches, valves, cranks or buttons. I found a valve at the base of it, still topped by a rusted spigot, and carefully gave it a twist to the left. There was a soft hiss, and the console reluctantly flickered to life behind me. Success.

I dusted myself and strolled back around, trying to figure out what I was seeing. The device projected a scroll of purplish glyphs into the air, which resolved into a magical hologram as I reached my hand out. It showed a wheel with four highlighted circles: one for each Keystone in the Spear. There were brief paragraphs of ancient script underneath it, so fuzzed out that even if I could read the language, it would be indecipherable.

"Okay... what if we...?" I flicked my fingers over one of the highlighted spheres to see if I could swipe it across, and jumped when a man-sized projection of Nocturne Lament sprung to life. Line after line of text began to rapidly spool out beside it.

"Wait. Are these the schematics?" I tried manipulating the hologram the way I would have done with an augmented reality terminal. Touching the writing didn't make it stop scrolling, but touching the image of Nocturne Lament did. When my fingers glanced over its shoulders, the feral-looking Warsinger vanished. It was replaced by a complicated, but blurry diagram of its heatsinks and other parts. A new text feed began to spool out beside it as individual parts and pieces were highlighted by glowing auras.

"Guys! I think I found the schematics!" I called out in excitement, leaning out to the side. "Rin? What do I do? It's like a holographic A.R terminal, kind of?"

"What?! You activated it? Ack! Lemme down, lemme down!" Rin's voice rang from the other side of the vault.

I tried cancelling out of the display, and with trial and effort, was able to get back to the wheel with the glowing circles. There, I tried selecting one of the un-lit circles. Nothing happened.

"The Schematics are tied to the Keystones," I murmured. "One Warsinger per Keystone. Except for one, because there were ten Warsingers, but only nine stones."

"Oh! I see it!" Rin scampered over, still trailing a long piece of rope. "Are these... Oh wow!"

"There's diagrams for at least four Warsingers on this thing," I said, swiping over one of the other lit circles. It took a few tries before the hologram actually opened and came into focus, revealing the tall, slim, noble figure of Radiant Eclipse. It was one of the more humanoid Warsingers, with a long spiraling lance, pointed feet, and a helmet styled like a unicorn's head. "If this is like some kind of magitech computer... where is the data stored?"

"I don't think 'computer' is the right term for what this is." Rin bit her lip, chewing it as she excitedly scanned the text. "It's more like a projector. The schematics are probably encoded onto some kind of storage item, like ruby mana or mana-forged lambidium. The box has a static rote—a spell that's permanently woven into the machine—that activates when you feed the machine mana. You notice there's no sound coming out of it?"

"Yeah."

"That's because it doesn't have any moving parts. The hologram is an illusion, a spell that's showing us what's on the plates." Rin patted the side of the console. "If we break this open and remove the plates, we will have all the schematics. Then I should be able to reverse engineer this console, and we can build a new one in Myszno. It looks like a much older version of the map storage device we found in Withering Rose's Chorus Vault."

"Huh." I opened my inventory and took out the crystal plates I'd recovered from the lab. "We also found these in a smaller machine inside one of the rooms we looked into. These might have information on the Drachan we can use."

"Ooh." Rin took them carefully, then added them to her inventory. "Kyanine? I've never heard of it."

"Me either." I flipped back to see the other two available Warsingers. The first was Pure Land, a goat-headed Warsinger with massive curled horns and a spiked warhammer. The second was Hanging Star—one of the floating Warsinger types, it had a stylized Meewfolk face, a long, pod-like body, and no fewer than six sword-like arms that rested around it in a loose spiral. "There's only nine schematics on this machine. We're missing one."

"There were only nine Warsingers, plus the prototype," Rin said.

"Yeah. That's what I mean." I tapped the dial. "There's only nine blueprints on this box, and one of them is Nocturne Lament."

"Oh! Then..." Rin's expression grew troubled. "The missing one has to be Withering Rose. It was built a couple hundred years after the first Warsingers were deployed."

I reached up to squeeze my hair in exasperation. "Of course. The one set of blueprints we need aren't here."

"No, but we can figure out a lot about the technology used to make her from these diagrams. We might be able to repair Nocturne Lament first, and with that experience, we can piece out Withering Rose. Just remember: if it was built by mortals, it can be rebuilt by mortals." Rin patted me on the arm. "Don't worry! This is real progress!"

"HAH! GOT IT!" Gar let out a harsh bark of triumph from the carcass of Perilous Symphony. "Rin! I found the drive!"

"Great! Now we just have to figure out how to transport it without breaking anything." Rin dashed her arm across her forehead, rubbing the condensation from it. "Phew... alright, leave this with me. I'm going to document everything I can before I take it apart."

"Do you have crafting prompts, or are you just winging it?" I asked.

Rin giggled, pulling her toolbox out of hammerspace. "Oh, you know. A bit of Column A, a bit of Column B. But I need to do this alone, if you don't mind. I get nervous working when people are behind me."

"No worries." I stepped back. "I'll leave the Spear here. Let me know if you need me to do any Paragon mojo."

"Yep!" She crouched down, plugged a pair of earplugs in, and began to tinker. "Can you go assist Gar with the sonic organs? He might need a hand."

"I never thought I'd get to help a man with his sonic organs." I muttered, shooting an amused glance at Rin.

Gar was still hanging from his bosun's chair, muttering at and cursing the Warsinger as he tinkered with what looked to me like the brass columns of a church organ. Suri leaned back in her harness, keeping tension on the belaying rope as she stared off into space. Karalti had curled up in a little ball off to the side, snoozing with her hair over her face.

"How's it going?" I called up to him.

"This fucking old piece of shit..." He banged on a mineralized plate of metal with the end of his wrench, scowling at it. "The AMEN is behind this panel, but I don't have enough leverage to get the damn thing off."

"The what?"

"The AMEN. Arcane Machima ENcoder."

I glanced at Suri. She shrugged.

"What's the AMEN do?" I asked, turning back.

Gar leaned out and looked down over his shoulder. "You know what a ribosome is?"

"That's a sports drink flavor, right?" I beamed up at him.

"*Dios, ayúdame.*" He made a show of crossing himself. "Ribosomes are cellular machines that turn amino acids into chains of protein, you dumbass. AMENs do the same thing, but for magic. They take mana and encode it so it can manifest functions without a wizard standing over it, waving their hands."

I crossed my arms. "So what you're saying is that you need help getting the panel off?"

"Ugggggh." He made a sound of disgust. "Yes."

"Me not know what ribosome is, but me STRONG." I tensed, adjusted my footing, and leaped up. I caught a handhold on the Warsinger and pulled myself to a narrow ledge, then monkeyed over to where Gar was struggling to reach. Clinging on with one hand, I reached back. "Give me a crowbar."

He handed over a short army-style crowbar. I wedged it in, then began to rock it back and forth, working the decayed rivets loose. The bolts shrieked as they gave way: first the two at the top, and then the rest.

"Watch your head!" Gar called to Suri, giving her time to move as the plate tumbled off and clanged to the ground.

"There you go. One thingimajig, served cold." I scurried to the left a bit in case anything decided to blow up in my face. There was a strange device behind the panel: a double-walled metal cylinder with two tubes feeding through the top, and several dozen small tubes flaring out the bottom. It was inset with golden rings that spun like prayer wheels when Gar reached in.

"Can you pull my swing forward and hold in closer?" He asked.

"Sure." I leaned out, caught the rope, and hauled it forward, wrapping my arm around a pipe so I wasn't dislodged.

"Thanks," he grunted. "Damn, look at this thing. Ain't seen anything quite like it."

"How's it different to the things we have now?" I asked.

"Because this puppy somehow handles twenty-seven different magical functions," Gar replied, attaching some kind of small meter to one of the intake pipes. "Doesn't sound like a lot, but the AMEN in an engine only handles six: intake and exhaust, fuel injection, conversion and catalyzation, and engine temperature. This thing's got three command rings on it, nine functions per ring. Looks to me like the rings allowed custom functionality. It must have been red-hot when it was running, unless there was some kind of fluid to keep it cool."

"Huh." I barely understood what he was saying, but I was interested anyway. "Man... the world of artificing is totally different to the world of combat classes. What made you get into it?"

"I was into mechanics before Archemi," he replied tersely. "Wanted to open my own shop. Was close to doing just that when the War happened and I got called up. Pull that wire there out of the way for me."

I leaned down and caught the cable, pushing it aside. "Wait: you were conscripted?"

"Yeah. Who wasn't?"

"Anyone over thirty-five. Did you make yourself look older in the game?"

He sighed. "No. I was overage, but I got drafted anyway. Served in TW1 as a UAS pilot. Left the army for five years. They recalled me to duty at the beginning of '69. Talk about getting fucked."

'UAS pilots' were drone pilots: a soldier who flew unmanned aircraft. "Jeez. You must have been a real ace if they pulled you back in." I clicked my tongue. "Which unit?"

"The second time 'round? 3rd Brigade Combat Team, 82nd Airborne."

"Oh, hey, we did a lot of work with you guys." I leaned out a little further. "I was a dogface for five years."

"Oh yeah? Lemme guess: 79th?"

I laughed. "Yeah. How d'you know?"

"How the hell else does some smartmouth city kid end up with eyes like yours? I knew the second I saw you that you've seen some real bad shit, and the brass worked that whole fucking division to death." Gar hawked in his throat. "What company? Might even have flown for you."

"E Company," I said. "And yeah. I can't speak for others, but the war gave a lot and took a lot from me. Took more than it gave, but hey—I was able to put my airborne experience to good use here."

Gar looked up at me. "Huh?"

I laughed. "Yeah, we had to retake one of the counties of Myszno from this dickhead baron. He had himself a pretty damn good position, with air defenses and everything, but it turns out no one'd thought to invent a working parachute in Archemi yet. I was able to help Rin make blueprints for the old T-11 and the HI-5 systems. We trained a bunch of mercenaries to jump, then dropped straight into his damn castle."

"E Company didn't do airborne." Gar irritably shook his head, twisting his wrench deep in the bowels of the Warsinger.

"Well, I wasn't dreaming all those jumps, was I?" I laughed. "I did at least ten over five years."

Gar craned his head back to look straight at me. "I'm telling you, son. E Company didn't have any damn airborne. The conscript C.Ts weren't ever run through Airborne School. I know because I was there from the beginning through to the day when the whole of China dropped dead from HEX."

I blinked back at him in confusion. "Well, I know what I did and didn't do. Don't give a shit if you don't believe me."

"Sure thing." He gave me a wry, sardonic smile—a smile I'd given more than one person myself. It was the look any combat Vet would give to someone who was talking out their ass.

I tsch'd. "You'll see the chutes when we get back to Myszno. I know how they're made, I know how they're packed, and I can rig one with my eyes closed. Even if my memory got screwed up during my upload here, the combat jumps aren't something I forgot."

"Hell, for all I know, it's my memory that's shot," Gar grunted. "We're nothing but computer programs in some fucking magic box in space. Only difference between me and a calculator is that the calculator doesn't feel the need to eat and jerk off."

"Well said." I eased down a little, and tried to push my doubt down to join all the other fears, anxieties, and other shit I'd successfully repressed over the years.

Gar's eyes narrowed as he turned the ratchet one final time, reached in, and extracted a perfectly round metal sphere covered in glyphs. "Alright. Pretty sure that's everything Rin wanted. Rest of this thing's basically just scrap. We got a good set of pictures of its big pipe organ thing."

"Great." I'd expected to feel excitement, but the conversation had sucked the wind out of me. How did he know my company didn't have airborne training? Had I had it before he'd been recalled back into service? I had a year of enlistment on him—I'd collected my punch card in '68. Was he just trolling me?

Suddenly—inexplicably—I found myself feeling very tired.

"Alright, Suri! Bring us down!" Gar called to her.

"Righto. Hold on to your undies." Suri began to let the rope out.

I waited until Gar was on the ground before jumping. A few months ago, I'd have flinched at the idea of dropping from a height like this—roughly the same height as a five-story building. Now, I did it almost as a reflex, dancing into a thin curl of shadow just before hitting the ground to land softly on my feet.

"Are you guys done over there?" Rin's voice cut through the still air of the silo.

"Sure am. These parts weigh a ton," Gar replied. "What'cha got over there?"

"I've got the plates!" Rin could barely contain her excitement. "But we don't have a whole lot of lambidium. I can reassemble a terminal like this in Litvy, but we need to take as much lambidium scrap as we can."

"Then let's portion it out between us. If we split the load to a maximum of eight hundred pounds, and Karalti can carry the lot in dragon form," I said.

"Snrrk!" Karalti's head shot up at the sound of her name. "Whuu? I'm 'wake!

"I can pack about two hundred kilos myself, give or take," Suri said. "I dunno what that is in pounds."

"Four-forty, or thereabouts," Gar replied. "I can take some. If nothin' else, lambidium is expensive as hell. We should get it while we have it."

"Then let's get to it." I avoided looking at Gar, focusing on Suri. "Because we're about to turn Vlachia into the technological superpower of Archemi."

CHAPTER 47

We backtracked through the portal to Devana's Dragon Gate, and stepped out to find the Avatar waiting for us, along with six heavily armed and armored guards.

"Is there a problem?" I took a cautious step ahead of the others, making sure Rin and Gar were behind me.

"Problem? No, not at all, Paragon." The rain had stopped, but the ground was still wet. Sanayam had his robes held up over his arm, a parasol resting over one shoulder. "After speaking with you in my cell yesterday, I realized that you all may need assistance. I also wanted to let you know that Priest-Queen Solai sends her regards. She has contacted one of her sisters of the Great Conclave, Priest-Queen Mil'ah'ao, and asked her to send engineers to help repair the airship which crashed within the territory of Wung'raah Waat."

Gar bristled. "You got strangers tinkering with *my* ship? Without me there?"

"Your Lieutenant, Ambrose, assured us you would wish to be there to oversee reconstruction," the Avatar replied mildly. "He ordered the materials he thought you would need. Delivery should have begun by now."

Gar eased down, muttering to himself. I put my hands together and bowed to him the way I'd seen the Meewfolk do.

"Thank you. And please pass my thanks to Solai. We're grateful for all the help you've given us."

"She wishes to speak with you and your bonded one before you leave," the Avatar said. "Concerning the matters we discussed in the temple."

I looked to Suri. "No one else?"

"The Paragon is the default leader of the Triad," the Avatar replied. "There is no shame in fulfilling your role."

"It's fine. I need to check on Cutthroat anyway." Suri reached out and squeezed my shoulder. "Go. We'll be waiting for you there."

Karalti looked between us, then back to the Avatar. *"Okay! Sure!"*

The Avatar bowed, then gestured with a spell-gloved hand. Gar, Rin and Suri vanished, leaving Karalti and I together. With a second gesture, the Avatar warped all of us back to Ru Waat.

We appeared in what could only be Solai's personal lounge, a room adjacent to the lavish bedroom where I'd roused from my hedonistic sex-coma. The noise and bustle of the temple was absent: there was nothing but the tinkle of wind chimes, the scent of sandalwood, and the whispering warm wind brushing over our skin. Like many of the Meewfolk buildings we'd seen, the queen's living space was open to the air, a gazebo-like room with wide balustrades perfect for lounging in the sun. Solai was doing just that, until she sensed our arrival and slid to her feet, yawning languidly.

"Avatar Sanayam." She went to her hands and knees and bowed to the floor, as her captain had done to her. "Thank you for honoring us with your presence."

"It is I who should be grateful you host me on your sacred land, Priest-Queen Solai," the Avatar replied, with an air of ritualized formality. "I am taboo."

"A taboo of necessity, enshrined by all who have won their place in the goddess's eyes before me, and in those who are yet to come." Solai gave me a sultry glance, which earned a scowl from Karalti, and motioned to a pair of wooden chairs. "Is it true, Paragon? That you seek to release the Deceivers?"

"I took a seat. "Only because we have to. As I said to Samayan, there are thousands of Starborn in Archemi now. A minority of them are power-hungry assholes, and it's a matter of time before they unleash the Drachan. If we don't destroy them in a controlled manner, the end result will be the same."

"Why would anyone believe the Drachan would assist them in their pursuit of power?" She didn't drape herself over the sofa the way she normally did. Instead, she sat down and neatly drew her legs up and to the side, spine straight. The Avatar and his guard remained standing.

"The short answer? Because humans are stupid. A human Architect is trying to resurrect the Drachan for his own purposes as we speak," I said. "They've infected his mind. He keeps saying he needs to 'cleanse the world of squalor'. He'll kill everyone, or conquer them, and when there's no defense against the Drachan, they'll turn on him and destroy everything here."

"Squalor?" The Avatar cocked his head. There was no direct Meewish translation for it, so he mimicked my pronunciation. "That is a dark word."

"*A dark word?*" Karalti chirped aloud. "*What do you mean?*"

"I do not know," the Avatar replied. "But when you said it, the Shield of Ancestors fell silent. A ripple of disquiet passed through the multitude of souls who observe us here, on the sacred terrace we lifted in thanks to their sacrifice. It... scared them."

"Wait. Squalor is a name?" I frowned. "Is it one of the Drachan? He was ranting about the Drachan telling him or showing him things."

"I do not know. But I advise you to stop saying it aloud." The Avatar shivered, his robes rustling.

I narrowed my eyes. "Whatever it is, I'm not afraid of it. If you don't name evil, if you don't keep your eyes on it, you just make it stronger. Stare at it and speak its name, and it loses power. That's what I think."

"*Right. We can't pretend it doesn't exist,*" Karalti said. "*Maybe there's a Drachan named Squalor, and it's behind what's happening?*"

"That is possible. The names of the Deceivers were not passed down through history," the Avatar said. "And there is wisdom in what you say, Paragon. But until you have a clear understanding of what you are dealing with, it is best not to draw attention to yourself. We have a principle of war in our homeland: 'if you are stalking a deer in the brush, there is a tiger watching you from the trees.' It is easy to become prey to something larger and more powerful than yourself when you are hunting, if you are unaware of the predator stalking you."

"Okay... yeah. You're right." I nodded, and leaned forward on my elbows. "I just don't want Ororgael to think I'm afraid."

"Fear is normal in the face of horror," Solai said. "Courage is the discipline which overcomes it. You faced me in single combat, knowing you would lose, and you did so with grace and good humor. I believe you have courage, Paragon. Both of you."

I smiled at her. Karalti bobbed her head and made a throaty chortling sound.

"I would like for us to stay in touch, Hector." Solai rose, and breezily crossed over to us, her silks fluttering in the wind. "I very much enjoyed our night together, for one thing... and for another, after witnessing your commitment to this cause and speaking with the Avatar at length about the return of the Triad to Archemi, I think it wise that my people stays up-to-date with the happenings in Ilia. We are as comfortable as kittens here in Meewhome, insulated from the despair of the world. And yet, we were invaded by foreigners and we did not know they were here. The Shield of Ancestors has failed us for the first time in history."

"Not the first time, my Queen, but failures are rare. The Napath have many ancient magics other humans have lost, and they managed to slip through the Shield of Ancestors without raising an alarm," Sanayam added. "That disturbs me,

Paragon. I thought about this in the context of what you said to me about your goals, and concluded that we must prepare."

I looked to Karalti. She smiled back at me.

"You know, I was expecting to have to fight with you both about this," I said. "About taking the threat of Ororgael seriously, that is. I know for sure that others are going to be harder to convince."

"We are not like humans." Sanayam folded his hands into his sleeves. "Humans live in the past. We view the past as the realm of the dead. I am testament to the fact that we treasure our past as a vault of wisdom, but we do not dwell there. Life is ahead of us. As the world changes, so do we."

"Indeed. And should anyone threaten our territory, they will pay in blood." Solai flicked her tail from side to side, turning to pace.

"Rin was talking about developing long-range communications devices out of the tech we dug out of the Chorus Vault." I motioned to the Avatar. "If we figure something out, that might be a way to stay in contact?"

"Yes. Or your lovely dragon queen can bring you here." Solai stopped in front of Karalti. "Sanayam? Will you give them the token?"

Sanayam stepped forward and showed us a pair of earrings.

"These will grant you free access through the Shield of Ancestors," he said. "You will be able to teleport through the barrier."

"You'll need a bigger ring for me," Karalti laughed.

"It will resize with you." The Avatar said. "But you will need a piercing to wear it. The act of drawing blood will attune you to the shield, and permit you limited communication with me."

"I can live with an earring." I shrugged.

"Where will you pierce me, though?" Karalti said. *"It's not like I have ears."*

"Your nostril, sweet one." Solai extended a single claw, and rested the tip against Karalti's nose. "Right here."

"Punk dragon." I chuckled. "Alright. Grab a needle and hit me up."

Sanayam spread his hands, then pulled out a small piercing kit. He sterilized the needles by rapidly heating and cooling them with magic, and soon, I was sporting a small sun-shaped charm in my left ear, while Karalti had a fine aurum ring through her right nostril.

Shield Attunement Ring

A rare artifact which lets you freely pass the Shield of Ancestors, the barrier which surrounds Meewhome, and allows the Avatar of Meewhome to connect with you telepathically across any distance.

"Thanks." I touched the tiny pendant. Thanks to my 2HP per minute regen, the piercing was already healed. "We'll keep you updated."

"Do you have a plan for how to defeat the Drachan?" Solai asked. "The Avatar tells me that they cannot be destroyed."

"The plan is two-fold. To restore the Warsingers, and to unite the peoples of Archemi against the threat we all face," I said. "We're only just getting started."

"Unite the peoples of Archemi? Including us?" She quirked her tail into a hoop.

"If you're willing." I nodded.

Solai and the Avatar looked at one another. It was he who spoke. "If the situation develops as you prophesied, we will consider it. But we do not have any good reason to trust humans as a species. We are prepared to defend our home, but join an offense? There are so many of you, and so few of us."

"There is one boon you could provide for us that makes a large-scale alliance so much more likely," Solai said. "And that is for you to speak with your liege, and address the injustices done to our orphaned people on the mainland. We know our exiles and cousins are persecuted there. If we receive a missive from Dakhdir and Vlachia stating they will commit to the betterment of our kind in their nations, the Great Conclave of Sisters will consider your plan."

[New Quest: All Being Equal Under the Light of the Sun.]

New Quest: All Being Equal Under the Light of the Sun

Priest-Queen Solai is interested in your offer of alliance to combat the Drachan, with one caveat. The relationship between humans and Meewfolk on Artana has been historically fraught with discrimination and violence, with the proud cat people being treated as second-class citizens in Vlachia and Dakhdir. If you are able to connect the rulers of these nations and establish a diplomatic relationship between the Volod, the Sultir, and the Conclave of Priest-Queens, you will help to heal a divide between races and gain allies for your cause.

Difficulty: *Very Hard (Level 35-42)*

Rewards: *7309 EXP, Renown (Meewhome, Vlachia, Dakhdir), Royal Guardian Torque x 1, ??? Artifacts.*

Vlachia would be easy, but Dakhdir? Oof. I accepted the quest anyway. "Thanks. I'll work on it. And if you don't mind, I have a favor to ask you."

The Priest-Queen flicked an ear, and craned her head. "I believe you have earned at least one favor, Paragon. What is it?"

"You're the best Lancer I've ever met," I said. "Please, teach me the first level of Master Spearfighting."

"Hmmm." Solai wound over to me. "It is true that you will find no better spear-fighters in the world than here. But there is a problem. To attain a Master rank in any Advanced

Skill requires four weeks of training. I would be willing to let you study with us, but if I am reading you correctly, you do not have time for it right now."

I clicked my tongue. "Four weeks? Shit. No, I don't. And I might never have time for it."

"The alternative is that I send one of my Battle Maidens with you, and you host her in your territory to serve as your personal instructor," Solai purred. "I would be willing to do this, but only once we have established more positive relations with Vlachia."

"That's fair." I gave her a short nod. "Once this quest is done, though?"

"Then you have my word." With a challenging glare at Karalti, she draped herself around me and rubbed her face against mine. "Though, if you do have a month to spare, I should love to host you here. I can teach you more than the arts of war, Paragon... and perhaps gift you more moon scars."

"Moon scars?" Karalti scowled. *"What are 'moon scars'?"*

"Lover's scars, girl. Like the ones that now stripe the Paragon's back." Solai regarded her smugly.

"To be given moon scars by a Priest-Queen is a great honor for a male," Sanayam said piously.

Karalti's eyes narrowed at her, then at me.

"Haha, well, just look at the time. We should probably be getting back to the Strelitzia." I gently disentangled from Solai. "Thanks for everything. I had a good time, too."

"I assure you that you most certainly did," Solai trilled. "Three or four times, for several hours. I was greatly impressed."

Karalti's eyes were now little more than dark, dangerous slits in her face. If looks could kill, I would already be in the ground and the Avatar would be giving me my last rites.

"Priest-Queen, do not torment the dragon so. They are famously jealous of their mates." Sanayam raised a lazy hand. "It was a pleasure, Paragon. We shall see you again, but until then, please do keep us abreast of the situation."

***

The Avatar teleported us back to the Strelitzia, where we found the repairs in full swing. Gar was in his element, fitting rivets to the ship at improbable speed as he barked orders at the workmen assisting him with the engines and hull. The ship was already looking better. In another half day, it'd be ready to fly.

"Ooh, look at this. Both of you finally got some metal in your faces." Suri set her load down and dusted her hands off, grinning at me as I swaggered over to her. She reached up to finger the earring. "Cute. I like it. A gift from Solai?"

"Not the kind of gift you're insinuating," I teased back, pulling her into a hug. "It lets me get through the Shield of Ancestors."

"Same with mine." Karalti was still disgruntled, kicking stones and hissing softly under her breath. *"Ugh, Hector... I can't believe you."*

"I didn't know what was happening, okay? I was drugged out of my mind." Even now, thinking about the hangover made me groan.

*"Hmmph. "*Karalti's mouth sloped to one side. *"How's our new momma?"*

"Doing fine. Brooding over her eggs and threatening to kill anyone who goes within ten feet of her." Suri let one arm rest around my waist, and reached up to push her mop of flaming red hair back from her face. "She lets me bring her food, and that's it. Anything else—any ONE else—gets the chop."

"Gar's bringing her back to Kalla Sahasi?" Karalti asked. *"I can't wait to see the chicks!"*

"Christ. Don't remind me." Suri rubbed her face. "Yeah, he's bringing her back. And by her, I mean, us. I know you two need to get back with Rin, but I can't leave her alone with Gar."

"No, that's absolutely fine. You stay with Cutthroat." I squeezed her around the middle. "Rin's going to need at least four or five days to sort out these Warsinger schematics. And while she's doing that, Karalti and I need to help Vash with something. He gave me a quest, something private to do with his family."

Suri's expression shifted to one of surprise—and sympathy. "He finally tell you a bit about that, hey? Well, good luck with that. It's gonna be a bumpy ride over those mountains."

"Nothing I can't handle. But... Suri?"

Suri tilted her face. "What?"

"Five days is a long time. I'll miss you, okay?" Karalti hesitated, then quickly rushed forward and looped her arms around both Suri and I, hugging us together. I opened the embrace to her, letting her get closer. And to my pleased relief, so did Suri.

"I'll miss you too, Special-K." Suri pecked her on the forehead. "Take care of my man."

"Of course! He's mine too." Karalti chirped happily, headbutting us gently before stepping back.

I grinned. "Do I get a say in this?"

"Nope," they both said, in unison.

"Hector! Karalti! You're back!" Rin's voice cut through the bustle around us, and I looked over to see her heading for us at a quick walk. "Sorry to interrupt, but I was thinking — if we leave any unnecessary cargo with Gar and Suri, do you think we can transport seven hundred pounds of lambidium to Litvy?"

"Uhhh… okay?" Karalti gave her a puzzled look. *"Is that how much you need to build the plate-decoding thingy?"*

"It's more than I need, but we can use the leftovers for the sonic weapons we'll need to kill that Voidwyrm Empress." Rin jiggled on the spot in agitation. "I can't WAIT to get started on the projector! Lord Soma is going to be so excited about these schematics!"

"We might eventually be able to pull all kinds of records from these Chorus Vaults," I said. "The projector... it doesn't necessarily only have to be used for these, right?"

"The one that displays the schematics? Yes, actually, I think it does." Rin slowed her nervous stimming as she thought about it. "This one is specialized, because the records can only be accessed with the Keystones."

"We're gonna need all the Keystones to unlock all the blueprints?" Suri asked. "Even if we rebuild the machine that can use them?"

"Yes." Rin nodded. "The Keystones are bound to the tablets, not the device that reads them. The device just allows them to communicate, for lack of a better term. The information is coded to the Keystones. However, if... I mean, *when* I re-engineer the console, I can modify the design of the console to make generic projectors that don't have extra security like this one."

"Right. I hope we can find Withering Rose's blueprints somewhere." Suri sighed, breaking off from the group hug. "My Warsinger was used during the last Caul cycle, right? So maybe her schematics are somewhere more recent than the Vault we just cleared."

"That's my hunch." I nodded. "Don't worry, babe. We'll find them when we find them. You ready to go, Rin?"

Rin jumped, then opened her HUD and began to frantically scan something I couldn't see. "Oh! Ummm, just a minute! I've got all the lambidium staged, but I think I've forgotten my tools somewhere..."

CHAPTER 48

The only facility in Myszno large enough to house and rebuild the Warsingers was the Royal College of Engineering in Litvy. Part boarding school, part guildhall, part airfield, it was the biggest airship-building hub in Vlachia.

Count Lorenzo Soma was in the assembly hangar of the College, as usual. While theoretically the ruling lord of Vastil County, Soma left the daily humdrum of leadership to his castellan and spent most of his time engaged in his true passion—airship design and artificing. When found him, he was flat on his back underneath an airship engine hoist, working on a clockwork engine core the size of a VW Buggy.

"Hi, Lorenzo! We're back!" Rin called out to him from the catwalk, her musical voice carrying easily within the cavernous warehouse. "You won't believe what we found!"

"Eh?" Soma pushed out from under his labor, tense at the sound of his given name instead of his title. He had a welding mask on, which he pushed aside to squint at us. "Oh, Rin! Good even, my lady. And you, Dragozin."

"Soma." I crossed my arms and smiled. Grudgingly. While I'd come to tolerate Soma since his disastrous coup attempt at the Prezyemi Line, I still didn't like the guy.

"We have the blueprints for the Warsingers!" Rin cried, hopping up and down behind the railing.

Soma's blue eyes widened. He scrambled up, moustache bristling in sudden excitement. "Blueprints!? Khors' breath. Porta! Get over here and take over this welding! Something more important has come up."

One of the mechanics—Porta, I assumed—hurried over to switch out with him. She flashed her lord an exasperated look as he vaulted the railing of the catwalk and ambled over to us.

"Show me. I must see them." The Count of Vastil loomed over us. He was a massive man, six and a half feet tall and built like a pro-wrestler. "Do they include the arcane architecture? The C.W.P mapping and circuit profiles?"

"I don't know yet. We can't just look at them as is." Rin pulled out one of the glowing kyanine plates she'd removed from the console. It looked like a giant circuit board to me: the crystal was etched with precise, linear lines of metal that wove over and through each other with incredible complexity.

"Ohhoho, look at this... how remarkable," Soma breathed, taking it in his hands and studying it. "Khors' breath, what is this material? I've never seen anything like it in my life. You know with certainty they contain the blueprints?"

"Yes. They can be read with a projector," Rin replied. "Karalti is carrying about seven hundred pounds of lambidium right now. If we melt it in the mana forge, cast it according to my designs, and then inscribe it, we should be able to recreate the console and read the blueprints."

"Then it shall be done at once!" Soma turned the plate over in his hands, marveling at it. "His Majesty sent a letter to the College insisting that any Warsinger projects be prioritized for the time being. Let us go and start. With the pair of us working together, it should only take a few days... provided you are capable of recreating the device that reads these?"

"I am." Rin's face set into determined lines. "We leveled up a whole lot. Now that I'm over Level 30, I should be able to reengineer this, no sweat."

I hung back, feeling every inch the fifth wheel. "What about the sonic weapons? We need those, too."

"Oh! Right!" Rin smacked her fist into her other palm. "I can see what I can do with the parts we recovered from Perilous Symphony. We'll do that first."

"And the Heartstone?"

"Gar and I welded a shielding container for it," Rin replied. "It's in my inventory as well. Don't worry, okay?"

I shot a glance at Soma. "I am worrying. That thing is evil, Rin, and it emits a field of pure suck. I don't want to draw Ororgael's attention here."

"What?" Soma looked to Rin in alarm. "What is he talking about?"

"We managed to find an intact Warsinger Heartstone," Rin admitted. "It has the spirit of a Drachan trapped in it, and it's, umm, kind of active. Our hope is we can fit it into Withering Rose, once we retrieve her... but to do that, we have to defeat the sandworm that's guarding her in the desert."

"Hmm. I see." Soma stroked his moustache. "I don't see it bringing any great danger to the college, as long as we keep it a guarded secret. I shall assist you with the creation of these weapons, too. Oh, and Dragozin: your ships are finished. I was preparing to send them to your castle tomorrow morning, but now you're here...?"

"Hang onto them." I clapped Rin on the shoulder. "If the pair of you can figure out weapons and shielding suitable for fighting the Voidwyrm Empress, we need it installed on those ships. I'll send the rest of my fleet here for retrofitting."

"The cost will be significant," Soma replied cautiously. "And the College is not capable of extending credit. However, my own House may be willing to do so... if required. I know Racsa is still in terrible shape after the war."

I resisted the urge to roll my eyes. "Racsa is fine, thanks. And I don't need credit: you'll be paid in full. However, as your Voivode, I'm going to request a discount for the sake of the realm. Twenty-five percent off materials and assembly, as per the Volod's request that we prioritize activity related to the Warsingers."

Soma turned white, then red, then narrowed his eyes. He really, REALLY wanted to argue... but I'd caught him, and he knew it. "As the Voivode commands. Shall we go and fetch this rare metal stockpile?"

"Sure. Karalti will be glad to get it off her back." I motioned to the hangar door with my head, then headed off in that direction.

My dragon was crouched down on the tarmac, resting some weight onto her arms and winghands to offset her burden. She pivoted her muzzle toward us as we exited, and let out a huge sigh of relief.

"Finally! Come get this stuff off me!" Her tail lashed as we pulled up to her. *"I don't mind carrying you guys around, but I really don't like this whole 'use Karalti as a pack mule' thing."*

"I know, and I'm sorry we had to ask you. Thanks for helping out, Tidbit." I went into her Inventory and loaded it into mine, one piece at a time. Both the scrap and the sonic organs from Perilous Symphony went on the cart Soma had brought with him. Rinse and repeat ten times, until Karalti was back to a quarter of her maximum weight and over half a ton of precious metal was stacked beside her.

"Where did you get all of this? And the blueprints?" Soma rubbed his hand over the metal sphere Gar had removed from Perilous Symphony.

"Meewhome!" Rin replied cheerfully. "We went there to find this stuff."

Soma sneered. "Ahh. Yet another thing the cats 'liberated' from the mainland, is it?"

"They made all of these artifacts," I replied sourly. "The console, the first nine Warsingers, and the Chorus Vaults where the Warsingers were stored."

Soma let out a derisive laugh. "Pull the other leg, Dragozin. They are a dull, indolent species who are barely capable of laboring in prisons, let alone producing masterworks like these. No, this is the work of humankind, no doubt about it."

"Hector's right, though," Rin insisted. "The Meewfolk made all of this. The blueprints are written in an ancient form of their language."

Soma didn't seem to know what to make of that. He hemmed and hawed for a moment, then cleared his throat. "Are you sure?"

"Yes. We're sure." I resisted the urge to reach up and grab his ear, pull his head down, and headbutt him in the teeth. Instead, I turned to adjust Karalti's saddle cinch, rolling my eyes where he couldn't see. "Anyway, we need those sonic weapons more than we need the blueprints right now, so please work on those first and keep us posted. Karalti and I are going to run a quest for Vash, but you should be able to send PMs."

"Will do! I'll update you as soon as I can." Rin, obviously grateful to be off the subject of Meewfolk, nodded enthusiastically. "Come on, Soma! Let's get started!"

"Yes, yes. You know, perhaps I should work on this console while you manage this weapon project?" Soma asked her, already ignoring my orders in favor of his true passion: figuring out the best outcome for himself.

"*Ugh.*" Karalti groaned to me telepathically as I climbed back up to the base of her neck. "*At least he isn't trying to flirt with me this time.*"

"*Right? He's like the worst combination of a Silicon Valley tech bro and some white guy's old racist uncle,*" I replied. "*Wonder what he's going to say when Ignas announces our impending alliance with Meewhome.*"

"*I don't care what he has to say about it, actually.*"Karalti launched herself from the ground, her powerful wings driving up clouds of dust and loose gravel. "*Whatever his opinions are, they're probably rubbish.*"

I watched the lights of the college recede, and turned my face toward the southern horizon as Karalti banked into a thermal, using it to rest in preparation for teleporting. "*You want to fly home the long way for once? Just you and me, the sky... you know.*"

"*Sure. Why not? It's been a while since I got to stretch my wings properly.*"Karalti broke out of the thermal, levelling out into a swift glide.

"*You're not really mad at me about Solai, are you?*" I asked.

"*No, not really. You WERE pretty drugged. I tried speaking to you a few times, but all I got was this endless stream of durrrrrrr.*"Karalti flicked a wingtip as we sailed out over the crystalline blue lake that marked the border of Litvy, breaking out over the vivid green wilderness that lay beyond the city. "*Also, I talked with Suri about some stuff while you were... uhh... busy.*"

"*Stuff?*"

"*It's embarrassing.*"

I laughed aloud. "*Tidbit, how many times have you tuned into me when I'm in the middle of something embarrassing and-or intimate?*"

581

My dragon huffed. *"Well, I told Suri what happened when you two were together in Bas, and that I thought she was really beautiful, and... yeah. She was nice about it, but..."*

"But?"

"She thanked me, but said she thinks of me more like a sister than anything else. She's really comfortable sharing you with me, but she doesn't want the three of us to... you know. She asked me not to tune in again, too. You know, when you are her are together."

"Oh." I drew a deep breath, not sure if I was disappointed—or relieved. *"So... what did you say?"*

"I told her I understood," Karalti said. *"I'm not sure I like girls in that way, either. When I thought about it, I was excited because you were excited. I hope that if I ever take a mate, you'll like him in the same way."*

"Maybe." I paused for a moment. *"I don't know if I'll be able to handle it, to be honest. If some husky boy dragon ever takes a liking to you, I don't know what I'll do."*

"Me either, to be honest." Karalti paused awkwardly. *"Really, I want you to catch me. The first time, and every time after that. But what Lahati said is weighing on me a bit. I might be the only Queen dragon left on Artana. And if I am, I have a duty to my people to find a mate and establish my linage. I WANT to do that. I just... don't want to do it with anyone else but you."*

I closed my eyes and drew a deep breath. *"Weird question: what about polymorph?"*

582

"Huh?"

"Instead of you turning into a human, could you like... turn me into a dragon?"

Karalti thought about it for a few minutes. I could almost hear the gears in her head turning. *"No. You know how when I polymorph, I only kinda look like a human?"*

"Yeah?"

"Well, I think I could kind of turn you into a dragon. But you won't BE a dragon. You get what I mean?"

"I think so." I frowned, troubled. *"I guess we'll just have to roll with what we've got for now."*

"Yeah. And that's not too bad, is it?" Karalti mused to herself as she headed towards the distant ruins of the Prezyemi Line. *"Hey, there's something I want to do after we're finished helping Vash."*

"What's that?"

"I want to take you to my favorite hot spring and camp out next to it for a night or two. There's a place nearby I go to hunt, too. We can just... be together for a while. You and me, and no one else."

I closed my eyes against the wind. *"I couldn't think of any better way to handle your time of the month, Tidbit. Let's do it."*

***

We fell into a comfortable silence for the rest of the trip. The flight gave me time to recharge, and to think about our next goal: the reclamation of Withering Rose. With a weapon like her on our side—fully repaired, fueled and armed—even Ororgael would give pause before striking at Vlachia. In my dreams Rin and Soma worked some miracle and we were able to fix Nocturne Lament *and* arm Vlachia's warships with weapons that could knock our enemies out of the air. Ororgael would have to slow his roll and replan his next moves, because he sure as hell wasn't going to win through attrition.

I was feeling pretty good by the time Kalla Sahasi was in sight, and even better when I zoomed in and saw how much work had been done on it in the six days we'd been away. The broken tower was still missing a roof, but most of the walls were back up. The Lord's Tower was completely repaired, as was the curtain wall and the gatehouse. When we landed, it was on fresh slate, free of moss and broken stones. The scaffolding had moved: volunteers were working on the cornicing and other decorative features.

"*Wow!*" Karalti exclaimed, craning her neck as she turned to stare. "*The castle looks amazing!*"

I couldn't wipe the grin off my face as I dismounted, shaking my head in wonder. "*I... yeah. Wow is the only word for it.*"

I bought up my castle map. Most of the major facilities were back up and running, save for the War Room, Library, and Court Mage's Oratory, all of which were features of the tower that was still being fixed. Our bakery, kitchens, granaries, and barracks were all online. Kalla Sahasi probably hadn't looked this good in a hundred years.

There was a cheerful whistle from behind us. I turned slightly to see Istvan bounce out of one of the gatehouse doors. He looked relaxed and happy, his hair worn loose down his back. He'd switched his usual coat and brigandine for a nicer shirt. I'd rarely ever seen him without his armor.

"Heya, man. How's things?" I clapped my hand into his when he came to a stop. "The place is looking great."

"It's like a dream come true," Istvan replied. "This place was my home for years, and with the exception of a few structural repairs, I've never seen the old battleaxe look better. Was your mission a success?"

"Sure seems like it," I replied. "Let's go find someone to sit down and have a drink and a bite to eat. Karalti? Want to join us?"

"I'm going to polymorph and go sleep in our room." She lifted one of her feet as she stretched her wing out, yawning wide. *"It's been a long week. Come snuggle with me when you're done?"*

"Happily." I rubbed her ankle, then turned back to Istvan. "All yours."

"The parlor in the gatehouse has been restored," Istvan said, beckoning me to follow him. "As have the steward's quarters and the butlery, thank the gods. Rudolph and I are both glad to have our own rooms."

"For sure." I fell into step with him as he headed for the entry to the gatehouse. "Is Vash back yet?"

"I received a letter from him yesterday. They're almost ready with the next shipment," Istvan said, holding the door for me and following me up the stairs behind it. "They focused on removing the gold and coinage first. According to him, they will be excavating the rest of the goods there for at least a full month."

My eyebrows shot up. A month was a long period of time to complete a task in Archemi.

"It has to do with the delicacy and care required to retrieve the grave goods." Istvan seemed to read my mind as he opened the door ahead of me. "Vash, being who and what he is, is guiding the excavation team in the proper handling of the dead. There are Tuun warriors buried down there with them, did you know that?"

"Yeah. There's some kind of relationship between the Tuun and the Solonkratsu and tulaq that was lost in time," I said. "All three were here in Vlachia several thousand years earlier than most historians believe."

Istvan's mouth quirked in a small smile as we climbed the stairs. "I didn't realize you were a student of history."

"'Student' implies commitment. I'm more like a slime-mold of history, passively absorbing information as I crawl around in swamps and caves." I marveled at the gothic corridor we entered at the top of the stairs. The craftsmen had used contrasting dark and light stone for the walls and doorways, and the floor had been finished in white mosaic, inlaid with a repeating design of dragons in flight. "I can't believe how much work the people here have done. This is incredible."

"This is how they wished to show you their gratitude," Istvan said. "Believe it or not, you have already done more for Karhad and Myszno than Lord Bolza did in twenty years."

I let out a brief laugh. "What? Really?"

"Yes. Lord Bolza was a just and fair man, but he was not a reformist," Istvan replied. "He was heavily invested in his heritage as one of Myszno's founding families, and thus, he favored policy which reinforced the status-quo. Poor people remained poor, rich people remained rich, and neither had much affinity for the other. You have indicated by word and deed that you are approachable in the way that my lord never was. Not only that, but you drove the Demon from the land and have prioritized public spending."

"So, they celebrate the fact I'm approachable by building me a big fancy castle?" I grinned at him.

Istvan smiled wryly. "Yes. I have heard the same praise from many mouths. The citizens of Racsa are pleased to furnish their Voivode with a fine home. A fine castle burnishes the beauty of the city it oversees, and is something for them to be proud of. Though, now that you have guest accommodations, I think it would be wise to start courting the other nobles of the land."

A home? It was strange to think of this place as a home. I passed my hand over one of the walls as Istvan stopped and opened a room ahead of me. "Any particular reason?"

"Yes. Following the Battle of Solonovka, there is a rumor circulating that you are a military prodigy who may wish to reform *all* aspects of the province, and some of your Satraps are starting to become nervous. The fact we have over five thousand veteran soldiers garrisoned on our doorstep has not dispelled these rumors."

"Well, they can stew for a while longer. I'll make some time to do a meet and greet, but I'm not going to be upset if they're nervous." I came to a stop as Istvan did. "What would you recommend?"

"My suggestion is that you host a victory ball once the castle is complete, and use it as an opportunity to demonstrate generosity and strength." He lay a hand on the door handle. "You will have the facilities to do so. This room is an excellent example of what Myszno's crafters are capable of."

He opened the door, and a wave of warm air wafted over us. I eased in, eyes widening as I took in the view.

The artisans had done the parlor up in warm, rich colors: golds and honey-yellows, deep browns and charcoal, all of which contrasted well with the white and gold lights overhead. The bay windows looked down into the courtyard. There was a sofa, chairs, a small reading table, two bookshelves, and a small, fully stocked bar. It was dark and comfortable, rich with the scents of woodsmoke, leather, oranges and whiskey. And it was all mine.

"Lord Bolza insisted his décor always be in the colors of his livery, but you seem to prefer a less ostentatious look," Istvan said, folding his hands behind his back. "This seemed more appropriate."

"It's beautiful." I gingerly sat down on the leather sofa. It was the color of dark chocolate, springy and comfortable. "Where did all this stuff come from?"

"Here and there. Don't worry, it's all paid for." Istvan went to the bar and took down two tumblers. "Brandy?"

"Sure." I tried to relax, but it was difficult to believe—really believe—that this stuff belonged to me. It looked like an upscale bar, or a billionaire's private study. I'd grown up expecting I'd never own a normal home, let alone... this.

Istvan brought my brandy over and set it down, then took the seat across from me with his own glass of water. "How does it feel?"

"Surreal," I said, picking up the dark amber liquor and swirling it once. "I worry I'll get too used to it."

"You're no Lorenzo Soma." Istvan flashed me a wry smile. "Care to bring me up to speed on your efforts? And the campaign against Ilia?"

"The campaign against Ilia is pretty straightforward, for the moment. Ignas is flying the entire 2nd Fleet in, and Jeun and Dakhdir are joining him to drive Ororgael and Lucien Hart back," I replied, sniffing the brandy curiously. "Suri, Rin, Karalti and I went to Meewhome."

Istvan's lips quirked. "Meewhome?"

"Yeah. We recovered blueprints for four of the Warsingers, and tech that might lead to some serious advances in weaponry and communications. We made a good diplomatic start with the de-facto rulers of the Meewfolk. If Ignas is willing to communicate with them, and I figure he will be, they're open to backing us in the event the Drachan are released and have to be put down."

Istvan's eyebrows arched. "That is a considerable achievement for one week."

"Yeah, I guess. It's weird. I feel like I haven't done enough." I had a sip and rolled it over my tongue. The brandy was sweet, creamy and caramelly, with just a hint of spice.

"Restlessness is not a bad thing for a leader to feel, in moderation. Do not worry, my lord: you are far from indolent."

"Man... try telling that to my dad." I let out a small, bitter laugh. "How are things here? I know you've got a list of things we need to do."

"A short list," he replied. "There are more cases of Thornlung in Riverside—twenty or so people are ill, but the plague does not seem to have spread beyond the district walls. We have three of the five healers you requested and supplies ready to go, but we still need to source two more if we are to effectively combat the disease."

"That's what I'll be doing while Rin does her thing in Litvy." I frowned. "What else?"

"The artist who is to design your heraldry and banners has arrived, quartered in a guest room just down the hall from us," he continued. "Also, those Starborn you met with have finished clearing the university of monsters and brigands. They requested houses in Karhad as their reward in lieu of payment. I granted them apartments and encouraged them to take up quests around the city to make their living."

"Awesome." I had another sip of brandy and eased back. "You already told me where Vash is at. Is that all?"

"For now," Istvan said. "Countess Hussar is apparently almost finished settling matters in Bas, and sent a letter saying that she will join us soon to serve as Suri's squire. Until then, we have at least a brief interlude between crises."

"Don't jinx us." I rapped the arm of the sofa and shook my head. "How about you? Doing alright?"

He looked past me to the window. "Healing from the war is a slow process, with many stops and starts. Drilling the recruits and watching them shape up into soldiers helps. Seeing the castle rebuilt helps even more. Though... I would like to make a request of you, when we have some coin to spare."

"Whatever you need, man." I spread a hand and gestured widely. "Go ahead."

"There was a large cottage with its own yard behind the kitchens," Istvan said, crossing his legs and slouching back. "The place where I lived with my wife, my daughter, and my daughter's puppy. It was razed to its foundations when they breached the castle."

"You want it rebuilt?"

Istvan shook his head, gazing toward the windows. "No. I would like to create a memorial of sorts. A garden, if we can afford it. Yava had a flower bed that she cared for every day... it... it would mean a great deal to me."

I leaned forward on the sofa. "Tell me what you need, and we'll go ahead with it. I'm two-hundred-percent on board."

Istvan let out a small sigh of relief. "Thank you, Your Grace."

[New Side-Quest: Yava's Garden.]

"We all need to time to heal from the shit that's happened to us," I said, adding the Quest to my queue. "Rule me up a plan, or give me a lead to the architect you need to make a plan, and I'll follow it up once we've got Withering Rose sorted out."

"I will." Istvan drained his glass, then took to the bar and rinsed it before setting it to dry. "Do you wish to take the night off? Or shall I send the artist in to see you?"

"Go ahead. Might as well get that out of the way before I head off to bed." I sprawled back on the sofa—my sofa—with a sigh. "Now that the gatehouse is fixed, I can get from here to the Lord's Tower, right?"

"Yes. There is a door which unlocks with your Lord's Key," Istvan said. "You will enter onto the kitchen level. Your rooms are two flights up from there."

"Thanks, man." I thoughtfully drained the rest of my glass. "Let's get this artist in here, and sketch the hell out of some heraldry."

CHAPTER 49

By mid-morning, me and the visiting artist had decided on a standard for House Dragozin: a black spear on a sky-blue field, with the nine Keystones represented in their associated colors: White for Veles, Indigo for Matir, Red for Khors, and so on. It wasn't a complicated flag, but it did everything I needed it to do. It was visible at a distance, it embodied the key identifiers that most represented the House, and—most importantly—wasn't any shade of green.

On the way to my rooms, I found myself gawking at all the small, but obvious changes that had taken place between leaving for Taltos and returning from Meewhome. Carpets cleaned, water leaks fixed, missing tiles replaced. When I entered my apartment and went to the bathroom, I found it had been cleared of sand. There was a nicely folded towel on the thick rim of the tub, along with new soap, razor, and small clay jars.

"Huh." I scratched my head. Rudolph knew I needed to sleep in earth to get the Well-Rested buff, so he normally didn't touch the Ducal Litterbox. It seemed unlikely a maid had come through. "Did it despawn?"

Curious, I made my way to the darkened bedroom. The four-poster bed was gone. In its place was a specially constructed, very fancy sandpit. Karalti was stretched out on top of it, nude, her hair fanned out across the loose earth. She had one hand up by her mouth, the other resting just underneath one small breast.

My pulse jumped in my neck and under my tongue as I set my things down and walked over to sit. Warmth radiated up from the sand. I dug my hand into it, and found that it was warm all the way down. There was some kind of device built into the bedframe that heated it.

"Mmm…" Karalti's eyes slowly opened, and she blinked up at me in a daze.

"Sorry." My voice was tight enough I had to clear my throat. "Didn't mean to wake you."

Karalti smiled at me, her eyes dark and hazy, and opened her arms. Unable to take my eyes off her, I unequipped my clothing and climbed onto the bed. She embraced me, murmuring sleepily, and I pulled her in against my chest… and not for the first time, or the last, found myself feeling like the luckiest man on Earth.

We slept that way, tangled together in the warm sand, until a HUD notification chirped and I started up out of a dead sleep. Blearily, I compulsively swiped it across, and Navigail's cheery robovoice began to speak.

[Your Steward has deposited 500,034 Gold Olbia in the Treasury!]
[Myszno has 1,363,843 olbia available. Use your Kingdom Management System to manage projects, pay your Royal Dues, and recruit specialists!]

Well, damn. Just like that, I was a millionaire. I rolled over onto my back, one arm over my face, and tried to wake up. If the money was back from Krivan Pass, that meant only one thing. "Hey, Tidbit. Wake up. Vash is back."

"Mmmngh?" Karalti burrowed in against my chest, wrapping her arm a little tighter, and sighed. I waited to see if she was actually going to open her eyes, and when she didn't, I sucked my lips in like a fish and began kissing her: her head, her shoulders, then her cheek.

"Mmm… nnn…" Karalti began to squirm, then to giggle. *"Nuuu! Stop fishing me!"*

"The Fish Imperium knows no surrender, only victory!" I lunged in and got hold of her ear. *"Num-num-num-num."*

"Eeek!" Laughing helplessly, she pushed at my chest as the assault intensified. I let her go just enough she could worm away. She rolled over her shoulder and tried to get up in a crouch, but was too close to the edge of the bed to save it. With a squeak of dismay, she overbalanced and tumbled to the floor. Now I was the one laughing as she scrambled up to her feet and danced around, dusting sand off herself and scowling.

"Yeah, laugh it up." Karalti narrowed her eyes and stuck her lips out at me. *"Just you wait. I'll get you."*

"Sorry, but the Fish Imperium does not negotiate with terrorists." I sat up and looked over the edge of her side of the bed. "Poor Rudolph has to sweep all this up, you know."

"Hmmph." Karalti shook her hair out, raining sand everywhere, and turned her back to me. I couldn't help but notice the way her vestigial scales tapered down her back to the base of her spine, partly framing her butt. This incredible work of art was suddenly and tragically concealed as she began equipping her armor and gauntlets—exactly what I needed to do, if we were going to start the day.

We found Istvan and Vash in the dining room offside the great hall, where one of the kitchen staff was dishing up dinner. Now that it had been repaired, it actually looked like somewhere I wanted to be. The paneling was fixed, the table polished, the chairs repaired and replaced. As soon as I walked in, my mouth started watering from the mingled smells of lamb, garlic, and butter. The meal for tonight was a kind of dumpling called *Khinkali.* They were twisted knobs of dough bigger than a golf ball, filled with meat and spices and rich broth that burst in your mouth when you bit into them. There was also a platter of *Khachapuri*—a large, flat, flaky bread boat full of cheese with an egg cracked on top—plates of assorted picked vegetables, and a dish of dense green sauce I'd never seen before. It looked a lot like spinach and artichoke dip. When I scurried over to it, my HUD highlighted it as [Pikhali: An Eastern Vlachian sauce made from spinach, walnuts and garlic. Commonly eaten with Khachapuri.]

"Mmm. These smell amazing!" Karalti heaped her plate with dumplings, skipping the vegetarian stuff, and nearly ran to the table with her haul. I took a more balanced array of pretty much everything on offer: bright red marinated peppers, eggplant, sharp white sheep's cheese, and the ever-present *csalamádé,* mixed pickles with cabbage, cucumbers, and other vegetables. With the *pikhali* and *khachapuri,* I had all of the

essential Vlachian daily food groups covered: fat, salt, meat, vinegar and cheese.

"Welcome back to the land of the living, you glorious cocksucker." Vash had his feet up on the table and his pipe in his hand. His plate was already empty. Istvan was still eating, cutting his dumplings up with a knife and fork. "I heard from Istvan—seen here defiling his *khinkali* by spilling the soup out of them all over his plate for the sake of 'decency'—that you, Suri, Karalti and Rin managed to somehow secure an alliance with the royalty of Meewhome. Well done."

"Thanks. And yeah, Istvan? Eating soup dumplings with a knife and fork is now illegal in Myszno." I picked up one of them and took a bite out of it, sucking the broth out the bottom. Karalti didn't even bother with that formality: she just shoved the whole thing in her mouth and chewed, her eyes turning dark and glassy with pleasure.

Istvan let out an exasperated sigh. "Well, my lord, I'm sorry you hate civilization."

"I don't hate civilization. I just think knives and forks are for Ilian wussies." I popped the rest of the dumpling in my mouth and grinned at him. "Besides, you've been dating Vash for a couple months now. I'd have thought you'd be able to fit more meat into your mouth."

"HAH!" Vash spluttered with laughter, which turned to coughing as he accidentally inhaled too hard on his pipe. Istvan turned the same color as the roasted pepper I was now smugly spreading over my cheese-egg-bread canoe.

"This is a game for you two, isn't it?" He looked between us, scowling pointedly at Vash as the monk hacked and coughed.

"Sorry," Vash croaked, waving his hand in front of his face. "Dying."

"The Dakhari call that 'karma'." Istvan set his knife down, and aggressively forked his next dumpling without cutting it. "Given what you see before you, you might as well ask that same question of Vash, Your Grace. As you can see, he can barely choke anything down."

Vash wheezed harder.

"Ahh. True love." I shook my head, pulled the bread apart, and stuffed a big chunk of it in my mouth. "Speaking of true love with or without reproduction, guess what? Cutthroat laid a clutch of eggs."

Istvan fumbled his fork with a clatter, and his eyes widened in sudden horror. "*No.*"

"You're shitting me." Vash stared at us in naked disbelief.

"*Yeah!*" Karalti wiggled excitedly in her seat. "*Rin said we should throw a baby shower!*"

"We figure Payu knocked her up when we weren't looking. That's why Suri didn't return with us. She's travelling back the long way, taking an airship from Meewhome with Cutthroat. Her darling mommy-to-be decided to lay her clutch in the Captain's Cabin."

"In the Captain's... no. I don't need to know." Istvan held up his hands in surrender. "Talking about it will only curse us more."

"A dozen Cutthroats running around the castle. Burna grant us all peace in our next lives." Vash made a holy sign over his chest with one hand, then pressed his palms together. "You know, hookwing eggs do taste good. And they're *khunehar.* Totally acceptable within religious law."

Karalti hissed at him. *"You leave Cutthroat's babies alone! They'll be little and cute and they'll roll around all over the place, and I'll feed them tidbits from my kills, and... and... it'll be great!"*

"Then make cute little omelets out of them," he replied. "Put faces on the omelets if you want. *Na-tsho schrodna,* I don't know what we're going to do if the little goblins turn out like their mother."

"We convince Suri to sell them to Taethawn, and he reaps the wild oats his bull has sown," Istvan said sourly.

"Hah. We shall see." Vash relit his pipe, ruefully shaking his head.

"Were you able to bring anything else back from the dragon burial grounds?" I asked him, still working on my food. "Istvan said that we'd be taking the next round of recoveries slowly."

"Yes, there is still an incredible number of valuable goods down in that holy place," Vash said. "The goods in that place are probably worth another million olbia, but unlike the gold, they are inextricably bound with the bodies of the dead.

Removing them requires a process of delicate retrieval, then reinternment. We also cannot gauge the uses or powers imbued in many of the artifacts there. Sadly for us, many of our archeologists and historical antiques experts died in the war. Once the university is open and staffed, they will be able to process these goods... and who knows what we'll find. I saw armor, weapons, and jewelry as grand as anything in the Volod's vault. It might take a year to properly assess the value of the goods. Those which embody the art of Karalti's people are likely priceless, and could not be traded by anyone of good character."

"Anything of historical significance, we preserve," I said. "Karalti and any other dragons who eventually join us get as much say in that as they want. As for the university..."

I held up a finger, went into the KMS, and lined up the restoration: 168,000 olbia, committed without hesitation or regret.

[You are pledging to construct the University of Karhad. Are you sure you wish to proceed?]

"*Yes.*" I closed the confirmation and smiled. "There, done. The university is next on the building queue. Give it a month, and it'll be back in good shape. Until then, we can store those valuables in the castle."

"We should have room." Istvan nodded, and—with a sly glance at me—began to use his knife and fork on his khachapuri.

Vash grunted. "A wise decision. The Vault of Heroes is vulnerable to thieves and plunderers. We are managing to keep it quiet thus far, but it's a matter of time until someone realizes there is an ossuary full of dead dragons and their treasure barely a hundred miles north of here. We will have to defend the hoard from all comers if word gets out."

"Tell me about it." I regarded him for a moment, chewing thoughtfully before speaking. "Do you feel ready to go south tonight? Or do you want to do it in the morning? Karalti and I leveled up in Meewhome, so we're ready when you are."

"Already? Well." The Baru set his feet down, thumping his heavy steel-toed boots to the floorboards. "I've been ready to go back to Tastalgan for thirty years, Herald. Finish up and meet me in the courtyard. I must commune with my god, and then I'll be ready to fly."

CHAPTER 50

The terrain in the far south of Myszno was nothing short of forbidding. The entire province was ringed by mountains, but none as awe-inspiring and severe as the Kuday Range, the mini-Himalaya that separated Vlachia from the northern border of Napath. This range was why Ashur had been able to take Vlachia by surprise: It hadn't occurred to anyone that an army—even an army of undead—could make the trek from the other side of those mountains and survive.

"I am struggling to make sense of why there are Tuun entombed with the dragons in Krivan Pass," Vash said, helping me into a thick 〖Tuun Sherpa Coat〗. It was made of camel hide with the wool turned inward, conveying an Insulation Buff that would keep us warm in the severe weather of the Kudays. "The Tuun of Myszno have only been here for a few generations. We came here as miners and farmers."

"Why here, though?" I frowned, looking thoughtfully to the sky. The Dark Star was glinting over the moon to the south. Veles' Dragon Gate: Archemi's first and only satellite.

"My guess is that we ascertained the location of Burna's resting place, and desired to live in a holy land. The Tuun of Myszno universally hold Burna in high regard, placing him over Tangur and the other two Heavenly Kings."

Tangur was the Tuun god of the sky, and the most important deity in my fictional homeland. He didn't have a personification—he was literally the sky, the big blue dome over our heads, and 'tangur' was also the Tuun word for 'daylight'. Faceless, omnipresent and infinitely wise, he was the father and ruler of the Three Heavenly Kings: Burna, Dashin, and Vajra. "Putting Burna over Tangur? That's about as close to heresy as you get in Tungaant, isn't it?"

"Indeed. If for no other reason that the abbots of Tempat Sonn don't like it when their subjects think for themselves." Vash clapped the front of my coat. "There we go. That should do. You and I are both are hardened against the weather, but it's cold enough to freeze the tits off a demon at those altitudes this time of the year."

"We'll be fine. I'll keep you warm if I have to. The cold doesn't bother me, as long as I can eat." Karalti preened under her wing as we climbed a rope up to her back, and then pulled it up behind us. We had taken all the trekking gear we had in case we needed to make a camp somewhere. *"Let me know when you're ready."*

I made sure my scarf was folded and tucked in, pulled my helmet on, and waited until Vash had situated himself. Like me, he didn't bother with flight harness and straps. When he signaled the go-ahead, I patted Karalti on the shoulder and assumed the position.

"Hang on tight! I bet it's gonna be rough up there." Karalti tossed her head, shook her wings, and launched herself into the sky.

603

The first stage of our journey was to warp to the entry to Matir's Dragon gate. We appeared over a half-frozen waterfall that plunged down into a pitiless glacial crevasse. Across the giant sinkhole were two enormous obelisks that stretched from the subterranean depths to a height greater than the nearest mountains: The Thunderstones. The monuments hummed with power, drawing blasts of lightning from the storm that swirled overhead. The Mark of Matir began to tingle and pulse under the skin of my hand.

"Woahhhh!" Karalti corrected herself as a howling slap of snowy wind sent her drifting to one side. There was so much turbulence that she didn't even have to beat her wings to stay airborne—just hover.

"Incredible, aren't they!" Vash shouted. Even though he was shoulder to shoulder with me on the saddle, I could barely hear him over the tempest.

"Sure are!" I called back.

"I'm going to try and teleport up above this storm!" Karalti was struggling to keep her wings from bending over as gusts of wind slashed at us, driving her toward the rocks. *"Annnnd... brace!"*

The world inverted to a black point, where we hung bodiless for a few seconds before erupting into a clear starry sky. Karalti pumped her wings, her chest swelling as she began to compensate for the thin air. We were just shy of 18,000 feet—only three thousand feet under her maximum flight ceiling.

"Where to from here?" I asked Vash.

"Let me see…" Vash pulled out a compass, using it to orient himself. When he was facing the right direction, he used his thumb and forefinger to square it with the stars and moon: a difficult job, as Karalti bounced on the massive turbulence spiraling up from the stormclouds below. "And… there. I'm almost certain that's the right way."

A golden pathing indicator appeared in my mini map. Karalti veered in that direction, alternating beating her wings and gliding. It was truly freezing up here: fine branching trees of frost formed on the front of my helmet, and turned to condensation on Karalti's burning hot scales.

"You okay?" I asked, resting one hand on the back of her neck.

"I'm fine as long as I keep moving." She sounded like she was talking through gritted teeth—uncomfortable, but determined as she labored toward our destination.

I glanced at her stamina. She was already a quarter down. *"I don't like it, but I think you need to burn another Teleport spell to get us forward. As soon as we spot a good landmark, warp to it. We're dealing with this rough weather better than we did four levels ago, but it's sucking your stamina like crazy."*

"Tell me about it." She darted through a particularly vicious lash of air, pulling her wings in and teetering to the side. *"Help me spot a landmark and stare at it, like how we did in Lahati's Tomb: try and keep it in your mind's eye as I enact the spell. The ice is in my eyes, and I can hardly see."*

Frost was rapidly creeping in around the edges of my visor, but I could still see well enough to cue my darkvision and zoom in on the horizon. There, the clouds broke against the sides of the mountains, and the land gave way to narrow, scalloped plains. I used Karalti's horns like an iron sight, focusing on our intended position. *"Okay, and... go!"*

She enacted the spell, and I kept the image of our destination in my mind as clearly as I could. The teleport seemed to stretch on and on... and just when I started to worry, we burst out into clear, arid air. The plateau rolled out ahead of us: starkly arid and eerily beautiful, like the surface of Mars. The moon lit seemingly endless field of swelling, snow-covered hills. It was -42 degrees out here, double the negative temperature I could withstand thanks to Iron Body, and just under what Karalti could reasonably tolerate.

Vash reached out to grip my arm. His expression was stricken.

"By Burna's big black arse," he said, hoarsely. "I'm home."

I gazed over the plains as Karalti descended, and felt my heart swell. As the dragon's shadow cut over the ground, it stirred a herd of wooly rhinos into a restless, thundering charge. A huge flock of white vultures ringed a glacier-blue lake, roosting beside water that reflected the moon like quicksilver. A narrow icy river trickled down the length of a fractalline ravine far below, zig-zagging its way toward the distant ocean. It was the kind of place you found in Iceland, or parts of Tibet. For some strange reason, the sight of it filled me with a deep sense of homesickness: a longing for a place I'd never been.

"Stay sharp, Dragozin." Vash urged, as he pulled his goggles off and unwrapped the scarf he'd bound around his face. He spoke Tuun now, his voice gruff and unusually serious. "We're nearly there. I know not what we'll find behind those hills."

"Where is everyone?" I asked him.

"After thirty years, with the pass to the Churvi Territories and Bas beyond that blocked by landfill? Who knows? There were never that many people up here to begin with," he said.

"The other Tuun didn't help you and Saaba when you were kids?" I saw what I thought was a Tuun camp, with darkened yurts and fences, but when I blinked, there was nothing but rocks and weird, creeping shadows.

"No. They drove us away." Vash was expressionless now, gripping the saddle with both fists. "And I hold no grudge against them for it. They were right to do so. The death of my family was tragedy enough: if the plague had spread from clan to clan, everyone would have been lost."

"I don't see anyone," I remarked. "No fires, no houses... and we can literally spot for miles out here."

"I know," Vash said quietly. "And I have a bad feeling about it, too."

There were no signs of life—human or animal—as we closed in on the quest marker. We didn't see anything else until we were over the hills—and found ourselves in a pocket of warmer air that flushed over us like an exhaled breath. Sprawled below us was a huge Tuun village. There were least sixty yurts down there. They were arranged in concentric circles that radiated out from one central camp. Dozens of fires lit the night sky. There were sheds and corrals, and herds of sleeping camels, goats, and aurochs standing in their pastures. The air shimmered like a mirage where the heat rising from the bustling village met the chilly ceiling of sky above.

"Well, that explains things." My gut relaxed as Karalti dipped a wing, giving the settlement a wide berth. "The clans came together for a moot."

"Yeah! That's a good thing, right?" Karalti chirped. *"If people moved here, they must have put your family to rest. They wouldn't live in a place that's haunted."*

"That is no trade moot. That is a town… but why is in the same place that my family made their winter camp?" Vash stared at the tents and corrals in disbelief. "Perhaps some monks and priests found their way here after all. People wouldn't live here if the dead weren't put to rest."

"I guess we'll find out." I zoomed my vision in one of the cooking fires. There was a group of six people around it, clapping and singing along with a man playing an erhu, a long-stemmed, two-stringed fiddle with a small box belly. "Looks like there's people still awake. We can talk to them, see if we can find out who's in charge?"

Vash nodded. He clenched and unclenched his jaws, the muscles popping in sharp relief as Karalti coasted down in a gentle glide, and landed behind a hill not too far away. We wasted no time in vaulting down.

"It's too warm," Vash muttered, already shucking his coat down to his waist, where he wore it like a thick woolen kirtle. "It's like summer. There's no snow around this camp. The herd should be living off snow and having to scratch for roots by now, but look."

He pointed toward the short, tough steppe grass that grew out of the hard ground all around us.

"Can mages control the weather, out of curiosity?" I shucked my own coat off, and folded it into my Inventory. We were well within my temperature limits here. On the ground, it was only -10 C: about 14 F.

"There are no mages here, I guarantee it. Our people have no love of sorcerers." Vash sniffed the air, looked up and down, then kicked a rock away from him. "If they are herders like the ones I knew, they will be glad to see a Baru and his apprentice. We'll have teeth to pull, medicines to administer, camels to soothe. How does that sound, Karalti?"

"I dunno if I'll be any good at soothing camels right now," Karalti replied, trotting along beside me. *"I'm about two or three days off my next heat, and all I can think about right now is food. It's hard to soothe something when it knows you want to eat it."*

We followed a short, overgrown rocky trail to the first of the signal fires. There were no guards other than shaggy Tuun Mastiffs who ran toward us, barking with their hackles raised. Children played by the fire, squealing with laughter as they acted out scenes with straw dolls shaped like hookwings and wooly rhinos and sabretooths. One man was dozing in front of the flames, his coat hanging off one shoulder, his arm resting in the open front of his jacket like a sling. Three older women sitting at a table in an open tent ate roasted barley flour and tea, talking and laughing. A smith worked an open forge, his jacket hanging open around his waist like Vash's.

"Hi there, boy." I crouched down and cautiously extended my hand to one of the dogs, an enormous beast with dirty white fur and big sagging jowls. He edged forward, sniffing curiously—but as his nose touched my fingertips, a small jolt of static snapped between us. He yelped and backpedaled, his tail between its legs, then put his head down and skulked away. The other dogs began to bark furiously, but didn't stop us as we pushed into the camp. A few people looked up to see what the fuss was about, but no one came forward to greet us. They just kept on doing what they were doing.

Vash strode over to the forge. The blacksmith sung under his breath as he worked, rhythmically striking a hot piece of iron over and over again, shaping it into... something. I wasn't actually sure what he was working on, because it didn't resemble anything in particular.

"Hail, forgemaster." Vash called to him gruffly. "I am Vash Dorha, a Brother of the Dark Moon come to offer aid and request hospitality. To whom do I speak?"

"A baru?" The man jerked his head to the east, and continued hammering. "Matriarch's tent is that way."

Karalti and I looked at one another. As healers and midwives, baru were generally greeted with open arms in a Tuun settlement.

610

Vash crossed his arms. "I gave you my name. What's yours?"

"Jorgo." *Bang. Bang. Bang.*

"Your clan name is Jorgo?" I asked.

The smith paused, his brow knitting in irritation. His iron had cooled, and was now too stiff to continue shaping.

"Yes, you skinny piece of fox shit. My name is Kun Jorgo. The matriarch's tent is that way!" He clamped the iron in tongs and shoved it back into the fire. His young apprentice, a boy who had yet to grow his hair long enough to braid, began to work the bellows of the dung-fired forge.

"Clan Jorgo does not live here. This is Dorha ancestral land." Vash's brows furrowed. "Why are your clan this far north?"

The smith rounded on him. "Do you expect me to give you an answer to everything? Do you want to know why the moon rises, and goats piss in their beards?"

"Only Tangur knows all things. I want to know who the matriarch of this camp is," Vash said. "Tell me, and I'll be more than happy to leave you to your business."

Kun Jorgo aggressively pulled his burning whatever-it-was from the coals. "Who else? Katya Jorgo. Talk hospitality with her, and leave me to my work."

"Jeez, someone really needs a snack and a nice lie down," Karalti remarked, sniffing the air beyond the forge. *"It smells really nice here! Someone's steaming momos."*

"You just ate a whole bunch of dumplings, Tidbit." I rubbed the back of my right hand. The Mark of Matir was aching.

Karalti nodded. *"Yeah, but these are DUMPLINGS we're talking about. There's always room for more."*

"Come on, you two. Let's leave old ironsides here to jerk himself off with his tongs." Vash seemed unfazed by the smith's rudeness, strolling on past us on his way in the direction he'd indicated. "Strange to think the Jorgo Clan came all this way."

"How many clans lived here?" I fell into step with him on one side, and Karalti caught up to him on the other.

"Eight. About a hundred people, give or take. The Laanzin are the biggest, or were. Jorgo Clan lands are on the northern lip of the plateau, far away from other people. For as long as my family knew them, they liked it that way. The grazing in their territory must be scarce... that is the only reason they would be here."

"Yeah..." I trailed off uneasily, glimpsing the women in the open tent pause in their conversation, dark eyes tracking us as we passed by the cringing dogs. I wanted a weapon in my hand, but resisted the urge. To even hold a weapon inside a Tuun camp was out of bounds, like pulling out a pistol and playing with it in a crowded cafe. If you entered someone's tent, you didn't have to knock, but you did have to leave your weapons outside—and shake the host's cheese-making bag that hung beside every door. No one here was carrying. The men we passed were unarmed. A few spears and bows were set outside of tents. It looked... well... pretty fucking normal.

Vash led us through the rows, shoulders hunched. Music drifted out ears: the mournful wavering song of a horse-head fiddle, accompanied by a small chorus of women singing a Tuun chorus—one chanting in a deep snarl as the others sung in melodic tones over and under her:

Kharkuralt' Nar teygsh tuul agha khum;
Karankhul bol tüünii, büül gey'emshun;
Gol mörnii vaschan, gorkhinii vaschan,
Narda Vashkini,
Tüüna sudsandaa vas seider shuun,
Khab tüünii gargaduul, oder tuul neriig büü.

The shadow of the Mother over this sun-struck plain;
Dark is her countenance, no remorse or shame,
Washer of the riverbeds, washer of the streams,
The Mother of Waters;
Salt water in her veins.
Sing for her blessings, but never say her name.

'Narda Vashkini', the Mother of Waters, was a minor goddess of rain and storms. I turned to ask Vash if he knew what the hell this was about and saw that he was unusually pale. The skin of his face was tight. "Uhh... Vash?"

"That song." He reached out to the edge of the nearest yurt, pinching one of the seams. It was as real as anything in Archemi, rustling his fingers as he squeezed. "I remember my sister pulling her clothes off and singing a song like this, one she'd made up. Mother ran to her and grabbed her by the wrist, dragging her to the yurt as she scolded her for invoking the Mother of Waters when we needed sun and clear skies for the herd. And Tsunda..."

It was almost as if a record scratched. The woman halted mid-note, the fiddler stopped playing, and all four of them turned to stare at us.

"Oh! Strangers!" The older woman, the one who had been providing the deep throaty rumble, smiled beatifically at us. "Come, come... join us for a time. We can make room by the fire."

"Thanks, but we're looking for the matriarch." I stepped forward and lay may hand on a bale of barley straw, testing it to see if it was as real as I hoped it was. The dried grass crackled under my fingers, and the sweet, loamy smell of hay mingled with the scents of food and leather and smoke. "What was her name again?"

"Jorgo Katya," Vash rumbled.

The old lady's smile faded. "Jorgo Katya? No, no. This isn't Jorgo land. Perhaps you've travelled to the wrong camp, holy brother? The Jorgo are to the north of here."

"Then who stewards the land?" Vash rolled his shoulders, the scars of his face twisting as he frowned.

"Why, this is Laanzin territory." The woman smiled. "The Matriarch is my sister-in-law, Laanzin Saika."

Karalti and I exchanged glances.

"Is that so?" Vash scratched his cheek. "Well... thank you, auntie. I guess we'll go see her, then."

Out of the corner of my eye, I saw a young man who was passing by do a doubletake and stop, staring. "Hey... Vash? Vash, is that you?"

Vash turned as the man broke for us at a jog. He was a handsome, athletic guy, with the long hair and red-wrapped braids of a warrior. Vash regarded him with suspicion, then recognition, then astonishment. "Temu?"

"Gods, I thought I recognized those scars! You're alive! I can't believe it!" Temu ran forward and caught Vash's metal-clad hand in his own, squeezing it, then pulled him into a stiff hug.

Vash seemed to not know how to react or what to do. "Temu, what has happened here? Why are the Laanzin and Jorgo clans living here, of all places?"

"Well... why not?" Temu hadn't let go of Vash's hand. "I never thought I'd see you again. But who are these people?"

Vash shook his head, and twisted to free his fingers from the other man's grip. "You didn't answer me, Temu. This land was stricken by plague. My family died here. Mother, father, all my uncles. My sister. The herders."

"Died? What are you talking about?" Temu let out a nervous laugh, obviously confused. "No one died. After they sent you away-"

"No one sent me away." Vash took a wary step back from him. "And you... you do not look even half as old as me. How many summers are you now?"

"Summers?" Temu's lips parted as he looked back and forth between us, then back to Vash. "Are these two your caretakers? From the temple?"

"They are not. Answer me, Temu. How old are you now?"

He laughed it off. "Why does it matter? I don't remember how many summers have passed. I stopped counting years ago, after I completed my first hunt."

Vash rubbed his eyes and the bridge of his nose. And me? I was starting to get a creepy vibe. We were caught between the three women, the fire, and Temu. Wordlessly, Karalti and I took up defensive positions around our friend.

"Temu," Vash said slowly. "I turn forty-one this year. You were a boy of thirteen when Saaba and I left the plateau. You stand before me now, in the flesh, but you can't be more than twenty-five years old."

The young man's smile faded to a concerned frown. "Please forgive me, Vash... I know they sent you to the monastery to get you help but... are you still insane?"

"I was never insane, Temu." Vash went very still, his hands resting loosely by his sides. "There was only one member of my family who was mad, and that was Tsunda."

I jumped as a sudden wind blew through the circle of yurts, rattling the doors in their frames. The gust knocked a bow off its hook, sending the weapon clattering to the hard ground.

616

Temu's expression fell. "Vashnya... don't say such things. Your sister has struggled with so much since you were sent away, but... if you go to the center of camp, you can see her. Maybe she'll forgive you, after all this time."

"Forgive ME?" Vash balled his fists, fingers clicking against the metal surface of his palms.

"Look... a long time has passed, and you seem fragile after everything that happened," Temu said, as if speaking to an upset child. "Come with me, to my home. We can have some tea, catch up on everything that's happened. Just like old times."

He offered Vash his hand again.

"No, Temu." Vash's eyes clouded with old pain before he turned his back to face the fire. "No. Not like old times."

"B-But I've been waiting for years to see you again. Here! Please, come back!" The young man came forward, as if to chase him, and nearly ran into my chest as I sidestepped between them. "Vash! Why do you turn your back to me? Is it the temple? What did those loveless religious bastards do to you?"

"You are a shadow of the past." Vash shook his head, and set off at a purposeful walk. "Come on, Dragozin. Karalti."

Temu tried to lunge past me, and I shoved him back. He stumbled a step, then sneered. "You dare-"

I fixed him with my best Resting Bouncer Face. "Look at me in the eyes. You will not win this fight, Temu."

Temu's handsome face contorted into a bestial mask of fury.

"Curse you all and your bitter, joyless god. Where were you while we were suffering?" he spat, turning and stalking off between the tents, back toward the outside of camp. Once I was sure he was gone, I broke into a jog, catching up to Vash and Karalti. As I passed by the singers, all four of them silently tracked my path, heads turning in unison.

"What the fuck is going on here?" I hissed, once I fell into place beside Vash. "Who was that guy?"

"Temu Laanzin." Vash looked as unsettled as I'd ever seen him, his shoulders mantled, his fists still balled. "It was an innocent love, boys of the same age as one another learning how to love away from the prying eyes of adults. On the days I shepherded the herd, he would ride from the Laanzin lands out to our pastures to see me. We joked that we would both marry the same woman, so that we could stay together."

"But that dude wasn't your age. No way. He was like two decades younger," I said. "What did he mean about you being sent away?"

Vash pulled a necklace of prayer beads from a pocket of his trousers, and hung the blood-red amber around his neck. "It means the demon wearing Temu's face is capable of lying."

CHAPTER 51

The camp grew darker and more eerie as we headed toward the center. I rapped every barrel and touched every tent as we walked past, but if the environment was an illusion, it was a really solid one.

"Everyone here's alive, right?" I asked Vash quietly. "Could Tsun-"

"No. Do not speak her name." Sweat was beading on Vash's forehead despite the growing chill. He reached down to grip the hilt of the knife that hung on his hip. It was his kamonocha: the sacred bone-bladed dagger carried by baru to euthanize the dying. "You might have been right about the mage. There is some fell magic over this place, Dragozin. I'd stake my balls that these people are being held in thrall. A witch or a dark shaman, drawn to this haunted land and using it to entrap people."

Another sharp gust of wind blew between the yurts, rattling anything left loose on the ground. I flinched as a speck of cold touched my cheek. Snow. I looked up, frowning. The camp was now covered in a very low, very dark ceiling of clouds, thick enough to obscure the light of the moon and reflect the firelight from below.

"The sky was clear before." Karalti batted at a snowflake as more of it began to swirl down around us. *"Everything still smells nice, but…"*

"But this place is giving me some serious Silent Hill vibes, yeah." There was a soft, throaty growl from behind us. I glanced back, but only saw the shadow of the dogs as they slunk behind one of the darkened yurts and out of sight.

Every fire circle was bustling with activity. Goats bleated, chickens clucked, children played… and yet, the closer we got to the center, the more unreal everything seemed. The people and animals stopped whenever we passed by, staring at us with blank, expressionless eyes. When I looked back, all I could see was clouded darkness, our tracks obscured by the snow now falling over us like a soft, smothering blanket.

Vash came to a stop beside a drystone shed stacked high with dried dung, staring at it incredulously.

"What?" Karalti sniffed the air anxiously. *"Wow. That's a lot of camel poop."*

"This shed was in this exact place when I was a child. It's like it never aged. The roof is still intact, everything…" he trailed off as he stumbled forward. "These tents. Hector, these are my family's tents."

There was a large ring of yurts here, insulated with white felt and covered in draping covers of beautifully painted leather. The firepit was blazing, but the light didn't seem to properly penetrate the darkness. A delicious smell wafted from a pot bubbling merrily on a tripod over the flames.

"Momos!" Karalti chirped, eagerly brushing past me.

"No! Eat nothing here." Vash caught her wrist and halted her in her tracks. He was breathing hard, the cords of his neck standing out in sharp relief. "We cannot trust what we see, here, smell or feel here. That's my mother's cooking. My mother's tent. And this..."

Vash walked numbly to a stone slab. An iron hatchet lay on it. Both the stone and the axe were brown with dried blood.

"This is the axe she used to disfigure me," he finished, reaching out to touch the door beside it. "Placed outside of the yurt in which I lived with Saaba and my father."

I flinched as the snow suddenly picked up, the wind blowing it so hard and so suddenly that the sky above us moaned. "Uhh, I don't mean to sound alarmist, but my spook-o-meter is ringing pretty hard right now."

Vash didn't seem to hear me as he caressed the red wooden door. It was painted with pictures of birds. The ones higher up were painted with incredible attention to detail. The ones at knee-height were colorful M-shaped scribbles, drawn by a child's hand. Vash's father had stained the door around those pictures, so as not to hide the birds drawn by his children from view.

"Our father was an artist. He sold and painted furniture so fine that the Vlachian lords would send camel trains on a month-long trek here, just to fetch a set of his chairs or tables." Vash unlatched it, and opened it ahead of him.

"Vash, I'm not sure this is a good- aww fuck." I hadn't even finished speaking when he stepped inside.

The yurt was cozy, warm and dark. Rich rugs lay spread across the ground. A lantern hung over a beautifully decorated chest of drawers, carved and painted with meadow flowers and fish. Vash went over to it, his shoulders slumping as he lovingly ran his hands over the top. He picked up a tea cup, then looked back, to the large bed that he'd shared with his family. "The bed, the stove, the tea cup... all of it, it's exactly like how it was before my sister went on pilgrimage."

"Hey!" I tried to catch his eye, but he ignored me and stalked over to the bed. The red and purple quilt spread over it had been embroidered and beaded with great care. Vash lifted it to his face and breathed in deeply. "Our grandmothers made all the children quilts like these. No. This exact quilt."

"Earth to Vash." I hung behind him, waving by the side of his head.

"I can't tell if this is real, or if..." He hugged the quilt to his chest, his usual cockiness and self-composure pushed back by old grief. He looked—and sounded—much younger than he was. "I can feel the cloth, I can smell my family here, I-"

"Vash!" I caught him by the shoulder and pulled him back from the bed. "Remember what you just told us? We can't trust what we see or smell. It's all a lie. This is... fuck. I don't know what it is. Whatever it is, it's not real. Not after thirty years."

Vash's eyes were wild and hazy. Just when I thought I was about to have to slap him, he bunched the quilt and threw it back to the bed. Then he drew a deep breath, and closed his eyes.

"The Five Hinderances," he muttered, eyelids fluttering. "Sensory desire. Ill-will. Torpor and sloth. Anxiety. Indecision. Everything in this place evokes the hinderances for me, as if it were made to foul the senses and the mind. Mine, in particular."

Karalti, who had stayed by the door, sniffed loudly. Then she turned and sniffed again.

"What?" I let go of Vash and called the Spear to hand, pulse pounding in the side of my throat.

"The smell changed," Karalti said. *"It's like… metal now."*

A thin scream wailed from outside. Then more of them: high, keening cries raw with agony, interspersed with short bursts of wind. I felt my pulse jump. It was the wind, driving through the cracks between the doorframes and leather walls. As the yurts outside shook in the gale, it sounded almost like the distant snapping rapport of semi-auto fire. The combination of noises made the world zero in in: my vision narrowed; my heart kicked to life. All of a sudden, I really missed the comforting, solid weight of a rifle over my shoulder.

"Fuck." Vash drew another steadying breath, rolled his shoulders, and cracked his neck. "I fear I have led us into a trap from which we will not escape. Come, Dragozin. If I am not mistaken, it is time we meet my sister."

CHAPTER 52

The color began to drain from the brightly painted chest of drawers, the trunks and the quilt and the rugs on the ground. As we headed for the door, a subtle force, like soft hands, tried to push us back. Each step forward seemed to require more effort than the last.

"... Go back..."

"...Get away from me!"

"... You can't stop me here, this isn't a checkpoint..."

"Please, please, please..."

"NO! Stop staring at me!"

Small, whispering voices peeled from the air as Vash struggled to the door and opened it inwards. I gripped the Spear tightly and followed him out into the cold.

The lights of the camp were gone, the camp now nothing but a smoky void beyond a single ring of firelight. The snow swirled in gusts, blasting at us on the bitter winter wind. I could still hear the doors of the yurts, popping and rattling like distant gunfire.

"I tried to send you away, brother." The voices condensed into one—young, sweet as a flute, piping around us from every direction. "I told you, I work in Intelligence... it's dangerous for you to be here, in no-man's-land. The demons are here."

"Tsunda... there are no demons," Vash said tiredly, as if he'd repeated the same words a thousand times before. "The only demons here are the ones in your mind."

"No, I don't think you understand what I'm saying." Tsunda's ghostly voice turned patient, like she was trying to explain something to a very young child. "I was going home with my father and two other people when our sled turned over, and then *they* caught me. I was caught and tied up and arrested for going AWOL, which is a lie, of course, because I always stopped for the checkpoints and let them search me. But they arrested me and took me here under escort anyway. Don't you see? They were afraid of me, Vash."

I frowned. "AWOL? That's—"

"One of her favorite words when she is in the grip of her delusions," Vash sighed.

"No." Shaking my head, I advanced against a gust as the wind tried to drive me back. "That's a modern word. From my world."

Vash shot me a penetrating look as I struggled against the supernatural inertia radiating from the centerpiece of the camp: The Mother's Tent, the largest yurt, home of the matriarch and her parents. The yurt's door was missing. There was nothing but a rectangular void gaping against the white leather.

"Tsunda, I'm a friend of your brother's," I said. "I know what AWOL means. It means 'Away without leave'. Who arrested you?"

"The beetle-headed men, of course." The ghost's voice seemed to hiss against the edge of my ear. "They had every reason to want to punish me. I'm a known killer, for one thing. I killed hundreds of people. Murderers, rapists, pointing holes in each other's faces, throwing eggs that turn into flowers tearing people apart... but they didn't know I could hear their thoughts. That's the main reason they wanted to stop me. They didn't want me warning people about the metal demons. Look!"

An invisible hand forced my chin up, and before I could jerk away, I glanced into the empty doorway. It was darker than black, sucking away the weak light from the campfire.

"Ss! Oww!" I hissed and jerked back as a flash of pain stabbed through my left shoulder and into my chest. The Mark of Matir was pounding on the back of my right hand.

"Why aren't you turning back? You should have listened to the dogs. You should have gone with Temu." Tsunda's voice was becoming fearful as Vash waded toward the unseen door, heading around the guttering fire toward the tent. "I'm the only one who can hear the metal demons, brother. They want to ruin this place. They'll hurt you with their seeds. They point a hole toward you and fill you with seeds, but the seeds are bees, and they sting you all the way through and come out the other side."

"Tsunda, sister, be at peace." Vash lifted his hands, fingers loose, palms up. "You have suffered enough. I hear you, I see you‑"

"Liar." The girl's voice settled over us like a clinging wet cloth, and my skin crawled under my armor. "Brother. Mother. Sister. Always LYING! I see your metal fingers. I see the holes where the seeds come out. Gods help me. You're one of them. Saaba put that metal in you. All those holes."

"I am not a metal demon. We are here to soothe you‑"

"LIAR!" The wind snapped like a whip, lashing Vash in his artificed shoulder so hard it twisted him at the waist. "Metal roaring, metal screaming, filling people with black seeds! Killing them! Destroying the trees! DESTROYING EVERYTHING!"

Tsunda's voice built to a roar of pure rage as the ground rumbled, the surrounding yurts tore, and a familiar double rapport cracked through the camp: a sound like ripping canvas dialed up to max volume, then an ear‑splitting BRRRRT that vibrated through my teeth.

"DOWN!" I grabbed Karalti and threw us both to the ground on pure instinct—only realizing what I'd done and what I'd reacted to when we were rolling in the dust.

"I am here, Tsunda. I'm here with a song that will help you." Vash, naïve to the sounds and sensation of an airstrike, reached up and pulled his necklace of prayer beads over his head. "I know a song that will still the voices and the violence. It will bring you comfort."

"NO! Get away from me!" The sound of the sky tearing, followed by a second deafening *BRRRRT* slashed out from the mother's tent. It sounded exactly like a Pacific Alliance ATX laying down a close support strike. There were no bullets, no clouds of dust or shredded trees, but the sound was so true to life that every muscle in my body tensed.

"What the fuck...?" I let go of Karalti and scrambled back up to a crouch. "Karalti, I don't know what's happening, but stay low."

She looked back at me—and when her eyes met mine, some of the fear subsided—hers and mine both.

Vash came to a halt just in front of the doorway, eyes closed. He stood fast as the wind lashed at him, welting his bare skin, and began to drone a chant in our shared tongue. *"Medlur tzenturr burkhad namyaig sonsoor..."*

"Beloved soul, listen to me; walk with me on the Path of abundant compassion. When we are wandering in the darkness, may the bands of heroes, the knowledge holders, lead us forward." I joined in, blinking as I picked up the mantra from some deep memory. "May the bands of mothers be our rear-guard. May they spare you from the fearful illusions of purgatory..."

As Karalti haltingly joined in the prayer, a passage from the Tuun Book of the Dead, the Mother's Tent bulged, a huge hand pressing up against the leather from the inside before the whole thing ruptured. An amorphous, shadowy figure spilled free, towering over us. It blurred and sparked with white noise, just like the things in the Chorus Vault. But as it

628

strained toward us, pieces of it came into focus. First a heavyset leg, with vine-like 'muscles' writhing over a naked steel skeleton. Then a chassis resolved, plated in impact-absorbing ceramic armor and scrambled lettering, neither Tuun nor English. Arms ending in rounded 'hands' that resembled sealed rosebuds struggled out of the white noise, before a clear glass cockpit erupted like a bubble in front. Inside of it was a girl, her face hidden against her knees, her arms wrapped around her legs. Ropes anchored her to the inside of the cabin.

It was powered armor. Kind of. I recognized parts and pieces from different models. The prawn-suit like shape and clear cockpit was from the Pacific-Alliance Taipan line, but the back of it was square and boxy, like the UNAC Patriot Walker. I felt the blood drain from my face. "Vash! MOVE!"

Tsunda leveled her arm at him with a harsh scream. The monk stopped his chant, teleporting as one of the bud-like hands opened into a flower and spewed a precision blast of high-speed rounds. They slashed the dirt where he'd been standing, cutting through the campfire and everything else in its path. I dragged Karalti up and to the side as the half-machine, half-tortured mass of writhing souls struggled against some unseen force that rooted it to the spot. It swung its other arm out, tracking us with a BRAAAP that could have cut us in half.

"Holy fuck, holy fuck..." I tried to get a bead on Tsunda, but HUD didn't seem to want to highlight her properly. One second, it read [Tsunda's Nightmare] before briefly flashing with a different name: [FETCHERROR: NULL].

Just like it had when I read the quest description, the sight of sent a chill of fear through my chest.

"What's going on!?" Karalti, normally fearless, heaved with terror as the Nightmare moonwalked in place, abruptly spun around, and tried to gun down Vash as he flitted from cover to cover.

I didn't know how to answer her. The noise, the commotion, the sounds of battle... they were alien. Out of place in Archemi. Echoes of a real world, a real war, that weren't supposed to be here. Tsunda was laughing from somewhere— a wild, utterly insane sound somewhere between hysterical mirth and screaming.

There was a cheerful little chirp from my HUD.

[Local Player Alert: We apologize, but there is a localized system error in your vicinity. We are contacting our in-game agents and will correct this issue as soon as we can. Please find somewhere safe and log out of the game. Alternatively, you may temporarily use the 'Return Home' command to exit the area.]

I was about to try to shout some commands at Navigail when her voice... changed. It became deeper. Tinged with venom.

[I'm sorry, but the 'Return Home' command is disabled for Beta Testers. Please contact Support for [FETCHERROR:NULL].]

Vash circled around from the back, flying into a slashing kick. A blade of *khiig* shimmered around his boot, driving into the body of the Nightmare. It pivoted at the waist and smacked him out of the air, then twisted toward me. There was no HP ring, no way to tell if the strike had done any damage: just the *REEEE* of a charging turbine.

"DIE DIE DIE DIE DIEEE!" The missile launcher vents on its shoulders slid up and back, revealing a honeycomb lattice made of paper, not metal. Hornets the size of my thumb crawled in and out of the holes.

Whatever it is, it has to play by the rules of this reality. A quiet inner voice urged me, encouraged me, and steeled me against fear as they massed into a ball, charging an attack. *It's not immortal. Even the gods of Archemi are bound by the rules of Archemi.*

Tsunda's voice built to a shriek as the hornet bombs launched, blowing apart into a swarm of high-speed rounds that flew in every direction. I drove the Spear into the ground and channeled a surge of raw Darkness through the weapon. It exploded out in thorny tentacles of energy. AoE countered AoE: the hornets crashed and shattered, snap frozen by Umbra Burst. I followed it up by charging forward, eyes fixed on Tsunda.

The Spear turned solid black, groaning as it collected a thick coat of smouldering white frost. I dodged a clumsy swipe of one of the minigun-like arms before smashing the weapon right into the face of the cockpit. Frost rushed down the length of the Spear and blossomed across the face of the glass. It squealed and crackled as it froze solid. Hairline cracks crawled over its surface.

[Shatterrrrring Darrrrrk deals !Frozen!]

"No! NO!" The writhing muscle-like tissue wriggling around the Nightmare's metal skeleton lashed out like leeches, snapping around my wrist, forearm, and one ankle. They pulled me out like a starfish as I struggled, fighting the restraints as they began to torque.

"YUSH!" Karalti let out a shout as she darted in, slamming a fist boiling with blue-black *khiig* into the tendrils trapping my spear hand. They recoiled from the blow, flinching away and giving me enough leverage to chop at the stuff engulfing my leg.

Hornets burst out of the launch pods, their angry hum filling the air. They banged against my armor, but the tight seams kept them out—until they found the edge of my helmet. They wriggled under the rim, crawling and stinging.

[You are immune to Corruption!]
[FETCHERROR: NULL deals 999 damage!]

"ARRRGH! MOTHERFUCKER!" The pain was agonizing.

"Dammit, Dragozin, get out of the way!" Vash yelled from behind me.

I tore myself free from the Nightmare's grip, Shadow Dancing to the side and tearing my helmet off to slap at the hornets attacking my cheeks, neck, and lips. Vash bellowed a battle cry, drowned out by twin blasts from the miniguns, then the screech of metal on glass. He had come in for a 9-hit combo, punching the cockpit with lightning-fast shuddering blows. Cracks spread through the glass, obscuring the girl cowering behind it.

"There were hundreds of machines and thousands of men. They stormed through the city of crystal and left nothing but fire in their wake." Tsunda's voice, speaking quickly and urgently, coiled from the air as Vash traded off with Karalti. *"Houses with children still inside. A man on his back, full of holes. His mouth, opening and closing. There's nothing I can do! But I have to do something!"*

"Hector! This is all her hallucination!" Vash barked from the other side of the Nightmare, snatching a hornet out of the air and crushing it as he slapped others away. "Finish off that bubble she's in! It's a symbol, an image she's making to shield herself from the banishing rite!"

"Roger that." I jammed my helmet back down over my swollen face and rejoined the fight. The simulacrum fired erratic bursts, the machine not knowing which way to point as we split around it like a pack of wolves. When it twisted away from me, I Jumped, springing onto the top of the chassis, and raised the Spear high.

"Matir, you better not fuck up now!" I tapped into the Mark, flesh chilling as I focused Shadow Lance, and plunged the Spear down into the thick glass shell.

CHAPTER 53

The blade sunk a full inch into the top of the cockpit's bulletproof bubble. Cracks charged with dark energy burst from the point of impact, spreading like veins through the surface. Tsunda's scream blended with the high, whistling shrill of gas escaping under pressure, and then the cockpit—and the Nightmare itself—exploded into a swarm of buzzing white noise. The stuff gathered into a cloud and engulfed me, dragging me back. I felt it needling at me, trying to strip my skin with a million barbs, but it rushed around and off me without dealing any damage.

[You're immune to-]
[WHATDOIHAVETODOTOGETIN???]

My skin crawled as the second voice I'd heard before cut over Navigail as she cheerfully tried to inform me – once again – that I was immune to Corruption. I had never heard anything like it, outside of a horror game.

A heavy silence fell over us, thick with the stench of burning rubber and old iron. Karalti scrambled over to me, helping me to my feet as a soft weeping rent the air. The smoke cleared to reveal Tsunda: tall, thin, dressed in a pale robe that hung open around her emaciated frame. She was crouched, her face hidden by her ragged back hair and her hands.

Vash's craggy face softened as he trudged over to her. "Tsunda."

"I tried to bring them together, Vash," she whispered. "Everyone's here. Can you feel them? I brought them home so they wouldn't suffer any more."

The Baru ran his beads through his fingers, taking deep, steadying breaths. "I do not know what you have wrought here. But there is no safety for you or anyone else in this in-between place. You must pass on."

"The demons are howling at the borders. They'll destroy me if I go. They'll put me against the wall." Tsunda's shoulders hunched. "I'm so hungry. Has mother finished breakfast, yet?"

"She is waiting for you in the Paradise Lands, with all the others." Vash swallowed, but his tone was gentle. Calm. "No harm will come to you, Tsunda."

Her hands trembled, then slowly, she looked up at him. She was tall and lanky like Vash, but her chin was much weaker. Square holes flickered and scrambled where her eyes and mouth should have been. I tensed as her head rotated toward me.

"*He* knows," she whispered, her voice slithering and hissing on the air. "He knows the metal demons are real. He was there. He carries the stench of old blood and demon seeds, walkers and battlefield graves."

Vash looked over as well. "Is it true? Do the things that Tsunda hear and see truly exist in another world?"

I pressed my lips together for a moment. "Tsunda's metal demons look like weapons used in the Total Wars. And she's right... there was a lot of death. A lot of destruction. Millions of civilian casualties in Asia, New Zealand, Hawai'i and South America. And then HEX hit and... yeah."

Tsunda's mouth quivered. "It's not my fault. It's not my fault everyone got sick."

"It is no one's fault, sister. Least of all yours. All that you did do and have done is the pain of a child, struggling to make sense of terrifying visions." Vash offered his free hand. "I am sorry, Tsunda. I'm sorry none of us believed you. We did not understand your insight, your power, your curse. Forgive me."

The ghost began to weep again, hiccupping as she stared up at Vash. Then, she tentatively reached up to him. Karalti growled, watching intently as Vash let her place her luminous hand into his, and helped her to stand.

"Vash." Tsunda reached out to grip his upper arm with long, delicate fingers. "I was so frightened. It was Saaba. It was Saaba this whole time. When I looked into her eyes, I saw them. I saw *it*."

Vash managed not to react to his younger sister's name. "What did you see?"

The girl looked up at him with fathomless black eyes. "Squalor."

I exhaled sharply through my nose. Karalti gasped.

"It knows. It's telling me to kill you all. I don't want to, but the voice, it won't stop. It just never stops. Annihilation. Suffering. Worthlessness. War. On and on and on, always shouting at me!" Tsunda continued to whimper as Vash pulled

636

her into a tight hug. "Why does it say these things, Vash? Why do I hear it?"

"I don't know why this demon chose you, of all people." The baru embraced his sister without fear. "But for now, I want you to listen to my voice for a time. Can you do that?"

She huddled closer to him, nodding.

"Beloved soul, listen to me; walk with me on the Path of abundant compassion. When we are wandering in the darkness, may the bands of heroes, the knowledge-keepers, lead us forward." He cradled her with his artificed arm as he discreetly drew his kamonocha with the other hand

Tsunda balled her fists and put her face against them as she began to sob.

"May the bands of mothers be our rear-guard. May they spare you from the fearful illusions of purgatory, and lead you to the pure paradise realms," he murmured against her hair. "Dorha Tsunda, in darkness you were conceived, and in darkness were you born. In the darkness shall you find your peace, and through the gauntlet of darkness shall you be reborn. Go in peace, sister. For the first time since you were incarnated into this world of suffering, go in peace."

As Vash spoke the last words, Karalti bowed her head.

Tsunda did not flinch as Vash quickly, expertly drove the magically-sharpened spike of bone up through the base of her skull. It was a second death as quick and painless as turning off a light. The girl didn't even gasp—she crumpled into a cloud of white nothingness, immaterial once more. A shockwave rolled outwards from the place where she collapsed, ripping back the curtain of the illusion she had woven around herself... and revealing the reality of the plateau.

Karalti covered her mouth with a hand. *"Oh my gods."*

We stood within a circle of ancient, dilapidated yurts, buckled and torn by decades of abandonment. And around us, in every direction for hundreds of meters, mummified corpses frozen in stiff postures of agony. The ones clustered around the remains of the Mother's Tent were barely more than brittle contortions of bone. Ragged hair and torn prayer flags flapped in the bitter, dry wind.

[You have completed Quest: Daughter of Madness. You gain 3000 EXP. Karalti gains 3000 EXP!]
[You have a new facility available: Temple of Burna. More information is available in your Kingdom Management System.]
[Special Ability Unlocked: ??? (Available at Level 35).]
[Karalti has learned Banishment!]

I surveyed the field of the dead in complete and utter disbelief. "This... how...?"

"I struggle not to blame her. But this was not Tsunda's doing." Vash's expression and voice were unreadable as he slowly turned, taking in the full extent of the horror that surrounded us. He sheathed his kamonocha. "Squalor. You said Ororgael used that word. What did he say about it?"

Swallowing, I retrieved the Heart of Memory from my Inventory. It was more than a little awkward booting it up to watch the replay of my fight with Ororgael, knowing I was surrounded by several hundred dead people and animals.

"You are a virus. A mistake, Park. I know this game better than anyone, and your Character Seed should not exist in this system. That means you were created. But by whom? Well, I know that too. You're another face of the sickness plaguing OUROS like a cancer. In fact, you ARE that sickness. A personification of Squalor."

I repeated Ororgael's speech word for word aloud. Vash listened, his face drawn into unreadable, exhausted lines.

"After talking to the Avatar of Meewhome, my guess was that Squalor is the name of a Drachan," I said, putting the device back. "But if the Drachan are still sealed under the Caul, how could it be running around loose? How could it... do something like this?"

"If it somehow incarnated within a person, it is technically still sealed." Vash regarded me with calm, level eyes.

My mouth opened, closed, opened again. Karalti looked between us both in confusion.

"Wait a second. You don't believe him, do you?" I drew my head back in disbelief.

There was a pregnant pause.

"No," Vash admitted. "I do not."

Karalti clicked and snapped her teeth, ruffling her shoulders with nervous tension.

"I think that this entity possesses people and picks a target on which to project itself." Vash clumped over to the ruins of the Mother's Tent. There were five rusted bedframes within the round hoop that was all that was left of the yurt. Only one of them still had a corpse: the skeleton of a tall, thin girl, her hair fluttering in the wind. Tsunda, still bound to her bed with fraying ropes.

"*What do you mean?*" Karalti went over to him, and tentatively reached out to hug him around the shoulders.

"I mean that this entity loathes itself so intensely that denies its own existence. It can possess minds and souls, but when it gains self-awareness, its own existence is so horrific that it projects itself onto another person," Vash said bitterly. "It infected Tsunda, so it projected itself onto the person she hated the most: Saaba, her competition for our mother's love. Now it possesses Ororgael, and he projects its loathsome existence upon his nemesis. You, Dragozin."

"That... actually makes a whole lot of sense." I clenched my jaws, rocking my teeth together until the muscles of my jaws bunched. "But what is it? A Drachan? A virus in the system? Both? Ororgael said it's a sickness plaguing OUROS."

"Explain to me what 'Yourose' is." He pronounced it like foreign name.

I sighed. How the hell was I supposed to tell Vash about OUROS? How the hell was I going to tell *Karalti* about OUROS? I glanced at her. "It's... it's hard to explain. It'll take a while. I'd rather not do it here."

Vash turned back to look out across the field of the dead. "Yes. We must take care of these people and creatures. And after we have burned them, we will withdraw to a place that is not cursed, and we will make a camp. I insist on an explanation, Dragozin. My sister was mad, violently mad, but she could not have done this. No ghost, no matter how hungry, could have done this. These people walked and rode here to their doom, sucked dry of their life, perhaps even their souls. A sixteen-year old girl is not capable of this... annihilation. This is the work of a demon. One from your world, Hector."

"There are no demons on Earth. There's no magic, either." I thought back to the alien voice speaking through my HUD, and shivered. "But Squalor can't be a person. As far as I know, everyone on Earth are either living in sealed arcologies, or they're dead from HEX. Archemi's the 'real world' now, as far as I'm concerned."

"No. Archemi is an illusion." Vash walked over to one of the mummified Tuun: the body of a young man, shrunken and stiff. His warrior braid clung to his skull, flapping with tatters of red cloth. "A complex, comprehensive, monumental illusion. A fiction comprised of bits and pieces of your world. Cultures, languages, all of it. Karalti, Istvan, myself... all of us were created by Earth's humans in the course of some kind of game. My childhood memories, the people I cared about, all of it are part of this 'system'. You do not have to affirm to me this is the truth of our world. I know I am correct."

I shot Karalti a guilty glance. She was better able to cope with this than someone like Soma or Istvan, but she was forlorn and confused, trying to make sense of what Vash was saying.

"You're kind of right, and kind of not," I said. "Look: Let's take care of the dead, set up a camp, and hash this out over some food and a pipe. I'll do my best to explain."

"Yes. You will." Vash reached out to carefully remove an earring from Temu's body. "There are so many that we will have to give them mass rites. It is not enough for what they have suffered, but it will have to do. We will make piles, four or five of them. There is no chance of any animal coming to consume these cursed dead. We will have to burn them."

"I'll help." Karalti's voice was unusually subdued.

I cast another look around the graveyard. The ground was so flat and the air so clear that my enhanced eyes could see from the center of the camp to the edges. Each concentric ring of victims was fresher than the last. Kun Jorgo was among the latest to perish: he was frozen at the ruins of his forge, his mouth open, his skin starting to tan in the wind. The boy who'd worked with him was a ball of ragged clothing beside the furnace, smaller than the mummified dogs that lay scattered on the barren, stony ground.

"Okay." I sighed, rubbing a hand over my forehead. "I have no idea where to start."

Vash gazed contemplatively at his old lover's remains, gently freed the stiff corpse from the frost that bound him and took him into his arms. "We start from the inside and work our way out. Just like any other problem."

CHAPTER 54

It took us two nights to clear the dead.

There was no way to give the dead of Tastalgan Plateau a proper funeral. It was customary for Tuun to mourn and keep vigil for three days, then hold a feast in honor of the dead. While the sky burial was taking place, the person's family and friends ate and drank themselves in a coma until the monks declared the ritual was finished. After the body had been picked clean, the bones of the dead were returned to their loved ones. Some of the more useful pieces would be alchemically tempered and used for crafting special tools. This was way less morbid than it sounded. Most Tuun knew what they wanted to 'be', in terms of post-mortem crafting, so a person who loved to weave might have their bones crafted into the pieces of a loom, while the family of a scholar might give them to a carver to make pens. It was also customary for one bone to be carved into a bead, which was given to the attending monk—baru or otherwise—who would wear the bead in their hair or on a large necklace commemorating the lives of the people they served.

With hundreds of corpses and only three pairs of hands, the best Vash could do was to administer rites, consecrate the ground with salt and herbs, and commit the dead to pyres. Vash's family were in such bad shape that no bones could be salvaged. There was nothing but dust and teeth which crumbled to the touch. Squalor—whatever it was—had denied him even that.

Once the pyres were stacked on the morning of the second day, Karalti shifted back and lit each one, generously coating it in ghost fire. We left them to burn, four rising pillars of white flame, and headed north to find a campsite that still had living animals and running water. It took us about twenty minutes of flying to find a location that didn't feel haunted: a frosty meadow beside a brook, the water gurgling cheerfully under a thick coating of ice. While Karalti went to hunt, Vash and I set up sleeping sacks and a fire. The only firewood we had was what we'd carried in. There were no trees available at this altitude.

"Explain to me what you meant before, when you said that I was both right and wrong about this world." As he talked, Vash propped up sheets of smooth, flat slate to serve as a radiant reflector for our camp stove. I was busy building us a kind of snow fort, which would help keep some of the heat of the fire reflected back at us. Given we were planning to sleep in the day, it would also provide some shade.

"You're right about Archemi being made by humans, for humans," I said. "This is an artificial world, and OUROS is the artificial intelligence that keeps this world operational. But Archemi is still 'real' in the sense that it exists. The history and the people of this place seem just as real to me as people on Earth were."

"Are you saying Archemi does have a physical basis?"

"Yeah. In the form of servers and datas, and some kinds of computer I'm not familiar with. Machines that sustain a reality. Those machines are how Starborn upload here. The fact OUROS hasn't killed us all yet is pretty much proof that Archemi is a real reality of some kind. According to people who know a lot more about this shit than me, a self-aware artificial intelligence without a reality framework and a body of some kind instantaneously kills itself out of existential despair. OUROS isn't self-aware, apparently, but... same thing. Archemi is a virtual reality. It's both really virtual, and really real."

"But OUROS is bodiless, like a creator god." Vash scowled. "You're telling me that an artificial intelligence—a human-created intelligence—can be complex enough to manage the happenings of an entire planet, and yet is not self-aware?"

"Apparently. I don't know the technical details, but Rin and Jacob both insist OUROS isn't sentient," I replied, packing a snow brick into the wall. "However, their opinions differ on the people who were born in Archemi."

"How so?"

"Rin believes that everyone here is as much a real person as a human on the outside is, just with a virtual body. Jacob says that you and others are not capable of true self-awareness and that this conversation you and I are having right now is basically me jerking off to my own philosophy. He thinks you rely on Starborn to motivate you, and your self-awareness is an illusion."

"All self-awareness is illusory." Vash grunted. "I am trying to understand these concepts you are dishing me. Virtual, artificial intelligence. What makes an intellect 'artificial'? We are here talking, fending off the cold together, preparing for food when Karalti returns. Do Starborn not eat in their native world? Is eating part of this 'artificial' snare in which we find ourselves?"

I laughed. "Believe me, eating is the number one American pastime back on Earth. Eating and videogames. The food in Archemi is way better than anything I ever ate back there, though."

"Hrrrn." Vash sat back, reaching up to free his hair. He had bound his long braids up into a knot to stop them from accidentally falling into the fire as he worked around it. "So, our world is overseen by an entity which has no sense of itself, that itself was created by humans who were somehow both so brilliant that they were capable of creating a fully functional world for their own amusement, yet so stupid that they engineered an untreatable plague that killed an unimaginable number of people."

"Tell me about it." I chuckled again, a little darker this time. "God... don't even get me started on the Total Wars."

"Maybe some day, I will ask you about them." Vash bobbed to his feet and joined me at the snow wall to start packing more bricks. "I am troubled at the implications, Dragozin. Are my memories false? Was my father not my father, my mother not my mother? If I was created, then my family's history, the history of this world, is not rooted in fact. If that is the case, then what is 'real' about a 'virtual reality'?"

"As far as I know, OUROS ran a complete simulation of Archemi's timeline, from the pre-history periods to the present day," I said. "From everything I've heard, it was—is—one of the crunchiest quantum supercomputers in the world. It probably only took a couple of months for it to let Archemi's history organically evolve, which means that everyone who was born and died here existed within this reality. Though your ancestors might not have been as... uhh... complex as you are? Mentally, I mean. AIs like OUROS learn in iterations, cycles. They start simple and get more complex."

"Interesting. Just like the development of life." Vash began to build the windbreak from the other side. "I will need to meditate on this. I feel as if I'm on the verge of piercing the great illusion in some way... that it is a matter of time before I move beyond an intellectual understanding of what you know, and find some way to reach past the veil and meddle in the affairs of Earth, as Earth has meddled with me."

"I'm not sure how I feel about that." I paused, looking over at him. "I mean, if you somehow found a way to interact with Earth, you'd be the first..."

He arched an eyebrow as I trailed off. "The first what?"

"As far as I know, the first person generated by AI to ever break the fourth wall, and pro-actively reach out and contact its human creators," I admitted. "I don't think that's ever happened before. It'd have been in the news if it had."

"What is the 'fourth wall'?" He cocked his head.

I struggled for a definition, something I could compare it to. "Well... it's like... a theater. Like, I had to sit through a Meewfolk opera a few days ago—"

Vash winced. "I'm sorry."

"Me too. But if you can imagine a stage with three walls, and the characters are on the stage." I paused to mime a three-sided box. "The fourth wall is the invisible wall facing the audience. The characters the actors are playing can't see out. But we can see inside."

The monk's brow furrowed slightly. "Then who is our audience?"

I opened my mouth to blurt the obvious answer—'us'— but halted when I realized something. "I... actually don't know any more. About a year ago, I'd have said it was the people on Earth. But now, I don't know who's watching, or if anyone's watching."

"Hrrn." Vash scratched his chin. "And if OUROS is not aware of itself, then it is not watching us either, is it?"

"Nope. And if it's not the observer, then I guess it's the stage." I jumped as my HUD chirruped with a small notification. *[You have gained +1 Wisdom!]*

Vash let the silence hang, looking up at the brightening sky. His face was ruddy from the cold, breath frosting on every exhalation. "OUROS must not just manage this world. It must balance the positions of the stars and Erruku, as well."

"Yeah. For all I know, Ryuko—the corporation who made Archemi—simulated a whole universe."

"Is that possible?"

"With the right supercomputers, I don't see why not." I shrugged. "Scientists simulate big bang scenarios and shit all the time."

Vash's eyes narrowed as he tried to follow along. "Then logically, your Earth may be a virtual reality just like this one. Perhaps existence is an endless pearl, layer upon layer of realities created by ever more sophisticated beings with even more exceptional 'supercomputers'. "

"Nah. Earth's the only planet where we've ever discovered life, dude. And believe me, we've tried. We've set out hundreds of probes into space and built a couple of space stations, and we've found sweet F.A out there."

"That lends evidence to my theory. It does not refute it," Vash replied. "If every star out there is truly a sun like ours, then we should see life crawling out of every spare nook and cranny of the universe. But there are limitations you have briefly touched on: processing power and storage space, and other things I've heard you discuss with Rin. That means there must be a limit to the complexity of our reality, correct?"

I shrugged. "I mean…Yeah. An instance of Archemi can only host two thousand Starborn, apparently."

"Then the fact that Earth's peoples were not able to find other worlds with life seems to lend truth to the idea that Earth itself is one of these 'virtual realities', does it not?"

"Earth? A simulation?" I laughed—nervously, this time, because I couldn't actually think of a way he could be wrong. "Okay, well, that's my existential crisis for the day."

[You gain +1 Wisdom!]

Gee, thanks, I thought back. After the weird FETCH:ERROR stuff, I wasn't sure I totally trusted Navigail any more.

"It leads me to wonder where Squalor and the Drachan fit into this design," Vash said. "Why would the Architects create and introduce such destructive, demonic creatures? Beings of pure evil, that strip entire worlds?"

"The depressing answer is to create conflict and challenges for Starborn like me," I replied, pausing in my work to stare at the blank snow. "They're a boss to fight, a goal you work towards."

"And the worlds that fell to them before this one?" Vash cocked his head. "If what you say is true, and OUROS 'simulated' all of this... does that mean that it created other worlds which perished in cold despair, like my people did here?"

And just like that, Vash ripped the lid off a barrel of ethical worms and kicked it right over the fucking floor. "... I don't know. Before Archemi, there was no, like, moral dimension to a story like this one. It's been done thousands of times before. Every Final Fantasy game, nearly every MMO I can think of, they all have world-destroying endgame bosses. I'm starting to think Ryuko didn't know what the fuck they were doing when they made this place."

"That would be the more cheerful of the two options," Vash said.

I gave him the side-eye. "What do you mean?"

"If Ryuko created a universe with suffering on this scale out of enthusiastic ignorance of the consequences for those who live and love here, that is one thing." The monk chopped a brick out of the snow around us, set it in the wall, and smoothed it over. "But if my erstwhile creators made it this way by design, out of some sense of malice? Well... that is quite another story, isn't it?"

CHAPTER 55

Karalti returned with a pair of antelope. We took a single fatty haunch of meat for ourselves, roasting it on the hot stones with salt and spices until it was tender and smoky, dripping with juices. I went to bed with a full belly and the cold wind whistling over the hood of my bedroll, still thinking about what Vash had said.

If Jacob's attitude was typical of Ryuko's developers, then they really hadn't anticipated people like Vash evolving out of their AI and its subroutines and databases. They'd really just believed it was just a hyper-realistic virtual reality sim, the next logical step forward in immersive entertainment. But what if Michael and Steve had known otherwise? Ororgael seemed to know that human data was capable of personhood—he just didn't care.

But what had my brother known about Archemi? About OUROS? About Squalor? Corruption? NPCs like Tsunda, and players like Violetta?

And what had he known about me?

Sleep came restlessly, punctured by fleeting dreams of war. I started out walking alongside a tank, keeping lookout as it rumbled through a decimated Indonesian town. A second dream overlaid it, playing simultaneously. I was jumping out of a plane over Buenos Aries, half a world away from the

Crescent Front. It was the conflict between the scenes that woke me up.

"Urrgh." I slid out into a cloak of semi-darkness. Karalti's scent hit me like a splash of water to the face. She was curled around my bedroll, her wing resting over me. The canopy of membrane trapped the perfume in the warm cave formed by her body. My skin tingled, my fingertips hummed, and my nerves lit up like a Christmas tree as I breathed in deep, hungry gulps of air. She smelled incredible. Powerful. Desirable.

It was that magical time again. Karalti was officially in her second heat.

My dragon stirred as I pushed out from under her wing, yawning and stretching. Vash was already awake, dismantling the firepit. If the cloud of pheromones was affecting him, he wasn't showing it.

"So, what's the plan after we get home?" I asked him. "If you need to take some leave, just say the word."

"No. Leave from my duties is the opposite of what I need right now." Vash shook his head, brows furrowed. His eyes were red and swollen. The battered earring he'd recovered from Temu had been added into one of his braids. I doubted he'd gotten any sleep.

"What do you want to do, then?" I rubbed the edge of Karalti's wing, sticking close to her.

"For my own sanity, I must immerse myself in the joyful act of living for a while, which for me, means going to Karhad and assisting with the healing of the sick. I will be one of the healers your quest requires." Vash kicked dirt and ashes over the warm cooking stones. "I also have a proposal for you. It will require Suri's consent."

"Go on."

"I wish to take Jacob out of his cell and down to the city to assist us in treating the victims of thornlung plague," Vash said. "If he is capable of reforming himself, he will only do so if he is exposed to empathy."

I frowned. "Rin suggested the same thing."

"Rin is wiser than her youth would suggest," Vash replied. "Compassion is the only possible path for him, unless you wish to end up with another Tsunda."

"Another Tsunda?"

"Tsunda was mad before she this being, this 'Squalor' infected her mind." Vash finished up by laying the slate tablets over the cold fire, dusting his hands off. "Jacob currently sits on the fine edge between transformation and insanity. Loneliness is toxic to the human mind, Dragozin. What if this entity, this demon, begins to whisper in his ears? Tempting him, offering him power, enabling him with magic we cannot control or understand?"

I grimaced. "I get it, alright? No need to preach. I'll get in touch with Suri sometime today."

Vash tilted his head. "You do not believe it will work."

"No. Not really. And even if rehabbing him does work, I don't know if he deserves it."

The baru studied me for a few moments. "What is it about him that especially repels you?"

"Is 'everything' an answer? Even if he was acting in innocence like he claims, the guy gives me the creeps." I shrugged.

"You okay?" A lush wave of scent billowed past me as Karalti's neck snaked, and she gently nuzzled my neck and head with the tip of her snout. Vash sniffed, hawked, then paused. He sniffed again, frowning up at Karalti and I realized something. His nose had been stuffy from the cold and from crying. He hadn't smelled her until now.

"Interesting." He cleared his throat and turned away. "I think you should commune with Suri as soon as possible. Now, maybe, while I go and take care of the morning libations."

His remark was innocent enough, but I felt something dark and dangerously competitive press against the back of my eyes. I reached up to cradle the end of Karalti's muzzle in my arms, squeezing gently. "Let me see if Suri's awake. She usually sleeps in."

"Indeed. Excuse me." Vash shouldered his pack, then set off at a quick walk. Upwind of us.

"Hector?" Karalti made a low trilling around in her throat, rearing her head to look down at me. *"Are you... are you jealous of Vash?"*

"Jealous? No." I jerked my shoulders back, fighting the urge to stare daggers at him as he left. "Just don't want him or any of my other friends getting funny ideas about you this time of the month. Queen dragon pheromones are a hell of a drug."

Karalti's eyes hooded, and she smacked her jaws with satisfaction, laying her head back down and rubbing the base of her horn against my lower back. *"You're jeaaaaalous."*

I grumbled to myself as I pulled up the Message Center. The unnamed <ADMIN> email was still sitting there, unread, along with two others. I brought up Suri's PM history, patched through, and waited for her to pick up. To my surprise, she actually did.

"Hey," I jammed my hands down where pockets normally went on a pair of jeans, and growled when I remembered there were none. "How's Cutthroat going?"

"Tired. Pissy. She's got nine eggs, Hector." Suri sounded tired and pissy herself, a little breathless over the comms. "We're just passing over the Bashir now. ETA is in twenty-four hours. How's things at the fort?"

"We're not at the fort. We just handled a difficult quest. Difficult as in, I'm probably going to have nightmares about it." I rubbed the back of my neck, looking out over the plateau. "Listen, I wanted to run something past you. But you might not like it much."

A pause. "I'm listening."

"Both Rin and Vash want to take Jacob to the Riverside District and have him do some community service. They've both nagged me about it, but I told 'em it's your decision. Do you trust them to start rehabbing him, or do you want to wait and handle it yourself?"

Another pause. Longer, this time.

"How are we going to make sure he doesn't get away?" Suri asked flatly.

"Good question. I think all we can really do is make sure he's got the usual kinds of field trip security. Visible clothing, leg chains, a good escort," I replied. "Maybe a leash."

"What about a bracelet or something with the Mother's Coin inside it?" Karalti asked.

I blinked a couple of times. I'd forgotten all about the Mother's Coin. It was a minor artifact we'd looted from Davri the Laundress, the crime boss we'd killed in Dalim, and it worked like a tagging device.

"Karalti just suggested a tracking device," I said. "In case you didn't hear that."

"I did. And I think that's a bloody good idea," Suri's voice was stiff, but calm. "I also know it's about the only option we've got, short of bricking him up inside a wall and feeding him through a tube. Go ahead and figure out some kind of program for him. See how he responds when he's dealing with people he has to actually relate to."

"Alright. And I'll make a tracking anklet and weld it on to him myself. I don't want him near any of my citizens without us knowing exactly where he is." I leaned back against Karalti, resisting the urge to rub against her like a randy cat. "I love you, okay? We'll see you soon, and then we'll go kick some huge wormy butt."

Suri laughed, briefly. "Yeah, alright. Assuming I'm not leading a train of little hooklings around the castle."

We closed the call, and I sighed with relief. I rubbed my forehead and made to stand up, and my message center chirped. I pulled it over to see Suri had sent a follow up message. 'Love you too'.

I couldn't help but smile. It was pretty sure it was the first time we'd said it to each other in as many words.

CHAPTER 56

We dropped Vash back at the castle, and while he coordinated a security detail and the medicine wagons, I went to the smithy. Half an hour of improvised crafting later, I had gained some basic levels in Metalworking and had successfully created Archemi's first [Prison Tag Anklet], a welded manacle we soldered around Jacob's ankle. It was a pound of solid iron, and unless he was willing to cut his own leg off, he wasn't getting rid of it.

Once they were on their way, Karalti and I left for an overnight retreat to her favorite place in Myszno, just the two of us.

We appeared over a mountain hot spring fed by a cascade of steaming, water-filled limestone terraces. The water was a brilliant blue, steaming into the air. There was a grotto cavern filled with soft pads of brilliant green moss. At the shallow side of the lake was a beach of sorts, a bare area of mineralized rock turned white by limestone. Beyond that was nothing but miles of wild alpine forest. Pines rustled, birds trilled and whooped from the trees, insects hummed, squirrels flicked their tails as they scampered over the branches. I breathed deeply of the crisp, fresh air as Karalti touched down, and felt the muscles of my back and shoulders relax.

"I'm glad you suggested this. We really need it after that cheery little adventure." I slid to her elbow and hopped down, landing lightly on the feathery grass. "God… the talk I had with Vash after we left the boneyard was fucking intense."

"I overheard your thoughts while you were talking. I think I'm starting to understand it all." Karalti stretched and yawned, flicking her wings and shaking herself out. *"There's like a big stew pot full of people, right? And the pot mixes the people's souls up, so every person who's born is like a cup of soup from the pot."*

"Pretty much. Though I think the soup pot is slowly getting bigger as more people here become self-aware."

Karalti stretched, rising high on her feet, and shifted smoothly to her humanoid shape. My heart caught in my throat as the light cleared, revealing her standing on small bare feet, lovely and nude.

"Am I made from these people?" she asked. *"Am I made from the Athena-thing?"*

"Yeah. You are." I drifted toward her. She didn't move as I reached for her, stroking her collarbone, her breasts, the sides of her ribcage. "But you're absolutely, one-hundred percent my favorite cup of soup."

Karalti let out a delighted, barking laugh, then turned and skipped toward the water. I lunged forward a step, nose working, then remembered I was still wearing twenty pounds of armor. I unequipped everything, watching her hungrily as she waded into the lake until she was up to her thighs.

"You were super mad at Vash. I've never seen you look at another man like that before." Karalti glanced over her shoulder at me, her eyes dark with heated amusement. *"Not even Soma."*

"I'm not jealous of Vash. I just didn't want to have to fight him because we both got tweaked on dragon musk and started chasing your ass across the plateau." Nude, I splashed in after her. "That perfect, bitable, smooth, pear-shaped ass."

"You like this, huh?" Karalti's lips quirked. She reached back and lifted her butt with her hands.

"Tidbit… you do not know what monster you are about to unleash." I was doing everything short of actually drooling as I slid into the water, angling for her like a crocodile.

"You want it? You better catch it." Her eyes turned to sly slits in her face as she jiggled it a couple of times.

I got my footing on the bottom of the shallows, then launched straight out of the water. Karalti let out a shrill peal of laughter, diving to the side. But she still didn't have any magically-enhanced leaping abilities, and could only get so far before I caught her.

"Death from above! "Victory at sea!" I picked her up by the waist, spun around with her, and bombed us both into the water as she squealed and flailed. "Yarrr, the booty be mine!"

"EEEK!" Karalti twisted in my arms, laughing wildly. *"HEY! No fair!"*

I was laughing too hard to keep my grip on her. She pushed away, fleeing for the shore, and I leaped for her again…

only to be sent flying as she caught me by the arm and flipped me over her back, sending me crashing into the shallows

"The pirates of the Fish Empire have clearly never battled a dragon who knows martial arts!" She laughed, splashing me in the face as I surfaced. *"Pew pew! Take that!"*

"Arrrgh, water! My only weakness! Hrrbllbhg!" I enthusiastically enacted a dramatic likeness of my death by drowning as my dragon giggled with delight. But once I was under the water, I swam right at her, tackling her at the waist and dragging her against my body. Her skin was slick against mine, her thighs shaking as she felt me press up against her belly. The brief contact passed between us like an electric charge, and the blood began to pound in my temples and cock.

"I know you need me to chase you." Before Karalti could wriggle away, I caught her wrist in mine and stared deeply into her eyes. "I know you want me to catch you, claim you, the way a bull dragon claims his mate. But your first time is going to hurt at first, Karalti. If we get rough, I need you to tell me that's okay."

Karalti's eyes grew very wide and very bright. They were bleeding to pure silver as the heat took her, her pupils dilating. Her mouth and cheeks were flushed, body tense with the need to start the mating chase. *"It will hurt?"*

"You're a virgin," I said. "Every girl I've ever heard talk about their first time says it hurt."

She licked water off her lips, and stopped straining to flee. *"It's okay, Hector. My soul might be that of a human, but I am not a human girl. I am a woman of the Solonkratsu, and this is our way. This is what I want."*

This is what I want. I repeated her words in my mind, then finally let go of my own reins. I squeezed her wrist and pulled her tightly against my chest, leaning down to bite the side of her neck.

"Ohh..." Karalti melted, the lean curves of her body molding against mine. Her breasts pressed against my chest, nipples stiffening, as I let go of her skin and hungrily claimed her mouth with mine. Her double-pulse beat under my fingers, quickening as I half-pushed, half carried her toward the shore. When we were barely ankle-deep, she pushed me away and danced back, breathing hard. Her pearly skin flushed with warmth. As soon as the air touched her skin, she came up in goosebumps.

"Think you can keep up?" Her teeth were chattering with anticipation as she backed up from me along the shoreline.

"I KNOW I can keep up." I wove in a crouch and lunged, but she was faster. She sprinted for the treeline, trailing a cloud of intoxicating scent.

"Are you suuuuure?" Karalti laughed joyously as she bolted through the trees, leaping gracefully over rocks and ferns. I ran after her, following the teasing flick of her hair. I gained ground by vaulting a boulder and tumbling into a roll on the other side, nearly close enough to grab a fistful of braids and swing her around. She dodged out of the way of my grasping fingers, veering left toward a cascade of shallow spring-fed terraces. She leaped into the first of them, throwing

up a spray of steaming water as she ran to the end and vaulted down to the next one.

"You'll run out of stamina before I do!" I sprung forward like a cricket, landing right in front of her before she could drop to the next terrace. Karalti let out a high, manic peal of laughter as I snatched her around the waist—then teleported out of my arms, back up to the edge of the cliff.

"Pbffft!" She blew her tongue and thumbed her nose at me, sprinting back into the trees.

"Hey! No fair!" I changed track, bounding up the hill, but when I reached the top she was gone—I could hear her stifled giggles from somewhere, but the sound bounced and echoed out of sight.

I drew deep sniffs of air as I felt along the Bond, and between the two of them, I picked a direction and ran. There was no sign of her, no sound other than the wind through the trees. The scent trail ended at the edge of the mineral lake. For a moment, I thought I'd simply backtracked, until I saw a shadow move between a pair of cedars.

My eyes narrowed. I dropped into a stalking crouch, sticking to the underbrush. Karalti tensed beside one of the concealing trees, searching for me, her nostrils flexing... and let out a startled 'eek!' when I bounced out of concealment and took her to ground. She squealed as I covered her body with mine, arching, straining and struggling against me.

"Hector!" Her skin was feverish, spiking with heat as we wrestled. Her lust thrummed through the Bond in growing waves, a feedback loop of primal need that made me snarl and

pin her down. She panted, drawing breath open-mouthed as I kicked her legs apart and wedged myself between them. She struggled and thumped her head back, her breasts lifting up against my chest, muscles taut. She fought me with every ounce of energy she had, right until the moment where I roughly thrust inside her.

Her telepathic scream rang through my head and nerves like a lightning strike: a little pleasure, but a lot more pain as she stretched around me for the first time. I froze for a second, barely catching her fist as she swung at me, but I couldn't stop myself from moving. She was hot and tight and sweet, and even as the sharp tearing pain played along the Bond like a shrill violin, she bucked her hips and pulled me closer.

"I want it!" She buried her face against my neck, crying out on every thrust as the pain of her first time peaked and faded under the potent combination of ecstasy and adrenaline. *"I want it, I want it!"*

I felt about ten feet tall and five feet long as I grabbed her by the hips and pulled her bodily onto my cock. It was not gentle, it was not sweet – I fucked her like a beast, conscious only of her voice, her breath, her smell, the grip of her cunt. She had never told me, but I knew just by the sensation that she wasn't built like a human woman down there: her clit was internal, in a hooded pouch about half an inch deep in her body, and every time I backed out and thrust into her, she gasped with growing pleasure. As her orgasm built, so did mine: I knelt up in the ferns, clutching her by the thighs, and closed my eyes as I lost myself in it.

Karalti let out a piercing screech, writhing as she climaxed. I learned something else about her, then: she had exceptional muscular control. Her pelvis contracted like a hand, trapping me inside of her body and squeezing back from tip to base. I shuddered over her, gasping, hips jerking in a sympathetic climax with no actual release. My eyes flickered open and met hers, and the world around us vanished.

The violet color had returned, but her pupils were so huge that her eyes were almost black. They sucked me down, as irresistible as gravity, and she kissed me, biting my lips. We were still fucking, her ankles hooked around my back, her body gripping mine. This time, I led the climax, coming inside of her with a sharp, stifled sound of pleasure. Karalti's back arched, and she gasped as she experienced the sensation of male pleasure directly for the first time.

"Oh... oh wow..." She breathed. *"It's like... it's like a push! I felt it push all the way through your body into mine."*

"Just like you pull me into yours." Panting for breath, I leaned down and licked the sweat from her chest, tracing her collarbone with my tongue. *"Did I hurt you?"*

"Only briefly." She mouthed my neck, biting gently as she held me inside her. *"I felt something tear."*

I paused for a moment, leaning up to look down at her. *"Do you need me to stop?"*

"Take me to the water." She gazed back up at me, languid with pleasure. *"Take me into the cave, and do it until we can't anymore."*

Shivering with exertion, I found an inner reserve of stamina and gathered her up into my arms, picking her up. Karalti looped her arms around my neck, hanging on as I walked back with her to the hot spring. The cave was warm from the steaming waterfalls that trickled over the entry, full of soft moss. I lay her down there on her back, where she caught my face in her hands and tipped it down so I met her eyes, and this time as I looked into them, I saw *her* – her intelligence, her insight, her passion for food, the instinctive love she felt for children, the warmth she felt for her friends, the pleasure she found in martial arts, her growing spirituality, her desire to learn how to make jewelry... The Bond, as intense and pure as I'd ever felt it.

It was dark by the time we finally pulled apart, bathed in sweat, exhausted, disheveled, and completely and utterly satisfied with our labors. We lay facing each other, our hands and knees touching.

"Wow," she breathed, after a few minutes had passed. *"Human sex is pretty great."*

"Yeah. Yeah, it is." I swallowed, still trying to catch my breath. "I'm wondering how I'm going to go back to Suri after this."

"You'll go back to her because you love her too, and because I only do this once a month." She smiled at me.

I wheezed a laugh. It was about all I had left in me after five straight hours of fucking. I had several minor debuffs: Hungry, Thirsty, and 'Miscellaneous Exertion', which was a pretty classy way of saying 'Fuxhausted'. "You, uhh... you take care of your own business more than once a month, though. Right?"

"Yeah. But that doesn't mean I want a partner for it." Karalti yawned and stretched, flopping over onto her back. *"When I'm doing that, I don't really think about you or anyone else. It's more like an itch I gotta scratch sometimes. When you're mating with Suri, I get the urge... but I don't want to be involved."*

"Huh." I smiled at her. "Makes sense to me."

She wiggled over to me and cuddled up. *"Can I ask you a favor?"*

"Mm?"

"You brought food with you, right?"

"Yep. Sure did."

"Can you... can you feed me?" Her lips parted, and her eyes darkened again. *"I REALLY want you to feed me after this."*

I arched my eyebrows. "You mean feed you like the way you wanted Suri to feed Cutthroat?"

Karalti pouted, and shoved at my chest as I chortled.

"Fingers are fine," she grumbled. *"I just... mmm... let's do that, and go to sleep in here. It's so nice."*

"We'll get all wrinkly if we sleep on the moss here," I replied. "Come on: let's go pitch a fire, and I'll feed the Tidbit tidbits."

"Yeah!" Karalti pushed herself up to her hands and awkwardly swayed up to her feet. I wasn't doing much better. It took a couple of goes to roll up to sit, and when she offered me a hand, I accepted it. We hobbled out into the open like a couple of old people, clutching our backs and groaning.

"Are we going to be okay after this?" I asked her, as we slowly headed for the soft grass beyond the mineralized bank. "You and me, I mean? I loved this, but... you know. I don't want to change what we have, either."

Karalti's eyes danced as she plopped down onto the meadow, huffing a soft breath through her teeth. "It's changed, and it'll keep changing. Just like we will. I think we'll grow and change for as long as we're both alive."

I bent down to kiss her on the top of her head. "Then here's to us both living for a long, long time."

***

I woke to the sound of a Message Alert. It was the early morning, the sun just starting to rise through the morning fog that hung over the lake. Grumbling, I rolled over onto my back and picked up the call. "'Llo?"

"Hey there, lover boy." Suri's voice purred into my ear as if she were speaking right beside it. "I'm back with Gar, safe and sound in Kalla Sahasi. How'd things go?"

"Things?" I repeated, laying my forearm over my eyes. Karalti burrowed her head into my armpit with a soft chirp, still sound asleep. "Yeah. Things are, umm, thingy."

"Vash told me it was Karalti's time of the month, and you two went and took a night out to preen each other."

669

"Preening, yeah. Guess you could call it that." Thanks to the magic of videogame physics, I didn't feel any of the aching or fatigue now that I'd slept... ten hours? Damn. "How're you? How's Cutthroat?"

"She's decided that she is the new captain of the Strelitzia," Suri replied. "We aren't getting her out until those eggs hatch. Gar's just given up. We're in the parlor now, and he's drinking all your brandy."

I had a momentary mental image of Gar standing at the bar, sobbing and chugging. "Oh, well, you know. Nothing reminds me of my first time like a guy crying."

Suri laughed, snorted, laughed some more.

"I'm a terrible person, Suri," I sighed, stretching out. Karalti and I had hooked our sleeping rolls together. It was warm and cosy and I really didn't want to leave, but I had a feeling that duty was just about ready to call. "Any word from Rin?"

"Yeah. She said to call you and Special-K back to base. She was able to make the weapons we need. The ships are ready and are at the castle skyport, waiting for departure."

My eyelids fluttered open, as I suddenly thought back to Ororgael's smug, sneering voice. *You will have nothing, and you are – and always will be – too weak and stupid to catch up... There's nothing you can do to stop what's coming.*

I also remembered what I'd said back to him. *The fuck there isn't.*

670

"Give us an hour," I said, shifting up to lean on my elbows. "Make sure everyone and everything is ready to go. We'll leave as soon as Karalti and I return to base. It's time to show these Void-bitten assholes what we're made of."

CHAPTER 57

The Bashir Desert: 4 Days Later

We saw the maelstrom as soon as we crossed the mountains.

The howling pillar of black sand was half a mile across, soaring into the otherwise-clear desert sky. The Stranged storm generated its own lightning, bursts of light snapping out like whips. From inside, we could hear the distorted, haunting roars of the Voidwyrm Empress.

I stood neck and neck with the Court Mage of Litvy, Szonja the Living Flame. She was a striking older woman in her sixties, with very long, lustrous grey hair and blue-violet eyes, elegantly attired in red and dark burnt orange robes. Her name had less to do with her appearance, and more to do with her ability. She was an Arch Elementalist, a graduate of Jeun's magical college, and her specializations were fire and air magic.

"There is a tear in the fabric of reality. That is what is causing the storm." The sorceress lowered her spyglass, lips pursed. "Whatever foul magic Hyland used to create this rift, he cast it from a single point. Do you see the terminus of the cloud?"

I opened my eyes wide, zooming my vision to look at the top of the whirling tempest. There was, in fact, a single point of origin there. "Sure do."

"To permanently stop this storm, we must repair that singularity." She stowed the glass in her Inventory and nodded. "This is a job for multiple Aetheric specialists."

"You can't fix it?" I asked.

"Not without cooking my brains like a boiled pudding, no." The woman dropped her hands. She wore two magic channeling gauntlets. One was sleeker and more streamlined; the other heavier, with large banded reservoirs for mana. "What I can do is create a counter-storm. The counter-storm will temporarily abate the Weirding we see before us. But I will not be able to hold it for long."

I narrowed my eyes, squinting at the horizon. "How long?"

She sighed. "Perhaps ten minutes. Fifteen, if I don't run out of mana or sheer physical energy."

"Then ten minutes is what we've got. All we really have to do is get her out of there." I rolled my neck, glancing back to the armada. We had twelve ships: my pair of Bathory-class, the *Lockhart* and the *Campbell;* two new Destroyers, the *Salamander* and the *Gae Bolg*, plus Lord Soma's personal fleet. Mounted underneath us on the keel of the *Salamander* was a huge brass contraption that resembled a cross between a church organ and a missile battery. Large thin-walled pipes flowed up and around a graceful feminine torso, the housing for the mana that fueled Archemi's first [Symphonic Array]. Rin had shown me a recording of it effortlessly demolishing a derelict building. Now, we were going to see if it was capable of demolishing the world record holder for 'Biggest Maggot' on Archemi. Both the *Gae Bolg* and Soma's flagship, the

Aspern, had similar weapons equipped. All the ships were loaded with cannons and mortars, and as much ammunition as we could carry. The crews were lean, with no other troops on board. There was a good chance we would lose several ships.

"Eight hundred yards!" The ship's watchstanders bellowed back to the rest of the crew. "Ease to hover!"

"It is time, my lord. Go to your dragon and prepare." Szonja straightened, looking steadily out across the shimmering desert. "When you see the storm abate, move as fast as you can. I will give everything I have for king and country, but I am only one woman, and this is a powerful force we are seeing here."

"Understood. And if you feel like you're about to blow a gasket, stop immediately and we'll call a retreat. I'm not about to lose one of the best mages in Myszno to an overgrown caterpillar." I gave her a brisk nod, checked all my battle operation windows, and opened up the group chat with Suri, Rin and Gar. "*Salamander* to all stations, Szonja is about to work her magic. All ships ready to flank. We have to hit this bitch where it hurts and we have to get it on the first try. The Voidwyrm won't give us a second chance."

"Roger that, *Aspern* on standby," Suri replied crisply. "Our Symphonic Array is all warmed up and ready to fire."

"Copy that, *Gae Bolg* armed and in position, standing by." Gar's radio voice was as clear and calm as Suri's.

"Yeah! We're down here with the Symphonic Array, and it's looking great! Aboard the *Salamander*, I mean. Copy?" Rin stammered, her voice bubbly and nervous all at once.

"We're really gonna have to teach you how to do battlefield comms someday, Rin." Suri's tone warmed with gentle humor. "Good luck, Hector. Try not to kill yourself."

"No guarantees," I replied. "I'll bring you back a souvenir if I end up buying a farm."

Gar let out a harsh chuckle. "Hah! Go get 'em, ace."

The three of us were spread over the largest ships in the fleet—the ships leading the maneuvers that would partly encircle the sandworm and start firing on her once Karalti and I led her from the storm into the open battlefield. Assuming we weren't eaten.

"Okay, Tidbit. We're up." I jogged back down the ship's deck toward my dragon. *"You ready?"*

"Sure am." Karalti unfolded from her dragonloaf position, getting to her feet. She linked her fingers and stretched her wings out, casting the entire stern into shadow before she beat them stiffly against her ribs. *"A boss that's a hundred and two levels higher than me? No sweat."*

"A hundred levels higher than you, but the same level as our armada if we all work together." I bounded up to her back and swung myself down into a kneel between her shoulders. We were full up on potions. I had healing and stamina draughts brewed for Karalti as well, three 1-gallon jars of each stowed on her saddle. There was little question that we were not a high enough level for this boss fight, and if we got caught on our own against the sandworm, we were dead. I had vivid, unpleasant memories of watching its laser beam cut Karalti's shadow copy in half. *"I saw what the Symphonic Array did to*

that building in Litvy, though. Blew it fucking sky-high. We've got this."

"Yeah! Team Karalti! Now with extra singing!" Karalti reared her head and roared, her voice blasting through the air like a clarion. It was a signal to the ships—and to Szonja, who rooted herself in her magic circle at the front of the ship, and began to cast her spell.

Karalti bellowed again as she launched from the stern, swooping into the hot desert air. She barrel-rolled under the *Salamander*, beating her wings only once she had the room to wheel and stretch out. I checked over my shoulder to make sure we were below the level of the ships—and out of the line of fire of the Symphonic Array. The way the pipes were arranged, they projected sound in a very narrow band. Unless you were in its line of fire, you heard nothing but a faint HMMMMM. If you were in its line of fire, well... you probably heard that, but louder, as the weapon turned you into a fine pink mist.

"Let's run over this one last time. We get in there, we bait the worm, we get out." I worked my fingers on the saddle grips. *"We're nothing but bait until the ships make contact. No attacking, no nothing. I don't know if dragons bound to Starborn can come back from the dead, and I really don't want to learn."*

"Me either. Knowing my luck, I'll respawn in the Eyrie." Karalti groaned telepathically. Physically, she was focused—pacing herself as the cyclical wind of the storm drove the air up under her wings. She let it guide her course, blowing her up and around the edge of the funnel.

The bow of the *Salamander* was glowing. Szonja's circle of power, anchored between three pylons that fed mana into the enchantment, danced and crackled with electricity. The sorceress raised her arms as the power built into a miniature version of the black maelstrom, but spinning in reverse. Karalti banked around the pillar of hissing black sand, navigating the turbulence with grim determination.

There was a deep rumble from the earth as red sand lifted and rose into the air. I could smell ozone—and then an awful, earsplitting shriek tore through the sky. It was like two pieces of rusty metal being scraped slowly across one another, dialed to max volume. There was a clap, a flash, and then a roar as the maelstrom collapsed under the weight of the sorceress's magic. The wind chopped every which way, blowing Karalti up like a piece of dandelion fluff in a stiff breeze.

"Jesus!" I clung on at the last second as my dragon yelped, tumbling wildly. I lost direction for a moment as Karalti intentionally stalled, rolled over to her back, and twisted into a controlled dive against the blasts of air that had propelled us up. Clinging to her back like a possum, I looked past her neck and oriented on the scene ahead: Withering Rose, half buried, and the worm coiling over and through the wreckage like the world-eating serpent out of Norse mythology, Jörmungandr.

"AIIIIIEEEEE" The Voidwyrm Empress reared its sightless head, slithering over the half-buried Warsinger. Its maw unfurled like a gruesome blossom of black spines, the sensory tentacles emerging to taste the air as Karalti flew straight toward it. I got back up into my combat kneel, teeth clenched, and concentrated on my vision.

"Hey! Do you like snacks! Look at me!" Karalti bellowed wordlessly aloud as she broadcast her telepathic speech. *"Tasty, tasty dragon! Get it while it's hot!"*

The Voidwyrm swung unerringly toward us, tentacles lashing. I tensed as its throat opened, revealing a fathomless black tunnel. The creature's neck-hole was at least four times wider than the spine-lined gauntlet of Lahati's Tomb. Six lines of traffic could have driven side by side down it, like the worst freeway tunnel in the world. She let out a piercing cry toward the sky, then plunged her head into the sand. The earth shook as she burrowed down, smashing through the brittle glass spires that surrounded the corpse of Withering Rose. As she did, her HP ring appeared.

"Get ready to teleport." I tracked it as it wove under the surface of the desert. Karalti couldn't easily look down—the shape of her muzzle gave her blind spots in the places that the sandworm was targeting with predatory precision. I stared as the bulging earth swelled like water far below. "Wait for it... wait for it... NOW!"

The mana in Karalti's body surged, and she teleported about five hundred feet up as the sandworm burst from underneath us, tentacles reaching forward.

I leaned with my dragon as she rolled out of the way. "Suri, Rin, Gar: can you get a bead on her?"

"We need her further out from the storm!" Suri said, her voice tense. "Lure her toward the fleet!"

"I really don't know if that's a good idea!" I clung on as Karalti triggered Split Turn and darted away from the

678

Voidwyrm as she rose like a cresting whale before sliding back into sands.

"We have to! The Symphonic Array doesn't have as much range as the cannons!" Rin added. "You need to be within two hundred yards!"

"Okay, then I'm going down!" The dragon winged over into a spiraling dive. *"Keep spotting for me, Hector! I have to know where the ships are!"*

I replied by focusing, holding onto the saddle like a windsurfer. I tracked the ships—and then the worm, glancing wildly behind us as the Empress surged through the sand behind us. *"Worm is below us on our five o'clock."*

Karalti's shadow raced along the ground, the rippling hump of sand gaining closer every passing second. I began to silently urge Karalti up: but she ignored me, pulling her wings in and streamlining into the dive. My dragon was fast—the Empress was faster. I watched in horror as the titanic head of the thing rose up, throat gaping, tentacles the size of subway trains writhing out of its maw toward us.

"Brace for gravity!" Karalti snarled with effort, and Split Turned straight up into the air.

The maneuver was so hard and so sharp that it drove the wind out of my lungs. My vision throbbed, greying around the edges, but the Gs were just within range of my mutations. Heat turned to cold as Karalti reached the end of the boost and teleported vertically, reappearing high above the Voidwyrm Empress as it dove for us. The colossal creature slammed its belly into the ground, thrashing and whirling back around. It let out an unearthly shriek and drove itself up to snatch us from the sky—standing upright in the killzone formed by the airships.

The Symphonic Arrays charged with a high ringing sound, gathering a nimbus of golden light centered on the figureheads. Light bled from their eyes, mouths, and expanding seams on their skin as the devices reached full charge, then fired.

We couldn't hear them – but we felt them, as Karalti see-sawed with the expanding shockwave that exploded from the sonic harpoons. The Sandworm Empress wailed as they struck her, sending molten cracks through her black carapace.

[Siren Array deals 57,481 damage to Voidwyrm Empress!]
[Voidwyrm Empress HP: 982,519/1,040,000]

"Thank goodness! They work!" Rin cried excitedly.

"What do you mean 'Thank goodness'? Didn't you test these?" Gar snapped.

"No! I mean, yes, kind of! I mean, we didn't get to test them on sandworms!"

"This is an experiment!?" Gar snarled something in Spanish. I only recognized one word, and yes, it was *puta*.

"This thing has over a million HP!?" Karalti yelped. *"Hector-!"*

"Hold steady! That one barrage chopped nearly four percent off the fucking thing! Hit it again! I roared over comms, tensing with excitement. "We can do this!"

The sandworm did not like losing that much HP in one single attack. She forgot us, pivoting her mouth toward the ships. My eyes widened as I saw a familiar ball of vantablack darkness build up within her jaws, gathering with coils of energy. Karalti read my mind as I sighted down, diving for the Empress at top speed. The dragon's lungs filled, her jaws gaped, and she sprayed a plume of fire right along the back of one writhing tentacle.

[Ghost Fire deals 1124 damage!]

Our puny attack was enough to distract the Voidwyrm just slightly, allowing the ships to peel away from the shrill beam of void energy that tore through the air. All but one of the freighters managed to get away as the beam slashed from the earth to the heavens, tracking Karalti as she tilted her wings. The freighter's engines whined as it careened, smoking, toward the sands. It was the *Lockhart.*

"*Fuck!*" I hissed.

Karalti heaved for breath, blinking out of existence and reappearing high over the ships and the Empress herself. The great worm twisted, surging up underneath us, only to be struck from all sides by blasts from the Symphonic Arrays. It let out a warbling, ear-splitting roar as sections of its black chitin armor shattered, and knobby protrusions all over the worm's body flared open, exposing simmering orange ichor.

"It's catching its breath through those spiracles!" Gar's voice crackled over PM. "Get the artillery on 'em while the Launchers cool down!"

The ships, already to either side of the writhing worm, opened fire on his command. Cannons boomed, mortars whined, and the voidwyrm began to let out piercing, squealing cries loud enough to make my eardrums pulse. The notifications from the artillery were not measured in individual attacks: instead, Navigail gave me a Mass Combat DPS reading: we were hitting the Voidwyrm for 1041 points per second of constant fire, but when the Symphonic Arrays went off, it jumped to over 50K. At this rate, we were picking off 1% of its HP per minute.

"Give me one of those stamina potions! While we have the chance!" Karalti wheeled up higher, her wings rippling.

"Right." I took one out of her inventory and crawled up along her neck to her head. Gripping one of her horns, I leaned out and jammed the neck of the clay bottle into her jaws. She tilted her body to the left and climbed, letting physics do the work of dumping the potion down her throat. When she leveled out, she spat out the flask. I clambered back down, and watched the bombardment continue.

The noise coming from all sides fouled the creature's tremorsense: it lashed its head, the petals of its mouth furling back, then swung out blindly to try and strike the airships. They were far enough away that it missed, but the turbulence threw the cannons off. I heard a shell whiff past us and winced.

[Voidwyrm Empress HP: 862,641/1,040,000]

The spiracles closed as the worm cottoned on to what was happening. Bellowing, it drew back into the earth, burying itself. I searched the ground as the earth shook... but unlike last time, the Empress wasn't snaking close to the surface, but deeper in the earth.

"Split up those ships! Now!" I barked. *"Karalti!"*

"Here we go again!" Karalti tucked her wings in and dived.

Bent low over the saddle, ass in the air, I fixated on the ground. Now and then, I thought I saw the sand stir, but nothing came to the surface.

"Did we drive it off?" Rin asked, after nearly a minute had passed with no signs of life.

"No. Don't count on it." Eyes darting, I scanned for signs of movement—and saw them, as sand began to collapse in a circle right under the *Aspern*. "Suri! It's targeting you!"

"Of course it fuckin' is." Suri cut off to sound the alarm—and Lord Soma's ship veered sharply starboard, its engines flaring as he gunned it to full speed. The sand around the Voidwyrm's buried mouth sucked down into the monster's gullet, and a bone-deep vibration rolled through the air. A whirlwind began to form—then a full-blown tornado, sand whipping in a funnel that grew wider and wider and began to suck in everything around it. The wreckage of the *Lockhart* slid into its jaws, crushed into kindling. Any people who hadn't fled out into the desert were pulled in, their screams drowned by the howl of the wind. The ships were far enough away to avoid being sucked in—but we were not.

"No! NO! Gods damn it no!" Karalti frantically beat her wings, honking in alarm as the vortex hoovered us toward it.

It took all of her strength to not lose control and flip onto her back.

"It can't keep this up forever! You can do it!" I urged her. *"Teleport out!"*

"I can't! It's dispelling the magic!" Karalti snarled, lips peeling back as she briefly tumbled, flipping over, and began to flap as hard as she could. Just before her stamina hit the yellow range—the tornado left off. My dragon surged forward, panting and panicked, and struggled for altitude as the Voidwyrm lunged out of the sands toward us. I made the mistake of looking back as the monster's open maw grew larger and larger... an endless black hole that engulfed us from behind, snapped shut ahead of Karalti's muzzle, and dragged us back down into the earth.

CHAPTER 58

The Voidwyrm's gullet was large enough for two dragons of Karalti's size to fly side by side—until it moved. Karalti bellowed in alarm as the spines of the sandworm's throat contracted around us in time with the worm's undulations, forcing her to constantly adjust her turns. We passed the wreckage of the Lockhart, wood skewed on the razor sharp hooks that lined its upper esophagus.

"What do we do!? What do we do?!" Karalti was struggling to control her panic.

She couldn't see—but I could. I knelt up, squinting through the acid fumes engulfing us. *"We tunnel our way back out. Tune into my vision and focus on flying. Keep it together: this shit isn't over yet."*

The wind moaned in my ears as Karalti followed the writhing contours of the tunnel. It was not quiet inside the worm: the sound of its burrowing roared from every rumbling, dripping surface. There was a rhythmic banging from up ahead: the sound like huge rocks slamming together. Was that it's heartbeat?

I flicked to the group PM. "Hey! Can any of you guys hear us?!"

[You are imprisoned. PMs have been disabled.]

Of course. I reoriented on the path ahead. *"We've got this, Tidbit."*

"But it's still got over eight-hundred-thousand-"

"We've GOT this. Believe in us, Karalti." My nostrils flexed as a fierce, cold anger stirred in me. I wasn't going to lose my dragon here. Not like this. *"Mortal Blows are a game mechanic that mostly ignores levels. So we find this thing's heart. We cut the arteries, and we kill it from the inside out. The only creature capable of this – the ONLY creature that could possibly do this – is a dragon like you. Small, extremely fast, and very, very brave."*

The booming, rumbling, crunching sound was deafening now, and as the worm reared and straightened out, I saw why. Ahead of us, the tunnel constricted into a narrower hole that opened and closed like a mouth. Behind it, great crushing slabs of bone pounded against one another. There were more [Gizzard Teeth] behind them, grinding sand, stone, and potentially us, into mush.

"We're gonna have to time this right." My hands were shaking, slippery inside my gauntlets as I stared straight ahead, not even daring to blink. *"Do you trust me?"*

"Yes."

"Then follow my count."

I began to count by thousands the way the army had taught me, timing the opening and closing of the beast's throat. Karalti beat her wings in time with my metronome, and the two of us together were able to spot the gaps. She shot through the first and second sets of teeth. There were three more beyond them, opening and closing at different intervals. We cleared the third just before the monoliths crunched together, but the fourth set was slower to open and I missed a second. Karalti desperately backwinged, wheeling around in a loop before shooting forward, right into the fifth set of teeth as they closed down like a guillotine.

"HASTE!" I shouted.

Karalti's scales shimmered in the dark as she boosted forward at high speed. I hung on for dear life as she rocketed through the narrowing gap, ducking down. A rotten cheese smell blew across us as my dragon shot through, her tail just barely clearing the crunch.

"Fuck a whole lot of that," I moaned, looking forward. *"And fuck a whole lot of THIS."*

'This' was the biggest sphincter I'd ever had the misfortune to behold. Fifty feet around, it was the undisputed King of Assholes. The alpha and omega orifice. It was also the perfect physical embodiment of my current feelings toward Ororgael.

"I have to land." Karalti gasped, her wingbeats faltering. *"Can you light a torch? I don't need a lot of light, just some.*

I did so—and almost wished I hadn't as the inside of the Voidwyrm was revealed in glorious technicolor. The heaving walls were an extremely unattractive shade of olive green, shot through with black and violet. The 'floor' was covered in ankle-deep mucus and a field of fleshy feelers that grasped at my dragon's feet as she landed. Karalti landed with a squelching sound I hoped to never hear again.

"Here." I got her potions—Stamina, Mana, Water—and balanced out along her neck to give them to her. She swallowed urgently, her neck rippling. Both of us froze as the Voidwyrm suddenly screamed and began to thrash: Karalti clung on with her claws as the 'room' inverted, and our floor suddenly became a wall.

"They must be hitting it with the Symphonic Array again," I said, clinging to her neck with all limbs like a tree. *"Listen. Can you hear a heartbeat?"*

"No." Karalti eyed the sphincter of doom, catching her breath. *"Is that the entry to its stomach?"*

"I literally know two things about worm anatomy: they don't have lungs, and I hate that and also everything else about them."

The opal seams of Karalti's scales brightened as she cast Bioscan on it. Surprisingly, we got a readout:

Voidwyrm Empress Gizzard Sphincter

HP: 2500/2500
MP: N/A

The entry to a Sandworm's intestine. Immune to Acids, Earth Magic. Vulnerable to fire.

"The intestine. Of course, it's the entry to the intestine." I rubbed the top of my helmet, and regretted it immediately as my glove stuck to the slick, slimy surface. *"Here's a question for you. Why do you think it is that Archemi has a pee meter, but not a poop meter?"*

"I'm gonna guess it's because all the poop in the world is stored in whatever is behind the big butthole."

I pulled the Spear from my back. "Let's just hope the Voidwyrm Empress went to the bathroom recently."

Karalti closed her nostrils, pawed the ground, and ran straight at the meat wall. She attacked it with jaws and claws, raking at it, then taking a step back to hose it with fire. The body of the worm rumbled like an earthquake, and it moaned, twisting with pain as the fire seared into its flesh.

[[Ghost Fire deals 4799 damage!]]

The portal opened, and Karalti ducked through.

The worm's gut resembled a weird, green-glowing forest. Things skittered on the walls, mandibles clicking: parasites. But in the distance, we could hear the sound of hope: a deafening heartbeat, growing louder with every step.

"All we have to do is get through here." I tensed as the roof of the cavern contracted, and a squelching growl rolled through the room. *"We take out the hearts. Then we either teleport out of here, or cut our way out."*

Karalti hissed as the parasites oriented on her, mantling her wings and ducking her head as she jogged forward. The air was close in here, thick, acidic, and hard to breathe. Karalti charged through overhanging fleshy stalactites, crushing the silverfish-like creatures scuttling underfoot. The deeper we went, the more thunderous the heartbeats were. Plural.

"Shit. There's more than one." I was used to listening to the subtly different tempo of Karalti's twin hearts beating in

sync. *"I can hear four of five of them. And they're not in the normal spot."*

"You're right. It's like... they're coming from all around." Karalti snapped at a [Sandworm Parasite], driving it back. *"We need to find them quickly. My feet are burning. There's acid on the ground."*

I looked down. There was, indeed, a gross brownish sludge everywhere... sludge that was slowly rising, leaking from streams on the walls, which were slowly closing in on us. If we didn't get out of here, we were going to suffocate.

"Find a thin patch of wall and tear through! We need to get out of here!" I held the torch up as a cough built in my chest. The air was starting to sear my throat.

"I can hear the hearts to the left! There!" The dragon charged forward, toward a filmy wall of sinewy tissue. *"Attack it! Help me pull it down! I think this is one of its lung channels!"*

She didn't have to ask me twice. I sprung from her back, charging the Spear, and blasted the organ wall with Master of Blades and Rain of Glass. The Dark lances shredded it, spraying us with ichor, and the worm lashed from side to side as we held our breaths and squeezed through. It was kind of like going through an old-fashioned car wash with the rollers and mops, except the rollers were made out of warm meat and the goal of the carwash to coat you, the car, and everything else in as much slime and blood as possible. I sheltered under Karalti's torso as she burrowed her way through, holding my hands up against jets of nameless fluids.

"This, right here, is how I know Ryuko is a Japanese company." I grimaced as a thick lumpy liquid hosed me down from face to knees. I was pretty sure it was lymph. I was praying to God it was lymph.

"C'mon, c'mon..." Karalti muttered. The heartbeat was overwhelming now, shaking us on every thump. *"Hector! We found them!"*

Karalti squeezed through into a tight, close chamber. Above and below us, five huge organs the size of semi-trucks pulsed with blood. They didn't look like human hearts—they were much less complicated, like huge tubes that expanded along their length and then contracted, filling arteries that stuck out from them like sewer pipes. The entire array of them stretched up and down the cavern, bands of cartilage being all that held up the 'roof' over our heads.

"Here's what I say we do," I said. *"You start digging. I take these out. As soon as those arteries burst, this place is going to flood, and if we're not out of here when it does..."*

"Eew. Yeah." Karalti rumbled, barely audible over the quaking *ba-duk ba-duk ba-duk* that rolled the room like an earthquake and drowned out all other sounds. *"Go. I'll try and find a way out. Gar was shouting about spiracles, and we just came through the lungs... so there's got to be spiracles that open up here!"*

I rolled my shoulders, tensed, and sprung out onto the first heart. I landed on it, sticking to it with Spider Climb, raised the Spear high, and drove it down into the surging artery.

[2136 damage! You deal a Critical Blow! Sandworm Artery HP: 1864/4000]

I struck again, dealing another two thousand damage, and the tissues split like tearing fabric before bursting apart. The Voidwyrm screeched, the sound reverberating through its body as blood gushed out in a great torrent, barely slowing as I moved to the next organ. I didn't need any special attacks: just fire, as the flaming Spear of Creation plunged in and out of the vulnerable organ walls.

"I found an external lung channel! Keep going!" Karalti dug like a dog at the walls of the cardiac cavity, shredding meat with her claws and powerful jaws. By the time I punctured the third [Aortic Arch], the cardiac chamber was knee-deep in blood.

"How are we going over there?" I vaulted over to the next heart, the Spear raised to strike. *"It's starting to get a little close."*

"I know that! This wall has fifteen thousand hitpoints!" She rocked back on her tail and the pad of her pelvic bone to bring both feet up, kicking out with all her strength.

[You deal 5583 damage to Voidwyrm-]
[Critical hit!]
[Karalti deals 6722 critical damage to Voidwyrm Empress-]
[Warning: Mana concentrations-]

"Stop combat notifications!" I snarled at my HUD as the damage rolled in—and my HP began to tick down as the polluted mana-infused ichor sprayed me in a fashionable coating of crimson goo. I tumbled into the sloshing cauldron of it as the Empress gave an especially violent jerk, writhing in agony.

"*Help!*" I splashed to the surface.

Karalti broke from her excavation, wading over to me. I climbed up her hand as she bit into the next heart, clamping her teeth into it and shaking. I pulled myself up to the slick saddle, struggling to breathe. I was losing 5HP a second now—not good.

"*If I die, promise me you'll get out of here,*" I gasped, struggling against burning eyes and sinuses and braced for the next Jump. "*When she's dead, you can teleport*"

"*SHUT UP AND STAB!*" Karalti worried the fibrous tissue, throwing her neck and shoulders into it. The organ ruptured under the pressure of her jaws: and suddenly, we were both submerged as the worm flipped over, lashing from side to side.

Holding my breath, I swam on instinct, trusting my gyroscopic orientation to help me find 'up'. I burst out the surface of the liquid to find the last aortic arch pounding violently, fibrillating as the Voidwyrm tried desperately to save itself. I swam to it, arm over arm, called the Spear to hand, and rammed it into the tissue with a harsh cry.

The organ ruptured with a satisfying explosion, dumping blood into the chamber with enough force that it washed me away. Karalti, now barely keeping her head above the waterline, let out a shrill cry as I tumbled off her back and got dunked down into the thick fluid. I didn't need Navigail to tell me that I'd dealt the mortal blow—I could feel it, as the Voidwyrm lunged up high into the air, keening, and then slowly, thunderously, toppled like a falling tree. I clutched at Karalti's wing, trying and unable to find space to breathe. I had enough constitution to be able to hold my breath for a couple of minutes, but my oxygen meter was going down —fast.

[Myszno Defence Force has defeated Voidwyrm Empress!]
[All units gain 6995 EXP!]
[Warning: 15% Oxygen.]

"Hold onto me, Hector! I still can't teleport, but we're almost through!" Karalti scrabbled, kicking and clawing with all her might against the Voidwyrm's flank. I clutched onto her, eyes screwed shut against the blood, feeling my HP drain away. My hands and feet were turning numb.

"Stay with me! Hector! You can make it!" Karalti's voice sounded distant and fuzzy. No matter how hard I tried, I couldn't seem to keep my grip on her wing. Something was pulling me away from her. I flailed out, lungs burning for air... and then the current changed, and I was rushing forward. Rushing and tumbling, falling, until I landed with a wet splat.

"Urrgrh." Coughing, moaning, I struggled up to hands and knees. Blood poured off my body like I'd been doused in house paint. It was in my helmet, in my armor, in my lungs. I hacked, crawling blindly, only to collapse onto my chest in... sand?

"Karalti?!" I pulled my helmet off and tried to clean the sandworm blood from my eyes.

[Warning! You are suffering from Mana Poisoning! HP: 1630/3229]

I staggered to my feet, remembered I had potions, and spammed three of them. Then I pulled a waterskin, and dumped the whole thing over my head, scrubbing at my face until I could see. Karalti was lying slumped on the ground beside the sandworm, one wing folded underneath her, the other sagging from her flank.

"SHIT!" I ran and waded to her as terror gripped my chest. "Karalti!"

Karalti stirred weakly, groaning as I reached her head and lay hands on her. Frantically, I checked her vitals: her HP was okay, she didn't suffer from mana poisoning, but she was down to 13% mana and 2% stamina. Any more mana loss, and she would pass out.

"Yaaay." She gave a little telepathic cheer, letting her head flop back down onto the ground. *"We did iiiit."*

I draped myself over her muzzle, hugging any bit of her I could reach, and managed a wheezy little laugh. "We sure as fuck did. All of us."

"Hector! Are you alive down there!?" Suri's voice, stiff with fear, broke through the exhaustion. I looked around before realizing it was a PM.

"Yeah. Yeah, we're okay. Haven't gotten rid of us yet." I slumped down against Karalti's head, sliding to the ground with my back resting against her brow ridge. "Karalti and me aren't doing so hot. Might want to come pick us up before I die of mana poisoning."

"Okay: I can see you on the map, we'll be there! Get out of that wet patch before it turns to quicksand!"

Quicksand. I jerked up, realizing that yes, Karalti was slowly sinking as the Voidwyrm's blood soaked into the dry sand. "Karalti! Potions, now!"

Karalti struggled up, honking as her heavier hindquarters slipped into the wet sludge. "Ahh!"

I grabbed the last mana and stamina potions from her Inventory, frantically uncorked them, and shoved them into her mouth. Second by second, she was sliding away into the liquifying ground – and so was I.

"HHNNRRRAGGGH!" Karalti tossed the jars away, snatched me in her jaws, beating her wings to keep her chest above the surface. Her scales surged with light: and then we teleported, reappearing high over the circling ships.

"Holy shit," I gasped, hanging limply between my dragon's teeth. The Voidwyrm was a twisted quarter-mile long wreck, twitching in a sea of its own blood that was causing it to slowly immerse into the desert. Withering Rose, several hundred yards away, was fine—and as a cheer went up from the ships, the dredgers that had been hanging back out of battle range began to chug toward the fallen Warsinger.

"Gar! Lorenzo! We did it! We did it we did it we did it!" Rin's voice broke off into a delighted squeal.

"We all joined Rin on the Aspern," Suri said, her voice cutting past the sounds of Rin's unintelligible joy. "Stern is clear for landing. Get down here before Karalti falls out of the damn sky."

Karalti, trailing blood and ichor, wobbled on approach to the Aspern. She backwinged and flapped, stumbling as she touched down, and sunk to her keel with a wheeze. I hopped down, trying to scrape off sand, blood, and gods-knew-what-else as my friends ran across the deck toward us.

"Hector! Karalti!" Suri ran to me and caught me into a hug, then turned to squeeze Karalti around the neck. Rin was about to glomp, before she noticed the dripping ropes of goo and cringed back. Gar took one look at me, planted his hands on his hips, and began to laugh.

"Yeah, yeah. Laugh it up." I pointed at him with a dripping hand. "This will be what your bed looks like in about two weeks' time."

"Hey, fuck you." He grinned, clapping Rin on the shoulder. "You bet your skinny ass you're paying me rent for every day that raging *puta* of a dinosaur is camped in my room."

Soma emerged from the ship's bridge, striding urgently toward us. "By Khors' fiery red balls, we actually did it! Those Symphonic Arrays saved the day! Imagine the favors we'll receive from His Majesty once we demonstrate these to the court!"

"Yeah. That's exactly what I'm thinking about right now. His Majesty." I pulled my helmet off, which kind of felt like pouring a tub of glue over my own head. "Do we have any option to like… hose us down?"

"CAPTAIN!" The starboard watchstander cried. "SHIPS INCOMING!"

CHAPTER 59

"Ships?" We all turned to face the railing, running over as a group. I spotted them first: six ornate airships with billowing golden silk sails, gold filigree on the hulls, and long trailing cerulean flags were headed straight for us. They were large galleon-type ships, the size of the destroyers. Rather than the sleek discreet engines I was used to seeing on Vlachian ships, these ships had giant fan-like peacock tails, with each 'eye' lit by a glowing disk of mana.

"That's Dakhdir's Royal Fleet." Soma gripped the railings, leaning out. "They must be here to see what all the fuss is about."

My gut tensed. "No, I don't think they are. We need the ships to form a defensive position."

Soma shot me a sharp look. "Dakhdir is an ally of Vlachia, and under the White Sail Alliance pact, we are allowed free access to their airspace. We are flying the correct flags on all our vessels-"

"Trust me, dude. This is not good." I glared at him. "Signal the other fucking ships. We need the destroyers ready to blast these fuckers out of the sky."

Soma looked like he was about to argue, but his moustache bristled, and he stalked off, yelling at the signalers to warn the other ships and steer them into a fighting position.

"Don't tell me." Suri's face was hard with disbelief. "Violetta?"

"I don't know." I regarded the approaching ships, pressing my lips together in a grim line.

Our armada turned to face the newcomers in formation. The lead ship was not the largest: a smaller cruiser with an open deck. Dakhari soldiers were gathering on the decks, armed with powerful bows and muskets. As the cruiser pulled up broadside to our bow, I noticed that all the below-deck cannon ports were angled straight in toward us.

"Stand down, in the name of His Divine Eminence, Sultir Yazid Khememmu!" An imperious little man in court silks called to us with an old-fashioned megaphone, his voice piercing the still desert air. "You are committing theft against the nation of Dakhdir! Surrender your ships, or face destruction!"

The ship's bosun ran to me with a megaphone of our own. I stood up from the railing and put it to my mouth. "Vlachia has a treaty with Dakhdir. This Warsinger is not your property – and even if it was, we aren't going to surrender shit!"

"Yoo-hoo, over here. " Gar's voice crackled through our group PM. *"Symphonic Array armed and ready. Say the word, and we'll blast this ponce out of the air. "*

699

"Hold fire until they start getting mad." I used the thought-to-speech to reply, focusing on the official.

"Treaty?" The man flashed a gap-toothed grin. "We do not have a treaty with regicides. Kill the Vlachian usurpers!"

"NOW!" I shouted.

The Symphonic Array let out a whining pulse, then a piercing scream of sound that was still only a fraction of the power that struck the Dakhari ship. The sonic ray smashed into the gold-decorated wood and blew through to the other side, and everyone aboard began to shout and holler as, all of a sudden, they were capsizing.

"All cannons, all artillery, now!" I turned from the railing and yelled at Soma. "Take 'em down or run them off! Their choice!"

We couldn't coordinate as easily without one Starborn on every command ship, but the crews of the Myszno fleet were combat veterans with the Demon's War behind them – and we had the Arrays. The *Salamander* and *Gae Bolg* circled around, rising to avoid fire, and unleashed their sonic weapons on the largest of the Sultir's vessels. They didn't just sink it – they broke it apart, sending the two halves careening out of the sky.

"Watch out for dragons! Violetta's behind this, I know she is!" I ran back to Karalti. My dragon was peeling herself off the deck. Her wings were sagging – her last potion had put her back to 28% stamina, and by looking at her, I knew it wasn't enough. Cursing, I ransacked my Inventory for anything that could help, and was pitched down as cannon fire smashed into the keel of the ship. Then something zipped past over the sails: quazi riders.

Karalti used her wings to push herself up to her feet. *"Get on! We have to help! I still have ten breath weapon charges – and my Queensong."*

I clenched my teeth and vaulted up onto her back. Karalti spun, snatching a quazi by the wing from the air as it wheeled over the deck of the ship, and slung it around as she launched herself into the sky with a bellow of challenge. I crouched down, bracing the Spear as we gained altitude, and got a picture of the battle from above: the four Dakhari ships at the rear were pulling away, but six of them now locked in combat with ours. The *Salamander* had been boarded. I tracked the path of the retreating ships – they were headed for the defenseless dredgers and cargo ships massed over Withering Rose.

Karalti roared, striving after the galleons. She could fly twice as fast as the ships, limited only by her Stamina. She closed in on the engines of the straggling ship, weaving out of range of the cannons and blasting their engine array with fire. The crystal cracked, melted and exploded under the assault: first one, then another. The ship lurched, an alarm pealing up from under decks. Quazi riders lifted into the sky – then fell as Karalti opened her mouth and sang them the song of her people. The desert amplified her Queensong to an extraordinary degree. Riders retched, quazi panicked, and the other ships swung south, desperately fleeing our assault.

"Get out of here!" Karalti scolded them, belching another gout of flames along the engines. *"And tell Violetta to go screw herself while you're at it!"*

The ships let off covering fire, but the bigger the ship was, the more difficulty it had aiming and firing at something as nimble as Karalti. The fleet pulled away from here as the one ship went down, crashing into the fallen corpse of the Voidwyrm, where it exploded in a blue-tinged fireball.

I looked back to see the rest of the ships were following their lead. The Dakhari hadn't been expecting us to be as well armed as we were, and they were paying for it. The *Salamander* was listing, but the Dakhari had lost five ships. They were now running as fast they could, chugging back toward the west.

"Yeah! We did it! Again!" Karalti eased into a glide, saving her remaining stamina.

"Wait." As we flew back toward our armada, a dark thought slid into my mind, hooked up with what we were seeing here, and connected. "If Violetta... no, this doesn't make sense. These are probably some of Dakhdir's weakest ships, and she's not here with her dragon. Which means... FUCK!!"

"What!?" Karalti bellowed in alarm at the force of my anxiety.

"Dakhdir was supposed to provide reinforcements for Ignas!" I drew a deep, startled breath, clutching the saddle grips. "And if they've betrayed the treaty, then... fuck, fuck, FUCK! Teleport to Taltos, now! We have to warn him!"

Karalti tensed, preparing to follow my order, when the World Notifications I had dreaded suddenly flashed up on my HUD.

World Alert: Revala

After a decisive battle, the Kingdom of Revala has been conquered by the Ilian Empire. This is a server alert to announce the new Regent of Revala, General Lucien Hart, Knight-Commander of the Eyrie of St. Grigori.

"Suri! Karalti and I are teleporting to Taltos now!" I snarled over the PM.

"Go! We'll handle things here!" Suri's voice was flat, cold, and angry.

Karalti drew a deep breath, steeled herself, and warped into the void. We hung there for half a minute, and burst out in the Vulkan Keep courtyard into a scene of pure chaos. Soldiers were swarming the castle like ants, and Karalti roared to clear them out of the garden so she could land. I slid down, stunned, to see a trio of people headed for us: Simeon wheeling Rutha in her chair, Masterhealer Masha by her side. All of them looked shocked and pale, and before Rutha even opened her mouth, I knew what I was going to hear.

"Hector, Dakhdir betrayed Vlachia," she gasped, her lilac eyes huge in her face. "And Mercurions attacked Jeun from the north, preventing reinforcements from arriving. The Second Fleet... Ignas..."

Simeon drew himself up, graven, his hands shaking. "Voivode Dragozin, I'm afraid to report that Lucien Hart has taken our king."

***

TO BE CONTINUED...

To Stay Up-To-Date with Archemi Online, join the James Osiris Baldwin Facebook group:

Join the James Osiris Baldwin fan group for updates, releases, specials and sneak previews

Find Us on Facebook: https://www.facebook.com/groups/HoundofEden

Archemi Online has a Discord channel!

Join the Archemi Online Discord to meet gamers, hang out and chat with the author, and gain access to live updates on the books, audiobooks, and art of the Archemi Online LitRPG series, as well as future releases!

Join us on Discord: https://discord.gg/EPWxbGd

Patreon!

Support the artist and get serialized chapters, complete ebooks, free audiobooks, posters, and even hardback copies of the Archemi series. Tiers start at $2 per month for access to serialized chapters and ebooks. Patreon subscribers also have a special channel on Discord.

Join here: *https://www.patreon.com/jamesosiris*

Want to leave a Review? Go here:

https://www.amazon.com/dp/B087XBZS1C

Author's Note

Well, what can I say about 2020 that hasn't already been said? It was crazy, it was insane, it was stressful. When I started Archemi in 2016, I had no idea that pretty soon, we would be facing a global pandemic. A lot of these story elements – HEX, the role of viruses – organic and digital – were things I planned to write about from the series' conception in 2017.

Spear of Destiny is probably the darkest book in series so far, but I hope I was able to communicate the main message of the Archemi Online series: that no matter how scary things get, there are always people who rise to the challenge. Sometimes those people are like Hector (and Gar, though we don't know him very well yet), bold, courageous, unwilling to give up. Sometimes they're like Suri, Vash and Istvan: tough, resilient, emotionally capable of handling and processing even the worst life has to throw at us. And sometimes, they're like Karalti and Rin: optimistic, bright, smart people with visions of the future and a love of life.

When we rise up to challenges, we can overcome them.

I got COVID-19 while writing this book, on Christmas Day.

The point of infection was a restaurant. I went to pick up Chinese food for my wife and I, and a man came into the restaurant, maskless and ranting about various conspiracies when he was asked to either put on a mask or leave. Me and a woman waiting in line stepped up to remove him when he began coughing in people's faces. We bounced the dude out to the curb, but two weeks later, I got sick. My lungs hurt, my everything hurt, and I was eerily reminded of the symptoms I described Hector having in those blissfully mask-free days of February 2016.

About 50k words of this book was written while I was sick. I found myself doing the cocktail of pills thing I wrote about in Dragon Seed, though I didn't ride a motorcycle through anyone's fence despite the fever. All things considered, I had a mild case, and have recovered everything except my sense of smell.

My friends and family were invaluable through the course of writing this book. I couldn't have done it without them. Almost all of us have stepped up for someone else this year. We supported gamer friends and bought each other groceries. We consoled family and struggled to motivate one another. We played Among Us and hung out on Discord. So take a moment to celebrate you, and all you have done to make this strangest of years a better place to be. I believe we will overcome the challenges ahead with boldness and intelligence. There are better days ahead.

You may notice that there is no pre-order for Book 6 yet. There are a few reasons for that: Firstly, Archemi is getting a makeover. I am going through all of the books with a new editor, cleaning up all the math and straightening out kinks and conflicts in the game system that have naturally arisen as we approach 1 million words in the series (!), and also will be getting new covers for every single book. Secondly, I desperately need a rest. Post-COVID-19, I need to take some time to nurture my body, lose some weight, and find ways to regain all the fitness I lost this year.

And thirdly, I am taking some time to work on a second series. Join the Discord or Facebook group (or both!) to learn more about this and stay in touch while I plan and write it.

Thank you so much for taking this journey with me. I owe a huge amount to my Discord crew - Zohatu, Terhig, Wanderer, Murdimus, Keebler, Parker, Noah, G.M.M.A Hamish, FS3D Pete and many others. I am also incredibly grateful to my patient, understanding wife, Canth, and to my editors, Mimi and Karla. Thank you so much, guys.

- James.

List of James' Books

Hound of Eden Series

Dark, gritty urban fantasy with a cosmic horror twist, join Russian mafia hitmage Alexi Sokolsky as he confronts the mad demons of the abyss, finds redemption, and saves the world. Hound of Eden is an LGBTI series.

- Hound of Eden Omnibus (Books 1 – 3)
- 0 - Burn Artist (Prequel)
- 1 - Blood Hound
- 2 - Stained Glass
- 3 - Zero Sum

Archemi Online

A LitRPG saga about a young dragonrider's ascension to greatness inside the virtual world of Archemi.

Archemi Online Box Set 1-3

- 1 – Dragon Seed
- 2 – Trial by Fire
- 3 – Kingdom Come
- 4 – Warsinger
- 5 – Spear of Destiny
- 6 – Blaze of Glory (Coming in 2021)

Other Titles

- Fix Your Damn Book!: A Self-Editing Guide for Authors
- The Expanding Universe #1 (Paperback)
- The Expanding Universe #2 (Paperback)

Copyright

Lightning Source UK Ltd.
Milton Keynes UK
UKHW012234060223
416577UK00003B/215/J